OLIVI
FLAVO

D0364941

"Compulsively readable. . . ."
—New York *Daily News*

"With a dash of wit and just a touch of malice, Olivia Goldsmith revives that mainstay of summer reading, the Sex &
Shopping Novel. . . . You'll appreciate her wicked good
spirits and essentially compassionate heart and her ability to
write a nice hot sex scene or two."
—*Entertainment Weekly*

"Typical Hollywood . . . with a genuinely terrific ending."
—*Mademoiselle*

"[A] blockbuster novel. . . . perfect summer reading. . . .
what more could you ask for from the flavor of the month?"
—*Village Voice Literary Supplement*

"On Hollywood . . . no one can touch Goldsmith for gusto.
In *FLAVOR OF THE MONTH*, [Goldsmith's] latched onto
another theme. . . . Hollywood, which she masticates with
characteristic glee. . . . At the close, she pulls out all the
stops . . . in a wild, over-the-top way."
—*Kirkus Reviews*

"Deliciously juicy. . . . Goldsmith spins out a dizzying
whirl of subplots . . . and she enlivens each with a twist . . .
she perfectly conjures up the envy and insecurity, the toady-
ing and backstabbing associated with the celebrity circuit."
—*Publishers Weekly*

A Book-of-the-Month Club Main Selection

Books by Olivia Goldsmith

The First Wives Club
Flavor of the Month

Published by POCKET BOOKS

OLIVIA GOLDSMITH

FLAVOR OF THE MONTH

POCKET BOOKS

New York London Toronto Sydney Tokyo Singapore

A Pocket Star Book published by
POCKET BOOKS, a division of Simon & Schuster Inc.
1230 Avenue of the Americas, New York, NY 10020

Copyright © 1993 by Olivia Goldsmith

ISBN: 0-671-79450-7

First Pocket Books printing May 1994

10 9 8 7 6 5 4 3 2

POCKET STAR BOOKS and colophon are registered
trademarks of Simon & Schuster Inc.

Cover art by Punz Wolff

Printed in the U.S.A.

Acknowledgments

I would like to express very special thanks to Nancy Robinson, my secretary, critic, and friend. Without her cheerful and brilliant support, I would have surely drowned in the second revision. Not to mention the third, fourth, fifth, and sixth. Sincerest thanks also to:

Brendan Gunning for his peerless editorial assistance

Todd Harris of the William Morris Agency, who introduced me to Hollywood and taught me the maxim "the agent always gets screwed"

Dr. Michael Sachs, whose understanding of women and beauty is only matched by his brilliance as a surgeon

Dr. Richard Gulian for the time he made for me, explanations he went over, and invaluable help he gave with the technical aspects of plastic surgery

Bill and Ann Johnson for their early readings and their generous comments on the draft

Dwight Currie and Michael Kohlman for their friendship, humor, and the research help they offered

Ruth Bekker for her insights on the New York acting scene

Diana Hellinger for tireless enthusiasm and encouragement way beyond the bounds of friendship

Georgiana Francisco for her insider's view of L.A.

Jane Scovell, who knows everyone and everything, and is my pal

Ellen Hall, who helped in so many ways, and mailed out the manuscript, time after time

Bill Hall, who finally got the job done, and beautifully!

ACKNOWLEDGMENTS

Matilda Tucker, for her unconditional love and helpful suggestions for revamping chapter one

And, as always, Curtis Laupheimer and Justine Kryvin for everything

Lastly, special thanks to all the women in Hollywood, both actresses and those behind the scenes, who so generously shared their experiences and their pain. Your truth is stranger than my fiction. I only hope I have not betrayed your trust.

Note From the Author

"Call me Ishmael—and call me often."

I once knew a Hollywood agent, strictly small-time, who had that printed across the bottom of his business cards. Not that most people get the joke. And not that Ishmael Reiss did much business, but it wasn't because of the bad Melville allusion. Remember, this is the town where Bob LeVine, CEO at International Studios, once asked, "Hamlet? Isn't that the Mel Gibson vehicle?"

Writers—Melville, Faulkner, even Shakespeare—don't get much respect out here. You've heard the one about the dumb starlet? She was so stupid she slept with a writer to get a part. Of course, in the Hollywood food chain, writers are at the very bottom—the economic equivalent of career plankton.

That is, most writers—novelists, screenwriters, gag writers, or TV scriptwriters. But not all. I'm a writer, I chose to live out here, and I get respect. Well, it isn't mother love, but it beats the hell out of scorn and abuse. They may not like me, but they respect me, because they fear me. And I earn a lot of money.

Most people know who I am, and most people will say they don't like me. "Laura Richie, what a cat!" they say, and that's when they're being polite. But as long as they buy my books, I don't care. Anyway, they don't actually know me—I'm just a famous name to them.

I'm famous for writing about the famous—a kind of celebrity hybrid, like Robin Leach. Funny about his name, isn't it? People call both of us leeches, but they also call me "Richie the Bitchy." An unfortunate coincidental assonance. Hey, it could be worse—"Kitty Litter," for example. Still, those who call names also lap the stuff up faster than I can research and write it.

It takes a lot of work. And I take pride in my work. It's biography. It's fact, not conjecture, not hearsay, not my opinions and my prejudices. I've got plenty of those, of course, but I keep them to myself, at least as much as any writer consciously can. I do a careful and complete job. I'm a plodder.

Well, I admit that as a life's work it's not Rheims Cathedral or even a biography of George Washington Carver, or Von Hilshimer, or Churchill. But comparatively few people are interested in the greats. Or even the near-greats. They prefer the ingrates.

So, if writers get no respect and no interest, what does?

Beauty. America is a country that worships only three things: money, youth, and beauty, and if you have the latter two, you can parlay them into the former. Beauty is youth. Beauty doesn't die, or at least it gives that impression.

What is new is that for the first time in history, money can buy beauty. And that somebody did.

Beauty begets money, money begets power. Sometimes. And everybody wants to read about beautiful women.

I know. My first book was Marion Anderson: A Black Artist's Struggle. It was based on my doctoral thesis. It sold 2,216 copies. I'd worked on it for five years. But hey, she wasn't beautiful. My last book, Cher!, sold a half million copies. That's hardback. Multiply it times twenty-two dollars (of which I get 15 percent) and then call me names, if you want to. My banker calls me "Miss Richie." And for him I'd endorse my royalty checks "Richie the Bitchy" if it sold one extra copy. Plus, Bob LeVine and Mike Ovitz and April Irons return my calls. And invite me to their parties. It's nice to be noticed.

And it took long enough, to get to be a known commodity. A Laura Richie book sells. Fame. It's weird, but useful. Fifty-nine percent of Americans know who Donna Douglas is—she played Elly May Clampett in The Beverly Hillbillies—but they can't name even one Nobel Prize winner. Think about it. Hey, I didn't make this society, I'm only trying to live here. And I live well, and quietly. Of course, not too quietly. It wouldn't sell the column or the books. I've been on Donahue, and Oprah and Geraldo and Sally Jessy and a hundred radio call-in shows. But despite that and my picture on the back of my books, I still manage a private life. Know why? Because a writer—even a famous writer—could never be famous enough to lose all privacy. Actors, yes. Entrepreneurs, models, athletes, even notorious prostitutes, royalty (no matter how minor or spurious): they become celebrities. Women usually gain celebrity by being beautiful. Men because of their wealth or achievements. Funny how that works. Then the people who struggled up out of the morass of obscurity into the celebrity sunshine gain recognition but lose their lives to the public.

Because America is also addicted to fame. Celebrity is more important to Americans than achievement, but the public's adulation is a two-edged sword. They build you up but they'll knock you down, too. That's part of my job. Knockin' 'em down. Once I started writing celebrity exposés—ones that told the whole truth—I found a market niche that can never be filled. Because America wants the dirt on those they worship: the stories of abuse, bankruptcy, incest, battering, addiction, and pain. The ugliness behind the beauty. A grim fairy tale. My public. The seamier it is, the better they like it.

For women, the story usually begins with looks: a beauty in search of an audience. We are what we look like. But beauty isn't enough. For Jahne, Sharleen, and Lila, names that have now become legendary, it all started with lipstick. Well, more than a lipstick. A fight about lipstick. But I'm getting ahead of myself.

So, let me guide you through the story. Permit me to point out all the places of interest. After all, who knows celebrity or Hollywood better than I? I promise a great story and no one could tell it completely, from the beginning to the end, as I can. Because I was there. And there's never been a Hollywood saga like it.

> Laura Richie
> Halfway, Wyoming
> 199–

Obscurity I

"The first real problem I faced in my life was that of beauty."

—YUKIO MISHIMA

"The way I look at it is, folks, if you wake up and you're ugly, you know what real pain is. That ain't fun. So I don't want to hear from 'I think it's real difficult to be good-looking and be an actress.' . . . Give me a fucking break."

—DON SIMPSON

"If there is a defect on the soul, it cannot be corrected on the face. But if there is a defect on the face and one corrects it, it can correct a soul."

—JEAN COCTEAU

Obscurity 1

1

New York winters are not kind to Broadway gypsies, Mary Jane Moran thought, not for the first time that day. She fought a sudden gust of biting wind to open the heavy glass door to the unemployment office. She walked into the cavernous gray room, ignoring the various direction signs hanging by wires from the ceiling, and, as she had done every week for the last six months, took her place in an already long line, this time behind a very short woman. I just hope she's not a talker, Mary Jane thought.

Mary Jane released a deep sigh as she surveyed the familiar scene. There was the usual smattering of laid-off seasonal workers and blue-collar types, but, for the most part, she guessed that a lot of the applicants were very much like herself—young and energetic, probably talented. But in New York most talented people didn't earn their livelihoods in the arts. They suffered instead. She thought again, as she always did at times like this, of the old showbiz joke: The guy at the circus who sweeps up the elephant shit starts feeling really sick and goes to the doctor. After dozens of tests, the doc tells him he has good news: "Nothing serious, though very rare. Seems that you're severely allergic to elephant shit. Just avoid it and you'll be fine." "But I can't!" cries the guy, and explains his job. "So, quit," the doctor tells him. The guy is stunned. "What! And give up show business?"

Like the guy in the joke, Mary Jane couldn't quit, despite her growing allergy to elephant shit. She usually felt compassion for the down-and-out writers, the dancers, the actors and singers, but not today. Too much elephant shit, and I've got my own troubles, she thought, and began rummaging in her large vinyl bag. She dug out a Mounds bar and a dog-eared paperback copy of *Queenie*, resigning herself to the long wait.

The woman in front of her half-turned toward Mary Jane and said, "Hi. Rotten weather, isn't it?"

3

Mary Jane peered over the top of her book at the tiny woman in what looked like a child's tan car coat, the kind with rope-and-wood closures. She looked only a step or two above a bag lady: none too clean, and a bit dazed or crazed. Mary Jane's boyfriend, Sam, always called her a "dreck magnet," because every kind of dullard and maniac approached her for a handout or a conversation. Still, she couldn't bring herself to be really rude to this tiny woman. Secretly, Mary Jane identified with every old, lonely woman she saw. Fear of my future? she wondered, and shrugged. "Yeah, I hate it when it rains or snows on my reporting day. It makes the animals in their cages even more testy than usual," she said, nodding toward the bored bureaucrats behind the counter. Well, that was enough talk. No need to encourage her. "And I'm in no mood for anyone right now." Mary Jane went back to her book as the woman shuffled around in her oversized galoshes and faced forward, pulling herself tighter into her coat.

It was several minutes before Mary Jane realized she had been reading the same sentence over and over. Shit, she thought, I was a little harsh. The woman was just trying to pass the time. Tapping her gently on the shoulder, Mary Jane said, "Want a piece of gum?" The woman hesitated, looked at Mary Jane, then accepted and smiled. Her teeth made Mary Jane wince.

The woman unwrapped the Dentyne and popped it in her mouth. "I'm a little anxious." Motioning with one hand, she indicated the counter, yards before them. "I'm afraid of what I'm going to hear when I get up there."

Mary Jane laughed. "Join the club," she said. "I think I've blown my wad, but I figured I'd come back today, just in case they make a mistake and give me one more check."

The woman sighed, nodded.

"What do you do when you're working?" Mary Jane asked.

"I'm a writer, but I was working as a word processor at a law firm until I got laid off. And you?"

"I'm an actress," Mary Jane told her. "A currently unemployed but once-working actress. I had one big

4

chance off-Broadway three years ago, got rave reviews, you should forgive the cliché, then nothing."

"What was the show? The woman seemed genuinely interested.

"*Jack and Jill and Compromise.* I was with the show for over a year." Mary Jane felt herself grow depressed. "I haven't gotten any attention since then." Well, it was worse than that, but, she reminded herself, she didn't have to spill her guts to this complete stranger.

"Next!" they both heard at the same time. The old lady waved at Mary Jane as she shuffled off to the long counter before her. "Good luck," she said over her shoulder.

Mary Jane shifted once again on her cold and wet feet, watching as the interviewer began flipping through her files. She watched the old woman's face when the interviewer shook her head. Poor thing. What hole in the wall would she scuttle into? Had she really been a writer or was she just delusional?

After she watched the old lady slump and wander off, it was Mary Jane's turn at bat, time to receive the surly warning that her benefits ended in another two weeks. Mary Jane Moran walked out of the unemployment office at Twenty-sixth Street and Sixth Avenue and pulled her dun-colored down coat tightly around her big-boned body. Two hours and forty minutes in line for a hundred and seventy-six bucks. After pausing a moment in the doorway to gather herself together, she began the long trudge up to St. Malachy's Church on West Forty-sixth Street for the repertory-group rehearsal. Her moon boots, cheap foam covered in vinyl, squished in the icy gray slush puddles, sending new currents of wet cold darting through her feet. Then it started to snow. Great! she thought. Why not just crucify me and get it over with? She pulled the scarf that was wound around her head farther forward to help shield her exposed face from the big wet flakes. She pushed her mittened hands deep into the pockets of the worn coat and kept trudging uptown.

She was used to the cold. She felt she'd always been out in it. Mary Jane had been raised in Scuderstown,

New York, by her grandmother. Her parents had been victims of a car wreck. Mary Jane could only dimly recall the argument between her drunken father and mother, the lurch of the car, the screech of the tires, the shattering glass. Then nothing. Except she clearly remembered the cold—it had been a December night—and then how she shivered in the hall of the hospital, a shaken four-year-old probably in shock, who was ignored while the medical staff clustered around her father and her mother.

Her mother had died. Her father had been severely brain-damaged and sent off, eventually, to a veterans' hospital. But she, at four, had been reluctantly taken in by her father's mother, her only living relative, and spent her childhood and teen years in a ramshackle farmhouse in upstate New York, the unloved, unwilling guest of the bitter old woman. It had been cold in the winters, almost as cold indoors as out, and she hated the cold then as she did now. She thought of the old lady at unemployment in her thin coat and shivered.

At Herald Square, she noticed that the Christmas decorations were still up at Macy's. By December 1, she was sick enough of Christmas cheer but now, in January, after the holiday season she had just survived, she wished Christmas had never been invented. The looks on the people coming out of the department store supported her view. Everyone hates it, she thought. It's just that no one will say it and stay off the bandwagon when it rolls around. I didn't. She sighed, remembering the call from her grandmother. Another poor, unloved old woman.

"I'm sick, Mary. I think I've got the flu. I can hardly get out of bed. I wouldn't ask you if I didn't have to, Mary." Grandma only called her by her name when she wanted something. Otherwise it was simply "you." "Could you come up for a few days and take care of me?" *After all, you are a nurse*. Grandma didn't say it, but it was implied. And, despite the rage, despite every feeling that made her want to fling the receiver back onto its cradle, to get an unlisted number, to run away, change her name, and never go back, the old guilt prevailed.

So, on December 24, Mary Jane had gone by bus to the one person she wanted most *not* to be with. Christmas in

New York would have been glum enough, with Sam going to spend it in Sarasota with his parents, but being back in the shack outside Elmira, taking care of the sick old lady was a nightmare. It somehow made Sam's failure to invite her to join him even more hurtful. Was he ashamed to have her meet his parents? Mary Jane sighed.

Sam, wonderful as he was, was difficult. He'd been married once, when he was really young, and his wife had left him. That was his reason, he said, for hating marriage. Mary Jane didn't mind—not really. She had him, so why need a ring? But if they'd been married, wouldn't he have brought her to Florida? Wouldn't she know his parents by now? Any in-laws were preferable to her outlaw grandma. It had been a miserable Christmas.

And it wasn't as if Grandma had been grateful. She never was. Instead, she alternately coughed up phlegm and carped. "You've gained weight, I think. Look at me, skin and bone, but you, you've always been fleshy. On my food, on my pension, on my food stamps and Social Security, you got fleshy. Fleshy and conceited. Thought you were better than other people. Scuderstown not good enough for you. Nursing not good enough for you. Couldn't be a practical nurse. Had to get that useless R.N., then you don't even use it. Miss Actress. Got any jobs lately? Haven't seen *you* on TV or nothing. What happened to that show you was in?" It went on and on, unbearably, ceasing only when enough bourbon and Nyquil put her grandma out for the night. It had been almost more than Mary Jane could bear.

I should be grateful for being healthy, she told herself. I should be grateful that I'm smart. Not everyone is. For some reason, she thought of a high school classmate, Margery Heimann, who hadn't been able to name the capital of New York State, even though Scuderstown was only forty miles from Albany. That was dumb.

But, then, Margery was one of the prettiest girls in Scuderstown Regional High, and Mary Jane could imagine and did what it might be like to have all the boys follow you with their eyes and fight to sit next to you on the school bus.

That had always been part of Mary Jane's problem,

she figured: her imagination was too good. As a teenager she couldn't just sit there in the back of the gym at the pep rallies like the other lumpy farm girls, who seemed contented as cows. Mary Jane watched the cheerleaders, Margery Heimann among them, and could imagine what it would feel like to cavort in front of the crowd in those cute little skirts, and she was sure she would like the feeling. She also imagined, even then, how Lady Macbeth felt as she walked into the dark bedroom to commit murder, how Anna Karenina felt when she heard the train coming, and how Alice Adams felt when everyone ignored her at the dance. Oh, yes, even back then she could imagine *that* easily.

But *that*, she reminded herself wryly, didn't take very much imagination, since everyone at school had ignored Mary Jane. She had walked through the halls, a clumping ghost as far as all the boys and the popular girls were concerned. She was plain. Big nose. Beetle brow. Thick, lank hair. Thin lips. She decided then that there would be no easy way for her, no helping hand.

She'd have to do it herself. Boys wouldn't help her, her grandma wouldn't help her. She'd have to do it all herself.

And she had. Nursing school, on scholarship, to get out of Scuderstown. And then acting classes, and the almost hopeless round of agents, auditions, day jobs, cattle calls, small parts, and rejections. It had taken so many, many years to prove herself, but at last she'd had a hit, been recognized, been accepted, been paid to do the work she loved. And she'd even been loved by a man who was both brilliant and handsome. Yet somehow it seemed she was losing it all, that it was turning to elephant shit.

An icy wind blew down Broadway, forcing Mary Jane into a doorway, where she tried to get her breath and a moment's rest. Standing there watching people catching cabs, she once again asked herself that question, the one she knew the answer to, the same answer every time she asked. What am I doing this for? Give it up, the voice inside her, her grandmother's voice, said. You don't even have bus fare, your boots are leaking, your coat is five years old and coming apart at the seams, and you're walking through a snowstorm to get to your acting group, which doesn't pay anything but demands fifty hours a week from you. You must be crazy.

But she knew she wasn't. She was doing what she had always wanted to do. As a kid back in Scuderstown, acting had saved her life. She was in all the school plays, always in the character parts—Regina in *Little Foxes*, Mrs. Webb in *Our Town*—and she'd been good. Hell, she'd been better than good. She'd been *real*. It had showed her the real way out—out of Scuderstown and Elmira, out of her unbearable life. She knew her grandmother wouldn't pay for college or acting school, and she had no money, and no way of earning a living. She had been forced into nursing school, but she had hated it. It was acting she loved, had always loved. It was in acting that she lost herself, found friends, gained herself. But now, once again, she would be forced to nurse just to earn some money.

There had been a time, not so long ago, when she thought that the day jobs were finally over, that at last she'd be able to earn a living acting. She'd been cast in a little two-character play, *Jack and Jill and Compromise*. She played a dumpy, middle-aged loser sales clerk who does a one-night stand with a down-and-out salesman, and the two fall in love. It all took place with them naked, in bed, on an almost bare stage, and it had been what she had always dreamed of—the vehicle that moved her up into the modest success of a working actress. Then, wonder of wonders, it had been praised by the critics, it had moved to a big off-Broadway house, and for almost two years she'd played the role of Jill, the role she'd created. Best of all, it was sold to the movies, and one of the producers, Seymore LeVine, met with her, nearly promising her the role.

She'd dreamed, back in Scuderstown, but she'd never been daring enough to dream of the movies. So, despite her very real success, her grandmother, Margery, and all the rest of Scuderstown was unaware of her triumph. They were not off-Broadway denizens, to say the least. But a *movie*. Everyone would see her. It would be a

9

vindication, and, for the first time in her professional life, there would be some money in it. The play would bring her everything she'd ever wanted.

Because it had also been the play that had brought her Sam. He'd written and directed *Jack and Jill and Compromise*. He'd cast her and directed her and—miracle of miracles—he'd fallen in love with her. Then, almost six months ago, when Hollywood bought it, he'd negotiated to get to direct the movie. And he'd told her that she'd get to do Jill on the screen. It was a gritty, real, everyday tragic part. And it would be hers. Forever.

Sam had flown out to L.A. for the negotiations. He called her every night at first, then every other. Then, for almost a week, she didn't hear from him. She'd been nuts. At last, she got his note, "Forgive me. I did the best I could. I'll be back in four days."

Two days later, she read in *Variety* that Crystal Plenum was considering playing Jill. Mary Jane hadn't been able to get out of bed for twenty-four hours.

It was only her friend Neil Morelli who had gotten her through it. "They're assholes," he told her, while she lay, face down, silently weeping. "Listen, you remember what the Taoists say about this?"

"No. What?" she sniffled.

"Shit happens."

She sat up, wiped her nose. "Yeah," she agreed. "And Hindus say, 'This shit has happened before.' "

Neil smiled, his weasel face almost looking good. "Here, eat some of my rigatoni in pesto sauce. Crystal Plenum is a bimbo. She'll flop. Listen, *you* made Jill. *You* brought her to life. No one who ever saw you will forget that."

"Yeah. And no one will ever see me again." The sadness overwhelmed her, and she turned away to cry.

"Hey. You'll get another part. Remember what the critics said? 'Evanescent. Pathos without a scintilla of sentimentality.' Even fuckin' John Simon said you were transcendent, and he hates *everyone*. Fuck Hollywood. Fuck Sam. Fuck 'em all. Hey, while you're at it, how about fucking me?"

"Oh, Neil."

"All right. Maybe later, after you've wiped your nose again." He handed her a fresh Kleenex. "So, how about a blow job?" he asked as she took the tissue. She grimaced at him and blew her nose.

"There's a good girl. Still, the next time you *do* a blow job, I've got a little hint: don't use your nose, use your mouth, and don't blow, suck. Got it? It's guaranteed to improve your popularity. Might even get you a part."

Neil, her best friend, held her when she cried, made her laugh, fed her pasta. He was a great friend, but he'd been wrong. She hadn't gotten cast in anything since *Jack and Jill and Compromise*. Sam returned, shamefaced and guilty, and she tried to accept and understand. Of course he had no choice. Of course Hollywood wanted to cast the hottest woman in town, Crystal Plenum, in the part. And when Crystal Plenum accepted the role, Mary Jane tried not to resent Sam for rejoicing. For the last six months, she *had* tried to forgive him, while she watched his career surge forward. She *had* to forgive him, or she'd lose him. She loved him, and she knew he'd done the best he could. Hollywood simply didn't want fat, plain, almost middle-aged women on the screen. As far as she could figure, America didn't want them anywhere. Mary Jane shivered and pulled her old coat around her.

Sam had tried to make it up to her as best he could. He minimized the importance of the Hollywood trips for casting and preproduction prep, and he even began a new production—an off-Broadway revue that she'd be featured in. But he resented her depression.

She shivered again. The wind *was* getting colder. At Times Square, she walked west through the theater district. Ugly, tawdry, with old handbills peeling from older brick walls, dark, urine-reeking alleys—but the part of town she loved. It was Wednesday, matinee day, she realized as she noted all the late-afternoon activity under the theater marquees, the comely crowd preparing to face the storm and wend their ways home to Westchester and Long Island. Mary Jane looked up at the enormous sign over the Plymouth Theater announcing *Dead Stop*. She had auditioned for it. No dice. Now she thought with envy of all the happily employed actors sitting in the warmth of an after-show glow in their cozy dressing rooms.

Since *Jack and Jill* had closed, she had felt lost. And now she was afraid she might be losing Sam as well. He was all taken up with the movie, while she sank deeper and deeper into her misery. She watched him prepare for his trips to the coast, and she hated herself as she clung to him before he left and when he returned, as he would tonight.

Sam hated clinging. It was probably why he was meeting her at the rehearsal. A cling-reduction strategy. It would be the first rehearsal with Sam in weeks. He'd run the group for nearly four years. And with him out on the coast, they all felt lost. But he'd be back now, for a while, and she'd pull herself together. She'd pull herself together and not resent that he would soon be leaving her for months, and try not to feel that he was leaving her for good. He'd asked her to come, she reminded herself. Maybe I shouldn't have refused. The snow was turning to sleet. At least there would be no sleet out in L.A. No sleet and no work, she told herself.

At last, drenched, she crossed Eighth Avenue, passed the two black whores who stood shivering in a Burger King doorway, and came to the entrance of the parish house of the St. Malachy's Church. She pushed her way through the heavy wooden doors. Father Damien, the actors' priest, stood inside talking with a parishioner and turned a startled face to her.

"Mary Jane, you're soaking wet." The white-haired old man reached around her and helped her remove the snow-laden coat. He is always at hand to help an actor, she thought gratefully, and was moved by his concern. "What happened?"

"Father, don't ask. I'm an unemployed New York actress, and you're my guardian angel. That's all I know." Holding her wet, torn boots by the edges and throwing her old coat over her arm, she bumped open the door to the stairs with her wide behind and said, "They better have some hot coffee ready down there, Father, or there'll be blood on the walls."

2

Sam Shields unfolded his sweater and threw it down on the bed. His trip back from L.A. should have tired him out, but he felt full of energy. And flying MGM Grand was a nice way to travel: nothing but first-class seats, and no one but first-class people. The studio had picked up the tab, *and* sent him to the airport in a Rolls limo. That was the purest luxury—going top-drawer OPM—on other people's money. No more steerage for Sam Shields.

It was about time, too. Money—other people's or his own—was never a commodity Sam had much access to. Growing up on the North Shore of Long Island, in a tiny rented house that was always so damp that the wallpaper scrolled off the walls, where there was never enough money for proper clothes or a good cut of meat (but where there was always a bottle of Beefeater being poured by either his mother or his father), Sam had learned both what quality was and also how to do without it. Nice people wore Brooks Brothers, not suits from Robert Hall, so, if there wasn't money for a quality new blue blazer, he wore the old one until his arms had pushed so far below the sleeves that it looked as if he had rolled them up. His father, a failing advertising man, had once been a golden boy at Doyle Dane, back when that was *the* place for a clever Yalie to be. His mother had done her two years at Smith and then donned white gloves at Katie Gibbs. Both lanky and good-looking, he fair, she dark, they met at the office and married a month later.

What had it been like for them back in the fifties, when women wore hats and gloves, everyone drank Manhattans, and the city was a glistening pearl? Did they feel then the way he felt now, as if the world were opening up for him? He wondered if they had ever had a chance at the brass ring, and if they knew when, the exact moment,

13

they missed it. Because for the two of them, after the first
heady days of wine and roses, it was steerage all the way.
Copywriting was beneath Philip, but what could he do
that wasn't? He talked about writing, but he never did it,
and his wife never stopped resenting that. After a lot of
time and a lot of booze, Phil couldn't even write copy
anymore. And Sam's mother, that deb with a heart of
steel, must have realized that, despite her husband's ped-
igree and pretensions, she'd bet on the wrong horse.
Sam's parents reminded him of characters from a failed
Fitzgerald novel: those who lived at the edge of the beautiful social world but never got to the center. Nowhere
near it. And it was cold at the edge.

Sam hated Fitzgerald novels.

His parents had taught him to feel superior to everyone
to whom he didn't feel inferior; to look down on Jews, on
Italians, and especially on the Irish. Blacks weren't even
in the picture. He was taught to revere the Whitneys (his
father's distant relations), the Harrimans, the Vander-
bilts, the Roosevelts, and all their cousins, aunts, in-laws,
and dependents. And, as if he were the monied scion of
a great family, he was sent to Deerfield and Yale (both on
scholarship), his father's alma maters. Then he, too, had
toiled in obscurity, with the fear that he would fail as his
father had failed.

Now that had all changed. He smiled as he reached
into the suitcase and lifted out his crumpled jacket. It
was an old black linen one—he always wore black—and
much too summery for New York in winter. But it had
worked in L.A. *Everything* had worked in L.A. He and
April had clicked, the rewrites were coming along nicely,
and it looked as if they might go into production as early
as May. If they were lucky with casting, it could happen.

Ah, casting. There was the rub. *Jack and Jill* was a
gritty play, a slice of life. He'd seen it as *film noir*. Well,
he still did. Not that it didn't have humor, pathos, the
whole nine yards. But it was a dark story. A true story.
And aren't all true stories dark?

Well, his was. Long Island boy moves to big city,
starves, lives for the theater, writes good plays, is ignored, almost gives up, writes one more, makes good.

14

Sam shrugged, tired of unpacking, and dumped the rest of his dirty clothes onto a heap in the corner. Normally he'd leave the laundry at Mary Jane's. But not as things stood right now.

For the last two years, they'd lived together at her place most of the time, but Sam had been careful to keep his loft on East Nineteenth Street. It was important to him to have his own space to retreat to, and just as important for Mary Jane to know. It kept their boundaries clear. They were lovers, but he'd never made it a secret that he kept his options open.

He went to the other side of the loft and hit the flashing button of his answering machine. It whirred, then beeped, then clicked, and then Mary Jane's voice filled the room. "Not back yet? I hope your flight was okay. I've got to go down to Unemployment. In this weather! Call when you get in. I leave at eleven-thirty." The machine beeped. Sam looked at his watch. Twelve-forty-five. He'd missed her. Just as well. He shook his head. She sounded fine, but still made him uncomfortable. Guilty.

Because there *was* the dark side. And it was Mary Jane. Not that she was some *femme fatale*. Sam had to smile. Oh, he'd had more than his share of those: neurotic, haunted, narcissistic actresses who tortured him. He'd married Shayna when he was only twenty-three and let her torture him for four years. Then he'd been a wild man, but after a year or so of the bar scene he'd found Nora, to drive him equally crazy. Who was more beautiful, Shayna or Nora? Who was more selfish? Impossible to call. After Nora there'd been a string of lithe, perfect women, all with dancer's bodies, wonderful breasts, lovely lips, and tender, lying eyes. They'd either bored him or driven him crazy. Those were the two modes he'd known.

Until Mary Jane. At thirty-six, he'd just been beginning to think that he might be a failure, and his last play expressed that. He *was* Jack: desperate and afraid. Afraid of another soured affair, afraid of another big break that went nowhere, afraid that if this play went down the toilet he wouldn't have another in him. And in walked Mary

Jane. Talented. Oh, more than talented. She took the part; hell, she fuckin' *owned* the part of Jill. She made it live. Onstage, he couldn't take his eyes off her. Working with her was so exciting. There wasn't a nuance that escaped her. And she knew her craft. She could hit the emotional peak, then nail a gag with perfect timing, night after night. She always made it look new, fresh.

Offstage, of course, she was nothing to look at. He had never taken her down to meet his judgmental parents. He imagined the mother's eyes giving Mary Jane the once-over. Half Irish, half Jewish, and the worst of each. Sam could imagine his mother's grimace, followed by the tight smile that would never reach her eyes. Mary Jane would not pass muster.

But he found that she was someone to talk to. Unlike the beauties, she listened, she responded, she was warm, loving, and always honest. Sam groaned aloud. Yes, she was honest, and he valued honesty and truth, although he couldn't seem to manage much of either one lately. Jesus Christ, why was life like this? It was some kind of cosmic practical joke: you can't get what you want without sticking it to someone else.

Well, once upon a time, three years ago, Mary Jane *was* what he wanted. He had to keep reminding himself of that. Oh, it might have started as a pity fuck, but she blew him away. She was hot, and right there. She'd bailed him out with her warmth and her performance, and it was so touching to see how much she obviously loved him. He had been moved by her passion, and her gratitude, and when he compared it to the coolness and self-interest of Shayna and Nora and all those pretty, difficult girls that came before, he felt happy for the first time.

Mary Jane asked for nothing, and she gave him everything. If there was an imbalance in that, he had felt too comfortable to question it. Not that he hadn't had a few relapses. He'd slept with a few cuties, but it was pleasant, even powerful, to go back to Mary Jane. It let him off the hook with them. And he had promised her nothing. Absolutely nothing. He'd always been clear about that. Still, she grew on him. It became natural to stay at her house: it was comfortable there, with a soup always cooking on the back burner, and his laundry sorted and folded and even ironed. He'd had a chance to regroup, to lick his wounds. It was like going back to the womb. Her big body was motherly. And she believed in him the way his own thin, beautiful, wasted bitch of a mother never had. Mary Jane's belief and talent sustained him. They worked together all day, intense in the *Jack and Jill* rehearsals, and then they comforted one another at night. She might be the first and only woman that he'd ever really loved. He'd even been tempted to ask her to marry him. Not that he was the marrying kind.

She'd brought him luck. When the play hit, it was her performance that got raves, that drew in the crowds. They moved it to a larger theater, but were still Standing Room Only. He knew she was a cinch for the Obie. She believed *he'd* get one, or maybe two. They had: Best Actress, Best Play, Best Director.

So, instead of slitting his throat before he was forty, as he'd planned, he was flying out to the coast and making a movie. He'd held out for getting to direct it. His agent was sick about it: she didn't like to work for her money, but in this case she'd had to. No sale of *Jack and Jill* unless he, Sam Shields, got to direct. And, finally, Hollywood had gone for it.

But he wasn't going to get to enjoy the triumph. No. Because Hollywood was definitely not going to risk sixteen million dollars on a plain, fat, unknown actress for the lead, even if the role called for one, even if it was, as they said, "a small film." It was a part of the deal from the get-go. Crystal Plenum was interested. If she signed, it was a guaranteed money-maker. So he got to be the bad guy, to break the news to Mary Jane. Try being happy looking at spaniel eyes that followed you everywhere, spaniel eyes that said, "It's all right to kick me. I'm used to it."

He knew that she must resent the shit out of him, but she'd never say so. It was the one dishonesty she'd ever tried. She had simply accepted. And her voice on the taped message seemed fine, normal. But it didn't play. Jesus, how it didn't play. Thank God he'd never proposed.

So, here he was, sorting his own laundry in his own dusty apartment. Because he couldn't face those spaniel eyes. She hadn't landed anything else since *Jack and Jill* closed. Christ! That, at least, wasn't *his* fault. He was coming to believe that she *wanted* to be a victim. And that she was punishing him by not allowing him to enjoy his success.

The message machine beeped again. "Hi, Sam. It's Bethanie. I wondered if we could get together again." The breathy voice paused; then she giggled. "I mean I'd like to. I'll be home all day before rehearsal tonight. Bye."

Shit. The troupe had rehearsal scheduled. He had almost forgotten. Jesus, after the sun and studios of Los Angeles, he wasn't sure he could handle St. Malachy's basement tonight. And, to be honest, the revue he was throwing together, though a crowd pleaser, was really just a bone. The machine beeped again.

"This is Sy Ortis of Early Artists calling Mr. Shields. Please call our Los Angeles office at 555-0111." Sam raised his brows. Sy Ortis *himself* had called? Wait until my agent hears this: that I'm being called by the biggest power broker in L.A.! Sam thought of the old Industry joke: A writer comes home to find the police and the fire department at his house. A detective greets him with the news that his agent has gone berserk, come to his house, raped his wife, killed his kids, and burned the place down. The writer looks stunned. "My agent came to my house?" he asks.

Well, Sy Ortis hadn't quite come to his house, but he *had* made the call himself, not delegated it to some effeminate assistant. Sam played the message again, just to be sure. God, he thought, I really am hot. Well, he was happy with his representation, but he would call Sy back. He scribbled down the number.

There was one more message. "Hi, big boy. And I'm talking to your dick when I say that. Hope the flight was fine. Give me a call." Sam smiled. April Irons was so secure she didn't bother to say who it was. He'd better erase this tape. Not that Mary Jane came to his place often, but just in case.

The thought of her once again wiped the smile from his face. Because, despite April, despite the others, he did love M.J. He hoped she would decide to come to L.A., though he was ashamed of her. But he also knew that he needed her, now more than ever. Despite the heat, despite the shot he had at the big time, despite the buzz, or maybe because of it all, he was afraid. Afraid he'd lose his shot at the brass ring. Bungle it, and wind up living his life out in obscurity. Ah, well, he'd see M.J. tonight. That would be soon enough. And in the meantime, perhaps he *would* pay a visit to Bethanie.

3

Mary Jane went down the stairs to the cavernous church basement that, for the last fourteen years, had been used as a rehearsal hall and showcase theater. Thank God for the warmth, she thought, walked into the large room, and stood for a moment, taking in the delicious sounds of actors gathered for a production.

The vast room was low-ceilinged, with pillars breaking the big space into several areas. The walls were painted church-basement green, the floor a gray vinyl tile. Folding chairs of every design, color, and condition lined the perimeters of the room. At the far end was a small raised stage. A shabby deep-red curtain hung open, displaying the narrow backstage space and the klieg lights. Several people were already huddled in a small circle, running lines. Two women were adjusting the height of the lights, although the show was far from ready for lighting. Mary Jane spotted a table off to the side which held a big pot of coffee and several open boxes of supermarket cakes and chocolate-chip cookies. Thank God! Empty carbohydrates and caffeine!

Sipping from a chipped mug, chewing one cookie and clutching another, she finally smiled. Mary Jane loved the animation, the excitement, whenever actors gathered in a room. Despite all her years in the New York theater scene, she never took it for granted. An actor could *never* afford to take the opportunity to work for granted, even if it was, here, unpaid. Because this ensemble group was *good.* Sam ran it, wrote for it, directed it. After he'd come back from L.A. the first time, almost seven months ago, he'd promised everyone that his next trip to California was only temporary, and that he'd come up with the idea for this revue. After directing *Jack and Jill,* he'd be back. Sam could never be happy in L.A., the town of false happy endings. His work was too real, too gritty, too involved with the realities of living life in good faith. The troupe had already had a few minor successes, along with the major one of *Jack and Jill.* If the rest of the actors felt any resentment or envy of Sam, they lived with it. Because you never knew what casting agent or director might turn up in the audience.

She sipped the coffee again and felt herself thawing out. Everyone here is just like me, Mary Jane thought. She had known some of these people for almost a dozen years, and to her they were family. We're all broke or just hanging on, all more or less talented, and we're all determined to make it. Some would look and see a roomful of actors, but it was also a roomful of waiters, cab drivers, speech coaches, word processors, and bartenders. Everyone with a day job. What we do for love of the theater, she sighed.

"Mary Jane." She turned to see Bethanie Lake, the newest member of the ensemble, walking across the floor with a fresh pot of coffee. The girl glowed. Mary Jane watched the young woman as she swayed, balancing the coffee. Though she wasn't very good, she *was* very pretty. Mary Jane never would have voted her into the group, but Sam had lobbied for her. And Mary Jane respected his judgment.

Bethanie was so pretty, M.J. had to work hard at not resenting her. She was the type her grandmother had admired, while the old woman ridiculed M.J.'s own looks. Mary Jane had never forgotten her grandmother's childrearing: the poor food, the humiliation of the cheap, dirty clothes, the remarks and the scorn she got from Grandma and the other girls at school. But worst of all had been her own awareness that her grandmother had been right—cruel, but right—when she called her fat and ugly and a ridiculous dreamer.

She remembered sneaking into the dark, mildewed bathroom of the farmhouse to check on her reflection, hoping for some contradiction of her fears. She would turn on the light, a single sixty-watt bulb that extended from the wall over the bathroom mirror without benefit of a shade. She would open the shallow drawer in the chipped Formica vanity beside the sink and scrabble amidst the old hair clips, broken scissors, and half-used tubes of ointments, looking for the hand mirror. It had been a double-sided one, with a cracked magnifying glass on the back, two ancient rubber bands holding it together. Clasping it in her right hand, Mary Jane had to open the medicine cabinet so that it stood out from the wall, its age-speckled mirror facing the toilet. Then Mary Jane would climb up onto the commode seat and crouch there. It was the only way she could see her profile, and, awful as it was, it mesmerized her.

Each time, before she looked, she had paused for a moment, closed her eyes, and whispered one last prayer. Her heart always pounded, and her palms were always moist. Then, each time, she held the mirror in her left hand, angling it so that she could just manage to peer into it and see her profile reflected back at her in the larger, medicine-cabinet mirror. And each time her heart sank.

Her nose jutted out in a high arch from her forehead, her thick eyebrows almost meeting there. Then the nose flared out into a fleshy blob over her thin lips. Her chin, what there was of it, receded into her neck. Her cheeks were too full, formless chipmunk pouches. Except chipmunks were cute, she had thought. Chipmunks were attractive. Her face was unbalanced, horrible.

Each time that she crouched there and stared at her reflection, hot tears had filmed her eyes, as they did now. And each time she had, in the end, turned back to the mirror to face her enemy. Her eyes, still teary, big and brown, had stared at her from under the beetle brows. Windows to the soul, she'd thought. What good did it do her to have pretty brown eyes? So she could see how ugly she was? Nice joke, God.

At thirteen, Mary Jane Moran had known a few things. She had known that she was smarter than most of the kids in school. That wasn't hard in a place like Scuderstown, New York. Let's face it, she had been smarter than most of the teachers, too. But she hadn't let it show if she could help it. People didn't like you if you were smarter than they were. Her grandma had always called her "Miss Smartypants," and made it sound not like a baby word, but like a real insult. Mary Jane also had known that her grandma didn't love her. And she'd known that she was ugly, and probably would stay so. So, then, nobody would love her. Ever.

Now pretty Bethanie refilled Mary Jane's mug. What skin! She looked as if she'd just had sex! "Oh, bless you, Bethanie. How could you tell I needed it?" Mary Jane sipped the hot liquid and moaned with relief while Beth helped her arrange her wet garments on a chair behind her.

"So. Tell me. How was Unemployment?"

Mary Jane paused for a moment. Had she mentioned to Bethanie that today was her reporting day? She didn't think so. How had she known? Well, it wasn't important. Mary Jane shrugged.

"Pretty much as I expected, Beth. It's the end of my twenty-six weeks. The well's going dry."

"I'm sorry, Mary Jane. Is there anything I can do to help?"

She was very sweet, Mary Jane knew. Pretty, not too talented, but very sweet. Mary Jane had seen a thousand of them. They all had thin thighs and cute names. Bethanie was newly arrived in town, and filled with ambition and awe. Too bad that, despite Bethanie's face and body, she'd never make it. In New York you had to be able to read before you could act. But, hey, Mary Jane thought, you never can tell. There's always television.

"You can't help any more than you just did. Thanks for the coffee." Looking around the noisy room, she asked, "Is Sam here yet?"

"Yes, we've been here about an hour. Oh, we've come

up with a wonderful scene for you and me to do together."

We? Mary Jane thought, and sighed. Another starry-eyed actress in love with her director. Mary Jane had gotten used to it. She looked around for Sam, but he wasn't anywhere among the bustle that she could see. "That's great, Bethanie, I'd love to work with you. What kind of thing is it?"

"Well, it's sort of a spoof on a magic act. It could be good." Bethanie was all enthusiasm. "You know, I've wanted to work with you since I first joined the company. You're so, I don't know, so *professional.* I know I've learned a lot from you already, just watching you. I feel the older, you know, the more *experienced* actresses have so much to offer, like role models."

Great. Thirty-four years old, never been in a Broadway production, and I'm referred to as a "role model." Why doesn't she just roll out the wheelchair? That's it, Mary Jane thought. Today qualifies as the worst day of the year and it's only January. Stifling a groan, she turned as she heard Sam's voice raised over the buzz in the room. Just hearing him warmed her better than the coffee had.

"Okay, everybody, let's settle down. We have a show to do."

Mary Jane moved with the others to the circle of chairs in the center of the space, glad that her conversation with the deadly Bethanie had been interrupted. She looked over to Sam and smiled, and he nodded. She wasn't surprised. He had never been demonstrative in public. Well, he'd say hello later, at home, in bed. Now the work of improvisation, rehearsal, scripting, and more rehearsal would start up again. Together, this group of ragtags would create a polished theatrical work, a showcase for all their talents. They were working on an idea of Sam's —to do a spoof of a variety show as in the days of television, but to show the backstage story as well. The working title was *Snow Business.*

Mary Jane loved the idea. But, of course, that was why she loved Sam. He was brilliant. Funny, brilliant, and hers. So what if every now and then he was tempted by the latest little item? Sam had insisted, from day one, that theirs would be an open relationship. Mary Jane simply closed her eyes to his dalliances. Not that there had been any that she was *certain* of. As she took a seat, Mary Jane looked across the room at Sam, caught his eye again, and winked, but he didn't wink back. Well, he was being the serious director again, she thought. Remember, he comes home with *me*, not with any of *them*, she reminded herself for the thousandth time.

She loved watching him in the theater setting, loved drinking him in without his noticing. Tall and lanky, he moved with grace, like a dancer, Mary Jane thought. His usually pale skin was tanned from the California trip, and the two-day growth of beard and the black turtleneck sweater he favored reminded her, as always, of some Italian film star of the fifties. His long, silky black pony tail offset his slightly receding hairline. He was very aware of his hairline, and she sometimes caught him measuring it in the mirror. It may bother him, but not me, she thought.

He'd be leaving for L.A. soon. What will I do then? she asked herself. Though she'd forgiven him for not being able to cast her in the film, Mary Jane wasn't sure that she could bear to watch stoically while *Jack and Jill and Compromise* was made without her, and she doubted she'd get any work on her own in L.A.

"Let's face it," she'd said to Sam, "I'm not the L.A. type."

"That's *why* you'll get work," he insisted. "Character parts. I can almost guarantee it. You're so fucking talented, even the morons out there will see it."

"Seymore LeVine didn't see it," she reminded him.

"Oh, Seymore's just a producer. He's an asshole."

"It's my impression that it's the assholes who do the casting," Mary Jane had said dryly.

Sam had been more than disappointed; he'd seemed angry that she wouldn't say she'd come—angry and *guilty*, a lethal mix—so maybe she shouldn't risk the long separation. After all, Crystal Plenum had a reputation. And, to be honest, with Sam gone, Mary Jane had nothing going for her here. Worst of all, she wasn't sure she could bear being without Sam for months. He had made her life worth living.

Sam was handed a note by one of the troupe. He looked up, and that was all he needed to silence the room. "First an announcement," he said. "This Saturday's dinner will be at Chuck Darrow and Molly Closter's place, in the East Village, Sixth Street, past Avenue A. As usual, the hosts will provide the pasta, everyone else brings the wine, bread, and dessert." The tight circle turned to the couple and clapped lightly. Mary Jane almost always found the Saturday Movable Feast to be warm and homey. And Molly was her closest girlfriend. I'd hate to leave this. This *is* my family, she told herself, as she looked around at the friendly, bantering crowd, caught Molly's eye, and smiled. Then Mary Jane's gaze fell on Bethanie, but *her* huge gray eyes were staring at Sam, waiting for his next word. Has he slept with her? The thought was a little flicker of poison, like a serpent's tongue.

But she didn't want to think about that. She and Sam did have a strict agreement that he would never sleep with any of the women she knew, so even if he did sleep around it wouldn't seem real to her. She'd only heard of his infidelities by innuendo. One "friend" or another mentioned vague things from time to time. But she'd never discussed it with Sam.

And why should she? she thought. She wasn't 100-percent sure, and, anyhow, he loved *her*. That much she knew. He had nurtured her acting craft, encouraging her for almost three years. And still was. If it had hurt her when he insisted she'd get character work in L.A., it had also buoyed her. She'd never be an ingenue, but he still believed in her.

Still, what was that in Bethanie's gaze?

I've got to stop this, Mary Jane said to herself firmly, letting Sam's voice bring her back to the business at hand. Anyway, if anything was up in that department, her pal Molly Closter would let her know.

"We have four scenes in front of the curtain put together so far for the revue, and six backstage scenes," Sam began telling the now attentive group. "We still need a few more variety-act skits to round out the show. I have an idea myself, but I would like to hear some of yours."

Before anyone could answer, the door from the stairs crashed open and Neil Morelli came bounding in. "I got it! I got it!" he screamed.

The group rose as one and ran to him, everyone hugging and talking at the same time. Neil Morelli, Mary Jane's best friend, obviously had gotten the TV pilot he had read for last month! Another one of us has made it, thought Mary Jane as she ran to him along with the others. Neil might be a little crazy, but he had a good heart. He was one of the cleverest comedians she had ever known. And she had known many—a few in the biblical sense.

The congratulations bubbled on. Taking her turn, Mary Jane threw her arms around Neil's skinny neck and said. "Oh, Jughead, I couldn't be happier if it happened to me. You deserve it."

Neil managed to scoop her up and gave her a little twirl. "Thanks for all the rehearsal time you gave me," he said. "How 'bout a French kiss?" He planted a loud wet smack on each of her cheeks. The crowd laughed; he bowed, then turned back to her. "You're next, you know."

Mary Jane smiled wanly at this. In all her years of trying to get jobs as an actress in New York, every time someone else made it, he or she always said the same thing to her: "You're next." But she never was. She thought that *Jack and Jill* had been her shot, but the phone wasn't ringing off the hook.

Sam, the only one who hadn't crossed the floor to Neil, did so now. "Good luck," he said, extending his hand. Neil took it—reluctantly, it seemed to Mary Jane. They weren't great friends, but had always tolerated one another, if only for her sake. Sam smiled at Neil, his eyes cold. "We're all very happy for you, Neil. Now, if no one objects, let's get back to work. I have an idea for a short skit for the show. A magic routine."

Everyone groaned. Magic! Mary Jane thought. Well, I guess it could be worse. It could be a mime act.

"Hey, this is a democracy. I'll let you all judge. Then I'll decide." Everyone laughed. "Mary Jane, Beth, Neil. Front and center. I'm going to walk you through it."

Sam outlined the blocking of the skit to each of them. Neil was the magician; Beth and Mary Jane were to play the obligatory assistants. Neil, always ready to take center stage, gave up his moment of glory and, stripping out of his coat, did the walk-through, not knowing where it was going. As Sam directed, Neil placed Mary Jane in the imaginary box and said "Ta-da." Mary Jane did the classic one-arm-in-the-air, one-on-the-hip gesture of the magician's assistant. She got a laugh. Sam grinned at her. At the cue, Neil threw a sheet over the box. Then, ad-libbing, Neil went into an abracadabra spiel, playing to the crowd. Selling it. Meanwhile, Sam grabbed Mary Jane's hand, pulling her from behind the sheet. Without urging, Bethanie quickly took her place.

Then, with a big flourish, Neil pulled off the fabric. Bethanie perfectly aped Mary Jane's ta-da movements. The members of the troupe sat in silence for a moment, then erupted into laughter. At the sidelines, Mary Jane stood still. She wasn't certain what had happened. But fear flickered somewhere around her stomach. What was the joke? Then someone said it out loud. "I get it. 'Before' and 'After.' "

Mary Jane stood as if rooted to the spot, stunned by the realization. Her cheeks reddened with humiliation; tears stung her eyes. She was afraid to look at Sam, or anyone. How could he? she thought. Why? Why? Sure, she was a trouper about her looks. The part of Jill was that of an unattractive woman. Everyone knew it. She herself made self-deprecating jokes. But this was different. He knew how she really felt. Was that cheap joke worth her pain? Sam couldn't be so insensitive as to think that this wouldn't hurt.

She forced herself to scan the throng. They're my friends, she thought, my family. And they're laughing at me.

But not everyone was laughing. Molly Closter was looking at her with pity. And now so was Bethanie, who blushed and turned away. Mary Jane also felt a hot flush of shame. Pity felt worse than ridicule.

Then Neil Morelli held up his hands and called out Sam's name. The group's reaction calmed. Sam looked over at him as the group followed suit.

"I don't get it, Sam," Neil said. "I mean, what's so funny?"

Sam opened his mouth, but before he could explain, Neil interrupted. Mary Jane could see he wasn't having any of it. And he was starting a roll. Oh, no, Neil, she thought. Let it go. Don't be a hero for me. Just let me sit down, creep away.

"A transformation? Short, dark Mary Jane turns into tall, blonde Bethanie? Jeez, it's politically incorrect, but, even worse, I don't think it's very funny. I mean, it's been done. Wait a minute, Sam. I got a better idea. Let's change the scene just slightly, so it's not such a cliché. I think we can get a better laugh. A role switch. A *woman* magician, Sam. And *you* go in the box. She says 'Ta-da,' you disappear, and, in *your* place, Rick here pops out."

Mary Jane, like all the others, looked over at one of the newer troupe members. Rick, the kid with a full head of golden curls and a body sculpted to perfection. Mary Jane saw Rick dip his head down a bit, then shrug. Some of the group laughed, and Molly Closter and another woman clapped.

Sam looked coldly at Neil, then smiled. Despite her shame, Mary Jane could see Sam was raging behind his pasted-on smile. Everyone watched Neil as he walked casually across the room and took his coat from the back of a chair. "Come on, Mary Jane," he said, as he began to put it on.

Mutely, she shook her head. That would make this all worse. She'd been waiting for Sam to come back from L.A. for two long weeks. She had so much to discuss with him tonight. And she wanted him to hold her, to be with her. Where would she go if she left Sam and her family? If she took this too hard, if she let them see her shame, she could never come back. Now Neil was pushing her into a corner. She backed away and shook her head again.

"Well, all right, then," Neil sighed. "But I'm out of here for good." As he reached the door to the stairs, he turned and spoke only to her.

"I meant it, Mary Jane. You are by far the most talented actress I've ever met. You *are* next," he said, and closed the door behind him.

4

In the search for an obscurity capital of the world, Lamson, Texas, would be a major contender. Grim and seemingly endless, Interstate 10 stretches from El Paso to San Antonio and has got to be one of the most depressing, dismal drives in the whole United States. Each dot on the map is an excuse for a town more dusty, faded, and dead than the one before. I, Laura Richie, know that, because I had to stop at so many of them, doing this research. But Lamson doesn't even rate a dot on the map. And in Lamson, the most obscure homes were in the trailer park beside the highway.

Sharleen Smith jumped off the dented yellow school bus and began to walk quickly along the dusty highway. She kicked small stones ahead of her with the toes of her Keds, puffing the dry dirt in low clouds around her feet. She turned off the main road and away from the other students, down the littered side street, toward the haphazard collection of decrepit trailers at the end, pulling at the red ribbon holding her pony tail as she went. She shook out her long, white-blond hair, running her fingers through the loosened mass.

The groan she usually felt in the back of her throat, the groan she usually let out as she neared the tin box of a trailer she shared with her brother and father, was replaced today by a low hum of pleasure. Today nothing could bother her. Not even Sueanne Skaggs, who'd come to school on Monday in a new T-shirt. It had Sharleen's picture on it and a line below it that said, "Just say no."

Sueanne had given one to all the boys on the football team. But Boyd, the captain and Sueanne's ex-steady, *he* didn't wear *his*. And none of the team would dare to if he didn't.

Sharleen couldn't quite figure out why Sueanne and all the girls hated her. Of course, she was poor, and she knew she was ignorant. Maybe even stupid. But she was really pretty. At least she *thought* that she must be. Momma had always told her she was. But then Momma had left a long time ago.

If she was still pretty, the girls didn't seem to like her for it. Maybe it was her clothes. She tried to dress like the others, but she and Dean didn't have much, and that was a fact. Still, her red sweatshirt was clean, and her hair ribbon was pressed, and her jeans didn't have no more holes in 'em than the other girls'. But it seemed like they *bought* their jeans with holes, while hers came naturally. That made all the difference, she reckoned. Sharleen winced for a moment. Even with the thought of Boyd glowin' in the back of her mind, it didn't feel good, knowing the other girls hated her. But the boys sure didn't.

Sharleen skirted the trailer next door, ready for the snarling dog on a chain, remembering, too, when the pit bull used to run loose. Six years the dog had known her, but it still reacted with fury when she approached. Only her brother, Dean, could quiet the beast down. Well, Dean could make any animal love him. "Shut up, Wally," she told the snarling dog, feeling sorry for the creature. She knew what it felt like to be trapped and beaten. Poor Wally; its owner, a nasty biker, had never dignified the animal with a name. Only she and Dean called the dog Wally.

"Oh, shoot." Her father's aged pickup truck stuck out from behind the end of the lot. The angle at which it was parked and the door left open told her that he was not only home but also drunk. She sighed. Nothing ever changed in Lamson, Texas. She paused for a moment, right there in the dusty road, and took out the Bible her momma had left her. She opened it blindly, then let her eye fall on the page. It was in Psalms, the prettiest part of the Old Testament. It was Psalm 21, and she read it through. All right, she told herself, then went to the door of the trailer and opened it quietly, not wanting to wake him if he was passed out. "Please, oh, Lord, let him sleep," she prayed. She didn't want tonight to be ruined.

His smell hit her as she stepped inside, a rank mixture of body odor and beer. She could make sure he had fresh-washed clothes, but she couldn't make him change them often or take a shower. Luckily, though, there wasn't a sound in the trailer. She realized he must be in a stupor, because she also smelled the overlay of cheap bourbon he drank only when he was into a real bad bender.

She turned on the light in the cramped living room where she slept. She sighed with relief to see that her father had made it to his own room in the back and by-passed the convertible sofa bed.

Sharleen welcomed this time alone. Dean worked over at the feed-and-grain store after school let out. Tugging off her sneakers without untying them, she stepped out of the worn jeans and pulled the bright sweatshirt over her head in a single motion. Taking a towel from one of the hooks she used as a closet, she tiptoed toward the bathroom for her few luxurious moments of privacy. But before going in, she pressed her ear against the thin door of the room her father slept in, to confirm what she knew. Yep. His snores rattled like a snake in a bucket.

She closed the equally flimsy door to the tiny bathroom, and once again bemoaned the broken lock. Sharleen had no privacy. Though Dean was supposed to share the bedroom with their father, he most often wound up sleeping on the sofa with Sharleen. Not that she minded. She would feel safer now if Dean were home, knowing that *he* would keep an eye on her father while she showered. Still, Dean in his own quiet way demanded a lot of attention. Perhaps it was better like this. She reached into the cramped bathroom and turned on the water, hoping that there was some. Lamson Trailer Park's well occasionally went dry, or the pump broke. When she felt the first sting of the stream, she adjusted the temperature, pulled the cheap plastic curtain on the shower stall aside, and stepped in.

She let the water fall on her head and down her sleek hair to her shoulders. Her hair turned darker as the water ran down it to her breasts. Her nipples hardened as the water touched them. She turned slowly with her eyes closed. The water played at the small of her back, her buttocks, down her long, tapered legs to her feet. She felt good. *Well, I might not be smart or rich or anyone important, but thank the Lord I'm pretty.* Bein' pretty made Boyd like her. She was just like Momma, who had been pretty. Men liked Momma. All men except her daddy.

Sharleen could still picture Momma. She didn't have a photo of her or nothin', but she remembered her real well. Thinkin' of those times made her sad. She could still remember hiding with Dean in the red dust under the trailer, listening to her daddy and her momma above, hearing Momma being beaten. It had been a familiar sound, an awful sight, terrifying, but in a way even more terrible to think about. Sharleen still remembered the last time. Momma had come back from the laundry where she worked, still in her pink uniform, her hair batted up under the hairnet, tiny tendrils twisted at her temples, limp from the heat. Old tennis sneakers were on her feet, small holes at each pinky toe, worn by the three-mile walk each way between the laundry and the trailer. Down by her side she carried a plastic bag, holding the white shoes she polished each morning. She looked real tired, but when Dean showed her the tiny pup he'd found that day, she'd smiled.

Until Daddy had come home.

Sharleen and Dean had so often hidden from their dad, breathing into each other's ears, blocking out the sounds of the screams. The gentle hum of their breaths had always calmed her. She hummed now. She closed her eyes, letting the water run over her. It was almost as comforting as Dean's hand, the comforting rhythm he used as he stroked the back of her head, their bodies pushed tightly against each other. That day, the day of the puppy, had been real bad. She thought of how they rocked in rhythm with their breaths. The memory of the warmth of his body against hers, the fear that was a knot in her throat, now made her moan softly. His hand always went to her secret place and held it as she moved against him. The rocking caused them both to utter long slow moans. The sounds from the rest of the trailer, the fighting and the screams, would seem far away.

They spent that night in the dirt under the trailer, while the screaming continued, followed by silence. Somehow, the silence was worse, and they trembled until they finally slept.

Sharleen remembered their last morning together. Momma had come to find them. "Sharleen, Dean. Are you there, kids?" Her voice was a whisper. Sharleen knew without being told that they were not to wake their father.

"We're here, Momma. Dean, come on, let's get up."

Dean had rolled over and crawled out from under the trailer. Sharleen followed, brushing the dust off her as she started up the steps. Momma stopped just inside the door, and Sharleen saw her in the light. One side of her face was swollen and red. Her right eye was black and blue and puffy. The other was swollen shut. Dean froze, and Sharleen tapped his shoulder gently. Nothing else she could do.

"Go wash up, Dean, but be quiet," she said. "Don't wake him."

When Dean went into the bathroom, Sharleen went to Momma and put a hand up to her face. Her mother winced and drew back. Sharleen had never seen her hurt so bad.

"Momma, it's bad," she said gently, as if breaking news to her mother. "You're hurt *real* bad this time, Momma."

"I know, honey. It feels real bad this time."

"We gotta go to the hospital, Momma."

"No, honey. We'll just ask Jesus to take care of me and the puppy." Momma took out a shoe box, the puppy lying twisted inside it. Sharleen didn't have to ask. Momma knelt, and so did Sharleen, who first got her mother the little Bible. Then Dean joined them. Sharleen even now remembered how he looked at the box and how his eyes got big, so very big.

33

"Is it sleepin'?" he asked.

"No, Dean. She's in heaven now, with Jesus. She's Jesus' puppy now." Dean knelt beside them, and their mother whispered some words.

After breakfast, only Frosted Flakes and water 'cause there was no milk, Momma walked Sharleen and Dean to the school bus. Sharleen saw that her mother had put on her one good dress. It was bright blue with a white collar.

And she was carrying a cardboard suitcase. Sharleen knew then that her life was about to change, but couldn't imagine it getting worse. As Dean moped alone up ahead, their momma spoke real serious to Sharleen. It made Sharleen feel like a grown-up.

"Sharleen, honey, Momma's got to go away for a while. I can't take you two with me, but I'll come back for both of you as soon as I get a job and a place for us to live. You know you wasn't my natural-born daughter, but I love you like my own. Dean is my blood, but I got to leave him, too. He's only your half-brother, but I want you to love him like a true sister. I've only been your stepmomma, but I love you like flesh." She handed Sharleen the little Bible. "Keep this now, till I come back. No, honey, don't cry. You got to be strong. Jesus is going to watch over you. I promise you that. You talk to the Lord, and he'll take care of you while I'm gone." She paused, wincing at the pain in her face. "I want you to promise to take care of Dean. He ain't as smart as you."

Sharleen listened in silence, knowing that there was nothing she could say. She'd known all along that her momma could not live through any more beatings. Her momma had no choice. Sharleen was glad she was getting away. And, being such a good girl, she didn't stop to think that there would be no one for her now. No one except Jesus, who she couldn't see, and Dean, who she had to take care of.

"Don't say nothin' to Dean until tonight. I don't want no fuss," Momma said.

Sharleen nodded, and she and Dean got on the school bus. She turned around in the rear seat to look back at her mother. The frail woman raised her hand and waved twice, then turned very quickly and walked along the main road in the opposite direction, toward the Trailways bus stop near town. Sharleen had turned forward in her seat after she lost sight of her mother. She wouldn't cry. She just wouldn't. Because, once she started, she thought, maybe she'd never stop. She had bit her lip, then turned to her brother. "Dean, I'm going to take care of you now," she told him. He said nothing for a while, then just leaned his head against her shoulder and closed his eyes.

"It was a real good puppy," was all he said.

Sharleen remembered it all, standing there under the thin trickle of the shower. She hadn't heard anything, lost in the memory of her momma and the sensation of the falling water. But suddenly Daddy was holding open the shower curtain with his shaking hand, his odor filling the steamy stall with his intrusion.

"What the hell are you doing?" her father growled. "Wakin' me up. You crazy?"

She jumped at the voice and backed up to the rear wall of the tiny tin shower stall. Her practiced eye measured her father's condition. Drunker than ever. It had been eight years since her momma had left, and her daddy had been mean and drunk for all of them. But he'd never done *this* before. Please, Lord, she thought. Please.

"Daddy," she managed to breathe, trying not to show her fear. "Wait a minute and I'll be right out." She squeezed past him while he watched her nakedness. She took the towel off the peg on the wall and, feeling less vulnerable with it wrapped around her, walked toward the living room to the safety of her clothes and the outside door.

She heard the motion before she felt it. His hand fell like a stone on her wet head. Then he grabbed a handful of hair and he pulled her back, back toward the smelly den of his bedroom. The towel fell, leaving her bare. She screamed at the suddenness and the pain, and tried to stop him by holding on to the slippery handle of the old refrigerator. He reached around her and, with his free hand, wordlessly pried her fingers loose.

She went limp out of instinct, hoping he would have to loosen his grasp, reposition himself to carry her, but instead he just pulled her along the floor by her hair. The first words escaped her lips since the struggle had begun. "Noooo!" she shrieked. "No, Daddy, no!"

He stunned her silent with a slap of his broad, callused hand, hitting flat across her face. "Don't start with that, you little tease. I know what you are. Heard 'bout them T-shirts over to school. Struttin' yourself around in those tight pants. Tossin' your hair like some kinda Jezebel."

As he dragged her down the hall, she went limp again. Then her father scraped her over the threshold of his door, and he let her fall at the foot of his bed. Holding a sheet around her, she started to scramble to her feet.

But he was too fast for her. He lashed out, quick as a striking snake, and threw her over his knee, viciously ripping away the sheet.

"I'll teach you some respect for me if I have to beat it into you," he told her. Face down in the rank bedclothes, she tried to struggle off his lap.

"Please, Daddy, no. I'm sorry," she cried, but his hand slapped her across her bare buttocks, hard. "Please!" she cried again, but he hit her harder. When she tried to struggle up, he put his other hand on the back of her neck, pushing her head so hard into the mattress that she could barely breathe.

Her bare butt already stung, but once he had her pinioned helplessly he slapped it again and again and again. "Little slut," he cried. "Tease. Just like your mother. How many of them boys you fucked? Boyd Jamison and who else? No-good little slut." He grabbed one of her reddened buttocks and squeezed it viciously. Sharleen screamed at the pain and the shame of it.

"Don't you make one sound," he warned her, swinging away at her again, and, despite the unbearable hurt, she didn't. After a time, he slowed down, then he stopped, but he still kept his one hand on her neck, pinning her. She felt smothered, and had to tell herself to keep breathing, small little breaths, despite the choking feeling in her throat and chest.

Then, with a chill of horror, she felt her father's hand move up between her legs, touching her *there*, in her private place. He grabbed a handful of her hair, there,

36

down below, and tugged it. "You let the boys up under your skirt?" he asked, his voice thick.

"No, Daddy," she choked out.

His hand blessedly moved away, but then it was back to cup her right breast, hanging down over his left knee. "You let them touch your titties?" he asked.

"No," she cried again. His hand closed over her nipple, and he pinched it between his thumb and forefinger. The sharpness of the pain shot through her. "You sure?" he asked.

"I'm sure," she sobbed.

"Good," he told her. "Be sure you don't. Else you'll be a whore like all the rest of 'em." He stood up, tumbling Sharleen, naked, onto the floor. He looked down on her with disgust.

"Get yerself decent. I'm going out," he told her, and was gone.

Sharleen stumbled out of the close room and returned to the shower. The hot water had run out, but she hardly felt the difference. She stood in the cold flow, let it run over her back until the hurt cooled a little, then stepped out and carefully patted her raw skin with the thin towel. Thank God, Dean wasn't home, she thought. At sixteen, he weighed 185 pounds and was six-foot-two. She knew that Dean could hurt the old man, and once again knew she could never tell Dean of this. But Daddy was getting worse and worse. She flushed with the shame of it, feeling again her father's hand on her body. Worst of all was what she had felt against her belly while he hit her: her father had pressed his erection against her. She was afraid for herself, and also for what might happen to Dean if he knew. He'd fight their daddy, and then Daddy would kill Dean. He needed her to protect him, and she had promised her mother that she always would.

She put her hands up to her forehead, pulling back her hair as if she could pull the ugliness from her mind, and began, slowly, to dress in the skirt and blouse she had carefully made for what she was hoping would be an important occasion. With a trembling hand, she managed to put on lipstick in front of the flyspecked mirror nailed

37

to the kitchen cabinet, then stopped for a moment to will herself to calmness. Lord, grant me this, she prayed. She had looked forward all week to her date with Boyd Jamison tonight, and wasn't going to let *anything* take away from it.

Sharleen took yesterday's meatloaf—mostly bread crumbs, not meat—from the refrigerator, cut off two big slices, and placed them in a pie tin. She scooped out the rest of the leftover instant mashed potatoes and added them, as well as a small can of creamed corn. She covered this all with aluminum foil and left it in the oven, then wrote a note to Dean telling him how to warm up his dinner and that she was going to the dance at the school. She didn't mention anything about Boyd or a date.

Turning back to the mirror, she examined her neck to make sure there were no telltale signs of her father's attack. There were none, except her sore behind and her still-trembling hands. On the outside, Sharleen looked just perfect. So she left the trailer to wait for Boyd, in front so he wouldn't have to sound his horn.

5

Theresa O'Donnell has been world-famous for over thirty years. We know about her movie career, her mansion, her disastrous marriage, her failing career, her brilliant comeback, her slide, and even more than most of us would like to about her famous drunks. But it's hard to remember that only three years ago no one had heard of her daughter, Lila Kyle. Our fascination with the life-styles of even the rich and fading let us in on Theresa's latest album attempt, the perfume she was launching, and her troubles with the IRS. But not her daughter. And Theresa liked it like that.

A reader who didn't already know what was going to happen to Mary Jane and Sharleen might wonder how these two females are linked, and whether Laura Richie had not—as we say in the trade—lost control of her ma-

*terial. But you, gentle Reader, are savvy enough to have
known from the beginning how these two are to be bound
in a knot of fame, sexuality, and merchandising un-
matched by any circus since the days of P. T. Barnum.
And of course you would be wondering about the third
part of the trinity, the most famous—or infamous—of
them all.*

The Rolls Corniche purred through the west gate of Bel
Air, moved up the hill effortlessly, swung slowly into
the gently curving driveway, and came to a stop under
the porte cochere. Lila Kyle opened her door, jumped
out, and strode up the wide, cracked Carrara marble
steps, through the enormous carved wooden door, slam-
ming it behind her. She looked about at the once-grand
foyer, the huge crystal chandelier, the curving staircase.
"It's not home, but it's much," she murmured to herself,
and headed upstairs. Her mother's housekeeper came
into the gallery from the dining room, the expression on
her face a combination of surprise and anger, just as Lila
hit the first step to her bedroom suite on the floor above.
"Lila," Estrella called out from below. "Don't slam
the door. I've told you a hundred times."
Lila stopped, her hand holding tightly to the alabaster
banister. She turned slowly toward Estrella, swinging her
stuffed handbag over her shoulder. Lila wasn't only the
daughter of a world-famous mother. Her father had been
Kerry Kyle, the matinee idol of the forties and fifties. She
was going to have to get into it with this bitch—*again*.
When was Estrella going to get it? Glaring down at the
Mexican woman, Lila said, "Are *you* telling *me* what to
do, Estrella? In *my* home?" Lila walked slowly back
down one step, paused there, then said, "You're way out
of line. Anyway, you're only the *housekeeper*, you
know? Hired help. And I'm *not* nine years old, for chrissakes." Lila watched as Estrella's face flushed. It was a
look that was becoming increasingly familiar to Lila. Like
that teacher in school she'd had to straighten out that
time. Or the saleswoman at the Rodeo Drive boutique.
Panicky. Embarrassed to be reminded that they were
only staff. Which was all they were. Because Lila had

decided a long time ago that you couldn't buy these bitches' friendship, but you *could* demand their respect. Too bad her mother had never learned that lesson.

When she was satisfied that Estrella was in her place, Lila turned and began to retrace her steps. As she continued to walk up the stairs deliberately, she called over her shoulder, "And send me up something to eat after my swim. You know, something I'll enjoy. Give it some *thought*, Estrella."

Lila walked through the sitting room of her suite and through the double doors to her bedroom. She tossed her bag on the bed, wiggled out of her tight jeans and three-hundred-dollar silk jersey T-shirt, and walked into the bathroom. Without pausing, she turned on the sauna. While it was heating up, she moved to the huge walk-in closet and took down the chenille robe she favored, threw it around herself, then went down the hall to the bedroom on the opposite side of the house to look out over the pool. It was the room her two "sisters," the wooden dummies that Theresa had made famous on her TV show, shared. The puppets lay in their twin beds, staring at the ceiling. She wrinkled her nose at the smell of mildew that had gathered in the unused room. Why the fuck does she have to let it go like this? Lila thought. It's not that the Puppet Mistress's money was gone—Lila knew it wasn't. But Theresa was getting creepy, letting help go, not keeping things maintained. Jesus, Estrella and Perez were the only household help they had, and most of the time Estrella just sat on her fat brown ass and watched TV with Theresa. The bitch is losing it, Lila thought. Well, that's not *my* problem. So long as the money is there.

Leaning out the window, she was able to see the entire pool area. From up here, it didn't look too bad. It was when you got close, and saw the cracks in the pool tile, or the overgrown weeds next to the pool house, that you knew that Theresa was ready for more than just her fucking close-up, Mr. DeMille. One of these days, Lila figured, Bill Holden's corpse would be floating out there.

The house had been built by a very big star in the thirties. In those days, before he'd gone out of style and bankrupt, the actor had set the standard for wretched excess in Hollywood, which most people in this town today had succeeded in topping. At the height of her career, Theresa O'Donnell had bought the place, and restored the house and grounds to their former splendor. But that was a long time ago.

Now Theresa O'Donnell, like the guy who'd preceded her, was over the hill. No more musical-comedy roles, no more movies, no more stupid TV shows or even recordings. Still, she held on to what she had—a hefty income from very carefully managed investments—but the glamour life was gone. Some people had said that Theresa was gone, too, but not Estrella, her resident fan, or the circle of aging men—the Court of the Faggot Queens, Aunt Robbie called them—who loved to come over to Theresa's and dress up. Jewelry, makeup, wigs. Dresses and shoes. Trying on and changing. Imitations of Judy Garland being topped by Bette Davis. With the final coup de grâce: impressions of Theresa singing her theme song, "The Loveliest Girl in the World."

Lila scanned the lounge chairs around the perimeter. Good, she thought, no one's there. I'll have it all to myself. None of the usual bunch of her mother's hangers-on and moochers (although Lila knew that even they had been thinning out the last few years). Those few who remained were falling apart as badly as the house. But there was a new development: the faggots were being replaced by what Lila thought of as the Cinema Dweebs. All those young guys with glasses and hollow chests, who came from places like Akron, and wanted to write a book about the symbolism of breasts in Frank Tashlin's comedies of the 1950s. They ogled Lila and worshipped her mother. A lot of good it would do them. All Theresa wanted was to sit in the screening room and watch her old movies endlessly. *The Lady's in Red, Cruising Down to Buenos Aires.* All the old crap that Lila herself used to watch. And, of course, *Birth of a Star.*

At least Kevin was different. He might have come to interview Theresa, but once he'd seen Lila he had stayed to talk to her. He was working on his film masters at

UCLA, but he didn't look like a Cinema Dweeb. He looked great—tanned, fit, and very handsome. And he was smart. He came from back east somewhere, and he'd read like a million books. He gave her *East of Eden,* and she read it, even though she'd seen the movie. Kevin was interesting. And now that she'd dropped out of Westlake, Lila was bored.

Kevin paid attention to *her.* He played tennis with *her.* He jogged with *her.* He took *her* down to the Long Beach Marina and sailed out to Catalina. Stuff her mother was too old or too drunk to do. He was polite to Theresa, but he listened to all Lila's complaints about her, and he agreed. And sometimes he put his arm around Lila, though he never did anything more.

It felt good. He was taller than she was—the Dweebs came only up to her chest—and even more athletic, and it felt okay—just to be held. That was all she wanted, and that was all Kevin asked for.

Still, when Theresa had cooked up the idea of their marriage, Lila had been enraged. Kevin was her secret. Just for her. And, after all, she was only seventeen, too young to get married. Plus, it was none of the Puppet Mistress's goddamn business. It was embarrassing. Kevin might not be that interested in her. But, without even telling Lila, the Puppet Mistress spoke to him and got it all settled. At least *she* thought she had.

Just as she thought she had the reception all arranged. Theresa chose the date—to coincide with the start of the hiatus of the television shows—so they would have the biggest attendance possible. And the caterer was to be the one used by Jack Wagner's wife for all her parties. Theresa was knocking her brains out trying to make a decision between Ed McMahon and Pat Sajak for master of ceremonies. Lila could tell she had begun planning this as the beginning of another comeback caper. But Lila also knew there wouldn't be any reception, not to mention a comeback. Because Lila wasn't going to perform for the Puppet Mistress yet again, just so that Theresa could make a splash with Industry people. If Theresa wanted another job, let her get it herself.

But marrying Kevin was Lila's ticket out of this mausoleum. Lila didn't know where Kevin was now, but she assumed he was up at the tennis courts with his instructor. Even though Lila was starting to feel bored, she was glad to have him occupied for a while. Sometimes she just had to be alone. People, even Kevin, closed in on her. She wasn't in the mood. The Puppet Mistress had promised her that this would be accepted by Kevin, after the wedding. It had better be. Lila padded on her bare feet back to her room, and stripped down to her panties to sit in the welcome dry heat of the sauna. The thick door made her feel safe. Sweat began to bead the top of her chest and drip down her beautiful breasts. She'd been taking hormones that Theresa had gotten for her since she was ten, but on her sixteenth birthday she'd also had implants—her mother's sweet-sixteen gift to her. Now they were perfect—round and upthrust, with tiny pink nipples that pointed high. They hadn't hardened with scar tissue or anything, the way some girls' had. Still, she didn't want anyone touching them but herself. She thought about Kevin again, and getting married. He hadn't squeezed her breasts. He'd never tried. Or done anything worse. Sometimes she felt he understood something about her that she didn't know about herself. Maybe that was enough.

More than anything, Lila wanted to get out of this crazy house, away from her mother and the madness and the fights. She needed Theresa to support her until her own money became available. But that might not be until she was twenty-one. One more disservice her father had done her, a trust fund that wouldn't kick in for another four years. She was dependent on her mother till it did. And the only way her mother would let her go was if she were married. "A girl needs a man around, honey. Keeps the wolves from the door," Theresa had said. "And it looks bad, a girl your age moving out on her own. No one can say I didn't look after you, that I haven't been a perfect mother."

Well, that was it. Theresa and her image—God knows, Lila wanted out of the house. But Lila was also afraid. Kevin was the best of the guys she'd met, and better than Mother's court, other than Aunt Robbie, of course.

Kevin wasn't as mean as the others, maybe because he was young and good-looking. The rest of the Court of Dweebs or old and flabby fairies were ugly ones at that. Something happened to them when they reached a certain age, Lila thought. Something that made their mouths form into perpetual sneers. She wasn't going to wait around to see that happening to Kevin, though. This was only a temporary solution, after all. Until her trust fund kicked in.

But, God, I don't *want* to get married. I want to get the fuck away from here, but I don't want to get married, Lila thought. Kevin's nice and all, and very understanding. She could *talk* with him—nothing too deep, but she had no one else to talk to at all. Except Aunt Robbie, but he was older, and he also loved her mom. And Kevin liked the old movies—like she did—and enjoyed them without having to figure out symbolism and all that shit. That was something else they had in common. Mother had told her that Kevin would never force her to do anything. He would be very gentle, Theresa said. Or, if she wanted, he would leave her alone. He understood.

Sometimes Lila felt as much like a puppet as Candy or Skinny. Once she had hated them, had been jealous of them. Now she could almost feel sorry for them.

Slowly, she sat up and rubbed her skin roughly with a thick towel, then walked out of the sauna. She went to her bureau and opened a locked drawer with a key that she kept on a chain around her neck. She took out the three bottles of pills and arrayed them on the top of the dresser. She didn't have to look at the labels—she'd memorized them since before she was eleven, for chrissakes. She knew each one by shape and color. And she had the dosage schedule down pat. What to take on what days. She took them out of the bottles, went to her bathroom sink, and swallowed the combination, washed down by a glass of water.

One of them—the one she had to take least frequently —always left a bitter aftertaste. Lila rinsed her mouth out with mouthwash, then returned to the bedroom, locked all the vials away, and pulled out the black Versace bathing suit she liked best. Inching on the tight spandex over her underpants wasn't easy, but at last she stared at herself in the full-length mirror and managed to smile. Then she left the room and headed for the pool.

Lila lay back on the chaise longue, the water droplets pooling around her on the white canvas cover. She felt the tension easing out of her, the effect of the hot sauna and quick swim. A shadow fell over her closed eyes, and her heartbeat quickened.

"Kevin?" she asked, opening her eyes, shielding them with her hand against the late-afternoon sun.

"No, mees, just Perez."

Lila recognized her mother's latest (and oldest) yard-man. "Have you seen Kevin?" she snapped.

"No, mees. He was here 'bout an hour ago, but he leave. I don't know where." He continued, "Eet's okay I treem the hedges here, Mees Lila?"

"With this whole fucking place falling apart, you have to work *here? Now?* Go find yourself something else to do. This isn't showtime, for chrissakes." Perez gave her the creeps, the way his eyes followed her whenever she was outside. He always seemed to be working right around her. She had told the Puppet Mistress to set him straight, but Lila guessed that she hadn't: *no one* worked cheaper than Perez. But Lila couldn't tolerate him.

Kevin was usually in the pool at this time of afternoon. He'd play tennis for an hour in the morning, then two more hours' practice in the afternoon with his instructor, one Theresa had hired, then he'd swim the pool for fifty laps. She liked that about him, the way he took care of his body. Exercise. Vitamins. They had *that* in common, too. And she liked to watch him in his tennis shorts, his Speedo swimsuit. He would come over to her in the afternoon on his way to the bathhouse to change out of his tennis clothes, and bend to kiss her as he went by, leaving the salty taste of his sweat on her lips. Sometimes, before she'd left Westlake, he'd pick her up after school. Every girl in school hated her for that. He *was* gorgeous.

But now Lila was lonely. Where the fuck was he? She stood up and pulled her robe closed. She decided to go back into the house, maybe go look for him. As Lila neared the door, she thought better of it. She didn't want to run into her mother, so she curved around the side of the building, past the solarium, intending to go in through the kitchen and up the back stairs to her room. The door to the unused solarium was closed, but the transom was open, and a mumble of voices came filtering through. Perez? she thought.

The low laugh was familiar and welcome. She twisted the knob and pushed in the door. "Kevin?" she asked as it swung open. In the half-light of late afternoon, there were figures moving in the shade over by the rotten wooden potting table.

"Kevin?" she asked again. And then she saw clearly. He was leaning over the table, his strong arms bracing him, and he was naked. His tennis instructor was behind him, his back and bare ass to Lila, and he was moving, his white shorts in a puddle at his feet.

"Do you like it?" Bob asked, as he made another thrust with his hips against Kevin's bare ass. "Tell me you like it," Bob teased.

"Yes," Lila heard Kevin laugh. "Yes, you bastard." He grunted then, and so did Bob.

Lila felt the coldness stab at her heart and lungs. She stopped breathing for a long moment. The grunting continued, and then a groan. More than anything else, it was the disgusting sounds they were making that immobilized her. She made a sound herself. Kevin was the first to notice her.

They separated, slowly, breathing hard. Lila was breathing hard, too. She thought she might throw up. Kevin reached for his tennis shorts and said, "It's not what you think, Lila. I love *you*, baby."

But Lila was already screaming. "I could kill you both," she cried, her voice a shriek, sounding unnatural in her ears. The horror, the *meanness* of it was more than she could bear. "I trusted you, Kevin. We were supposed to get married. *But then you do this!*" she screamed.

"Calm down, babe. Just calm down. Hey, I thought you knew, that you understood. I mean, this isn't a *sur-*

prise to you, is it?'' Kevin held out his hands, palms up, waiting for an answer.

Bob zipped up his white shorts, smoothed back his sweaty hair while looking at his reflection in the glass wall, then stepped past Lila. It appeared he had seen all this before. Turning to Kevin, he said, "Same time tomorrow? Call me," and left.

Lila stood there, shocked into silence until her breathing slowed. "I despise you, you fucking faggot." Lila turned to the door and opened it for him. "You're no different than those disgusting old nellies that hang all over my mother. I should have known. I want you out of here. Now."

Kevin stepped back, as if slapped. Then his face hardened. "Yeah, you're right. You *should* have known. And Theresa told me you did, that it was all taken care of. Freedom and respectability for you, a nice income for me. I guess we're *both* fucked. *None* of us gets what we want now. Not even your mother." He shook his head and walked through the open door. "It could have all worked out. But—*someone* fucked up. And it wasn't *me.*" He was about to close the door behind him, then stopped, reconsidered, and smiled. "No hard feelings?"

Lila pushed the door shut on him, then stood in the same spot for what seemed like a long time. She wasn't shaking, not a tremble. It was just that she couldn't seem to move, to think. At last, from behind her, from the door now open at the other end of the solarium, she heard Theresa's voice. "Better take him as he is, pet. He's the best *you're* ever going to do."

Lila spun around. "Oh, my God! Why didn't you tell me? You lied to me. I hate faggots, you *know* that. You said he didn't *want* that. You said . . ."

"What I *said* was, he doesn't want *you.*" Theresa paused. "Just the good life. I said that he'd leave you alone. You'd be safe with him. We both would."

"Why didn't you come right out and tell me, then?"

Theresa, as she so often did, ignored the question. "It was a one-in-a-million deal and you blew it. I did it all for you, Lila."

"But it's *my* life!"

"And *my* money! And *my* house, and *my* clothes on your back. You wanted to drop out of Westlake. Okay, I let you. You want to move out? I was letting you. But not without someone around to take care of you. Not to live some wild kind of life and start rumors. So I arranged it. I set it up. I found him, I paid him, and *this* is the thanks I get? After all I've sacrificed to keep you safe. To give you security."

"Spare me, Mother. Next you'll be telling me Candy and Skinny are more grateful than I am." Lila took a deep breath. She wouldn't cry. She was too angry, but the anger was cold. It had frozen all her tears. She looked at Theresa, the wreck of a star. "The truth is, you're jealous of me. You're jealous, and you have been for a long time."

"Jealous! That's a laugh! *I'm* Theresa O'Donnell. *I'm* a star. *I'm* famous. *You're* the one who's jealous of *me!*"

"I can get famous, Mother. You can't get young!"

Quick as a flash, Theresa struck out and slapped Lila, hard, across the face. Lila gasped, reached up to her cheek, took a step toward her mother, towering over her, then stopped. Her voice became low, deep, and frightening. "You will *never* do that again. I'm certain of that. Because, if you do, I'll kill you. And you're not worth it. I'm *sick* of you. Sick of your constant manipulations. I'm not a puppet. For chrissakes, I'm not even your goddamn *daughter.*"

Theresa's face went ashen. "Don't you *dare* say that to me. Or to *anyone. Ever!*" Specks of spittle had formed on the corners of Theresa's mouth.

Lila turned to go. "I'm leaving." She turned her back and began to walk back to the house.

"Don't you *dare* leave! Where are you going to go?" the Puppet Mistress screamed behind her. "You can't be on your own. You don't have a dime. And who's going to take *you* in?" Lila heard her mother's voice shrieking now. "Don't you *dare* leave, Lila. You have no place to go."

Sobbing now that her back was turned, Lila kept on walking away.

6

To understand this story, you've got to know Neil Morelli. Everyone knows him now, but no one knew him before that big Emmy award night. Now he's infamous, but back then he was just another stand-up comic trying to get a break and a sitcom of his own. Mary Jane's best friend, and a guy dying for recognition, he was one of the hungry hordes of New York entertainers trying for a ticket to the big time.

When Neil Morelli left the scene of Mary Jane's church-basement humiliation, he went on to work. Maybe someday she'd get wise—and notice the man in her life who really loved her. Now he couldn't be depressed about it. Bouncing off the elevator into the law firm's offices on the twenty-eighth floor of the Rockefeller Center skyscraper, he passed the receptionist behind an enormous cherry-wood desk. She sat amidst antique Sheraton tables and English hunt prints on the silk-papered walls, but he raced down the hall to the Word Processing Department. After working as a temp for three years in some of the most prestigious law firms in New York City, Neil had arrived at what he called his Ethnic Inversion Proportional Decorating Theory. He thought of it again as he rushed down the hall—the more Jewish or Italian partners in a firm, the more WASPy the furnishings—laughing to himself as he usually did. After all, a stand-up comic had to be his own best audience. With more than half of the partners here at Minster and Creed either Jews or guineas, the place looked like the queen herself supervised the decor. Yeah, he cracked to himself, but which queen?

Grinning, he opened the door at the end of the hall and walked into the fluorescent-lit interior, three rows of computer workstations, six stations in each row, spread out before him in the windowless room. The noise level and the Spartan Formica work areas were in stark contrast to the sedate richness seen by clients. Ah, backstage at the law office.

Well, no more backstage: it would now be a soundstage for him. He had been waiting for this moment for three long years.

Dana was sitting at the supervisor's desk in the front, as usual. Neil breezed by her with an airy "Hi," dropped his backpack on the floor next to his desk, and waved a general hello to his co-workers. He saw Dana lower her glasses to the tip of her skinny nose and beckon him to her desk with an exaggerated curl of her index finger. At that moment, she reminded him of the nun in the fourth grade at St. Dominic's, Sister Helga. Neil had succeeded in getting his classmates to refer to her as Sister Hell Bent. Once the old crow had stood him up in front of the class and asked him where he thought his shenanigans would land him. "Show business," he cried, and the whole class laughed. The laugh was worth the beating he got later.

Now he waited for Dana. Like Neil, she considered herself in show business. Unlike Neil, she was kidding herself. A string of failed auditions did not constitute a career. She'd tried to be an actress, but she'd been both stupid and lazy, and now she was bitter. During his first days at the firm, she'd been warm and the soul of sympathy when he bombed over and over. It was only when he kept it up that her attitude changed. And Neil *had* kept it up, for over seven years now, doing a stand-up comedy routine at every club in town, starting with open-call nights only, midweek. He'd honed his material, worked all the way to weekends in the better clubs, and he had felt Dana's envy every time she asked him how he was doing.

If the envy had been mixed with respect, Neil supposed he could have tolerated it. But when Neil got his first paid gig, Dana's attitude took a turn for the worse. If once they had shared a camaraderie, from the night he got the twenty-five dollars for his bit at a retirement dinner on Long Island, Dana withdrew and seemed to take a perverse pleasure in making his job at the law firm hell.

Because, while he'd moved up the club circuit, she'd only moved up the scut-work ladder. Now she was Queen of the Scut Work. Third-shift manager of a word-processing center. Big deal. But it gave her enough power to guarantee that any really shit typing got assigned to him. Statistics. Tables. Footnote corrections. Neil swore she saved them up. Twenty-five bucks, for chrissakes, Neil thought. She's made my life miserable over twenty-five bucks.

But it wasn't just the twenty-five dollars. When he'd gotten the shot on *Letterman,* she'd begun the crucifixion. And since she'd gotten wind of the pilot, she'd been murder. But no more. Neil smiled to himself.

"You're late—again," Dana warned as she neared his desk.

"I know. I'm sorry," Neil said. All eyes were on him, though typists' fingers continued to fly. He made sure his face showed the proper contrition. No gags, no funny lines. He knew how to play an audience. He turned to the crew at their monitors. "Hey, guys, what's the difference between a vulture and a lawyer?" They were ready for the gag. "One's a lice-ridden scavenger that lives off the unfortunate." He took a beat. "The other's a bird."

The crowd went wild, but Dana didn't even blink. "That's the third time this week, Neil, and today's only Wednesday."

Neil kept a straight face. The line's good and the bitch doesn't even know it, he thought.

Dana lowered her voice. "I can't keep covering for you with the day manager," she said. A total lie. The day manager only knew what Dana told him. "I'm talking to you as a friend, Neil. Let's face it, this pays a lot more than retirement dinners, Letterman's scale, or free drinks at The Comic Strip."

That's the good girl, open wide. For weeks now, it had taken all his willpower not to mention the sitcom pilot again. She must have figured it died, like her hopes. She wouldn't see this one coming. "I know," he said. "But I won't be doing retirement parties for twenty-five dollars anymore, Dana."

He could see her cheer up, the sick bitch. "So, you're

finally giving it up. Well, I can't say I blame you. I know you haven't had many bookings lately. You're better off here. *This* is your bread and butter."

Now, this is getting too sweet, he thought. Time for the old one-two. "Oh, I also won't be working *here* anymore." The typists' fingers slowed down. Some actually stopped typing altogether.

"What? Why not?" Dana asked.

"Because," he said, standing, then stepping back with his arms stretched up overhead, "I GOT A TV SHOW IN L.A.!"

The other word processors, a motley crew of losers and misfits, applauded and stamped and shouted their congratulations. Only Dana looked nonplussed. So Neil waited for silence, returned his face to its somber look, and spoke to her in a normal tone. He didn't need to shout. The whole room was still. Not a key was struck. "I'd like to give you fifteen minutes' notice. I quit," he said, as he grabbed his bag and began to walk to the door. Dana's jaw dropped. He turned around and decided to give you his co-workers one more lawyer joke. He'd been doing one a day for six months, saying he believed it to be his equivalent of a marathon. "Why does New York have all the lawyers and New Jersey have the toxic waste?" he called out to the room. Everyone but Dana had stopped working and was smiling at Neil in anticipation.

"WHY?" they yelled.

"Because New Jersey won the toss," he told them, and opened the door to gales of laughter. Before he stepped out into the hall, he turned for a final time to Dana. She had managed a smile, but it was forced on tight lips, her face rosy with envy and humiliation.

Pay-back time. "Keep punching them keys, Dana." Neil smiled. "Remember, it's *your* bread and butter." He closed the door and walked down the hall to the elevators, whistling.

Neil let himself back into his apartment, dropped his bag and the mail on the kitchen table, and took a beer from the refrigerator. He didn't normally drink, but today he was celebrating. Recalling Dana's face as he closed the door, he raised the bottle of beer in a toast, took a gulp, then made an imaginary checkmark in the air with a moistened index finger. He pushed one of the packing boxes off a kitchen chair and sat down, flipping through his mail. Bills, more bills, and a funny postcard from his sister, Brenda—the lesbian. The wall phone rang beside him, and he reached up and grabbed the receiver while continuing to sift through the envelopes.

"Hello."

"Hey, Neil, I finally got you. Where've you been?" the cheery voice asked.

"Who's this?" Neil asked, his tone sweet.

"Nate."

"Nate? Nate who?" Neil asked in the same syrupy voice.

"Nate. Nathan Fishman, for chrissakes. Your agent." Nate's voice had lost a little of its friendly tone.

"Nate *Fishman*. Well, holy shit," Neil said, now pretending excitement. "I didn't recognize your voice. It's been so long. You must have gotten my—what, twenty, thirty messages, right?"

"Listen, Neil, I've been busy. But I heard the good news. I hear you got the pilot. See, kid? I said stick with me. We did it."

Neil's voice dropped. " 'We,' you scumbag? 'We'? Where was the 'we' when I heard about the gig? Where was the 'we' when I wanted to get in touch with the producers? Where was the 'we' when I begged you to lend me the plane fare to fly out to L.A. to test? No 'we,' Nate, unless you're talking 'we we.' Because you pissed on me, Nate. And now you're fired."

There was dead silence at the other end of the line for a minute, then a forced laugh. "What do you mean, fired? This is a gag, right, kid? After all I did . . ."

"You didn't do shit for me, Nate. We had lunch a couple of times in the past year—*both* of which I paid for, by the way—I signed something three years ago, and you've been collecting ten percent of everything I earned since, including my fucking word-processing job *and* the two-fifty out of the twenty-five dollars for my first gig. I booked the jobs, not you. You never got me a job, and most of the time you didn't return my phone calls. But you cashed my checks, right on time, every month.''

"So you get a break and then walk away from me?" Nate's voice rose with indignation.

"You're a loser and a slime bucket, Nate. Think about it.''

"I'm a loser? *You're* the fucking loser. You're going to L.A. to make a pilot? Big fuckin' deal. They make five hundred pilots a season, asshole. What makes you think yours is going to go network, or even get syndicated? You'll be back here in a month, pounding on my door.''

"I just picked up my messages from my answering service,'' Neil yelled, holding up two pink slips as if Nate could see them. "And guess who they're from? Sy Ortis. 'I'd like to talk to you about representation at your earliest possible convenience.' *Sy Ortis,* Nate. Early Artists. That's why they call the firm that. They get the talent Early, when we're just about to take off. *Two* messages, Nate. And I think they deserve a call back! So fuck off, small time.'' Neil banged the receiver back on the hook, took a deep breath, then made another invisible checkmark in the air.

He sat in silence for a moment, trying to regain his composure. Now the bastards were coming out of the woodwork to take credit for having discovered him. Well, fuck them. I did it myself. I'm the one that knocked on doors and took the abuse. I'm the one that got stiffed for pay by the worms that run the clubs.

He thought of Sal Condotti at Horizon's Star the other night. After Neil had finished his act, Sal had come up to him and offered Neil his hand.

"I always knew you could do it, Neil. That's why I gave you weekends so soon after you started. I could tell quality." Sal pumped his hand. "So, whenever you want to break in your new routine, just let me know. I'll give you a Saturday night—and top billing.''

"Gee, thanks, Sal. I sure appreciate that. And could I get a raise, too? Could you let me have maybe fifty-*five* dollars instead of fifty?" Neil had kept a smile on his face.

"A raise? *You* should be paying *me*, for chrissakes," Sal had said automatically. Talk money and he always went into his "what-I-done-for-you" routine. "*I* gave you your break, and now you want to soak *me* for more money?" Sal smiled but shook his head sadly.

"Not *more* money, Sal," Neil said. "*Some* money. You haven't paid me for the last three weeks. I mean, it's just as easy not to pay me fifty-five dollars as it is not to pay me fifty, right?"

Sal laughed and slapped Neil on his back. "You're a riot, Neil. Okay, let's say fifty-five dollars. Would that make you happy, kid?"

Neil stared at the ceiling for a moment, as if considering Sal's offer. "Nah," he said, and stepped away from Sal. "But I tell you what would make me happy. I'd be happy with a hundred dollars at Catch a Rising Star." Neil began to walk to the door. "And that's what I'm getting Saturday night *there*, Sal. Fuck yourself, Sal, you cheap wop. Drop in and see my new routine, if they forget to lock the cage."

Sal's smile disappeared, and his voice went very low. "Hey, *gumba*—don't burn all your bridges. You might need them when you cross the Styx into Hades."

"I'll never be playing the sticks again, *paisano*. And that includes this toilet," Neil had said, and walked out onto Second Avenue.

Remembering it now, Neil made another checkmark in the air of his kitchen, and smiled to himself. They were adding up, he thought, and then remembered to add Sam Shields to his list. Neil felt bad leaving Mary Jane and the troupe, but it was a pleasure to toss his success at Sam in front of the rest of them. The self-important bastard acted as if the group was his personal property. Humiliating Mary Jane in front of them all. *And* cheating on her left and right, not that Mary Jane would let herself see it. Neil sighed.

Why does someone like Sam wind up with someone like Mary Jane? he thought, for the seven or eight millionth time. She isn't beautiful, but she's a good friend and an enormously talented actress. She's a woman with a soul, who loves a man without one. Neil could never get over the fact that Sam's arrogant artiste shit worked so well on women. The black clothes, the fakola creative moods. When the guy is six-foot-two and good-looking, why did he bother to use a shtick to get laid?

Neil had seen a dozen guys just like Sam Shields. Guys who'd gone to an Ivy school but pretended to be from the streets. Guys who wrote plays about blue-collar characters, but who wrote dialogue with words like "plethora" and "facetious" and "cosmology." Neil *was* a street guy —his dad had been a minor capo in one of the New York families—and he hated the suckfaces from places like Exeter who liked to talk "dese," "dems," and "dose." Neil watched Sam pull his tough-guy act out of his ass, and watched the women fall over and spread their thighs. It made you lose respect for them.

For a short, skinny, homely guy, Neil had managed to joke his share of women into bed, but he could never treat them cruelly enough to make them love him. And because he loved Mary Jane, he could never treat her cruelly at all.

Hey, he told himself. None of that self-pity, now. Neil stood up abruptly, went into the tiny bedroom, and began to toss the contents of bureau drawers into an empty packing box. Mary Jane was the one bridge he was *not* going to burn, he thought, and went to the phone to leave a funny message on her machine. Maybe this last humiliation in front of the troupe would be enough. Maybe Mary Jane would finally wake up and smell the Sanka.

7

Sharleen was happy, happier than she ever had been. Going out—well, "sneaking out" would be closer to it— with Boyd was real nice, and they'd been dating for almost a month now. Just like a normal girl. Just like they showed on TV. And he was nice. Real nice. Just sitting beside him here in his red Trans Am convertible felt good. Then the car crunched along the stony dirt road and, when the lights picked out the outline of the trailer ahead, Sharleen felt the feeling fade. She reached across Boyd and turned off the lights, then put her finger to her lips. He stopped the engine, and the silence of the Texas night fell around them. Sharleen laid her head back on the seat and looked directly up at the star-filled sky, stretching like a blanket from horizon to horizon. What was it she had felt? Different? Special. She felt special.

Since Sharleen had begun dating Boyd, she'd started to see just how special she was to him. She saw it in his eyes, which reflected her own face back at her.

They sat in comfortable silence for a moment. Sharleen was grateful that Boyd didn't start pawing her the moment he turned off the engine. That was one of the things that made him different from the other boys at school. He was such a gentleman at the party tonight. The other boys seemed so childish in comparison to Boyd.

"Did you have a good time, Sharleen?" he asked.

She turned her head so she could see his profile in the dim light. "Oh, yes, Boyd, I sure did. I had a wonderful time. Thank you."

And she had. She held in her arms the stuffed animal he had won for her in the dunking-for-apples game. When he handed it to her, a fuzzy poodle-dog, she knew what it was about him that made him special, too. He said, "I remember you said you once had a puppy that died." Boyd *listened* to what she said.

"Sharleen, you're the prettiest girl in the school, you know that?" he asked now. Sharleen blushed with pleasure, then became uncomfortable at what might be coming next.

"And you write the prettiest poetry. That poem in the school paper was good. It really was." He turned sideways to face her. Sharleen tensed at the movement. "You're not like other girls. You're . . ." He paused.

"Sharleen," he said softly, "would you be my steady?" She turned her head to face him and studied him closely. Boyd was the richest boy at Regional, the only boy who had a new car, not a secondhand. He was a senior, but had a very boyish face, kinda like Dean's.

But he made her feel two years older instead of two years younger. Sex with him was something different. Scary but good, in a way. She reached out her fingers and touched the outline of his square jaw. She could manage one night out with him each week, but more and Daddy would surely find out. Plus, Dean would be alone so much. But how could she explain any of it to Boyd?

"Boyd, I don't want to go steady with nobody. It's not that I don't like you, Boyd. I really do. But I can't go steady with anyone right now." She felt his hurt and disappointment and rushed to relieve it. "Couldn't we just be friends for a while, Boyd? You know, just do things together? I mean, like go for rides and talk? Once in a while. Without all the fuss? I surely do like you."

If she went steady with him, she'd have to wear his ring. Word would get out. And her daddy might make trouble. Dean would feel left out, or maybe even jealous. She leaned forward and kissed Boyd on the lips, barely brushing them. She lingered there, her lips against Boyd's, not moving, not touching anyplace else. Then, gently, she pulled away.

"Sharleen, I love you. I'll do whatever you want. I just want to be with you," Boyd said, and he seemed relieved at last to be saying these words to her.

She heard the whoosh of the falling wood first, then the thud of the bat on the back of Boyd's head. She saw him then, stumbling around to her side of the car, the baseball bat still grasped in his hand. Boyd slumped forward, his head bumping against the wheel. There was blood, a lot of blood. In a moment, the seat was covered with it.

"You filthy bitch," her father snarled. "Giving it away to strangers. Get out of the car, you whore."

Sharleen's wide-eyed gaze fell first on the bloody head of Boyd lying against the steering wheel, then back to her father as he grabbed crazily at the door of the car, not able to open it in his frenzy. She threw herself back, trying to clear the car by scampering over the seat, then over the far side, but he jumped across the back fender and his hand fell on her ankle, pulling her with such force that she lost her breath. The scream died in her throat;

her breath gasped from her. Instinctively, she knew that he had gone over the edge: she was going to die.

Her daddy's grip left her ankle while he tried to get ahold of her arm. She used her last moment of freedom to kick out with both legs, succeeding in knocking him off balance. She got down off the car trunk and ran toward the trailer.

"Dean! Dean!" she screamed. "Help me, Dean, help." Then her father was on her in a leap, forcing her to the ground.

"You little cunt! Jest like your mother. Slut! I'll show you. Fuck every boy that comes walking by." He wrenched her over, straddling her at her waist, then slapped her hard across the face, stunning her. She knew he would kill her now, or worse.

"Deannnnnn! Help meeeee!" she screamed as loud as she could, and, with that gigantic effort, slackened her body. He used the moment, and quickly had her skirt up and blouse ripped open, his body pressing the breath out of her lungs.

"The Lord is my shepherd; I shall not want," she began to pray. "He maketh me to lie down in green pastures." It was going to happen, like she always knew it would. Like she'd always been afraid of. She closed her eyes and felt his rank breath against her face. She heard the sound of his fly being unzipped. "Yea, though I walk through the valley of the shadow of death, I will fear no evil," she whispered.

She didn't see the bat, or Dean holding it, or the arc it made before it connected with her father's skull. But she heard the sickening crunch, felt him tumble off her, and heard her father's last fluid gurgle. Not until she opened her eyes, managed to scramble up from the dirt, and saw him lying there, his blood spreading over the ground, did she realize he was lifeless. And she was glad.

She pulled down her skirt, looked at Dean, who now seemed paralyzed, then ran to Boyd. She didn't have to touch him to know that the blow from the baseball bat had killed him. His face was calm and serene, in spite of the mass of red-and-white pulp strewn on the seat of the car. He never knew what hit him.

She turned back to Dean and put her arms around him. "Dean, thank you. You saved my life. He would have killed me."

Dean was still staring at the body of their father. Dean didn't move, didn't blink, didn't even seem to hear her.

His stillness frightened Sharleen, forcing her to take command. "Dean, listen to me. He killed Boyd. Look, Dean." She forced him to the driver's side of the car. "He bashed in Boyd's head with the baseball bat, Dean. He was going to kill me, too." She stood very close to him, circling him with the warmth of her arms, reviving him, a frightened animal, with her closeness and the familiarity of her smell.

"You saved my life, Dean. Now, listen to me, and I'll take care of both of us."

He nodded, then looked at her. "He killed our puppy, Sharleen. He hit Momma. He was hurting you, Sharleen. He was hurting you."

"I know. But I'm okay now. You have to be okay, too."

He dropped his head on her shoulder and began to cry. "I'm okay, Sharleen. I'm okay. I didn't want to do that. I didn't. But I'll never let anyone hurt you. Not ever."

8

Mary Jane sat swirling her coffee cup in circles on the Formica table in the kitchen. Through the small, grimy window facing the airshaft, she was able to see that the sun was out only when she craned her neck with her cheek on the pane. She took a spoonful of plain yogurt, wishing it had strawberry preserves in it, then pushed the container away.

Holding the mug in both hands and blowing across the top, she sipped mindlessly, and stiffened as she heard Sam in the next room: he often mumbled in his sleep, and now he cried out, then sighed deeply. She listened as he coughed once, then heard the bed creak as he turned over.

Mary Jane relaxed in relief. I can't talk to him yet, she thought. I've got to figure out last night first. What to say. How to say it. Where to draw the line, the line she would have to draw to preserve her self-respect. He really hurt me, she thought. And he did it in front of Molly and Neil and Chuck. In front of all of them.

As always, she found herself backing off from the confrontation, beginning to formulate excuses. Well, they *had* been going through a hard time lately. Guilt, shame, and anger—now, there was a nice pot of emotions to stew in. And though they'd talked about it—endlessly, it seemed—there was really nothing that could be changed. Sam had to take this shot and do the movie, she'd feel lost out there, and neither of them could force Hollywood to change. She just couldn't stand the thought of being without him.

But she couldn't stand the thought of going with him as nothing more than his unemployed girlfriend, either.

She knew he was angry at her for that—for not wanting to go. For abandoning him when he was so nervous about his first film. Maybe *that* was why he'd staged that humiliation last night. To "get her back" for not coming with him to L.A. Mary Jane shook her head. Whatever the reason, he was way out of line.

But perhaps it was more. Wasn't it Freud who'd said there were no jokes? Maybe the gag last night was Sam's way of transforming her. Maybe he wanted someone who looked like Bethanie Lake. Or maybe he wanted Bethanie herself; she certainly wanted him.

Mary Jane got up, walked across the tiny kitchen, stood in the doorway to the narrow bedroom. Sam lay, his hair spread out on the pillow, his long arm over the side of the bed. Just looking at the long, lean arm, the bulge of the muscle above the elbow, the downy hair on the forearm, made her weak, gave her pleasure. With his dark, shoulder-length hair and tomahawk nose, he reminded her of a sleeping brave.

Since *Jack and Jill and Compromise* was sold, after she was passed over, it seemed as if Sam was angry—

angry not at International Studios; not at Seymore LeVine, who had promised Mary Jane the role; but at Mary Jane herself. He couldn't bear her grief—"moping," he called it. He'd become impatient, easily irritated. And he took it out on everyone. On her, on Neil, on Molly, on everyone. The scene last night had just been his most extreme way of showing it.

So he was going out to L.A. Big deal, she told herself. It was only for one film, *his* script. Sam had always said he wasn't interested in Hollywood—he was a Broadway gypsy, too. Maybe he was frightened about going. Still, it was no excuse for last night.

She sipped at her coffee and then sighed. Her mind kept running in circles, like a rat in a trap. Well, she felt trapped. Last night especially. She had lasted through the rehearsal, then avoided coffee with him and the others, come straight home, gone to bed, and pretended to be asleep when he came in, much, much later.

She picked up her coffee mug, pulled her old terrycloth bathrobe around herself, and went into the living room. She put a disk on the CD—a recording of the sounds of the rain forest—and sat in the recliner, closing her eyes. To the sounds of a brook and bird calls, Mary Jane took the deep breaths she had learned in yoga class. I can't let this get out of hand, she thought. Not like the other times. I must be clear about what happened, and how I feel.

As always, she felt a part of herself wanting to let it go, to chalk last night up to his enthusiasm for the show, a momentary lapse of taste, *anything,* so long as she didn't have to confront him. But the hurt had been so blatant. The looks of pity on Molly's and Bethanie's faces flashed again before her eyes. And again she thought, How could he? Tears began to sting her eyelids. No, she *had* to confront him.

Sam's voice from the bedroom broke into her thoughts. "Any coffee, babe?"

"In the coffeepot," she called back. Let him get his own fucking coffee, she thought. I've spoiled him by bringing his coffee to him in bed every morning. I'm so pathetically grateful for his attentions that I serve him like a faithful dog. Not today, she told herself, and she wiped the tears away quickly. Then a thought came to her. Maybe he would apologize. All on his own. Blame stress, blame jet lag. Give her a good, contrite act of repentance and save the day.

Sam came into the living room. "Can I get you a refill?" he asked. Oh, he knew he was in trouble. Otherwise he'd never have noticed her empty cup. As Sam placed his mug down on the scratched old coffee table in front of the Salvation Army sofa, she could feel his uneasiness. Well, at least he had the decency to feel some remorse. He reached over to lift her cup.

"No thanks. I don't want any," she told him. Sure, she told herself. Try a little passive aggression; that's right up your alley.

She watched him attempt to be casual. Well, clearly there would be no apology; she would have to begin. She reminded herself not to lash out at him, to talk calmly about her feelings. She didn't want this to deteriorate into a shouting match. She hated arguments. They'd had only a few, but those had been whoppers. Each time he slammed out the door, she feared she'd never see him again. She watched him now as he picked up the newspaper.

"Sam, I need to talk about last night."

"What about last night?" His eyes didn't leave yesterday's *Post*, which, she noted, he was reading as if it were tomorrow's.

"C'mon, Sam. About the magic act. Jesus, that was mean. You hurt me."

Sam looked up, his face a blank. Oh, Jesus, she thought, not the little-boy-lost routine. "Hurt you? What are you talking about? What does hurt have to do with casting? I'm trying to do a show."

Christ. He was defensive already. She sighed. Why did otherwise normal men find it impossible to admit they were wrong? Why did they have to get so blind and stubborn? "But to hold me up to ridicule and humiliation that way . . . that was so unnecessary. Were you *trying* to hurt me?"

Sam placed his mug down with a thud. "Now, wait a minute, Mary Jane. What I did was try to put together a skit for a show. It was a funny bit. If you don't like your part, I'll recast it. You're blowing this all out of proportion. *I* didn't humiliate you.''

She couldn't believe that he was going to try and stonewall. It made her even more angry, as if he were ignoring an elephant in the room with them. ''I was held up to ridicule because of my looks. Tell me that's not what happened. And tell me it's not humiliating.'' His face remained blank. He's not going to cop to this, she thought, a sick feeling in her stomach. And if he doesn't, we'll have to break up.

''Mary Jane, get a grip. I needed to cast a 'Before' and an 'After.' It was a classic old gag. And you were there, could do for the 'Before.' Hey, this is no discovery. You weren't passed over for Jill because you resemble Michelle Pfeiffer.''

Mary Jane felt her stomach cramp—as if she'd been punched in the gut. Sam picked up the paper again. ''I don't want to have to take the rap for your feeling bad about your appearance. I've told you, you look fine to me. We've been through it a hundred times. Own up to your own feelings, and don't project them onto me.'' Sam got up and went to the kitchen. She heard him pour himself more coffee but could barely look up as he returned to his spot on the couch. She took a deep, shaky breath.

''I'm not *projecting*, Sam. I'm hurt. Everyone there last night either laughed at me or pitied me. And I can't stand either.'' But that was nothing compared with this. Compared with his pretending it hadn't happened, and throwing the blame back on her. She felt her eyes fill, her throat close. She wouldn't allow herself to cry. Not now.

Sam stood in the doorway, looking in at her. ''You know your problem? You're paranoid,'' he said, and walked to the bedroom.

She got up and followed him. ''Paranoid? What are you saying, Sam? That you *weren't* insensitive? That I *wasn't* hurt?'' Mary Jane was raising her voice, her anger pushing back the lurking tears .

Sam turned to her, standing in the doorway, and looked up at the cracked plaster ceiling. ''Okay, Mary Jane. Now you're not paranoid. *Now* you're getting hysterical. I can't talk to you when you're like this.'' Calmly he pulled on a pair of socks and struggled into the black sweater that lay on a chair next to the bed. ''I'm going out until you've cooled down.'' He tucked his T-shirt into his jeans, and pushed into his cowboy boots. Grabbing his black leather jacket from the closet, he turned back to her. ''And don't play the misunderstood martyr, Mary Jane. That doesn't work anymore.''

''Sam, don't go. Not till we've sorted this out,'' she said, her voice raised.

Sam strode to the door and put his hand on the knob. ''It's not my issue. *You* do the sorting. Then stop screaming like a banshee,'' he told her.

''You bastard!'' Mary Jane cried. ''You always do this. How did it start out being a discussion about my *feelings*, and wind up with me being the shrew who chases you out of the house?''

''Maybe because I have feelings, too,'' he said calmly.

''And you're not understood here, so you're going to take them to Bethanie, right?''

Sam stopped, stock-still, at the door, his hand still on the knob.

''That does it, Mary Jane. Now you've gone too far. You *are* a fucking paranoid.'' He went through the door and slammed it behind him.

Mary Jane stared at the back of the chipped old fire door, the Fox police lock jerked out of its slot on the floor by the violence of Sam's slam. ''Oh, shit,'' she wept, her voice too low for anyone else to hear.

9

Lila opened her eyes, straining to see the clock in the gloom of the heavily draped guest room. The small green number said 11:17. She squinted and saw the even smaller ''A.M.'' She couldn't have known that, because the fabric over the windows shut out the light. The entire room was swathed in silk, and looked like some kind of tent from the Arabian Nights, complete with camel saddles and brass lamps.

She lay still, trying to get it together. The dream lurked behind her eyes. She strained for a moment to bring the images back, but could only feel the horror, so she willed the pictures away.

The days and nights had merged into one long searing burn, broken only by the blessed blackness of sleep. It was when she first moved her head that she realized the pillow was damp. She must have been crying in her sleep, she thought. She turned her head to avoid the clammy spot, as she raised her hand to her forehead. What day was it? Tuesday? Wednesday? How long had she been here?

Seven, maybe eight—no, nine days. Nine days ago, she had come running here to Aunt Robbie's from her mother's house. The picture of Kevin bent over the potting table snapped into place. The headache sprung fullgrown again. The memory of the animal sounds curling from his lips accompanied the picture. The scene brought spasms of nausea to her stomach. She swallowed hard against the urge to retch.

A low whirring sound came from the other end of the one-level contemporary house Aunt Robbie had built in Benedict Canyon. The sound, familiar to her, grew louder as it neared. Then it stopped, and Lila heard Aunt Robbie fiddle with the door handle before swinging it in. It had to be Robbie. José, Aunt Robbie's houseboy, normally left her breakfast tray outside the door.

" 'Suffering was the only thing made me feel I was alive.' " The words were sung by Rob's deep basso voice as he rolled into the room, Chinese-red lacquer breakfast tray held chest-high before him. Aunt Robbie came to an abrupt stop at the low hammered-brass table. He put the tray down and reached up to pull the drapes back from the windows, suddenly flooding the room in a bath of sunlight. Again he sang Carly Simon's line from the song: " 'Suffering was the only thing made me feel I was alive.' "

"Shut up an' go away," Lila growled.

"Come on, Sister Miserere—novena's over. Nine days

of pissing and moaning over a man is all the good Lord allows." With surprising grace, Robbie sat down on the camel saddle, his mauve-trimmed flowered satin caftan billowing around his feet, hiding the roller blades he wore. "Makes me feel light on my feet," he had once explained to Lila. Now he grinned. "Come on, I had José make this especially for you." Robbie poured thick black coffee from a small antique Russian samovar he swore had been given to him by his first john—who was most assuredly one of the deposed Romanoffs.

"Lila?" he asked, and paused. When, after a few moments, there was no response, he leaned over and picked up a mallet and banged the brass temple-gong to which it was attached. She jumped. "Listen, girlfriend, get the fuck over here this minute." He slapped the filled Limoges coffee cup onto the brass tray.

Her head ached with the echoes of the gong. "Don't do this to me, Aunt Robbie. Please," Lila begged.

"Now, now. No whining. It's time you and I had a little chat." He patted a stack of cushions beside him. Robbie's voice softened. "Come sit next to your old but ever-so-attractive auntie."

Lila sighed, sat up, and moved with effort to the cushions. It was exhausting, so she dropped down, then put her face in her hands and began to cry. "Robbie, I can't bear it another minute." She cried soundlessly, and he let her until she wiped her eyes with the sleeve of the peignoir he had given her the day she arrived. After a few more minutes, she looked up and took a sip of the coffee Robbie handed her. "What am I going to do?" she asked for the thousandth time in nine days.

"What do you *want* to do?" he asked. Aunt Robbie reached across the table and touched Lila's chin with his stubby, crimson-nail-tipped fingers. Lila knew that he loved her as much as he had loved her father, though she shrank from his—or anyone's—touch. Still, his gentleness and soft voice showed his concern.

"Honey-girl, I know how hard this is on you, how confusing. But you can't let yourself just melt away. I'm serious, now—nine days *is* long enough." Robbie stood up and rolled again to the window, touching Lila's arm lightly as he passed. "You haven't been out of this room since you got here."

"I hate her," Lila said.

Robbie turned from the window and faced her.

"She was the one who set up the marriage. My own mother. She said he'd never bother me. But she didn't tell me *why*. *I* didn't know until I walked in on them that he was . . ." Lila's voice trailed off. She didn't want to offend Aunt Robbie, although she knew she could always be honest with him. "Well, *you* know," she continued. "Not only was it *disgusting*, it was *deceitful*. He said he loved *me*."

"Well, maybe he does. There are different kinds of love, you know." Robbie was standing at the full-length mirror now, patting his red-dyed hair in place. "If I curled up in bed every time one of *my* boyfriends dipped his wick in another inkwell, I'd be a fat mental case by now." He made a full spin on his skates, then considered his reflection once again. "Actually, I *am* a fat mental case now, but you get my point."

Lila got up from the low cushions with what felt like an immense effort and sat on the chair in front of the vanity table. She stared into the triple mirrors. She picked up the Victorian silver-backed brush, and began to run it through the accumulation of knots at the back of her usually silky red hair. "What I don't understand," she said, as she strained against a tangle, "is how my own mother could have absolutely no regard for my feelings. She manipulated me into this engagement, but she didn't do it for *me*." Lila dropped the brush, helpless against the snarls, and turned to Aunt Robbie, who was now sitting on the end of the bed, legs crossed, one skated foot swinging slowly.

"It's called narcissism!" Robbie said. "I've known your mother a long time and I love her, but I can't say I've always liked her. Still, Lila, you have to try to remember there are reasons why people are the way they are." Rob's foot stopped moving. "Do you know anything about her childhood?" he asked.

"Oh, give me a break! Are we going to start that bit

about how she went to her first audition in L.A. through — the snow without shoes?" Lila snapped.

"You know, Lila, the only training for *being* a good parent is *having* a good parent. She didn't, so she raised you the same way she developed a career—by the seat of her pants." Lila angrily stood up and started walking toward the door. "No, wait, you've got to hear this," Robbie continued. "Do you think you could do any better raising a child than she did, Lila? Given the way *you* were raised?"

"*I'm* not having children."

"But if you did?"

"I'd like to think I would do better," Lila said.

"That's my point. So did Theresa. And she *did* do better than her folks did to her." Robbie got up.

They both stood in silence for a moment; then Aunt Robbie skated back over to the open window. He looked out at his lover, Ken, who was cleaning the pool wearing only a tiny chartreuse Speedo swimsuit. Suddenly Robbie shouted to Ken: "Mary, what did I tell you about wearing that marble bag? You look ridiculous!" He turned back to Lila as if there had been no interruption.

Lila had to smile and look, too. She could see Ken moving the pole of the pool vacuum slowly up and down on the sides of the pool, as if he hadn't even heard Robbie's voice. Someone else was with him, she could see.

"Look at this, Lila."

"Like I haven't seen Ken in his bathing suit before," Lila said, more grumpily than she felt. "Why don't you leave him alone? You know he never listens to you." Lila paused, looked at Robbie's getup, and then laughed. "And how can you say *he* looks ridiculous?"

"No, I don't mean Ken. Do you see that girl sitting on the chaise longue talking to Ken?"

"You mean the little black kid?" Lila asked.

"That's Simone Duchesne, the star of the TV show *Opposites Attract*. And she's no kid. She's twenty-two."

"*That's* Simone Duchesne? But I thought Simone was the same age as her character—about six or seven."

"Yeah," sighed Robbie. "So does everyone else. She only looks like a kid. She has a benign tumor on her adrenal gland. It stunted her growth. It *could* have been removed by simple surgery when it was first discovered, but her parents—who, by the way, managed her—decided against it. Now it's too late.''

"Why?" Lila asked, though the feeling in the pit of her stomach told her she already knew.

"They say they were too poor. But, hey, if she'd grown normally, she would have outgrown the TV role. The parents chose the money instead.''

"Poor kid. I mean, woman," Lila said and shivered. "So is she after Ken?" she asked.

"Oh, no, she's asexual," Robbie said. "Her parents robbed her of that, too, when they wouldn't allow the surgery. No, she's just become attached to Ken, follows him around like a puppy dog. You know what a good listener Ken is. They met on the show. Ken did the lighting for it." Robbie came away from the window. "She'll never get hired for anything else. What a life, huh, Lila?"

Lila couldn't answer, allowing the silence to speak for her.

"Some things are worse than being the child of a star. Like *being* a child star. Robbed of her stature *and* sex life *and* money by her greedy parents. Ken tells me Simone sees a shrink five days a week, and has started a lawsuit against them. But, no matter how the lawsuit turns out, she'll still wind up the loser."

"I know how she must feel," Lila whispered.

"Tsk, tsk. Do you, Miss Self-Pity? Look in the mirror. I don't mean at the puffy eyes and pale face—that'll go away in a couple of hours. I mean, look at *you*. What do you see? Not a black female midget."

Lila studied her reflection for a moment. "I know I'm beautiful, Aunt Robbie, and that men want me. But *I* don't want *them*. Then my mother picks the only man that doesn't want *me*. And I don't really want *him*, either.''

"Do you want girls, then?" Robbie asked, gently.

Lila shuddered and turned her head quickly, as if slapped. "No! I *hate* women."

Robbie tsked again. "Doesn't leave much choice, do it? Well, if it's any consolation to you, you come from a family with a long line of gender confusion. Your father was the only man I ever loved—nothing personal against Ken—but your father didn't know if he was coming or going. He spilled his seed all over Hollywood. 'Boys and girls together, me and Mamie O'Rourke,' " Aunt Robbie sang. "Theresa was the one who wore the pants in the family. You might take a lesson from her. As fucked up as she is, she *did* make one good decision in her life, once she realized that he would always make her unhappy. I don't like what that decision did to you, but it saved her sanity. She decided, since her love life wasn't going to be her career, then she would make her career her love life." He paused. "That was what she wanted, and she went for it. What about you, Lila? What do *you* want?"

Lila stared at her reflection in the mirror for a long while before she spoke. Without taking her eyes off herself, she said, "I want everyone to love me—but always from a distance."

10

Seven and a half miles outside Fort Dram, Texas, Sharleen stood at the side of Interstate 10, the white-hot glare of the sun beating down on her head, the steam of the blacktop burning through the thin soles of her sandals. She knew it was seven and a half miles, because she had walked every flat sizzling inch of them. So had Dean, and he had carried their bag as well. When they had first begun to walk, it seemed like the best thing to do. After only three miles of their last ride, Sharleen had begun to suspect that maybe the truck driver was being too friendly to her. They'd gotten out fast. Maybe he meant no harm, and maybe she had been too quick to get Dean away from the guy, but when the trucker had taken her hand and asked if she wanted a chance to steer, she'd become afraid that somebody might get hurt.

Yes, it was the right thing to do, she reasoned. It's what Momma would have told her to do, if Momma had been there. But even with her momma so long gone, Sharleen would still never want to do anything that might bring shame down on her momma's head. All those things her daddy had said were a lie. She made a silent prayer: Thank you, Lord, for getting us out of Lamson and to Fort Dram, and for getting us out of that truck and on this here road that's burning my feet, instead of staying in the truck and maybe ending up burning in Hell. The thought that maybe Dean and she would go to Hell for what they had done to her daddy came to her. But surely Jesus would understand. "Dear Jesus, forgive us. It won't happen again," she said.

Dean was struggling along beside her, sweat rolling off his forehead and down his face, his white T-shirt now gray against his muscular chest, damp both from walking and carrying the one suitcase they had between them. He had broken at least two of the Ten Commandments, but Sharleen couldn't see Jesus not forgiving Dean. And if Jesus sent Dean to Hell, Sharleen was surely going to beg to go right with him. Not, she thought, that Hell could be too much hotter than Interstate 10 outside Fort Dram, Texas. A white Chevy sped by, its wake more like a gust from an open oven door than a breeze.

"Sharleen!" Dean called out. "That was a New Hampshire tag! Ain't never seen one of them! What does it mean—'Live Free or Die'?"

"Means they don't cut you no slack in New Hampshire, I guess," Sharleen told him. Since Dean was a little boy, he had sat beside the highway, watching for out-of-state tags. Dean's ambition was to see all fifty license plates. At home, he'd sit beside the highway for hours, though not much passed but local Texas plates, and the others often flew by too fast to decipher. Still, Dean was real patient.

"Now I got me fifteen, Sharleen: Texas, Arkansas, Oklahoma, Florida, New Mexico, Arizona, New York, Ohio, Colorado, Indiana, California, Tennessee, Mississippi, Louisiana, *and* New Hampshire!"

"That's real good, Dean." She wondered how far it was to the next town, and how far that town was from the one after that. She couldn't remember how many miles across Texas it was to the border. For a moment, she felt so overwhelmed by fatigue that she wasn't sure she could take another step.

But she had to. And she had to risk taking another ride. Because they had to get out of Texas, and maybe even out of the country. And if a trooper or even a local sheriff drove by, she was sure that she and Dean would be in a world of trouble.

They had carried their father's body over to Boyd's Trans Am along with the bat, then pushed the car behind the dumpster. Sharleen said a prayer, best she could, and asked God to accept the two souls. But she didn't imagine even Jesus could forgive her daddy, and she knew she never could. Then she and Dean lit out, stopping only to take Momma's Bible, some clothes, and the few bills and change that they had saved in the place under the kitchen cabinet. They'd walked all night, gotten a ride to Fort Dram, slept all the next day in a park next to the post office, then caught another ride, the ride that hadn't worked out. Sharleen knew she had to make a plan, a good plan, but all she kept thinking, over and over with each step, was "Father, forgive them; for they know not what they do."

She heard it long before she saw it. The car's engine sounded strong and sure as she squinted against the light to catch a first glimpse. Out of the waves of heat rising from the road they had just walked, Sharleen could make out a silvery glint. Before she realized it, it was near, the first car they had seen all afternoon that wasn't going so fast it was almost a blur.

Without a word, the two of them got into their positions. Dean stood at the edge of the road, one thumb out in the air, the other thumb tucked passively onto a belt loop. Sharleen sat on the suitcase, shaded slightly by Dean's shadow, and slumped down, elbows on knees, to hide the obvious curves of her body.

It was a Pontiac, she could see. A big car, tinted windows shut tight against the heat of the day. Sharleen caught a glimpse of the driver as he came to a stop just beyond where they stood. Old guy, maybe fifty or sixty. Another plus. And he had a dog with him. Would a pervert have a dog? She hoped not. They both rushed up to the lowering window on the passenger side and peered in.

"Where you headed?" the old guy asked.

"Montana," said Dean.

"California," said Sharleen. They had answered together.

The driver laughed. "Confused, ain't you?" he asked, smiling.

"No, we know where we're going," Sharleen spoke up. "First we're going to California, then, later, to Montana. Where are you headed?" she added, deciding that this ride might be okay. She saw Dean reach out to the dog, a big black Lab.

"To California and beyond. Hop on in," he said, and reached across the seat to open the front passenger door. Sharleen eyed Dean, then opened the rear door and sat in the back. Dean pushed the bag onto the seat next to her and got in the front beside the dog, just like she had told him to. With the doors closed, it became immediately, blessedly cool.

Sharleen looked around and noticed the driver's large satchel on the floor at her feet, along with a beat-up five-gallon can. Overflow from the trunk, she thought. Must be going to be away a long time to have this much luggage. She leaned her head back on the soft headrest and felt herself sink into the plush upholstered seat. The cool breeze from the air conditioner came wafting back to her, drying the sweat from her damp shirt, the chill making her nipples hard. Dean turned back to her for a moment and grinned.

"What's your names?" the driver asked as the car gathered speed.

"I'm Sharleen, and this here's my brother, Dean," Sharleen answered, touching her brother gently on the shoulder with one hand while straightening her messy hair with the other. "What's yours?"

"Dobe Samuels is as good a name as any, I figure. Named the dog Oprah 'cause she's fat and black and smart. No disrespect intended."

They rode in silence, Dean petting Oprah, Sharleen

74

lulled by the air conditioning and the motion of the car. Blessed relief, she thought as she thanked the Lord for their good fortune. She noticed the back of Dobe's neck and saw that he had a fresh haircut. The collar of his cotton shirt was clean and pressed. Sharleen checked the rearview mirror to see if he was eyeing her and was satisfied to see he wasn't but seemed instead to be staring at the long stretch of road before them.

Hanging from the mirror was a small plastic-coated sign that said, "My boss is a Jewish carpenter," written in a sort of churchy print. Who's his boss? she wondered, then realized what it meant. He's a Christian, she said to herself, and felt the last of the tension leave her body with a sigh. Thank You for this message, she prayed.

Then a car pulled up behind them, real close, almost like it was following them. She felt her stomach lurch, just like it did when David Janssen was almost caught on each episode of *The Fugitive*. Sharleen turned around, looked, and was grateful to see it wasn't a cop car. But maybe it was *plainclothes* police: she felt her heart begin to pound.

"I'm doing sixty-five and the guy is on my tail," complained Dobe.

"The dirty dog," Dean agreed, then looked at Oprah. "No disrespect intended," he added.

Dobe laughed. "Oh, she don't take offense easy." Dobe patted Oprah, and her heavy tail thumped. "Guess a dog is the only thing that loves you more than you love yourself." The car behind them pulled ahead to pass, and kept right on going. Slowly, Sharleen's heart stopped pounding.

They drove for a long time, the Pontiac easily eating up the miles that Sharleen had dreaded walking. They were far from Lamson. They looked like a family on a vacation drive. And maybe no police would notice them now. They'd be out of Texas in no time. Maybe it would all be okay.

Dobe was the first to break the long silence. "Need to stop at that station up ahead," he said, as he slowed to turn into the isolated filling station.

Sharleen became immediately alert. "Are you going to

75

get gas?'' she asked. Did he expect us to pitch in for it? she thought. With only sixty dollars between them, Sharleen and Dean could not afford gas, and only an occasional something to eat.

''Well, you'll see,'' Dobe answered. He drove the car past the single, rusting pump and came to a stop. He got out of the car and greeted the figure of a young man almost obscured by the shadows on the porch.

''Howdy,'' Dobe called, then opened the rear door to the car, reached in, and took out the gallon can that was beside Sharleen. Dobe left the door open, told Oprah to stay, and took two steps toward the young man on the porch. He was sitting on a straight chair, tilted back, his feet on the railing. Sharleen noticed that the guy, who was wearing coveralls, hadn't said anything.

''Could I trouble you for some water?'' Dobe called out, holding up the empty can so the man on the porch could see it.

''What about gas?'' the man asked.

''Don't need none. Just water.''

''I *sell* gas.''

''I don't need gas, young feller. Just water.'' Dobe smiled broadly, takin' no offense, even if some was intended.

Sharleen then got out of the car and stood with her hands tucked into the back pockets of her jeans. ''We'd be much obliged,'' she called out. In the many towns they'd lived in, she had known a lot of ornery backcountry trash. She didn't want no scene now.

The man on the porch put the chair right and placed both feet on the floor. A shaft of sunlight caught his long, horselike face, and she watched as his small eyes opened wider.

''Sure thing, ma'am,'' he said. '''Round the side. He'p yourse'f.''

Dean jumped out and went with Dobe. ''What do you need water for, Mr. Samuels? The car's not overheating.'' Dean was almost as good with motors as he was with animals.

Dobe reached down and picked up the brass spigot of the hose, turned on the water, and placed the spigot in

76

the can. "Son, you're about to see a miracle of modern science," Dobe told Dean as his eyes watched the water climb to the top.

"What kinda miracle?"

"I'm going to pour this here water into my gas tank, then drop in a magic tablet, and I'll have instant gasoline."

"You can do that?" Dean asked, his voice gone high with amazement.

"Sure. Just watch."

Dean called over to Sharleen. "Hey, Sharleen! Dobe's gonna make his car run on water. He got a special pill." Dean was wearing a grin as wide as a wave on a slop bucket and watching Dobe's every move.

Sharleen eyed Dobe as he started walking back to the car, straining to carry the gallon of water. What kind of foolishness is this? Sharleen wondered. Is Dobe one of them guys that make themselves look smart by teasing Dean? There were enough of them back in Lamson. She'd play along, but try also, as she always did, to protect Dean's feelings. Still, she felt disappointment in Dobe, funning Dean like that. "Why, sure he can, Dean. And he's the only one in the world can do it, too." Sharleen didn't show any surprise until Dobe actually began opening the gas tank.

"Mister," the man in the coveralls said, as he came down the two steps from the porch. "If'n you mix water in with yer gas, you ain't driving this car out a' here. I bet you five dollars you cain't do such of a thing." He stood with his hands in his pockets, grinning for the first time since they pulled up.

"That wouldn't be a wager, young feller. That would be pure theft," Dobe said as he tilted the water can into the gas tank. Dean and the coveralls man both gasped.

"Whoa, don't do that, mister! You're going to ruin your car."

Dobe ignored the stranger's protest and finished pouring in the water, then called out to Dean: "Son, get me the box of tablets out of the glove box, would you?"

Dean nodded eagerly, ducked into the car, and carried a box to Dobe, who placed it on the hood and opened it.

77

Both Dean and the good ole boy drew closer, eyeing the array of red, horse-sized capsules. Dobe took one out and held it up to the sun, then slowly, as if performing a ritual, dropped the capsule into the gas tank and shut it.

Dobe leaned toward Dean and tossed him the car keys. "Start 'er up, son, while I get us a couple of Dr. Peppers." He walked past the yokel toward the soda machine just as the engine coughed into a roar.

Sharleen looked back at the idling car, then toward Dobe. She wasn't sure what was happening. What was in them pills?

"Where'd you get them pills, mister?" The gas jockey's voice was filled with awe. He was as surprised as Sharleen herself.

"I made 'em," Dobe said, walking back toward the car with four cold Dr. Peppers in his hands. "I invented a way to make gas out of water." Dobe passed two bottles of pop to Sharleen and Dean, then gave a third to the gas pumper.

"My name's Samuels—Dobe Samuels," he said, also offering the man his hand. "What's yours?"

The young man accepted the pop and the hand. "Eb Cloon." Eb walked over to the car. "How many miles to the gallon can you get on it?"

Dobe took a long drink of pop, then said, "Ain't quite like gas that way. One gallon of water and one of these pills is the same as three or four tanks of gas."

"Three or four *tanks?*"

"Sharleen, have we stopped for water before today?" Dobe asked.

"No, this is the first time," she answered.

Dean was excited. "Sure didn't," he said proudly. "And this mornin' I started in San Antonio."

"What's they made of?"

"That's the funny thing, Eb. If I may call you Eb?" Eb Cloon nodded. "Made from stuff around the house. Nothing you ain't got in your kitchen cupboards right now. But I sure ain't gonna tell you any more than that. Lots of folks purty interested, I can tell you."

"How much do them pills cost, anyway?" Eb asked.

"They're not for sale, young feller. I'm on my way to

show my invention to one of them big oil companies."
He took another gulp of soda and turned to walk back to
replace the empty. "Can't say more, but they're mighty
interested, I can tell you that."

"I'd buy me a couple of them pills, if the price was
right," Eb offered.

Sharleen watched Dobe rack the empty bottle and then
raise his head skyward as if considering. "Will you promise not to try and copy the recipe?" Dobe asked. Eb
nodded agreement.

"Well, I *could* let you have a few at five dollars apiece,
but you can only have ten of 'em. We got to get to California, then on to Montana," he said, and turned and
smiled at Sharleen. He had a nice, friendly smile. "That's
if you let me have some more water for my dog. She's
gettin' powerful thirsty."

"Well, sir, I'll take them," Eb said, and turned and
almost ran back to the house to get the cash. "Take all
the water you want," he shouted as an afterthought.

"Now, remember," Dobe said after he gave a pan of
water to Oprah, watched her lap it up, and handed Eb ten
red capsules, pocketing the crumbled wad of dirty bills
that made up the fifty dollars. "One gallon of water and
one of these pills will last you as long as *three* tanks of
gas. Mebbe four, but I ain't makin' no exaggerated
claim." Eb nodded. "Wouldn't want you to be disappointed."

Dobe told Oprah to get back into the car and sat down
in the driver's seat, vacated by Dean; and Sharleen again
slipped into the back. Dobe started the motor, lowered
his window, and extended his hand. Eb took it. "I'm sure
you'll get what you deserve," he told Eb.

"Mr. Samuels, I sure do thank you. Wait'll Pa sees
this," Eb said, and stepped back, grinning.

"Don't mention it," Dobe said. "I only wish I had
more to give you." He put the car into gear and pulled
out, waving friendlylike at Eb as he did.

Dean was only silent for a little while. "Mr. Samuels,"
Dean said when they returned to the highway, "you're
going to be rich when you get to California."

Sharleen caught Dobe looking at her in the rearview

79

mirror. "I'm already rich enough, son," he said, patted Oprah, and winked at Sharleen.

Sharleen woke early, while Dean slept on beside her in the single bed they had shared, leaving the second bed untouched. She got up slowly, so as not to wake him, and went into the tiny bathroom of the motel cabin. The crisp, clean sheets on the bed when they got in last night had felt so good that she had moaned with pleasure as she slid between them. Tired, full, and happy, both Sharleen and Dean fell immediately to sleep, Dean's arm wrapped protectively around her. She touched the green-plaid bedspread on the bed as she passed, wishing she had had one as nice as that when she was a little girl. The solid-green drapes with the green-plaid pullbacks framed the light coming in the window. The gray hooked rug felt soft and warm under her feet as she padded barefoot to the bathroom. All of it was so nice and clean—jest like a room in the Sears Catalog. It was the nicest room she'd ever been in. This was the fourth motel they'd stayed in, after almost a week on the road with Dobe, and Sharleen still couldn't figure out the danger. The Lord had surely provided. And, as if it were a sign, Sharleen had found a Bible at each of the motel rooms.

They'd traveled more than a thousand miles, Sharleen figured, and they'd finally left Texas yesterday. Dobe stuck to small roads, and sometimes he doubled back a bit. He also stopped for water three or four times a day —because he was experimenting on mileage, he said. And at each stop he topped off the tank with water and sold some of his pills. It seemed so easy that Sharleen had come to accept Dobe's offers of meals and a place to stay—and he hadn't tried to touch her or nothin'.

Sitting on the bathroom stool, Sharleen looked around the tiny, spotless white-tiled room. There were two towels for each of them, also two new, tiny, wrapped pieces of soap. They were really nice, and it seemed such a waste to use 'em just once and leave them. She longed for the neatly wrapped little soaps, but she wouldn't steal nothin'. She finished, flushed the toilet, then stepped back with a giggle as it made a strong whoosh noise, then went silent.

She pulled back the white shower curtain and turned on the water, amazed at how powerful the spray was compared with the trickle she was used to in the trailer back in Lamson. There were two *more* tiny bars of sweet-smelling soap here, *and* a little bottle of shampoo. Dobe had told her they came with the room and she could keep them, but still she hadn't liked to. Just in case.

This place must be very expensive, she thought, but she couldn't tell. She had never been in a motel before this week. This place seemed a little nicer than the other ones, but all of them were a treat to her. And Dean was in hog heaven.

Back in Lamson, Dean's biggest treat, aside from sightin' a new license plate, was always watchin' the *Andy of Mayberry* show. He'd seen all of the episodes many times by now, but he was never bored by them. He loved Aunt Bee, laughed at Gomer, and got frustrated with Barney, the deputy. It seemed to Sharleen that Dean liked Opie most of all. Well, she figured, in a way he *was* Opie—a motherless country kid in a small town. 'Cept his daddy was no Andy Griffith. Now, on the road, more than anything else he was missing the nice Mayberry people. So, when they pulled in last night, and there was a TV running the episode of Aunt Bee's pickles, Dean was soothed and happy.

Before she fell to sleep last night, her thoughts were how lucky she and Dean were to have met Dobe, and to eat in nice restaurants and sleep in clean beds. Now she added having hot showers to the list. As she patted herself dry, she happened to look out the bathroom window in time to see Dobe Samuels walking back from the gas station across the highway. He was carrying two gas cans. Oprah followed behind him.

Sharleen watched from the steamy bathroom window as he went to his car, opened the trunk, and, after a quick look in both directions, emptied the gas from the cans right into the trunk of the car! Then he closed the trunk cover and walked around to the spot where he had poured in the water yesterday. He knelt down and looked under the fender, then pulled something. Water rushed out and made a puddle around his feet. Oprah licked at it. Dobe reached into his back pocket, pulled out a handkerchief, and wiped his hands. Then he turned and began to walk toward Sharleen and Dean's room.

She ducked back, away from the window. What had she just seen? Sharleen felt her hands begin to tremble. She wasn't positive, but something about it all sure didn't seem right. She quickly pulled on her jeans and T-shirt and tried to open the door before Dobe knocked. She didn't make it in time.

Dean stirred at the sound of the knock, and Sharleen gave him a poke as she passed, indicating the bathroom behind her. She had to squint to make out Dobe's face, because of the strong early-morning sun behind his head.

"You kids ready for some breakfast?" he asked.

"I sure am," Dean called out, still shaking the sleep from his head as he walked toward the bathroom.

"Then meet me in the coffee shop in ten minutes," Dobe told them cheerfully, and turned back to the main building.

Sharleen waved at him as she closed the door, then yelled in to Dean, "Ten minutes, Dean. Make it snappy." While he washed and dressed, she neatly made the bed, dusted the room, and folded the towels.

The coffee shop was almost empty as she and Dean entered, except for a few truckers at the counter. Sharleen led Dean to the booth where Dobe already sat waiting for them, reading a paper. She slid into the seat opposite Dobe, and Dean sat beside her, his long legs sticking out into the aisle. The waitress came over, poured them each a cup of coffee, and freshened Dobe's.

"What would you like, kids? Anything you want, remember. It's on me," Dobe said, pushing aside the menu without opening it.

Dean suddenly came to life, brought around by either the coffee or the offer of food. "Steak and eggs," he said. "And grits. And pancakes on the side—*with* syrup."

Dobe laughed. "That's what I like to see, a man with no fear of cholesterol." He looked at Sharleen. "And a woman, too. Oh, and, miss?" he asked the waitress.

"Could I have a side order of bacon to go? Seems my dog gets surly if she don't get her breakfast bacon. She likes it crispy."

Restaurant bacon, just for a dog? Sharleen was awed. But then the scene at the trunk of the car came back to her. Maybe for Dobe money was easy come and easy go.

They ate in silence, the forks and coffee cups the only sounds at the table. Dean was finished first. He dropped his fork noisily, leaned back, and patted his stomach with two hands. "I'm full as a goose in a corn crib. I better walk around for a minute. I'll take the bacon out to Oprah for you, Mr. Samuels, if'n that's all right." Dobe nodded. "Sharleen, I'll be outside," Dean promised, and headed for the door.

Sharleen sipped her coffee, then placed it gently on the saucer. "Mr. Samuels," she began.

" 'Mister?' " Dobe asked, his brows raised. He smiled and put down his paper. "I think this is going to be serious."

"Dobe," Sharleen corrected herself. She would give him a chance to explain. "I know you're a very smart and kind man, but, well, with that gas pill, I can't help feeling there's something I just don't understand." Sharleen hesitated, not wanting to offend the man but also, if there was something not . . . well, not *right* about what he was doing, she had to know. She and Dean were in enough trouble already.

"What don't you understand, Sharleen?" Dobe asked.

It was best to tell him what she'd seen, she reckoned. "I saw you pouring gasoline into the trunk of your car this morning, and now I'm confused." Sharleen added quickly, "Not that I'm judging you or nothin', Dobe. It's not for me to judge anyone. But, you know . . ."

"I see," he said. Dobe's voice lowered, and he leaned forward and looked directly into Sharleen's eyes. "I respect you, young lady." He paused for a few moments, as if he was thinking of how to say something, then continued. "I can tell when people are in trouble, and I can see you and Dean—well, let's just say you might need a friend. And I see how you watch out for that boy, and how he looks out for you. It's nice. Real nice." He paused. "You know, God gave me a certain talent, and I use that talent to make money. I don't know why he didn't give the talent to everybody. And I never do evil to those that do good. You watch, and you can see that. You do, don't you?"

She thought of Eb Cloon, of the other men, of their meanness. She nodded. "I do understand—but maybe me and Dean better move on."

Dobe looked at her, it seemed sadly.

"Well, I sure would hate that. I got this gift, and the least I can do is share some of the Lord's bounty. Plus, sure is lonely on the road. Even with Oprah. So's I'm asking if you would be kind enough to let me take care of you and Dean as far as California. I can see Dean needs some taking care of."

Sharleen thought about how good it felt to have the comfort of a ride, good food, good beds. But Dobe was telling her that she *was* doing something wrong. Get thee behind me, Satan, she thought. But Dobe, with his kind face and crinkled eyes, didn't *look* like Satan. Was he lookin' for somethin' else from her?

"Dobe, you know me and Dean don't have no money. There's nothing we can do for you other than help with the driving. Nothin' more I'm goin' to do for you." There, she'd said it.

Dobe continued to look into Sharleen's eyes. "I respect that. You don't owe me nothing, Sharleen. I appreciate the way you get out of the car when we stop at a service station. You pretty up the scenery. That really helps me out. Without you, sometimes I don't think I would have even gotten the water. Or the attention. These ole boys can be right mean. All's I'm asking is that, when we stop someplace, you get out of the car again, like you been doing. Sometimes it takes a pretty face to get what a good Christian should offer by nature."

Sharleen lowered her eyes.

"Dobe, those pills don't work, do they?"

"They work for me, Sharleen. And I never sell too many. It isn't a big sting. Only people who want something for nothing buy them. I'll never ask you to lie—all you do is stand beside the car. I'm not putting you on the grift. I'll never ask you or Dean a question you can't answer honestly." He paused for a moment, then went on: "I'll get you both to California—and to Montana, if you want—well fed and well rested."

Sharleen sat for a long, silent moment, her hands clenched in her lap. "Okay, Dobe. Just so long as I don't have to lie, or do anything else that's wrong, we'll go."

Dobe offered his hand across the table and gave Sharleen's a firm shake. "You do me a great favor, ma'am," he said, then tipped an imaginary hat.

Dobe leaned back against the restaurant banquette and stretched, then smiled. "You know, I'm a lot older than you, and take kindly to women. I'd politely ask for your favors, but I know how it is between you and Dean. You're safe with me. Anyway, the last few years I've switched my affection from women to dogs. You can make a real fool of yourself with a dog, and she won't lose respect for you—in fact, she'll make a fool of herself, too." Dobe joined Sharleen in a laugh. Then he got a serious look on his face. "See, I have a practical problem. Never did like any woman on the grift. Con them, con me, I always found. But good women are too dependent and too shockable. Either don't want nothing to do with me or want what I got but don't want to know how I got it. Makes for a lonely life." He paused. They sat there together, the sun pouring in through the diner's window, in a friendly silence and a pool of sunlight.

Then Dobe leaned toward her. "Sharleen, when I went to wake you up this morning, I saw that you only used one bed last night. And that's your business. Just let me give you a little advice. What you do *ain't* nobody's business. But a lot of people you'll meet will think it *is*, so I don't think you should call Dean your brother no more. Sharleen, tell people he's your boyfriend. That's what people want to hear, so it makes it easier on you."

Sharleen blushed deeply, and her mind began to race. What was he talking about? But she knew, of course. All these years of being so close to Dean, their warm times in bed, the comfort they took from one another. But never was it ever spoken out loud by either of them or

85

anyone else until this moment. She pushed the shock of it from her mind. But she had to say something.

"He *is* my boyfriend," she said, returning Dobe's steady gaze as she felt the blood still rushing to her face. "I only say 'brother' so's people don't think we're living in sin." The lie felt heavy on her tongue. Now she'd broken another commandment.

Dobe sat back in his chair. "Sorry for the misunderstanding," he said, and lowered his eyes. Then Dean returned to the table, and Dobe stood up and stretched. "Time for us to hit the road. Let's have us some adventures." He clapped Dean on the shoulder, and Sharleen could see how the fatherly gesture pleased Dean. Their daddy had only touched Dean when he meant him harm.

As Dean walked ahead of them in the parking lot, Dobe leaned toward Sharleen and said, "He's a real enthusiastic boy, Dean is. And good-natured. I'd sure hate to see him ever lose that." He looked sideways at Sharleen.

"So would I," Sharleen agreed. Then all three of them got into the car.

11

Mary Jane sobbed herself into a light sleep. It had been four days without a word from Sam. She alternated between being frantic with worry and livid with rage. She ate two bags of Pepperidge Farm Milano cookies. She drank the end of a bottle of Jack Daniel's and started a new one. She passed out, woke up hung over, showered, drank, and slept again. She couldn't leave the apartment for fear he'd call and she'd miss him. Anyway, she had no place to go. She had Chinese food delivered—vile sweet-and-sour pork and moo-shu chicken—and ate it for lunch and dinner. Now, in their big bed alone, she tossed in her sleep. The ringing telephone roused her, and she rushed to it. Sam, she thought. Oh, thank God!

She made herself stand beside the battered black phone and wait one more ring before lifting the receiver.

"Hello." Not too breathless, not too pathetically eager, she hoped.

"Hi, Mary Jane. It's Neil. Are you okay?"

"Oh, Neil." It felt as if all the air was sucked out of her lungs. "No, no, I'm not okay. I feel terrible, as a matter of fact."

"Well," Neil said, "you know what Confucius says: 'Shit happens.' "

"Yeah, well, Protestants say, 'If shit happens, you deserve it.' "

"More Sam crap?"

"No less. He's gone walkabout. I haven't heard from him."

"You want to talk about it?"

"Spare me! Just cheer me up."

"I think I got just the prescription. You didn't forget I'm breaking in the new material at the Comedy Club tonight, did you? My last gig before the big time."

Oh, damn, Mary Jane thought. Of course she had. Jesus, she didn't even know what day it was. "No, Neil, how could I forget?" she lied.

"So you'll be there? I reserved a table right up front for you and the shmuck."

"Oh, *I'll* be there." She knew how Neil felt about Sam in general, how he'd feel about the argument, and she didn't want to go into it all with him. She sighed, miserable but loyal. She added quickly, "What time's the show?"

One more thing to do that she didn't feel like doing, she thought as she hung up. Midnight, her fat white Persian cat, jumped up onto the counter and pressed himself up against her, his squashed-in face expectantly looking toward her own. She opened the cheap, scratched metal kitchen cabinets. No more Tender Vittles. She searched the shelves until she found a can of tuna stuffed behind a box of stone-hard brown sugar. "Here," she told the cat as she opened the can, "knock yourself out."

She stumbled into the bathroom and turned on the shower, making it almost hotter than she could stand. She had just finished the first shampoo of her thick, heavy dark hair when the phone rang. She flung open the curtain, leaving the water running, and ran down the narrow hall, trailing soapy footprints. She slipped when she stepped into the kitchen, caught herself at the edge of the table, twisting her ankle, and lunged for the phone.

"Hello," she panted.

"Hi." Sam's voice was dead, cold, the way it always was after a fight, but it *was* Sam's voice.

"Hi." Well, Christ, *that* was stupid. "Are you okay?" she asked. Fuck. That was *pathetic*.

"Yeah. What about you?"

"I've been better."

"Listen, M.J., I'm sorry about the other night. I didn't think. You know. Coming back from L.A., and the negotiations. There's been a lot of pressure on me lately and . . ."

Oh, sweet Jesus! He'd apologized. Tears filled her eyes. "Hey . . ." she interrupted. "I understand. I do. And I've been thinking." She paused now, took a deep breath. It would be all right. He'd said he was sorry. She'd go with him to L.A. He'd still love her. And she could still love him. "I want to go with you," she said. "The part doesn't matter. *We* matter. I'll get my shot later. I'll just wrap up a few odds and ends here, stick Midnight in a box, and hop a flight to L.A."

There was silence at the other end of the phone. A long silence. "Sam?" she asked. "Are you still there?"

"Sure. Sure. I'm . . . I'm just surprised, is all. But that's fine. That's great. I'm just, well, surprised." He paused. "Look, we have to talk, M.J. Maybe I can come over tonight and . . ."

"I have to go see Neil," she interrupted. "It's his last gig."

"Oh, fuck Neil!" There, he was irritated again. "The guy's animus is scary."

She sighed. "I'd rather fuck you. Baby, it's been a long time to do without you. Listen, I *have* to go, but the show's at ten; I'll be home by midnight. How 'bout if we make up then?" She packed all the warmth into her voice that she could manage.

"Yeah. Fine," he said, and hung up.

She did, too, and as she turned she caught her own

reflection, her hair full of lather, her body naked and wet. She forced herself to look. Her breasts hung, like sagging water balloons, to the place on her rib cage where a small roll of fat had developed. It, in turn, rested on the swell of her round belly. Her *fat* belly, she corrected herself, which protruded over her pubic hair. Her hips were another monument to fat, the saddlebags visibly divided into three small but distinct ripples. Cottage-cheese thighs. Even her knees were ugly. She had let herself go and become a rounded, disgusting fertility figure. Even her thick, long hair, her one beauty, was starting to show gray streaks. She'd let herself go, something no actress could afford to do. No wonder Sam didn't sound happy on the phone, or eager to make love. Oh, God, how could anyone love me? she wondered. She was so very, very lucky to have Sam.

At a quarter to ten that evening, Neil saw Mary Jane come through the door of the club and try to adjust her eyes to the dark interior. He rushed over to her, hugged her, and cried, "Mary Jane, thanks for coming. Christ, I'm nervous. All the guys are here, waiting to tear me apart. Feeding time at the zoo. Jesus, they're so jealous that I've had to hire a food taster. Hey, you look great. Very Mildred Pierce–ish. When she's on the decline."

He was so kind. Even in the midst of his spritz, he took the time to notice. Mary Jane had been collecting vintage clothes for years. Neil always managed a riff based on the film or actress she dressed as. He always said she looked great, and Mary Jane always ignored it. But she didn't usually look as wrecked as this. Well, she'd done the best she could. He took her coat as he led her toward the small room at the rear.

"This place is larger than I thought, Neil," Mary Jane said. "How many people does it seat?"

"Seat? Forget about seats. We got *standees* here tonight. The entire bridge-and-tunnel crowd, plus every out-of-work stand-up motherfucker in the city. Them alone would fill Shea Stadium." Indicating the one unoccupied table in the front, he added, "The publicity about my pilot is paying off. But there's always room for you, Mildred. Boy, what a crowd!"

Bending to kiss her, Neil whispered, "Wish me what I need, Mary Jane."

Mary Jane patted Neil's cheek. "I do, Jughead. Break a leg. Now, get started, funny-man, and make me laugh." She followed the waiter to her table.

Neil was a good friend, and the crowd looked good, too. Hell, everything was rosy to her now that she knew Sam was waiting for her at home. After all, he had apologized. She shifted in her seat. The crowd was noisy tonight. It was the short break before the headliner, her pal Jughead.

For years, since they'd discovered that, among other shared tastes, as kids they both had read and collected Archie and Veronica comics, she had called Neil Jughead, and he'd called her Veronica. Now, with any luck at all, her pal would kill 'em. She felt her stomach tighten in nervous anticipation. He's good, she reminded herself. It will go well.

Neil had taken the three steps up to the stage and walked off into the wings. Now, after a rave introduction, he returned with a hand-held microphone, entering to a roaring welcome. He looked at her. "Hello, Veronica," he said. She smiled, and he was off on his spritz.

"Evening, folks. Good crowd. You all look very prosperous. You, sir"—pointing to a well-dressed man in the front row—"you look like you do all right. What do you do for a living?"

What was this? Mary Jane knew that Neil never stooped to working the crowd for his act. It was for hacks and amateurs, he said. Now he watched his mark in the audience, and so did everyone else. Mary Jane shifted, uncomfortable in her seat. Was Neil going to embarrass the poor guy?

"I'm an investment banker." The guy sounded wary but self-satisfied.

"You are?" said Neil. "And what did your father do?"

"My father?" The guy paused. Not so self-satisfied now. Embarrassed. Mary Jane hunched her shoulders.

"My father was a school custodian." There were a few titters.

"School custodian?" said Neil. "You mean a janitor, right?" Someone actually laughed, but the rest of the audience was silent. What's he doing? Mary Jane wondered. That's nothing to mock. He's shaming the mark. He'll lose the crowd.

The guy adjusted himself in his seat and after a pause finally said, "Yeah, you're right. He's a janitor," and managed to laugh himself.

"And did he get you your job?" The audience tittered, but more out of confusion than embarrassment. They were definitely uncomfortable. Where was this going? Mary Jane again asked herself nervously.

"How could he get me my job? I told you, he's a *janitor*. I got my own job."

"Me, too," Neil agreed. "We got something in common. I got my own job, too, which is weird, 'cause that doesn't happen much in show business anymore. I mean it. Like now there's a new generation of Fondas making it in the movies. Henry's *grandchildren*. Can you believe this shit?

"As far as I'm concerned, the *first* fucking generation of those bastards was more than enough. Then we had to have Jane and Peter. He was a fuck-up, and, let's face it, Jane was a dog." Some shocked laughter. "You think she got parts based on her looks or her talent? Get the fuck out of here! Even with her father's connections, she had to settle for *Barefoot in the Park*. And she had to marry Vadim to get cast in *Barbarella*. You think there aren't ten girls in the room right now better-looking and more talented than she was? But, hey, let's talk about Peter, a *true* no-talent degenerate. What the hell did he ever do? Now we got *his* kid, and we're going to have to watch *her* for another generation?

"They call them show-business dynasties. Get the fuck out of here! That isn't a dynasty. That *legitimizes* the no-talent dog shit. It ain't a *dynasty,* it's a *conspiracy*. This country is supposed to be a democracy, but we're fighting nepotism."

He paused and looked around the audience. "See,

91

America was supposed to be a meritocracy. It was what you *did*, not who you *knew*, remember? And it sure wasn't who your father was. Who the fuck was Thomas Jefferson's dad? Or George Washington's? The trick is, this isn't private enterprise. Hey, you want your son to join you in your plumbing business—aces with me. But this is *broadcasting*. This is television, radio. Airwaves that are owned by us all. But these fuckers have a lock on 'em. Nothin' left for us.

"See, show biz has lost that grand American ideal of rewards based on talent, a combination of hard work and talent. Tell me that Talia Shire was the best Connie that her brother Francis Coppola could buy. Well, maybe not, but his daughter was *perfect* as Mary in *Godfather III*, right? Get the fuck out of here!" The audience laughed. "Hey," Neil continued, "there were entire theaters that cheered when that bitch got shot down. Did anyone count the number of Coppolas in that movie? Of course not, because no one can count that high. You know, Coppola won a special lifetime-achievement award for putting more family members in a single movie than anyone else. And he had stiff competition in that category. Let me tell you about Anjelica Huston. No, *you* tell *me*. A big, ugly girl who can't act. John Huston put her in all his later films, 'cause Nicholson wouldn't marry her and she needed an income.

"What I love is when these bastards say they had to audition for the part, just like everybody else. We know how she had to audition for Nicholson. What I don't want to think about is how she auditioned for her father! Don't ask."

The audience was rolling now. Mary Jane saw heads nodding, the laughs were building. And the janitor's son shouted "Right on."

"I'm a working actor, and what burns me up is how rarely I get to work. Then you hear these assholes on TV telling Arsenio or Jay Leno how much harder it is being Debbie Reynolds' daughter, because people expect so much more from you. Get the fuck out of here!

"Hey, don't get me wrong. I have compassion. Being rich and having famous, powerful parents in the Industry *can* be a liability. And I'm sure Arsenio will schedule me as a guest so I can explain how being Nunzio Morelli's son made it *easier* for me, since people expected so little.''

There was a true explosion of laughter, and Mary Jane sighed with relief. Despite the bitterness, the hostility, in the routine, the crowd was going for it.

"Of course, in the music industry it's different. Wilson Phillips were a different story. I mean, even if they hadn't been the children of multimillionaire, drug-addicted, degenerate recording artists, I really do believe they'd probably be the same dog shit they are today.''

The audience was rolling with shock and laughter now. But Neil had no mercy. "Or the Nelsons. Oh, excuse me. Just 'Nelson.' Get the fuck out of here! They're the California white-bread visual equivalent of Milli Vanilli. But, hey, Grandma Harriet says they're her pride and joy. Well, that makes it all right for the rest of us, right? Shit, even *Ricky* was a lousy musician.

"Okay. So you're mad, too, but you say there's nothing you can do. You say the abuse is too rampant. You say you're just another man on the street. Get the fuck out of here! The solution to the problem, as I see it, is taking a simple action. Like the Boston Tea Party. Join the Neil Morelli Antinepotism League. You *can* make a difference. I say a few acts of terrorism could liberate the airwaves.''

Oh, sweet Jesus. He's gone too far now, Mary Jane thought. Some people in the audience "ooooh"ed.

"Oh, you think that's too extreme, huh?" Neil said, voicing her thought. "Well, let me just say one word to convince you: Sheen. Am I right? Marty, then Charlie and Emilio. *He* said he didn't want to use his dad's name to get ahead. Right! He must have used it to get an ass— that fat ass had to come from *somewhere*. So they make every movie a family affair, to keep it a secret. Get the fuck out of here! Waste 'em. The world will thank us, I promise you. Think of the alternative: Emilio might reproduce.''

The crowd was whooping now, and Neil, his hostile energy aflame, was playing them, pacing across the stage, punctuating his gestures with a Mick Jagger strut. Then he stopped dead and turned to the crowd, still.

"But one more thing. We can't be accused of sentimentality or favoritism. There are a *few* talented children of the stars. Think of the Bridges boys. Still, we gotta be fair. Waste 'em. And then there are the old standbys. Oh, I know. You'll beg for them. But hey, if we spare Liza Minnelli, we have to pass over Laura Dern or Tori Spelling, Melanie Griffith or Nicholas Cage. Of course, *he's* a special case. He's getting by on his good looks." He paused, got his laugh, and went for his tag line. "Get the fuck out of here!" he cried.

It went on and on. He killed them. Mary Jane looked over to the corner tables, where Belzer, Leary, Barry Sobol, and half a dozen other stand-ups watched. Even *they* were laughing. At the end of the set, Mary Jane rose while Neil was still getting his ovation and made her way back to the crowded, tiny area that passed for a combination dressing room and green room backstage.

Now Mary Jane waited while Neil accepted congratulations, drank down a Scotch, joshed with the guys, and greeted the heavyset woman that Mary Jane knew was his sister, Brenda. At last he noticed her. He moved toward her and planted a kiss on her lips. He smelled of sweat and alcohol. Neil rarely drank and could never hold his liquor; the adrenaline from the set, plus the Scotch, had made him high. But he was still sharp.

"You must be one of the Aristocrats," she said, quoting the old vaudeville joke, too dirty to repeat.

"Yeah," he said, getting the reference, "I've been fucking everyone onstage," he laughed.

"You're stinko," she told him. "In both senses of the word."

"*In vino veritas.* And in humor, too. That's why they laughed. Because it's true."

"But too much. Too mean. It's . . ." she paused.

"Bad taste? Mean-spirited? Provocative? Uh-oh. You know what happens to comics who err in that direction?" He took a beat. "They fill Madison Square Garden!" Neil took the towel from around his neck and patted down his sweating forehead. He stopped smiling, and, for a moment, his thin, almost weasellike face looked sad. "You didn't like it?"

"I did, Neil. I did. But I just worry. People might take you at your word. It won't endear you to Hollywood."

"Who cares about Hollywood? There isn't going to be one person in L.A. that I respect."

"Neil, *I'm* going to L.A."

He paused, shook his wet head like a spaniel, then recovered. For a moment, he looked serious, and tired. "Great news for me. Great news for Sam. Great news for you?"

She shrugged. Neil smiled at her, his burning energy surging again.

"Hey, we'll grab the bitch goddess by both teats, huh? We'll hang on hard and squeeze."

"Yeah, a regular Hollywood Romulus and Remus," she said dryly.

"Weren't *they* with the Aristocrats?" Neil asked. "Oh, no, excuse me. They were that dog-and-parrot act."

"Was Romulus the dog or the parrot?"

"I don't remember, but I know Remus was the uncle."

She laughed. She couldn't help it. He *was* funny, and he was her friend. He smiled, his weasel face lit up by the grin, his eyes narrowing. He put out both arms to her.

"We'll slay 'em, Veronica," he said. And he was half right.

"I worry about you, out there with those . . . those . . . Americans."

"Ah, fuck 'em if they can't take a joke. Anyway, I don't have to do sets anymore. I got a sitcom now. Let the *writers* sweat their guts out over the yocks." He paused, his toughness draining out of him like dirty water down a sink. "But you liked it, didn't you? You laughed?" He looked at her, needing her benediction. "I was funny, wasn't I?"

"Neil, you were a fucking riot."

Mary Jane left as soon as she could and splurged on a cab to get her back to the apartment and Sam as fast as possible. Aside from the debacle at the rehearsal and the fight that followed it, they hadn't been together since he got back from L.A. His body against hers was almost all she could think about. Just in time, she remembered the cat, though, and stopped the cab at the corner bodega to pick up Tender Vittles and a bottle of wine. What the hell.

She ran the three flights up the cold stairway, but when she got to her apartment, no light showed under the door. Midnight met her, his fluffy white coat silken smooth as he moved in figure eights against her legs. She scooped him up, flicked on the light, and called out to Sam. Had he fallen asleep? Had he not come? Her stomach tightened in fear.

She walked through the kitchen clutching Midnight to her, peeked into the empty living room, and then continued down the hall to the tiny bedroom. Maybe, she thought desperately, maybe he's asleep.

Sam was stretched out on the bed. And he seemed to be sleeping. Well, with jet lag and all, it was understandable. As always, Mary Jane was moved by his grace—his long body stretched diagonally across the bed, his feet relaxed over one corner, an arm thrown negligently over his head reaching the other corner. It was his length and leanness more than anything that attracted her, she thought. She longed for Sam's arms, for the comfort of his body pushing against hers. But he was tired. She'd let him sleep. There was always tomorrow. She began to undress in the dark.

But when she climbed into bed beside him, as quietly as she could manage, he turned to her. He buried his head in the soft flesh of her neck. "I'm sorry," he whispered. "I'm so sorry."

And all at once she *could* forgive him. Completely. His voice, husky with sorrow and maybe with lust, released her from her anger, from her pain. He was in pain, too, and she could free him. All it took was his apology, her acceptance of him.

Because she loved him so much. "That's all right," she told him. "It's all right."

"You love me?" he asked, his mouth close against her

ear, his deliciously warm breath tickling her. She felt her body warm to him.

"Of course."

"I need you, Mary Jane."

She pressed herself against him, her softness against his hard flesh. Pressing him at the shoulder, at the chest, belly to belly, thigh to thigh, she still couldn't get close enough, be close enough to him. Then his hands were on her breasts, and his mouth was on her mouth, and his body rolled onto her body. She felt his erection, and tears sprang to her eyes: tears of gratitude and pleasure. She had the power to excite him, and he loved her. He *needed* her. He had said so. And she needed his love, needed him so desperately that she was almost afraid to let her neediness show.

"Sam. Oh, Sam," she whispered.

"Promise you'll forgive me."

"I do, Sam."

"No, promise that you'll *always* forgive me. I need you to." In the dark, his voice sounded as desperate as she felt.

"Yes. Yes, I promise. I forgive you."

With a groan of relief or pain, he slid inside her. She shuddered, but he remained still, cradling her in his arms. Yet it was she, she felt, who was giving comfort, giving absolution.

"I love you," she said.

"I know," he told her, and it was only much later that she realized he had not told her he loved her, too.

The next morning, she awakened with a smile, reached across the bed, but found that Sam was already up. Quickly she rose, shrugged into her chenille robe, and walked out, barefoot, looking for him. Midnight, nestled at the foot of the bed, stretched and followed.

Sam wasn't in the bathroom, or in the living room. She didn't smell coffee brewing, but he must be in the kitchen, making it.

He wasn't. But there was a note propped on the old, scarred Formica table. He had gone! Fearfully, she sank onto the sofa and unfolded the paper.

M.J., First of all, your grandmother called while I was here last night. She's real sick and wants you to go upstate.

Also, I've given a lot of thought to what went down and I guess I feel that I was way out of line. I'm sorry.

I'm also sorry that I don't think it's a good idea for you to come out to L.A. You know how very, very special it was for us with Jack and Jill and how good things had been. I always told you that I wasn't the kind of person who compromised. Something's lost and I think it best not to go on without it.

> *My silks and fine array,*
> *My smiles and languish'd air,*
> *By love are driv'n away;*
> *And mournful lean Despair*
> *Brings me yew to deck my grave:*
> *Such end true lovers have.*

Then he'd signed his name and had added, "Try not to hate me."

Mary Jane stood there in the bleak little room, staring at the note. He fucks me, quotes Blake to me, and blows me off! she had time to think before the tears began.

12

The strangest interview I ever did was a brunch with Theresa O'Donnell out at her Bel Air mansion more than a dozen years ago. I showed up with a photographer for an "at home" shoot. It was the first time I had been to Theresa's home and the first time I met Lila Kyle.

Theresa was decked out in one of those lacy bed jackets and silky pj's. The kid was in a matching outfit. But so were Candy and Skinny, the two dummies that were featured on Theresa's TV show at the time. And the luncheon table was set for five. Cute gag, huh? Except the dummies were served, too. And they spoke up through-

out the meal. Theresa was a fairly good ventriloquist, but it was Lila I watched. The kid—she was five or six then —acted as if this were the most natural thing in the world. She called her mother "Lovely Mummie" and had perfect table manners. Meanwhile Candy picked on her. So did Skinny. And Theresa intervened when it got too rough.

I can't remember what provoked the final incident—I think Lila didn't want to finish her fruit cup. Theresa said she had to. Lila pointed out that Candy and Skinny hadn't eaten theirs. Theresa smiled, overly sweetly, and said it was too bad. Lila would still have to. So Lila dumped her fruit cup on Skinny's lap.

And Skinny called the child "a little cunt."

I often wondered what the rest of life was like for that little girl in that big house. But I didn't see her again until her birthday party almost five years later.

Lila remembered the party. It was a turning point in her life. And now, in the quiet of Aunty Robbie's house, as she faced the question of what she wanted, the party kept coming back to her.

Lila had given it a lot of thought. At least for her it was a lot. And when she tried, really tried, to think about what she wanted, what she wanted more than anything, it was to be a star. A powerful, important star. A star a lot bigger than her mother, or even her father, had ever been.

She wasn't sure if she could act—she didn't even care. She knew that what she could do was get people to look at her, to want to know her, to be interested in—no, fascinated by—her. It had happened to her before—she knew she could hold a room. She remembered her moment onstage, in the room full of stars at that party, when she sang "The Loveliest Girl in the World." She remembered the feeling in the room. Everyone stopped. They only wanted to watch *her.*

She shivered. Her mother's theme song gave her the creeps. She hated it. Lila Kyle knew that she was born to Hollywood royalty. But, like Princess Anne, or Margaret, or even poor Queen Elizabeth herself, Lila also knew that lineage didn't ensure happiness. Still, she wasn't going to wind up like Nancy Sinatra or her brother Frank, like Julian Lennon, or even Jane Fonda, who had never exceeded the reputation of her father. She, Lila Kyle, would be important in her own right.

Years ago, she recalled, she had sat before the mirror at the vanity table in her bedroom, watching Estrella's reflection as the woman stood behind her, when their eyes met. Perhaps they hadn't looked one another in the eye since then. "It's your *tenth* birthday, that's all I know," Estrella had said, in answer to Lila's question. "That's what your mother say." Estrella had turned Lila around while she inspected her from head to toe.

"But it's my *eleventh*," Lila remembered she had continued to insist. "I was ten *last* year." Lila wanted to cry but was afraid to ruin her makeup. Aunt Robbie had warned her about that all week, when they were rehearsing. "And eleven is too old for bows in my hair," she told Estrella once again. The woman shrugged. At times like that, Estrella still pretended she couldn't understand English.

Lila had been sure—*positive*—that she had been ten years old on her *last* birthday, the year *before*. Why were Lovely Mummie and Estrella saying she was only ten years old *this* year? Lila *remembered* her other tenth birthday. She remembered it so clearly. Unlike this birthday, there had been no big birthday party, only birthday cake with Aunt Robbie and Estrella, because Lovely Mummie and the girls had been too busy working.

But that was before Mummie's TV show was canceled, which must be a terrible thing, because Mummie had yelled all the time since then, and it was getting harder to understand when she spoke, even in her normal tones. Lila didn't know what "canceled" meant, but it sounded worse than sickness, or even death. And Mummie and Aunt Robbie acted as if it was. And so did the girls at Westlake. "Your mom's show was *canceled*," sneered Lauren Caldwell. "Some big star."

Estrella tightened the bow in Lila's hair and gave her a gentle prod. "Now," she said, "perfect." Estrella placed the brush back on the blue-mirrored vanity table and waddled to the door. Before she closed it behind her, she said, "Lila. Listen to Estrella. For the last time, you're *ten* years old, and your mother say you got to have a big bow in your hair. Please," she added, "don't ask questions. Promise?"

Lila had considered Estrella's request, then nodded in agreement as she always did. Even though Lila didn't really like Estrella, they both wanted the same thing: to keep Lovely Mummie happy.

Alone, Lila ran to her bedroom window and stood on tiptoe looking out, hoping that it wouldn't put cracks across the front of her new black patent-leather shoes. She strained to see the occupants of each of the limousines as they were pulling up at the door of her mother's house. As the cars disgorged their well-dressed occupants, Lila practiced naming the famous persons she recognized: "Miss Taylor, Mr. Stewart, Mr. Peck," she murmured. Her mother insisted she be polite and greet every one of the party guests by name. Some were famous, and she knew them from movies or TV, but the others were harder. And even more important. She had to get them all right. Mr. Sagarian, Lovely Mummie's agent. Mr. Wagner from CBS. And her business manager. And lots of fat, bald guys. All grown-ups, she thought. Lila didn't really have any friends at school, but, still, since it was her birthday, she wished some kids were here.

For Lila, it was a relief that there weren't as many parties as there used to be, back when Lovely Mummie was working. Lila could remember how she used to long to be with her mummie and Candy and Skinny on TV. Every Friday night, Lila would sit before the TV, watching her mother's show. She often played at being Cinderella: she had two mean stepsisters and a wicked mother who wouldn't let her go to the ball. *Theresa O'Donnell Presents "The Candy Floss and Skinny Malink Show."* Why couldn't she be on television with them? The Theresa and Lila show. Without stupid Candy and Skinny. Lovely Mummie might let her, *if* she was very, very good tonight, and *if* they got another show.

Except Lila wasn't so sure she wanted to anymore.

Mummie was home all the time, and sometimes Lila wished she weren't. It wasn't so much fun to be with her mummie. Maybe it would be different, though, when they got their new TV show.

"This is important," Theresa had said to her, over and over, as Theresa made the party preparations while rehearsing Lila. "If we can get Jack Wagner or one of those rat bastards interested, I'll just move to CBS and start over. Update the concept. Cut back on Candy and Skinny. More skits. Less singing. And bring you on. Wholesome. A family show. Like the Osmonds. No one wants these cops and westerns for their kids."

Lila liked the idea of cutting out Candy and Skinny. She hated the two puppets. When she'd been a little girl, Lovely Mummie had told her they were real—her real sisters. Now Lila knew they were only puppets, that Mummie made them speak, but even now, at eleven— she was sure she was *eleven*—she sometimes wasn't certain that the two were not alive. Still, she had done all she could in rehearsing and rehearsing with Mummie and Aunt Robbie to try to take their place, and that night she would do it.

Though all of it happened years ago, Lila would never forget a moment of it. She had left the window and run to the guest room, on the other side of the house, to look out once again at the decorations around the pool. Japanese lanterns were strung between trees, gently swinging in the warm evening breeze. The surface of the pool was dotted with cork disks holding lighted candles in clear glass containers, with scented gardenias floating among them. White-jacketed waiters were already moving through the colorfully dressed crowd. The sound of their chatter urged Lila down the stairs to join the fun, but, instead, she returned to her room to wait to be summoned, as she had been told.

She sat down in her rocker, and looked over at Candy Floss and Skinny Malink sitting at their usual seats at the tea table, both of them smiling like they didn't have a care in the world. Easy for you, she thought. "I'm the one that's got to be good tonight," she told them, part proud, part frightened.

The dummies' heads were tilted slightly, and Lila could see the place where her mother's hands went behind the dolls to manipulate their mouths and extremities. She'd never noticed that when she was little. Before, when she was little and stupid, she used to think they were real, that they were really her sisters. But that had been a big fat lie. A joke her mother called it. Ha ha.

Candy Floss and Skinny Malink had been part of her mother's life long before she had been. "I love these two as much as I love you," she'd say.

Lila sat and rocked, closed her eyes and tried to remember her lines and the movements her mother and Aunt Robbie had gone to so much trouble to teach her. She was sure she had everything right. She leaned across and arranged Skinny's and Candy's dresses just so, then fluffed her pink dress around her, taking care not to lean back too far for fear of crushing the big bow at the rear.

She jumped as she heard her mother, coming down the hall to her room, calling her name. "I'm here," Lila called.

"Girls, I've come to take you down to entertain our guests. Oh, how pretty my little babies look." Was Lovely Mummie slurring her words again? It made Lila shiver. Mummie patted both dolls' heads, then turned to Lila. "Let me look at you," she said, and frowned. Theresa O'Donnell watched as Lila turned slowly in front of her, waiting uneasily for her mother's comments.

"Lovely, just lovely," Theresa finally said, her frown dissolving into her TV smile. Lila breathed out and smiled, too. "How do you like my hair, Mummie?" Maybe she could take the stupid bow out. "Estrella put a big bow in it."

"Perfect," her mother said, "Exactly the right touch. Now, if only you weren't so goddamn tall."

Mummie looked more closely. "But what's that?" she asked, pointing to a locket. "A necklace? Take it off. Candy and Skinny don't have necklaces, so that's not very fair, is it?" Theresa stood and reached over to pat the dummies. "Don't mind," she told them. "Lila's taking it off now. Aren't you?"

Lila bit the inside of her cheek as she unclasped the

103

locket Aunt Robbie had given her for luck. She put it safely in the top drawer of the bureau. Oh, God, why did Mummie still talk to the dummies? Why did she still pretend like this?

"Lila," her mother said, becoming very serious. "There are a lot of people here who are *very* important to me. I want you to make Mother proud of her little girl." Turning to the dummies, she hummed, "And my other two little babies *always* make me proud." She kissed each doll on its painted wooden cheek and demanded of Lila, "You *are* going to be perfect, aren't you?" Lila saw her mother take Candy's hair in her fist and pull very hard, while keeping her eyes on Lila. She could almost feel how that must hurt. For once, Lila felt sorry for Candy, and, unconsciously, she reached up to her own hair. Lila whispered, "Yes, Lovely Mummie."

Then Theresa released Candy's hair, and gently patted it back into place.

"Smile, girls, we're on now," Theresa said as she took the dummies, each in the crook of an arm, and walked very carefully down the stairs, Lila trailing behind. Please, Mummie, don't trip again, she thought.

"I hate these fucking stairs," Lila had heard her mother mutter. "Elegant, my sweet Irish ass. Cross of Christ!"

As they reached the main floor, Theresa paused and took a moment to command the attention of the crowd. "Hi, everyone. Tonight I'd like you all to meet my other little girl, Lila, who will be making her debut right here with us."

Candy leaned forward and said, "Her debut and retirement in one performance."

"Candy, that's not nice," Theresa scolded the puppet.

"Not nice but true, it seems to me," said Skinny on the other hand. The crowd laughed, and Lila's heart quickened at the sharp barbs from the two. This hadn't been in the rehearsals. She wanted to tell them to shut up, but then she remembered that it was her mother who'd said those things. And it was her mother who'd told her over and over: "Don't be mean to your sisters, they're your bread and butter."

"She wouldn't be Theresa O'Donnell's daughter if she couldn't sing and dance with dummies, would she?" Mummie said. Everyone laughed again and looked at Aunt Robbie Lymon, Mummie's stooge on the TV show. "No, no, everyone, not *that* dummy," she laughed. "Now, please, come with us into the ballroom."

Lila walked up to the raised platform at one end of the room and was helped up by Aunt Robbie, who whispered to her: "Hey, kid, don't worry about anything. Just do it like we rehearsed."

Sitting on a small chair next to her mother, Lila waited until Aunt Robbie finished playing the introduction. Candy and Skinny each sat on one of her mother's knees, their heads turning, scanning the crowd. The music stopped, and Theresa spoke.

"Skinny, Candy, who's that other pretty little girl sitting on the stage? Is she with you?"

Skinny and Candy looked at each other and shrugged their shoulders. "I don't see any pretty girl on the stage," Candy said. "Do you, Skinny?"

"Nope," Skinny said. "I just see you and me pretty little girls, but I don't see no *other* pretty little girl."

Lila's toes tingled cold in her shoes. This wasn't the opening to the act. Mummie had forgotten the opening. Oh, no. Oh, my God. Aunt Robbie had told her what to do if her mother forgot her lines.

"Well," Lila said, "I see *one* pretty little girl and *two* dummies."

Both of the dolls turned their heads to Theresa at the same time, then toward Lila. She was aware of the laughter from the audience and was surprised at how good that made her feel. She noticed how her voice sounded in the big room, and made a point of remembering to speak to the back of the crowd, just like Aunt Robbie had taught her.

"Excuse her, folks," said Skinny. "*She's* hoping for a notice in *Variety*."

"*I'm* not the one whose acting is wooden," said Lila. The crowd laughed again. Lila preened. But Lovely Mummie looked flustered.

As the routine continued, more or less according to the

script, her mother forgot some lines, but Lila filled in. She got caught up in her interchange with Candy and Skinny. She remembered to hold her head just like dolls did, just as she had imitated so many times while sitting in front of the television set. She moved her jaw just like Candy, and kept her arms immobile like Skinny, while reciting her lines. Then, at last, it was over, and all she had to do was sit there while her mother sang her famous song.

When Aunt Robbie began to play the music for Mummie's song, Mummie just kept on smiling. It was a strange smile. The audience murmured, a sound like wind in the orange trees. Why wasn't Mummie singing? She was supposed to sing her song, "The Loveliest Girl in the World." Aunt Robbie began the intro again, and Lila understood what he was trying to say to her. So, desperate, Lila began to sing her mother's closing song. She sang so hard, she didn't notice that the whole room had grown quiet, and every face was on her, even her mother's. She sang with all her heart the famous final words of the song. Lila had never rehearsed it, but she had watched her mom's movie *Birth of a Star* so many, many times that she knew it perfectly. When it came time for the last bar, for the high note, she closed her eyes and made it easily.

When she opened her eyes and looked at Aunt Robbie, he was standing at the piano, applauding. The audience suddenly came alive, shouting, clapping, and whistling. I did it! she thought. I remembered every word and motion and then, when I had to, I even remembered Lovely Mummie's song. And they like me. She looked toward her mother, a smile of achievement on her face. Her mother looked back at her without expression, holding Candy and Skinny down by her sides . . . like dolls. She *never* did that. Lila was confused, but continued to bow to the audience and accept their applause.

Then, at last, Mummie stepped forward, stood next to Lila, smiled broadly, and bowed. She led Lila off the stage, turned, and took the last bow alone, holding Candy and Skinny in her arms like infants. Ignoring the cries of the crowd for an encore, she said, "Thank you, everyone. It's past the girls' bedtime. But you will be seeing us again." Floating on a cloud, Lila waved as her mother led the way through the crowd.

Mr. Wagner put his hand on Theresa's arm as she was passing, and the audience stopped chattering to listen. "Jack, darling, how nice of you to come," Lovely Mummie said so everyone could hear, kissing him on the cheek. "What did you think of our little family entertainment?"

"A perfect performance. It gives me an idea for a TV show. Interested?"

Theresa smiled broadly at Mr. Wagner. "We're always interested in television, Jack. We'd love to do another show, wouldn't we, girls?"

Lila's heart jumped. Did he mean *her*, too?

"I mean Lila, Theresa. The kid's a natural. We'd start her with a half-hour after school, see where it goes." He leaned down toward Lila. "How about it, kid? Want to have a television show?"

"Oh, yes, Mr. Wagner"—remembering to say his name. Then she saw the expression on Lovely Mummie's face, and knew that something was wrong. "I mean, I don't know. I'll have to ask my mother." She just knew that she had better get away from Mr. Wagner, and not hear any more about a television show. She could tell that Lovely Mummie didn't think it was such a good idea.

Her mother closed the door of Lila's room behind her and leaned against it, Candy and Skinny dropped in a heap like dirty laundry at her feet. Lila looked at her, apprehensive.

"Just who do you think you are?" Lovely Mummie growled.

"What do you mean, Mummie?"

"You humiliated me tonight, before everyone who means anything in this town. And in front of Mr. Wagner, of all people. 'Oh, yes, Mr. Wagner,' " she mimicked. Stepping closer to Lila, she screamed, "You humiliated me," and swung her open hand across Lila's face. Lila fell against the puppets. She was stunned, both by the blow and by the words.

"Mummie," she sobbed, "what did I do wrong? I remembered the words when you forgot, Mummie. And I was good, wasn't I? Mr. Wagner said so." Lila was confused.

"Shut up, you little traitor. I didn't forget my lines. I never do." Lila saw the spit spray from her mother's mouth as she yelled. "You deliberately stole my song." Theresa grabbed a handful of Lila's hair and pulled her toward her. Lila, sobbing, pleaded with her mother to tell her what she had done wrong.

"Everyone was laughing at me, you little brat. You couldn't wait to humiliate me, could you? You must really hate me, to deliberately steal the scene, making me look like a fool." She was screaming, in a frenzy. "I'll never be able to get a contract now, because *you* fucked it up. Wagner would have asked me if it wasn't for you."

Theresa picked up the two dummies and shook them in Lila's face. "Are you trying to take their place on television? Do you think you can make their money?" Mummie didn't wait for an answer. "No, you can't, and you never will. Just remember this, *I* got the talent. Not *you,* Lila. *Me.*" Her mother swung a hand at her face again, but Lila pulled away with a sudden effort.

Lila shrank back into the corner of the room. Her mother, breathless, paused. Then she brushed her hair out of her face, and her breath came more slowly. She went to the vanity mirror and fussed with her hair, patted down her gown. "I'm going to return to my guests now. I'm going to look those people in the eyes and pretend that my daughter didn't humiliate me in my own home. You're to stay in your room until I tell you you can come out. And I want you to think about how you've ruined my career tonight."

Then Theresa had turned and left the room, a doll in each arm, shutting the door behind her with a crash. Lila had slumped to the floor and let the tears flow. What did I do? What happened?

She wasn't sure of anything, except that she would never sing again.

And since that night, Lila never had. There was something else about that night, though. It was the first time Lila had known it was the Puppet Mistress who had made the mistakes, not her. But still, she was punished. I did it *right*, Lila had told herself after her sobs subsided. They *liked* me. They applauded. The audience liked *me*, not Theresa O'Donnell. Mr. Wagner liked *me*. And despite her burning cheek, despite her tearing eyes, that had felt very, very good.

Lila put her hand up to her cheek now. She could still feel her mother's slap. She'd never sung since then, but now she knew what she wanted. She wanted that audience, and she'd have to get it. The first step was getting some money. The Puppet Mistress was not going to give her any, or help her move forward in her career.

So after eleven days in the darkness of Robbie's guest room, here she was at Moody, Shlom, and Stone. Her dead father's lawyers. Because, even if he was dead, her father could help. He had left her money, and through these lawyers she could get it. Still, Lila was intimidated, and Lila wasn't intimidated by much. Never having been to a lawyer's office, she wasn't prepared for the size or the sumptuous furnishings. Whenever there had been any business about her father's estate, Mr. Shlom had come to the Puppet Mistress's house.

Now Mr. Moody came out to the reception area himself, and seemed genuinely glad to see her. "Lila Kyle. Bart Moody." He shook her hand. "I've met you before, but there's no way you would remember," he chuckled. "You were two months old, I think." He led her into a corner office, decorated like something out of some corny *Masterpiece Theatre*. She sat on the leather club chair opposite his desk, crossed her legs after hiking up her skirt, and smiled across at her father's lawyer.

"You'll forgive me," the old man said with a laugh, "but you've certainly grown since the last time I saw you."

Lila laughed, and faked a rearrangement of her skirt, as if demurely trying to cover too much exposed thigh. It worked. She noticed him looking at her legs. Well, it couldn't hurt, she thought. "And *you* haven't changed a bit," she giggled.

He blushed. "I see you've inherited Kerry's Irish blarney. And the combined good looks of him *and* Theresa.'' The lawyer paused, and in that moment remembered himself. He cleared his throat. ''But enough of that. What can I do for you?''

''As I told your secretary yesterday, I wanted to talk about the current state and provisions of my trust fund. The one my father set up for me.''

''Yes, your father was very specific; although not exactly a prudent man in many things, he made sure you would be provided for.''

''Yes, Mother told me all about that.'' Screw him, talking about her father. Her father had been a fuckin' *star,* not a fat-ass lawyer. Well, she'd keep it together. ''That brings me to the reason I came to see you. I feel that I can't be a drain on Mother any longer. I need to be independent, and to devote my energies to acting. I've decided that's what I really want to do. But I understand that I can't get an income from my trust fund until I'm twenty-one.''

Mr. Moody, the jerk, shook his head.

''Well, I thought, maybe, you might be able to make an exception for me, since I am doing *exactly* what my father wanted for me—*and* my mother, by the way. So could you, you know, let me have money now?''

The jerk smiled at her, but it wasn't a nice smile. It was an aren't-you-pretty-for-a-stupid-girl smile, and Lila wished she could reach across the desk and kick the old bastard in the nuts. ''I'm sorry, but the terms of the trust are very specific, and I'm bound by law to adhere to them.'' He put on reading glasses and looked down at a file of notes. ''I'm afraid that my late partner Bernie Shlom used to handle this, and I'm not quite filled in yet. How old are you now, my dear?'' he asked, when he looked up.

''Eighteen,'' she lied. Well, close enough.

''Ah. Time flies. I hadn't realized. Well, there *is* a provision for you to receive income from the trust after your eighteenth birthday.''

Lila smiled. Thank God. Maybe the old wrinkle bunny wasn't so bad after all. ''Yes? When can it start? Right away?''

He reached into a side drawer of his desk and took out a yellow legal pad. Looking across the desk at Lila, he said, "I *could* draft a request form asking that you receive benefits immediately."

Lila gave him her sunniest smile, then grabbed the paper and pen from Moody's hand and scribbled her signature. This was easier than she had thought. "There!" she said. "Could you fill that in and do it?"

Again he gave her that annoying grin. "Well," he said, "first we'd have to petition your father's executor to give you your benefits now."

"And who is the executor?" Lila sighed. What bullshit.

"Well, here," Moody said, and handed her a paper. Lila looked down at the paper, then up at Bart Moody's face. She was trembling, but was determined not to lose it. "My mother? Why does she have to give her permission?"

"It's a provision of the trust. If you would like to receive income before your twenty-first birthday, your marriage or your mother's permission is necessary."

Lila sank back into the chair, her arms folded across her chest. How could her father have done this to her? Withhold her *own* money, and give *Theresa* power over it—and her. Why, he hadn't even *liked* Theresa!

Lila leaned forward, one hand on her hip. "Let's forget about Theresa for a minute, Mr. Moody. What about getting a loan—like an advance on it, then? Can you do *that* much for me?"

The old man shook his head, looking forlorn. "The only one who can help you is your mother," he said. "I'm afraid we couldn't touch the fund without her permission."

Lila jumped up. "My mother can't even help *herself*. Have you seen her in the last ten years? She's a drunk. A crazy, booze-soaked, washed-up nut case. She's not going to give me permission for *anything*. I need that money to get away from her."

"Now, Lila, you're only eighteen. The legal age of inheritance is just three years away. Then you . . ."

Lila leaned over Bart Moody's desk, and stared into

his face. "Three years? Do you know what L.A. can do to a woman in three years? I'm new *now*. I could be hot. I can be someone. I could be dead in three years, for chrissakes. I need the money *now*."

Bart Moody stood up and walked to the door. With his hand on the doorknob, he said, "Then I suggest you have this conversation with the only person who can get that money to you now." He opened the door. "Good day," he said.

She was so angry, so frustrated, that she walked down the stairs rather than wait for the elevator. Now what? What the fuck *can* I do? It's not like Westlake gave any career counseling to their students. That would have been ludicrous. Most of the school's graduates were going to walk into jobs their parents got for them, if they were going to work at all. And even if they had job counseling, how did you counsel someone on how to become a star?

She had to have money. She needed a good car, manicures, facials, clothes, a decent place to live. Lila reached the parking lot, and stopped. It was going to have to be Aunt Robbie. How long can I stand him? she wondered. How long will I be able to beg money from him? He wasn't a rich man, and certainly couldn't afford to keep Lila in clothes.

Well, she'd have to economize. Right. Facials only once a month. She'd do her own pedicures. Ask for a comp on her haircuts. Get an allowance from Robbie, promise to pay him back, and live within a budget.

It was that or crawl back to the Puppet Mistress.

No fucking way!

13

"What time is your flight?" Mary Jane had asked Neil to be polite. She couldn't stand to talk to him, or Molly, or anyone. Sam was gone. Flown to LALA Land. Her life felt unlivable. It wasn't quite bad enough for suicide, she thought dully. Only bad enough to wish you'd never been born. She hadn't bathed or changed or cleaned the place since Sam left. Perhaps she'd leave it just as it had been then. Stop the clocks. The whole Miss Havisham bit. Neil was calling from some other century.

But Neil, with all his hustle and excitement, meant well, so she pretended to be interested. With Sam gone, Neil leaving, and a trip up to her grandmother's to look forward to, Mary Jane felt like death on toast.

"Nine A.M., from Kennedy," Neil had said when she asked. "Will you come see me off?"

Mary Jane hesitated. She had been afraid of this. It would be the fourth send-off of friends in a year, all going to L.A., all with contracts tucked under their arms. And she'd heard through the grapevine that Bethanie had gone off tucked under Sam's arm.

Had he known when he made love to her that he was leaving her? Or had that only come to him afterward? Or had he meant only to say goodbye, then rolled into her arms as a knee-jerk reaction? Had Sam met someone in L.A.? If so, why was he taking Bethanie with him? Did he simply need someone, anyone? Had her initial refusal soured him? Did he love her? Had he ever loved her?

They were unanswerable questions. Perhaps Sam himself could not have told her. But that didn't stop her from asking herself, over and over, why. Why? Why?

Now she had to cope with Neil's departure. Mary Jane hated airport goodbyes, hated the interminable subway-and-bus ride, the cheapest transportation back to the city. An hour and a half, at least, wasted, when she could be home, lying in bed, eating Entenmann's chocolate donuts and watching videos. God, she couldn't disappoint Neil, though. Well, she'd bring some donuts and a book with her. Or maybe splurge and take the Carey bus back to town. "Sure, Neil," she'd said. "What time are you going to catch the bus?"

"The good news is: no bus. Hey, the producer's paying my way by limo. The bad news is the time. Pick up at seven in the morning," Neil had told her. Mary Jane moaned audibly, then Neil quickly continued, "We'll have breakfast at the airport after I check in." She had heard the gratitude in Neil's voice when she agreed. Aside from his sister, who did he have to see him off? "Thanks, Mary Jane," he had said just before he hung up.

But that was yesterday. Commitments look different at ten after six on a Sunday morning. She yearned to get back into bed, to become once again oblivious to everything. To avoid the temptation, Mary Jane sat on the tattered sofa in her living room, sipping a steaming mug of coffee, conscious of the total stillness in the apartment. She'd never felt so tired or so alone.

Mary Jane hadn't thought about it till now, but she had been the only handkerchief-waver each of those other three times friends went off to succeed, and she was sure she would be the only one today, too. It couldn't be she was the only friend that all these people had. That was true of Neil, of course—he was much too angry a loner to have many friends—but the others had been outgoing, popular types on the theater circuit in New York. Maybe other friends hated goodbyes more than she. Or maybe, she realized with a jolt, other people were too lazy, too self-involved, and too goddamn envious to share in their friends' good fortune. Maybe she, too, was envious, she thought.

She dressed slowly, forcing the good cheer she didn't feel. It was Neil's triumph today, she thought. She wasn't going to let her feelings about her own career interfere with Neil's success. Maybe she *had* driven Sam away. Tears began to fill her eyes. "Oh, Christ!" she told herself, standing up and almost spilling the coffee. "Get on with it."

Mary Jane was down at the door in front of her building at seven on the nose. While she waited, she studied herself in the reflection of the glass entrance door, and ran her fingers through her thick, almost black hair. At least her hair was nice. But she had to do something about the gray. The denim wraparound skirt made her hips look even bigger, but Neil had commented once on how much he liked her in it. It made her look exactly like Veronica in the Archie comics, he had said. Veronica had given him his first hard-on. So Veronica was who he was getting today, Mary Jane thought, and tried to smile to herself.

She also had on a Laura Ashley print shirt, cream-colored with tiny pink rosebuds and a Peter Pan collar that she had found in a thrift shop on Third Avenue uptown. Very Veronica. On one collar tab she wore a small gold circle pin, and a ridiculous charm bracelet on her wrist, both plastic, both from Woolworth's. Plus, a school cardigan with a letter on it. Penny loafers completed the costume. Now Mary Jane smiled at herself again.

She had just switched her bag to the crook of her elbow, like schoolbooks, when she saw the dark blue Tel Aviv sedan turn the corner from Tenth Avenue onto Fifty-fourth Street. Neil was at the open window as the car came to a stop, and yelled out, "Veronica!"

"Jughead," she called back, and did a tiny pirouette to give Neil the full effect before she got into the car.

"You're crazy, Mary Jane," Neil said, laughing, as the car pulled away from the curb. "That's why I love you."

"*I'm* crazy," Mary Jane said in mock surprise. "*You're* the one with the Veronica fetish. I never knew anyone who was in love with a comic-book character before."

"What I felt had nothing to do with love," Neil leered. "I wanted to get her into the back booth at Pop Tate's and do the horizontal boogaloo."

"Other boys jerked off to *Playboy*. You always had to be different," she laughed. She turned and eyed Neil from head to toe as they sped downtown along the East River Drive to the Midtown Tunnel. Pink raw-silk shirt, the top three buttons open, white slacks, white Gucci loafers, no socks. On someone else it would look good. "Looks like I'm not the only one who visited Wardrobe," she said. "Let me guess. You're going to a party costumed as Robert Evans."

"Hollywood *is* a costume party," Neil said, and laughed. "So what do you think? Will I fit in?"

"Just a minute," she said, and began to rummage through her handbag. "You're missing something." She extended a small, gaily wrapped gift box. "Bon voyage," she told him, and handed it over.

Neil opened the wrappings roughly, then shrieked with laughter as he held up the wide fake gold chain with the huge Capricorn medallion suspended from it.

"*Now* you'll fit in," Mary Jane said, and secured the garish chain around his neck. She patted the medallion so it nestled against Neil's exposed skinny chest and sparse chest hairs. "*So* L.A."

"Actually, I think they're now into the fake cowboy stuff again, mixed with wire-rimmed glasses. But, hey, I'm a traditionalist." Neil laughed.

At the terminal, Mary Jane watched from the sidewalk as the driver pulled Neil's bags from the car trunk. Neil's usual angry frown was gone, and he had a smile on his too-wide mouth. His ferretlike profile would put Jamie Farr to shame, she thought, but, God, she was going to miss him. "Let me help you," she offered.

"Nothing doing," he said. "Stars never carry their own luggage." He signaled to a skycap, who was able to check him in and tell him the gate number for his flight. Once inside, Mary Jane let Neil take her arm and lead her across the near-empty waiting area to the coffee shop.

The waitress poured coffee for them, then took their breakfast order. "And two Bloody Marys, doubles," Neil added before she walked away.

"Why, Jughead, what would Pop Tate say? Are you trying to get me drunk?" Mary Jane asked coquettishly.

Neil leaned across the table and took Mary Jane's hand. "Come with me, Mary Jane," he said softly, his voice serious.

Oh, not this, she thought. Not now. I have no strength

to be brave. I used it all up being a good sport. Mary Jane tried to keep her tone light. "Sure, that's just what Hollywood needs: a fat, ugly broad who can't get a job, because the beauties can't get them, either." The waitress came and placed their drinks in front of them. It was the distraction she needed. "Here's to you, Neil, and your success." She clicked her glass against his and took a sip.

Neil took a gulp, then put his glass back down. "I mean it, Mary Jane. Come with me now. I could buy a ticket on my credit card, and we'll be gone. Just do it."

Mary Jane shifted in her seat. "I can't do it, Neil. You know that."

"I love you," Neil said. "Now that you've split from Sam, I can say so. I love you. I dream of you almost every night. I want to touch you all the time. I want to take care of you."

Mary Jane felt the tightening in her chest. Oh, good Christ, it was too much. It was impossible. And, in a way, insulting. A cosmic message: Sam was too good for you; this clown is all you get. But Neil wasn't just a clown. He was her friend. She looked over at him and saw his pain. "Neil, I thought . . . I thought we were just good friends. I didn't know." She began to cry. "I'm so sorry, Neil."

"If you won't do it for me," Neil said, "then do it for yourself. You have a unique talent, Mary Jane. You could get work out there."

She tried to get control of herself, mopping her eyes with the damp cocktail napkin. "Neil, if I didn't get cast in the movie version of *Jack and Jill and Compromise* when I'd originated the role on the stage, I'm never going to get a role in the movies. *Jack and Jill and Compromise* was my only chance. I know that now." She saw Neil's face fall, the dejection causing his eyes to turn down at the corners. His sadness was more than she could bear. She didn't want him to leave New York so glum. And she prayed he didn't feel about her what she felt for Sam. "Hey, Neil," Mary Jane said. "What time is it when your best friend dresses like your fantasy?"

Neil tried to smile, but didn't answer.

"Time to get out of town," Mary Jane said, and patted his hand.

Neil sighed. "Okay," he said. "So I get out of town. What about you?"

"What about me?" Mary Jane asked. "I have the theater group, I have friends. I don't know, maybe one of these days I'll even get another successful play. And when Sam comes back . . ."

"Forget Sam."

"Don't, Neil. I've asked you before." Mary Jane felt her color rise. They paused, looking intently at each other as they listened to the boarding announcement on the public-address system. "That's your flight," she said, and was grateful that this scene was ending.

Neil picked up his carry-on bag from the seat next to him. Without looking up, he said, "Forget Sam, Mary Jane. He was never good enough for you. He was just a nice tall body and perhaps a dick the size of his ego. And he stuck it into anything that walked."

Mary Jane got up quickly. "This isn't the time or the place, Neil. I didn't want to hear this." She began to walk toward the exit.

"I'm sorry, Mary Jane," Neil said as he caught up to her. They stood in silence next to the security desk leading to the boarding gates. Neil dropped his bag and turned Mary Jane around by the arms to face him. "I *do* love you, Mary Jane. But I wouldn't be a friend if I didn't tell you what I think. I don't dislike Sam because he's with you. I dislike him because he uses people, and he's used you. His play would have folded in a minute, just like his other plays, if your talent hadn't held it together. And I think, Mary Jane, that you just fell for a pretty face. Don't be shallow. I'm not so great to look at, but I think you ought to look twice."

"I wish you hadn't said that." Mary Jane looked intently into Neil's eyes. "Goodbye, Neil, and good luck." Mary Jane turned and began to walk away, choking back the tears of sadness and anger.

But Neil pulled Mary Jane toward him again and hugged her. "I won't ever forget you, Mary Jane," he said, then kissed her on the lips. It was a real kiss, his tongue darting into her mouth, his lips wet against her dry ones.

Mary Jane froze.

Neil let her go, then picked up his bag. "Am I still a frog, or have you turned me into a prince?" he asked, his voice hard.

"You've always been a prince to me," she told him.

"That's the first lie you ever told me," he said. "You know what? I'm tired of playing a supporting role in your life. I'm ready for the lead. Why is it that I called you 'Veronica' but you never once called me 'Archie'? It was always 'Jughead.' Sure, Jughead had the lines, but Archie got the girls. I could see you as Veronica, Mary Jane, but not once, not once could you look past the surface and see me as Archie. Every time you called me 'Jughead,' it hurt. Every single time. Well, I'm sick of that role. I'm trying out for Archie's part. And if I've failed the audition, fuck you!" Then he turned, walked up to the security desk and dropped his bag on the conveyor belt, moving through the security check. He didn't look back.

In just another moment, he was gone.

Mary Jane stood at the curb outside the terminal, waiting for the Carey bus that would take her back to the city. She dabbed at her eyes with a tattered tissue, then dropped it into the trash barrel beside her. She looked up and saw the bus pull into the pickup lane. She turned back to the trash barrel, took off the stupid charm bracelet and pin, and dropped them in, too, then boarded the bus without looking back.

When she got back to her apartment, Midnight greeted her, along with a yellow Western Union envelope. What fresh hell is this? she wondered, and tore it open. Am I being evicted, or has the IRS decided to audit penniless actresses this week? She pulled out the message.

YOUR GRANDMOTHER DIED THIS A.M. PLEASE COME TO ELMIRA NO LATER THAN TOMORROW TO MAKE ARRANGEMENTS. PLEASE CALL ASAP. EDWARD ROBINSON. ROBINSON'S FUNERAL HOME.

Mary Jane stared at the message. Her grandmother was dead. After all those false alarms and miserable complaints, when Mary Jane had finally decided to ignore the old woman just for once, then the old woman dies. Tearless, profoundly tired, Mary Jane stared at the slip of paper. Her grandmother was dead.

And, with a pull deep in her gut, Mary Jane realized that she envied her.

14

Sharleen's fear had begun to recede, lulled by the comforts of Dobe's car and the easy living. And, she thought, if the police were looking for her and Dean, they wouldn't be lookin' for a family. Together, the three of them did look like a family. It was pleasant in the car. Dobe told funny stories, and Dean kept them busy with license plates. "Look! There's an Oklahoma. 'Oklahoma is O.K.,' " he read off the tag.

"Never struck *me* that way," Sharleen said.

"Well, at least they're not making exaggerated claims," Dobe said mildly. "Not like Louisiana."

"Sportsman's paradise!" Dean told him proudly.

"Depends on what you consider sport," Dobe said grimly.

They stopped in gas stations, and each time Dobe filled up with water, sold a dozen pills or so, and they moved on. They spent more than a week in Arizona, then moved up to Nevada. And at each state line they crossed, Sharleen said a prayer and drew a deeper breath than she'd been able to breathe before.

That night, in yet another motel, this one outside Carson City, Nevada, Sharleen knelt in prayer and thanked the Lord for all the blessings He sent her way, and for His help in taking care of her and Dean. And she thanked Him again for Dobe, who was a gentleman and a Christian. As always, she prayed for the souls of Boyd and her daddy then. Sharleen stood up and walked to the night table, opening the drawer. Again there was a Bible. God *must* be leading them. But she was starting to think there might be a Bible in every motel room, just like there were towels and soap. She walked to the bathroom door, knocked, and called in to Dean.

"They got another Bible here, Dean. Almost ready?"

"What are you going to read tonight?" Dean asked from behind the door.

Sharleen took the black-covered book and put it aside. "I like reading from Momma's," she said, as she placed the motel's Bible back into the drawer of the nightstand, picking up their mother's tattered copy instead. "I don't know just yet, Dean. You know I like to open it without any plan, and just let the Lord and Momma give us their message."

From the time Dobe had spoken to her about Dean, she had been mulling over what he had said. The lie that Dean wasn't her brother troubled her, but not as much as the fact that he *was* her boyfriend. And her half-brother. It all seemed so complicated. Dean in many ways was like a child, but he also was her protector. She took care of him, but she needed him, too. He was her family. At home in Lamson, she could keep the problem out of her mind. On the road, their relationship troubled her far more.

Dean came out of the bathroom. "Read me the one about Daniel with the lion again, Sharleen. I like that part. I don't understand some of the other stuff."

Sharleen sat at the edge of the bed. Dean was sprawled the length of it, wearing only his jockey shorts. He had his eyes closed, his hands behind his head, and a small, peaceful smile on his lips. Sharleen looked down at him, marveling as usual at his beauty and the perfection of his body. He reminded her of an angel, a frightened, gentle, loving angel, and it was her responsibility to take care of him, to see that his gentleness and beauty would not be destroyed by the harshness of life. Sharleen knew she wasn't too smart herself, but at least *she* was smart enough to make sure that they both got along without getting in too much trouble with some of the wicked people that roam the earth.

Sharleen flipped the pages of their mother's dog-eared Bible, then stopped and opened to a page. "Tonight's reading, Dean, is from Deuteronomy, chapter ten, verse nine. This is in the Old Testament, Dean, before Jesus was born." Sharleen looked closer at the passage, and saw that the scripture she had chosen had been marked in pencil by their mother, as many had. "Dean, guess what! Momma liked this passage, too, and marked it. So let's see what she's telling us from the Lord."

Sharleen leaned back on the bed's headboard, the Bible opened on her lap. As she settled in, Dean turned his face toward her, rested his forehead against her thigh, and threw one hand across her legs. He kept his eyes closed.

"This is the place Momma marked," Sharleen told Dean. " 'Wherefore Levi hath no part nor inheritance with his brethren; the Lord is his inheritance, according as the Lord thy God promised him.' "

Sharleen closed the book slowly, holding a finger in it to keep her place. "Levi hath no part . . . with his brethren." She thought of Dobe's advice to her about Dean, of her shame, and she got gooseflesh all up her arms.

"Go on, Sharleen. It sounds real pretty."

"Dean," she said very gently. "This is a message from Momma."

"She says things in her book so pretty, Sharleen."

"Momma is telling us something, Dean. Sit up and listen."

Dean opened his eyes and pulled himself up to a sitting position, also using the headboard for support. "I can't understand what Momma tells us in the book, Sharleen. She don't talk like she used to back home."

"These aren't Momma's words exactly, Dean. These are the words of God. Momma just tells us where to look in the book. And tonight she told us to look at these words because they tell us something. Something very important. It says Levi has no part with his brother."

"Only Levi I know is dungarees. What do you mean, Sharleen? Who's Levi?" Dean asked.

"It don't matter who *he* is. He just ain't supposed to have no part of his brother." Dean looked at her, and slowly, very slowly, she saw the fear come into his clear blue eyes.

Sharleen put her arm around Dean's shoulder and stroked his white-blond hair, so like her own. "Dean, Momma is telling us we got to sleep in separate beds from now on. Now that we're growed, it's time we slept alone."

"But why? *Your* name ain't Levi. It don't say *Sharleen* don't have no part with her brother. And why should Momma want us to sleep alone now? She always tucked us in together back home. Why's she saying now we got to sleep separate?" He sounded petulant, almost on the verge of tears.

"Because we don't just sleep. And it ain't right, what we do. Brothers and sisters ain't supposed to share the same bed. They ain't supposed to touch each other like we do."

Dean's face crumpled. It pained Sharleen, right to her heart. "You mean we can't be close and feel good no more?"

"That's right, Dean. We can be close friends, but we can't make each other happy in that way no more." Sharleen thought again of Dobe's comment. About seeing how things were between her and Dean. Before he had warned her, she had tried real hard not to think too much about it, it had felt so natural at night to be close to Dean, safe and happy. Why, they had always been close like that. She couldn't sleep any other way. It was their secret. But Dobe was a good man, and smart, and now Momma sent this word from the Bible. That's twice now she had been warned.

Sharleen rose from the bed and pulled the covers over Dean's body. She noticed the bulge in his briefs, and quickly covered it.

Dean continued to cry. "But the dreams, Sharleen. I get so scared. I can't go to sleep without you holding me, Sharleen. I never had to before."

Sharleen thought of her own, more recent bad dreams, but bent over him and kissed him on the forehead. "I'll be right here in the other bed, right beside you. Nothing bad's going to happen to you, not as long as we do what God wants us to do." She pulled back the covers of the other twin bed and slid in, then turned off the light, leaving her mother's Bible on the table between them. "Now, just say your prayers and go to sleep. The Good Lord will watch over us. And don't forget to pray for Boyd and Daddy, and especially for Momma, and thank her for her guidance."

Dean sniffled. "Okay, Sharleen. I will, if that's what you want."

They lay in silence for a long while. Sharleen knew she would not be able to sleep, but hoped that Dean would finally drift off. And she prayed he wouldn't dream. Not one of the real bad ones anyway. She continued to lie there, wide awake, as Dean's breathing slowed. She missed his warmth beside her, but now she knew what Dobe had meant. Still, it was hard to relax without Dean next to her. Silly, because their daddy couldn't hurt them now. It mustn't be right to be with Dean. Hadn't Momma's message practically said that exactly?

Eventually, she heard Dean's breathing even out into sleep. She tried to sleep herself, and dozed a little, but just as she became aware of the first streak of light on the horizon outside her window, she heard him.

Dean had started to thrash in bed, whimpering. "No," he moaned. "No, please!" Sharleen couldn't bear it, but forced herself to stay in her own bed. It will pass, she thought.

But Dean's cries grew louder, and his movements in the bed more violent. "No! Daddy! Please!" he cried out. She knew he was having one of the bad ones, but she was resolved to do the will of God. It was torture, though. Dean writhed, groaning. She picked up Momma's Bible on the nightstand, hoping to find words of comfort. She clicked on the small light over her bed, and ran through the pages of the Bible. Dean quieted down, but he still wept in his sleep. Sharleen closed her eyes and prayed. "Oh, Lord, please help me do the right thing, and give Dean peace in his sleep. Momma, help me." She, too, began to cry softly, and once again opened the Good Book, to Psalms, her favorite. But once again Dean moaned, a deep, pained cry.

She flipped a page or two and stopped at Psalm 133. "Behold," she read in the dim light, "how good and how pleasant it is for brethren to dwell together in unity!"

She stared at the page, running her finger over the text, over and over. Then Sharleen put the book back on the night table and said in a whisper, "Thank you, Lord." She got out of bed and went over to Dean. She touched him gently to make room for herself, and got in next to him. She put her arms around him and whispered in his ear, "I'm here, Dean. Everything is going to be all right now."

Dean had wakened as Sharleen came into his bed. Without opening his eyes, he nuzzled deeply into Sharleen and said, "Don't never leave me alone, Sharleen."

Sharleen rocked him gently in her arms. "No, Dean," she promised, "I never will."

15

Mary Jane was suddenly and completely awake, but she knew the effort of opening her eyes was beyond her for the moment. She lay there, her body fitting into the familiar depression of the lumpy mattress. Her skin quickened from the cold in the damp, unheated room.

She allowed her eyes to flicker open for a moment, saw as much as she could bear, then shut them again. Oh, God! No. She hadn't meant to wake up. At least not here. Couldn't she do *anything* right? She was a nurse, for chrissakes. She was lying on the bedspread, no blanket, still wearing the black dress she had worn to the funeral yesterday, now twisted about her body. One black pump lay on its side at the bottom of the bed.

The funeral. I came back here after the funeral yesterday. And then . . . ? And then I had a drink, she remembered. And that was as far as she could go for the moment. Another chill ran through her body, this one forcing her to sit up, the sudden movement making her lightheaded. She turned to the edge of her bed, very slowly now, and lowered her feet. She sat there for a moment, gathering her resources for the next movement. And then, without warning, she vomited.

When she was done, Mary Jane looked around the sparsely furnished, unadorned room, feeling like an intruder, even though this was the bedroom in which she had grown up. Hell, she'd felt like an intruder *then!* Her eyes fell on the closet door, knowing the remains of her childhood were in cartons in there. The smell of mildew mixed with the smell of her vomit. Slowly, she stood, tottered over to the bureau, and wiped up the mess with an old tattered towel. She opened the half-rotted window sash and dumped the fetid rag outside.

Even after all these years, it still hurt that her grandmother had packed all her belongings into boxes the week she went away to nursing school. Mary Jane could never bring herself to go through the boxes of old clothes, clippings, yearbooks, and memories, but she still resented her grandmother for erasing all signs of her presence. The resentment lingered now, even after the old woman was dead.

Mary Jane wrapped a robe around herself for warmth, closed the bedroom door behind her, and walked down the worn wooden stairs, her stockinged feet making shushing sounds as she moved. For a moment, in the silence between steps, she could almost hear Snowball, her old black cat, walking at her side, thumping down the steps to join her at her lonely breakfast, his tail swishing back and forth in excitement. That cat—long dead—had been her only comfort growing up. Now Midnight was her only friend back in New York. Well, she told herself, not much has changed.

She walked into the kitchen and looked around at the chaos, resenting her grandmother even more for her slovenly ways than for the poverty of spirit that engendered them.

She picked up the coffeepot from the stove, filled it with cold water and coffee, and placed it on the flame. She waited for it to percolate while she recovered from the effort, seated at the stained white-enamel table, her chin in her hands. Her eyes swept the mean room, coming to rest on the stack of empty soup cans off in one corner. The shelf over the cracked porcelain sink held a few chipped plates and mugs from the five-and-ten; the wallpaper was faded and bulging in spots, probably from the many leaks the house regularly sprung each spring. The green-and-brown-enameled stove stood on six metal legs, the surface dark from layers of grease untouched for years. The linoleum was worn through before the sink and the stove, exposing older, tattered linoleum and the gray splintering wood underneath.

She looked out the grimy window at the steel-gray day, and the other pieces of the day before began to slip into her consciousness. The funeral, the burial. The few people in the church were there out of neighborliness, even though Mary Jane's grandmother had been anything but neighborly. Only one other person made it to the grave, Mrs. Willis, Grandma's closest neighbor, who lived a mile away.

After hearing the first thud of dirt from the shovel hit the cheap, unfinished pine box, Mary Jane had settled the bill with Mr. Robinson and gotten back in the rental car she couldn't afford. She drove Mrs. Willis back home. Then she returned to the desolate farmhouse. Yes, and had a drink.

And another. And another. And cried. At least I cried, she thought, as she poured out the coffee. But I didn't cry for my grandmother. I cried for me. And then, she admitted, she'd walked into her grandmother's room and taken every pill on the nightstand, washing the whole collection down with the Chivas she'd brought with her from New York. She planned never to wake up, never to face another bleak morning. Because at thirty-four she knew she had had her shot—an important part, a special man—and it was over. If a fat, plain actress couldn't make it by thirty-four, should she expect it would be better at forty-six? At fifty? I've ended my great expectations, she thought.

But her suicide obviously hadn't worked. The irony of it—a nurse who couldn't find the right prescription for

127

suicide! There had been a lot of pills, then the rest of the Chivas. Then, at last, blessed unconsciousness, unconsciousness that she hoped was permanent.

But she'd awoken to this: the ugliness and filth of herself and her surroundings. *This* is what I came from, and, despite all my work, *this* is all I am. Trash from trash.

There wouldn't be another Sam, or another part like Jill, or another friend like Neil, or another theater group like the troupe. She sat at the table, too sick, too tired even to cry. She remembered the Dorothy Parker suicide poem and added a stanza of her own:

> Pills taste awful;
> Vomit stinks;
> But I've had a crawful—
> The suicide thinks.

The coffeepot began to bubble as she walked into the pantry to look for something she could eat to calm her sick stomach. Saltines, maybe. She surveyed the contents of the shelves, mostly squat mason jars containing the dried peas and beans and preserved vegetables her grandmother had religiously put up every year but never used. Rows and rows of aged tomatoes and carrots and string beans. The short wall of the room held perishables, each tightly enclosed in a baggie with a red wire twist at its neck. Her eyes fell on some crackers; she knew that this was the only solid food she could manage. She took the plastic-bagged box from the shelf, untwisting the tie as she walked back to the littered kitchen table.

She poured a cup of the coffee, reached into the box of crackers, and removed the opened portion. She bit into one tentatively, tasted its mustiness, spat it out, and pulled out one of the other waxed-paper sleeves. She was about to open it when she noticed it was already unsealed at the wrong end. Through the opaque wrapper, she saw something. Something grayish-green.

A mouse? She almost dropped the packet, but it didn't move, and she looked more closely. No. Not a mouse. Mary Jane tore open the wrapping and sucked in her breath. A rubber-band-wrapped bundle rolled onto the table. Mary Jane stared down at it for a moment before she croaked the word out loud.

"Money!"

The bills had been so tightly rolled, it took her some time to get them unfurled and laid out in denominations on the table: all $637. The shock of the discovery forced her to sit back in the creaking chair. Where had this come from? For an instant, she wished her grandmother had known about the money, then realized the truth . . . her grandmother had put it there!

Oh, no, Grandma, she thought. Why? What did you hope to do with this money? Then, at last, Mary Jane cried for the crazy old woman, mourning her grandmother's missed opportunity of spending this money, which Mary Jane guessed must have taken a lifetime to save.

As her tears abated, she sipped her now lukewarm coffee, trying to think. How long had it taken the old woman to save over six hundred dollars on her egg money, her vegetable sales, her Social Security? Mary Jane wondered.

She realized she had never thought about her grandmother's finances before. She'd always accepted the fact that they were dirt-poor. Grandma had told her over and over how she, Mary Jane, lived out of Grandma's charity —"when I haven't even enough for myself." But was that the truth? Surely her grandmother had received Aid to Families with Dependent Children after Mary Jane's mother had been killed and her father incapacitated. And hadn't her grandfather, long dead, been with the railroad? Had there been a pension? What about the V.A.? Was there a pension from the army for her dad? It also had never occurred to her that her grandmother had made extra money from leasing out her grazing land to farmers. The belief was always that that rent was barely enough to pay the mortgage, but could there be more? And had the mortgage been paid off? Like a dreamer, waking up, she shook her head. It was probably a crazy idea, but Mary Jane stood, dropping the opened crackers to the floor. She walked to the pantry.

Mary Jane ripped open the other package of crackers.

Nothing. Of course not; silly idea. Look at this place. Worse than Miss Havisham's. Dust and cobwebs everywhere. Grandma was dirt-poor. But what if there *is* more? she thought. What else is in the pantry? In the house?

Trembling, she began to pick up each mason jar of vegetables, to study their contents through the dusty glass. Halfway down the row, the heft of one of the jars in the back was different. She returned to the kitchen, washed off the dirt, and looked. Hurriedly, she released the vacuum seal with effort, reached in, and removed a plastic-wrapped bundle: another roll of bills. Her heart thumping in her chest, her hands shaking, she counted out the money. Almost two thousand dollars.

She poured a fresh cup of coffee and slumped into the chair, her heart still pounding. More than two thousand dollars! And if there was this much, there was more.

Looking down at the growing stack of bills, Mary Jane knew with certainty: My grandmother never loved me. She took me in when my mother died and my father went into the V.A. She was the only family I knew, but she never loved me. No wonder I always felt like a burden. She remembered, as a child, when she asked for something, as children do—money for the movies, candy, a toy—the words of her grandmother's refusal. "No, can't afford it, not now that there's two mouths to feed. Now that I'm saddled with you."

So she had soon stopped asking, and even stopped expecting. She expected nothing, and felt everyone was "saddled" with her, as if she were some unspeakable burden. And when she lost her scholarship because she'd had to take a night job while going to nursing school fulltime during the day and her grades had dropped to B's, she accepted without questioning what her grandmother had said: "Can't help you out. I can barely feed myself."

Mary Jane crashed her fist down on the table. The old woman had lied. Where had this money come from? What if there's more? She stood up and looked around the room, at the ridiculous stack of empty soup cans that had been washed out and saved for no discernible purpose. She kicked at the pile, sending them clanking across the floor, kicking at each one, bouncing them off the walls, stomping on some as they rolled along the floor.

Goddamn you, Grandma. How could you? I was a good girl. How could you have withheld this money? How could you not have loved me, not even a little?

Mary Jane's eyes fell to a bubble in the faded wallpaper over the sink. She reached out and felt a bulge and, now with purpose, took a knife and cut out the square. She peeled back the paper and exposed sheets of the kind of plastic found in photo albums. Through the shiny surface, Mary Jane saw the certificates. Bearer bonds. Old ones. She counted them. Eleven thousand dollars' worth of bearer bonds!

She tore the house apart. It took her hours. The backs of pictures, the lining of upholstery, the floorboards, the rest of the preserves. In the freezer she found almost four thousand dollars frozen in an ice block. In the bathroom there was $760 in an old—a very old—Modess box. As she tore and smashed and cried, as she searched every inch of the filthy, nasty little shack she'd been forced to grow up in, she sobbed.

That night, Mary Jane picked up the bundle of cash and bonds, over sixty-seven thousand dollars' worth, and started upstairs to her room. Her step was slowed by exhaustion from the search, from the anger, and from the tears. As she passed the thermostat at the foot of the stairs, she looked at the setting: sixty-five degrees, the highest her grandmother ever allowed it to be set. With a snap she pushed up the setting to seventy-five, and continued upstairs with her bundle, knowing that now, at least, she would be warm.

16

In twenty-five years of covering the Hollywood water-front, I—Laura Richie—have learned one thing for sure: There are faces that the camera loves, personalities that come alive, project, expand under attention. It isn't simply a question of looks, although being photogenic helps. But it's much more than that, much rarer than that: Sophia Loren had it, Gina Lollobrigida did not. Gary Cooper had it, Gregory Peck did not. Burt Reynolds had it, Tom Selleck does not.

You can't learn it, or practice it. It's just there, like your breath. People want to watch you. You have an intrinsically riveting persona that plays on screen. How? Why? Nobody knows.

And it isn't acting. There are some great actors who didn't have it. Back in the thirties, the Schencks and Goldwyns and Warners called it "star quality." It's as good a term as any. And believe me, dear Reader, it's as rare as, and more valuable than, a black diamond.

Lila pulled her old Mustang convertible into the parking space behind the low gray building in West Hollywood. She jumped out and, throwing her bag over her shoulder, walked quickly to the side entrance and up the flight of stairs, her red hair flowing in the breeze behind her. She could tell from the chattering voices that the door to the classroom was still open. I'm on time, she thought. Lila hated to be late for acting class. George Getz took perverse pleasure in singling out late arrivals and haranguing them about their responsibility to the "company," as he called his pretty little collection of wannabes. Not that he could ever succeed in making Lila feel uncomfortable. On the contrary. George was usually so busy fawning over the daughter of Theresa O'Donnell that Lila felt like she might lose her lunch.

She looked around the cavernous, windowless room,

at the gray-tweed carpeting that went halfway up three walls. Several stacks of putty-gray folding chairs were piled to one side. Next to them were mounds of soft cushions. One wall was entirely mirrored. Lila walked past a knot of young women who greeted her by name as she sailed by. Just like Westlake. She was still the popular girl, and it was still because she didn't give a shit. She didn't look in their direction, but gave a general hello as she opened the door to the ladies' room. Inside, she pulled a brush through her silky red hair to get out the tangles caused by the wind lashing around her as she drove her convertible with the top down. Well, Ken's convertible, actually. Aunt Robbie had talked Ken into lending it to her. She actually hated the Ford, and the maroon color clashed with her hair, but beggars couldn't be choosy, so they said.

The door opened behind her and, in the mirror, she could see one of the young blonde women rush in. Bandie something, Lila thought, and turned her attention back to her own hair. She was friendly; they were all friendly, because once they had watched her mother and Candy and Skinny. Now they felt they knew her, and that maybe the famous Theresa O'Donnell would help them. Yeah, like she could help herself! Or her own flesh and blood!

"Oh, hi, Lila," Bandie cooed as she dropped her bag on the table in front of the mirror and began to rifle through it. "Guess what," she said. Not waiting for Lila's reply, she continued, "I got a commercial. A *national* commercial!" Bandie applied the melon-colored lipstick she'd finally found. "I can't believe it," Bandie said. "There were sixteen callbacks, and *I* got it."

"Congratulations," Lila said. Even though money was a problem for her, she'd *never* do a commercial. Yet she knew that for one of her classmates to get a commercial was a big coup. The income from a national ad could go a long way toward easing the financial strain brought on by acting classes, elocution lessons, singing lessons, and dance classes. Not to mention clothes, cars, personal grooming, personal trainers, orthodontists, hair coloring, colonics, and a touch of the surgeon's knife from time to time. But Bandie, like so many of the others, actually considered commercials real acting jobs. For most, Lila knew, it would be the closest thing to performing before the public that they would ever get. Lila shuddered. *She'd* never sell floor wax or douches on TV.

Lila remembered when her mother was asked to endorse some crap—a detergent or something—on television, with Candy and Skinny. Theresa had gone apeshit. "Stars don't do laundry *or* TV commercials," she had screamed at Ara Sagarian, her agent. Lila had heard many of Mother's definitions of stars through the years, and filed all of them away. The Puppet Mistress was a manipulating bitch, a drunk, a pain in the ass, and a total nutcake, but she *had* been a star. And that is what Lila wanted to be, a *star*, someone who never carries cash; always arrives by limousine; never opens a door; doesn't smoke in public; never refuses a request for an autograph; remembers everyone's name; never wears a gown publicly more than once; addresses her directors as "Mister," encourages others to address her as "Miss"; does not socialize with the technical crew; never makes her own reservations; shakes hands in greeting instead of kissing; calls her *producers* by their first names; has a secretary; never drives her own car unless it's a fun one; has favorite charities; attends other stars' performances; knows how to turn a man down without rejecting him; arrives late and leaves early; sits in the best seat at a party and waits for *them* to come to *her;* does not serve herself from a buffet table; knows how to read a contract; and is never offstage.

And that is what she aimed to be: a bigger star than her mother. So no fucking commercials.

She turned to Bandie. "What's the product?" Lila asked pleasantly, like she cared.

"A premium bathroom tissue," Bandie said with a look of triumph.

Deliver me, Lila thought. "Congratulations," she said politely, and put her brush back in her bag.

"I called Mr. Getz immediately. He's *so* proud of me."

Great. Their acting coach was proud his student was selling ass-wipe. Lila sighed. Robbie had *sworn* that Getz had connections, and Lila had to start someplace. She went back out into the open room and dropped down onto one of the cushions. She looked around at the other participants and was struck once again by the number of beautiful men and women in the room. It was an L.A. cliché. They were a plague, these perfect-looking mannequins. Here assembled in one room was the handsomest boy from Debbins, South Dakota; Lake Winesha, Wisconsin; Portland Bay, Oregon; Charleston, West Virginia; Cudahy, Iowa; Woodbridge, Massachusetts; and Shreveport, Louisiana; as well as the most beautiful girl from Shadley, Mississippi; Goochland, Virginia; Barre, Vermont; Standish, Rhode Island; Black Springs, Ohio; and Enid, Oklahoma. Their looks had made them special, had been a passport out of the backwaters they'd crawled away from, but here in Hollywood even the best looks only guaranteed a waitressing job, a parking-valet job, a blow job. Lila shook her head.

A door opened at the end of the room and a paunchy man in his fifties entered, his long, gray hair pulled back into a pony tail. There was some hesitant clapping from a few of the recent enrollees, then silence as George Getz plopped heavily down on a cushion one of the students had brought for him. The semicircle re-formed around him. Only Lila didn't move. Lila studied George as he sat cross-legged, poring over some notes. His paunch rested on his legs; his white, scrawny legs were like matchsticks extending out of his khaki safari shorts; black leather sandals shod his feet. He was wearing a faded, white "Save the Whales" T-shirt, which stretched across a distended stomach. His rimless glasses were thick, so his small eyes appeared open in amazement all the time.

Well, it was Aunt Robbie who had suggested George Getz. Robbie's opinion about acting teachers was well known. He felt that either you could act or you couldn't. If you couldn't, no one could teach you how; if you could, all you needed was someone to show you a few of the tricks to develop your craft, and George, he felt, was at least capable of *that*. Plus, he was still plugged in to a few of the older producers and directors.

Now George looked up, calling the class to order by

letting his eyes drift over the faces in the room. Lila could feel the tension in the stillness. Everyone was here to learn from this man, but they all knew that there was a high price to pay, besides the tuition. George rarely praised anyone's efforts, and took great delight in humiliating the youngsters' least competent attempts.

"Everyone, spread out on the floor . . . get rid of the cushions . . . make sure you have a large space around you. . . . This is going to be a group effort. Bring your focus within, close your eyes, do your breathing exercises." The class responded to his instruction, the only sound the hypnotic breathing of the group. Personally, Lila thought it was a load of crap. "Now sit up, keeping the eyes closed. Bring your legs to your chest, hugging them. Breathe. Breathe. Now, focus. I want you to convince me that you are vanilla ice cream melting in the sun. I want you to *be* vanilla ice cream melting in the sun. Forget about time. I will tell you when to stop. Begin."

Lila slowed her breathing. What an absolute pile of dog shit! Lila supposed that good acting came from the ability to visualize and then represent an intense inner experience of a character, but ice cream? Anyway, she wasn't planning to be an actress. She was planning to be a star.

The silence was broken by George's voice. "Corey," he said, "continue with the exercise, but don't open your eyes. Class, open your eyes and look at Corey."

Lila did, then sighed. She knew what was coming, and resented the ridiculous interruption just to satisfy George's egotistical rants.

"What do you see, class? Keep studying Corey. Do you see vanilla ice cream melting in the sun? NO!" he suddenly shouted. The class jumped. "He looks like a mound of mashed potatoes. And mashed potatoes don't melt, do they, Corey?"

Corey opened his eyes and gave George an apologetic smile; then his face colored as he saw the entire class looking at him.

"So that, boys and girls, is an example of how it's *not* done." George looked around. The others looked away, but Lila boldly returned his stare. "Ah, Lila, would you come up to the front? I want *you* to demonstrate how you did it. Watch *her*," George said, and stepped back.

Lila had become used to being singled out by George in this way. But what the hell was this ice-cream-cone dreck? Instinctively, Lila knew how to center attention on herself. She pushed conscious thought from her mind, and slipped easily into the mood. As a sop to George, she relaxed, first her neck, then her shoulders, then her arms. All eyes were riveted on her. And she could keep them there by force of will. Moments passed; then she became aware of George's voice breaking the silence. *"That's* vanilla ice cream melting in the sun," he said, turning to the class, then turned to her once again. "Lila, have you worked on Portia's soliloquy yet?"

"Of course, George." It had been their assignment last week.

"Then do it for us now, if you will, Lila. I have need of some *real* acting today." George leaned back against the wall and closed his eyes. Lila's classmates shifted their positions to get comfortable, as if another body angle could make their envy stop hurting.

Lila rose, ran the first couple of lines in her head, and then flipped the internal switch on, the switch that made her a magnet for the eyes. She hadn't understood much of the monologue, but Robbie had coached her, and the direction was etched into her brain. She had performed the scene for Ken, and he'd loved it. Now, without hesitation, Lila became a Shakespearean heroine, the strange words and their melody welling up out of her. She was a good mimic and remembered where Robbie had dipped his voice and caught his breath. But it was her energy that mattered. She turned it on, a lantern of glowing energy. For a moment, she noticed the faces of some of the people in the audience. They were mouthing her lines, eyes turned up to her in envy and adoration. In that instant, Lila loved them all, these desperate, sad, pretty, lost little people, and poured out that love in every word and gesture. She wanted to give them a piece of herself, to give them something they did not have, could not have, would never have, so she reached across the open space and drew them into her heart. She spoke the words not to the group, but to each individual. Admiration was good, but only when she was safely up onstage.

When at last the final lines came, the room was silent. Then, as she came out of character, they burst into applause and shouts. Lila smiled dryly, bowed deeply once, then returned to her seat, avoiding the eyes of her classmates. The good feeling ended. She felt almost empty— no, dead—inside. Bandie, sitting beside her, reached over and patted Lila's hand in congratulations. Lila snatched back her hand and touched her throat to hold back the disgust that bubbled up in her mouth like bile. Contempt popped up goose bumps on her forearms.

George praised her. "Only four months with me, and see how she's applied herself. You should all learn from her example. That's the Getz method." After his plug, he moved to another topic, his voice droning on. She looked at the class out of the corners of her eyes while they now paid rapt attention to George. As if they could learn to be what she was. She almost laughed. They were all beautiful, she thought, but she knew that *she* was the best in the room. She also knew that looks alone would not make her a star. Nor her connections through Theresa, *if* she could somehow manage to use them, nor Aunt Robbie, nor poor George. And talent wasn't enough. Deep, deep inside, Lila knew she had something special, something that drew the attention, the interest of others. But that something had to be showcased. Sitting in this class week after week was not going to do it, either. Half the room hoped that Sy Ortis would suddenly walk in the door one day and discover them. Well, she had news for them: he wouldn't. So now the only thing she had to figure out was the same trick these lamebrains were working on.

How to make it happen.

17

Mary Jane left her grandmother's the next day, and stopped at Mr. Slater's, an Elmira lawyer, to discuss selling the house and its contents. She had her grandmother's will—she'd been left the house, but in trust for her father. Her father, the man whose drunken driving had killed Mary Jane's mother and turned himself into a vegetable! She told Slater to probate the will and sell the place off as soon as possible. Then she drove across the state line, into Massachusetts, and called in the bearer bonds. Finally, she began the long drive back to New York. How could $67,411 (all of it undeclared and tax-free) make her life worth living?

What did she want? It wasn't enough money to buy a house in the Hamptons, or even a co-op in New York. It couldn't buy her a business, and anyway, she didn't want one. She could use the money to live on, but what would happen when it ran out? Back to Elmira, the Chivas, and a handful of pills?

In her whole life, it seemed to Mary Jane, she had wanted only two things: Sam, and a career as an actress. Well, the money wouldn't bring Sam back. And it wouldn't buy her a theater. She kept on driving down the Thruway, the radio playing some stupid seventies disco music. She stopped for coffee at a disgusting roadside rest stop, sat down at a table, and thought some more. And then it came to her. What she wanted, what she truly wanted and needed.

She needed to be beautiful.

Why hadn't she thought of it before? She had the talent to succeed as an actress—her reviews for *Jack and Jill* proved that—and she had the love to succeed with a man. After all, despite her looks, Sam had wanted her. It was only her outer self, her mortal coil, that offended, that limited her, that ruined her. She had tried to kill it, but with it would have gone all the rest—her talent, her ability to befriend, to love.

As she sat at the orange Formica table, while the cars flew by on the Thruway, she felt her hands on the Styrofoam coffee cup begin to tremble.

Why couldn't she use the sixty-seven thousand dollars that lay in the bag beside her to buy a new face and body? Become a new person, at least on the outside? Throughout all of history, men had had the money and could buy women's beauty. A Nell Gwyn could move up from the streets and trade beauty for wealth. Now, for the first time, a woman could buy beauty for herself. She, Mary Jane Moran, had the money to buy a new face, perhaps even a streamlined, perfect body. She knew the technology was there. It could be done.

She felt the trembling move from her hands up her arms to her whole body. She tried to breathe deeply, and hoped no one would notice, but the fat, distracted mother with three cranky children at the next table, and the old man with what looked like a wife with Alzheimer's across the aisle, had other things to do. She pushed away the coffee cup and closed her eyes for a moment. Could this thing be done? Did she have the courage to do it?

The trip to New York passed in a blur. She shut off the radio, put the pedal to the metal, and sank into a strange state, between fear and elation. She hadn't been a nurse all those years for nothing. So, when she got back to New York, with the sixty-seven thousand dollars in cash, wrapped in plastic, stuffed into a canvas Channel 13 tote and hidden safely in the back of her closet, she began her research. She knew about Dr. Walden at Doctors Hospital, of course, and John Armstrong at Columbia Presbyterian. They were the Park Avenue plastic surgeons that the *beau monde* employed for the subtle but critically important nips and tucks they all required. They had great reputations, but Mary Jane required a lot more than that.

She told no one about the money or her plan—if it was a plan. In fact, she didn't see any of her friends. She'd have to do some research first. She called Nancy Norton, an old classmate, now a nurse at the Mount Sinai Burn

Pavilion. After burns, major reconstruction was often necessary. She also spoke to Bobby Watkins, a black actor who moonlighted as an emergency-room nurse and saw lots of trauma cases—smashed up from accidents. She sat for hours in the library at Cornell Medical Center, poring through *The Lancet, The Journal of the American Medical Association,* and the specialized plastic-surgery bulletins. She cross-referenced all that with research in the AMA's who's who.

It came down to four men: Robert Ducker of Miami, who had developed dozens of innovative techniques when he worked in Haiti and the Dominican Republic, on poor patients, who couldn't afford to sue; William Reed, who practiced out in L.A. and was purported to be the best nose man in the business; John Collins, a Park Avenue type; and Brewster Moore, chief of plastic surgery at Cosmopolitan Hospital in New York. He'd been an army doctor, worked on Vietnam vets, and had been chief plastic surgeon at the hospital for close to a dozen years. But he was the only one without an extensive private practice. He was known in the medical profession as "the doctors' doctor," and the word was that he corrected the errors other plastic surgeons made.

Mary Jane lay in bed—her bed, which was now so big, so empty, with Sam gone—and stared at the ceiling as she thought it out. Midnight kneaded her stomach, purring deeply with satisfaction, and she stroked him as her mind turned her plan over and over. Was it really possible to stop being plain old Mary Jane, her talent hidden under a bushel of body, and emerge as someone not just better-looking, not even just pretty, but beautiful? Was it possible that now, at thirty-four, she could belatedly join that sisterhood of women who turned men's heads when they walked down the street, who entered a room and caused a stir, or even a momentary silence, who inspired lustful dreams, romantic fantasies, simply with a look, a smile, a toss of the head?

What would it feel like not to always have to compensate for her looks, not to have to work against her formless cheeks, her big nose, her absent chin? Never again to see the wince when she walked into a casting call, met a director, was introduced to a man? What would it be like to play the ingenue, to be sought after by men, not to be invisible, as she so often felt, but to be undressed by their eyes, the way they did Bethanie and those other beauties?

Was it possible? How much art and science would it take to sculpt her formless putty into a classically chiseled profile, to raise her pendulous breasts, thin her thunder thighs, flatten her wattled stomach, remake her into the image that men called beautiful? How much would it cost? How long would it take? How much would it hurt? Could it even be done?

Her medical background gave her a basic understanding of the names and techniques for most of the procedures she'd need. But would a surgeon be willing to perform them all? And she knew that it had to be not just a surgeon but an artist, willing to work for months, maybe longer, willing to take her seriously, willing to undertake a transformation, a reconstruction, but on someone undamaged by burns or disease, functionally adequate but needing to be beautiful.

They might think she was frivolous, or a nut. She knew she wasn't the former, but she wasn't sure about the latter. Maybe she was crazy. Still, she had decided. What else could promise so much possibility for the better? The money, Grandma's money, wasn't enough to fix her life in any other real way. Sure, she could pay off all her charge cards, take a trip with it, but then she'd come back to this life. And she wouldn't live this life, the one she'd been dealt.

Since she was in New York, she'd start by making appointments with both Collins and Moore. Her hands actually shook as she dialed the old rotary phone—probably the last one in Manhattan—she still had and made the appointments. It wasn't easy. She had to use the name of a hospital administrator she knew to get an early appointment with Collins. First Collins, then Moore. Then she'd see.

Dr. Collins' office was in a very impressive building on Park Avenue at Sixty-fourth Street. The lobby was marble-floored in that patrician pattern of checkerboard black and white squares that ran diagonally. The floor shone so that it looked wet, and the brass buttons of the doorman were as shiny as the polished nameplate on the office door. Intimidated, Mary Jane walked in, ashamed of her lumpy down coat and her bulging black bag.

The secretary-receptionist didn't make her feel any more comfortable. The woman was thin, blonde, and beautiful, her hair done up in one of those complicated French braids that Mary Jane could never get her own hair to hold. She wondered if the woman had been worked on by Dr. Collins. If not, he was guilty of false advertising.

She waited almost half an hour, filling in the usual forms. Her hands were shaking. At last, the woman led her down a long, thickly carpeted hall to Collins' inner sanctum. He rose when she entered, seeming to take her in from top to toe.

"Well, Miss Moran, how can I help you?"

Mary Jane cleared her throat. "I'm an actress," she said.

"Really?" Did his voice rise at the end of the word, almost as if he didn't believe her? Quickly she outlined some of her credits. "The problem is, I can't get work. Because of how I look," she told him. God, this was hard. She looked at him. His face was impassive; his eyes were attentive but cold. She couldn't go on.

"You were thinking of surgery?" he prompted.

"Yes."

"How old are you?"

"Thirty-four. Almost thirty-five," she admitted.

"What exactly did you have in mind?"

"Everything. Whatever it would take!" she burst out.

"I don't understand. Rhinoplasty? Or . . ."

"Whatever it would take to make me beautiful," she cried.

The man looked at her and sighed. "I am a doctor, Miss Moran, not a magician."

She spent two days in bed, and very nearly didn't go to the appointment with Dr. Moore. But she decided, in the end, she could manage one more humiliation before killing herself.

Dr. Moore's nurse, Miss Hennessey, was one of those battle-axes that Mary Jane had seen in hospitals for years. A commuter from Queens, no doubt, and a real yenta. "The doctor doesn't do body work. Exactly what are you thinking of? Procedure-wise?" she had asked over the phone.

"Seeing the doctor," Mary Jane had told her, and it shut the woman up, even if it put a sour tone to her voice. When Mary Jane showed up at the office, the sourness had moved up to Miss Hennessey's face. She silently ushered Mary Jane into the Spartan office. Brewster Moore was a small, dark man, no taller than five six. She noticed his hands—very small and soft-looking—before she sat down. His skin was pale but healthy, with a pink glow, set off by his black hair and dark-brown eyes. He was wearing a dark suit with a white shirt and blue tie. She'd never seen anyone who looked as clean as he did.

She looked up at him, a slight man with a receding hairline and a cool, blank, professional manner.

She sat before Dr. Moore, her eyes downcast, her hands dangling in her lap, feeling worse than she had felt at Dr. Collins', more nervous than she'd ever been before any audition. Christ, what were the lines that would get her this part? What would win a surgeon's empathy and compassion? If any surgeons had either.

"How can I help you?" he asked, and, to her complete surprise and shame, she burst into tears.

She cried for a long time, while he sat silently and still, except for pushing a box of tissues toward her. At last, after gasps and nose blows and eye wiping, she finally looked up, her shame washed away by her flood.

"I'm an actress," she said.

He nodded, attentive. There was no wince, but no other expression, either.

"I'm very good." She reached into her coat pocket, took out a now crumpled résumé. "You have to believe that," she added.

He looked the résumé over, then looked back at her. "Many of my patients are very courageous, Miss Moran.

It takes a lot to walk in these doors. Why don't you tell me what you want?"

So she did. Calmly. In as professional a manner as she could. She ended with the disappointment over *Jack and Jill and Compromise*. "So, you see, I need surgery. I need a lot of it. For my business. But I don't know what's possible, and I don't know what it will cost."

He looked at her, as he had throughout. At last he spoke. "I understand your problem, Miss Moran." He stood up, walked around the table he used as a desk. Gently, he touched her under the chin, raised her head, turned it, first left, then right.

"Flesh isn't stone, Miss Moran. It's not predicable. It moves, it drapes, it scars. Your face lacks definition. There are no planes here"—he touched her cheeks—"and here"—he placed his finger under her nose—"there is no decisiveness. Your brow is too protruding. Your chin is weak. Your nose joins your upper lip without the recess we define as beautiful. Of course, the chin and nose present few real problems, but surgery can't really alter the shape of the face, or the head itself. And beauty depends on the relationship of so many of these separate parts." He paused. "Certainly I can make improvements. But I'm not sure I can promise you beauty. And I'd caution you to avoid any surgeon who tells you otherwise."

She thought of Collins' words, licked her lips, took a breath, and spoke. "Doctor, I'm not looking for a magician, but I'm also not here for a little profile-contouring. I don't want a cute little snub nose. I don't just want some 'improvement.' I'm looking for an artist. I've heard about you. I've seen your work. I think you can do what I want."

"Thank you. I've seen your work, too. You were brilliant in *Jack and Jill and Compromise*. You *are* very good."

"But can I *look* good?"

"There is a very narrow standard of beauty in the commercial sense," Brewster said, looking out the gray window at the gray day beyond it. "There is an aesthetic intolerance in this country for the ethnic, for the imperfect, for the unusual. Although, of course, beauty actually is unusual. That is why we venerate it, I suppose." He sighed, as if he were tired of thinking about a very old problem, one he had reviewed a thousand times before. He turned back to her. "I worked with cadavers all through my internship and residency. I dissected almost four hundred noses, trying to determine what the magic formula was. What made a nose beautiful? What magic proportion, what relationship to the rest of the face, what line, what curve was responsible? Then I reconstructed each one, striving to achieve that perfection."

Had he achieved it? She wanted to ask him, but she was far too afraid to, afraid that she'd hear that he had failed.

He turned back from the window. "In my opinion, society is sick. They have created a false, an almost impossible vision of female beauty and then induced women to attempt to achieve it. All of them fail. I have some of the most beautiful women in the world in this office, and they're frightened because they feel they aren't quite beautiful enough."

"That's hardly my situation," Mary Jane said dryly.

"No, it isn't," he agreed bluntly. "But most plastic surgeons feed off this sick society. Women who have been made neurotic, who feel their breasts should be bigger, their noses smaller. Or who have husbands that believe that. Or who *want* husbands who believe that. The medical profession's fed off the illness of society for years: we are banishing the natural, creating the supernatural."

"Why do you do it, then?"

"Well, it isn't my main practice. Mostly I do reconstruction. But there *is* a fascination in the work. I'd lie if I said there wasn't. And, of course, the money is very, very good. I can charge what I like. It is, after all, elective."

"For some people," Mary Jane said flatly.

"Well, for my face-lift clients, for example. Seven thousand dollars, and I can do it in under two hours. That might buy faces for two of my clinic kids. Or a new operating room for our little Honduran hospital."

"You work in Honduras?"

"Yes. Lots of gunshot wounds. I prefer impoverished, underdeveloped countries. No face lifts in Honduras. There, living long gains you respect, and surgery is only for important issues, not breast enlargement and nipple placement."

"No silicone-breast cancer cases?" Mary Jane asked.

Brewster Moore shook his head. "Dow has always been an enemy of the people. Clearly disturbing data on silicone implants were already published in 1979. But it appears that women in America would rather risk cancer than live with small breasts. And doctors would rather collect fees than be scrupulous. The deadly search for beauty."

"All right, doctor," she said, looking directly at him. "Now we both understand the situation. So. What would it take to make me truly beautiful?"

The doctor looked out the window. "There would be a great deal of surgery involved," he began. He turned back again and looked at her. "And there would be body scars. Scars that would never fade and couldn't be disguised. Keloids might form and disfigure you. I don't do body work, but I can recommend those who do." He paused. "And there would be discomfort. No, pain. Real pain. Undeniably. And it would take time. Time for multiple procedures, and healing in between. There are no guarantees. Work on this scale is difficult. And costly."

"But you could do it?" she asked. "It would be possible?" Her voice caught for a moment. She stopped there, took a breath, and continued. "They all told me you were the one. That you work miracles. You can make me beautiful?"

The doctor folded his hands over the file on the otherwise barren desk. "Too soon to tell. I need to see preliminary X-rays and the results of a complete workup." Gently he touched her head, moved it left to right, right to left. "But it may be possible."

She sighed, then drew her breath again. "Would it take more than two years and sixty-seven thousand dollars?" she asked.

"I'm not sure. Perhaps. That's assuming, of course, that it can be done at all. Why do you ask?"

"Because that's how much time and money I've got," she said, and pushed her purse across the desk to him. He looked at the battered bag. Then back at her. For the first time in the interview, he almost smiled.

"I'm glad you have the money, though it's a bit premature. I don't consider this frivolous surgery, Miss Moran, but the clinic would never underwrite it. And it *will* be expensive. *And* you will be incapacitated for periods after the procedures. You certainly couldn't work."

Mary Jane laughed. "I don't get to work now." The laugh sounded almost as bitter as she felt. "But it won't cost more than I have?"

"Perhaps. I don't know. But we can cross that bridge when we come to it. For now, I'd like a series of detailed X-rays, as well as your dental records. And I'd like you to think about the seriousness of what you're proposing. Then we can meet again."

"Yes, yes. Thank you. Thank you, doctor."

"You're welcome, Miss Moran."

"So, you want a deposit? I mean, should I give you a check or something?"

He looked across the table at her, another appraising look. "Give me forty pounds," he said, and for a moment she thought he was talking about English money. For the first time in the interview, Mary Jane felt the color rush to her cheeks as she blushed hotly. "We can't even see what we're working with until you lose that weight," Dr. Moore told her. "Then we'll get a better idea."

Forty pounds! She knew she had always been chunky, thick through the waist, fat thighs—but forty pounds! She'd really let herself go. The misery over losing the part, over losing Sam. Forty pounds! That would bring her down to about 115. She hadn't weighed that even back in high school in Scuderstown. Christ, it was hard to face ten—how would she lose forty?

Still, if that's what it took, she'd do it. She'd quit eating, she'd exercise, she'd fast if she had to. She'd show her commitment. She was going to change herself, her life. She nodded, and rose from the chair.

"Forty pounds, Miss Moran. Then we'll be able to see what you're made of."

Mary Jane nodded again, and managed to stumble out of his office.

18

"Where're we going?" Dean asked, excited by the surprise Dobe said he wanted to show them.

"You'll see, young feller. It's just a few miles more."

Sharleen sat forward, leaning both arms on the back of Dean's seat. "Now, what do you and Oprah have up your sleeve today, Dobe?" she asked, and smiled. She was sad that she and Dean would be going their own way tomorrow, when they got to Bakersfield. Dobe had been a perfect gentleman for the whole trip, and never once asked her to lie or behaved improperly toward her. But Sharleen knew that what Dobe did wasn't right, and, anyway, it was time she and Dean stood on their own two feet. She wasn't sure how they were going to do that exactly, but the good Lord would provide. Hadn't He gotten them to California?

Of course, they were sinners. They'd broken two commandments that Sharleen knew of for sure, and she prayed to Jesus every night that they'd be forgiven. But she also remembered her momma's last words—and she had to take care of Dean.

She didn't know how she would have managed without Dobe. He'd broken a few of the commandments himself, she felt sure. She thought of the story of the traveler who fell among thieves and was rescued by the Good Samaritan. But what did the Bible say when the Samaritan and the thief was the same person?

"Up my sleeve?" Dobe was asking her now with exaggerated surprise. "Why, young lady, would you think *I* have something up my sleeve?'' he asked, looking at her in the rearview mirror, his eyes wide.

"Sharleen, that ain't right. Now, you apologize to Dobe. He's been mighty good to us," Dean said, half-turning in his seat. "Anyway, Oprah don't have no sleeves, do she, Dobe?"

"I'm sorry if I hurt your feelings, Dobe," Sharleen said. She patted Dean's shoulder and smiled. Dobe brought his eyes back to the road and slowed down. "Here we are," he said.

"Look at all them cars!" Dean cried out. The glittery sign over the building read "Honest Abe's—Ten Acres of Used Cars." Dean jumped out of the car after Dobe, and Sharleen followed.

Dobe waved to a man behind the picture window and started to walk down the long rows of cars, the multicolored pennants flapping in the warm California breeze over their heads. Dobe came to a stop in front of a car that had "Special—$1,999" scrawled in white paint on the left side of the windshield. "Seems it's time to buy a car," Dobe said. "This looks like a California model." It was sporty—a Datsun 280Z, and it was silver.

Sharleen stood by Dobe's side as he and Dean studied the car. Dean walked around it in circles, patting the roof, kicking the tires.

"It's a beauty, Dobe," Dean said. "And it's silver. Like your car. Like the Lone Ranger's horse."

"It sure is pretty," Sharleen said. "It's one of them foreign cars, isn't it?"

"But what do you want with another car, Dobe?" Dean asked. "The one you've got is real good. There wouldn't be much room for more'n you and Oprah in there."

"It's not for me. I was thinking maybe you would like it."

Dean's eyes opened wide. "Me?"

"Sure, why not? Oprah and I wanted to get something for you and Sharleen here as a going-away present, seeing as how you been good enough to keep an old man company." Dobe turned to Sharleen. "And you'll be

150

needing a car in California. I hear they arrest people out here that don't own one."

Before she could speak, before she could refuse, "Welcome to Honest Abe's," they heard a voice behind them say, and they turned to see a short, pudgy man with a big belly walking toward them, wearin' an Abe Lincoln stovepipe hat on his head. "If I can't help you, I won't hurt you. Oh, it's you again, Mr. Samuels. And is this the son you were telling me about?" Honest Abe asked Dobe, pulling his eyes away from Sharleen.

Sharleen went over to Dobe and touched his shoulder. "You've been so good to us already, Dobe," she said softly. "We've been living like rich folk since we met you, and eating better than at a country funeral. And you've been a perfect gentleman. You don't need to give us no present. You give us enough already."

Dobe looked down at his boots. "It would make me very happy, Sharleen," he said. "This has been a real nice time for me. It's like you're my own kids. And you've been a big help. You earned the money."

"Sharleen," Dean said, "this here car's a beauty. You know, I could put her into top shape if anything goes wrong." She could hear the yearning in his voice.

"But if I'm overstepping my bounds," Dobe continued, "just say so, and no hard feelings."

Tears filled Sharleen's eyes. Not since Momma left, not for such a long time, had anyone been this good to her, taken care of her. After a moment, Sharleen said, "Thank you, Dobe. We'd be grateful. And we'll pay you back someday."

Dobe turned back to Abe. "This could be the one," Dobe said, as he took Abe by the arm and walked him away from them, talking into Abe's ear as they strolled.

When he came back, he tossed the keys to Dean and said, "Well, son, let's take her for a ride." Dobe opened the front passenger door for Sharleen, then got in the tiny back seat with Oprah and leaned forward. "How's she feel?" Dobe asked Dean as they turned onto the main drag.

Dean floored the accelerator, then let up. "She's a beauty, Dobe. Great pickup."

"And she's all yours now, kids. Makes sayin' goodbye a bit more cheerful."

Sharleen wondered if they did some kind of police check when you bought a car. She wondered if the Lamson sheriff had put their names in one of them computers, the kind that tracked you down. But as Abe went over the car with Dean, Dobe took her aside.

"Seems to me, Sharleen, from the first time I saw the two of you, that you was on the run." He put his hand up. "I don't know nothin' and I don't want to know. But I know how it feels. I truly do. Anyway," he continued, "I put the car in my name. Well—in the name Dobe Samuels. Clean as a whistle. Consider it a loan. Someday I may ask you for a favor. I'm sure you'd do it for me. And keep your own nose clean, huh?"

Sharleen swallowed and nodded silently. Then she leaned over and gave Dobe a big kiss on his sunburned cheek.

When they got back to the motel, Sharleen and Dean loaded their suitcase into the back seat of the Datsun. Dobe stood with his hands in his back pockets, while Dean fussed over the car, proud as a coon with a catfish.

"Sharleen, could I give you a little more advice?" Dobe asked, his voice quiet so it wouldn't carry.

"Why, sure, Dobe. You're a smart man. And a good one, too."

"Well, you're more than pretty, Sharleen. You're beautiful. And life can either be too easy or too hard for a beautiful girl. Now, you ain't the type to make it too easy for yourself. But don't make it too hard, neither." Dobe looked into Sharleen's eyes. "If you got to say yes to somebody someday, Sharleen, just make sure it's for the right reasons."

Sharleen nodded, not quite sure what Dobe meant, but figuring that, like some of the Bible's meaning, it would come to her later. She stepped on tiptoes and kissed Dobe again on the cheek, then hugged him tight. "Thank you, Dobe, for being so good to us."

Dean came over and put his arms around Dobe. "I'm sure going to miss you. Now I got no one but Sharleen to

152

talk about license plates with. And thank you for the car, Dobe. And for the food. And the beds.'' Dean's face got red, and he knelt down to Oprah and put his arms around the big dog. "You take care, hear?'' he told her. She licked his face.

Then Dobe called to the dog, and she got into his car next to him. Dean shut the door, and Dobe turned the big silver Pontiac out of the motel parking lot onto the street. Sharleen turned around and waved a kiss to him. Dean blew his nose.

"He been real good to us, Sharleen,'' Dean said. "I was going to ask for some pills for the gas tank, but since he never offered, I thought it would be greedy. Right, Sharleen?''

"Right, honey,'' she told him, and put her arm around his shoulders.

19

Mary Jane sat at the battered desk before her front window, looking out onto West Fifty-fourth Street. Since she had met Dr. Moore, two days ago, she had hardly managed five hours of sleep. She had unplugged her answering machine and had spent the time both pacing and lying flat across the old double bed in the back bedroom, staring at the cracked plaster of the ceiling.

How, she kept asking herself, how could she do this thing? That she *would* do it, or die in the attempt, she knew. But how could she manage to survive the transformation she was contemplating? And not just the physical one. Plain, almost homely, all her life, how could she learn to act the part of a beautiful woman? For without action, she knew, no role could be successfully played. How many pretty girls had she seen who never believed in their own beauty, and couldn't make anyone else believe in it, either? And how many unextraordinary women had she seen who could project an aura of beauty despite only average looks? It wasn't enough to get the exterior right, the costumes, makeup, and posture. She would have to perfect the persona of a beautiful woman. How could she, a female who had had absolutely zero faith in her looks, act the part of a beauty? Would she be ridiculous? Would she fail? Once again she stood up and paced the tiny front room. What misgivings did a fat old caterpillar have as it started to close itself into its cocoon? Did it have a genetic script for its upcoming role as a butterfly, or did it ad-lib? Well, she had no script, and since she'd never been good at improvs, she'd have to create one.

She walked back to the desk and stared down at the spiral-bound notebook in front of her. On the first page she had written four headings: "Financial Plan," "Social Plan," "Career Plan," and "Physical Plan." She had determined that she wouldn't leave the dark apartment until she had considered all the problems of each category and come up with solutions. She had always been good at observation and imitation, the tools of an actor's craft. And she would use visualization, the tricks she had learned in therapy, to feel her way to her new role. But how you went about becoming a new, successful, beautiful person when you were an almost middle-aged, unattractive failure wasn't going to be so easy to visualize.

One thing she knew: she couldn't go through the process in front of her friends (or her enemies). If all the world was about to become her stage, she knew that she couldn't undermine her new role by letting people peek into her dressing room. Molly, for instance, would tell her that she was wonderful just the way she was. If Bethanie had been around, she would, no doubt, have felt superior and acted supportive. It made Mary Jane's skin crawl to think of that. Father Damien would suggest the power of prayer, or maybe some Prozac, which had helped him out of a depression. Chuck would probably suggest primal therapy. Neil, if he had forgiven her and if she could reach him out on the coast, would just crack wise and make her laugh. But Mary Jane knew that all the affection of friends and primal screams in the world wouldn't change how she looked or give her what she wanted. Unless she took this drastic step and succeeded, she'd never get a leading role again. Sam or any other man worth having would never love her as she was. Her friends were wrong when they told her otherwise, and their kindnesses or lies were useless. The Mary Jane that her friends knew had died alone in that grim farmhouse in upstate New York.

She jumped up from the desk again and recommenced her pacing. If there weren't already holes in the old tweed carpet, she would be making them now. She wrapped her arms around herself and continued walking to and fro. She would have to disappear, she decided. It wouldn't be all that hard: just move and leave no forwarding address. New York was a big city. After all, she had no family that would try to reach her. The fight with Neil would be a good excuse not to keep in touch. Who knows, perhaps he never meant to call her again anyway. Sam, obviously, had no plans to try to see her. So all she needed was a relatively believable pretext for disappearing. Well, she'd always been a theater gypsy, as they all were. She could simply tell Molly, Chuck, and her other friends that she'd gotten a job doing stock, then go away and not return. Perhaps, afterward, when she was out of the chrysalis and knew that she could fly, she could call them up, explain everything, and see them again. But not now. If they judged her or dissuaded her, she wouldn't have the courage to go on, and if she didn't make this change, she didn't want to live anymore.

God, it all sounded so melodramatic! She had to smile to herself, but it was a grim ghost of a smile. She walked to the mirror, the small, scratched one that hung over the bookshelf, and stared into her own dark eyes, her pale, shapeless face. She shivered. She felt as if she were staring at the head of a corpse.

She turned away and moved back to the window, then reached into the top drawer of her desk and scrabbled around for her checkbook. If she was going to do this, she had better figure ways and means. The torn blue plastic check cover had her name stamped on it in faded gold. She'd paid four bucks extra for that. Well, she wouldn't have four bucks extra for a long, long time to come, *and* she'd need a new name. She threw the cover into the wastepaper basket. She opened the ledger side and looked at it. She had a balance of $1,471. She also had her old passbook savings account. She opened the book to the last entry: $3,054. Plus whatever the interest was, not that it was ever much.

Of course, that wasn't counting her grandmother's money. That she had already put in a safety-deposit box at the Bowery Bank. She would need it for the operations, and she was determined not to touch it for anything else. But since she didn't want to have to work during the next year or so (and probably wouldn't be able to during recovery), she would need a lot more than the cash in her two accounts to live off of, no matter how cheaply she lived.

Well, she could start with a tag sale. Of course, since she'd mostly always been broke, she had decorated the apartment with Salvation Army purchases, thrift-shop finds, and discarded furniture from off the street. She couldn't raise anything on that stuff. But she could sell her books and her record albums. She would get rid of her stereo, and her TV. That would bring in a few hundred. And her vintage clothes would have to go.

For a moment, she felt a pang. Over the years, she'd collected the old silk dresses, the alligator bags, the taffeta petticoats by relentlessly searching out quality among the crap at flea markets and auctions and thrift stores. She'd lovingly hand-washed and pressed them all, stitched up seams, and mended tears. But hadn't she collected and worn it all to distract attention from her appearance? Hadn't it been a pathetic ploy? See my clothes, don't see me. Some of her stuff was worth money. Well, she wouldn't need the clothes now, she told herself. She'd give Molly the cashmere forties jacket that Molly had coveted, and bring the rest of it down to a dealer she knew in SoHo. It would give her another few thousand at least.

And she could sublet the apartment and get key money up front. There were hundreds of kids in the theater district who would want it. She'd guarantee them two years, but they'd actually be getting it free and clear. She picked up her pen. Under "Financial Plan" she wrote:

1) Have tag sale
2) Sell books/records/clothes to dealers
3) Put up flyers/run ads for sublet

She did a quick calculation. That would give her perhaps a total of eleven thousand dollars. But she owed some money, too. She added to her list:

4) Pay off MasterCard balance
5) Pay off Nurses' Credit Union

The only other asset she had was her IRAs. She looked in the bottom drawer of her desk for the Merrill Lynch statement. She had a total of just under eight thousand dollars salted away, but if she cashed them in there'd be tax to pay. And then she wouldn't have a dime of retirement money. Oh well. What the hell good would eight thousand bucks be when she was sixty-five? Probably wouldn't pay for a month in a nice rest home by then. And who would want to live this life up to retirement age? She was gambling for high stakes, so she'd better ante up everything, or give up now. She picked up her pen again.

6) Cash in IRAs
7) Close bank accounts. Open new ones.

Since the tellers knew her at her branch, she didn't want them to comment on her changing looks, bruised eyes, or bandages.

8) Set a daily budget for food, carfare, etc.
9) Stick to the budget
10) Don't buy anything
11) Find cheap weekly hotel rental

She'd thought it out. A shared apartment, maybe up around Columbia, would be cheapest, and she wasn't likely to run into her old friends up there, but she didn't want the hassle of roommates with their questions and curiosity. Still, she needed people around, just in case

157

there was a medical emergency. A single-room-occupancy hotel would do the job: transients wouldn't notice her, and the desk would ask no questions as long as they were paid. Maybe there was something out in Brooklyn or Queens that would be a few steps up from a welfare hotel. If, in the end, she had to work a little, she'd see if she could do night shift. She'd cross that bridge when she got to it.

Under "Physical Plan" she wrote:

1) Lose weight
2) Exercise

She stopped and had to smile. Well. Easier said than done. But she'd live in a place without a kitchen. There would be no temptation to cook up a pot of pasta with a little garlic, basil, and olive oil. No sneaking Mounds bars. And this, meeting Dr. Moore's first specification, would be her only job right now. With the pressures of her work and the relationship off, all she had to do was focus on this.

She'd been fifteen pounds overweight her whole life, always fighting it, losing it, and gaining it back. She'd been a size ten when she should have been an eight. Then, in the last year or so, the pounds had really started to creep up. But forty pounds! How long would it take to blitz that off?

In the margin of her notebook, she used some of her mathematics from nursing school. There were about thirty-five hundred calories in a pound. If she lost two pounds a week, took in seven thousand calories less than she expended, it would take twenty weeks before she could see Dr. Moore again! But if she went down to a lot fewer calories than that, she knew she'd be constantly hungry, and probably binge.

She would have to make it up in activity. But she hated exercise classes, and she couldn't afford a health club now anyway. She would simply have to walk the weight off. Walking was aerobic, she liked it, and it didn't cost anything. It also kept you out of trouble, as long as you didn't eat éclairs as you walked. She crossed number "2) Exercise" off her list and replaced it with

2) Walk a minimum of 10 miles per day

At twenty city blocks per mile, that was two hundred blocks! Almost from the George Washington Bridge to Greenwich Village! Well, she could work up to it, and she could walk a different route every day. With determination, she could lose the weight in four months. As a nurse, she knew that any faster wouldn't be safe or lasting.

She also knew that she would have to be as concrete and specific as possible in writing her plans. Otherwise, she might as well simply write down "Become a famous great actress and win the love of a wonderful man" and be done with it. She picked up her pen again and added

3) Plan each day's meals in advance
4) Write down everything eaten
5) Keep no food at home

Under "Career Plan" she had quite a bit to put down. But, then, she had done all of this once before.

1) Create new resume
2) Write to West Coast repertory companies
3) After surgery get new head shots
4) Choose new name

If she changed her name, created a new identity, she'd have to give up her Equity card. She had worked so hard to get one, and it had been such a validation of her that it seemed, of everything so far, perhaps the hardest thing she'd have to relinquish. It was the big question that separated the pros from the tyros: "Are you Equity?" She thought of all the audition notices that stated "Equity Only." She shrugged. Well, so it goes. Equity membership hadn't gotten her where she wanted to be. Putting together a phony résumé was nothing. She knew enough defunct theatrical endeavors, and could drop enough names, to make anyone believe she had played Eliza Doolittle in the Oak Bluff, Missouri, Dinner Theater revival of *Pygmalion*. Or Emily in *Our Town*. Or Laura in *The Glass Menagerie*. Too bad she'd never gotten a chance to play those roles: always the character actress, never the ingenue, she reminded herself bitterly. But now that would change.

Of course, she'd have to leave off her triumph: creating the role of Jill. And she'd have to drop off mention of her equally precious Obie. But she could bring her talent along. That and good looks should be enough to justify one more assault on the mountain.

But she would also have to work on creating herself anew. She would have to study up on how to play the part of a beautiful, hopeful, successful young woman. Well, she'd read interviews with them, and she'd watch films with those kinds of characters. She knew how to do research for a role; this would be her greatest challenge, more difficult than playing fat, frumpy Jill.

Mary Jane stretched her back against the oak mission chair, then stood up. Outside, dusk was beginning to fall, and people had begun to troop by, all of them coming from the east and walking west from the subway exit toward their homes. Would they have a family waiting? Would there be a nice hot meal, a hug, and maybe a few laughs after a day of hard work? For a moment, she felt self-pity begin to settle on her like a wet, cold mantle. Courage, she told herself. But what if she couldn't lose the weight that imprisoned her, holding her tighter than a shroud? What if Dr. Moore wouldn't take her on? Or what if he did but failed?

She *would* lose the weight, Dr. Moore *would* take her on, and, if he didn't, some other doctor would. But what if you simply fail again, and this time without the excuse of your looks to blame everything on? After all, who do you think you are? How many pretty girls try to make it and wind up waiting tables in San Diego? How many job openings are there for new stars? Who do you think you are?

And there, in the deepening dusk, she heard her grandmother's voice. "Want a part in the senior play? Who do you think you are? Auditioning for drama school? Do you think you're Sarah Bernhardt? Who do you think you are? Who do you think you are? Who do you think you are?''

She held her hands up to her ears, her grandmother's voice too loud to block out. "I don't know who I am, or who I'm going to be, but I'm not who I was!" she shouted. "I'm not who I was!"

20

The afternoon sun cast long shadows across the veranda that encircled Aunt Robbie's pool. Lila was on her stomach on a chaise longue, her bikini top open so she could get the full warmth of the sun, though she was so covered in sunscreen that a hydrogen-bomb explosion probably wouldn't even pinken her. She wasn't turning into some lizard-woman. Her silken red hair, coated with a thick layer of conditioner, was wrapped in a towel. And soon José would bring her a huge frosty glass of lemonade, made from real lemons and diet sweetener. He even put a leaf of real mint in it. Heaven. Staying here at Robbie's, though it was a drag in both senses of the word, definitely had some benefits. And Aunt Robbie was as gung-ho about her career as she was. "Decide what you want, then grab it by its nuts," he had delicately said. So she'd have to start doing some nut-grabbing soon.

There was no longer any doubt what she wanted. She needed a movie, a movie more wonderful than anything her mother had been in. A vehicle to catapult her into the public eye. Lila heard the soft padding of someone walking toward her. She opened her eyes in a squint and saw Aunt Robbie, sans roller blades, a huge, floppy straw hat on his head. It was odd to see him waddle instead of glide.

"Why, Aunt Robbie," Lila asked in her best Southern accent, peering down at the bare feet that stuck out from beneath the hem of his aquamarine-and-pink caftan, "whatever has become of your skates?"

Aunt Robbie dropped heavily down onto the chaise next to her. "That bitch José. He hid them on me, I'm sure of it."

"Why would he do that?" Lila asked. She had become used to the daily battles between the two of them. In fact, she occasionally even enjoyed listening to the two queens snap at each other.

"He hates the skates. He says he's embarrassed for me. Can you believe that?" Rob tugged the caftan skirt down around his legs. "So I said, 'Honey, if *I'm* not embarrassed, why should *you* be? After all, this is *Hollywood*.'" Robbie laughed, extending his flabby arms to the air in general. Then he lowered his eyebrows and tried to make his pudgy face menacing. He called out in a theatrically loud voice, "If he doesn't get them back to me today, I swear, I'm calling Immigration," then leaned his head back on the chaise, adjusting the rim of the hat to shade his eyes.

"And what, may I ask, are you doing out here broiling?" Robbie said, looking over at Lila's near-nude figure slick with suntan oil. "Don't you know about the holes in the ozone layer? You'll get skin cancer. If you up and die on me, I'll kill you. Keep that in mind. And no mourning. I look like shit in black."

"I need to work on my tan."

"You need to work on your judgment, it looks like."

"This is *Hollywood*," Lila mimicked. "And this is what people do in Hollywood."

"No, my dear, they do more than that. They also try to build careers." Robbie turned his head toward the house and roared, "José!"

The small, dark-skinned man came out of the kitchen door, wiping his hands on a frilly apron while mincing toward them. He stopped in front of Robbie and put one hand on his hip.

"Wha' chu want, Miss Thing?"

Robbie ignored José's attitude and said brightly, "I'd like a frozen margarita, José, please, and bring another diet lemonade for my date here." Then Robbie flicked his hand, and José turned and sashayed back to the house.

"Now, it's time we did some more career planning. Aunt Robbie has been thinking a lot about your future, Lila, and I have a couple of ideas."

Lila had heard all this before from Robbie. He meant well, but so far his ideas hadn't panned out to anything. He was out of touch in a business that didn't want to hear about yesterday's news. Much less, news from the fifties. "A film?" she asked in mock excitement. "Is one of your friends doing a film?"

"Give me a break, girlfriend. You'd be very lucky to do television."

"I'm not doing television," Lila grumbled, and sat up, allowing the top to fall from her perfect breasts. Robbie certainly didn't care. "I want to do a movie. Television brings you too close to the public. There are no real stars on television. Just celebrities."

"My goodness, what a pair of knockers!" Aunt Robbie said. "A little decorum, please."

"Look who's talking!" she snapped, but turned away for a moment, then made a face at Robbie and tied her top behind her. "You've said television is second-rate yourself. You always say so to Ken," she added.

"That's because Ken *works* in television. But I'm only suggesting television as a starting point. A lot of stars got their start on TV."

"Name one."

Robbie thought for a moment. "Rob Reiner."

"He's not a *star*—he's a director, for chrissakes," Lila said. "So is Ron Howard. Anyway, name a *woman*." She paused. "Don't even bother racking your brain, Aunt Robbie. There are just no stars on television."

"Carol Burnett."

"She's not a star, she's a has-been. And no one ever paid to see her in the movies."

"Shelley Long."

"Who?"

"The blonde from *Cheers*."

"Exactly. Name one of her *films*. Forget it!"

"Sally Field."

"Oh, my God. Gidget goes to work in a factory. She *never* had any draw. Aunt Robbie, these women have no glamour. They aren't anything. I've got to get a *film*. A major one."

"Mary Tyler Moore."

"Oh, fine. What has she done? *Ordinary Movie?* If Redford hadn't directed it, it would have died like a dog. No. No TV!" Lila was beginning to lose her patience. "Come on, Robbie. I want to be like my mother was. I want to be *bigger* than my mother was. You know exactly what I mean."

José returned with their drinks and a bowl of macadamia nuts. "Well, we're jumping ahead of ourselves, Lila. You've got to have an agent first," Robbie said, popping a handful of nuts into his mouth.

"Who do you suggest, Robbie? One of your little friends? First assistant to the first assistant of something? Spare me, Robbie. I'm thinking bigger than that."

"All your thinking hasn't done you shit, has it, honey? It's time to stop thinking and start *doing*. I happen to know just the man for you, and he's a big thinker, just what you want."

Lila paused, then said, "Wait. I know what you're going to say."

"No, you don't."

"Yes, I do. Don't suggest Ara. He's my mother's agent, he's a hundred and four, *and* he has the breath of a sick dog. Plus, he'll never see me because Theresa wouldn't stand for it. Anyway, he's got a foot in the grave."

"I swear, it's morbid how paranoid you are about your mother. If she were so goddamn powerful, don't you think she would have scared up a part for herself by now? She's not going to stop you. And Ara is only eighty-one, and if he has one foot in the grave, then the other foot is firmly planted on Hollywood and Vine. Ara Sagarian is so well connected that he'll be getting work for his people even *after* he's dead."

"But I hate him," Lila said.

"Of course you do," Robbie said with exaggerated patience. "He's an *agent*. But he's handled Jimmy Stewart,

Frank Sinatra, Joan Crawford, *and* your mother, of course. And he still has lots of biggies. Hagman and Michael Keaton, I think. Lots of others."

"Oh. J.R. and Batbore. *Now* I'm impressed."

"Well, laugh if you want to, but Ara Sagarian is very big on television these days. Says it's what the studios were like in the forties. And I don't see anything else on your horizon, Miss Thing. I can get you in. Then you just charm him."

"Well, maybe I could go talk to him," Lila conceded. Then she laughed. "Should I just walk in and tell him I want a starring role in something? That I won't take television, but that I really want to be a movie star?" Even though she was the daughter of Theresa O'Donnell, the old man wasn't going to be exactly thrilled at another Beverly Hills brat knocking on his door. Still, if he *would* see her . . . Lila hated to admit it, but Robbie might have something here. And if Robbie could guarantee getting her in . . . Ara *was* big. The biggest contact Robbie had suggested so far. "You're certain he'll see me? I mean, not just a courtesy call."

"Oh, don't worry about that," Robbie said. "Ara's my godfather in the gay Hollywood mafia. He'd do *anything* for me. If you agree, I'll talk to him, just feel him out." Robbie leaned over the arm of his chaise and looked into Lila's eyes. "Just say you're willing to do some TV and I'll make the call."

Lila sipped her lemonade, then said, "Okay, Robbie, but only a miniseries and a starring role, even if it *is* my first shot out of the box. No crappy sitcom, no guest shots. I mean it."

"Jesus, Miss Thing! Aren't we the choosy one?" Robbie said, and rolled his eyes.

"Hi," Lila heard Ken call as he walked toward them from the garage. "I'm slaving under hot klieg lights all day, and you two are out here taking it easy?"

Robbie looked at his watch. "I didn't realize it was so late, Ward," Robbie said in his best June Cleaver voice. "It was just that the Beaver here was giving me trouble. Maybe you two can talk!" He turned and sashayed toward the house again, and was about to yell out for José when he saw the little man coming toward them, a frozen margarita for Ken on a silver tray before him. Robbie waddled back to his chaise.

"Well, it's about time, Maria. Ken, sit here and have a drinky." Robbie pulled up his fat legs to make room for Ken at the foot of the chaise.

"So what were you two up to?" Ken asked, after taking a sip of the iced drink.

Lila smiled at him. "I've been getting skin cancer and some career advice from my auntie, here," she said. "Both unwelcome."

"He usually gives good advice. Not very good head, but good advice."

"Oooh! Aren't you a little kiss-and-tell!" Robbie cried, and the two began to bicker.

Meanwhile, Lila decided. She would see Ara. After all, what did she have to lose? "Okay, Robbie," she said. "Set it up. But no assistant shit. With Ara. Himself."

21

Mary Jane gave herself a budget: nine hundred calories and nine dollars a day for food for the next three months. She spent the first two days of her new regime in bed, mostly sleeping, but once her exhaustion began to pass she knew that would never work. Home, in bed, was where she ate. She had to be out. She needed the exercise to drop the weight. And she had to lose the weight before she made another appointment with Dr. Moore or Miss Hennessey, his dragon lady. She needed some results to show him.

So on Wednesday, exactly two weeks after her grandmother's funeral, she bundled into her old dun-colored down coat and trundled heavily out the door, after a breakfast of one poached egg, two pieces of (dry) melba toast, and a small glass of tomato juice. It was a cool March day, but at least there isn't a cutting wind, she thought, and began walking east. West Fifty-fourth Street wasn't beautiful at any time of day, but it was particularly unlovely in the morning. Eleventh Avenue was still streaming with trucks, a few patches of filthy snow, covered completely in black soot, and littered with dog droppings, making nasty detours for pedestrians. She walked over to Tenth, past the dank tenement houses, then Ninth, with its bodegas and liquor stores, past the piles of restaurant garbage, to Eighth Avenue, and then over to Broadway. Christ, it was even worse here, she thought. The guys in straight business suits rushed by, clutching attachés, their faces grim, their eyes averted from the tawdry posters outside the grind houses and porno-book shops. Mary Jane wasn't sure who depressed her more: the civilians in their commuter ruts or the degenerates already clustering at the shop gates, waiting to get their sex fix for the morning. Jesus, imagine a porn-film audience at 9:00 A.M.! Who *were* those guys? She shuddered and headed south, moving quickly because she didn't want to find out.

She was getting cold, so she stopped at Seventh Avenue and Thirty-eighth Street, the heart of the fashion industry, for a cup of coffee—using up a dollar of her precious hoard, but at least not adding any calories. There was a tabloid newspaper at the counter that some garmento had left behind, and she thumbed through it. The usual stabbings, shootings, and child abuse. She turned to the gossip columns. They contained the typical mix of New York theatrical, society, and Hollywood names. Shirley MacLaine was apparently writing yet another book on yet one more of her past lives, while her brother was making the most of this one by sleeping with yet another starlet.

Then she saw it. *"Crystal Plenum loves her work so much that she's taking it home with her. Rewrites have started on the script of* Jack and Jill and Compromise, *a real hot property. Apparently so is Sam Shields, the director. Crystal and Shields have been seen at Spago, Mr. Chow's, and were even making nice over breakfast at the Polo Lounge."*

She felt herself flush, then go cold. She was afraid for a moment that she would fall off the stool at the counter.

She felt dizzy, as if she'd been spinning on it as she had when she was a child. It was strange, she thought, as she threw the dollar and assorted change on the counter and stumbled out onto the street. He was my life for more than three years, and now he's gone. She looked at her watch. Right this minute he's probably lying in bed, asleep beside Crystal Plenum, who's got my part. She didn't know which hurt more, that the woman had her role, her precious role as Jill, or that she had Sam.

She cried all through the garment center, down to Twenty-fourth Street. She kept walking, and finally paused long enough to go the bathroom and wash her face in the ladies' room at the Chelsea Hotel. The hip, tatty place which artists and writers had been checking in and out of for decades was grim as ever. "Well," she told herself, looking into the old, cracked mirror over the sink, "if Dr. Moore won't take your case, or the plan doesn't work, you can always come back here to the Roach Motel. Perfect for a successful suicide." She wouldn't be the first. It was the only thought that comforted her.

She walked down Seventh Avenue to Eighth Street, stopped in a used-book store, and browsed distractedly for an hour. She would learn not to think of Sam; she'd train herself starting now. She wandered over to Hudson Street. Then she had half a cantaloupe at a Greek joint (no cottage cheese—only forty calories, but an outrageous $3.50) and made her way down the Avenue of the Americas to Houston Street. There the marquee over Film Forum attracted her. It was a Mai Von Trilling double feature—both of which she had seen countless times before. Still, she loved those German movies of the early thirties, and Mai was surely one of the most beautiful actresses of all time. Mary Jane lined up along with the other losers who make up the crowd for the first show at art theaters. Still, for six bucks she'd buy four hours of forgetfulness, see some *real* acting, then walk all the way home and chew on some salad before she hit the sheets. And she wouldn't let herself think about Sam.

So her pattern was set: out of the house by nine, walking for almost eight hours, with a movie break and a cup of coffee (black) when absolutely necessary. She didn't call anyone, didn't return any calls, not even Molly's. After a week, she disconnected her answering machine. She found two kids to take the apartment, sold off her stuff, and found a cheap place to stay on East Nineteenth Street. But they wouldn't take cats. So she made one last visit to Molly, with the cashmere jacket in one hand and Midnight howling in his travel box. Oddly enough, it was giving up Midnight that made her more lonely than anything else.

Mary Jane walked, hungry, up and down Manhattan, without the courage to weigh herself, or to read another newspaper. Her room was grim. No place to hang out. She avoided mirrors and haunted public libraries, bookstores, and the shops with theater and film memorabilia. She splurged and bought a few cheap stills, black-and-white glossies of the faces she'd loved on the luminous screen. Could I get Jeanne Moreau's mouth? Garbo's chin? Mai Von Trilling's nose? Cheekbones like Hepburn —either Katharine *or* Audrey. She wasn't particular. But mainly she walked. And when she was too tired to walk anymore, she rested at Grand Central Station, or Penn Station, or any one of the lesser hotel lobbies—temporary homes of the displaced person in Manhattan.

As she walked, memories came back to her. Memories of her grandmother, of Scuderstown, of nursing school. But mostly she remembered Sam. Whole conversations they had had. The night they got locked out of her apartment. The day he cast her as Jill. The surprise birthday party she threw for him. The way he made love to her. Sometimes she walked with tears running down her cheeks. Luckily, it was New York, and no one even noticed.

And she discovered something: if you only had one purpose, it wasn't so hard to achieve it. When she had to cinch her jeans in three notches on her belt, she decided to call the Hennessey witch at Dr. Moore's. She'd show him the photos she'd collected, she'd get weighed by Yenta, his nurse. But had she lost enough? she wondered. Would it prove her commitment? Would he take her really seriously?

When she called, Miss Hennessey was cool, but without argument she made the appointment for a week later. For six days, Mary Jane really starved herself. Would he not see her again, not move her on for more X-rays if she hadn't shown enough willpower and commitment? She showed up almost an hour early, and paced the hospital lobby. At last, she had the courage to take the elevator up.

Stripped to a hospital gown, she stood barefoot on the scale while the nurse weighed her. Miss Hennessey fumbled, looked at Mary Jane's chart, and then moved the weights again.

"Can this be right?" she asked Mary Jane. "In seven weeks, you've lost twenty-one and a half pounds?"

"Have I?" Mary Jane said, and wondered if it would be enough.

When Mary Jane passed Miss Hennessey's desk and entered Dr. Moore's office, she felt as if she might pass out. By now he'd seen the preliminary X-rays. What if he told her that he couldn't give her the results she wanted? What if Dr. Moore said it was possible but chancy? Would she risk it? And what if he simply said he could do it? What then? She was determined to move forward, but she was, she had to admit, petrified.

Dr. Moore was standing before a light screen, looking at cranial X-rays. He looked up as she came in, and gestured at the pictures. "The face is endlessly fascinating," he said. "When I was looking for a surgical specialty, I had every intention of becoming a cardiac surgeon. It was where the hottest, smartest surgeons gravitated. But I found out there was a glut of them, and that I'd probably wind up practicing in Idaho. Then I was stuck, because, aside from the heart, I couldn't think of an area where I could make a living but that would never get boring. Until I talked to a plastic surgeon, and I was hooked." He looked back at the X-rays.

"Are those mine?" she asked. He nodded.

"Come over and take a look."

She moved to his side, surprised to find she was taller than he was. Wordlessly, she looked at the dark shadows on the film. She could not bear to have to ask him again, to form the words, to beg. As if he could read her mind, he answered without taking his eyes off the screen.

"Yes, I think I can make you beautiful. You're one of the lucky ones. For you, all it will take is time and money. Of course, there are no guarantees, and I need you to understand that and the extensiveness and risks of the program I'd outline."

She nodded, feeling as if she hadn't enough breath to speak. She was immensely grateful, not only for his answer but for the privacy that his averted face gave her. He was very close to her. He smelled of disinfectant soap and a very slight underscent—was it vanilla?

"I'd propose that we'd begin by working on the skeletal alterations: the bony superorbital ridge, which would have to be shaved down; the cheekbones, which require implantations; and the work on your chin to bring about a better proportion and relationship to the facial planes themselves." As he spoke, he touched the X-rays of her jutting brow and her cheeks, and moved his hands finally to her chin. Only then did he look at her, and she nodded her agreement. She still couldn't speak. "The skeletal work would take six months to a year, depending on your rate of recovery. Then we would move on to the soft-tissue work."

"What's that?" she managed to croak.

"The movement and realignment of your skin on your new skeletal frame. Blepharoplasty, for one thing, though I would propose only a modified eye-lift. You don't have bags under your eyes, just some sagging on top. We only need to melt the fat that is deposited above, at your eyelids, and we can do that with a procedure I invented. I'll insert a needle here"— he touched her eyelid very gently, but she winced—"and heat it, melting the fat away. That will give you a very clean, well-defined upper eyelid. And almost no incision, so no visible scars."

He touched her neck, gently fingering the skin. "We'll need liposuction here, and then we'll do a fairly aggressive lift. I'm not talking about simply stretching the facial skin, but actually separating the skin from the fascia all the way down to about here"—he moved his hand to her breast bone—"then peeling it back, pulling it taut, and excising the excess before reattaching it."

"That leaves scars," she said.

"None that you will see. I reattach the skin *above* the hairline, into the scalp, so that natural hair growth will cover almost all of it."

"Then you'll have to shave my head?" she asked, horrified. Her thick mane of hair was the only naturally beautiful thing about her. Sam had loved her hair.

"No. We succeed in sterilizing it. I've never had infections at the scalp."

He moved to his desk and indicated a chair. "I'm glad you've already done so well on the weight reduction. It demonstrates to me not only the resilience of your tissue but also your motivation." He peered at her. She tried not to squirm under his gaze, wondering what imperfect feature he was assessing. But at the same time she felt grateful, and also close to him in a strange way. Finally, here was one man from whom she had nothing to hide.

Once again, as if he could read her thoughts as well as her bone structure, he spoke. "You know, there is a great intimacy in a project like this. In a way, it is a mutual seduction, and then a marriage. We will work together: a great deal will depend on your tissue, your ability to communicate what you want, to follow a regimen, and to heal; the rest will depend on me and my talent. Facial surgery is a gift. Beyond technique, there has to be a vision, and an ability to see the possibilities. And for me to do my best work, I have to be in love with the project."

"And are you?" she asked. Outside, the rain was pouring down, and the only noises were the heavy dripping at an outside eave and the humming vibration of the frame of the light board against the clip that held her X-ray.

"Yes," he said, and she felt a tightness in her chest. "It's a challenging, fascinating project." He came closer to her, very close. "Have you ever smoked?"

"No."

"Good. Now you never will. Also, no sun. None at all. Never. Sunscreen at all times."

She looked out at the freezing rain and the overcast day. "At all times, doctor?"

He smiled. "Well, not at night. Also, no alcohol."

"Not even wine?"

"Not even beer. Well, let me put it this way: I know you will, so be very moderate. It's not good for your skin. I can see you've lost weight, and the sun has done little damage to you so far."

"I never could afford a vacation, and tar beach didn't appeal."

"Well, *that* was good luck." He paused. He took her hand in his and for a moment, she thought he was going to get personal, to give her a kind word. Instead, he pinched the back of her hand, then watched as the little ridge of skin he had made resolved itself back into the relative smoothness of her wrist. "You still have remarkable elasticity for a woman your age. That helps. What's your diet like?"

She told him.

"Fine. But I want you to eat more raw vegetables. A lot more water, too. Hydration is critical for skin. And to keep this somewhat unnatural weight and the benefits of surgery, you can only eat two spare meals a day from now on. You are trying to attain an unnatural ideal, one that is almost impossible for a woman to maintain beyond adolescence. Now that large breasts have been added to the lanky, extremely thin model that's been in vogue for years, almost no woman naturally has that shape to begin with."

"Do you give young, thin models those breasts if they want them?" she asked.

"I don't do body work. Only facial surgery. And I don't know any male surgeon who does a good job on breasts. I recommend a woman doctor: Sylvia Wright. It makes sense that a woman would have a better feel for breasts than a man." He smiled. "But Wright won't do implants. Nine years ago, reputable journals were reporting problems with silicone. Anyway, you won't need

173

implants. Yours would only require a restructuring and lift.''

She looked down at her drooping chest. Despite the weight loss, or because of it, her breasts looked worse than ever. Well, she told herself, one thing at a time. The important thing was, he would take her case. And that she believed he could work miracles.

22

Sharleen pulled the Datsun that Dobe had bought for her and Dean onto the gravel parking lot in front of the aluminum-sided diner there on Ming Avenue and braked to a halt alongside a row of battered cars, pickups, and semis with trailers. She sat in the car, the *Bakersfield Times* in her hand folded open to the want ads, and thought about what she was going to say.

Darn, she thought, they all said "experienced." Eight diners today said "experienced only." Then each of the disgusting diner owners had made her a proposition, if she really wanted the job. She thought of Dobe, of what he told her about being beautiful. Maybe she could have handled the men, but she didn't want to get into another situation with Dean.

Anyhow, how much experience do you need to serve eggs and hash in a truckers' diner, for heaven's sake? I've eaten in enough of these places to do the job in my sleep, she told herself. But she hadn't been sleeping. No work, no money equaled no sleep. What could she do? Unless she let these guys touch her, or told a lie, she didn't know what she'd do. If only she had experience that wasn't a lie.

She snapped her fingers. That's it, she thought. I've had experience *eating* in them for months; maybe that's enough experience for anyone.

Sharleen strained to look at her face reflected in the grimy rearview mirror. She pinched her cheeks the way she remembered her mother doing when she couldn't afford makeup. It brought a bright-pink glow to her face.

Sharleen squeezed her lips together, bruising them to a cherry red. She felt along the top edge of her white Mexican blouse, and gave a tug to pull it up; it did keep falling off one shoulder.

"Oh, Lord, help me with this," she prayed.

She sprang out of the car, locked the door, and gave her cowgirl belt a cinch to pull it tighter. Sharleen sucked in her breath and encircled her small waist with her hands. Just right, she thought.

She rubbed the front of her high-heeled sandals against the backs of her tightly blue-jeaned legs and, deciding she was ready, walked resolutely toward the front door. She swung her hips and her straw bag just a little, in case the boss was watching her approach. Might as well walk like she felt good, even if she didn't.

Before she could put her hand on the knob, the screen door swung open, and the fattest man she had ever seen stood before her.

"I've been expecting you," he said. "Or I should say, I've been praying for you." He stepped aside, holding the door open to let Sharleen squeeze past. She paused, then shrugged and walked into the cool, noisy interior. She saw that all the men plus both women customers and the waitress had turned to look at her. So she *had* been noticed as she came up the walk, she thought.

"My name's Jake and this is my place. Jake's Place. Get it?" he asked as he led her past the few occupied tables to the semiprivacy of a rear booth.

Sharleen couldn't keep from smiling. "Sure thing, Jake. And I bet you guessed I'm here about the . . ."

"You're hired. Now, get rid of that newspaper and have a cup of coffee with me and tell me all about yourself." He walked behind the counter and came back with two white mugs of coffee and a tray of donuts.

"Wait a minute, Jake. What do you mean, I'm hired? You haven't asked me if I had any experience yet. Your ad said 'experienced.' " Maybe she wouldn't have to lie, or flirt, she thought with relief. A man as fat as Jake wouldn't be chasin' her around counters.

Jake leaned his huge, beefy arms on the table between them and smiled. "Lady, I could see you was experienced the moment you started to walk toward the place. Hell, everybody in here could see it." Sharleen could feel her face flush. Anyone could see she was embarrassed. But Jake didn't. He just looked down at his coffee, reached over to pick up a donut, and continued. "And everybody in here said you was hired before you got to the door."

He indicated the few businessmen at the tables and booths, and the truckers lined up at the counter. "They're my regulars, and I like to keep them happy." He took half the donut into his mouth and mumbled, "So, you're on. What's your name?"

Sharleen sat back and laughed. The Lord sure did work in mysterious ways. She looked around the place.

There were rows of wire-stemmed white plastic flowers, now gray from dust and grease, along the bottom of the front window. The tables in the middle of the floor had flowered oilcloth covers, with a fake potted plant in the center of each, surrounded by the sugar pourer, salt and pepper shakers, napkin dispenser, and a bottle of barbecue sauce. The booths along the walls were high-backed and deep. The seats were upholstered in orange vinyl, broken in spots, their stuffing pushed back in with silver-gray duct tape. The jutting tables were blue Formica, chipped here and there. Each booth had a miniature juke box with a flip-card selection of records, a mixture of country-and-western and fifties hits, Sharleen was sure.

Her eyes went to the long blue counter that seemed to join both sides of the room. Big trucker butts hung over the stools, the bodies above them huddled over bottomless coffee cups. The noise level was high; the topics of conversation were baseball, road conditions, and hunting. The two women customers in the place talked only to each other.

A stocky woman in a pink polyester waitress uniform plodded back and forth to the kitchen, carrying armloads of meat-and-gravy dishes and pie, all the while shouting orders to the Mexican cook dripping sweat in the tiny kitchen. An open slot in the wall held the waiting meals under hot lights.

Well, Sharleen thought, it's better than McDonald's. At least there'll be tips. Now Jake wiped the donut crumbs off his rubbery mouth with the back of his hand. "What's your name?" he repeated.

"Sharleen, Jake. And when do I start?"

23

COSMOPOLITAN HOSPITAL

Patient:	Mary Jane Moran	Insurance:	None
Age:	Thirty-four	Address:	749 East 19th
D.O.B.	Sept. 22, 1958		New York, NY

Date:	July 22, 199-	
Procedure:	Abdominoplasty	
Physician:	Silverman	Cost: $7,425.00
Date:	Oct. 18, 199-	
Procedure:	Face lift & submental lipectomy	
Physician:	B. Moore	Cost: $4,300.00
Date:	Jan. 11, 199-	
Procedure:	Buttock lift, flank resection	
Physician:	Silverman	Cost: $3,830.00
Date:	April 21, 199-	
Procedure:	Blepharoplasty	
Physician:	B. Moore	Cost: $1,540.00
Date:	Sept. 28, 199-	
Procedure:	Lipectomy—batwing arms	
Physician:	Silverman	Cost: $1,950.00
Date:	Feb. 28, 199-	
Procedure:	Mastopexy	
Physician:	Wright	Cost: $4,300.00

Patient:	Mary Jane Moran	Insurance:	None
Age:	Thirty-four	Address:	749 East 19th
D.O.B.	Sept. 22, 1958		New York, NY

Date:	April 1, 199-	
Procedure:	Dermabrasion	
Physician:	B. Moore	Cost: $1,750.00
Date:	June 3, 199-	
Procedure:	Rhinoplasty	
Physician:	Moore	Cost: $4,100.00

—From the files of Laura Richie

After all the preliminary workups had been finished, Brewster Moore set up a schedule for her. He suggested other surgeons for the tummy tuck, the breast lift, and the liposuction. He would supervise their work carefully. Many of them worked with him at the clinic he had founded for indigent children.

"Isn't that work depressing?" Mary Jane asked.

"Less depressing than talking to a socialite begging for her third face lift," Brewster Moore snapped. "Would you like to see my other work?"

She felt properly chastised, and accepted his invitation. It was the only time in the weeks since she'd met him that he had offered anything about himself or his interests. She'd grown used to surgeons and their coldness, but he was unlike them—he had the surgeon's sureness, but beyond that he possessed an odd combination of formality, detachment, and compassion.

She discovered his secret on the tour. His clinic was his passion. There, from all over the world, were children who had been born with deformities so frightening, so monstrous, that many of them had been abandoned or left for dead. "Well, you can understand it," Brewster Moore told her matter-of-factly. "We are conditioned to respond to a baby's smile. Some of these children didn't have a mouth to smile with. Even educated parents have problems accepting this," Brewster explained. "Imagine what it was like for a peon in Peru."

He introduced her to Winthrop, a Canadian boy whose parents had died in a private-plane crash which he had survived, though he was burned beyond recognition. Now he had a new face, constructed from skin grafted from his back and thighs.

And Hilda, a blonde three-year-old who had been left at a Bremen church a day after her birth. In the year since she'd arrived, her harelip had been corrected, but she still required a nose.

And Raoul, a twelve-year-old from Honduras whose bright eyes and clever little drawings were his only means of communication, since he was born without a tongue or a lower jaw.

The ward and private rooms were cheerful, the equipment up-to-date, and the operating theater the most advanced in the country. "How do you pay for all this?" she asked as she looked around at the facility and the bustling staff.

Dr. Moore shrugged. "A bit of government funding, lots of private donations, and the rest comes from my fees. I do cosmetic work for some very wealthy and influential people." He smiled. "They support a lot of this."

"It makes me feel even more petty," Mary Jane said.

He stopped there in the hall and turned to her. "It shouldn't," he told her. "Don't buy that Puritan idea of predestination, or some outdated morality that says appearance is nothing but vanity. Some things have not changed since the beginning of time. Your face is your fortune. These children could attest to that."

She trusted him completely. So it was silly, really, she told herself. After all, she was a nurse and had been in hospitals for years. Still, hospitals made her nervous. And she was more than nervous before the first "procedure," as Miss Hennessey kept calling it.

Because, after all, she'd never been a patient before. "Healthy as a horse," she used to say, and slap her own wide flank.

The first surgery was a horror. The long ride on the

gurney, through the hospital corridors and on the elevator used by visitors, flower-delivery guys, and employees, had been humiliating. The orderly who wheeled her along pushed her as if she were a supermarket basket, and he must have been running for mayor of the hospital —he stopped and talked to everyone he passed. She actually was relieved when she finally got to the operating room.

Perhaps if it hadn't been *elective* surgery, perhaps if it had been life-saving, she wouldn't have felt the contempt that seemed to roll off the orderlies as they dragged her, one more piece of meat, under the knife. Plastic surgery, they seemed to sneer. Self-indulgent. Neurotic. Selfish.

She had lost thirty-eight pounds and her stomach had receded, but instead of being flat, it hung in a nasty pouch of stretched skin. That would be neatly stretched in the abdominoplasty. It was a fairly serious operation, but Dr. Moore wanted it first, to give her time to recuperate.

The abdominal surgery—involving both liposuction and a "tummy tuck"—was a major procedure.

"You've lost about as much weight as you need to," Brewster Moore told her. "But you'll have to keep it off."

"But I still look awful!" She raised her arms and swung them. Excess flesh waved back and forth.

"Batwing arms. Typical."

"Is that what it's called?"

"Yep. Descriptive, huh? Dieting won't help them. The rest is exercise, liposuction, and surgery. But your stomach muscles need to be tightened. So we'll actually cut and shorten the muscles and reattach them, slice off excess skin, and stretch the rest down."

"What happens to my belly button?"

"Well, it will be excised. Don't worry. I'll supervise everything. And Silverman will make you a very nice new one."

"A new one? How is it done?"

"It's just a staple from inside. Unless, of course, you want an 'outie' instead of an 'innie.' But that will cost extra."

Her eyes opened wide, until she realized that he was teasing her.

Despite being considered cosmetic, it was major surgery, with a seven-to-ten-day hospital recuperation, and was scheduled for seven-thirty on a gray Thursday morning. The night before, an aide had come in to—of all things—shave her pudenda. "All skin exposed to incision and its environs must be shaved, to reduce the chance of infection, and to make the removal of surgical tape and staples easier later on," the bored orderly droned. Her only comfort was that, at least for this one, she'd be unconscious.

The standard joke is that in a hospital they'll wake you up to give you a sleeping pill, but on the morning of the abdominal surgery Mary Jane was awoken at five-thirty and given an injection to relax her. The hypo worked, and she felt as if she were floating as she was lifted onto the stretcher for her ride to surgery. Oddly enough, the shot did little to ease her embarrassment at being in the elevator lying down while people in street clothes stood around her, pretending she wasn't there. No one looked her in the eye, and she had trouble stifling her laughter at how ludicrous the situation was.

Dr. Moore didn't do the surgery, though he had selected the doctor who would. Still, he came to visit her the evening before, and she was touched by his gesture. "Bob Silverman is a good man. You've got good tissue, and there should be little scarring. But for the mastopexy I've lined up Sylvia Wright. She has a feeling for breasts that no man I know has."

Mary Jane had giggled at his phraseology. And Dr. Moore actually colored. He was a very formal man, but Mary Jane was getting to know him and see the humor behind his formality. Dr. Moore smiled. He had a very nice smile. "You know what I meant," he said.

On the way in to the abdominoplasty, Mary Jane kept her eyes on the ceiling, following the overhead lights as she was wheeled along the halls. She knew she should be nervous, but, with the injection she had received finally kicking in, she at last lost all guilt, all shame, all nerves.

She really couldn't care less. The orderly parked her outside the operating room, in what felt like an alcove, but since she was disinclined to turn her head, she couldn't really tell. Time passed. She had no idea how long. Minutes? Hours? she asked herself. Or is it over? A nurse approached her and said her name, while inserting an IV in her arm. "We're going in now, Miss Moran," she said, and pushed the stretcher through swinging doors, into a pale-green room with huge, blinding lights overhead.

She was aware of a group of people in what looked to be camouflage, which she was able to remind herself was surgical green. They seemed to be standing around a table that wasn't there; then, suddenly, *she* was the table, and they were all looking down at her.

"Hello, Mary Jane," Dr. Moore's voice said from somewhere. "Are you comfortable?" She didn't expect him to be there at all.

"I'm very relaxed," she murmured.

"Count backward," the masked gas-passer told her. "Start at one hundred."

She tried to think of a joke, a wisecrack, but could barely manage the count. "One hundred. Ninety-nine." And then she couldn't remember the next number. . . .

Blessedly, it was over. "You can go to sleep now," the nurse said. Mary Jane started to say thank you, but never got it out.

She opened her eyes again later, but couldn't move. Her mouth was so dry that her tongue felt like sandpaper. The pain was worse than the worst stomach ache she had ever had. It felt as if she'd been stabbed. Mary Jane tried to call out to someone, but no sound came. She started to cry to herself, but the slightest movement increased the pain, so she began to whimper instead. The incision across her entire pelvis felt like a fiery slashed wound, and her whole midsection was knotted, as if she'd been kicked in the gut a million times. Then nothingness again.

She was aware she had slept. Or had blacked out. She opened her eyes once again, and now knew she was in her hospital bed. The pain was still there, but she knew that someone would do something about that soon, just as soon as she let them know she was awake. But she couldn't. She couldn't move a muscle. Not yet.

A hand touched her shoulder gently. "Hi, you want to wake up now? Come on, Mary Jane, wake up. How are you feeling?" The voice kept talking; she was being called to arousal, the nurse intent on getting her fully out of the anesthesia. Mary Jane tried to cooperate. "Water," was all she could manage to say. She also wanted to say "pain," but could only squeeze her eyes closed. The nurse understood, and Mary Jane blessed her as she felt a prick in her side and then—slowly, slowly—the pain ebbed. And Mary Jane felt fine. Her last thought, before she was gone again, was that she'd got one down and only eight more operations to go.

The incisions itched like crazy. But when the bandages came off, Mary Jane had a stomach as flat as a teenager's. She stared at it, fascinated. Was that her flesh? So smooth, so tight, so taut? She forgot about the pain, the cost, the knowledge that her excess flesh had been cut off and discarded somewhere.

Instead she simply contemplated her own brand-new navel.

The breast lift and reduction—mastopexy—seemed the worst, though actually Brewster Moore assured her that the pain in healing would be far less than the abdominal incisions had caused. "We're not cutting muscle, only fat. You have plenty of breast tissue; it is simply attached too low to your chest wall."

"I find this talk very titillating. Get it?"

Dr. Moore groaned. "Mary Jane, that is the most obvious pun I ever heard. Now, tomorrow Dr. Wright will make a new pocket of skin, higher up, fill it with tissue, and reattach the nipples centrally. . . ."

"Reattach the nipples? You mean you *cut off my nipples?*"

"Yes. I thought you understood that. From the material that Dr. Wright reviewed with you." Dr. Moore sighed. "She should have told you. But the scars are almost completely hidden in the areolae. . . ."

Mary Jane felt a wave of nausea. "But when they reattach them, do they work? I mean . . ." She stopped, embarrassed. "Will I be able to *feel* anything?"

"Well, you certainly won't be able to nurse, but sensation sometimes returns. But in my opinion the nerves do not regenerate. It's an important consideration. I thought you understood about it. Of course, you must decide if the sacrifice is worth it. And some women have reported *increased* sexual pleasure after the operation, because, I think, of their increased pride in their appearance. You know, the mind is the most important sexual organ."

"It's not my *mind* you're operating on, doctor."

"I know that. And I hope you know that I do appreciate how . . . courageous you've been."

"Hey, it's the kids like Raoul and Winthrop, or the ones who've lost half a face to cancer, who are courageous. But I appreciate the thought. And I'll make you a deal: Dr. Wright can cut off my nipples if she gives me perfect breasts and you'll give me a nose like Mai Von Trilling's."

"You drive a hard bargain, Mary Jane," he laughed. "I'll see what I can do." He turned to leave.

"Oh, and doctor? About those nipples." He turned to her, his face concerned as always. "You *will* be sure that Dr. Wright remembers to put them back, won't you?"

24

Hi there, Laura Richie here. While Mary Jane was struggling through her pain in New York, I bet you forgot all about me, back in Hollywood. No surprise. Hollywood is used to short memories. Nothing ever stands still. In this town, everyone in the business is either on the way up or on the way down. Like sharks swimming through the ocean, none can afford to stop. And, like sharks, all of them operate on hunger and fear. Hunger and fear are the fuels that generate the Hollywood agent-client relationship. The young up-and-coming starlets covet and

*fear agents as if they were gods in the pantheon known
as Hollywood. Agents can make or break careers.*

*But fear is a two-way street. Once they have become
established as talents and celebrities, stars have been
known to drop their agents in favor of even more powerful brokers. Every agent fears being dropped.*

Lila could smell that fear in Ara Sagarian's reception
room, and hoped that it was not hers. There were half a
dozen other young people scattered around the room,
one more beautiful than the other, each clasping a portfo-
lio while thumbing through the latest issues of *Variety*.
Only losers had to wait, and she hated waiting. But Lila
was sure none of them had appointments with Ara. She
guessed, too, that these were the flotsam and jetsam of
the Industry, who regularly made the rounds of agents'
offices, hoping each time for that brief five-minute interview that could result in an acting job, a walk-on role, or
even that coveted prize: representation.

Because in Hollywood an actor without an agent is an
actor without a chance.

"Miss Kyle?" the young secretary said, as every head
in the room turned to Lila. "Mr. Sagarian will see you
now. Will you follow me, please?"

Lila smiled, as if she expected to be treated specially,
and picked up her bag from the floor next to her chair.
She tossed it over her shoulder as she followed the
woman down the long, deeply carpeted hall. The walls
on either side were lined with scores of framed, signed
photographs. As Lila glided by, she was able to pick
out Frank Sinatra, Sammy Davis, Jr., Lucille Ball, Duke
Wayne, Joan Crawford, and a dozen others. "To Ara,"
began each autograph.

"There's your mother's picture, Miss Kyle. It was a
promo shot for *Birth of a Star*." Lila recognized the shot.
She had seen it dozens of times before, in her mother's
house. That and hundreds of others of her mother pa-
pered the walls of the Puppet Mistress's library and den.
"This is Mr. Sagarian's suite," the secretary said, and
rapped gently on the rosewood door.

Lila was nervous, but reminded herself that Ara Sagarian was not what he had been. He wasn't representing Sinatra or Davis or Wayne or Crawford or Ball now. Some of his clients were retired, and the other half were dead. He needed fresh blood, but not the blood of those losers waiting in the lobby. He needed a Madonna, a Tom Cruise, a Lila Kyle. A superstar, or someone with the potential to be one. He needed Lila Kyle. At least that's what she told herself.

"Come in, come in," Ara called out, as the door was opened and Lila stepped through it. How long had it been since she had last seen him? Five years? Ten? She wasn't prepared for the figure that came limping toward her. Once tall, even powerful, Ara Sagarian now was stooped and shorter. His left arm hung loosely by his side; his left leg dragged after his right. The left side of his mouth was partially paralyzed, and the words of his greeting sounded muffled. Everything about him seemed reduced from what Lila remembered. Of course, I was young then, and maybe he wasn't as big and as strong as I remember. But he'd certainly shrunk. And it looked like he'd had a major stroke.

"Mr. Sagarian, how kind of you to see me. I know how busy you are." Lila walked briskly toward him, her hand extended.

Ara shook her hand, then dabbed a linen handkerchief at the trail of drool that escaped from his mouth. His pencil-thin mustache was wet, too. "Not at all, my dear. I'm delighted to see you again. I haven't laid eyes on you since, let me see, you must have been seven or eight years old, and you performed a skit with your mother and her puppets at a party at her home." He looked at her appreciatively. "You've been busy growing up since then," he said. "Come sit over here." Ara indicated a seat on the loosely cushioned sectional sofa, and settled himself back into the plush down pillows.

"How is your charming mother?"

"She's very well, Mr. Sagarian. She sends you her love, of course. She's *so* grateful that you should take the time to talk to me about my career. As Mother says, if you can't get Mr. Sagarian to represent you, you're not in show business."

"Please, call me Ara. We're practically family. Now, what career is it that I'm to help with?" he asked, and wiped his mouth again.

"I'm an actress," she said, and suddenly felt very young. God, she *had* to make this happen. "That is, Mother tells me I'm a born talent, and has been pushing me for years to get into the business." Lila patted her skirt nervously in place and continued. "So I finally gave in. And here I am." Lila flashed her brightest smile.

"Here you are, indeed. And very beautiful, I might add. Now, what would you like me to do for you, my dear?" Ara asked.

Lila faltered. All the bravado she had felt on her way over here was slipping away. He was, despite his stroke, despite his age, so, so . . . so sure of himself. So courtly. She wasn't prepared to have to spell it out for him. He had to know what she wanted, and it certainly wasn't a date. Was he playing with her? She felt a flash of anger, but tried to stay calm.

"Well, I . . . I wanted to ask you if you would take me on as a client. You see, I was thinking of starting in television, but really I'm more interested in a career in movies." She rattled off a list of fake credits, though she'd never spent a minute before the camera.

Ara knitted his brows. "I'm so sorry to have wasted your time, Lila. I'm not taking on any new talent. This is nothing personal. I haven't in years, in fact. Had I known that was the purpose of your visit, I could have saved you the trip. But perhaps I could help you in another way. Maybe I could refer you to another agent?"

Lila was near panic. This was not going as she had planned. And she didn't want a referral to some has-been or wannabe agent out of the William Morris mailroom who had no more contacts than she did. Maybe flattery would work. "But I don't *want* another agent, Ara. I want *you*. Mother always said you understood the artistic temperament better than anyone else in town, better than any director." Lila dropped her eyes, as if to keep him from seeing her tears of frustration and disappointment. "I want to work with *you*, Mr. Sagarian."

"I'm sure you've given this a great deal of thought,"

Ara said, "and that your mother has prepared you for some of the pitfalls to such a career. But let me give you the history of an acting career in Hollywood. It goes like this: 'Who is Glenn Ford?' 'Get me Glenn Ford.' 'Get me a Glenn Ford type.' 'Get me a young Glenn Ford.' And then, 'Who is Glenn Ford?' I know that sounds a little cynical, but that's the way of this world." Ara wiped his drooling lips once again. "You've seen what your mother had to do to get on top and stay there as long as she did—as long as she has. Surely you don't want to have to go through that for the rest of your life?"

Oh, Christ, he wasn't going to start with fatherly advice now, was he? Why couldn't he just shut up, wipe his mouth, and send her over to Spielberg or Frears or even Robert Altman, for God's sake? She took a deep breath. She'd just have to lie. "It seems my mother has wanted this for me long before I wanted it for myself. I've been trained for the life by the mistress of the business."

"So, your mother is completely behind you on this?" Ara asked, raising his brows. "She's convinced you have the talent and the perseverance to handle such work?" Ara used his handkerchief once again before continuing. "Funny, I don't remember. But my memory isn't what it was. You see, I have great respect for Theresa's opinion. In the old days, she could pick talent like no one else. I have her to thank for the discovery of several very important talents I handle. It was Theresa who sent Marilyn to me, *and* James Dean. So, if Theresa thinks you have it, I would reconsider my decision. Of course, she must show a mother's favoritism, but she's no dummy. I'm old, and I haven't been well, and I've considered retirement. But perhaps, just one more time . . ." He paused.

Lila began to relax. What the hell. He was buying the lie, and she knew, if he sent her out for just one go-see, she could get a part, a foothold. She smiled. "Mother is one hundred and fifty percent behind me on this. We've spent many hours discussing the pros and cons of my decision, and she has been uncommonly candid with me about the business."

"Then excuse me while I make a quick phone call, Lila," Ara said, as he reached for the telephone on the coffee table in front of them.

Lila's heart jumped in her chest. Jesus Christ, could it really be this easy? she thought. He'll make one phone call, and I'm on my way? Whom will he call? Coppola? Sherry Lansing? Barry Levinson? Lila thanked all the gods of fortune and fame that she felt lurking over her shoulder, and stifled a smile of triumph.

Then she heard him speak. "Good morning, Estrella. Ara Sagarian here. May I speak to Miss O'Donnell?" He looked over at Lila and smiled a tiny, tilted smile, then wiped at the corner of his mouth once again with the handkerchief.

Lila stopped breathing for a brief moment. Oh, shit!

"Theresa, darling. How are you? I haven't seen you since my unfortunate hospitalization. It was so nice of you to come to visit. No. No. Not at all. But guess who I have sitting next to me at this moment, thanks to you." Ara listened for a moment, then continued. "Why, Lila, your daughter. Thank you for sending her to me, darling. I think I can help her."

Lila watched as Ara's expression changed while he listened intently to Theresa's side of the conversation, his expression becoming grave. Lila felt the blood rush to her face and her stomach tighten. Oh, God! What was the Puppet Mistress saying? She shouldn't have come here. She shouldn't have listened to Robbie!

"I'm sorry to have bothered you, my dear. I must have misunderstood. By the way, I will be seeing you at my Emmy party, won't I?" He paused again, nodded. "Good. It wouldn't be a party without you."

Ara hung up the phone and got to his feet. He stumbled over to his desk and opened the top drawer, removed a small vial, and took out a pill. He poured himself a glass of water from the silver carafe on his desk and swallowed the pill. Then he turned to Lila and finally looked her in the eyes.

"It should be very clear to you, Miss Kyle, that I was not born yesterday. You almost sent me up shit river without a paddle. Not only did your mother *not* send you to me, but she is decidedly *against* your choice of careers." Ara walked slowly around his desk to his chair and sat down. "She also believes that you have problems of an emotional nature that would prohibit you from ever living a public life. And that you don't have a shred of talent, and no experience. That she has begged you to go on to college, to pick some other career. But, frankly, none of that bothers me as much as the fact that you lied to me."

"Ara, Mr. Sagarian, please, let me explain." Lila's voice was tight with panic.

"There is no need to explain. I understand completely. But I will not help you, for two reasons. One, you jeopardized a very old, very lucrative relationship I have with one of my major stars, and, two, you underestimated me." Ara now held the handkerchief to his mouth as the drooling seemed to increase. "And for those reasons, Miss Kyle, consider yourself lucky that I'm only throwing you out of my office, and not out of the business." Ara pressed a button on his desk, and his office door was opened immediately. "Miss Bradley, please escort Miss Kyle to the elevator. And, Miss Bradley, Miss Kyle will *not* be making any further appointments to see me. Our business together is finished."

Ara Sagarian swung around in his chair and faced the window, picking up the phone as he did so.

Lila followed Miss Bradley, this time in silence. When they came to the elevator bank, the door opened to an elevator and Lila got in. "I'm so sorry, Miss Kyle," Miss Bradley said. "I always loved your mother." Then the door shut between them.

In the isolation of the swiftly moving elevator, Lila Kyle covered her face and cried.

25

If you have to pick a city to get lost in, you can't do better than New York. Mary Jane found it surprisingly easy to disappear, to melt out of her previous life and turn into a ghost. She spent almost all of her time alone. Those days of endless walking, spending nothing, eating nothing, speaking to no one, with no place to go but the room that she could not bear to call "home," seemed emptier than any life could sustain. But you have to make space if you want something new, she told herself, over and over. Since when is giving birth easy? Or being born?

And her memories kept her company. Memories of laughing with Neil, shopping with Molly, and hanging out with the troupe, and memories of Sam.

She couldn't forget him. In fact, it seemed that the longer the separation, the more often she thought of him. How he had cast her for *Jack and Jill,* the rehearsals, the start of their affair. What he said, how he looked. Perhaps it was because she was so lonely, but his memory did not fade. It got stronger.

Starving herself, exercising, undergoing surgery and recuperation were lonely occupations almost beyond bearing. But Mary Jane learned from it. She learned that she could survive almost anything, and that she could accomplish almost anything she wanted, if she kept to a single goal: she didn't think about meeting a man, making friends, getting a part, choosing what she would wear, buying a new book, or even eating a good meal. She focused only on the perfecting of her body, and the study of this new persona she hoped to become: a beautiful woman. And if the loneliness sometimes seemed almost to suffocate her with its blanket of New York isolation, at least, wrapped in it, she was safe from distraction.

By the third operation, she was more relaxed. She had seen the implants that would be inserted into her cheeks and chin. Dr. Moore showed her how they would be placed and where the incision scars would be hidden. She wasn't as fearful before the surgery, but the bruising and swelling afterward were so horrendous that she swore off mirrors for the duration. It was too frightening.

And, of course, she had to be conscious. It helped the surgeon better understand how the skin draped over her face. Brewster Moore had told her that, and she knew it, but she hadn't known how much it would bother her— seeing the gowned, masked faces, hearing the scraping of the bone as he worked on the ridge under her brows, hearing the drill that Dr. Moore used to cut away at her. But she was determined to move ahead with this plan, and she could see some signs of progress. She could easily wear size six now, and her breasts, though scarred, pointed up perkily under her blouse.

Well, she reminded herself, the oral surgery had been much worse. *That* wasn't any goddamn discomfort, and she'd demanded Percodan and gotten it. Eight teeth pulled—four wisdom teeth, four of the perfectly healthy molars beside them—so that there was room in her mouth for the others to straighten out. "It's not that your teeth are too big," Dr. Kleinman told her, "it's that your mouth is too small."

"I wish my grandmother could hear you say that," Mary Jane muttered, remembering all the times she'd been called a big mouth.

Her teeth had ached. Her jaw had been broken and realigned by Dr. Moore; then Kleinman, the master orthodontist, had begun his work. At least she hadn't been able to eat for weeks, and she'd dropped another nine pounds. When she had nothing better to do, she could now count all her ribs when she held her breath.

So she'd pop a Percodan, crawl onto the lumpy cot in her hotel room, and stroke her ribs like a washboard until the pain let up and she fell into a sleep too drugged for "discomfort."

But worse than the tooth pain had been the electrolysis. A Frenchwoman, Michelle, had worked over her hairline and eyebrows, following Dr. Moore's template, burning out hair follicles with a tiny needle inserted into her forehead. It was agony, and the smell made her want to gag.

"Easier to raise your hairline than surgically build you more forehead," Dr. Moore said. "And your hair *is* beautiful." It was the first time he had complimented her, and she felt herself flush with pleasure.

"My grandmother called it 'Indian hair.' It's so thick and heavy that I was ashamed of it."

"Medically speaking, your grandmother sounds like an asshole," Dr. Moore told her, and she had laughed despite the "discomfort."

She liked him. She liked him very much. And throughout the long, painful, boring hospitalizations, during the examinations in his spare office, even in phone calls to her, he treated her . . . kindly. With compassion. As if she was as serious a patient as Raoul or Winthrop, or the little girl who'd had her face burned off in a car accident, or the teenager who'd been kept in the basement by his parents, or some of the other horrors who waited in his office, hoping for a human face, a face he could give them to end their shame and isolation.

Still, even the steeliest determination has to grapple with financial realities. After eleven "procedures," Mary Jane had to face the fact that she was close to broke. She hadn't worked in almost twenty-two months, the longest "vacation" in her life. Not that all the surgery had been a day at the beach. Brewster had called her lucky—he said all she needed was money and time. Well, she'd certainly run out of the latter because now her money was just about gone. The only asset she had left was the farm up in Scuderstown, but in the more than two years since her grandmother's death it had been immersed in the legal tangle left by the old woman. Her grandmother had stubbornly left it to her son, Mary Jane's father, although he had been *non compos mentis* and hooked to machines at the V.A. for more than thirty years. Mary Jane had counted on that money's coming through by now. Leave it to Grandma to ruin my plans, even when she's dead, Mary Jane thought.

Slater, the Albany lawyer, was still trying to clear probate, but it was taking a long time, and his fees would probably eat into what little the farm would bring. By the time the money came through, Mary Jane, like her grandma, would also be dead of old age.

She tried to live on even less, and sold the engagement ring she'd had from her mother. But the four hundred dollars she got for it wouldn't last long. When she was down to her last thousand dollars, she had no choice—she went to Dr. Moore to tell him.

Mary Jane sat across from him, once more, in that austere office. "I have to stop the surgery for now," she said. She tried not to let her lip tremble, or show any emotion. She remembered the breakdown she'd had in this same chair the first time they spoke. "I mean to go on. It will just have to wait for a while."

"Why?" he asked.

"Personal reasons," she said. She really liked Dr. Moore, and she'd come to understand the compassion that he contained behind his formality, but she didn't want to discuss her problems with him.

"Well, I know this is a difficult thing that you are going through. Identity, self-worth, aesthetics, pain, anxiety, fear, scarring. It's a great deal that you are asking of yourself. If there is any way that I or the team can provide more assistance . . ."

She could see his concern. That he had done wrong. God, he must think she was having second thoughts! "I've run out of money," Mary Jane mumbled.

"What?"

"I've run out of money." She said it more loudly, more angrily than she meant to. They were silent for a moment. Brewster Moore blinked.

"Is that all? Jesus, I thought you were having regrets or some kind of mental problem. It's just the money?"

"Just?"

"Well, what I mean to say is that, as long as it's only financial, I think we could work something out."

"But I have to get a job. I'm really down to the bottom of my savings. And working isn't going to make me enough to pay my rent *and* surgical fees. I'll have to put everything off until my grandmother's estate comes through. If it comes through." Tears filled her eyes.

She'd put her life on hold for so long. How much more delay and disappointment could she take?

But Dr. Moore seemed unfazed. "Didn't you use to be a nurse?" he asked. "You could work for me now."

"With Miss Hennessey? No thanks." The nurse still gave her the creeps. And she felt the woman resented her growing relationship with Dr. Moore. Not that it was anything more than professional. Once or twice, Mary Jane wondered if she herself wished it *were* more. And if Nurse Hennessey had a yen for the doctor, too.

"Oh, she's not so bad."

"You say that because she worships you."

"Well, it's nice to have someone admire you, even if it's only Miss Hennessey." He laughed. "No, I was thinking perhaps you could work at the clinic with the children."

"Raoul and the others?"

"Yes."

She felt her stomach tighten. "I don't think so."

"I think you'd be good for them. I want them to see people who go through successful surgery. Of course, yours isn't as extreme as theirs, but, as a role model, you'll do. And they'd be good for you. Plus, I need the help and you need the rhinoplasty. A good exchange for everyone."

"But it will still take a long time to save up the fees."

"Tell you what. We continue with the procedures now, and you pay me out of your inheritance or future earnings. Meanwhile, if you're a clinic employee, I think I can get the hospital to waive its fees."

She felt tears come to her eyes again. He was being so kind. Was it just pity and charity on his part? Or professional pride in a project he wanted to see completed? She decided not to question it too deeply and simply be grateful.

And so they made the deal.

Now Mary Jane sat in a back booth at a Chinese restaurant, eating the dull steamed-vegetable dish before her. Even Buddha couldn't delight in this, she thought. She pushed the plate aside. Brewster Moore had explained it clearly—"to keep this somewhat unnatural weight and the benefits of surgery, you can only eat two spare meals a day." She was going in this afternoon for her first job at Brewster's clinic, and she was nervous. She knew that there he dealt with the most severe types of facial deformity. What would those poor, freakish patients feel if they knew that she, normal as she was, was also going through a series of surgeries?

She looked down at her plate. Eating had always been her solution to anxiety, but no more. Now it was steamed vegetables and a little brown rice, even under stress.

The placemat had the Chinese horoscope on it. She was born under the sign of the Dog—"Generous and loyal, you have the ability to work well with others. Compatible with the Horse and Tiger. Your opposite is the Dragon. 1910, 1922, 1934, 1946, 1958, 1970, 1982, 1994." She had been born in 1958. Well, she was generous and loyal, and she did work well with others—with Brewster, anyway, if not jealous Miss Hennessey. She looked up Sam's birth year, 1952. Yes, there he was—a Dragon. So, the Chinese knew their relationship was doomed from the start. It said he was robust and passionate, his life filled with complexity. He was compatible with the Monkey.

Despite the long months, despite the separation, despite the pain of what she was going through alone, she still thought of him. His smile. His long, slow hands on her body. His laugh, and the way he shook his head over a joke. Despite everything, she still missed him as badly as she had the first day he left her. Did he ever miss her?

She wondered what year Crystal Plenum was born. Monkeys were 1944, 1956, 1968. Was the bitch two years older than she, or ten years younger? What surgery had *she* had? What lies did she tell?

Well, Mary Jane decided, even if she did change her age, she was going to stay a Dog, if not in looks, then in Chinese horoscopes. But she wouldn't be a 1958 dog, she'd be a 1970 one. She thought she could pass for twelve years younger—the eye job and radical face lift seemed to have eliminated all wrinkles, and her skin's elasticity was such that she didn't have the stretched look that she had been afraid of.

It was the nose that still troubled her. She hated, as she always had, to look in the mirror. Now the fine cheekbones and the delicate chin that had emerged from under Brewster's scalpel seemed to mock the pendulous nose that still hung in the center of her face. In a way, she was uglier than she had ever been. She avoided all mirrors. There was a wall of them on the other side of the restaurant, facing her banquette, but she kept her head averted.

Dr. Moore had insisted that the rhinoplasty come last, after all the other work had settled. She trusted him, but, despite the lithe body that now looked good in tight jeans, despite the more feminine brow, the cheekbones, the improved hairline, the dental work, and even the colored contact lenses, the face that she glanced away from was barely attractive. Could the rhinoplasty fix all that?

Well, she sighed, the work on the ward should give her a sense of proportion.

And by the end of the first week, she realized it had. Brewster had asked her to come on as night nurse. There were few medical requirements—she simply administered painkillers to those children out of recent surgery and comforted all the children who were too frightened or restless to sleep. Brewster said they needed conversation and attention as much as anything else. "And they need to be looked at. So many people avert their eyes. Look at them. Not to stare. Just give them the gift of being seen."

"The gift of being seen." Yes, it was a gift, to be looked at approvingly. With her newly emerged slim body, Mary Jane had received wolf whistles. Only from behind, and only from some gross construction workers, but she'd be lying if she said she hadn't been thrilled. How long had she gone unnoticed? Thirty-six years seemed too long. She would look at the children and give them the gift of being seen, and she swore to herself she wouldn't wince.

There were dozens of kids, and all of them, beneath

the frightening failures of their faces, had the gift that children have: they were innocent and vulnerable and curious and alive. She had her favorites right away, of course. Sally, who was fourteen, and a victim of craniosynostosis: her skull had prematurely fused. She had undergone more than a dozen operations already to correct a frighteningly deformed head and jaw. And Jennifer, a three-year-old black girl whose brachycephaly gave her the pop eyes of a Crouzon's-disease sufferer. But of all of them, from the first night on, it was Raoul who drew her. Raoul, with eyes that had done all his speaking for twelve years. Raoul, born in South America without a tongue or lower jaw, unable to nurse, since there was no suction his poor deformed mouth could manage. Raoul, abandoned after his birth, who now tried, with a new mouth and tongue, to learn a new language. And Raoul, who made her laugh.

Raoul was twelve, and an active kid. He'd already had six major operations on his mouth and tongue, and was in for a seventh. He'd spent his first three years in a hospital, then his next two in an orphanage. But, despite all that, he had a strong spark of life and love. Raoul couldn't say much, but he could write and draw almost anything. Mary Jane played endless games of tic-tac-toe with him, and bought him a connect-the-dots book which so enchanted him that he designed his own. During her second week there, he gave her a picture to connect the dots on.

She picked up her pencil and followed his numbers. It was a nurse, complete, as she was, with comfortable shoes and a name tag. But when she got to the dots of the face, she realized it was a portrait of her, with her delicate cheekbones, almond eyes, and her awful, ridiculous nose. She nodded and tried to smile, then Raoul took the pencil. "LINDA MARY JANE," he wrote, and looked up at her with a face full of affection. She was confused for a moment, until she remembered that *linda* was Spanish for "pretty." She looked down at his ruin of a face. There was no irony there. He was the first male who had ever called her that.

Don't feel so sorry for yourself, she said. Look at

Raoul. And she did. Night after night. And in no time at all, his ghastly grin seemed normal to her. Normal and welcoming.

Often, in the early evening, Brewster Moore stopped by, visited with the children and the frightened, over-whelmed parents who came. He spent extra time with Raoul. Then he usually had a cup of coffee with her. She came to look forward to it. On the nights he didn't, she felt a strange disappointment. Oh, fine, she thought. My life has become so small that I am obsessed with my nose and in love with my surgeon. Perfect. Nothing wrong with that. But maybe I should think about getting a life.

Because she was, for the first time, drawn to nursing, to Dr. Moore, and to these children. The idea of abandon-ing them, as everyone else had, troubled her. Better move on before you get trapped, she told herself. Better move on before you lose your nerve.

So she decided, one night: after this surgery, it was California. However she came out, it was time to move on. For two years her life had gotten smaller and smaller. Now it was time to expand.

She'd need a new name. Her new age was twenty-four; she was still born in a year of the Dog, but it was a different year. And though she'd keep the same career, she certainly hoped that she'd be more successful than she'd been before, in her first incarnation. She was, of course, afraid she'd fail again, but it was time, she knew, to get on with it.

Once, of course, she had the new nose.

"Ever consider surgical improvement? I think if you had asked me that when I was twenty," she says, *"I might have said yes, but after seeing such bad facelifts, no."* Emma Samms was being quoted in an interview in *People* magazine. Mary Jane threw the magazine down on the floor. She was sick to death of reading about how naturally beautiful women kept themselves so. "Drink lots of bottled water," "Never eat red meat," "Simple yoga exercises and meditation to help you project your *inner* beauty!" Fuck the inner beauty. It had never gotten

her a date *or* a part. And it was a load of crap anyway. As if Perrier would alter your bone structure or clear up your skin! That new ingenue, Phoebe Van Gelder, had sworn she stuck to a macrobiotic diet, but Mary Jane knew, through Neil, the skinny bitch was on drugs most of the time, and had had a major nasal reconstruction. Sure, the Phoebe Van Gelder New Age diet: carrots and cocaine.

Over the last months, doing her research on beauty, she'd read all of the bullshit: "How to Lose Five Pounds This Weekend!," "Ten Tricks to Prevent Aging," "Top Models' Secret Makeup Tips for You." Yeah, the real tip was "Be young and tall and gorgeous with perfect bone structure." Well, Mary Jane knew the real secret to beauty now for the average woman. Beauty meant pain, expense, surgery, and almost full-time maintenance. It sure didn't leave time for the day job.

God, she was cranky, she admitted to herself. She glanced briefly into the tiny mirror she now kept in her purse. The bruising under her eyes was just about gone. She averted her face. It had been weeks now since the nasal surgery. She still wasn't pretty. If anything, her nose loomed even more hideously on her face. But Dr. Moore had explained it would take some time for the swelling to go down. Now there was only the final rhinoplasty left—the "refining," as Dr. Moore called it, that remained to be done on the nose. She noticed that Dr. Moore never referred to "your nose," only "the nose."

"Most cosmetic surgery needs to be done in multiple stages," he had explained. "For financial reasons—and emotional ones—most surgeons to the middle class don't bother. After all," he mimicked, " 'Missy does look *so* much better now, with that big bump gone.' But nasal tissue swells, and it sometimes takes months for the swelling to go down. Most surgeons are butchers. They break the nasal cartilage. It causes all kinds of temporary swelling. The only way to see the actual contour, to see both how the tissue takes to the cartilage armature and how the skin drapes the tissues, is to wait. And then 'refine.' Which often means a second operation. But most women don't want to undergo another procedure. Ergo, the instant nose. Now, with your face, on the other hand . . ."

Brewster explained that he had perfected a rhinoplasty procedure that didn't require the breaking of the nose. "And that means less swelling, no discoloration at all. But I didn't want to work on the nose until the rest of the armature was completed. And I want to wait for a second chance to work on the tip."

She'd been through the swelling, the taste of blood always in the back of her throat, the difficulty sleeping. "Refinement"? She laughed to herself, but even smiling hurt. Oh, no, she remembered. It didn't hurt. It caused "discomfort."

The last operation was surprisingly quick, less than an hour. Mary Jane got up off the table with little more than wooziness and a neat white pad of gauze taped over the new tip of her nose. After a night of restless sleep, she spent the next day packing her few belongings and telling the hotel she'd be leaving. Not that the ever-changing front desk staff cared. She worked her last week at the clinic, and said goodbye to the children. She did everything she could do to prepare for her departure, except take off the gauze.

Now the months of pain and waiting and Dr. Moore's kindness were over. Now she'd see the best he could do. The face she would live with. And she was afraid. So afraid that she couldn't do it alone. She left on the bandage, and avoided reflections in plate-glass windows; she'd long ago covered the medicine-cabinet mirror at the hotel. She simply had to trust this little man, the doctor, her only friend, and see what he had wrought. She made the appointment with the ever-cold Miss Hennessey for her final visit.

Now, at last, here in his office, the time had come for revelation. She was so nervous, she wanted to ask to hold his hand, but she was far too shy. As if he knew what she felt, Dr. Moore came up close behind her. He put his hands on her shoulders and walked her to the corner of the room. He had her face the wall mirror, and he lifted the last bandage from her nose.

She stared into the mirror.

A perfect stranger stared out at her. A perfect stranger. An oval face, with just a touch of squareness, firmness at the sides of the jaw. A broad, smooth forehead, thin, tapering brows, cheekbones that wouldn't quit. And the nose. The nose! It was long, but perfectly so, straight and long, with a thin bridge and wonderful sharpness where it met her upper lip. It was beautiful. It was all changed and beautiful. *She* was beautiful! All changed, except for her eyes.

Then, for a moment, she had the panicky feeling that her own eyes were staring out at her, trapped in a strange, lovely face, while her own, *her* face, on this side of the mirror, hadn't changed. Involuntarily she lifted her hands, and blinked as her fingers touched *her*, yet moved over the stranger's perfect face in the mirror. It was eerie, but it convinced her this perfect face was really hers.

He gave her plenty of time. She looked and looked, and was surprisingly unselfconscious in front of him, perhaps because he was staring as hard as she was. At last he broke the silence. "Are you satisfied?" Dr. Moore asked softly.

With difficulty, Mary Jane pulled her eyes away from the mirror and looked at him. "Thank you," she said. "Thank you more than I can ever say." She stared back at the mirror, the mirror that was now her friend. Gently she touched her face, her own face, again. Then she held out her hand to him. "You've given me a new life. Now I can leave. You've given me a second chance. I'll never be able to thank you."

He looked away; maybe she'd embarrassed him. But he turned back quickly and smiled. "Are you prepared for a new life?"

She nodded, proudly. "I've got it all planned. Even a new name."

He raised his eyebrows. "Galatea?" he asked.

It was her turn to smile, and she shook her head. "Jahne," she said. "I've always hated 'Mary,' but I was afraid to be plain Jane before. Now it will be J-A-H-N-E. Not plain at all."

"So, Jahne Moran . . ."

She shook her head again. "Not Moran," she said. "I'd prefer a new name. But with the same initial. I'd like to use 'Moore.' I mean . . ." She blushed. ". . . if it's all right with you."

"I'd be delighted. Truly. Quite a compliment."

"Something else, Dr. Moore." She paused. "Could I write to you? And Raoul? I mean just occasionally. I know how busy you are. You wouldn't have to write back."

"I'd be delighted. And I *would* write back." The little man smiled.

Jahne stood up. She found it was harder to say good-bye than she'd expected. She had a lot of feeling for this artist, this healer, this good doctor.

"I'm going to make one last visit to Raoul."

"He'll appreciate that."

"I hope that he recognizes me without the bandage."

"He's an artist. He can see deeply. He'll know you. But no one else will."

"Are you sure? Certain?"

"Mary Jane, you look twenty-four and magnificent. You have a flat stomach, thin legs, high breasts, and a perfect face. Not to mention Mai Von Trilling's nose. Who is going to recognize you?"

"No one," she agreed, and smiled.

"M.J., M.J.," Raoul yelled as he saw her from a distance moving through the ward. They were special friends. He drew her wonderful pictures, and she brought him little treats. She would miss him very much. His speech had improved a lot since she'd started working with him. As she got closer to him his face changed. The sparkle left his brown eyes, the smile slipped from the wreck of his mouth.

"*Buenos días,* Raoul," she said. "What's the matter?" For a moment, her stomach knotted. Perhaps she wasn't what she thought. Maybe he was disappointed with her looks.

"What is it, Raoul?"

"Did the doctor do this to you?" the boy asked. It was still difficult to understand him, but she had learned to. Now she nodded. Oh, God. Maybe Brewster had lied to her. Perhaps she didn't look as good as she thought. Raoul turned away.

"What is it?"

"You'll go now."

"How do you know?"

"Because now you are so beautiful," he said, and tears welled up in his eyes.

"Oh, Raoul," she breathed, and hugged him.

Mary Jane waited, listening as the phone up in Albany rang. Finally, Mr. Slater picked it up. "Mr. Slater, this is Mary Jane Moran."

"I'm sorry, Miss Moran, I've been meaning to call you. But there has been no progress on the probate. I was thinking perhaps that we could simply probate your father as the heir and get you both executor and power of attorney. That would . . ."

"Mr. Slater," Mary Jane interrupted, "I have a proposal for you. When the will is finally probated and the farm is sold, how much do you think it'll be worth?"

"Well, the market isn't good, but perhaps forty or fifty thousand dollars. Maybe less."

"Would you be prepared to take the estate in lieu of fees, and simply send me a check for ten thousand?"

She listened for a moment to the silence at the end of the line. Greed fighting with morality? "Well, that's quite irregular, and there is no telling when this might be settled and the farm sold. . . ."

"I know. That's why I'm willing to take so little. Is it a risk that you are willing to take?" She knew she had him hooked; she could tell by the tightness in his voice. All these small-town lawyers were alike. Now that it was in his interest to do so, he'd have the whole business cleared up in a week. Still, she needed the money now, to finance her new life. She held her breath.

"Well, I think I could see my way clear to do that."

Yes! "One more thing, Mr. Slater. I also need you to

do a legal name change for me. It's important for my career."

"That's no problem, as long as you're unmarried. I'll need your birth certificate and a few other documents, though."

"I have them, and I'll get them in the mail to you today, but I expect my check in today's mail as well."

"No problem," he told her.

And now there wasn't any.

Jahne walked up First Avenue, the sunshine glinting off her glossy hair, her stride long, a tilt to her pelvis that ensured an alluring twitch to her walk. I'll have to practice this, she thought. She might not have been born sexy or beautiful, but she *was* an actress, and she'd been watching the Bethanies of the world for half a lifetime. She might not *know* beautiful, but she could *play* beautiful, and now her old frame and face wouldn't make the portrayal laughable.

She stopped at the bank machine at Sixty-fourth Street, pulled out her card, and got on the short line of people already impatiently waiting. A plump, youngish man was about to pull out his wallet as she joined the line behind him. He stopped, his hand poised on his back pocket, and looked at her. Just looked. Then, "Please," he said, and indicated with his other hand that she should move ahead of him.

"Oh, no. That's all right."

"Please," he said again, and then colored to his receding hairline.

She glided ahead of him, accepting the tribute due to the lovely from the unlovely. She inserted her card and punched in her code, asking for her balance. Green numerals appeared on the screen: $694.18. She withdrew twenty dollars, then collected her card.

"Thanks," she said to the plump guy.

"Thank *you*," he breathed. She twitched by him, playing it, and walked up a block to Liberty Travel. The place was empty, just a single reservation agent at a middle desk. The agent was blonde and pretty in an obvious, big-hair way. Jahne walked up to her.

"Can I help you?" the woman asked, and gave her the head-to-toe once-over that attractive females reserve for the competition.

"Yes, please. My name is Jahne Moore. That's Jahne with an 'h' in the middle and an 'e' at the end of Moore. And I'd like a one-way ticket to L.A."

206

Discovery

———————————————— ■ ————————————————

"When love and skill work together, expect a masterpiece."

— JOHN RUSKIN

"In Hollywood 'breakfast' means maybe we'll do business, 'lunch' means yes, and 'dinner' means we're in bed."

— RICHARD ROUILARD

Discovery

1

By now, unless you have spent the last two years as a hostage in some hostile third-world country, you know why three women as disparate as Lila, Sharleen, and Jahne came together. But even you, hip Reader, don't know how.

Remember that I told you it was all because of a lipstick? An oversimplification, perhaps, but still the truth. It was, more accurately, an argument over a lipstick that set the wheels in motion.

For what seemed like a thousand years (but was really only a few decades), Hyram Flanders had to take back seat to his mother, Monica. Monica was the queen of cosmetics, the chairman of the board of Flanders Cosmetics Inc., and Hyram's boss as well as his mother. No wonder Hyram hated strong women.

Since he had taken over—at last—as president and CEO, Hyram had been searching. Not, as his mother had, for a new beauty product. After all, he knew all the crap they sold was basically the same. He was searching for a way to cut the advertising budget. Because beauty is sold through advertising, and if he could keep selling current volumes but cut the astronomical ad budget, he'd be a hero to everyone.

Well, to everyone but his mother. Monica said no to every proposal to cut advertising spending. It was as if she, too, believed in the ads, the way the consumer did. And Hyram had watched as the cost-of-sale grew and grew, while the market segmented into more and more pieces. Flanders carried twenty-three separate lines to appeal to the young, the very young, the not-quite-so-young, the middle-aged who didn't perceive themselves as such, the middle-aged who did. . . . Well, the list was endless.

It was Hyram who first talked to Les Merchant, head of the Network, about sponsoring a show that would ap-

peal to multigenerational women viewers. TV, unlike the movies, targets female audiences. Hyram and his advertising-agency rep, Brian O'Malley of Banion O'Malley, played with the idea. And Les Merchant, panicked at the Network's dwindling Nielsens, took the idea up with Sy Ortis, one of the hottest agents and packagers in Hollywood. Sy in turn reluctantly brought it to Marty DiGennaro, the director who could do no wrong (and who also never did TV).

Well, Reader, you certainly aren't surprised to hear that most, if not all, of what is broadcast on TV is spawned to sell you something. Perhaps you aren't old enough to remember the early days, when television-set manufacturers sponsored programs simply so there would be something to watch? Or after that, when shows were called by their sponsor's name? The Campbell's Soup Hour? The Hallmark Hall of Fame?

It still happens. It's just a little less obvious. Or sometimes more so. Plugs, endorsements, "infomercials," and all the rest. So, when Monica Flanders told Hyram, her son, that it was impossible to sell more than one consumer sector at a time, Hyram was convinced he had to find a way to do it. "Don't waste my time," his mother sniffed. "No woman will wear the same lipstick as her mother."

Which brings us to Sy Ortis. It is the agents who run Hollywood today. Agents control the stars, and put them together with the directors and screenwriters (also clients of the agents) in "packages" that they try to sell to the studios. Agents with a powerful stable of stars are the most envied, sought-after, and hated people in L.A. And among all the agents, Sy Ortis was the most envied, sought after and hated.

Sy Ortis stretched his little body, his feet lifted off the floor, his back arched against the black leather of the swivel chair that, with its eleven identical brothers, surrounded the electric-blue lacquer conference table. He turned from the glossy photographs laid on its shiny surface and the anxious faces that watched him. He stood up, walked to the window that overlooked La Cienega

Boulevard, and sighed. Christ, he was sick of incompetent assholes! And it wasn't as if Weinberg and Glick didn't know better. They were one of the two best casting agencies in L.A. He turned to Milton Glick.

"Let me explain it again, shmuck," he said to Glick. He spoke slowly, his high-pitched voice almost a whine. "Marty is a genius. And Marty wants three blank slates. New pennies. Fresh meat. Don't show me these twenty-six-year-old twats who've been selling it up and down Hollywood Boulevard for the last decade. Marty wants new. And what *Marty* wants, *I* want."

Glick licked his thin lips and nodded nervously, running his fingers through his equally thin hair, obviously replanted with even little tufts of curls that were plugged into his scalp. Sy turned away, not from any delicacy over Milton's discomfort, but, rather, at a queasiness that had always made his stomach reactive. Jesus, where did those hair plugs come from? he wondered. Milt's back? His armpits? His pubic hair? Why didn't the guy cover himself with a hat, so decent people didn't need to puke when they looked at him?

The room was silent. All of the young, trendy California go-go staffers looked down at their laps. As if, Sy thought, they had the answer in their crotches instead of their heads. Then Milton cleared his throat. "I think we can do it, Sy."

"Not if this shit is any indication," Sy snapped, and swept his arm across the table, dumping several dozen perfect, smiling, beautiful eight-by-ten faces onto the floor, decimating as many hopes with the gesture. None of the trendies moved.

Sy Ortis was, arguably, the most powerful agent in Hollywood, and one of the five most powerful men in the Industry. He'd scrabbled up the heap, he'd worked like an animal, he'd bled, and he'd performed bloodlettings. Most people in Hollywood would do anything he asked, just as a favor, gratis. And now he sat here in front of a bunch of morons he was paying to help him and got *nada*.

"Look," he said again slowly, as if each of them was mildly brain damaged. "Marty DiGennaro has never done television before. This is going to be the biggest show, the biggest trend since spandex. He's creating something totally new. He calls it a 'content-free show.' And the Network has given him carte blanche. *Carte blanche, for chrissakes!"* His face was red, his voice strangled. He'd negotiated the deal between DiGennaro and the Network, and it was unbelievable, unprecedented. But Marty had insisted on total secrecy, so—irritatingly—nobody could admire Sy's handiwork. No one ever really appreciated what he did. They called him "the most powerful man behind the scenes," and with secretive, paranoid clients like Marty, he'd had to stay there.

Sy now swept the worried faces quickly with a frustrated look. He'd try again. "So we're trying to do a *new* thing. Get it? That means no sitcom hacks, no refugees from Budweiser commercials, no rat-burgers from slice-and-dice flicks. This is Marty DiGennaro we're talking about, not Roger Corman. Marty wants fresh blood, and you've been given the exclusive to get it for him. Do you understand what that means?"

The little man was breathing hard, his voice rising almost to a scream. Christ, he couldn't breathe! He reached into his jacket pocket and pulled out his inhaler, thrust it up against his mouth, and sucked on it like a greedy infant at the breast. Not another asthma attack! *Madre de Dios,* it's the pressure, he told himself. And the smog in the Valley today didn't help. City of Angels, my butt hole! he thought angrily. With this air quality, it was only the Angel of Death who worked here. But, this was where the business was, and Sy hadn't become the most influential agent in the Industry by breathing calmly in Scottsdale, Arizona.

It wasn't just Milton and the shitty job he'd done, Sy admitted to himself as he gasped for breath. It was this whole new Marty DiGennaro project. Marty was, maybe, the most prestigious big-money film director in Hollywood; he was class *and* cash, and then he gets this crazy yen to stoop to television. *Television.* The ghetto of the entertainment industry, with the Kmart of plots and the Walmart of actors. But Marty wanted TV. And with this nutsy idea: an MTV-type, hip, freewheeling show about three girls hitchhiking across America. What the fuck? Marty was a genius, and Sy's most powerful client, but the thing made Sy nervous. "I want freedom from plots," Marty had said. "I'm so goddamn sick of telling a story. Let's forget stories. Let's do something new."

New! NEW! Christ, why not just say "dangerous," "risky," "a money-loser." If DiGennaro got his kicks from losing big at the high rollers' table in Vegas, that was all right with Sy; why the fuck did Marty have to pull this gambling shit with his career? Talent! Go figure. Talent loved to fuck with your head.

Then, to make things worse, Marty wouldn't use any of Sy's clients. An entire stable of stars, all of them willing to stoop to TV just to work with Marty, and Marty says no. A whole show to be cast, deals to be made, favors to extend, percentages to collect, and Marty says, "Bring me someone new." Sy was ready to suck his own dick over this one. So here he was, in the offices of Weinberg and Glick, pulling on his inhaler and looking for an unopened can. 'Cause if he didn't cast it soon, Marty would go to the outside, and Sy would lose control of the casting. Just the thought of losing control made Sy suck a little harder.

At last, his breathing calmed. The frozen trendies still sat there, useless as tits on a monitor. He turned to Milton, still nervously licking his lips. "Milton," he said. "These girls are gonna be big. Enormous. They'll be on the cover of *TV Guide* and *People,* they'll be on *Tonight* and *Arsenio* and *Letterman.* They'll host *Saturday Night Live.* And that's just for starters. If everything goes right, they're going to be a fuckin' industry. So I want them new and fresh. No nudes in *Penthouse.* No past jobs as weather girls in Kankakee. No porno, no agents, no bounced checks, no husbands, no *problems.* New and clean, so we can tie 'em up nice and neat. So, Milt, don't insult my intelligence. Don't piss up my back and tell me I'm sweating. Get me some new faces."

Sy turned and walked to the door, then spun on his neat little foot at the doorway. "Because, if *you* don't, Milt, Paul Grasso *will.*" Sy saw Milt wince at the mention

213

of his ex-partner, now his bitter enemy. "You've got till Tuesday."

"I'll do it," Milt assured him, but Sy was already down the hall.

If Sy Ortis had been the bully of the meeting at Glick's casting office, he knew he was about to be bullied at his next one. But in a lineup that included Les Merchant, the head of the Network; Brian O'Malley of Banion O'Malley, the largest advertising firm in the world; and Monica Flanders and her son, Hyram, he knew he was the smallest fish. He shrugged. One could do worse than be a guppy in *that* pond. There would not be a person in the room whose net worth was under fifty million dollars.

And there was nothing Sy respected as much as money. Thinking of the raw power of—say—fifty million dollars made him almost weak in the knees. Someday he'd have a net worth of that, and then he wouldn't take shit from anyone. Not that he had to take much now.

Sy, as usual, was on time, but, surprisingly, so was everyone else. The difference between big business and show business: big business had the discipline to keep to schedule. Sy smiled as he shook hands around the table. No one smiled back. Another difference.

The meeting was being held at the L.A. conference room of Banion O'Malley, and Sy was there to represent his client Marty DiGennaro. Both had decided it was best this way. After all, the deal had been consummated, but it was best to keep both the sponsor and the Network happy for as long as possible. Anyway, today the pressure was off Sy. It was Merchant's and O'Malley's dicks on the table. Sy almost smiled at the thought as he took his seat.

"Well, gentlemen. And Madame Flanders, of course," Brian O'Malley began. He was a big Irishman, his bulk carefully disguised by a Savile Row suit, his chins almost camouflaged by the Turnbull and Asser shirt he wore. Monica Flanders, the object of the meeting, who must be in her eighties, made a dismissive gesture. O'Malley nodded. "I think you're going to like what you see."

"We better," Monica Flanders said, and looked to her

son, the president of her international cosmetics firm. He nodded. Les Merchant, a tall man with a huge head of white hair, cleared his throat. Sy had been told that today was only a formality, that Flanders Cosmetics was in, and that Hyram had sign-off power. But he could see everyone sweating, in case the old *puta* didn't approve.

"Well, you know the demographics," O'Malley continued, and as he spoke a wall behind him lit up, as if from within, and a bar graph in glowing neon colors was projected onto it from some invisible source. "We are looking at a more and more fragmented female market, with the largest segment the aging baby boomers, flanked by two smaller segments of makeup-buying women: the menopausal and older, and the younger, teen-to-thirties segment."

He turned himself to look at the chart, and as he did so, the "menopausal and older" bar disappeared. "Discounting the older women, who are largely either brand-loyal, limited by shrinking purchasing power, or taken out of the consumer market by disease and death, we have the lion's share in the other two segments."

Sy noticed Monica Flanders wince when O'Malley mentioned death. Now her son spoke. "Brian, the lion's share means everything, not the biggest piece. Anyway, we know all this."

"Yes. But the point is that the aging-boomer market has been lagging in its purchase of cosmetics, although their spending has increased somewhat on anti-aging-care products. While the youth market has simply not had the purchasing power of the boomers at their age. This has spawned the need for narrow, expensive, targeted print and television campaigns, increasing per product-line cost-of-sale."

"Brian, may I remind you that narrowly focused campaigns were something *you* sold us almost a decade ago?" Monica Flanders said.

"And for a good reason. There was no alternative. But what if I told you there was a way to reach forty or fifty million women, week by week, in both the youth and boomer markets, with a single campaign?"

Monica Flanders wrinkled up her face in impatience

and disgust. "I would say you were crazy. DAUGH-TERS DON'T BUY THE SAME LIPSTICK AS THEIR MOTHERS."

"But what if I told you they would?"

"Gentlemen, I'm an old woman, but I know my business. Brian, how many shades of lipstick does Revlon produce?" The man paused, then shrugged. "One hundred and seventy. Their best seller is Wine With Everything. Estée does ninety-five. Their best seller is Starlit Pink, but ten years ago it was Rosewood, and fifteen years ago it was 'Frosted Apricot.' Even Chanel has to make sixty-eight colors. Because the nature of the market is fragmented. AND DAUGHTERS DON'T BUY THE SAME LIPSTICK AS THEIR MOTHERS." Monica Flanders stood up. "Hyram, would you call for the car?"

"Mother, wait just a moment more. Please."

Monica looked at her balding, paunchy, sixty-two-year-old son and shrugged. Silently she sat down again.

"Mrs. Flanders, what if there was a show, a weekly television program, that attracted a huge female audience of both young females and the aging boomers? What if we could put together a program whose demographics guaranteed *both* groups?"

"If wishes were horses, most people would be buried in horseshit," she said. "The youth market watches young people. *90210*. And the older market watches movies of the week. Or *fortysomething*. Or the fat housewife." She shuddered at the thought of Roseanne Arnold, pulling her aristocratic shoulders together around her ears like the ends of an ermine stole.

"What if there was a show that featured young women . . ."

"Boomers wouldn't watch it," she said flatly.

"But what if it were set in the sixties, when the boomers also were young?"

She sat, still and silent for a moment. For almost half a century, Monica Flanders had been selling beauty to American women. She had started by cooking creams in her own kitchen and now had a lock on almost a third of the annual six-billion-dollar market. She knew what

216

worked, what didn't, and still had the best ear for naming new products in the business.

For the first time, Les Merchant spoke. His Network had been losing audience to cable and Fox for the last ten years. But in this project he saw a resurgence for the Network. He was ready to gamble everything on it. Still, for something of this size he needed a powerful partner. Hyram had already agreed, in principle, to sponsor the show, but Les was no fool, and he knew he needed Monica's full support. "Monica, think of it. A quality project, with beautiful young girls. To make the older women long for their youth, and the younger ones long for beauty. Exquisite girls, irresistible girls, Monica."

She hated to be wrong, but she hadn't gotten this rich by being stupid. She sat, silent and still, the only movement in the whole room the blink of her eyes. She sat for a minute—then two. Then three. No one spoke. Probably they didn't dare to breathe. "It could work," Monica acknowledged, dipping her ancient head. Despite the surgeon's art and the expert maquillage, she resembled nothing so much as a tiny painted monkey. A very powerful painted monkey. O'Malley smiled, and Les Merchant continued.

"We have an exclusive. Marty DiGennaro will direct. A million and a half budgeted for each episode. And new talent."

"How many girls?"

"Three. They are hitchhiking cross-country."

"I want a blonde, a brunette, and a redhead. I want exclusive three-year contracts with each for print ads. They model the new line. We won't pay more than five hundred thou for each modeling contract, but we add smoke so we can tout them as million-dollar deals. We do a new line. We include both makeup and skin care. The girls wear nothing else, on camera or off. And no hitchhiking. It's trashy. Put them on motorcycles. That's sexy. Plus, we get the male audience. We sell them the fragrances for their girlfriends at Christmas."

"What fragrances, Mother?" Hyram asked.

"The new fragrances. Named for the three characters. What the hell are their names?"

"Cara, Crimson, and Clover," Sy volunteered.

"Perfect." Monica grinned.

"But, Mother! The cost! Developing and launching three new scents in a year! I never planned . . ."

"If *you* don't have the time, Hyram, *I'll* do it," Monica snapped.

Les smiled at Brian O'Malley. "Shall we show you some storyboards?"

"Show Hyram. I'm tired." Once again she stood up. She began to push away from the table, her age-spotted left hand clutching her gold-topped cane. But she stopped for a moment and turned back to them. "We have approval on the leads. No drug addicts. No whores. Clean. Get them from Canada if you have to. I understand they still have some virgins up there."

Then she turned her Chanel-clad tiny back on the men and left the room.

2

After Jahne picked her one suitcase from the luggage carousel at LAX, she headed toward the rental-car counters. In her purse she had a little less than six thousand dollars of the money she had received from Albany. May as well get the cheapest deal I can, she thought. In New York, a car was an expensive luxury, and in her years there, she had gotten out of the habit of owning one. But she knew, here in L.A., it was a requirement. She moved toward the group of businessmen standing at the Budget counter.

"Here, let me help you with that." A tall, gray-haired man in a blue suit and a deep tan moved to help her with her bag.

"Thank you," she said, and she flashed the smile that she found now worked so well.

"Bob," the executive said to his companion, ahead of them in line, "let the lady through."

"Oh, it's really not necessary." She played it as Audrey Hepburn had in *Breakfast at Tiffany's*—ladylike but knowing. A woman stood in front of her, also waiting for the attention of the rental-car clerk. She was a dumpy woman, stuffed into a size-fourteen sage-green suit. It was not a good color for her.

"Can I help you?" the man behind the counter asked Jahne.

The dumpy woman whined. "*I* was here first," she said, and shot a look of deep dislike at Jahne.

"Yes, she was," Jahne agreed.

Reluctantly the clerk turned to the piqued woman. "Have you a reservation?" he asked.

"No."

"Then I'm afraid I can't help you," he said smugly. "We're all out of cars except for customers with confirmed reservations." The woman stomped away to another counter.

Then, with a smile of relief, the clerk turned back to Jahne. "Now, how can I help *you?*" he asked her with a smile.

"I guess you can't," Jahne said. "I wanted a car, but I don't have a reservation, either."

"What kind of car did you want?" he asked.

"The least expensive," she admitted.

"Well, for you I just may be able to find one of our specials. How long will you need it?"

"Two weeks would be fine," Jahne said, and despite her guilt, she flashed him another Audrey Hepburn smile.

The Star Drop Inn had only two advantages: the room was clean, and it was only $286 weekly, paid in advance. It was one of those modular buildings that looked as if it had been dropped onto the black tarmac that surrounded it. The gray-haired old woman at the front desk had told Jahne it was a no-frills kind of place, and she certainly had not been lying. Jahne's room, number 29, was ten feet by nine feet, with room for two twin beds, a built-in shelf for a nightstand between them, a hanging rack in the wall across the way, and a television riveted to a bracket that was chained to the wall. There was also a fiberglass bathroom not much bigger than an unopened coffin. But it was clean and it did have double locks on the door. It seemed to cater to transients and tourist families mostly, but there were no fights and not much noise at night. Also, she had noticed a nice-looking, long-haired blond guy that lived in Room 28. She could do worse, she supposed.

Jahne lay on one bed, the other one covered with copies of *Daily Variety, The Hollywood Reporter, Weekly Variety,* and several other trades. She sat with a pen and legal pad that she had bought for $1.29 at the Jiffy Mart on the corner; on one side of the page she listed every audition, open call, or look-see; on the other she wrote notes to herself about what they were looking for. It was odd, after all her years of reading the trades, to be focusing now on those casting notices looking for young, attractive ingenues.

It was thirsty work, and she longed for a cold soda or beer, but there wasn't even a vending machine at the Star Drop Inn. She'd walk across the hot parking lot to the convenience store in a minute. The page was almost full, although Jahne expected little from cattle calls and the like. Still, she had carefully arranged a pile of head shots and attached résumés to the back of each. Before she left New York, she had spent almost two thousand dollars of the precious Albany money on a photographer, and she had to admit he had done a brilliant job that justified every penny. Her mane of dark hair emerged from a backlit drop behind her; her face appeared perfect. Even now she stared, mesmerized by the picture. If she couldn't get in to see people, at least she could leave this calling card behind.

She turned the page of *The Hollywood Reporter.* Ratings for all the season's new television shows were listed. Quickly, she looked up *All the President's Chakras,* Neil's show. Once again, it lagged at the bottom of the long list. She sighed. She'd watched it a few times, but it was almost too awful; she could see the desperation in Neil's eyes during each close-up. It was ironic that he and Sam were the only two people she knew out here, and it was impossible to call either of them—one because he loved her, and the other because he didn't.

There was a knock at the door, and she jumped. She looked quickly to see if the chain lock was up. It was, and she went to it, grateful for the protection. She opened the door slowly. Outside, the tall, blond man from next door stood awkwardly leaning against the wall. "Hi, I'm Pete Warren," he told her. He held up a beer. "Want one?"

"No thanks." He looked like a nice kid, twenty-two or -three, with the kind of beautiful teeth you seemed to see only in California.

"Hey, no strings attached. It's just an extra beer," he said. He handed it in through the crack and turned away. "See ya," he said. His shoulders were broad, and she could see his back muscles move under the T-shirt he wore.

"Thanks," she remembered to shout at his back, then shut the door. Gratefully swigging the Coors, she wondered if Pete Warren ever would have noticed Mary Jane. Certainly not, she decided. The beer was a good omen. But being pretty and young-looking might only be enough to get a cheap car rental and a free beer. Drinking again from the bottle, she wondered if any of the casting agents and assistant producers would notice her on her rounds. She patted the head shots for luck and hoped so.

If the last two years—and all that preceded it—had been like a nightmare, this felt like a dream. L.A. was so sunny after the darkness of New York—the beach, and the boardwalk in Venice, and the nonstop sun. But the main difference was her. She was so L.A.—with her heels on she was tall and slim and perfect, except for a few gray hairs. Just waking up felt great. Getting dressed felt great. Putting on her makeup felt great. Aside from the occasional itching of her scars, she felt wonderful. Hopeful.

And that, really, was the difference. In L.A. there was hope.

Jahne established a kind of pattern to her days. Each morning, she drove to the track at the junior high school and ran three miles, then came back to the Star Drop, showered, threw a banana, skim milk, and brewer's yeast into her blender, and drank it while she applied her makeup. Then she dressed and spent the morning following up every lead she could. At one o'clock, she'd either go to Dim Sum and eat the lunch special at the outdoor café, or she'd stop at Chin Chin and have their shredded chicken salad. And in both places she only had to wait ten minutes or less. Men would come to sit beside her. They'd make her offers: offers to buy her lunch, to take her out to dinner, to introduce her to their agent. They'd offer to show her Malibu Colony or their condo or a part of their anatomy. In a way, their offers shocked her. Not because she was a prude. It was simply getting used to all the attention. Although she had always presumed that her looks had affected her life, she knew now that they had ruined it. When you were young and beautiful, everything was easy. For the next ten years, at least, she would never have to eat another meal or have another drink alone.

All she had to do was do her face, find a crowd, sit down, pick out a man, and stare at him till she caught his eye. With eight out of ten, she noticed, all it took was a smile to get them to come to her. She perfected a look: a sort of pouty "You-know-what-I'm-thinking-about" expression that hooked them like trout. Then there was one out of the ten who needed a serious look, not a smile. She started to be able to pick them out. They usually wore black.

There was the one man in ten who didn't respond at all, but she figured there had to be a few gays and honest married men in the crowd. She didn't take it personally. After all, after years of starvation, L.A. was a feast!

It all got her hormones running. How long had it been since she'd been with Sam? Since any man had touched her?

But even though she was horny and she looked twenty-four, she was thirty-six, and the lines that men threw at her almost made her laugh out loud. They were "producers" or "good friends of producers" or "working for an independent production company" at some undisclosed job. No one was in insurance or data processing or banking. Everyone was "in the Industry." She talked and laughed and flirted. She considered it good rehearsal time, but she made no friends and she didn't give out her number. She could tell that none were for real. And it was too much of a strain to act the part of a beauty by day and also in the evening. At night, she needed to recuperate.

Pete Warren, her neighbor at the Star Drop, continued to stop by. He was twenty-four, from Encino, and working as an assistant cameraman. His dad was a projectionist at one of the studios and gotten him his union card. He was sweet—very Californian and very, *very* young. He came over most evenings, and they drank a beer or two and watched some TV. He was only at the Star Drop until the sublet he had arranged while he was off on location ended.

It was easy to be with him, but it was odd. Pete presumed she was his age, and she did not tell him otherwise. But she had forgotten the differences between twenty-four and thirty-six, between New York and California mentality. He struck her as a child, although a sexy one.

It was Pete who told her about the Melrose Playhouse —a hip theater group in West Hollywood. His sister was a lighting designer there and could get Jahne an audition, if she wanted one. She did.

So she spent her days making the rounds, dropping off her head shot, begging to be seen. She actually got an appointment for an audition at the Melrose Playhouse, and a callback from one cattle call she'd shown up for. She wound up as background in some beer ad they shot on Venice Beach, but it was something. It encouraged her.

So did Pete. He became her friend. At the end of the day, she looked forward to telling him her adventures. He was optimistic and supportive. He was sure she'd get a part eventually. And he didn't hustle her or crowd her like all the other men who hit on her daily.

Finally, Pete tried to kiss her, and she pushed him away. He didn't come back the next night, and she was sorry. His absence made her realize that she was lonely, and that his strong arms and big hands curled around the beer bottle had been a pleasure to look at. All of him was a pleasure to look at. When he knocked on her door two nights later, she gave him her best smile.

"How ya doin'?" Pete asked.

"Fine," she told him.

And he walked in, handing her the obligatory bottle of Coors. He sat on the edge of her spare bed. "Jahne, can I ask you something?"

She nodded.

"Don't you want to sleep with me?" he asked.

She smiled. "I don't think so," she said.

"You're not goin' out with anyone else. Don't you like me?"

"Sure I do, Pete. But not enough to sleep with you."

"How much more would you have to like me?" he asked. He wasn't belligerent. He didn't sound angry. Just confused.

She laughed. "I'm not sure."

"Jahne, I really like you. I thought maybe you'd like to move into my place when I go back there."

"Oh, Pete, I hardly know you. And you don't know me."

"Well, it would be a good way to get to know each other." He stood up and gently put his long arm around her shoulder. He bent down and kissed her. She felt a pulse of excitement. His arm felt so good, so warm, across her back. It had been so long. He kissed her again, and even though she knew she shouldn't, she kissed him back. It was irresistible. His flesh under his T-shirt felt warm and smelled young. For a moment, but only for a moment, she thought of Sam. Then she let Pete push her back gently onto the other twin bed.

3

After more than a week of sulking and licking her wounds in silence, Lila was speaking to Robbie again. Well, arguing and screaming more than speaking, but at least they were communicating.

"I've never been so humiliated in my whole life!" Lila was yelling.

"Oh, *sure* you have," Robbie said. "You just don't want to remember when."

Lila narrowed her gorgeous eyes. "I could *kill* you! You act so important, so sure. As if you know people. As if you can open doors. Yeah! George *Getz!* Or the *exit* door at Ara Sagarian's! That's all you can do for me."

"Lila, calm down!" Robbie snapped. "How was *I* supposed to know that Ara was going to call Theresa? *I* didn't tell you to lie. That was what screwed it up. He might have taken you on if you hadn't lied to him. *My* advice was good."

"Don't you blame me for this! It was *your* plan, and a really stupid one. My mother is still Ara's pet. You're a fat, faggot has-been. No. A never-was. You just hang on to anyone who *was* famous. Like my mother." A terrible thought occurred to her. "I know you still see her." Lila stopped yelling for a moment. Perhaps Robbie was scheming with the Puppet Mistress! Maybe they both set her up. For a moment Lila felt sick and dizzy. She clutched the edge of the mirrored coffee table in front of her.

"Lila, I see your mother because she is my friend, and she needs me. You need me, too."

"I don't need anyone," Lila spat.

Ken walked into the living room, a pained expression on his face. "I wish you'd stop it, the two of you."

"Look, I have a new idea," Robbie said, ignoring Ken. "We forget agents for a minute. We focus on getting you

225

a part. The right part. Then you'll have your pick of agents. Even Ara Sagarian.''

"I'd ice-pick Ara," Lila said. "But someday I'll see him crawl."

"Hey, maybe by next week. He can hardly walk now," Ken joked.

Robbie shrugged, as if Ken were a bothersome insect. "I want Lila to start her acting career in television. I'm sure we can find her a little *something*." Robbie turned to his lover. "Tell her to listen to me, Ken. That's where she'll get the most exposure, but *she* says stars don't do TV. Like she's a star!"

Lila gave Robbie a murderous look. To defuse the bomb, Ken broke in. "Why not, Lila? If Marty DiGennaro would consider doing television, so should you." Lila and Robbie looked at Ken in silence.

"Marty DiGennaro doesn't do television," Lila said.

"He does now," Ken said smugly.

"Marty DiGennaro would do television?" Robbie asked.

Ken nodded.

"How do *you* know?" Lila demanded.

"Don't you keep up on the business end of the business?" Ken asked. "In an interview in *Variety* last month, he said he sees television as a whole new medium. The way he envisions it, television since the cable revolution is more exciting than film, with more creative possibilities."

"Why would one of the top movie directors consider doing TV?" Lila asked.

"Search me. But he is. I know it for a fact. He's talking to a network, and Marty DiGennaro has his fingers on the pulse of the Industry."

"God, what I wouldn't give to work with him," Lila breathed.

"Does he actually have a show lined up? Scripts? Actors?" Robbie asked.

"Must have. They are lining up technicians. He asked me."

"Marty DiGennaro asked *you* to work on his TV show?"

"Well, not *him*. Dino, his AD, asked me."

"I'm impressed." Robbie whistled. He looked at Lila, made an I-told-you-so moue, then lay back down on the sofa, pulling the broad brim of his hat down over his eyes. "I rest my case," he said. "For a fat faggot has-been without connections, I guess I have a few tricks left." He lay there in silence. Then he had pity on her. "Maybe we could get you in front of him. Through Paulie Grasso. Or maybe through Dino or another of those Italians of his. And I know a typist over at Zeller, Moss-bacher. They handle DiGennaro's legal affairs. Maybe we could check out his contract. And I once had a fling with a guy over at Ortis' office. He's Marty's agent. Maybe I could confirm this with him."

Lila didn't say anything for a moment. What the fuck. And maybe television might work. It all depended on how she was positioned on it, but maybe.

"Christ, what I wouldn't give to work with him," Lila repeated.

"What's the show?" Robbie asked.

"Oh, it's all top secret. Something about three girls traveling across the States together."

"*Three* girls?" Lila asked, and for no reason at all she thought of Skinny and Candy.

Paul Grasso wearily looked up from the restaurant table, across at the still-talking director. Yahta, yahta, yahta. Christ, he wished it was back in the days of silent movies, just so he didn't have to listen to this whiny little Jewboy. Well, he guessed, even then the people *in* the Industry talked. It was only that the *audience* didn't have to hear them. Sure. He'd be willing to pay not to hear this *strunz*. Paul sighed. No such luck. He was paid to listen to A. Joel Grossman. Well, he might be paid.

"We need someone absolutely fresh. *Totally* exciting. But not in the expected way. There's a look—a vision, almost—that I'm trying to capture, an innocence that's *so* knowing, a purity that *understands* defilement . . ."

Paul tuned him out again. Yahta, yahta, yahta. Like everyone else, this A. Joel Grossman wanted fresh, beautiful cooze to sell his product. Why didn't he just say so?

And why was his name *A*. Joel? And why did the guy talk in *italics,* for chrissake? With all that *emphasis* he sounded like a fuckin' faggot. All these fuckin' stupid commercial directors were the same: couldn't just *do* the fuckin' job, had to act as if it was art, as if the shit that sold Buicks and shave cream and, in this case, denim jeans was actually important. Christ, didn't they know that no one gave a rat's ass? The biggest acting jobs in Hollywood were those performed by directors like this one. Paul couldn't believe he was reduced to buying the little fuck an overstuffed sandwich here at Geller's deli.

Christ, the whole Industry was overrun with annoying little Jews. Spielberg, Ovitz, Zeller, Ortman. April Irons, and Paul's own ex-partner, Milton Glick. You couldn't buy a property, draw up a contract, cast a movie, or sell the distribution without a Jew involved.

Okay, he was bitter. He'd admit it. But just because he was bitter didn't mean that he wasn't also right. There had been a time, back when he was working with Milton, when he had been an insider. When they were riding high, and when casting the next big picture seemed to matter. But that was long ago. Milt and his prissy Jewboy ways. Nervous in the service about the gambling, as if I'd ever welshed on a bet. Paul Grasso's marker was still good all over town. But he pushed me out. Christ, then Milton and all of them just closed ranks and hung together. Clannish.

Well, Milt was a pussy, and this little director was a pussy. They were all pussies. He didn't know a single Jew who could take a punch, except maybe Jimmy Caan, and he was so weird, maybe he didn't count. Paul looked across at the kid director, who was still talking. Yahta, yahta, yahta.

". . . and the campaign is *based* on that. The essential female. We need to cast this with great sensitivity. There must be a sense of *responsibility* here. The *image,* if you will, is more than an image. It bespeaks . . ."

Holy shit. Did the guy actually say "bespeaks"? What the fuck was with him? Thinks he's the fuckin' Sir Ralph Richardson of commercials, or what? No, probably wants to be the next Spielberg. Wake up and smell the coffee, jerkoff. There was room for one skinny, nerdy Jewish director of TV commercials to become a giant, but the job's been filled. Go back to Jamaica Estates or wherever the fuck back east you came from. In Grasso's opinion, these guys were always bragging about their contribution to the arts and sciences. Hype and bullshit. Aside from agents and lawyers, the twin scourges of the earth, he felt their biggest hit was pastrami. He bit into his deli sandwich appreciatively.

". . . subliminally. Because this is really more than just a commercial. We're saying a lot not only about the *product*, but about *ourselves*."

Paul stuffed the last bit of his pastrami sandwich into his mouth and nodded. Let the jerkoff ramble. But the jerkoff had stopped. He was looking at Paul. Now, *now*, when his mouth was crammed with pastrami and rye, the miserable little Hebe motherfucker wanted a response. Paul gulped. Christ, the hard edge of the rye crust was going to choke him. His eyes watered.

The guy reached out and patted his hand. Paul managed to swallow down the mouthful. Jesus, *was* this kid an actual faggot or something? Paul needed the work, but not that badly.

"Thank you for sharing my vision," the kid said. "I can really appreciate an honest reaction like that. And it means a lot that you can still cry over something that to others may seem jejune."

What the fuck was the little bastard talking about? Holy shit! Did he think I, Paul Grasso, was crying over his conception of a designer-jeans commercial? Paul looked around the restaurant. Who else was going to witness his humiliation? It was too much. Paul took a deep breath and stood up. If he hadn't blown every available dime he had on his last junket, he would tell this A. Joel to fuck himself. That was absolutely his last visit to Vegas. Absolutely.

He tried to smile at the kid director. "I think I know what you're looking for. Let's go look at the girl," he managed to choke.

* * *

229

Paul Grasso looked over the pink message slips scattered across his desk. Mostly creditors, and an ominous message from Benny Eggs, a "creditor" who broke legs. Nothing else, except for this one from Robbie Lymon. Paul wondered what that old queen wanted. A favor, no doubt. A. Joel cleared his throat, restive. Paul turned to the overweight woman in toeless high-heeled sandals who stood at the door of the Grasso and Associates conference room, tapping her foot nervously. "She's in the can," she explained to Paul, gestured toward the bathroom, and then shrugged. Paul looked down and noticed the chipped magenta nail polish on her big toe peeking out of the shoe, and the horny, yellowish toenail, complete with a visible sliver of dirt. He shuddered. What a pig. But he'd seen the girl, and she was a honey. Maybe the solution to young Eisenstein's problems. He looked back at A. Joel, kid director.

"I think you'll like her. She's got something undefinable." Yeah, the best ass and the flattest stomach in Los Angeles. Plus a perky pair of ta-tas. Face was okay. Only so-so, really. Pretty enough to get her voted prom queen, but less than average out here. Still, for a jeans commercial with no closeups, it was ass that sold. And for this soft-core crap that was passing as an ad, she'd be perfect. Too bad the little bitch was only fifteen. Or maybe less. The mother had the girl's birth certificate, but Paul had been through *that* shit before. When they were underage, it made all kinds of problems with the L.A. County Bureau of Child Welfare. Try to arrange a tutor for a two-day shoot! Still, for this ad it was probably worth it. Anything to get the kid director, this A. Joel Whatever, off his back. Also get Benny Eggs off his back. And put a few bucks in the bank.

The girl walked in. She hung her head, but despite the lousy posture Paul couldn't help but again notice the ass, the long legs, the nice pair of jugs. She had to have an eighteen-inch waist—nineteen tops. And this kid wasn't fifteen yet. He prayed she was already fourteen. He shot a look at his client. At last, the little cocksucker was silent, staring. Grasso smiled to himself. Well, this would make a nice little fee. Yeah, he hadn't lost his touch yet.

"Could I have a right profile?" he asked, and the girl slowly turned. Her hair, a medium brown, obscured her face, but the angle revealed the soft curve of her buttocks, emphasized by the taut stomach.

"So, Adrienne, could you look this way?" The girl said nothing, but she raised her head.

"Mrs. Godowski, I'm going to have to ask Adrienne to take off her shirt and slacks." He'd informed the mother from the get-go.

"She'll do anything you need her to, Mr. Grasso," the woman told him in liquid tones, then turned to the girl. "You heard the man, Adrienne."

Very nice, very maternal, Mrs. Godowski, Grasso thought, while Adrienne began unbuttoning her blouse. It was a cheap blue thing with a line of limp ruffles down the front. She shrugged out of it, letting it fall to the ground in a heap. She was wearing a red lace bra, an underwired job that served her tits up like grapefruits on a platter. Grasso eyed his client. So far, so good.

The girl kicked off her shoes with a practiced movement and put her hands up to the zipper of her tight white jeans. She pulled, and the only sound in the room was the metal noise of her fly opening. She began, ungracefully, to struggle out of them, but the zipper must have caught her underpants, for they slid off as well. From the waist down she was bare. There in the conference room, leaning with one hand against a file cabinet, she seemed unfazed, uncaring, revealed: her perfect flesh rose up in a white fountain from the jeans crumpled at her feet. There wasn't a mar or a ripple to spoil the perfection of her ass, her thighs, her belly.

This was what size fourteens in Tenafly, New Jersey, dreamed of looking like. *This* is what sold jeans. The girl looked blankly at the two men. Paul Grasso turned expectantly to his client, the kid director.

"She's too old," A. Joel Grossman said.

4

Sharleen juggled the plates along one arm down to her palm and grabbed the coffeepot with the other hand. She rushed from behind the counter toward the three police officers in the corner booth, her heart pounding.

"Okay, boys," she said with forced cheerfulness, "pot roast and mashed for you, chili and onions here, and chicken-fried steak for the good-lookin' one in the corner." She placed the dishes all around and poured coffee, trying not to make eye contact. The men began to rearrange their mismatched orders without correcting her. Sharleen hoped that Jake didn't notice she got the orders wrong again. North, south, east, west. Well, she'd never been good with maps. "Sorry, fellas," she said quietly. Police just frightened her. She was as rattled as a china cup in a buckboard.

The young officer in the corner was staring at her, she realized. She ducked her head back down, but she knew he could still see her face.

"Haven't I seen you someplace before?" he asked. She kept her hand from shaking and filled the last cup with coffee, then tried quickly to clean up the spill she made.

"You sure have, every time you been in here," she joked.

"No, I mean before, outside of here."

Sharleen felt her face go white, but dared herself to raise her eyes and look directly at him. Now she needed to spread a little grease to move him right along to another idea. "No, handsome, I don't think so. I'd remember *you*."

The other man at the table whistled and one stomped his feet. She turned to go, but the cop reached over and held her round her wrist. "Yeah, I seen you before. You're wanted by every police officer in the state."

Sharleen felt her hand turn cold. She tugged it away.

"Me?" she said weakly. "I think you're thinking of someone else."

"No, I'm not, honey, I'm thinking of you. All the time. And so are all the other cops in Bakersfield. We all want you." The other two officers began to laugh.

"He's in love, honey," the fat one told her. "Can't you tell?"

Sharleen let her breath out. "Well, then, fellas, that makes two of us. I'm in love with my husband," she said, and walked through the swinging doors to the back.

She leaned against the greasy wall inside the over-heated kitchen. Carlos, the cook, looked up at her, raised his eyebrows, then looked away. She went to the sink, poured a glass of water, and drank it in a gulp. Get a hold of yourself, she thought. Forget about Lamson. It was already a long time ago and far away.

She walked back through the swinging door, pushing her damp hair up off her neck, and picked up a napkin at the counter to wipe away the perspiration, unaware that her upraised arms lifted her breasts and pushed them invitingly forward. As she lowered her arms, she noticed a man at the end of the counter staring at her. Oh, Lord, no more today, she prayed. Why am I such a target for trouble? She sighed, dropped her eyes, picked up a menu, and walked toward him.

She saw that he watched her as she approached. But he's not like the other guys that come in here, she thought. This one was fifty, plain, with little eyes behind thick glasses, but he didn't look used up the way most men his age did. Thinning hair combed straight back, deep, cultivated tan, a white linen jacket crumpled loosely over a gray silk T-shirt, white pants. He wasn't a businessman, and he wasn't a salesman. Sharleen couldn't describe *what* the guy was, but she knew he was not your run-of-the-mill Bakersfield truck driver.

"Menu?"

"No thanks, I know what I want. Two scrambled eggs, no toast, no potatoes, sliced tomatoes on the side, black coffee."

"Sure," she said, and began to walk back to the grill to give Carlos the order. But she'd already forgotten it.

She turned back to the guy quickly and noticed his eyes still on her. "How did you say you wanted your eggs?" she asked. With a tremor, she heard Jake sigh from behind the register. Jesus, in your mercy, make me a better waitress, she prayed.

When Sharleen had placed the food down before the new guy, she turned to filling the sugar pourers now that the diner had started to quiet down. The guy ate quickly and called out for more coffee. While she was pouring it, she noticed him reading the nameplate on her breast.

"Sharleen," he said. "Pretty name. You an actress, Sharleen?"

Sharleen half-turned to him. She laughed. "Actress? Oh, no, not me. I'm just a waitress." She put the coffee-pot down on the counter and went on. "But I've worked in the rodeo once. Went all over the Southwest. That's kinda like show business, isn't it?"

The guy laughed, but not unkindly. "Yes, I suppose it is. But I meant, have you ever acted on the stage?"

She laughed again and turned back toward the kitchen. "Nope."

"Never made a commercial, been in a movie?"

"Dream on."

"Never even had your picture in a magazine?"

"Once some guy at the rodeo took my picture, but he never sent me one. I never done nothing like that."

"Would you like to, Sharleen?"

Sharleen paused. She didn't want Jake to get on her again about how she talked too much and didn't pay enough attention to her job, but this guy was interesting. He was different. He talked different. Soft, like he was a money person. But best to be careful.

"What are you doing in Bakersfield?" she asked him. "Out looking for actresses?"

"As a matter of fact, I was, but I had car trouble. I'm waiting for a tow." He turned, and she saw a white Mercedes convertible, one that Dean would give ten bucks just to touch, parked out in the dust. "But this must be your lucky day."

"Yeah?"

"My name is Milton Glick, and I'm trying to cast actresses for a TV show. I think you might be right for a part. Interested?" He waited for it to sink in.

He must think she was dumber than Dean. Next he'd tell her he'd make her rich. "How much does it pay?" she asked.

Milton leaned back, but almost slipped off the stool. He seemed to be enjoying himself. "A lot," he said. "More than you ever dreamed of."

Sharleen stepped closer to him. "What do I have to do to get this job?" she asked, her head tilted slightly to the side, her arms crossed over her chest.

"Nothing," he said, moving away from her, standing up to pay his bill. "All you have to do is come to this casting office next week and meet some people for an interview." He continued placing bills down on the counter from his wallet. "No guarantees, but you really could get a part on a TV show."

He handed Sharleen his card and said, "This is for real, Sharleen. And there are no strings attached."

She accepted the engraved card and said, "Okay, Mr. Glick. If I decide I want to be a TV actress, I'll give you a call." She walked away quickly as Jake, frowning, started over to her.

"Do it, Sharleen," Glick said to her retreating back, "if you want to be very, very rich."

5

Jahne moved out of the Star Drop Inn with Pete's help. Not into his place, though. She'd found an apartment to share with two girls. It had been a tiring move, and after she and he got her new bed in place and made up, she fell into it gratefully. She slept—alone, for Pete had an early call the next morning—the sleep of the justly tired.

The next morning Jahne opened her eyes, stared at the sunny, cracked blue ceiling, and smiled. Oh, yes. California. Her new place, off Melrose Avenue, to be precise. And the room in the apartment she was sharing with the two other actresses in the troupe.

It had all been so easy, but it was so very odd: everyone's birthright on the whole planet since time began was a face, a body, and a name. She had changed all three. In a way that could never have been done before. It was audacious, painful, risky. But it had already paid off.

She smiled and stretched. *Everything* was different now. Not just her name and her face and her body, but everything. Each morning, she woke up with a smile on her pretty face. She jumped out of bed. Dressing was a pleasure. Everything, anything looked good on a beautiful girl who was five foot six and weighed 121 pounds. Jeans slid over her thin, long thighs. T-shirts clung to her perfectly rounded breasts. Looking in the mirror was a gas, but being looked at was even better.

Men stared at her. Her every movement seemed to fascinate and delight them. She'd taken to tossing her head, arching her back in a stretch, all those bits of body language that she used to despise in other, pretty women.

But it was irresistible now. It got such a reaction, how could she refrain from crossing her legs and pointing the toe, enhancing the leg line? Or just licking her now beautifully pouty lips? She knew how to play sexy. And she knew that now it played.

She also knew that women watched her. Not so directly, but they watched her just the same. Now she was actually in the contest, not just an observer. In fact, she might be a major contender, and they sized her up out of the corners of their eyes. Better hair, better nose, better breasts. She could feel their cataloguing, weighing, judging.

Always before, the Bethanies of the world had simply written her off, choosing to ignore her or befriend her, but in either case the choice was a condescension. Jahne didn't mind if now some of the women hated her for no reason other than the potent one of her appearance. She felt it was an honor, an acknowledgment, and she'd live with it.

Because, for a woman, being beautiful—a real knockout, which she was—opened more doors than Aladdin's lamp or a trust fund the size of Onassis'. Look at poor Christina, for chrissakes. Killed by her homeliness and her father's and the world's view of it. Too bad *she* hadn't met Dr. Moore.

Best of all, the audition Pete's sister had gotten her had been worth the trouble. It was a bit dicey, she knew, to bother with stage acting here in L.A., where the camera was king. But the Melrose Playhouse in West Hollywood was hip enough to have an audience that included agents, casting directors, and even a few producers and directors. And what could be better for her, a stage actress, than a Hollywood debut on stage? It wasn't as if anything else had come her way.

And she'd easily gotten the part. It was the lead in a revamped version of *A Doll's House*. The characters had been updated to a successful Hollywood producer and his dependent starlet wife. Oddly enough, Ibsen's old themes of male domination and female dependency still worked. Sad, really.

The irony was that she, a woman who had never had the luxury of depending on a man, would get to play Nora. Well, it was a part to kill for, and she was delighted that she had snagged it, even if it only paid $175 bucks a week. Less than New York unemployment. But if she was lucky, it could bring her to the attention of people who mattered.

Jahne stood, throwing off the crumpled sheet. She slept in a long, shapeless white cotton nightgown, and had a cheap white terry robe that she used as a bath towel as well. The one thing she was having trouble adjusting to was the scars, and she intended neither to expose them nor to look at them much herself. In the shower, she simply faced into the spray, and the rest of the time she kept clothed. She continued putting on the vitamin E and was grateful that she'd never developed keloids. But even now the scars itched. Sometimes she felt they must glow in the dark. She always kept the lights off with Pete, and if she ever wanted to sleep with another man, she'd figure out how to cross that bridge when she got to it. But it didn't seem likely. Because right now she was, despite her thirty-six years, behaving like an adolescent. She liked the game far more than the scoring.

Hector, the artistic director of the playhouse, was gay, thank God, and not the slightest bit interested in her except professionally. But he appreciated her, and not just her looks. She'd been cast after her first audition. Hector was *not* a genius, and listening to his lame stage direction was painful—it made her miss Sam.

Well, to be honest, everything made her miss Sam. That was the only other fly in the ointment: the memories, the things they had done together, came back, replaying like an endless loop in her head. Weirder than that, now that she was here in California, where he was, new things made her miss him. She shook her head. Here is an orange tree. I'm standing under it, and I could pick one right off that branch. Maybe, right now, Sam is standing under an orange tree. Those were the stupid kind of thoughts that ran through her mind continually. She had to laugh at herself. Yeah, and I hope an orange the weight of a cannonball falls on his head. But she did miss him, and the idea that they'd never stand under an orange tree together brought tears to her eyes.

"God, I am an incorrigible masochist," she said aloud.

The thought that plagued her most was . . . Well, she hated to think about it. If she'd looked then as she did now, would Sam have left her? If he wouldn't have, does that mean that he'd still love her? Or, since he left her, did it mean that he never had? What would he think of her looks now? Was her beauty enough to keep him from wandering, to keep him forever satisfied? Would he even know her?

Oh, it was ridiculous to think about! Yet the thought kept coming back. And behind it another, even more insidious one: When people liked her now, when Pete pulled her to him, when other men smiled, and women submitted to her beauty, did they want Mary Jane Moran or Jahne Moore? If the world hadn't liked her before, should she like it back when it responded now? She groaned, and pushed the thoughts from her mind. She'd gotten exactly what she wanted, but she still knew how to make herself miserable!

She finished dressing and, now clothed, looked in the mirror. Her new looks stared back at her—long, lithe, perfect. She was smart enough to know that she didn't know how to dress—after all, when had she the time, money, or motivation to learn?—so she kept it simple. Her wardrobe consisted of three pairs of long-legged, slim-cut Levi's and a few white shirts, a couple of turtlenecks, and a great hot-pink cashmere sweater. It and her boots had been her only splurge. She'd bought the softest, most supple pair of brown, tall leather boots, with three-inch heels. When she slipped those on, she got the perfect height and tilt. She buckled a brown leather belt around her waist and was ready for makeup. Not that she really needed it. But she wore it, always, because looking her best was part of her role, and she was always onstage. She was playing the part of a beautiful young girl, and she never stepped out of character.

Only at night, after she made love with Pete and lay quietly in his arms, could she, just before she fell asleep, relax. Their lovemaking was athletic. Pete lacked the subtleties of an older, more experienced lover. He rammed himself into her, and didn't really seem aware of what a woman needed. But he made up for his gaucherie with his enthusiasm. After the first orgasm, he'd get hard again quickly, and then he gave her all the time she needed. She rode him to exhaustion. There, in the dark, with his delicious young body beside hers, she could wonder at who she was, and where unhappy Mary Jane had gone.

In the daylight, she had no time for that. She'd developed a simple, easy-to-apply face, as well as theater makeup and some more extreme maquillage for evenings or events. Not that she had anyplace to go. She found the crowd at the playhouse both dull and clannish. But, after all, they were all fifteen years younger than she; though she looked the same, she was not what she appeared. She watched the pretty girls date the wrong guys, do the wrong things, set the wrong goals.

She knew now what she'd needed to know then. She could see through the bullshit the way a thirty-six-year-old in sheep's clothing could.

6

Sam looked up from the storyboards that were splayed across his desk. It was dark. The L.A. twilight had quickly turned an inky, smoggy mauve. His light was probably the only one on in the long, low building.

Seymore LeVine, one of April's flunkies, had given him this production office and Rita, his secretary. While he worked on the picture, this little bit of Hollywood real estate was his. He looked around at the low ceiling, the whitewashed wooden walls. Once this had been the Writers' Wing at International Studios, back in the days when dozens of writers had been employed turning out three films a week. Who had worked here? Benchley? Agee? Had Bill Faulkner dropped by for a sip of bourbon and branch? What had been written in this room, and, more to the point, would *he* ever write anything here?

Sam shook his head, trying to concentrate. Only halfway into production of his first film, and he was already worried about his next job. That way madness lies, Sam told himself, but he couldn't help but worry. He had already pitched two of his plays to April, and she had passed on both of them. Sam could see what happened to a director and a producer here at the studio after their job was through: they gave up their offices, the parking spots with their names stenciled on, they packed up their tents and moved on.

But Sam didn't want to move on. In the almost two years he had spent getting *Jack and Jill* through development hell and into production, he had come to want to be a part of this town. And what was there to go back to? The thought of New York, its coldness, its grayness, chilled him. The pretensions of the troupe, his little off-off-Broadway productions. Could he settle down to that very small life, writing alone in a dark room for hours every day? What would he write about? The story of a neophyte in Hollywood, in over his head?

Sam Shields knew he was in over his head. Even though he finally had the screenplay for *Jack and Jill* under control, and even though he was doing the best he could to learn the technical part of movie producing, he was. And it wasn't just the film. Women were driving him crazy, and he wasn't coping well.

The fact was that he was more than scared. He was terrified. Since they'd begun principal photography on *Jack and Jill*, there hadn't been a night when he could sleep without waking up at three-fifteen, in the morning darkness, fear gripping his belly. He had been running over budget and behind schedule almost since the first week, and April had twice come down on him fast and hard.

Her first angry phone call had shocked him. After all, they had been, briefly, lovers. But then he had started sleeping with Crystal, during the first week of rehearsals. When April called, he expected a scene over that, not the budget.

"What the fuck do you think you're doing?" April's voice had asked coldly. Sam was ready with his excuses: he and April had no commitment; this new affair had simply happened, a chemical thing between him and the actress; he was wrong and he would apologize. April Irons was not a woman to offend. In fact, Sam could admit to himself that he was afraid of her.

"I'm sorry. I didn't mean to hurt you, April. This thing just happened." It sounded lame, even to him. He'd have to try harder, to . . .

"What the fuck are you talking about?" she demanded.

Was it possible she didn't *know* about the affair? Sam was not that naïve. Everyone on the set except Crystal's husband knew, and April never missed a trick. And if she had missed this, Seymore LeVine would be sure to fill her in. Seymore was officially associate producer, but "corporate snitch" would be a more accurate title. His father was chairman of International, and April's boss. April *had* to know about him and Crystal. Wasn't that what this call was about? But perhaps she wanted a confession. Some women were like that.

"Crystal and I, . . . well, it just happened."

"Oh, Christ! That! She sleeps with all her directors. Who cares? But why the fuck are you two days behind schedule already? Do you know what that costs? We haven't even begun location shooting yet. Seymore figures we'll be delayed at least a week."

Sam tried to recover and switch gears. "Take it out of my salary," he told her.

"Nice offer, but it's already twice your entire salary," she retorted. "Don't you know what a day of studio time costs? Those union cocksuckers will eat us alive if you let them. *No* overtime. I mean it. What the fuck do we need rehearsal time for anyway? This isn't Broadway."

"Mike Nichols always rehearses on the set. As an actress, Crystal needs to . . ."

"You, Sam, are no Mike Nichols. And Crystal is no actress. Just get the shit on film, okay?"

She'd hung up.

Since then, terrified, he had barely managed to keep to the budget. He might or might not be a Mike Nichols, but April was right that Crystal Plenum was no actress. She was a star, which, Sam was only now beginning to appreciate, was something different. She had fought him every step of the way as he tried to coax an actual performance out of her. She wanted to play the part of Jill in full Hollywood makeup, with perfectly manicured hands and good clothes and soft focus. She'd begged for the role, she'd fought for it, but then she wanted to change it, make it over into another Crystal Plenum vehicle.

But one that would surely fail, and take him down with her. It was only now, when he had something to lose, that a paralyzing fear of failing, of fucking it up, came over him. Crystal and all the rest of it seemed overpowering. It was only in bed that he could master her, calm her, coax her into giving it up, letting it go. He'd hold her, caress her, and tell her over and over and over again how she could do it, how great she could be. Night after night, in bed, he would convince her to be the role, to play the loser, to go it straight, that she had the talent, that she could act.

And then, each morning on the set, her hairdresser,

her makeup man, and her costumer would begin again. Decked out for the part, she'd refuse to be filmed. "Jesus, I look like shit," she'd say, staring, almost mesmerized, into the mirror.

"You look exactly like Jill," Sam told her.

"I look *old*," she retorted.

"You look perfect. You're tired. You're lonely. Your life isn't working. That's how you look."

"We should use a wig." She tugged at the dark roots of her blond hair. "It's so thin. I knew I shouldn't do this with my hair."

"Crystal, no wig. This is really perfect." He put a hand on either side of her face and forced her to look away from the mirror, away from herself, and at him. "This is really perfect. You're going to wow them all. You're going to give the performance of a lifetime.".

"Really?" Sometimes, when she looked at him this way, asking a question, he could see the child there, the little girl who had always been so pretty, who counted on being pretty. Who felt she had nothing but pretty to give.

"Really," he told her, and tried not to think of the half-hour that had been wasted.

When Crystal had seen the first dailies, there had been a crisis that lasted two days: she had cried so hard that night and the next day that they couldn't shoot anything then, or even the following day, until the swelling around her eyes and nose had gone down. "God, I look so old. I look so awful," she kept moaning.

"You look like a normal middle-aged woman," Sam had told her, but she had cried harder.

"I'm *not* middle-aged!" she almost screamed.

"No, but Jill *is*," he reminded her.

"I can't do this!" she had cried. "This shit works for Farrah Fawcett, but I don't want to spend the rest of my career playing beaten women in made-for-TV movies. Oh, God!"

So he calmed her, he loved her, and then he made a new rule: no one saw the dailies except Seymore, Sam, and the cinematographer. He closed the set. He watched the budget. And he made love to Crystal twice a night. It was a vigorous schedule, but he managed to do it.

And, despite all the pressure, all the problems, all his fear, he felt that, at last, he was in the center of things. That here, now, he was converting his vision into something that millions, not just hundreds, would share. And that this vision would last as long as celluloid. In a small way, he was becoming immortal.

New York seemed long ago and far away. He still became uncomfortable when he thought of his promise to return. But the idea of a ragtag bunch of actors in a basement no longer had any appeal. He'd put off returning calls to Chuck until the calls had almost stopped coming. They would feel betrayed, they would say he had sold out, but they were losers who had never gotten a shot at this. If they had, they, too, would grab it.

Because now he was a player. At least for now, he possessed an office at International Studios. He possessed a secretary, and he had taken Crystal Plenum, the movie star, as his lover. He possessed her, too. It was still hard to believe. It still bothered him that she was married. But Crystal had explained that the marriage was over in all but name, and it did not seem to complicate their affair. Nor did her four-year-old daughter.

It meant, of course, that he'd had to unload Bethanie, but that had been a mistake from the beginning. After all, he'd promised her nothing, and she'd gotten herself a ticket to L.A. and a place to stay. She'd even snagged a small continuing part on *Houston,* one of those dying prime-time soaps. She should have no complaints. But of course she did. They always did.

Except Mary Jane. She flickered across his mind's eye again. In all the time since he left New York, guilt and something else had stopped him from calling her. What's gone is gone, as his father used to say. But after all this time, it surprised him how he still thought of her, missed her. They would have had a lot of laughs over the ridiculousness of L.A. And somehow all the other women in his life seemed to drain him. Only Mary Jane had filled him with confidence, and more. She had comforted him.

But it was just as well he hadn't contacted her. Not now, with this thing with Crystal going on. It was too much to run on the side; it had become a full-time thing.

The film and Crystal's performance had become his whole life; the set and locations and cast and crew were their world. During the months of preproduction and the last two months of shooting, he hadn't known any other.

Yes, the pressure was intense, but the reward, he hoped, would be worth it. He was eking out a performance from Crystal that would startle. Her name would ensure box office; his direction would do the rest. His work would be seen. And now, if he could just find the time to write, he'd be all right.

7

Jahne left the stage of the Melrose Playhouse after her final curtain call, the applause still echoing in her ears. The adrenaline from her performance made her almost skip backstage, passing Beverly, the stage manager, who thrust a newspaper under Jahne's arm as she passed. "A review on page thirty-six. Read it and cheep, Jahne. You should be happy as a lark."

Jahne closed the door to her dressing room and leaned against it, trying to catch her breath. Really, what she wanted to do was laugh out loud. Today was her fifteenth performance as Nora in *Doll's House*. Each night, her curtain calls had increased. Tonight she'd had eight—count 'em, Jahne—*eight* curtain calls, and she was delirious with joy. This was what it was all about, after all, she told herself. The applause, and the love and respect of the audience. And so what if it was only a West Hollywood theater with an audience who couldn't tell Ibsen from Ionesco. She hugged herself to keep from crying out with joy.

She got undressed and stood in front of the full-length dressing-room mirror. She placed her hands on her hips, and turned first one way, then the other. Her once low, pendulous breasts were reduced and high, her nipples pointing to the ceiling. Funny to think they had been cut off and placed there, giving the illusion of an even perkier bustline. Catching sight of some of the scars, she quickly jumped to check that her door was locked. She had made it a point to lock it whenever she was dressing or undressing, and found that, of course, it was. She didn't take any chances.

The incision line across her lower abdomen had already begun to fade, from angry red to a light-brown line just above her pubic hair. But the two scars that cut down the center of her breasts, from the nipples to the rib cage, were still an angry pink. She put vitamin E on them all every day, but they still glowed. The lines around her nipples were hard to see, but when she lifted her arms, the scars from elbow to armpit were obvious. So were the ones on the insides of her thighs, and the ones below her buttocks. No one except Pete ever saw her naked and she still insisted they do it in total darkness.

Dr. Moore had said she had "good tissue," and he was right. All the incisions had healed quickly, and the scars were fading. But they would always be there. They reminded her of New York, of what she had been, and of what her life had been like. She hated to look at them.

She put on a cotton kimono, dimmed the rheostat, and continued to study herself. You're beautiful, she told her image. Beautiful and talented. Finally, both. She dropped down into the battered chaise longue provided only for the star and snapped open the newspaper Beverly had given her. The paper was folded to the theater section, and Blitstein's review jumped out at her. "The history of the Melrose Playhouse," he wrote, "is, for all intents and purposes, the history of theater on the West Coast. And while it isn't the Lunt-Fontanne or the Winter Garden on Broadway—Melrose can boast many consistent successes. And all can envy the discovery of great talent that has been the design—not luck, you will note—of this great Western American theater. Once again the MPH makes history, not only in its courageously updated production of *A Doll's House*, a play without peer, but also in its choice of leading lady. Jahne Moore is the consummate actress, and beautiful beyond words. As a Hollywood wife, trapped by the Beverly Hills life-style but longing for freedom from her gilded L.A. cage, she evokes pathos and compassion—a difficult trick since she is so lovely and her life so enviable. But Moore's talent overcomes the obstacle and, while the adaptation of the play is flawed, her performance is flawless.''

Jahne read on, feeling her jaw drop, in spite of the fact that the review was so similar to the others she had received since the play opened. In fact, some of the others had not been as positive about the play as this, but all agreed that Jahne Moore was a major acting talent. This, however, was Blitstein in the *L.A. Times*. It would draw the Hollywood crowd.

She crushed the paper to her in a burst of intensity, then immediately unfolded it and straightened out the kinks. This was going in her scrapbook.

The crackling noise of the paper covered the light tapping at the door. She stopped, and heard the noise. The knock was gentle, but nonetheless it startled her. She jumped for her longer dressing gown and called out, ''Who is it?''

''It's Marty,'' a voice said. ''Marty DiGennaro.''

Jahne smiled to herself and opened the door. The cast had taken to teasing her about her success, and had been playing a series of practical jokes on her. ''I never heard of any Marty DiGe . . .'' She stopped, the doorknob in her hand. He stood, a small man, outside the half-open door. Holy shit! ''Mr. DiGennaro, I'm so sorry,'' she said. ''I thought one of the guys was playing . . . You know how the crew gets when we're working on a hit. I mean, of course *you* do.'' She almost giggled now. If Marty DiGennaro didn't know about hits, who did?

''May I come in?'' he asked, his eyes crinkled into a smile. He was small, ethnic, a real New York Italian. He walked across the room and slid into a straightback chair, not saying anything, simply looking at her. Jahne didn't have a clue what to do, so she looked back. The silence stretched out.

''Mr. DiGennaro, please excuse me, but I feel like Fanny Brice did when she opened her dressing room door and found Nicky Arnstein. I'm a little giddy. Can I get you something to drink? Anything?''

''No, nothing, Jahne. And please call me Marty. I had

to come back to see you . . . to tell you what a wonderful performance you gave tonight. I have to admit, I didn't want to come to the theater—I was dragged here by friends who raved about you. It's been my experience that when friends say, 'You must see so-and-so, she's great' . . . well, I've been disappointed so often.'' He paused, continuing to look at her, his dark eyes so intense she almost felt they were piercing her flesh. She thought of Superman's X-ray vision. Could he see the scars under her wrapper? The director smiled. ''Tonight, I wasn't disappointed. You're as talented as everyone is saying you are.'' He chuckled. ''I agree with the theater critics one hundred percent, for a change. What an honor to see you perform.''

He began to rise, and Jahne found her voice. ''I don't know what to say. I mean, thank you, of course. But you must know what this means to me. More than anyone, you're the person in the business whose opinion I respect. To have *you* say those things . . .'' She paused. ''Thank you.'' She laughed; then her voice lowered, and she grew mock-serious. ''You really *are* Marty DiGennaro, aren't you? Not some celebrity look-alike. This isn't a practical joke?''

''Hey, who'd want to admit they looked like me?'' Marty laughed, stepped through the door, almost out of Jahne's life. But he hesitated, turned around for a moment, reached into his pocket, took out a business card, and handed it to her. ''Call me tomorrow. My private-line number is written on the back. I'd like to work with you.'' Then he was gone.

Jahne stood at the open door for a moment, watching Marty's back as he walked away. ''Hey, Susan,'' she called to the stagehand; then she yelled to Pete's sister and the rest of them. ''Beverly, anybody. Listen!'' Several of the cast stopped what they were doing and looked toward her. Mary came rushing over. ''Listen,'' she announced to everyone, waving the business card in the air. ''Marty DiGennaro just told me he'd like to work with me.''

Beverly's face broke into a grin as she turned to the

248

rest of the crew and winked. "So who's Marty DiGennaro?"

After the performance, Jahne usually spent her evenings alone, except for the once or twice a week that she went over to Pete's place. They had fallen into a pattern: he'd make a couple of burritos, they'd drink a beer, watch the late news, and then make love. His body was strong, his face was handsome, and he was both enthusiastic and gentle. He never spoke while they made love, and he never protested over Jahne's insistence that they kept all the lights off. If he felt any of her scars in the dark, he never mentioned them.

But tonight, after the visit from Marty DiGennaro, she insisted they go out to dinner: her treat. "After all, it's through you that I found out about the auditions."

They went to a cheap Italian joint on Melrose. As a celebration, she ordered a bottle of Chianti.

"What's that?" Pete asked.

"Italian wine," she told him, and nearly sighed. Well, after all, he *was* young and Californian. How could she expect him to know about European wine? Bistros with candles stuck in Chianti bottles? Still, his youth and inexperience sometimes made her lonely.

"Do you think he really meant it?" she asked him, both playing the coquette and also truly frightened about it. "Does he have a part in mind for me? Will I get it?"

"Sure you will," he told her.

His certainty would have reassured her if she could have trusted what he based it on. "Why?" she asked. She wanted his dissection of her strengths and weaknesses. She wanted his analysis of the Industry, and of Marty DiGennaro specifically. "Why?" she repeated.

"Because you're so pretty and so smart," he said simply. She felt her mood begin to slip. He hadn't reassured her.

They ordered dinner, and she tried to keep the conversation going, but she felt her excitement draining out of her, slowly. She kept drinking the Chianti, annoyed that his glass remained full.

"Don't you like it?" she asked.

"Not much," he admitted.

"Well, then, order a Corona, for God's sakes!" No wonder she never went out with him, she thought. He was impossible. She wondered how long this relationship could last. And she wondered if she could do without his comforting physical presence. She looked across the table at him. "What's wrong?" she asked.

"Nothing," he said, and shrugged his wide shoulders.

"Oh, come on," she pushed.

"It's going to be like my sister told me: you are going to get real successful and then you're going to drop me."

She was stung by the accusation. And the fact that she had just been thinking of breaking it off made it worse. She had always been a loyal person, the type who was left, not the type who left others. To her own surprise, she felt tears spring to her eyes. Pete had been kind to her, but his fear of losing her was the first sign of deeper affection that he had shown. Like a sweet and friendly big dog, Pete had kept her company. Now he expected to be forgotten.

"Maybe they'll need a cameraman," she said softly. "I could talk to Marty, if he hires me."

"Oh, he'll hire you," Pete said sadly, but he smiled. And, smiling, he reminded Jahne of a grinning golden Lab, or some other slow but affectionate puppy.

Paul Grasso sat in the grimness that was his office. The open pages of his desktop appointment calendar flipped back through the printed months, stirred by the sudden breeze that fluttered through the semifunctional air conditioner below the dusty window. The motion brought Paul's eyes down from the ceiling, where they had been searching the cracks for solutions. He took his hands from behind his head, brought his reclining chair back up to a sitting position, and began to rearrange the pages, grateful for any activity. But the emptiness of his daily booking sheets reproached him, proving the validity of the worries that had been occupying him.

Nothing! *Nada!* Not a fucking thing new in months. Okay, to be honest, in almost a year. Thirty years in the business, but that counted for shit. You're only as good as your last deal, and that one was too long ago. Christ, he hated the Industry!

At least he did at times like this, when he was scrambling like a wetback for every scrap of work he could get, just to keep his head above water. It hadn't always been this way, of course. He used to be the best. He and Milton Glick, his ex-partner, were *the* casting house for quality television, movies, you name it. No bullshit commercials, no exploitation flicks then. Then there was a different babe every night. An office with a view. And the high-roller suite in the Sands, where he could really let himself go.

Hey, he'd *been* a high roller. Paul Grasso. Rolling in it. Christ, he was good. *Was?* The word chilled him. Was he himself talking in the past tense already? Holy shit, he couldn't let it get to him. Because, despite the split-up with Milton, despite his current lousy business, he wasn't a has-been. He'd told Milton, the day he walked out the door, that Milton would run him back to *him*. Milton cried, said he, Paul, was running him into the ground, but Paul was sure Milt would come back. He needed *me* to make it rain. To bring in the really big ones. "What are a few gambling debts?" he'd asked. "C'mon. Loosen up, Milt. Without me you'll sink."

Except Glick didn't sink. He kept on swimming, hooked up with that fat prick Weinstein, and now Weinstein and Glick Casting, Inc., were center stage. You needed to cast a quality movie, call Weinstein and Glick. That was the word on the boulevard. You need to cast a shit jeans commercial, call Grasso, then blow him off. It was Paul Grasso who had sunk.

So here he was, back to nickel-and-diming. It wasn't that he wasn't making some money; that wasn't it. But what he made just covered the vig. And he hadn't made one of those big hits on a really big deal like he used to. But he'd close on one of them soon, he told himself, then pay off Benny Eggs and the other sharks and be back on the comp list. Christ, he *had* to close on something big soon. Because, if word got out that Paul Grasso had lost it, then it would be all over for him. The sharks would close in for a feeding frenzy. And he couldn't let that happen. Not for himself, but also so that stiff Milton Glick would never be in the position of laughing at Paul Grasso. *No one* laughed at Paul Grasso.

His secretary buzzed him to announce that Lila Kyle was here, his two o'clock. "Tell her to wait." This is how it's been going. People asking for favors, useless dreck kids of stars hoping for a bit part, or producers wanting freebees.

Now he'd have to waste time and bullshit Theresa O'Donnell's kid. Well, he couldn't turn Robbie Lymon down. Theresa and he had a lot of history.

He was also mildly curious to see what the child of beauty Theresa O'Donnell and swashbuckling grade-B movie hero Kerry Kyle—more handsome, some say, than Tyrone Power, and a hell of a bigger swish—looked like as an adult.

He buzzed his secretary to show Lila in, reminding his girl to buzz him again in exactly fifteen minutes. She knew the drill. He had decided that fifteen minutes would be polite enough. Jesus, even if the kid was Julia Roberts, he had nothing for her. As the door opened and Lila walked in, it took Paul a moment to get to his feet. He shook her hand, then gestured to a chair in front of his desk. Jesus Christ! What a beauty. Tits out to here, legs down to there, and a cascade of red hair that ended at her perfect butt. And none of the sloppiness, the casualness of the kids of today. This girl was turned out. She was finished, with the high gloss of a pageant winner.

"Lila. Lila Kyle. I didn't know that was your name. I always thought your name was O'Donnell until Robbie finally told my secretary the other day. Lila Kyle. I'm speechless. You sure have grown up. How old are you now? Twenty-one, -two?" He laughed at how ridiculous that sounded. "Jeez, you're beautiful, Lila."

"Thanks, Paul. You haven't changed much. Still smoking smelly cigars, a little wider around the waist, but still a fine specimen of a man." Lila smiled and crossed her sheer-stockinged legs.

Yahta, yahta, yahta. Flash a little cooze. Not that it will help. Well, turn up the heat so she doesn't get pissed or tell her mom I molested her. "Lila, I always knew that you would wind up more beautiful than your mother and father. And just call me 'Uncle' Paul!" Jeez, maybe he shouldn't mention the fairy. Never know how much these Hollywood kids knew. He sat forward, elbows resting on his desk. "You were a gorgeous little kid, but, well, pudgy, not filled out, no height, you know? But, hey"— he opened his hands at the evidence sitting before him— "a raving beauty."

He thought of Kerry Kyle, a raver, and smiled again as he watched Lila's expression at the compliments. Not a blink. Listening politely, but she already knows all this shit. Okay. Move on to the family yahta yahta.

"How's your mother, by the way?"

"I'm not here to take a stroll down memory lane with you, Paul. Neither of us is the type, so I'll get right to the point. I have a business proposition that will be good for me *and* for you."

He sat back and lit the cold stub of a cigar that had been resting on the edge of a chipped Steuben ashtray. Christmas gift from Milt. He needed the activity to give him a second to think. This was not coming off as your average Bel Air brat looking for a job. She'd read too many detective novels. Who'd she think she was, Mary Astor? He released a mouthful of smoke and said, "Okay, what can you do for my business?"

"First get me in front of Marty DiGennaro."

Paul smiled broadly, and crossed his hands on his belly. Same old yahta yahta after all. He knew his ground again. Was she in love, or did she want DiGennaro to make her a star, or both? "And how's that supposed to help *me?*"

Lila sat forward in her chair. "Marty DiGennaro is going to be making a TV series, and he's looking for new talent. Old-fashioned, virgin talent."

Paul laughed out loud. "My ass, you should excuse the expression. You got him confused with Barry Levinson.

Marty DiGennaro does not do *television series*." He said the last words as if they were street smut. The kid had shit for brains.

As if she could read his mind, her face changed. "I haven't tried for three weeks to get an appointment with you so Paul Grasso can treat me like I have shit for brains. If you listen to me, you might learn something—okay, *Uncle* Paul? Marty DiGennaro *is* going to do a TV series; he has the story, the concept, the Network, everything—except the leads. I *saw* the contract. You doubt me?"

He nodded. You could keep a secret in this town, but not a big one. And this would be *very* big. The girl flushed, bent down, and rooted around in her big white leather bag.

"Here," she said, and dropped papers on his desk. She sat back and waited for Grasso to look it over.

It *was* a contract. It looked in order. What a deal! Paul realized he was losing face, but she had him pinned. Christ, he'd played cards with Marty once a month for years, with Johnny the Jump and the other guys from back home. They used to let go in Vegas together regularly, though not for a while now. Was this legit? And how did *she* know, how did *she* have the motherfucking contract, while he was in the dark?

"If Marty was going to do television, he'd have come to me, Lila. No way he's having someone else do the casting. And no way I don't know everything he does. Him and me, we go way back."

"Right, Paul, except Marty DiGennaro doesn't look back, he looks forward. He needs three leads. New faces. All new." She pointed to the wall of mostly black-and-white head shots of actors Grasso had gotten roles for. And not one of those pictures was less than three years old. "Why would Marty come to you for casting? What have you got that's hot? Why should he?"

Paul's intercom buzzed, and he snapped into the speaker, "I don't want to be disturbed." He was about to go bananas. Either this broad knew what she was talking about, or she was nuts and making a fool outa him. She sat waiting for him to say something, not dropping her gaze. No, she's not nuts, he decided.

"Okay, *if* this is true, and *if* I get you an intro to Marty, and *if* he likes you, and *if* you get cast, how's that gonna help me?"

"Right now," Lila went on, "your old pal Milton Glick has got the exclusive for casting the series. Ortis gave them the shot. Anyhow, the word is Weinberg and Glick showed up at a meeting with Sy Ortis last week with nothing but their dicks in their hands, and Ortis goes apeshit. He threw every résumé and picture and video in the garbage. Things got tense." She smiled, licked her lips, and recrossed her legs. Paul was beginning to see Lila in a new light. She was tougher than Mary Astor. And the mention of Milton's name threw Paul into a real slow burn.

"So now," she continued, "they're standing knee-deep in dog caa-caa, and unless they come up with some girls, they can kiss this deal goodbye. You know, it's not a good idea to fail Sy Ortis." Lila put an exaggerated frown on her face, taunting. "But *you* should already know all this, Paul, shouldn't you? I mean, you *are* tight with Marty DiGennaro." Lila waited.

Grasso's mind was working quickly now. She wanted tough? He'd play tough. "How am I supposed to get you to him? I mean, every cousin is trying to get Marty to meet some chick or other. And what if I do? You're nice pussy, Lila, but Marty has it thrown at him from cars. What have you got?"

"I've read every word ever written on Marty DiGennaro, genius director. He grew up living in the world of old movies and movie stars. You know what his personal collection of first-print classics is like? Probably the finest in the world. And guess which one is his favorite, Paul?"

Paul shrugged his shoulders, pretending it wasn't important, but knew it was. Why don't I know what Marty's favorite old movie is? he thought.

"Does *Birth of a Star* ring a bell?"

Right! She was right. Marty *had* talked about it. He

loved Theresa O'Donnell's first big hit. Yeah, Paul remembered now. Marty had once said he had seen *Birth of a Star* fifty-two times, or some crazy-ass number like that. Because of *Theresa O'Donnell!* Said she was one of the last natural beauties with talent in Hollywood. Yahta, yahta, yahta. Paul never listened to that movies-as-art bullshit. But it rang Marty's chimes. And here was her kid—a natural beauty—sitting across from him.

Now the kid stood up and leaned over Paul's desk, looking down at him. "All I need is to see him over dinner. An hour with him. Make it happen, Paul. You're not slipping, are you?"

Paul was beginning to feel the old feeling again. This had dropped in his lap. But I *could* make this happen, he thought. "So I get you in front of Marty. Then what?"

Lila's tone turned patient. "Then leave the rest to me, Paul. I'm a big girl now. And, believe me, when we pull this off, Marty will be very grateful to you for doing what Milton couldn't. *Very* grateful. The show will need lots of cast. A weekly series. An hour. Think of it." Paul did, and licked his lips. "So call Marty DiGennaro, invite him out to dinner, with me as your date. Just one thing. Don't tell him who my parents are. Not one word. That's a must."

"You crazy? That's your draw."

"Listen to me: don't you dare mention my name. I'm a woman you're dating. Tell him I *hate* to talk business, and that you just want to fuck me. I'm another Beverly Hills Industry brat who hates the business. No ambition, no talent, no illusions. Got it?"

"Sure, but why?"

"It's important for *Marty* to discover *me*. He might not even look at me if he thought you were pushing me or I was hungry. I'm with you because you're trying to get into my pants. And you can't. Okay?"

"Sure. Okay."

She started to exit, then paused and returned to Paul, who was still sitting at his desk. She bent over and kissed him on the top of his head, then walked back to the door. As she opened it, she said, "Nobody keeps head shots on their walls anymore, Paul. They date you. Get rid of them. You're getting yourself a second chance."

Paul stared at the closed door for moments, then looked at the phone. Make it happen, he said to himself. Shit, make it happen, he ordered, and picked up the receiver. He punched in Marty DiGennaro's private number from memory.

Sharleen lay on the lumpy bed, listening to the sounds of Dean's breathing beside her. It was usually comforting to hear him so close in the night when she couldn't sleep, but tonight it was driving her crazy. She didn't want to put on the light. When she did yesterday morning, she saw the cockroaches scampering for safety. She wished she could put off tomorrow forever. The red neon haze from the motel sign pushed in through the holes in the torn shade. Sharleen knew that soon it would be replaced by the red light of dawn, the dawn of another bleak day.

She got out of bed and tiptoed into the bathroom, closed the door, and sat down on the covered toilet seat. The odor of mildew stung her nostrils, so she shook a cigarette loose from the pack on the vanity, lit it, and leaned back, releasing the smoke in one long, white trail. That skunk, she thought. Jake didn't have to fire me. I wasn't as good a waitress as Thelma, but he hardly gave me any time. It was only a month, for Lord's sake.

It was Thelma, she knew. Jake said as much. Sharleen sighed. Women seemed to hate her, no matter how nice she was to them. The same thing had gotten them fired from the rodeo. But she'd been nice to Thelma. It hadn't worked. She was afraid I would take her fat husband from her, Sharleen thought with wonder. If only Thelma had known how repulsive Jake looked to her. But if she'd told Thelma that, Thelma would have been offended. Sharleen sighed, dragged again on the cigarette, and coughed. She didn't really smoke. She'd only bought them because she was worried, and her momma always said that they soothed. Well, they were makin' Sharleen sick as a cat.

She and Dean had toured with the rodeo. Dean was great with the animals and the motors, but when guys came on to her—and they always did—Dean got into fights. So they'd had to leave. She'd worked in Burger Kings, and once, for over a month, they'd been so broke that they lived out of their car. They'd been tired and hungry and dirty when she got this job at Jake's, and now she'd lost it. She took another drag on the cigarette and choked.

Well, never mind; now what do I do? No job, Dean earning two-eighty-five an hour pumping gas. Lord, show me the way. Sharleen continued to smoke while looking up at the ceiling.

It was disrespectful to the Lord to smoke and pray at the same time, she thought, so she stubbed the cigarette out carefully, threw it into the uncovered toilet tank, and then knelt on the dirty linoleum floor, her head bowed over the seat.

Oh, Lord, I know we have sinned, and I know you have sent us into the desert, she began. But, please, dear Jesus, I am so very tired. Tired of the dirt, tired of runnin', tired of these old clothes, tired of bein' afraid, tired of the nasty motels, the torn towels, the greasy food.

Tears began to form on the lower lids of her beautiful azure eyes, pearling up and rolling down her perfect cheek, beside her lovely nose, landing on her pink, plump upper lip. Like a child, she licked them away and continued.

Oh, please, dear Jesus. Show me the way. She reached for her mother's Bible, which she kept in the medicine chest, then sat back on the toilet with the book on her lap. I'll open it and it will tell me what to do, she told herself. She wiped her face with the back of her hand, wiped her nose, too, then sniffed and took a deep breath.

With a swift motion, she inserted a fingernail into the Good Book and opened the binding. It flipped open to the New Testament, first page of the book of Acts.

She stared at the large-print heading on the page. Acts.

Acting. She looked up to the flaking thin ceiling of the bathroom.

What had that guy Milton said last week? I could get a job on TV and make a lot of money? But it couldn't be for real. She stood up and quietly made her way out to the dresser in the bedroom, picked up her straw bag, and crept back into the john. Rummaging around, she found the little bit of paper she was looking for. "Milton Glick, Weinberg and Glick Casting, 25550 La Cienega Boulevard, Hollywood, California."

"The Lord works in mysterious ways," she murmured.

It wasn't a comfortable drive from Bakersfield to L.A. for Sharleen. The Datsun's air conditioning wasn't working right, and she and Dean got lost twice. When she'd called, Mr. Glick had given her directions, but they didn't make sense, and she'd never been a good map reader. Plus, Los Angeles was so much busier and bigger than Bakersfield.

They got lost in a section of town that looked pretty rough. When they finally got on La Cienega, she sighed with relief. She had gotten all dressed up—a nice skirt from J C Penney, with a new blue blouse that had white lace with silver spangles on the cuffs and neckline. She had her old white pumps, but she'd covered the scuffs with the shoe polish she had used on her waitress shoes at Jake's. She thought she looked nice, but when she got out of the car she nearly cried. The skirt was all rucked up, and the wrinkles wouldn't smooth, while the blouse was wet up her back and under her arms. Her face was flushed with the heat, and her hair was lank from the humidity.

"Dean, you wait here, now, okay?"

"Sure, Sharleen. You gonna get another job?"

What if this guy was a crook? What if he was lying, and he tried to rape her? What if they were Mafia or worse? Her hands shook as she closed the car door and looked in at Dean. "I hope so, honey."

She walked toward the office-building door. It looked big, and new, with marble floors and glittery metal edges on everything that wasn't glass or mirror. The chilled air hit her with a blast as she moved through the revolving doors. She felt goose pimples raise on her flesh. Well, she was nervous. What would they do if she didn't get this job? She clutched her patent-leather purse. She had only seventy-six dollars and some change from tips left.

What if Mr. Glick was like them other men? Just makin' come-ons to her, lookin' for trouble? She remembered Dobe's words of warning. As she stepped onto the elevator, punching the button for the twelfth floor, she prayed that she'd get some honest work.

"Do I have to pray to Yahweh to get some honest work out of you?" Sy Ortis was asking Milton Glick.

"Sy, I know you're going to like this girl."

"I better. And Marty better. Because otherwise he's casting that nasty New York twat, and you are shit out of luck." Sy was furious about Bethanie Lake, a nobody from the East Coast that Marty was considering. She was already represented by Judy Priestly, so Sy would be cut out. And if *he* was cut out, Milton would be, too. He could guarantee that.

Sometimes desperation can alter perception. Even if Sharleen Smith had not been one of the most beautiful young women on the face of the planet, she might have been perceived as such by these two desperate men. But as she was ushered into the conference room, she had never looked lovelier. The cheap clothes, the messy hair, the flush all contributed to an air of irresistible youth and sensuality.

"Mr. Glick?" she asked. "Remember me? Sharleen, from Bakersfield."

"Not originally from Bakersfield," Sy Ortis replied. "Unless that's a fake accent."

"Do I have an accent?" The men laughed.

Sy Ortis stood up and walked over to her. No one had offered Sharleen a seat, so she stood there. Sy walked around the girl, then looked over at Milton.

"Almost white-blond. And no roots. Monica Flanders will like this one. Well, this is at least a possibility," he said to Milton. "The hair. It's your hair, Sharleen from Bakersfield?"

"Well, of course it's my hair." Except she pronounced it "hay-er."

"Give her a script," Ortis ordered Glick, and Milton rejoiced. He handed the girl a blue-covered binder, showed her where to read.

"We'll run some lines, okay? You read the part of Clover."

"Okay," agreed Sharleen, but it sounded to them like "Oh-ky." Milton read a line, and Sharleen stumbled through the next one. Then Milton read again.

Sy barely listened. He knew that Marty primarily cared about the way things looked, and this looked good. Was the kid wearing any makeup? It didn't matter. He could see this one would put lip gloss on her butt to please. He could draw up the Flanders contract and probably get her to sign for less than a hundred thousand dollars. Perhaps he could charge her an equal amount in finder's fees.

Excited but too experienced to show it, Sy picked up the phone and punched in some numbers. He stared blankly into space as he listened to the car phone at the other end ring, then be picked up. He said "hello," then punched them onto the speakerphone and put the receiver down.

"Marty?"

"What, Sy?"

"Marty, do you want to say hello to your new Clover?"

"Sure."

Sy motioned to Sharleen with an uplifted hand. "Say hello to Mr. DiGennaro," he told her.

"Hello, Mr. DiGennaro."

Marty snorted, the noise accompanied by crackles of transmission friction. "Where did you get that phony corn pone from?" he asked.

"From the mouth of the most beautiful virgin you'll ever meet." Then it hit him. Were they playing with jailbait here? A greedy parent could fuck up any deal.

"*Madre di Dios!*" He turned to Sharleen. "How old are you?"

"Nineteen," she said, but to all three men it sounded like "Nan teen." On the speakerphone, Marty laughed again.

"You're pulling my thing."

"Get over here and take a look for yourself," Sy told him. "Let her pull it." Milton Glick smiled for the first time that month.

"Sy, I'll personally kill you if I have to get on the freeway at this hour for nothing," Marty threatened.

"This isn't nothing," Sy promised.

They spent the next hour running the lines with her. Sharleen began to worry about Dean, but she was afraid to ask them if she could go. They wanted her address, to know how long she'd lived in Bakersfield, where she was from, if she had representation, and if she was married. Lots more questions, too. Sharleen thought of Lamson and lied. Talked about Arkansas and Oklahoma. She prayed she was saying the right thing. She had been standing in the shabby white high heels now for over an hour. Her calves were aching.

"Please," she finally asked, "kin I sit down?"

"Certainly," said Milton Glick.

Sy Ortis realized the girl had been afraid to ask to sit down until now. He took a deep breath. "Milton," Sy said, "she's perfect."

By the time the third man arrived, Sharleen was worn out. She was afraid to ask if she had the job, what it paid, and if it would last for more than a week or two. She read the lines as she had been instructed and tried not to be put off by Mr. DiGennaro, who prowled around her, sometimes close, sometimes farther away, occasionally crouching, once even pulling up a chair, jumping onto it, and staring down at her.

"Incredible," he said at last. "She doesn't have a bad angle. You know how easy that will make shooting her?"

Sharleen heard the word "shooting" and took a step

backward. Maybe these guys *were* mobsters. After all, "DiGennaro" sounded like a Mafia name. She licked her lips, gathered her courage, and finally asked a question.

"So do I get this job or not?" she asked.

"Oh, I think you do. I truly think you do," Mr. DiGennaro said.

10

By now you've probably forgotten Neil Morelli. Why not? So did several million people who tuned him in for the brief time that he starred in All the President's Chakras.

I—Laura Richie—had interviewed Neil back before the show came out. He was as high on his success and as cocky as any actor I've ever met. He talked about how he was "gonna kick Seinfeld's ass." He was driving a fancy car. He was dating his costar, a blonde bombshell who needed a reading for every line she had to deliver. It wasn't a pretty picture.

It wasn't that the concept of the show wasn't funny. It was. It was about a loony astrologer who had the President's ear and had been named to the newly created Cabinet post of "secretary of astrology." The show, All The President's Chakras, *could be really wacky, if only the writers could write jokes. But they couldn't. What can you expect from guys whose writing credits included* Charles in Charge? *Neil knew he could do better. In fact, he had, but no one would even read his suggested changes, never mind admit that the lines weren't working. It was a script from Ortis' group of hacks, and they were losers, skidders, and bums. But Ortis represented him, too. So what the fuck was up?*

Neil had gone to the producer over the director's head and shown him some of his proposed changes to the script. Okay, maybe he hadn't been diplomatic. Maybe he had tried to push his bantam weight around, but the guy had overreacted.

"Get the fuck out of my office," Lenny Hartley had yelled, throwing the script back at him. *"And you're off the lot for the rest of the day,"* he screamed. *"I make the decisions around here, not you. You guys are a dime a dozen, so, if you can't do what you're told today, don't come back tomorrow."*

That was the part that really frightened Neil. He was supposed to be the star of this little piece of shit. So where was the star treatment? He thought he had made it, that he'd finally gotten to a point where he'd get some respect. Some power. Wrong again, bean head. As he drove out through the gates of the lot he shivered, thinking about not being able to come back there. He had finally arrived, finally made it to Hollywood, burned all his bridges. There was no turning back.

But the script was lousy, and the President was an empty suit of an actor, while the other lead, the First Lady, was played by a dumb bitch who had fucked her way into the part. In fact, she'd fucked Neil. If she didn't make it on this show, she could always arrange to get another shot the way she had gotten this one. But what about him? If it flopped, where could he go? And as it looked now, there was no way that this bird would get picked up for the entire season.

Neil knew that it was make-it-or-break-it time for him. Maybe he shouldn't have screamed like a maniac at Sy Ortis' secretary; maybe he should have spoken again to the guy, the mini-agent in Sy's office, Brad or Tad or Todd or Ted, who had been assigned to him. But that guy was another know-nothing, do-nothing, a schmuck in Armani who specialized in taking meetings and fucking the dumb broads banging down his door.

I did a bit in the column about the trouble. But, hey, that's nothing new. There are over four hundred pilots shot each year. Only about two dozen of them make series. Of those, only one or two go on for more than a year. Not great odds. Neil was just a statistical probability.

Change is a bitch. Not all change, of course. Let's face it, it's not so tough getting used to living in a beach house, driving a BMW, having a cleaning woman who does your

*laundry and cooks your meals and irons your clothes.
It's not so hard to take, after a lifetime of deprivation.
Accepting those changes hadn't been a problem for Neil
Morelli. The house in Malibu and the BMW, the pretty
girlfriend, the sex in a hot tub—and the cleaning woman
—it was like he was born to them. No, they weren't the
changes Neil hadn't adjusted to.*

*It was the new changes he'd had to deal with the last
few months, since his series was canceled that were the
bitch. Getting used, once again, to a crummy apartment
in Encino, dirty laundry that didn't get washed by itself,
and working a day job.*

Fucking *working* again, like a slave, for fucking assholes. For tips! Neil Morelli returned home from his gig
exhausted and miserable. When *All the President's Chakras* was canceled, Neil wasn't surprised, since he had
known almost from the beginning that the scripts were
crap, that the writers were fourth-rate. In fact, he had
prophesied that it would be a catastrophe, unless major
revamping was done.

But knowing the show was going to flop sometime in
the future was no preparation for the devastation when it
was actually canceled. For the first few weeks after the
cancellation, he spent his time on the phone with anyone
at Ortis' office who would listen. Todd, Tad, Brad, et al.
After a while, Sy Ortis' office said the inevitable: "Don't
call us, we'll call you." And the great man didn't talk to
him at all. Not once. That was something out of a thirties
movie, for chrissakes. Who the fuck was Sy Ortis anyhow?

He tried, as he always did, to joke himself out of it.
Remember, he told himself, what the Muslims say: if
shit happens, it's the will of Allah. He also remembered
Woody Allen's line about Hollywood: "It's worse than
dog eat dog: it's dog doesn't return other dog's phone
call." But jokes didn't help. There was no Mary Jane or
anyone else to laugh with him. Then the isolation and
inertia set in. He knew he needed to do something. His
money was running out, he had no plans, his agent had
dropped him, and he couldn't—wouldn't—go back to

New York with his tail between his legs. So he did the only thing he knew how to do. He continued to work on his routine. He wrote and rewrote. But writing funny when you feel like used cat litter isn't easy. The routines weren't coming, and when they did they didn't work.

Overnight, it seemed, he had gone from Malibu to Encino, from a leased BMW to a used Honda, from starring in a TV series to working as a waiter in a comedy club. It was like getting broadsided by a car. The months had passed, and all he could say was "What happened?"

Shit happened is what happened, he thought. Or, as the Hindus say, this shit all happened before. Problem was, he was no Hindu.

Neil tossed his white shirt and black bow tie on the pile of clothes next to the convertible sofa that he never bothered to close and fell across the bare mattress. While he lay on his stomach, he kicked off his scuffed, black Gucci loafers with the holes in the soles and heard them thunk onto the pile of dirty clothes beneath them. He welcomed the sound—the only sound at four in the morning.

The musty odor of the mattress filled his nostrils, forcing him to turn on his back. There was no one he could share this with, no one who wouldn't gloat. Even his sister, Brenda, would just offer him some money and sympathy, tell him to come home. Christ! He felt as shamed as a beaten dog. As he lay in the silence of the night, he thought, as he often had, of Mary Jane. *She* was the only one who would understand, who could comfort him. There wasn't anyone else who understood him, or whom he understood. If she still did, he thought, after all this time.

But when he had tried to telephone, only a few months after he arrived in L.A., he found her phone had been shut off. The couple of cards he sent her had been returned. She'd moved and left no forwarding address. Neil still missed her. Missed her more, in his failure, than before, in his success.

He got up and unbuckled his trousers, let them drop to the floor, kicked them to the far wall, then tossed along his shorts. He plodded into the bathroom, turned on the hot water, and went back outside to the joke his landlord called a kitchenette, took a beer out of the refrigerator, and waited the ten minutes it took for the shower water to begin to run hot. He pushed the collection of old newspapers off the only chair in the room and flopped down, stretching his feet out before him. He was relieved that it was night, still not dawn. He hoped he would be asleep before the daylight crept into the room and illuminated all the nastiness that was now mercifully hidden. Hidden, but lurking.

He knew the hole worn in the acrylic carpet was still there, just inside the front door, something Neil had thought was a scientific impossibility—to wear out an acrylic carpet. And there in the darkness was the crack in the wall over the kitchen sink that had been caused by a leak from upstairs. And the grease on the stove burners. And the penetrating smell of decay everywhere. That even the darkness couldn't hide, but the malty aroma of the beer he held just below his nostrils covered it. Thank God.

He went back into the bathroom, turned on the overhead light, and tested the water. Hot; it took exactly ten minutes, the only reliable thing in his life. He adjusted the temperature slightly, then pulled back the sticky, stiff shower curtain and stepped in. He reached for the soap, and cursed when he realized he was down to a sliver. The shampoo would be almost gone, too, he knew, so he washed quickly and got out of the soap-filmed stall. The towel he plucked from the back of the door smelled, but at least it was *his* smell. He rubbed himself roughly, tossed the towel onto the damp stack on the floor, and went back to the other room.

He reached into the fridge for another beer, but was greeted only by a Diet Coke and a rotting apple. Neil slammed the door and flopped back down on his bed. He closed his eyes and prayed that tonight he would be left alone. But he knew he wouldn't be.

He breathed quietly for a while; then, just as he was beginning to drowse, he heard it. The words seemed to come in through his left ear, piercing his brain and shocking his spinal cord. It was him doing his comedy routine at the club tonight, and he would have to relive it even if he didn't want to.

It had been like this for several months now. Every evening, he went to work and waited tables, waiting for his spot in the last of the three nightly shows. Then it was back here, shower, go to bed, and, before he could sleep, listen to the routine all over again. He always used to record it, but he didn't need to now. It ran in his head, over and over. Some nights, it was fairly good, and Neil slept relatively peacefully. Other nights—most nights—he had to scream out that it was all wrong, then get up and write and rewrite the routine until he got it better, adding here, deleting there. Then back to sleep, maybe, for a few hours, until it was time to report to the club to wait tables and do the rewritten routine. Finally, home again for the private reviews, as he began to call them.

At least tonight's review was good. He listened to the piece he had added about Hollywood agents, and he could hear the crowd laughing. Yes, this bit wasn't bad. After a drought for months, he was onto something. This was good and I'll make it better. I'm going to get my second chance, he thought. He stretched out, exhausted, on the nightmare of a mattress. I'm not always going to live in a dump in Encino, he told himself. Someday, he thought . . . someday . . . I must do my laundry.

And he slept.

11

Jahne tried to keep calm as she drove over to the television studios. Her Toyota was vetted by the guard at the entrance, who checked her name off a list.

What do you do to prepare for the chance of a lifetime? *She'd* gone to the best hairdresser in L.A. Viendra was a man who wore a tight little red dress and size-eleven slingback pumps. He'd looked at Jahne's heavy hair. "What have we here?" he'd simpered. "How about a crew cut? You've got the face for it."

"No cut. Can you just cover the gray?" she asked. The white strands stood out against the darkness of the rest of her head.

"Hmm." He considered, did a tiny dance around her chair, and shook his head. "No. It would dull the rest of it. Nothing worse than dyed black hair. I have a better idea. We highlight it with blue."

"Blue?" she asked, and her voice must have quavered, but he explained it all calmly. The blue would make the black look darker and yet give a luster to the whole mane. She agreed to try.

Now she tossed her hair in front of the rent-a-cop. It did shine beautifully. "Go right into Building Three," he told her. She drove across the lot. Once the place had been Desilu, the soundstages where *I Love Lucy* and so many pioneering TV shows had been filmed. Before that it had been Selznick International Pictures. Jahne turned a corner and there, in front of her, was Tara, the plantation house from Selznick's *Gone With the Wind*. She gaped like a Hollywood tourist, but then she saw the sign —Building 3. She remembered now that Selznick had used the building as his offices. She was going in there. Not like a tourist, but as a working actress, the way Ingrid Bergman and Olivia de Havilland and Vivien Leigh had done. She pulled the rented Toyota over and took a few deep breaths. Her hands were shaking. Playing this part was a lot harder than she expected. She pulled down the vanity mirror in the car visor and stared at her reflection. She *was* beautiful, if a little pale. Her hair glistened like a raven's wing. She thought of Pete's voice whispering in her ear—"You're so beautiful. You're just so beautiful." And certainly Marty DiGennaro wouldn't have invited her here if she wasn't.

"You *are* beautiful," she whispered to her reflection. "You *are* beautiful. And you *are* talented. Go show him that. Go show him how pretty and how talented you are." Her hands still trembled. "Don't be afraid," she told herself. "This is an adventure." She took a deep breath. Her own voice didn't help her much, but the echo of Pete's came back to her again: "You're so beautiful." She could believe *that* voice.

She got out of the car and walked up the path to Building 3, then followed the receptionist's directions to the suite where Marty's offices were. A pretty woman with a crew cut met her outside the door. Did *she* go to Viendra?

"Jahne?" she asked. "Marty's waiting for you."

Wordlessly, Jahne followed her down a long hallway where dozens, hundreds, even thousands of actors had walked before. You are Jahne Moore and you are talented and beautiful, she had time to tell herself fiercely, and then was ushered into his office.

Marty DiGennaro was crouched on a big leather sofa, surrounded by a tangle of cables and cameras and lights. As she entered the room, he leapt up and took her hand. He was so nervous and small and wiry, he reminded her of a whippet as he bounded off the sofa, across the room, and then onto an ottoman.

"Sit down, Jahne."

She slid into the low beige leather chair across from him. He made a gesture with his hands to the several people crouching amidst the tangle of equipment. "This is Bill, Steve, and Dino, Jahne. If you don't mind, we're just going to talk, and they're going to tape us."

Oh, fine, Jahne thought to herself. She wondered what he would do if she said she did mind, but that was not in the cards. She felt her hands and armpits go clammy with sweat. She knew she could impress him at an audition, or even a cold reading, but playing Jahne Moore was not so easy for her. She tossed her head, shrugged, and smiled. "You're the boss," she said.

He laughed, a high-pitched giggle. Since the time he'd had two movies that were each grossing ten million a day, he'd been called "the Boss" by much of Hollywood.

"What do you know about the sixties, Jahne?" Marty asked her.

"You mean hippies and flower-power kind of stuff?" she asked.

"Exactly!" he said with such a high level of enthusiasm that she figured that it had to be faked.

"Well," she continued, "I guess it was the Beatles era." She quickly calculated how much it was likely a twenty-four-year-old would know about the period. And how to play a little with Marty's head. "Wasn't Paul McCartney a Beatle before he was in Wings?" she asked innocently.

"Ouch!" Marty yelped, and one of the guys behind the camera groaned. "Makes you feel old, doesn't it, Dino?" Marty asked. "What else do you remember, Jahne?"

"Well," she said, another punch line prepared, "Bobby Kennedy was president until he was shot." She smiled into the camera and licked her lower lip. "And wasn't there a war someplace?"

It took them a minute to see that she was putting them on. Then belly laughs from the guys, that giggle from Marty. "Okay, okay. Very cute." Marty smiled at her. He stood up and walked to her left, over to the window. She turned her head to look at him, but the camera remained on her. Well, if this was her screen test, she could play to a camera as well as to an audience at the Melrose Playhouse.

"Jahne, I am a child of the sixties, and I am obsessed with it. But I think other people are, too. Baby boomers who lived through the sixties, and the younger generation that wishes it had. Do you know what a PIQ is?"

"No," she admitted.

"It stands for Program Idea Quotient. Every year the HTI—the Home Testing Institute—asks television viewers to rate program ideas. The networks use the results to make forecasts of audience levels. My idea for a sixties show was tested. It scored the highest possible points, both with the sixteen-to-twenty-five-year-old group and the thirty-five-to-fifty-year-olds. *That* never happened before. I want to do a show that is set during that era. I can exploit the music and the style of the time, and I can bring in the political upheaval as well. This is Clinton country. There's a lot of opportunity for nostalgia, but it is more than that. There are a lot of parallels to today, and I think I can bring those out." He moved back to the seat across from her. She nodded, tossed her head, and watched the camera pan as she turned her head to follow him.

"You ever see *Easy Rider?*" he asked.

"Sure. That was Jack Nicholson's first movie, wasn't it?"

"Yeah. Well, I want this project to be a new take on that kind of pilgrimage: finding oneself; finding America. And I want three girls to do it. Three girls on motorcycles."

"Sounds interesting," she said. Jesus, she had never been on anything bigger than Neil's motorbike. She crossed her legs, smiled at the camera, and said, "I wish I had worn my colors."

Marty smiled. "I have a lot of ideas. I want this show to look different than anything else. We'll use a single camera and film it—no videotape at all. And we'll use a lot of locations. These girls will cross America. I'll use smears and sneaks and follow focus. It's not going to look like any other TV show. I have some of the best technicians in the business already signed up."

Jahne nodded, although she didn't have a clue what a sneak or a smear was.

"What kind of makeup do you wear?"

She blinked, paused. Why? Did she have a visible scar? Was there something he, a great director, saw on her face that others didn't? "Just some regular base. Lancôme, I think. And blusher . . ."

"Any objection to signing an exclusive with a makeup company to only wear theirs?"

"No." She tried not to show even a flicker of her relief.

"Hey, Dino," Marty said. "How are we looking?"

"Looking good, boss," Dino told him.

Jahne flashed the camera another smile. "So what next?" she asked.

Marty handed her a dozen unbound pages. "How about reading this? The part of Cara."

She picked up the script. A young girl talking to another one about her ex-boyfriend, about her parents, about society, about life. Kind of cornball, but sweet. Over it all, that veneer of toughness that a kid needs to protect herself from being thought a kid.

She looked up. "Okay. Who reads with me?"

"I'll feed you the cues off camera," Marty said.

So she began. She pitched her voice a little higher than usual, to get the youth, but it made her tough act so much more poignant. And she took the monologue about her father really fast—almost gabbled it—as if she had to say it aloud but didn't want it heard. She ended the scene—where she asks, "Do you know what I mean?"—with a whisper and a look right into the camera. She knew it was a good reading. A real good reading.

But was it good enough?

Dear Dr. Moore,

Well, you were a great doctor to my now great body, but how will you do as a psychiatrist? I have so much news that I don't know exactly where to start.

I'm glad you got the clippings—I try not to care too much about what critics say—but the one in the *Times* brought in a lot of L.A. people, including Marty DiGennaro! No, I am not making that up. He came backstage to compliment me, but that was only the beginning! He asked me to do a test, and, yesterday, he asked me to be one of the stars in his new television show.

Okay; I know what you're going to say: did I go through all that agony and you do all that work merely so I could become the next Vanna White? But, Dr. Moore—Brewster—*this is Marty DiGennaro*. And the series is truly innovative. It's called *Three for the Road* and I've seen the first couple of scripts. It's wacky! Three girls (yes, I'm passing for a girl!) go cross-country together by motorcycle. The trick, though, is the terrific dialogue and the wonderful visual concepts—great crosscuts, fades, camera angles. It's evocative more than linear.

Oh, Jesus, I just reread that. Do I sound like I've gone Valley girl on you? Listen, I am very excited, but it's not a done deal yet. Marty (that's me, calling Marty DiGennaro "Marty"!) has said he needs to cast all three of the leads to see how we play off one another, but I should get my agent to begin working on the contract! When I told him I didn't have an agent, he nearly plotzed! (How many exclamation points have I already used in this letter? I'm afraid more than my quota.) Anyway, he said he'd set me up with Sy Ortis, his agent. *Sy Ortis!* (Absolutely my *last* exclamation point.) Only the most powerful agent in the business.

Anyway, I've also heard that Ortis is a lying scumbag, and that he dumps anyone who doesn't regularly deliver. Not your Mister Rogers type. But, then, the neighborhood isn't much like Mister Rogers'.

Speaking of neighborhoods, I've been looking for a place of my own—just to rent, of course—and Roxanne Greely (the real estate agent to the stars) has shown me a really adorable two-bedroom bungalow overlooking the water. She got my name from Marty. All these famous people seem to know each other. I won't tell you the rent, because you'd kill me, but I'm not signing any lease until my contract is signed first.

And talk about money—I can't even imagine it. They're talking $33,000 per episode, and the contract is for eighteen of them! I can't multiply that high. The first check I'll write, though, will be one to finish paying off your fees, and I want to thank you again for waiting and believing in me.

There is one fly in the ointment. I have to sign a contract with Flanders Cosmetics to be their spokesperson. I hate the idea of selling anything, but I have to to get the job—well, they do promise me a quarter of a million dollars to do it!

Dr. Moore—Brewster—you know that I owe all this to you. You know who I really am—fat, plain, old Mary Jane Moran—and so you know all that I owe you. I can never thank you enough.

Right now, the really strangest thing is how this being beautiful works: it's like having a superpower. Just because of how I look, I'm able to melt barriers, draw people to me, and leap buildings with a single bound. All right, I can't do that last one, but I sure can do the others. It's wild.

How is Raoul? Has the reconstruction around his nose worked? The gifts inside are for him. Send him my love. Save some for yourself, and say hello to the other kids for me, too.

Anyway, I feel like a kid—but a happy one—in a candy store. Write!

Love,
Jahne

12

There are a few restaurants in the studio zone of L.A. that are more theater than the Melrose Playhouse ever was. One, of course, is Morton's, where the star-makers dine. Word is that Peter Morton loses money on the place, but keeps it running so he can be part of the scene. Then there's Le Dôme, known to the hipper crowd as "Le Dump." Very much the center of the gay mafia. The young stars eat at The Ivy—all salads and little vegetarian crêpes at fifty bucks per head for brunch on a Sunday. And then, of course, there's Spago.

Tourists are always disappointed by it. After all, it looks a lot like a suburban carpet store from the outside. But inside, the stars do twinkle. And it was where Marty chose to meet Paul Grasso for dinner.

Marty sat down at the banquette as the headwaiter pushed the best table in Spago back into place. After making the obligatory stops at stars' and star-makers' tables, Marty had managed a Hollywood hug for Wolfgang, the owner, and graciously stood until the maître d' had seated Marty's date, Bethanie. Only then could he turn his attention to her. "Sorry for the delay, but you know how it is here." He scanned her perfect face, her shapely shoulders, her deep cleavage, her baby-fresh skin, all lightly, evenly tanned.

"You look beautiful tonight, Bethanie," he said automatically, thinking once again that they all looked alike, the California wannabes. He was considering her for *Three for the Road*, but he had his doubts. She was pretty, even beautiful, but there was nothing *unique* about Bethanie. He'd just found the blonde—well, Sy and Milton had found her—an incredibly fresh girl, Sharleen Something, and *so* fresh she'd be fabulous. With Jahne Moore virtually signed up and vetted by the Flanders and Banion O'Malley crew, he had a brunette already. *She* was intense and brilliant; she'd be good contrast to Sharleen. Was Bethanie the last member of this trinity? He needed a redhead, and Bethanie was a blonde—but Bethanie would be more than willing to dye her hair another shade. Hell, she'd be willing to *shave* her head if it got her the spot. But she was no virgin in any sense of the word; she had been on several crappy television shows, and he really couldn't call her a new face anymore. Casting would be everything on this project, and he had to decide, because time *was* running out.

He removed a silver cigarette case, the one actually used by Cary Grant in *The Philadelphia Story,* took out a Dunhill, tamped it on the antique cover, and placed it between his lips. Marty didn't actually smoke, never inhaled, but he'd always loved props. A flame appeared at the cigarette's tip, held by the lurking captain, and he pulled at the end enough to light it.

Tonight was going to be quick and easy, for old times' sake. It might even be fun. He made it a point to keep up his old friendships—no one would ever be able to say that Marty DiGennaro had forgotten his old pals—but lately he preferred not being around Paul Grasso. Paul's gambling had gone too far, it had begun to show on him, the way an alcoholic's drinking inevitably became apparent. Marty had seen enough, in this town of swingers on the decline from too much drugs, sex, money, and the wrong people in their lives, to be surprised by anyone's skid. But with Paul, it was different. He had known him from the old neighborhood, back when they were kids. So he tried a little harder with Paul, although he knew from experience that no one could stop a skidder.

Paulie could still make Marty laugh, however. That was the one thing that Paul consistently gave Marty: funny stories, and hilarious memories. And since Paul hadn't asked him for anything on the phone when he'd called, Marty was going to assume the best: Paul just wanted a night out with an old friend. Paul had never begged Marty for work. He had too much pride, and he knew the risk he ran if he tried that.

Also, Paul had reassured Marty that Paul's date was not a wannabe. Paul raved about her beauty but emphasized that the kid was wealthy in her own right and, being from some family in the Industry, hated the business. Paul just wanted to get in her pants. Typical Paulie Grasso. If she's as beautiful as Paul says she is, he should be peddling her to every producer in town instead of spending all his energy trying to fuck her.

Bethanie broke into Marty's thoughts. "Who else is coming, Marty? Anyone I know?" What that translated into was "Anyone who can help me? Anyone I can use?" But Marty could be tolerant of a woman, as long as she was beautiful. And Bethanie *was* beautiful.

"No, I don't think you know him. An old friend, Paul Grasso, and his date." You wouldn't know him, Bethanie, because he hasn't done anything for anyone for a long time.

Marty looked at the old gold Patek Philippe watch, the one he'd bought at the Errol Flynn estate sale. On the back was engraved "To E.F. from his S.T." He'd often wondered who the S.T. was. His most amusing conjecture was Shirley Temple. As he looked up, his attention was drawn to the entrance to the room, the direction, he noticed, in which the other diners were also looking.

A woman—a very beautiful woman—was standing alone, her small black silk bag held in two hands in front of the skirt of her black chiffon dress. She at first appeared to be all magnificent legs, the illusion, to his trained eye, created by the shortness of the dress, the subtly shaded sheer black hose, and the dyed-to-match black *peau de soie* shoes. But she was also tall—God, so tall she made him hard! The top of her dress had a tight, low bodice, held up by the flimsiest spaghetti straps, straining at the fullness of the breasts. And, God, she was tall! Six foot, maybe, but a lot taller in those shoes. And what color would you call that hair? Not red, not *just* red. Her hair was deeply toned, but much more alive than any auburn. Her only apparent jewelry was a single diamond on her neck, and sparkling diamond earrings. In a town where beautiful women were a dime a dozen, where every waitress had been a Miss Tennessee runner-up, where perfection was ordinary, she was a knockout, a heart stopper. There was also something familiar about her, something that he knew. Had they met? Surely not —Marty never forgot a face. And certainly not one sculpted as cleanly, as precisely, as that.

Though he could see she was completely aware of the attention she was getting from the room, he could also see that, unlike the beautiful women he had known and observed, she truly seemed not to care about it. There was a calm—no, an aloofness—that held her apart. Then a man turned away from the maître d's desk and took the woman by the elbow as they were led into the room.

Holy shit! The man, Marty realized, was Paul Grasso. *She's* with Paul Grasso? Marty laughed quietly to himself, keeping his eyes on them as they came toward him. Why, that old son-of-a-bitch! This one was definitely *not* Paul's usual—typically, a Las Vegas showgirl or a tart just off the bus from somewhere. Paul's definitely in over his head. And as Marty stared, once again came that nagging familiarity. I know her *somehow,* he thought, or maybe I just want to.

Bethanie, along with every other pretty woman in the room, had watched the spectacular entrance. Now she was talking to him. Babbling on and on.

"What?" Marty asked.

"I *said,* 'Who are those people who just came in?' " Bethanie knew she couldn't afford to whine, but she almost was. After being dumped by that bastard Sam Shields, she had no intention of letting Marty get away. She knew the rule of Hollywood survival—"Fuck upward." Only someone as powerful as Marty could afford to fuck someone beneath him. She and Sam, just breaking through, needed more powerful partners, like Crystal Plenum and Marty DiGennaro. What she didn't need was competition from this Amazon.

"Why don't I introduce you?" Marty stood, extended his hand to Paul, and kept looking at the young woman who reminded him of someone. "Paul, good to see you. This is Bethanie Lake, Paul Grasso. He's one of my oldest friends."

Paul's handshake was vigorous, his good mood apparent. "Marty DiGennaro, Lila, and Bethanie . . . Lake, right?"

"Yes," Bethanie answered, but her displeasure was evident in the way she bit the word off. Shit! Who needed a bitch who looked like this one sitting across from Marty all night? she asked herself. Why was she so unlucky?

The maître d' had pulled out the chair for Lila opposite Marty, and she smoothly slid into it.

"I have to apologize for making Paul late, Mr. DiGennaro." She turned her eyes to Bethanie, then Marty, and smiled.

"Marty. Please call me Marty, Lila. And it's very nice of you to take the responsibility for Paul's lateness. Except I expect him to be late." Looking at Paul, smiling, he added, "Paul and I go back a long time."

Marty noticed Lila looking intently at Bethanie, who was now sitting up stiffly on the banquette. "Bethanie Lake. Didn't you create the role of Leora in *Houston* last season?" Bethanie nodded, perhaps a bit defensively. "You left that show just in time," Lila continued. "After that, the writing went downhill."

Marty noticed Bethanie relax slightly beside him, but he kept his eyes on Lila. In fact, he couldn't take them off her. Gracious, very gracious, he thought. Everyone knew that it was the stupidest move Bethanie could have made, to leave a successful TV series to try to do a mediocre movie that fell apart. Her agent and manager tried to talk her out of it, advising her to wait another year. But she wouldn't listen. A standard case of biting off more than you can chew. Bethanie *wasn't* ready, and it had really fucked up her career. Unless he gave her another shot. As he looked at the divine redhead, he suspected Lila knew that, too.

Marty forced himself to speak. "I've ordered a California merlot, if that's okay with everyone," he told them, as the waiter poured.

Lila held her hand over her glass. "Actually, I'd prefer

a Manhattan, if it's all the same to you." She turned to the waiter and said, "Straight up, with a twist," then dropped her eyes and snapped her purse open. Marty nodded to the waiter, then noticed the cigarette Lila held to her bow-shaped lips in the long fingers of her left hand. Nobody smoked in California anymore! She was a trip. He immediately pulled out his rarely-used Dunhill lighter, and beat the waiter's hand to Lila's cigarette.

She inhaled deeply, holding her cigarette hand straight up with its elbow cupped in her other. Where had he seen that gesture? God, it was driving him nuts! She raised her face to the ceiling and released a long, slow stream of white smoke, then dropped her head and stated to no one in particular, "I hope no one minds if I smoke."

He knew her, he was *sure* he knew her. Her gestures, her voice. It was maddening really, the familiarity of her, mixed with the utter strangeness. Yet how would he have forgotten her? He hated to stoop to the oldest line in the book, but he felt compelled. "I seem to know you from somewhere," Marty said, "but have we met before? You look very familiar."

Bethanie, her wineglass to her lips, choked, put down the glass, nearly spilling it, and coughed to clear her throat.

"Something tough to swallow?" Paul asked her, and gave her a smack on her back.

Lila smiled, raised her lovely brows at Marty, allowing the gesture to speak for itself. "Westlake School for Girls?" she asked. She looked away as if bored. "No, I'm sorry to say. We've never met." Then, looking back at him, she added, as if she had almost forgotten her manners, "But you're very nice to ask." Oh, Christ, Marty thought wryly, you can take the nerd out to Hollywood but . . . He watched her as she sipped her drink, holding the glass by its stem. It accentuated the length of her fingers, and he felt a tingle in his groin at the thought of those same fingers wrapped around another stem. But he was still perplexed.

"Do you act? I'm sure I've seen you in something." She was just so familiar . . . yet so distinctive.

"The one thing I do *not* do is act. My mother tried to push me into the business, but I won."

"Hey, I thought we weren't talking business tonight, *gumba*," Paul reminded Marty. He picked up his menu. "So, Beth, what's good?"

Bethanie looked away, but only for a moment, from Marty and Lila. She knew she couldn't afford to. Marty studied Lila some more, ignoring both Paul and Bethanie. "What did your mother do, Lila?"

"About what?" she purred.

He laughed. He was enjoying this woman, and he could see that she seemed to make Paul more like his old self. Only Bethanie was definitely not at ease tonight. She was way out of her league. Well, he thought, almost sympathetically, she *was* losing the chance of a lifetime. That could make *anyone* uneasy.

Marty smiled at Lila, and returned the conversational ball over the net. "About life, liberty, and the pursuit of happiness. And about a paycheck—or perhaps she was born rich?"

"She was born poor and made herself rich. And I was born rich and intend to stay that way. I just haven't yet figured out a way to do it. My mother had talent. I just resemble her." With a dip of her head, she indicated to the waiter she wanted a refill. Marty marveled at the familiarity of the gesture, sinuous, almost dramatic, yet still natural. Lila looked at him. "Now, *you* were born poor and became rich, and *Paul* was born poor and became rich, and then poor, and then rich again," she said, poking Paul gently in his side. She laughed, the noise a deep purr.

"*You* could act, Lila, I keep telling you," Paul said. "Your mother wasn't wrong about everything, remember? I knew her when. You're just like her. Even when she was on the balls of her ass, I had to sell roles to *her* harder than I had to sell her to the *producers*."

Then the light dawned. Of course! The resemblance was there, not only to her mother but to her fabulous father, too, a guy who had always been too beautiful to be a man. Marty smiled, placed his wineglass on the table, and said, "Theresa O'Donnell's daughter." He was almost embarrassed, but it would have been a lot easier if Lila had cooperated. She obviously was not the typical "my mom's a star" kid.

"I'd prefer that people say *she's* Lila Kyle's mother, but I haven't yet figured out how to make that happen. Anyway, I'm Kerry Kyle's daughter, too." Looking around the table, she said to no one in particular, "I'm famished. Would someone slaughter me a fatted calf?"

"Days and Knights, 1949," Marty said. It was a great old line from Theresa's first movie. She'd played a vaudeville hoofer.

"Nineteen forty-eight," Lila corrected. "But how did you know that? It's a little obscure for someone who's as current as yourself." He saw the surprise in Lila's face.

"It was *shot* in 1948, but it wasn't *released* until 1949."

"Well, I'll be damned," Lila said, obviously impressed.

"And I believe it was in that movie that she first met Kerry Kyle." He watched Lila sit back in her chair, her surprise growing. Picking up the menu, he looked over the selections and said, " 'I believe there are no more calves, my dear. Would a thigh do?' "

Lila's small shriek of delight pleased him. He knew not only Theresa's line, but also Kerry Kyle's response. Now Lila leaned over the table, took his face in both her hands, and kissed him on the forehead. The skin where she had brushed it tingled. "Oh, thank you!" she cried. Bethanie made a noise that sounded to Marty like a snort.

"I used to watch it whenever it came on television," Lila was saying. "It's how I got to know my father. He died when I was little. And I watched all my mother's films, over and over. I think it made me miss her less when she was away. But how do *you* know those lines?"

The waiter, who had been discreetly standing at the table for some time, finally cleared his throat. They ordered, the appetizers were served, and they ate and chatted. Or, rather, they ate while *he* chatted. About every film, about the fifties and sixties in Hollywood. Marty finally paused as their meals were placed before them. "It's sad, you know, that that era has passed. But I'm so grateful that I have some of the original prints from those times." He chewed and thought for a moment more. "Ted Turner, of course, should be horsewhipped."

Paul, who was never very interested in anything except gambling—who was playing the main rooms in Vegas, and how could he make some fast money—asked, "Why, what did Ted Turner ever do to you?"

Lila became indignant. "Ted Turner took Gainsborough's *Blue Boy* and had someone change the color to green!"

"So what?" Paul shrugged. Marty looked at him and shuddered. Watching Paul eat was a lot like watching a horror movie: you wanted to cover your eyes, but you couldn't look away. Marty tried to explain. "Eh, *gumba*, what Lila means is, you don't change a work of art once it's been created. Turner is taking hundreds of classic black-and-white films and putting color into them with the use of computers. That's *batz, capisce?*"

"Yeah, sure, Marty; okay, it's crazy. But, you know, I'm not so sure. I can't remember wanting to watch too many black-and-white movies lately. *Shadows and Fog* didn't pack 'em in."

Marty and Lila laughed. Bethanie jumped in to join them. But her laugh sounded more like a death rattle, Marty thought. He could feel her urgency to join the conversation somehow.

"So, Lila, what was it like growing up the child of Theresa O'Donnell and Kerry Kyle?" Bethanie asked. "You must have received a lot of special treatment."

"Well, to be honest, when I was a kid, I didn't think I was different from anyone else, really. I was alone a lot. And when I was old enough to go to school, I was going to school with other kids like myself—you know, Tori Spelling, the Nelson boys, Cary Grant's daughter—so I still was like everyone else." Marty watched Lila break a roll in half and butter a small piece.

"High school was the same. Well, not really; by then I was reading more about life outside the Hollywood ghetto, but, still, none of it seemed very real to me. I guess I was too sheltered," she said, and nibbled at the roll. "But I also took a lot for granted. I *do* remember a couple of really exciting times." Marty saw her look around the table to be sure everyone really was interested. "Once, Uncle Cary played Santa at my house and I sat on his lap. I knew *immediately* he was Cary Grant. My mother had every one of his movies at home, and every movie magazine had pictures and stories of Cary Grant. He had silver hair, he wasn't young anymore, but he was still gorgeous. Still, I was so disappointed, because in *that* role I wanted the real thing, not any old actor. I cried and said, 'You're not Santa Claus, you're just Uncle Cary.' I got off his lap and wouldn't return. I couldn't understand then why all the women laughed so hard."

Bethanie said it for everybody. "Cary Grant came to *your* house and played *Santa Claus* for you?" After a pause, however, she laughed a forced, throaty laugh, said, "Oh, come on, Lila," then took a dismissive sip of her drink.

Lila appeared almost embarrassed, her translucent white skin momentarily flushed pink. Her beauty was not lost on Marty's professional eye; for most of the evening, he had been looking at her as if through a camera's lens. She's more beautiful than her mother, has the eyes of her father, skin like Merle Oberon, a voice like Lauren Bacall, and the body of Ann-Margret, except taller. What a package!

Lila shrugged one shoulder. It was an elegant movement. "That's what happens when I talk about my childhood. People get jealous."

Bethanie suddenly wasn't laughing. "Jealous? I'm not *jealous*. I just don't believe you. I can't picture Cary Grant putting on a Santa Claus beard and having some snotty Beverly Hills kid sit on his knee. Why would Cary Grant do that?"

"Because he wanted to fuck my mother. And that was the deal," Lila said. "Anyway, that wasn't so much. When one of the Mankiewicz kids locked himself in the bathroom, *they* got the Three Stooges to do a show on the lawn so he'd come out. Of course, they worked cheap by then."

Marty gave up on Bethanie at that moment. He found himself staring intently at Lila. What he saw was more than beauty. She had poise, intelligence, and—instinct told him—talent. Plus a face that could move through a camera lens and be welcomed in every living room in America. And every bedroom. He wondered if she and Paul had set him up for this, with the reluctant-virgin bullshit. But what if they had? Selznick had never complained when his brother shlepped Vivien Leigh over the night that shooting for *Gone With the Wind* began. Marty could take a lucky break however it came. "Lila, I think Paul's right. I'd suggest you think seriously about acting on TV."

"But TV is crap," she said.

"Not when *I* do it."

"*You* don't do TV."

"I do now. And I'm going to change it for all time."

Marty watched as Lila, keeping her eyes on his face, put down her fork and stared. Finally, she spoke. "You're not kidding, are you?"

"No, I'm not. And in fact, if you give me a call tomorrow, I might even have an idea for you."

Lila put her hand to her throat and tilted her head back, letting her long, red hair cascade over the back of the chair. She seemed to be searching the ceiling of Spago for words.

Paul Grasso, quiet too long, said, "For chrissakes, Lila, just say 'Thank you, Mr. DiGennaro' and then kiss my ass for taking you out to dinner."

Lila smiled and said, "Thank you, Marty. I'll give you *my* number." Then she turned to Paul Grasso. "But it's a little too soon for any ass-kissing, Paul. After all, I haven't even had dessert yet."

13

After the *Jack and Jill* wrap party, Sam Shields drove home from the studio alone. He was exultant, because he knew the picture in the can was good, and had the potential to be great. He had the wonderful feeling of all creators when they look upon their work and find it good. His words had been made flesh, and the flesh was delicious.

Of course, it hadn't been accomplished without a certain amount of pain and suffering. And compromise. Well, that was appropriate for a work titled *Jack and Jill and Compromise,* he told himself. All of life was a compromise, after all. Wasn't that the home truth he was trying to express? And also trying to live?

For a moment, only for a moment, he thought of Mary Jane Moran's transfiguring performance as Jill. Filming the part she had created had brought her image back to him over and over again. There had been times in New York when he had felt that her face, her plain muffin of a face, had actually lit the stage. Well, he had managed to coax a good performance out of Crystal Plenum. It might not be as intense, as sensitive as Mary Jane's, but it was good. Crystal had never worked as a stage actress; it was only now that she was in her thirties and off a long string of ingenue roles in films that she wanted to try *acting*. And, Sam told himself proudly, he *had* gotten her to act.

He smiled as he drove the BMW onto the expressway. Even now, months later, when he was a soon-to-be-successful director, he was surprised that he, Sam Shields, was sleeping with a movie star. Crystal Plenum.

And, he had to admit, it was a thrill to look down at that perfectly exquisite face as he made love to her. It was a face he had already seen in ecstasy on the screen as Mel Gibson, Warren Beatty, Kevin Costner, and other stars had made love to her. Now he was doing it in real life. Her silken skin, her perfect breasts, her long legs—

all for him. It certainly enhanced his pleasure, knowing that she was probably one of the three most beautiful, most desired stars in the country, maybe in the world. And *he* possessed her.

He possessed her and her image in the cans of film. Immortality in tin. There was still so much to do, and to learn. There was the cutting and editing, the soundtrack had to be laid down, the final looping done. Even the credits had to be designed and laid in. And it would be a lot easier to learn the next batch of tricks of the trade without the entire cast and crew as his audience. From now until release date, he and a handful of pros would work without witnesses to any foolish question he asked or mistake he made.

And then—the release. He caught a glimpse of his reflection in the rearview mirror, and the stupid smile of triumph was still on his face. Well, why not? He had done well, and he was almost sure he'd get another shot at directing. For a moment, he felt a small shiver of anxiety tarnish his day: he had no other vehicle that he felt he could sell as a film.

The fact that he hadn't written a word since he came out to L.A. shouldn't worry him. After all, working on *Jack and Jill* had been a full-time job. But the idea of finishing this film and retiring to a quiet corner of his rented house and writing alone for a year did not excite him. Well, he'd cross that bridge later. Meanwhile, he had a triumph to prepare for.

And he had to admit that showing the film to his mother and father would be a sweet part of it. They had never been much interested in his stage career: to them, theatrical success meant Broadway. Now they were impressed. He'd had them flown up from Florida for a week during the shoot. They'd stayed at his Laurel Canyon house, swum in his pool, come down to the studio, watched him direct on the soundstage. His mother, perfect and immaculate as ever, still more than pretty despite her age and the toll that drinking took, surveyed it all coolly. He longed for some warmth, some sign of approval: a hug, a kiss, a loving look. Finally, at the airport, his mother had looked up at him with tears in her eyes and a tremor in her voice and said, "You're not like your father." It was hardly an embrace, but Sam took it as a benediction.

His father had taken his hand and, out of earshot of his mother, had simply gestured at his son's linen suit, the L.A. sunshine, the palm trees, the limo they had taken to the airport, and said, "Don't fuck this up for yourself." Not exactly a vote of confidence, but an acknowledgment, of sorts.

And if there was one thing Sam was determined not to do, it was fuck this up for himself. It was a funny thing: the higher he rose out of the muck of oblivion into the sunshine of L.A. success, the more determined he was not to sink back even half a step. He wanted not only success but all its trappings: the right table at the Polo Lounge, a house account at Morton's, people to take his calls immediately. He didn't care too much about the money—that was nice—but he did want the power and all that came with it.

Now Sam drove along the winding road to Laurel Canyon. His own driveway was hidden by the scruffy undergrowth and pine trees that passed as naturalized landscape out here. His leased house was small but choice, cream-colored adobe outside, and inside decorated in the Santa Fe style, complete with Indian artifacts, colorful serapes and rugs, big unglazed pottery. Giant stands of cattails and reeds grew around the tiled patios and pool area. He passed by them now, walked into the living room through the glass doors facing the sapphire blue-tiled pool, and threw his jacket onto the sofa. As always, he headed straight for the bar but stopped, as always, to turn on the answering machine. He listened as he poured out an Absolut, threw in a few ice cubes, and sat down to enjoy his two fixes of the day: his single drink and his messages.

The tape rewound, making its usual beeps and squeaks. Then it clicked into forward. "Hi, Sam. It's Bethanie. I've got a real shot at a Marty DiGennaro project, but I've run into a little snag, and I wondered if I could use your name? Look, could you please call me at . . ."

Sam, with his remote, fast-forwarded to the next message. He'd broken that off long ago and could smell a ploy for a get-together a mile off. But what if it was true? Sam admired Marty DiGennaro more than any other American director. Well, Bethanie knew that, was using that. It was bullshit. He'd forget it.

"April Irons' office. Could you please call her back at seven this evening at . . ."

Sam jotted down the number quickly. He had planned to spend the evening with Crystal, celebrating the wrap, but he could call April on his way over.

"Sam, it's Molly. I haven't spoken to you lately, and I just wondered if you're all right and if by any chance you've heard from Mary Jane. . . ."

Sam sighed and fast-forwarded over the rest of the message. The hell with her. Molly and Chuck had been guilt-inducing and tiresome, resenting him for leaving them behind, a reminder of how small his life had once been.

Another beep. "Sam, it's Crystal. I won't be able to make it tonight, I'm afraid. Some other time."

For a moment, he felt a stab of disappointment. Disappointment and something else. Was it fear? But Crystal had a complicated life: a kid, a husband. She had canceled at short notice before. Still, he backed up the tape and replayed the message.

"Sam, it's Crystal. I won't be able to make it tonight, I'm afraid. Some other time."

It made him uneasy. After all, he *knew* dialogue. He was a playwright, for God's sake. There was something about the line. It was formal, too formal. And the "some other time"—it sounded so perfunctory.

He played the message yet again. Goddamn it, it *wasn't* his imagination. He could *tell* when something was wrong. He was intuitive. That's what made him such a good director. He lifted up the phone receiver and dialed Crystal's number. Her au pair answered and tried to blow him off, but he managed at last to have Inga put him through.

"Crystal, about tonight," he began quickly. "April just called and I've got to see her. Could we cancel, or could you come over later?"

"Didn't you get my message?"

"No. I just walked in."

"Well, I said I couldn't make it."

"Great. That's convenient. I'll call tomorrow."

There was a pause. "I don't think it's a good idea, Sam."

He felt his palm go wet, making the receiver slippery to hold. For a crazy moment, his mother's face, as he'd last seen her at the airport, flashed before his eyes. He literally shook his head to rid himself of the image, to hear Crystal's voice clearly. "Listen, Sam, it's been great, but I think it's run its course, don't you?" he heard her say. "I mean, it's silly to beat around the bush, isn't it?"

His mouth was as dry as his palm was wet, but he managed, calmly, even rather coldly, to ask one question. "Just like that, Crystal?"

"Well," she said, her voice tight with impatience, "after all, the shoot *is* finished. The movie wrapped, Sam, didn't it?"

14

Lila awakened early the morning after she'd signed the contract to play Crimson along with the exclusive Flanders Cosmetics deal. Her picture, along with those of the other two bimbos, had made the third page of *Daily Variety* and Army Archerd ran an item. She poured a glass of orange juice and, carrying the cordless phone, took it out to the veranda. The money from the cosmetics company would come in handy. Of course, she didn't plan for a minute to wear that cheap crap, but so what? Anyone who knew anything wore MAC and she'd keep wearing it. But she'd use the money. She'd get a good car, some new clothes, *and* a place of her own. Plus, she would start her payback plan. And she knew who she'd start with. She reached over the Princess phone beside her bed and dialed the number. "Ara Sagarian, please. This is Lila Kyle."

After a pause, Lila said, "I *know* what Ara said, Miss Bradley. But if you let him know that I'm calling him because I have to make a decision about representation, I think he'll talk to me. No, I'll wait."

Lila didn't have to wait long. "Good morning, Lila. I'm a little surprised to hear from you again."

"Mr. Sagarian, I've presumed terribly on you and I'm very sorry. I'd like to make it up to you. I'm not going to ask any favors, except for advice. You know I got the part in Marty DiGennaro's new TV show? Well, I've practically signed with Sy Ortis, but I was hoping that you would approve before I did. There's a million-dollar contract involved. Is it the right thing to do?"

Lila listened to Ara breathing at the other end. It was a long moment. Would he take the bait? "You don't owe me anything, Lila. This is show business. I'm just happy for you that you got the part, and that you have such prestigious representation in Mr. Ortis."

"You're a real gentleman, Ara." She just let the hook dangle. He bit and asked the question. She smiled. "No, I still haven't signed with Sy."

"Lila, this is an important step. Let me take you to lunch today, you know, to make up for the way I treated you. Can we say the Polo Lounge at one?"

"Great. I'll see you then," she said, and hung up smiling.

For years, the Polo Lounge had been the place for power-broking breakfasts and lunches. But when the Beverly Hills Hotel closed for renovations, others had abandoned it, even after it reopened, refurbished. Ara Sagarian had not. Ara prided himself on his loyalty to anything excellent.

Ara was seated at what was once the most sought-after corner table when Lila arrived at ten after one. He stood with great effort to greet her, and Lila graciously kissed his deflated cheek.

"Thank you *so* much for the invitation, Ara. I was afraid I had really alienated you." She leaned forward. "I couldn't bear that. I think too highly of you."

Ara smiled. But he was too curious for chitchat. "Lila, how did you get Marty DiGennaro to give you the part in his new series?"

She threw back her head and laughed. "Blood will tell, Ara," she said.

After a moment, Ara joined her in laughing. "Well, it looks like you have done very well on your own. It hardly seems as if you need representation at all."

"Except, as you know, there's a lot more to be done. I'm certain Marty's series will be a major hit, and that will bring in endorsements, movie deals, licensing—millions, I'm told. It's not just a new series, Ara. It could be an industry. Les Merchant at the Network is really throwing everything into this. I need someone I can *rely* on. Someone I can be *sure* would watch out for my best interests. The way you did for my mother." Lila lowered her eyes. "Is Sy Ortis the man, Ara?"

He reached out an ancient claw and took her hand in his. "I'd be afraid to tell you yes, my dear," he said.

Lila fluttered her lashes.

"I was afraid of that! You know, I didn't like what you did to me at first, but after my ego repaired, well, I respect the loyalty you showed my mother. Even though she doesn't bring you in much money anymore, you still stood up for your client." Lila looked directly into Ara's eyes and added, "I like that." Lila watched as Ara adjusted himself in his chair. He took up a spotless linen handkerchief and delicately dabbed at his mouth, wiping the spittle away. The next move was his, and she could see he knew it.

"I'm not sure you can expect the same commitment from Sy Ortis," he told her gently. "But you say you haven't signed with him yet?"

"No, I haven't," Lila said blandly, and picked at her salad.

"Well, then . . ." Ara faltered. Lila remained silent. She wouldn't want to make this one bit easier for him.

"Well," Ara began again. He licked his lips. Yes, Lila thought. *Yes.* The old bastard is going to go for it. He's not so old or so sick that he can pass up the action. When was the last time he signed on a *new*, hot talent? "Since

292

you haven't yet signed with Sy Ortis, perhaps it's time *we* talked about a relationship." Ara dipped a spoon into his gazpacho and brought it unsteadily to his mouth. "Let's see, there are the endorsements, as you say, and future movie projects. There's already a lot of buzz on this project. We should start putting out feelers for something for you to do during your first hiatus. And there'll be contracts, contracts, contracts. Oh, the list is interminable. By the way, has anyone read your contract with Marty yet? You should have all sorts of options in it. There are a number of 'what-if' situations that one couldn't possibly anticipate, unless, of course, one had been through it with others for years and years."

"Unless one was someone like you?" Lila asked, just to set the hook firmly before she began reeling him in.

"Not someone *like* me, my dear. *Me!*" Ara said, and dabbed at the corner of his mouth.

"But I thought Mother wouldn't let you take me on. She'd be furious," Lila said.

"*I'll* handle Theresa," Ara told her. "After all, she's not so active now, and there would be no conflict."

"I'm afraid it would come down to an 'It's her or me,' Ara," Lila said, and she felt a delicious thrill. Would it really be this easy?

"Theresa would never be so foolish as to force my hand in that way."

"I'm not talking about Theresa, Ara. I'm talking about myself. If you were to be my agent, you would have to drop Theresa O'Donnell."

Ara put his spoon down and held the linen napkin to his mouth. He stared at Lila. For the briefest, most horrible moment, she felt the line go slack between them. But the bait was too rich, the hook too deeply set. Ara, the dying old shark, had smelled fresh blood in the water. Lila almost laughed out loud as she watched him struggle and then succumb. "I understand, Lila. Of course, I'll do it as delicately as possible."

Lila gave Ara a brilliant smile, then turned in her seat and called over a hovering waiter. "Bring Mr. Sagarian a telephone." Lila continued to look at him as the phone was jacked in and placed at his good right side. "I'm not particularly concerned with the delicacy, Ara, but rather the timing. I'd like you to show me some loyalty. Now, Ara. Call her *now*. You know her number."

Ara, staring at Lila almost mesmerized, picked up the receiver, dialed the number, then reached into his pocket and pulled out yet another pristine handkerchief to wipe the drool from the corner of his mouth. At last he tore his eyes away. Had she actually seen shame in them? Lila sat back and listened, the smile still on her face. "Theresa, please," he almost whispered, and Lila imagined Estrella going to the Puppet Mistress with the phone. "Theresa," he asked. "It's Ara. And I'm afraid I have some bad news." Lila listened to Ara's side of the conversation as if it were a wonderful dream. It was a more sumptuous sweet than the Polo Lounge's famous white-chocolate mousse.

When Ara had finished and hung up, Lila leaned over to him and patted his good cheek. "Now, that's taken care of," she said with satisfaction. "What would *you* like for dessert?"

15

It was a rat race, Sy Ortis thought as he drove his Bentley Turbo R out of the canyon. And there were a lot of different kinds of rats. Sy always thought of "RAT" as an acronym for "Regulars," "Assholes," and "Talents." It was his little code, his theory of life, almost.

The Regulars were in the vast majority—all the poor nine-to-five working stiffs, all the guys in dull businesses, the insurance agents, the waitresses and waiters, the IBM salesmen, the guys who worked in tool and die shops—all of them were Regulars: consumers of the dream machine that Ortis helped to create. Regulars watched other people's dreams and nightmares on big screens and small ones while they lived their boring lives, too unimaginative even for good dreams of their own. In Hollywood, they were called "the flyovers"—the masses between the coasts.

"Talents" were Ortis' clients. The special people, the ones who dreamed big enough to entrance the Regulars. So many Regulars, so few Talents. Christ, how boring was it when most people started in with "I had the most interesting dream last night"? Balls. It was only the Talents, with their weirdnesses, their visions, their little streaks of eccentricity, that really *were* interesting. Ortis worked with the most interesting people in the world. Writers who wrote down great dreams, actors and actresses who looked like great dreams, directors who could put the two together and create great dreams.

Yeah, sometimes the Talents were difficult, sometimes they got fucked up on coke, into bad debt with the IRS, into trouble with their marriages, but, hey, they *produced*. Sy knew how to handle Talents. And he had almost nothing to do with Regulars.

It was the Assholes in the middle that gave him trouble. The ones who *thought* they were Talents and wouldn't fuckin' let up on you until you had to crush them and wipe them off your shoe bottom like the dog shit they were. Sy's biggest problem was unloading an Asshole he'd mistaken for a Talent, and his worst nightmare was the revenge of a Talent he'd treated like an Asshole.

That Morelli character was giving him trouble now. A definite Asshole. Got the pilot, fucked it up, couldn't go the distance. So why didn't he just crawl back into the hole that he'd crawled out of? Instead of fuckin' driving Sy crazy with his phone calls and his crazy letters and his ambushes outside the office. Him and every other Asshole.

But Morelli wasn't *really* a problem. Sy was virtually certain the guy was a true Asshole. As long as the fucker didn't have a gun, Sy could give two shits what the little weasel thought or said.

April Irons, on the other hand, *she* was a Talent. A big Talent. So big that now she almost ran International Studios, one of the last big ones in the movie business. And Sy, to his eternal shame and grief, had mistaken her for an Asshole. He'd fucked her bad on a Marty DiGennaro deal, back in the days when you could fuck April over and live, and the bitch would never forget it. Christ, back then how was he supposed to know that gashes could run studios?

So, though he would go to a screening of Crystal Plenum's latest movie, produced by April, he knew he'd be seated back with the dog shit. That was despite being Crystal's agent and, he reminded himself, the most powerful man-behind-the-scenes in all of Hollywood. It was just that April was powerful in front of the scenes, too, and the bitch never forgave, never forgot.

Of course, neither did Sy. But he was at the mercy of his Talents. It was an agent's lot in life. And it pissed him off big-time that Marty, his guy, his resident genius director, was not only doing this stupid television gig, but had gone out and hired one of the little bitches for the goddamn thing without even consulting him. Marty's latest "find" was already represented by that dying old dragon lady Ara Sagarian, or so he had heard. Ara had represented her mother. Now there was nothing Sy could do about it, except suck his own dick. Instead, he reached for the inhaler on the seat beside him. He'd make Milton Glick pay for this. Okay, Milt had brought in the blonde and they'd tied her up, but Marty himself had also found the other actress, the Melrose one. Sy absolutely *had* to sign *her:* two out of three would give him the majority of representation, if not the unanimity he had craved.

Well, at least Glick *had* come through with that hillbilly. It had been and, he saw, would continue to be, easy as pie with her. Sign here, do this, move there, smile nice. Why couldn't it always be so easy?

The phone in his car rang and he winced, reached over, and lifted it from the receiver. Jesus, he hated to talk on the phone and drive at the same time. It made him nervous, and that made the asthma kick in worse. He sighed. "Hello?"

"Mr. Ortis? It's Michael McLain on the line," his own secretary's voice told him. "Can I patch him through?"

"Yes." There were a series of clicks and squawks. Sy

almost went up on the divider at the Burbank exit. *Jesús Cristos!*

"Mr. Ortis? Michael McLain is on the line." This time, it was Michael's secretary. Michael still made *you* hold for *him*. Well, those days will be ending soon if he makes another goddamn flop like *Akkbar*.

"I know that, goddamn it!"

"Hey, you old Spanish son-of-a-bitch. How goes it?" Sy swerved to avoid a Toyota Tercel that nearly cut him off. Sure. He was driving a nine thousand dollar piece of shit. What did he care. Sy almost dropped the phone, recovered it, and tried to inhale.

"What's up, Mike?" he asked. He knew that Michael hated to be called Mike.

"Listen, I wondered about what was going down with Addison and that script I liked."

Sy sighed. No way that Rex Addison was going to star Michael in his next action picture. For chrissake, Rex was only twenty-eight. He *grew up* watching Michael McLain movies. To Rex, Michael was an old fart. And the bullshit about Michael always doing his own stunts was bought by the civilians, but Rex was savvy.

"Jeez, I think we can do much better than *that*," Sy said. "The script has no style, no cachet."

"Fuck the cachet. Addison's last three had *legs*. I can give it the style."

In a pig's ass. "Listen, Mike, I have something much better. A buddy flick. Something I saw this week that's perfect."

"And who's my buddy?" Michael asked, suspiciously.

"Ricky Dunn."

"Who?"

Michael knew perfectly well who Ricky Dunn was. He'd had two unbelievable big ones. *People* magazine had voted him "the sexiest man alive." Sy slowed to avoid an old man just in time. "He's signed to play a rookie architect in that new Benson thing."

"Great. And I'm the geezer who shows him how to build a skyscraper? Fuck that."

"Michael, there comes a point in a man's career when he has to broaden . . ."

"I get top billing. My name alone over the title."

Sy knew it was impossible. Hell, Michael probably knew it was impossible. Although you never could tell: these guys' egos were so big they often lost touch with reality. Sy reached for his inhaler. "Listen, *compadre,* why would you want to cut off your nose that way? Might as well bring in all the Ricky Dunn fans, too." Sy knew that there was no way that Ricky would give up top billing. Why should he? Michael, on the other hand, hadn't had a solid hit in three years. He should be grateful for a chance like this. Sy knew he had to move him in that direction. Because if he could sell Michael on this, he could make a fortune off of packaging the deal—he also represented his client Benson and the crappy script.

"Mike," he began in a reasonable tone, "this is a real opportunity. Bob Redford asked to see the script."

"Look, don't start to tell me that playing second banana to a new kid on the block is *broadening,*" Michael screamed.

"Look at Paul Newman," Sy began again.

"Paul Newman is almost seventy fucking years old. I'm forty-six."

"Michael, you're fifty-three, and everyone knows it but you."

"Look, I still act as well as I ever did. I still fuck as well. *Better,* even."

"I, thank God, would have no way of knowing that," Sy said. He slammed on the brakes, nearly hitting his head on the windshield and almost rear-ending the motherfucker in the Benz in front of him. *Madre di Dios,* the roads had been taken over by assholes! And he was driving a car that cost more than most people's homes. He sighed. "Listen, just do me a favor. *Think* about the Ricky Dunn movie. It's just what you need now."

"Fuck you!" Michael screamed, and hung up on him. *Sangre de los Santos,* did it have to be this hard? Michael had been in a slump lately, and he was aging, but he was still important, and Sy wanted him as a client, at least for another year or two. Sy felt himself begin to gasp for air and reached across the seat again to his inhaler. Okay, he admitted to himself. He was upset. Normally he didn't let little things like this bother him. After all, he was riding high. He was the consummate deal-maker in Hollywood. April Irons might be powerful, and very visible, but she wasn't in his league. No one was.

Back in the twenties, it was men like Lasky and Mayer who ran the Industry: the big studio bosses were sultans, with the power of screen life or death over their stable of performers. Then, in the late forties, things began to change. The stars began going independent, and the studio system began breaking down. But no star, no matter how popular, had overwhelming power. It was only by controlling dozens of them that Warner or Mayer had stayed on top, and none of the studios today could afford to pay dozens of big stars.

But agents didn't pay stars. They were paid *by* them. It was a perfect setup. The more talent you represented, the more power you had, and the more money you made. So a series of superagents arose. In the forties, it was Lew Wasserman and Leland Hayward; in the fifties and sixties, it was Lew Wasserman and Ara Sagarian; in the seventies, it was Lew Wasserman and Sue Mengers; in the eighties it was Mike Ovitz. Now, Sy thought with a smile, laying down his inhaler, now, it's me. The next Lew Wasserman.

He told himself he should be happy. More than happy. Rich. Because Sy Ortis had a secret. Well, he had many of them, but he had one very big secret. It was that he had also kept the bodega, as his grandma used to tell him.

When he was little, it was his grandmother who had raised him and his five sisters. Tía María, as everyone in the neighborhood called her, ran the local bodega, and the rest of the neighborhood. And it was his grandmother who had taught him more about business than Wharton ever could have.

"*Pepito*, if I was Rockefeller," she'd say, staring deep into Sy's eyes, "I would be richer than Rockefeller. You know why?"

He shook his head.

"Because I'd also keep the bodega."

Now Sy, on his way to being as rich as Rockefeller, had come up with a bodega of his own. It was too hard to make a living simply by peddling bodies to producers and taking his percentage while they got rich. Sure, when it worked, it worked big. But Sy understood from the very beginning in the Industry that he should also try to keep the bodega.

So he did. He had started a dummy corporation—two, actually. One of them sold scripts—all bought cheap, mostly useless—to many of his stars' development companies and to studios. The other bought up merchandising rights from his clients for as little as one dollar, and sold them for a hell of a lot more. A conflict of interests? Perhaps. But very, very profitable. And nothing had ever been as big as the potential on this deal with Flanders Cosmetics. The girls signed up for *Three for the Road* were going to be pitched like a product to America, and unless he was *loco en la cabeza* they were going to be bought faster than condoms in a whorehouse.

Now Sy was only a few blocks from his office. He sailed through a red light and turned onto the wide avenue. He sighed with relief. Well, sometimes it was easy. At least that cornpone blonde had been signed easily, and could be big. Real big. Sharleen Smith. She was an extraordinary-looking girl. Glick had pulled that one out of his ass.

But it was still a constant struggle to stay on top of the slippery pile. Sy mourned the fact that he'd lost the redhead. He tried to take a deep breath. One step at a time. All he had to do today was sign this New York actress of Marty's, convince Michael McLain to do the Ricky Dunn movie, and then eat April Irons' dirt at the premiere. That, and manage to breathe.

Jahne sat across the desk from Sy Ortis, watching him while he talked on the phone. Christ, she hated these smarmy bastards. Flesh peddlers, she thought. Pimps. An evil in the Industry, but, she admitted reluctantly, a necessary evil. She didn't want to be here. But Marty had suggested she see Ortis. And what Marty suggested, Jahne would do. On the set, off the set, anything Marty said, she did. Well, *almost* anything.

"That was Michael McLain," he said. No apology for

keeping her waiting, as if the name alone was explanation enough. "Now, where was I?" he asked.

"You were telling me what you would be able to do for me if you were my agent." Jahne paused. "Let me ask, how long have you worked for Michael McLain?"

"With Michael," Sy corrected. "Maybe ten, twelve years. Why?"

"That means he came to you as a big star already. You didn't discover him, make his career. It was already on track." She watched Sy adjust the sleeves of his shirt under the Armani jacket. Although Sy's firm was called Early Artist Recognition Ltd., they didn't usually spot new stars. They exploited the hell out of established ones. Some people said Sy had insisted on the name so he could call himself the duke of Earl.

"He was working, if that's what you mean. But he wasn't rich, which is where I come in. He could have made a good living for life without me, don't get me wrong. But rich?" Sy chuckled to himself. "Nah, that was *me.*" He looked into her eyes. "And I could do that for *you,* too—may I call you Jahne? Rich *and* famous." He kept his eyes on her, and a smile on his face.

Jahne knew that he was right. He *had* made Michael richer and more famous. And other people as well. And wasn't that what she wanted, after all? Money and fame? Those gave you power to get the roles you wanted. "The money is, of course, important. Enough to make me independent. But fame? Well, I'd like to have enough of a reputation as an actress to be able to pick and choose my roles, take only the ones I want. *That* would make me happy."

"You mean like Meryl Streep?"

Was that a sneer Sy had on his lips? "Exactly. Like Meryl Streep," Jahne said.

Sy got up from behind the desk and came around in front, then sat with one buttock on the corner, his hands folded in front of him. "Except, Jahne, no one ever really gets to that point. Not even Meryl Streep. She has choice among some roles, but, nevertheless, she took the part in *She-Devil.* You remember that big bomb? And *Death Becomes Her?* Worse. Now, why would a talented, established actress take a role like that, risk her box office?" Sy leaned forward. "Let me esplain." For a moment, his accent slipped. "An agent is more than a contract negotiator. He should be a career maker. Someone advised Meryl wrong, and, talented as she is, she still didn't have the objectivity to really know a hit when she saw it. Someone like Meryl will bounce back. But maybe not quite so high as before."

Jahne was beginning to see his point. It was, after all, pretty much the point Marty had made when he suggested she see Sy. "So that's where a good agent comes in?" she asked, saving Sy from having to point out the obvious.

"Exactly. And not just a good agent. A good *businessman*. Someone who can see the big picture, who has enough of an overview of the Industry to know where placement should be, and with whom, and when. And someone who can read the fine print of a contract. Protect your interests. And that's me. That's what I do. That's what I do for Michael McLain and all the others." He swept his hand across a wall of pictures of famous people. "And that's what I will do for you. Just say the word," he said, his hands open, waiting for Jahne's answer.

Jahne was committed to acting, but she was no fool. She put aside her prejudices and extended her hand to Sy. "It's a deal," she said.

"Michael McLain on line one, Mr. Ortis," his receptionist said over the intercom.

Sy kept his hand on the phone for a moment before picking it up. Shit, he thought, this is all I need. *Now* what the fuck does he want? Although the meeting with Jahne Moore had, in the end, gone very well, and he now had her as a client, he was pissed. It always got him pissed, pitching a new client. And she'd been uppity. She needed to be brought down a notch or two. By the time they agreed to sign on the bottom line, she had pushed his ass as far as it could go, taking all the fun out of the triumph. Now Michael would drive him nuts. He sighed and lifted the receiver.

"Michael, you're calling to say you're going to do the Ricky Dunn movie, right?"

"Maybe. I just thought of something we haven't discussed yet. Okay?"

Sy leaned his head on one hand, suddenly feeling tired. "Do you want me to guess, or are you going to tell me?"

"I get the girl. Not Dunn. *Me. And* my name above the title? Right?"

Now Sy's head fell forward onto his hands. This guy is going to fuckin' kill me. "I'll have to talk to his people."

"You *are* his people! Anyway, I get top billing *and* I get the girl. Then I'll consider it."

"Michael, it's a very special screenplay. You won't be the main love interest, you understand? We can't have the Olivier of the screen making love to a nineteen-year-old. It would be *ludicrous*. Your fans expect someone more sophisticated for you." Sy felt his wheeze coming on. Now he was really winging it. "You know," he continued, "the name above the title is usually for the guy who gets the girl. But your name will be bigger—way *bigger*—than his."

"What the fuck do you mean, 'ludicrous'? I fuck nineteen-year-olds all the time, Sy. You should know that. I got them coming out of the woodwork, for chrissakes. Ludicrous!"

Sy was feeling pushed. Normally, no matter how much he wanted to push back, he was usually able to control it. But not today. Maybe if that little bitch Jahne Moore hadn't just sat there, forcing *him*—Sy Ortis—to make a sales pitch, like a fuckin' new kid on the block. Jesus, twenty years in the business and a snotnose like her can sit there and interview *him*. But for Michael he needed patience.

"It's ludicrous when there's a thirty-four-year age difference. It would be like watching Sean Connery fuck Drew Barrymore, Michael."

"*I* fucked her," Michael said.

Jesus, Sy thought to himself. Was it true? And who cares? "You did, huh? You're *amazing*, Michael. Think you can fuck anyone you want, right?"

Michael laughed.

"How about a real challenge, Michael? I bet you can't fuck all three costars in DiGennaro's TV show. They're all kids—maybe nineteen, twenty—but I bet you can't."

"And when I do? What do I get?"

"I'll guarantee your name above the title in this project."

"And if I don't? . . ."

Sy laughed for the first time during the conversation. "You do *this* movie without top billing, *and* the next two I tell you to."

Michael paused.

"Hey, what's the matter, Michael? There isn't any real problem for you here, is there? Not Michael McLain, questioning his prowess?"

"You got a deal, you prick. All three."

"Right you are! But I want proof, Michael. Not just war stories. Proof!" Sy hung up. If Michael McLain made Jahne another notch on his belt, it should take her down a notch or two. And if he didn't, well, he'd have to make Sy's movies. Sy breathed deeply for the first time that day. *Now* he felt better.

16

Hollywood, like Dante's hell, has many levels. And rarely, if ever, do they mix, except at work. I—Laura Richie—have been on stage sets, TV sets, movie sets, and location shoots, and, believe me, that is one thing that never changes.

The technical staff, the boom operators, the other sound men, the camera crews, the lighting designers, the gaffers and best boys and grips all belong to one level. The suits, those businessmen in charge of production, budgets, the front office, publicity, marketing, and the like, all belong on another.

Then there are the extras: part of the talent, but not really belonging to it. They play the small roles, the crowd scenes, the background, the color.

And there are the stars. On a successful TV show, the set is built for them, the schedule is designed for them, the catering caters to them. Well, everyone caters to them.

Lastly, there is the director. Even on the shows where stars actually rule, the director is still on the highest level. But remember: that it is only the highest level of hell.

The hell is trying to take three hundred people and get them to the right location with the right clothes and the appropriate weather to have the right light, the right script, the right performances, to ensure that whatever is being taped or filmed or (God forbid!) performed live gets performed according to the director's vision. At least that's the theory. And on the soundstage of Three for the Road, *Marty DiGennaro was going to ensure that that theory was put into practice. He was going to create a show, a wonderful show, that transcended anything that had been done on television before. And to do it, he had only to concentrate on that one thing. Wasn't it Lanford Wilson who had said that style was nothin' but always concentrating on one thing?*

Marty had the vehicle for a hit. He had the first three scripts, the cast, and the crew. The only thing, the one thing he might lack, just a little, was concentration.

Because, since he had met Lila Kyle, it seemed he couldn't get her out of his mind.

Marty DiGennaro looked across the bustling soundstage, his laboratory for dream-making. Even now, after all his years of success, it was hard to believe all these toys were his. A funny-looking little Italian kid, growing up in Queens, he'd been too puny to play with the tough kids of his neighborhood. And he'd been lousy in school, a failure with girls, bad at sports, even bad with his hands. He'd escaped, whenever he could, to the safety of the darkness of the movies. The Roxy, the Corona, the Flushing Loews. They'd been his haven, his home, and it was a daily miracle to him that they'd given him this life, this almost perfect life.

The success, the money, the perks, the opportunity to make movies of his own. All unbelievably lucky. It was only in his private life that things weren't absolutely perfect. Because it was hard, maybe even impossible, to know who his friends were. Even Joanie, his soon-to-be-ex-wife, had benefited from him, had built her career on his contacts. He hadn't minded that, but then, when he wanted the child, and wanted her to stay home with Sasha, she left him.

Now women, other women, virtually *any* woman was more than available. Eager, even. Too eager. Because, despite his success, his power, his enormous wealth, his contacts, he knew he was still Marty DiGennaro, a skinny, funny-looking Italian kid who was bad with his hands. He suspected all those women were disappointed in his sexual performance, all merely faking their response. Lovemaking was, too often, a burden. And the parade of anonymous lovelies that he'd started seeing since his marriage broke up were rarely asked to return or spend the night. Work, work, and more work was all there was for him. For, just like back in Queens, the only place he was comfortable was in the movies—on a set or a soundstage, except instead of watching magic, now he made it happen.

Go know.

This was Marty's mantra in show business. It was the punch line from an old borscht-belt joke. A guy goes to the doctor for a complete physical. After a thorough exam, the doctor, an old Jewish type with an accent, says, "Mister, you are in top condition for a man of your age. Lungs, heart, colon, all in great shape. You're a lucky man, in peak physical condition. You could live another hundred years!" The guy thanks the doctor, gets dressed, walks out the door, and drops dead of a thrombosis on the doorstep. The doctor looks at the corpse, shrugs, and says, "Go know."

Go know.

Hollywood marveled at Marty's unbroken string of hits. They wondered what the secret was to his magic formula for picking them. Marty knew the secret.

There was no magic formula.

If bankers wanted to believe this wasn't the biggest crapshoot on the face of the earth, let them. But Marty knew how dangerous a game it was. Still, no matter how dangerous, he was getting tired of it. He'd always been a thrill seeker, and putting out another movie, getting another Oscar nomination, or even winning one was beginning to pall. So he'd started gambling in Vegas. But that thrill had died, too.

So then he'd thought of TV. The vast wasteland. The thing called a medium because everything on it was so very average or below. Yet watched. Watched and watched. What if he, single-handedly, could help one of the dying networks, the dinosaurs that were having the living shit kicked out of them by MTV, by cable, by home videos? He could be a hero to Les Merchant, but, more important, he could have autonomy and a vehicle that didn't have to prove itself every fucking time it came out of the gate. He could take hours developing characters over seasons, instead of minutes in that precious 120. What if he put together something that had never been seen, never been done before?

The idea had intrigued him, and when he ran across the remaindered copy of *Three for the Road* by that obscure woman Grace Weber from Jersey, he knew he had his stepping-off point. He'd bought it for a song, and now, for the first time in years, he was excited by a project. Excited and scared.

He reminded himself that all he had to do was concentrate. He had the scripts, the cast, the crew. Still, he was frightened. Because, if he fell flat on his face, all the jealous bastards in town (and they were *all* jealous bastards in this town) would dance on his grave. But frightened felt alive; he was in the game.

He reminded himself that he had everything he needed for another huge hit. And then he reminded himself of his mantra.

Go know.

Jahne and Pete arrived at the studio separately. He had been grateful for the job, and accepted her explanation that it was best to be discreet about their relationship because Marty seemed concerned.

But was that really her reason? she wondered. With

excitement and nerves churning her stomach, she knew that having Pete on the set was just an extra complication, one she wished she did not have to consider. Her relationship with him was BTN—better than nothing—but little more than that. He was a warm body in the dark, a generous sex partner, a nice kid, but no one who could ever know her.

In a way, now, the relationship made her more lonely than if she had been alone. Because how could she explain how she felt? How could a young kid like Pete, honest and clean and simple, understand what she was going through? There was no way to explain it to him. To be honest, she could barely explain it to herself. There were so many feelings that swirled through her, minute by minute, that she couldn't keep up.

Right now, on the first day on the set, she knew what she felt. It was a single feeling, strong and deep, and it left a metallic taste at the back of her tongue.

She had never been so frightened in her life.

Sharleen stepped out of the trailer she had been assigned as her dressing room and placed her hand on the director's chair that had her name stenciled across the back; her other hand held her mother's small Bible. Until this moment, none of it had been real to her: the contract, the publicity-photo sessions, meeting all those important people. Not even the dressing room. But *this* was real. She tried to remember; no, she had never seen her full name printed out, except in her own handwriting. She wished Dean could see it, but she couldn't have him come to the set. She'd have so much to tell him about tonight.

"Miss Smith," the man with the headphone said. "Mr. DiGennaro would like to see you at the cast meeting."

She realized she was being spoken to. "Oh, am I late?" she asked, jumping up.

"No, Miss Smith. Miss Kyle hasn't gotten here."

Sharleen walked gingerly across the floor, stepping over lighting cables and electrical tape, afraid to put her feet down for fear of upsetting something. There was a lot of bustling, and people with clipboards, and other people with headsets on, but they weren't listening to Walkmen. Everything looked confusing to her, but she was sure it made sense to *somebody*.

"Sharleen," Mr. DiGennaro said, coming toward her. "I'm sorry we kept you waiting. I'd like to introduce you to everyone."

"Oh, that's all right. I was just sittin' back, like a hog on a barrel, looking around. It's kind of like a circus I seen back home once. Everything happenin' at once. 'Cept in the circus, at least they had a ringmaster keeping that organized." She turned back to the chaos she had just passed through. "Does everyone know what they's supposed to do?" she asked.

Marty laughed. "Yes, that's *my* job. I'm the director —a lot like a ringmaster—and I'd *better* know what everyone's supposed to do, or I'm out on my ass. This is Ted Singleton, he's in charge of special effects; that's Dino, my right-hand man; and Bob Burton from Wardrobe; Jim Sperlman, lighting technician; the tubby one is my new AD, Barry Tilden; over that side, Charley Bradford, technical consultant from Harley-Davidson . . ."

"Whee, Mr. DiGennaro, please! Give me a minute to catch my breath. I don't know what any of them jobs is, so, if it's okay with y'all, I'll just try to memorize your names for now. Heck," she said with a laugh, "I don't even know what *my* job is yet, but I'm here to learn. I'm Sharleen," she said to the group, and took a seat at the conference table. "Howdy." She wondered why Lila and Jahne weren't here yet. She had met them already, of course, but she was a little afraid of seeing them again today. *They* were *really* beautiful. Lord, she asked herself, how have I been picked to stand beside *them?* Sharleen looked around at the sea of faces and smiled. She was very pleased to see them all smile back. They're all so nice over here in Hollywood, Sharleen thought. Much nicer than in Bakersfield.

Jahne Moore didn't have to be called to the opening meeting twice. She knew that today's first impression was very important. It would set the tone with Marty, with the other two leads, and for how she would be treated by the crew for the duration of the show. Marty was already there, and, Jahne was sure, so were all the other departments, but the last people to arrive at these meetings were usually the stars. Costars, she corrected herself. Jahne wondered about Sharleen Smith and Lila Kyle. She hadn't seen either of the girls since they had met at the publicity party that announced their signing. She had liked Sharleen, and knew instinctively that Sharleen was no threat. Lila, she was afraid, might be another story. But maybe I should wait and see, she told herself, before I form *any* opinions.

The meeting was held on Soundstage 14. Marty DiGennaro met her halfway across the floor of the huge hangarlike space, took her by the arm, and escorted her to the table. "Sharleen, you've met Jahne Moore, your costar?" Then he introduced her to the rest of the crew, and Jahne made it a point to shake each one's hand. She knew how much any production was a team effort. And how much she'd depend on them. She might be a costar, but if *these* people didn't do their jobs right, *no one* looked good. Pete was there, sitting behind Jim Bert, head cameraman. He smiled at her, but was discreet enough not to do more.

Jahne joined the group at the meeting. "Hi, Sharleen," she said, sitting next to her. "How are you doing?"

"Jahne," Sharleen leaned to her and whispered, *"how* I'm doin' ain't the question. The question is, *what* am I doin'? And *here?* Don't tell anyone, but I think I'm asleep and dreaming this."

Jahne laughed and touched Sharleen's arm. Yes, she liked Sharleen. *If* she was sincere. Sincere or not, she was breathtakingly beautiful. She was to play Clover, the Texan, to Jahne's Cara, a New Yorker. Jahne listened to Sharleen chattering comfortably away to a couple of the lighting guys, as if she'd known them all her life. I just hope she keeps that innocence, Jahne thought, then laughed to herself. Fat chance. This is Hollywood. The girl was going to need more than the little book she was clutching to protect herself. Especially with *that* body.

Jahne looked over at the only empty chair at the table and saw who it was everyone was waiting for. Lila Kyle.

She still hadn't come out of her dressing room. Jahne had heard Lila arrive on the set, but where *was* she? It's not as if there were costumes and makeup today. It was just a preliminary meeting, to get to know everybody. She saw Marty lean toward his assistant and whisper something to her. Clare nodded her head, stood up, and walked in the direction of the dressing rooms. Give me a break, Jahne thought. Lila isn't playing "star," is she? Not this soon? And not with Marty DiGennaro?

More than anything, Jahne was a professional. In the past, someone might criticize her talent, her appearance, her interpretation of a role, but *never* her commitment to a project. She prided herself on always being on time, knowing her lines and her blocking, and believing that the director had the final word.

The murmuring died down slightly, and Jahne looked toward the approaching figure. Lila Kyle was walking slowly across the set, through the taped-down cables and lighting apparatus, every movement choreographed, Jahne could tell. Lila wore tight black leather pants, black high-heeled boots, and a black leather jacket with zippers and enormous shoulders. The boots and the shoulder pads didn't seem excessive on Lila's six-foot frame. On the contrary, in a strange way, Jahne felt that Lila's height and bone structure demanded them. And she was certainly in character for her role: Crimson, the runaway rich girl from San Francisco.

Lila came to a stop at the end of the big table as Marty stood to greet her. Before he could make any introductions, she kissed him on the cheek and turned to the rest of the crowd. "Hello. I'm Lila Kyle," she said, her voice resonant. She paused and took a beat. Jahne looked around. Every man had stood. Well, I'll be damned, Jahne thought. Now, how did she get them to do that?

Lila sat down, her mother's favorite famous movie line echoing in her ears: "Don't fuck with me, boys." Okay, they got *that* straight, she thought, watching the men take their seats. It was one of the tricks she had learned from Theresa, coming to the sets with her when Lila was a child: how to make an entrance. Be the last to arrive.

And let them know you're a lady. It makes them drop their guard. And their jaws.

Marty was introducing everyone at the table by name. Lila didn't look around, just kept a small smile on her lips. She had met Sharleen and Jahne before, but hadn't seen them in street clothes. Lila let her eyes fall on Jahne, who was sitting on one side of her, listening to Marty like he was God. She knew Jahne had real New York acting experience behind her, but, besides her looks, nothing else. And she was short—despite the boots she wasn't more than five six or seven. The *blonde* didn't even *have* acting experience. A waitress, for chrissakes, but definitely another beauty.

I don't have anything to worry about, Lila assured herself. Because while Marty insisted they were three *co-stars*, Lila intended there to be only one *star*, no matter *what* Marty DiGennaro said.

Lila felt Sharleen's hand on her arm, and turned, coolly, to look at her. "Those pants are beautiful. Where'd you get them?" Sharleen asked.

"I had them made. They're from Florence," Lila said. It didn't hurt to be a *little* friendly.

"Maybe you'll give me Florence's phone number," Sharleen said. "I'd like her to make me a pair, too."

Lila blinked, then forced a smile. This one's too good to be true, she thought. Her eyes fell to the Bible on the table in front of Sharleen. Puh-leeze.

"Florence, *Italy*," she said, and Sharleen blushed. Lila looked around at the table. "What do you call three blondes sitting in a circle?" she asked. All the faces looked at hers expectantly. "A dope ring," she told them, and was rewarded with a big laugh.

Only Jahne Moore didn't join in. She turned to Sharleen. "Florence, Italy, is a city that's famous for its leather," she explained to the blushing girl. "But most people pronounce it the Italian way: Firenze."

Well, fuck her, Lila thought.

Marty DiGennaro sat back and looked around the table. The meeting was going very well, very well indeed. He smiled to himself. Everyone he talked to in the business tried to give him advice. The biggest problem he was going to have, they said, was trying to direct three gorgeous women who had never worked television before. There was no way, they said, he was going to be able to maintain the right balance that would keep them all happy. Now he chuckled. He wondered if they had said the same thing back in the thirties to George Cukor when he was filming *The Women*. If Cukor could direct Joan Crawford, Paulette Goddard, Rosalind Russell, *and* Majorie Main in the same film, for chrissakes, he knew he could direct these three.

All of them were gorgeous, and all of them would look great on screen. But he also knew that one of them was born for the camera, not only because of her beauty, but also because of that certain way she looked back at it. Monroe had had it; she could look into a camera and into the eyes behind it, into the eyes staring back at her on the screen. She saw into the future and men's souls at the same time. And didn't seem aware of the gift.

Marty looked at Lila now. *She* had the gift, but, unlike Monroe, she knew it. Which made her dangerous, and probably difficult to control. But oh so exciting.

Cukor controlled his brood mares. Kept them in line, had them pulling as a team, but each stepping to her own beat at the same time. Like Clydesdales. And he had pulled off the coup of a lifetime. An all-female movie.

And Marty would prove he could do it, too. After all, he *was* Marty DiGennaro, and this *was* only television.

17

After work, Jahne went home exhausted. Most nights, Pete called and asked to come over. Jahne hoped it wasn't just snobbery that kept her from revealing their relationship, but, to be honest, there wasn't much of a relationship. He was kind and cooperative. He made love to her and he held her close, and she needed that, but they shared very little else. Pete's idea of conversation was to comment on the television shows that he always switched on for background noise. He was as comfortable as a warm bath, and about as stimulating. So different from Sam.

She pulled her mind away from the subject. It was madness, an obsession with her. The fact was, she had slept with Pete for all the wrong reasons: out of boredom, loneliness, horniness, and need. She'd behaved the way men do, and now she had to make it right. Poor Pete would pay the price.

When the phone rang, Jahne sighed. She knew it would be Pete. She hated to put him off another night.

"Jahne?"

"Uh-huh." She tried not to sigh into the receiver.

"Can I come over?"

"I'm awfully tired, Pete."

"Me, too. Those tracking shots really take it outa ya. But I only want to see you for a minute. I think we have to talk."

It was such an unusual request from him that she agreed, and in less than ten minutes he was at her door. She moved to the sofa but, instead of following her lead, he continued standing, though he leaned against the wall. "Jahne, I'm no Einstein, but I think I got the picture. You don't want to talk to me on the set, and I understood that. I'm grateful for the job, too. But my dad explained how it is. You're going to be a big success with *Three for the Road* and you don't need a techie hanging around your neck. You can date whoever you want now, and I can tell you don't want me."

Jahne stood there, silent. He was goodhearted and sexy and kind to her. How could she tell him that it wasn't his job but his age that made him inappropriate? And how, in good conscience, could she string him along for her own convenience?

For the first time it occurred to her that, in his inarticulate, young, California way, he loved her. It had been so long since anyone had that it was hard for her to consider it. But who, exactly, did he love? A reconstructed body?

A beautifully designed face? Certainly he did not know who she was in any deeper way.

"Maybe you're right," she said, and she let him go.

Jahne had never thought much about money. Of course, she had never had much to think about, until after her grandmother's death, and then all of that had been carefully earmarked for Dr. Moore, the hospital, and other expenses. She had worked in the theater, both for pay and for free, and had managed to eke out whatever else she required from nursing, when she had to.

Back in New York, she'd always kept her expenses low: a rent-stabilized walk-up, Con Ed, the phone and answering service. She'd had a virtually empty savings account, a MasterCard she'd gotten when she'd opened her first account at Chemical Bank, but she'd never had binges on credit. She'd lived frugally, even marginally, and imagined it was fine, a part of *la vie bohème*. After all, she'd never known anything else.

Now, for Jahne Moore, the money was rolling in in swells, each wave larger than the previous one. First the Flanders Cosmetics check had come. Jahne still felt uncomfortable about plugging a product, but she'd had to sign to get the part, though she'd only agreed to one year, not the three they wanted. And the money was glorious! She'd sent off what she owed to Dr. Moore, and, despite taxes, Sy's agency and finder's fees, and legal expenses, she'd had over ninety thousand left!

Then, when Jahne got her first paycheck—almost fifty thousand dollars—and realized there would be another one in two weeks' time, she was staggered. When she had signed the contract with Sy, she had seen that she was paid thirty-three thousand an episode, but somehow, in the excitement, she hadn't had time really to focus on it. She'd just opened an account at California National and deposited it and the Flanders check. But as check after check came rolling in, she began to feel uneasy.

Now she stared at the bank balance on the latest monthly statement. Two hundred and seventeen thousand six hundred and sixty-three dollars and forty-seven cents! It was unbelievable. And, Jahne knew, it was only a start. Even though the series hadn't yet begun running on the Network, Sy Ortis had already forwarded her several new scripts for future consideration: they were lousy made-for-television quickies, but not one of them paid less than $250,000. A quarter of a million dollars for five weeks of work! She shook her head. With all of her New York scrambling, Mary Jane had never made more than thirty-five thousand in any year of her life.

Ortis also wanted to talk to her about authorizing a line of leather goods, jeans, and wallpaper, of all things, along with *Three for the Road* dolls—sort of biker Barbies, as she understood the deal. All of it, tawdry and ridiculous as it was, meant a lot more money. And though she had no intention of doing *any* of this proposed crap, she understood that she had fallen—or climbed—into a money stream that wouldn't stop flowing for some time. Look at Jaclyn Smith or Kate Jackson—since their first TV hit, they'd always had at least a TV-movie-of-the-week or a sitcom gig. Even Suzanne Somers and Farrah Fawcett at least had exercise-equipment ads to fall back on. What had Mary Jane ever had to fall back on but bedpans? And both nursing and New York acting had been hard work. This stuff was insultingly easy. And lucrative.

It was all unreal to her: just as she had felt the unfairness of never being able to live off her craft in New York, she felt the unfairness of receiving the gigantic amounts of cash for very little craft here in L.A. Was it simply her looks that had entitled her to this enormous windfall? It was ironic that she had bought them for about 15 percent of her income so far. Not a bad return on investment, she thought, smiling to herself.

Well, at least I'm not burdened by much financial guilt, she thought. After all those years of famine, she supposed she could deal with some years of fat, although not of the physical kind.

But what must it be like for those actors who never went through the struggle she had? Those who hit it big, fast, and early. No wonder they so often drifted into drugs, excess, and bankruptcy. The guilt would be difficult, the burden of responsibility too unmanageable. Even she, with years of experience, stared at her bank balance now, feeling both helpless and exalted, and wondered what she would do with all the money.

Of course, she could simply blow some of the money. She could finally afford nice clothes and had the body to wear them well. She could have another spending spree. But was that what she wanted to do? She probably would need to find a nicer place to live. But she didn't want to *buy* a place out here, and she wouldn't spend a lot on a rental. She stared again at the bank balance. Maybe she should give some to charity, or use some of it to help actors and playwrights? But how could she do that? I mean, you just don't send a check in the mail to Molly and Chuck or the latest off-off Broadway writer.

Well, she could send a check to Father Damien. His church had given shelter and an outlet to a lot of New York actors. And ten thousand dollars would mean a lot to him and almost nothing to her. She decided she'd do it. But should she give money to individuals? Endow the arts? As she continued to stare at the bank statement, she realized that, though she had suffered when she chose to live that way herself, she had *chosen* to live that way, and it made all the difference. As Mary Jane, she had never much felt that state-supported arts programs and private grants were good things. No, she wouldn't become a philanthropist to culture. What she *would* do, she decided, was find herself a pleasant little bungalow in Birdland. The Hollywood Hills was an area where the streets were named for birds—Oriole Drive, Robin Lane —and, since a lot of gays had moved there it had another nickname, the Swish Alps. They had converted middle-class two-bedroom houses into chic, tiny shangri-las. She'd rent one, furnished. For her it would be total luxury. And let's face it—things with her two roommates were getting tense. Although both girls spoke only of their pride and happiness for her, both had also already asked for loans *and* guest shots on the show. She felt that each one looked at her and asked herself, Why her and not me? She felt she was a constant goad to them, and she knew resentments would flare at any moment.

She put down the bank statement. That was it, then. She'd get a nice place of her own. And she'd put some of the money into a money market—nice and safe. But what about the rest?

Then she thought, unbidden, of what she could do, what she had to do.

She remembered her own agony at her adolescent reflection back in Scuderstown. And she'd been normal, if unlovely. But all that was coming her way now was coming because she was beautiful. What must it be like, how deeply damaging, to be born deformed? It was unimaginable, yet tears sprang to Jahne's eyes as she felt herself an imperfect infant in Lima, Peru, or a monster-faced toddler in Guatemala. Well, then, this was something she could do.

She stood, walked to the desk, and pulled out writing paper. The burden of the money had lifted. She took out her checkbook, and scrawled a check for one hundred thousand dollars. "Dear Dr. Moore," she wrote, and smiled as she added the dash and "Brewster."

> *I remember you once estimated that $20,000 was the cost for a mobile Interplast unit for a month. I enclose five units, which I hope gives, by my reasoning, about fifty kids their faces back. Try not to make them all look like me.*

> *Your grateful friend,*
> *Jahne Moore*

18

Sharleen looked down at the light-green check in her hands and blinked. She had to be careful counting all these numbers. It was hard to imagine how much was hers. She looked up at Mr. Ortis. "Just for wearing some lipstick? What do I do with it?" she asked.

"Put it in the bank."

"Which bank?" she asked.

"Your bank," Sy Ortis answered.

Sharleen laughed. "Mr. Ortis, I don't have no bank."

She and Dean had moved around so much, and they'd never had much money. Banks and schools and police stations—official places like that—made her nervous. She kept their money tucked in Momma's Bible.

She noticed Mr. Ortis lean back in his swivel chair, his eyes on her, then lean forward again and lift the phone.

"Tell Lenny to come into my office." He hung up and looked at her. "Honey, we're going to fix you up. I got a guy who's going to take care of everything—bills, investments, taxes—everything."

There was a polite knock at the door; then a tall, thin man with a serious face came in. He looked over at Sharleen, and his face didn't move a muscle. Sharleen smiled anyway. "Sharleen, this is Lenny Farmer. I'm making him your business manager." Sy looked up at Lenny and indicated the check in Sharleen's hand. "Set up a business account for Ms. Smith and draw up the necessary papers. Get power of attorney. And have Anita give her a cash advance." Sy turned to Sharleen and smiled. "So you can do some shopping for yourself today," he explained. "And now that the money is coming in, we'll find you a house, lease you a car, set up charge accounts at some of the better stores, arrange for credit cards. Whatever you need. You tell Lenny. You won't have to give another thought to money. All you have to do is spend it."

It was a load off her mind. For a moment, Sharleen wondered if it was really okay to trust Lenny Farmer—or anyone—with all that money. But, after all, there would be more paychecks. More than she and Dean could spend!

Sharleen walked out the door of Mr. Ortis' office building and across the parking lot toward Dean, who waited patiently in their Datsun. The brown manila envelope that Anita, the bookkeeper, had given her felt heavy in her hand as she swung herself in next to Dean. Before speaking, she broke the seal on the envelope and looked inside. "My, my, my," she murmured.

"What's the matter, Sharleen?" Dean asked. Sharleen had already explained to Dean how she was making a television show, just like Andy Griffith. She was never sure just how much Dean understood about what she told him. Of course, Sharleen was not understanding much of this herself, she admitted.

"What's the matter?" Dean asked again.

"Nothin', honey. Not one dang thing." Sharleen patted Dean on the shoulder and smiled. "I just got myself my first couple of paychecks, so let's go shopping. It's a lot of money, Dean. So what would you like more than anything else in the world?" She sat facing Dean, watching him search for an answer to her question.

"I don't know, Sharleen. I don't want anything. I got you, and a car, and we got a real nice apartment now. And I ain't hungry no more." He paused. "I don't know, Sharleen, I guess I don't want nothin'."

Sharleen urged him on. "Sure you do. I know there's something you've been wanting for a long time. Think, Dean."

Dean's brow knitted in thought. "Well, I always wanted a dog. A puppy. You know, a Lab. Maybe like Dobe's."

They had gotten a cat—a fat black stray that Dean had already named Oprah—but Sharleen wasn't sure about a dog. Still, why not? "Well, let's go then. What are you waiting for?" she asked, waving them forward with her hand.

Dean's eyes opened wide. "You mean it? We got *that* much money?"

"Dean, since I started playin' this part of Clover, we got more money than the richest man in Lamson."

Dean stepped on the gas and screeched out of the parking lot. "Wheeoo!" he screamed, as the sudden acceleration pulled them back into the bucket seats, the squeal of the tires quickly fading in the wind behind them.

The pet shop was not unusual for Los Angeles, Sharleen realized. *Everything* in this city was the best. The salesman—dressed in a gray suit, a white coat like a doctor, sleeves rucked up to his elbows, shirt collar buttoned, no tie—came from behind the desk. "What may I show you today?" he asked.

320

"We'd like to get a puppy," Dean blurted out.

"We'd like to see maybe a black Lab, if you got any."
Sharleen looked around the showroom as she spoke.
Nothing in here except those pictures on the walls of dogs
all brushed up. Bet they even smell pretty, she thought.
"Where do you keep the dogs?" she asked.

"You're in luck. Our collection is usually shown by
appointment, but since we had a last-minute cancellation,
we can present several to choose from today." He
pushed a button on the desk telephone. "Lisa, please
bring in the black Lab we were going to show Mary Tyler
Moore." He looked at Sharleen appraisingly. "And also
the setter, and the golden retriever," he added, *sotto
voce*.

Moments later, a young woman in another spotless
white doctor's coat opened the door and pushed in a cart
holding a basket of three puppies. Good Lord, Sharleen
thought as she noticed the huge blue satin bows on each
of them.

Dean hunkered down beside them. She watched him
as he breathed carefully on the face of each puppy, closing his eyes as they licked at his mouth and cheeks.
"Please, mister, take them bows off them. That ain't natural," he said. "Kin I touch them?" he asked.

"Sure!"

He dipped his hands into the basket. "Hey, Sharleen,
look at these guys. They're all beauts." He looked up at
her wordlessly. "I can't choose one and leave the others."

"Oh, Lord," Sharleen said to the salesman. "Why did
you have to bring out all three?" She patted her purse
crammed now with her mom's Bible and the manila envelope of money. It felt good, reassuring, and Mr. Ortis had
promised her another one, just as big, next week. She
looked down at Dean, who had the setter on his lap and
was holding the Lab, while the retriever was on the floor,
pulling at his sleeve. Dean laughed. "We'll take *all* of
'em," she said, and took the manila envelope from her
bag.

"*All* of 'em, Sharleen? Can we? Really?"

"Surely can. But what will we name 'em, Dean?" She

looked at his face, so happy. It made her want to cry. Neither of them spoke about the pup their daddy had killed.

"Can't name her Oprah now," Dean said, patting the black Lab. "But let's name the blonde one Clover!"

"That's it, Dean," Sharleen said, and began to laugh. "She's Clover, the black one is Cara, and the red one is Crimson. Just like on the show!"

Back in the car, Sharleen spoke over the yapping coming from the boxes in the back seat. "We got one more thing to do, Dean. Let's go to the supermarket, get some puppy chow, and fill that fridge and freezer at home. What do you say?"

The store was almost the size of the football fields they'd seen on TV. "Where do we begin?" Dean asked, bewildered.

"With an empty basket," she said. "Then we go up and down the rows and take anything—you hear me, Dean?—*anything*—we want from the shelves, as much as we want. Like that TV show where contestants have to fill their baskets in five minutes, and the one with the most wins? Let's do it like that. I'll take one and start at that end. You take the other and start here. I'll meet you in the middle. Okay?"

"Okay!"

"Ready, set, GO!"

Dean won. He was in the middle first, with the most. He had three baskets in tow. He even had stuff crammed *under* the baskets on the frame. "Sharleen, I never knew supermarkets could be so much fun. It was hard work, but let's do it again." He was puffing, trying to catch his breath.

"Sure thing, honey. Tomorrow, if you like. But that's not all yet. Now comes the real easy part. Paying for it."

19

Hollywood has always been a town where PR rules, where even the slickest operators will sometimes buy not only their own PR but the PR of others. I—Laura Richie —certainly know it and benefit from it every day: invitations to parties, press junkets, gifts, and even the always-tempting "consulting assignment"—just a legal bribe to help in the successful launching of a bum movie or a new TV show. Most publicity is bought, one way or another.

The strangest thing about the way Hollywood operates is perhaps the way PR (which everyone buys whenever they can) is so often believed by Industry suits and producers when it's bought by someone else. Once there is buzz about a film or an actor, the buzz seems to take on a life of its own. It is sometimes strong enough to create a success. Is it because the suits have no judgment? Is it because everyone is always desperate for a success? To steal the mantra of Marty DiGennaro, go know.

There was certainly the beginning of buzz about Di-Gennaro's Three for the Road, or 3/4 as it was being called by the insiders. Of course there were a lot of angles: three fresh faces, the revival of the sixties, and, most important, DiGennaro's debut on television. Twenty years in Hollywood had led me to believe that in this case the buzz was the real thing: not purchased PR but real excitement over something that could become the biggest hit of the season or any season. And that Lila Kyle, Sharleen Smith, and Jahne Moore were stars in the making.

Making a TV show was hard work. Jahne thought she knew about hard, from her off-Broadway and repertory work, where she'd sometimes been her own wardrobe mistress, run lights, and even had to move scenery from time to time. But this weekly TV show had a killing pace that made off-Broadway look like a day at the beach.

The weeks took on a pattern. She got her script only the night before taping began, read it, and began learning lines. The next day, she was on the set and in makeup by 6:00 A.M. Then Marty liked a run-through, and scenes were blocked, but there was almost no time for rehearsals. By the evening of the first day, a few scenes had actually been shot. She had to know her lines, make her marks exactly, know where the camera was; then, and only then, if she had any energy left, she could act. By seven each evening, she was wrung out, exhausted, and grateful for the limo and driver that got her home most nights by eight. Then she had a little (*very* little) something to eat, worked out, and fell into bed, only to start again the next morning. Each week, it went on for six days straight. On Sunday, she collapsed to rest, but Sunday evening she had to learn the new script. Try emoting after a couple of weeks of that schedule! Jahne had a new respect for the TV actors she and Molly and the gang at St. Malachy's used to mock.

She still saw Pete on the set, and he seemed to have become like all the other crew members: helpful and pleasant but standoffish. Well, she told herself, she couldn't have it both ways: to use him for affection when she wanted it, and to keep him in the background all the rest of the time. She supposed it was just as well that they had split: she had no energy except what she marshaled for work. In the evenings, she lived like a nun, and if she was often bored and lonely on the set, his presence there would not have helped that.

Then, one evening, she tuned in *Entertainment Tonight*. They were doing a segment on *3/4*. But before it came on, they led off with a shot of Crystal Plenum and Sam Shields. She sat, paralyzed. *Jack and Jill* was on location. She sat, and watched them interviewed. She sat, and gaped as Crystal Plenum played Jill in a clip from the movie.

And it was as if a vacuum opened up in her. A vacuum that sucked all she had gained right through her and left nothing: nothing but jealousy and emptiness.

In the vacuum, dreams and memories of Sam continued to haunt her. He rejected you, she told herself. He lied to you. He broke promises. But though all that was true, he had been passionate, fascinating, intense. He had really listened to her, really looked at her, really *known* her. He'd been capable of producing art, of discussing acting, theater, films, and of making her laugh. When she had free moments—on the set, or at home—the thought of Sam's laughter, *their* laughter and jokes, crept up on her. It robbed her of her concentration. It distracted her. But thoughts of Sam kept her company.

Because working on the TV program was a little like what the army must be like—all "hurry up and wait." It was exhausting always to be on call, always to have to be ready, waiting to go, and then at last actually to begin shooting, only to be told that a light needed adjustment, or a boom was down, or continuity had forgotten a prop, or a shadow had changed. A minute of screen time could take an hour to film, sometimes more. It was backbreaking, serious work.

In fact, on the set, the only laughing was done at Sharleen.

Jahne and Sharleen were poised on their bikes before one of the cycloramas used on the soundstage for *3/4*. As usual, there had been a lighting problem, and now that it had been fixed, as usual, Lila was making them wait. Jahne felt her makeup running, her forehead beginning to shine. At last, Lila sashayed out, without an apology.

"Lights up," Dino shouted, and the spots they had been setting were switched on.

"Hey, guys," Lila called out to the crew. "Do you know how a blonde turns on the light after sex?" There was an attentive silence from the fellows behind the lights and camera. "She opens the car door," Lila said, and smiled only slightly at the laughter that gusted out from the dark.

Sharleen blushed to her hairline. Jahne felt sorry for her. "Are you about ready now?" Jahne snapped at Lila. "Or do we have more stand-up to listen to?"

"*I* won't blow my lines eight times," Lila said, another dig at Sharleen. It was true. Sharleen got flustered and blew her lines fairly often. Jahne knew the girl must feel in over her head. Lila's hostility didn't help.

"Come on, now. Settle down," Marty told them as he replaced Dino on the set. Lila looked him over coolly, then threw an incredibly long leg over her Triumph. Once Lila had learned that the other two characters had Harleys, she had insisted her character would have the only Triumph.

Marty DiGennaro was no dummy, and even though he wasn't asking for much in the way of performances, Jahne could see that he had something simply in the juxtaposition of the three of them, so similar and yet so different from one another. It was the undeniable sexy and visually interesting combo of the motorcycles and the women, the hardness of steel and chrome, the softness of the three girls. After working with him for a couple of months now, she didn't actually like or trust Marty, or even knew what he was doing, but she respected his talent and shrewdness.

Talking of shrewdness, Lila Kyle was one cute cookie. Jahne had seen the type over and over in New York, the steal-the-scene-at-any-price ambitious starlet, but California seemed to raise these traits to the tenth power. Maybe it was the fault line, or the plethora of crystals, or just what Californians still seemed to call "vibes," but it was clear that Lila, totally beautiful, was also a total narcissist; no one else existed on the set, unless he or she was there to do something for her. Yet the crew loved her. And Lila had certainly seemed to win most-favored-nation status from Marty. Even when she wasn't being filmed, Marty's eyes followed her wherever she went. Jahne wondered if the two of them were playing hide-the-salami together.

Sharleen was the opposite. If Lila acted as if everyone was there to do as she wished, Jahne noticed that Sharleen would do what virtually anyone told her to. Even the grips and gofers bossed her. She called them all "Mister" and seemed absurdly grateful for the smallest thing —Jahne heard her thank the makeup man three times when he powdered her just before shooting started. Jahne still hadn't decided: was Sharleen for real, or was it the most complete hokum Jahne had yet seen? And what was it with that Bible? Sharleen sat there, in between takes, with it in her lap. Was she a born-again starlet?

Jahne felt she herself was fitting in nicely. Her character, Cara, was the smart one, the most cerebral of the trio, and the rest of the cast seemed to accept that about her, Jahne, because she played Cara. The crew seemed to like and respect her already, and she had established an easy, bantering relationship with Marty. She noticed, though, that he became irritated if she asked too many questions about what was going on. Discussions about motivation, or even the point of a script, were not welcome. Marty was a control freak. He had pictures in his head that he wanted to get on film. Her job was to do as he said. It was a far cry from her days with Sam and *Jack and Jill*. Marty said "Jump," they all asked "Where?" and then jumped. Except Lila, who sometimes felt the need to make a scene. Jahne found it all exhausting. She, after all, wasn't really twenty-four, despite her unlined face and what it said on her bio.

But, to be honest with herself, she was starting to feel disappointed. She had hoped that, with Marty at the helm, they would have an exciting ensemble, and a new kind of television. Certainly on the first score she was disappointed: Marty was the Boss, and only interested in moving them across the sets and locations in response to some internal vision that he never shared. But perhaps it *was* art they were making—art that would also be a commercial success.

In the few episodes they'd already taped there wasn't much *acting,* Jahne thought ruefully. Just as well, because neither Lila Kyle nor Sharleen Smith appeared to be an actress. They did each have something, though, Jahne readily admitted that. The camera loved them, and both had a naturalness that played. Jahne was afraid she, a more traditional actress, actually might not play as well, and that she didn't have the stamina to keep it up.

More than the demands of the script, the camera, and Marty, Jahne was afraid of Wardrobe. For the first fitting, she had been terrified of entering the room. How much would she have to expose? How much of her body scarring would show? She wore her usual Gap outfit—slim jeans and a white shirt, cowboy boots, and under her clothes a thin Lycra jumpsuit. It masked everything, a bit. But if they looked for them, the scars would show. Would they ask her to strip? Hesitantly, Jahne had walked in. She'd already met Bob Burton, head of wardrobe, and his assistant, an older woman whose name she'd forgotten. He did ask her to take off the clothes. She kicked off her boots, slipped out of her jeans, and shrugged the soft shirt from her shoulders. She stood, exposed like a silvery eel, wearing the smooth body stocking. She held her breath. Would she have to go further? What then?

"I've got the stuff laid out. Why don't you and Mai start on this?" Bob asked, lifting up a pair of bell bottoms, and left the room.

Mai, the old woman who was wardrobe mistress, turned away from the cluttered table that also served as her desk and came toward Jahne, measuring tape in hand.

"Some numbers for designer," she said, in a heavy accent that reminded Jahne of the cartoon character Natasha from the old Rocky and Bullwinkle shows. If she hadn't been so nervous, Jahne might have been tempted to giggle.

"First here," Mai said, rolling the "r," and encircled Jahne under her arms with the tape. The old woman then had to hold the tape at arm's length, her finger marking the spot. She nodded, made a mark on her pad, and next circled Jahne around the bust line. Then she stopped, looked at Jahne. "You are sveating," she said, bluntly.

Jahne was, like a horse, from nervousness. She shrugged. "The lights," she said.

"Bad for costumes," Mai said, then only shrugged again. She continued her measuring, while Jahne continued to perspire. "Vat you vould like?" Mai asked. "A towel, or I should put up air conditioner?"

"Please, yes, put up the air conditioner." Jahne knew that it wasn't the heat of the room that was causing her to perspire. But maybe the air conditioning would help. The old woman continued measuring and making notes. So far, she hadn't asked Jahne to strip, and perhaps she wouldn't. Jahne finally broke the silence, to take her mind off the process. "What are the costumes like? Have you seen any of the sketches?"

"Humph," Mai snorted. "Costumes? Cheans! Cheans and T-shirts, that's the costume. For this they need a designer?" She shook her head.

Cheans? Jeans! Jahne laughed. "But I bet they're beautiful. Marty DiGennaro wants everything perfect."

"Oh, yah, they are beautiful. And the shirts. Silk. And *your* color vill be blue. Best color for television camera. Vhite no good—drains face," Mai confided, then stood back from Jahne and asked, "That's good, no? You are definitely blue."

Jahne thought about it for a moment. Mary Jane had never worn blue. It somehow looked wrong on her. But now, with her hair highlights and her colored contact lenses, Jahne Moore's best color *was* blue, she suddenly realized. She smiled down at Mai. "Yes, blue *is* my color."

Mai smiled. "You are perfect veight. Not fat. But camera makes ten pounds fat, so ve must compensate. But don't be too thin. Like the redhead. Unnatural. The blonde will go soon to fat. But you vork hard to keep so, Mai can tell."

Mai couldn't tell *how* hard, Jahne thought. And so far, Mai wasn't able to tell what else Jahne had done to get this body. She thought back to New York, not only the operations, but the starvation diet she had placed herself on. The one she was *still* on. To those long, lonely afternoons in New York, going to cheap movies, trying to keep her mind off food. Eating nothing, or almost nothing, walking, walking, walking in the cold, in the rain even, afraid to go home, afraid to eat, afraid to rest. Her only interests were in losing the weight and watching old movies. Here, in sunny California, where everyone was thin and tan and happy, it was hard to connect with that other world, that other life. But even here she was afraid to eat. Coffee and fruit for breakfast, cottage cheese and salad for lunch, a small piece of chicken and a steamed vegetable for dinner. Or, if she had a beer, no dinner at all.

Jahne didn't like to think of those New York days, but something about the woman now kneeling at her feet nagged at her and brought New York back. Something about the movies. What was it? Certainly there were a lot of lonely old immigrant women in the movie theaters she had frequented, though this one, Jahne could see, had once been beautiful. Despite the wrinkles, despite the sunken cheeks, the bones of her face were still there. And the nose, the cheekbones, were still . . .

Jahne looked more closely.

Here, in the Wardrobe Department, looking down at the old woman's face, Jahne made the association. She remembered not the old women in the art-theater *audience*, but the young woman on the *screen*, the painfully beautiful star, the one who had starred in those prewar von Sternbergs, the only woman of the time who could compete with Dietrich, the woman who was, in Jahne's opinion, more beautiful than Dietrich.

"My God! You are Mai Von Trilling!" Jahne cried.

The woman shook her head and smiled, a small, polite smile. "No, no," she corrected. "I *vas* Mai Von Trilling."

20

April waited for her latest secretary to usher in the moronic journalist from the *L.A. Times* who was doing some puff piece on her. She had no time for this bullshit, but after she was featured on the cover of *West Coast* as the winner of the world's-worst-employer contest, scoring lower even than the South African diamond mines, Public Relations had suggested this as a counter. So she'd waste a valuable forty minutes with a jerk from the press.

April Irons was her own greatest invention, and, like any great invention, she worked well. In fact, some people said that work was all she did, but she didn't give a rat's ass what people said. You didn't get to run a major movie studio by caring about what a bunch of hard-ons said.

Running production at International Studios made her the *capo de tutti capi*. She got to green-light all the other producers' projects, as well as produce a few of her own. She had power: power over them, and power to do what she wanted, as long as the bottom line looked good to Bob LeVine and the International stockholders.

At forty-four (though all the publicity put her three years younger), April Irons could, at last, *do* what she wanted and *be* what she wanted. After all those rocky years, hustling for a few dollars to produce some book or play that she'd managed to option for a buck three-eighty, she'd finally gotten a few credits under her belt. Not that any of the sons-of-bitches in the Industry had helped her. She'd spent four years working at Warner's, doing coverages of every piece of shit that came in the mail sacks, trying desperately to get the ear of someone, anyone that mattered. She'd begged for a job with Ray Stark, with John Huston. And she got them: carrying bags. *Nona: A Life* had been the low-budget hit that was her breakthrough, and she'd done it without anyone's goddamn help. She'd used all her savings, the sixty thousand dollars her grandfather had left her and the money from a second mortgage that her mom took out on her house in Brookline, Massachusetts. When April finally got distribution from an independent, she was down to paying for prints with her MasterCard advances. But the critics ate it up, and it had legs: first the young and the hip, then the suburban intelligentsia. Finally, Orion picked it up, and even the mall rats got to see it. Then she'd followed it up with *Request*. She'd gotten Angela Blake to do her first nude scene. April had been able to get good distribution for it. *It had done eight million its first weekend, and the fucker only cost four.*

And that, my dear, was the trick. She'd gotten out of independent producing and into a studio, working with other people's money—money she didn't have to raise. And she had the formula. Be very smart, be brave, work your balls off, and never let the motherfuckers tell you no.

Now she looked at the journalist sitting across the coffee table from her. They came in three varieties: overly ambitious ass-kissers who wanted a job as a *quid pro quo* for good press; normally ambitious ass-kissers who simply wanted access and to get to do another story again someday; and, lastly, the bitter ass-kissers, who would grill you and misquote you just to get a byline, a few bucks, and some mindless spleen vented.

All Hollywood called her the Iron Maiden. The real joke was that half of them also called her a nympho, while the other half called her a dyke. Which doubled her chances of getting laid, but *that* was *never* a problem. Certainly not now that she had so much power.

The reporter, a rumpled-looking kid in his late twenties, shambled in and nervously took his seat. She made an attempt at a smile, asked the girl to bring them some coffee, and looked at him attentively. They began with the usual half-assed questions: was it hard to be a woman in this business, what accomplishment was she proudest of, what trends did she see? She answered, her mind going over her afternoon. She wanted to freshen up before lunch, when she was meeting Sam Shields. It looked like *Jack and Jill* would work, and she was considering signing him up for another movie.

She was also considering him for a more personal job: her consort. She was sick of the pathetic men she'd been seeing: the ones outside the Industry bored her, the ones inside took advantage. But Sam Shields had amused her. He had a detachment that attracted her, a stupid East Coast snobbery that she found naïve and old-fashioned. Plus, he was a man who actually liked women, and there were few enough heterosexual men who loved females around.

Maybe Sam did not love them exactly—what man ever *really* loves a woman?—but he liked those things about women that women like about themselves. Softness, gentleness, complimentary colors. Femininity. Femaleness. April had enjoyed their brief affair. Of course, then Sam had gone after Crystal Plenum, like . . . like every man had gone after Crystal. And, as usual, Crystal had reciprocated. April expected it, knew Crystal had fucked every director she'd ever worked with. And April didn't really give a shit. Hey, whatever was good for the project.

But now the picture was over, and, as she knew so well, so was the love affair. Crystal would be reconciling with her husband/manager and then moving on to her next affair. And Sam would be ready for something new. April decided that something would be her. He looked right, he might be the new, hot *auteur*, and they would make a good team. Maybe even a marriage. Because, at forty-four, it was time.

April decided to give the kid with the pencil another three minutes. Then it was off to lunch with Sam at The Grill. "Any more questions?" she asked him brightly, pulling out her dark-red lipstick to freshen her immaculate makeup.

"Well, actually, I read recently that, before you fired your last secretary, you spent a month calling her 'Bitch' instead of her name. Is that true?"

April stopped, her hand with the lipstick frozen in midair. Hadn't anyone briefed the little putz that there would be no questions of this nature?

She turned her gray eyes on him coldly. "Get this straight," she told him. "I *never* called that cunt a bitch." She stood up. "You can go now," she said.

The drive to The Grill was taken up with a call to Public Relations to deal with the *L.A. Times,* so she had only a moment or two to prepare herself for Sam. He sat, waiting at the bar, his long body curved into a sulking question mark. Well, Sam was definitely the dark type. It was why she liked him. She was sick of California sunshine and businessmen.

"Postpartum blues?" she asked Sam as she approached the bar. One of the independent producers who had recently pitched her was sitting on the stool next to Sam, and he immediately vacated it for April. She took it without acknowledgment, and waited for Sam's answer.

"Isn't that what women get after giving birth to a baby?"

"Yeah, but directors get it, too, after they've given birth to their baby." Sam didn't answer, just stared sullenly ahead. "If I have to get my own drink, then what the fuck am I sitting here with you for?" she asked sweetly.

Sam tried to shake himself out of his blue mood. "I'm sorry, April. What would you like?"

"To drink?"

Sam looked at her. "Yes. Or whatever."

"Get me a Stoli iced. Then get yourself a real drink instead of beer, for chrissakes, and let's sit over there, at my table." April walked away from the bar and Sam followed with the drinks, his now a vodka also.

"So, are you taking me to the premiere?" she asked. She tried to sound casual.

"If I have to go, there's no one I'd rather go with than you."

"Of course you have to go. And it's for a good cause."

"You mean the kids' charity it benefits?"

She laughed. "No. I mean International's stockholders."

"Just tell me one thing: are you *always* thinking about the business?"

"Let me tell you a couple of things. One of them I already did: Directors get depressed when their movie is finished. It's natural. Everyone gets depressed when the shoot's finished. That's why we have wrap parties, to try to soften the blow." April took a sip of her drink. "The other thing, Mr. Broadway, is, every director fucks his star, and every star fucks her director. It's never love, and rarely even respect. It happens because it gives a level to the communication between director and actress that they wouldn't have without it. Sometimes it shows on the screen. It's good for the picture."

Sam grinned and shook his head. "You're a real piece of work, April. I appreciate your loving concern, but how come you're so worried about me? I'm a big boy, I can take care of myself. If I'm down, I'll get back up. And one actress doesn't a love affair make. Don't have any illusions, April. A good fuck is a good fuck. And when it's over, it's over."

April was surprised by how much she liked this guy. This was almost fun. "So why the doom and gloom?"

Sam paused, sipped his drink, put it down on the table, and looked directly at her. "I have some decisions to make. I have to decide on my next job, whether I'm going to stay out here or go back to New York. . . . I have a lot on my mind."

"Well, let me give you some more to chew on. How would you like to do another movie for me?"

"You rejected my plays."

"I didn't say your *plays*. I said a movie."

"What movie?"

"Forget about that, and just answer the question. How would you like to work with me again?"

Sam let a grin cross his face. "I'd rather eat broken glass," he said, still smiling.

"I don't know how to take that. It means yes if you like eating broken glass, and no if you don't. So which is it?" She was smiling back at him now.

"I've got to give you this, April. You *do* know how to get things done. I've never worked with anyone who was so on top of things. Seymore was a shmuck. But getting a decision out of you is a pleasure. Watching you arrive at one is also a pleasure."

"So I'll take that as a yes. And I've made one of my famous decisions. I want to do a remake of *Birth of a Star*. I managed to snag the rights to it. I'd like you to direct it."

Sam stopped smiling, looked away, and shook his head. "I don't do remakes."

"Did you ever see the original?"

"No," he admitted, a little sheepishly.

"Good. So for you it won't be a remake. It'll be original. Now, will you do it?"

"You have a script?"

"You want to write it?"

"I swore I would never work on someone else's story."

"You changed your mind. Hey, it's a classic. Guy on

335

the way down falls for girl on the way up. Love affair. Disaster. But we set it all modern. Liberated. Nineties.''

"Who for the male lead?"

"Michael McLain."

"Michael McLain? Jesus Christ, April, the guy is over the hill."

"Exactly. It's called typecasting, and a brilliant stroke of genius, if I do say so myself. Plus, he's cheaper than he used to be, and reliable. I hear there's trouble on his latest deal, a Ricky Dunn movie that might not happen. After *Akkbar*, if it falls through, he's got to give this everything he's got or he's out of the arena."

Sam thought for a moment. "Who for the female lead?"

"Suggest someone."

"Don't know. But if we're getting McLain 'cause he's really on the slide, let's get someone really on the way up. *Cinéma vérité*."

"Like who?"

"Maybe Phoebe Van Gelder. Or the girl who was featured in that last Redford thing."

"It's a possibility."

"Or how about one of the girls from the Marty DiGennaro thing? They're getting beaucoup publicity, and I think they're going to be hot now."

April looked at him, nodding in thought. Wasn't one of them the daughter of Theresa O'Donnell? She'd starred in the other *Birth of a Star*. That would be good for lots of press coverage. "I don't know. Television isn't the movies."

"Only movies are the movies. But the casting would be *perfect*. They're new, they're fresh, and any one of them would be great juxtaposed against the old harlot Michael McLain."

"Plus, it doesn't hurt that they're gorgeous and very fuckable, right? But can they act?" April laughed. "I'd rather go with a movie neophyte than a TV star."

"But one of them might be able to make the transition easily."

"Sure, that's what they said about Tony Geary."

"Who?"

"My point. The balding guy from *General Hospital*. Luke of Luke and Laura. Tried the big screen."

"I never saw him."

"Neither did anyone else."

Sam sighed. "Well, there's a lot of talk about the show and them now. Wouldn't it be a good thing to check it out?"

"Talk is cheap, especially talk *before* the show is out. But if you're interested, I could get an advance copy and we could screen it."

"Come on. No one can even get in there. DiGennaro is a nut about secrecy."

"I can get it."

It might even be interesting, she thought. And if it pissed off Marty, it might be worth it. Yes. Yes, it certainly might be.

Sam turned his body toward April, and looked at her. "Do you know everyone and everything?" he asked.

"Everyone and everything worth knowing," she told him, and slowly licked her blood-red lips.

21

Lila came back to Robbie's house from a long day of househunting with a dreadful headache. She climbed into bed and prayed he wouldn't bother her. She rubbed her forehead and tried to adjust the pillow so that her neck was supported. The Malibu sunlight had made her eyes water and intensified the pain at her temples. But now, at least, she knew her stay here was ending. She'd have the chance to get away from Robbie and his constant prying and badgering. She'd rent the Nadia Negron house—the home of the silent-film star who had played the lead in the very first *Birth of a Star*. It was more than a coincidence—she was destined to live there.

Because she needed a place of her own. Marty DiGennaro and 3/4 were only a stepping-stone to the larger career she wanted. It was nerve-racking not knowing if the show was any good or not. If it came out and flopped, she knew that the Puppet Mistress would do a victory dance. And that Ara would dump her. Even Robbie would be disappointed in her.

Well, if she had her own place, she could have more privacy, more control. And maybe, just maybe, she could bear to let Marty DiGennaro touch her, if that was what he wanted. But first she had to make sure he wanted her badly. Really, really badly. And she knew how to do that.

There was a knock at the door, that annoying whisper of a knock Robbie used when he wasn't supposed to be knocking at all.

"What is it?" Lila asked, exasperated.

Robbie rolled in, the cordless phone in one hand, his face an exaggerated moue of excitement.

"It's your director," he whispered.

Inwardly, Lila smiled. But she only winced before Robbie. "Oh, God. Not again. Why didn't you say I was out?"

"Because it's Marty DiGennaro, the biggest director in Hollywood and your boss. That's why. Can't you make an effort, for heaven's sake?"

Angrily, she reached out for the receiver. She wondered what pretext he would use now. A private screening? An extra run-through? Since shooting started, Lila felt that Marty had become more and more insistent on seeing her outside of work. But she had to make sure it was only her that he wanted. Not just any of the three of them.

"What is it?" she asked into the receiver.

"What's the matter, Lila? You sound ill."

"I have a headache."

"I'm sorry. I wouldn't have bothered you if I'd known."

"That's all right. What is it?" she repeated, but she did feel a little better.

"I wanted to know if you could have dinner with me. But not if you don't feel well."

"Call Jahne or the dumb one. You could eat with them."

338

"Oh, come on. Are you really sick? Would you like me to bring over anything? Advil or chicken soup?"

"No thanks, Marty, I'll be fine. I'll see you tomorrow."

"Okay. But I hope you feel better soon."

"I doubt it," she told him.

But by the time she'd hung up and Robbie left her, Lila found her headache had gone away.

22

The uncharitable in Hollywood would call Michael McLain a pimp, but they would do so quietly. He was too powerful and well connected to insult to his aging, pretty-boy face. If you asked for Laura Richie's opinion —and why shouldn't you?—I would agree, but I would add that he was a dual career pimp. Like Sy Ortis, Michael McLain had decided to try and keep the bodega. As a young actor, he had foreseen that the tides of stardom did not flow predictably. If he could have a fallback position, something that kept him in the public eye for those times when his current movie did not, he would be far better positioned to weather the storm.

And what better position than a recumbent one? Michael's policy was to bed the hottest Hollywood newcomer. If his first career was being a movie star, his second career was making love to, and headlines with, the most beautiful, wanted women on the planet. Nice work if you could get it, but work it was. Michael had schooled himself not only in his sexual techniques but also in those dozens of small wooing gestures and comments that made him irresistible and indispensable to the girls who became the Hollywood flavors of the month.

And if, when the flavor lost its tang, he moved on, who could blame him? Everyone else did the same. That was the nature of a flavor of the month. After all, who wants a steady diet of Pecan-Walnut Fudge? Certainly not Americans. They want their Cherry Garcia to be followed by Cashew Rocky Road, and after an addiction to Rain Forest Crunch, a switch to French-Mocha Praline is not only pleasant but necessary. After all, he never promised them forever. In fact, Michael McLain was very careful; he never promised them anything.

Michael now lay on the portable massage table that his therapist had set up for their weekly session. Clear plastic tubes lay on the table beside them. "Roll over," Marcia told him. Each week, she administered a high colonic to Michael, as well as another two dozen stars and spouses of stars. Michael insisted on the clear tubing, to be sure that she flushed out enough material. "A clean colon is a healthy colon," he always repeated. His crazy sister had turned him on to Marcia, and for once she made sense. The time he spent on the table was the time he used for thinking, and he found that, despite the discomfort of Marcia's hose pushed up his butt, the satisfaction in watching those toxins flushed past his line of sight soothed him. He did his best thinking then.

Now he was considering how he might proceed. There was no doubt in his mind that he could win the bet with Sy and have all three of the girls from the new show. To accomplish it would not be easy. Still, Michael was a veteran of difficult campaigns and almost never took no for an answer. Plus, the prize was so alluring. Not the women—long ago, Michael had begun considering them more work than treats—but star billing over that little prick Ricky Dunn. The kid was as hot as Michael had been twenty years ago. Everything Ricky touched turned to box-office gold. If Michael could maintain star billing over Ricky and also get fresh exposure to that sixteen-to-twenty-one-year-old crowd, he knew that he could really score.

So how could he score with the three new TV pussies? He felt a sudden cramping in his gut as Marcia turned on the water. "Hey, watch it," he told her sharply.

"Sorry, Michael."

He shifted on his knees, his butt still raised high in the air. He felt the pressure as the water continued to press up into his intestine. "Ouch," he cried, and looked toward the plastic to see if more than the usual feces was breaking away.

"Sorry, Michael. Have you been eating red meat?"

"No, goddamn it." He was sick of being blamed for her incompetence. He hadn't eaten red meat since 1981, for God's sake. A lot of other therapists would die for the chance to do *his* colonics. "Watch it," he told her, and tucked his knees tighter under his chest.

He considered the girls. He had seen that Sharleen, the blonde, would be no problem. He'd done some checking, and it seemed that she was living with some kid, but that didn't trouble him much. After all, he didn't want a *relationship* with her. With the right setup, it seemed like it wouldn't take more than a couple of dates to be photographed together. Trash like that would probably be willing to do it in the limo. That would give him a witness for Sy Ortis, in case he needed one.

Jahne Moore, the dark-haired one, seemed a little more problematic. Word on the set was that she and Lila Kyle did not get along. Should he let her and Lila know that he was pursuing both of them? Let them do the work of pursuing *him?* If they didn't like each other much, did they dislike one another enough to be jealous? Would they compete for him the way they competed on the set?

He grunted as the suction in his gut intensified. Nah, he didn't think that approach would work. Jahne Moore was a New Yorker, playing at the serious-actor bit. Maybe he could work on that. After all, when he first came to Hollywood, he had made some arty-farty films. But had little Jahne Moore ever heard of them? They were two decades old now, probably older than she was.

Of the three, it was Lila Kyle who troubled him most. He doubted she could be easily impressed with the star razzmatazz. Of course, with only an unaired TV show to her credit, she was not a star yet. But she'd watched that game her whole life. He had heard not only about her bratty behavior but about how Marty DiGennaro had begun to cater to it. If so, Michael would have to come up with something even more attractive than copping all the close-ups on your television show. That was a tall order. Michael smiled. Maybe Lila would like the part of the female lead in the movie with Ricky Dunn. Of the three, Michael figured Lila was the only one worth pursuing into a relationship. Yes. If he made a film where Ricky got the girl, but *he* got her in real life . . . She would be striking in photographs, of course, but, more important, even if the TV show went down in flames, she was the newest generation of Hollywood royalty. Pictures of him with Lila would help him stay forever young. Michael smiled. More than twenty years ago, he had had a brief fling with Theresa O'Donnell—it was his older-woman phase. She'd been a maniac in bed. Like mother, like daughter, Michael thought.

The noise of the colonic device subsided. "All finished?" he asked.

"Clean as a whistle," Marcia told him.

Sharleen heard the baseball bat as it connected with her father's skull. Thunk. Thunk. She shut her eyes and turned away and heard a siren. No, it was a phone. She was dreaming that a telephone was ringing. The sound of the phone pushed through the haze of sleep, until she realized that she was awake, and the ringing telephone was the one on the floor next to their bed. She turned toward the sound, and saw the green illuminated dial of the clock: 8:53 P.M. She and Dean were in bed by eight most nights. After all, she had to be up by five. The three puppies at the foot of the bed snuggled more deeply into the blanket. She moved Dean's paint-splattered arm from across her waist and placed it gently by his side, then leaned over the side of the bed and picked up the phone in mid-ring. "Hello?" she muttered, then cleared her throat.

"Hi, is this Sharleen?"

"Yes," she said, sleepily. Who was it? Only Sy Ortis, Mr. DiGennaro, and Lenny, her business manager, had her new, unlisted number. Oh, and Dobe, if he was picking up his mail. This voice wasn't any of theirs, and Sharleen didn't know anyone else that might call her. But the voice *was* familiar. She pushed her fuzzy brain to try and think.

"This is Michael McLain. Did I get you at a bad time?"

"Oh, *come on*." Had one of the guys on the set gotten her number? Barry Tilden, the new assistant director, was always teasing her. *"Sure* it is," she added, sarcastically. After all, she wasn't a fool. Then she heard the laugh at the other end of the phone. Oh, Lord, it did *sound* like Michael McLain—just like in that scene in his movie *The Last Stranger*, where he's challenged by the bad cop and, even though he knows he's going to lose, he laughs.

"If I'm getting you at a bad time, please . . ." His voice trailed off.

"How did you get my number?" And, more to the point, why would Michael McLain—if it *was* Michael McLain—be calling me? she thought.

"Sy gave it to me. Sy Ortis. He's my agent, too. I know it must be an intrusion," he said, but it didn't sound like he meant it. There was a slight pause; then he added, his voice lower, "Do you mind?"

"Are you *really* Michael McLain?" Sharleen asked. He laughed again. There was no mistaking it. Sharleen sat up, her back against the bare wall. Dean continued sleeping, unaware. "Mr. McLain, why, no, I don't mind. But are you sure you got the right person?"

"If you're the Sharleen Smith that's the star of Marty DiGennaro's new TV show, I do." Then that laugh again.

"Costar," she corrected. She wanted to be fair. "There is no star." Dean stirred in his sleep next to her in the bed. He was exhausted from painting their new house all day, he had collapsed into bed before eight, too tired to eat anything more than the Big Mac she'd brought home for him. And Sharleen was happy to join him. She was tuckered out each night, too. She'd finished six straight days of shooting, but thank the Lord tomorrow was her day off. "Mr. McLain, could you hold on a minute?"

"Sure," he said.

Sharleen laid the receiver down and slipped out of bed. They were so rich now, she had a phone in the living room, the kitchen, and even the bathroom. Turning around, she pulled the sheet up over Dean's back, then tiptoed over the plastic throw-cloths scattered around, hoping the crackling sound wouldn't wake him. She walked into the bare living room, closed the bedroom door behind her, snapped on the wall switch, wincing as the six bare bulbs in the light fixture hanging from the ceiling cast a harsh light, and sat cross-legged on the floor next to the extension phone, her shorty pajamas leaving her behind bare against the cold floor. Was Michael McLain really on the phone, or was this a joke or even a dream? She rapped her knuckles sharply on the phone. Her knuckles hurt. It was no dream. Picking up the receiver, she said, "Thanks for waiting, Mr. McLain. I just needed to get comfortable." She put her sore knuckles in her mouth.

"Michael, please. Are you alone?"

Sharleen looked around the large, empty room. "As a matter of fact, I am," she said. Well, Dean *was* sleeping in the bedroom, wasn't he? He wasn't there, so she was alone, she told herself. Anyway, this must be business.

"Good. Then how about having dinner with me?"

"Dinner? *You* want to have dinner with *me?*" If this *was* Barry Tilden with another one of his gags, boy, she'd sure look foolish. "I mean, sure. When?"

"How about tonight?"

Sharleen looked down at her shorty pajamas. "But I already ate," she said. Anyway, it was nine o'clock. Normal people ate at five or six. She didn't mean to turn Mr. McLain down or be rude. Could she go out and leave Dean? But could she say no to Michael McLain, if it really *was* him? Well, she had said no, she realized, and sighed.

"Okay, how about a drink, then?"

"I don't drink, neither." Sharleen paused. "But, if you like, maybe we could have some coffee."

"Great idea," Michael said. "I'll pick you up in twenty minutes. You're over in the Valley, right?"

"Yes. But maybe you should make it thirty minutes, if you don't mind," Sharleen said. "I need to change what I'm wearing."

Sharleen hung up, then sat motionless for a moment, her hand still on the receiver. This couldn't be happening to me, she thought. Michael McLain just doesn't call up strange girls out of the blue and ask them out. But this was Hollywood, and she was going to be a television star once the series came out, she reminded herself again. And *nothing* can be stranger than that. She jumped up quickly and ran across the shiny wood floor to the bedroom. She wasn't so careful not to make noise now; she had to find something to wear. She pulled the plastic off the floor lamp, and turned it on. Looking around the room at the boxes and suitcases through the opaque covering, she decided to start with the big brown suitcase she had bought on a shopping trip with Dean, and filled the same day. She pulled it out and began to go through the mass of new clothes, finally settling on a powder-blue silk shirt and a pair of white jeans.

Sharleen dressed quickly, then went into the bathroom and washed her face. She applied the liquid-base makeup the way Marcel on the set had shown her. Then the smallest amount of blusher, right above her cheekbone. She brushed her hair quickly, pulled it back in a pony tail, and tied it with a blue scarf.

As she walked through the bedroom again, Dean just barely raised his head. "What are you doing up, Sharleen?" His voice was groggy with sleep.

"Go back to sleep, honey. I have to go out for a while. It's business."

"You work too much," Dean mumbled, and his head dropped back onto the pillow. She stroked his back, then, seeing that he was breathing deeply again, walked quietly out of the room, switched off the light, and closed the door. In the living room, she put on the strappy sandals she'd held dangling from her hand, and left the house. She'd wait out in front for Michael, to avoid having Dean disturbed by the car's engine or a honk. It reminded her of those nights she'd waited for Boyd Jamison. Standing there in the dark California-soft night, Sharleen felt a momentary thrill. This was their property now, a nice house of their own, with a garden and a pool. And, Momma, she thought to herself, I even got a date with your favorite movie star.

Sharleen sat on a chair just inside the wrought-iron gate that looked out onto the curving driveway. Lenny had found them the house, and it was real nice, plus Dean loved the yard. She waved at Bert, the security guard in the development, but kept herself from blurting out that she was waiting for Michael McLain. Glaring headlights caused her to close her eyes for a moment; when she opened them, she saw the most beautiful limousine pulling up at the front door, black and shiny with chrome that shone like silver. It wasn't a regular limo—it was some kind of English car or something. Maybe it *was* silver, she thought. For a moment, she wished Dean were here to see it. But, she reminded herself, that could lead to trouble.

She saw Bert approach the car and lean into the driver's door even before it hardly stopped, taking off his cap as he did. Meanwhile, from the back, a man got out and turned toward the front door, and Sharleen felt her hands get cold. Michael McLain. It really was him. Then he was standing in front of her, smiling. Sharleen finally spoke. "You *are* Michael McLain," she said.

Michael took her hand in both of his, as if to warm her, laughed, and said, "And *you're* Sharleen Smith."

Sharleen giggled, and took her hand back from him to cover her mouth. "Of course you are. We are. I mean . . ." She stood up, still looking up into his famous blue eyes. "They *are* real blue," she said.

"Everything about me is real," Michael said, and took her by the elbow to lead her to the car. Bert held the passenger door open as Michael handed her in; then Michael crossed in the headlights, and his driver held open his door. Then the driver pulled the car out onto the boulevard.

"Where are we going?" she asked. Not that it mattered —she'd go anywhere with Michael McLain.

"Wherever you want," he said. "Still want a coffee?"

"Sure. Do you know a place?"

"I know just the one. West Hollywood. Around La Brea?"

"Never been there."

She saw Michael look at her again. "You *are* new in town, aren't you?" Without waiting for an answer, he continued, "The shops on Melrose Avenue are different from any of the other places in L.A. Most of them will be closed, but we can walk around and look in the windows. Everybody does."

"What's it like?" she asked. And what will it be like walking on the street—in public—with Michael McLain? Sharleen felt giddy.

"They have the hottest shops in town. You'll see some of the prettiest boutiques, and *the* latest designs. Not that you need them. You're perfect just as you are."

She blinked at the compliment, flustered.

Then he began asking questions. Questions about the show, about her costars, about her life before. It was real nice, if only she hadn't been nervous not to mention Dean, or her daddy or Lamson. But he made it easy. He seemed so interested. Slowing down after turning onto La Brea, Michael said, "Here we are. Let's park and walk."

Sharleen had never seen anything like it. Even on Rodeo Drive. There was a shop all filled with leather— even a leather bikini. Maxwell's had clothes by Japanese designers. Sharleen felt like she was in a new world.

"I have to bring you back here when they're open," Michael said, as they passed a store with a sign outside that read "Twist." Sharleen looked in the windows and agreed. The clothes were all tight and flouncy, both at the same time. "No one over twenty should wear this stuff. It's scary on them. But they'd be great for you," he added.

Sharleen felt her face begin to flush, and spoke before the blush became noticeable. "Look at the name of *that* store," she said quickly. " 'Wacko'! I like that."

Michael slowed down, looked over at the sign and laughed with her. "Let's go to Jackson's Place and have some cappuccino," he said, and took her elbow in the palm of his hand. There was something about the way he held her, something hard. For a moment, Michael's touch made Sharleen feel that old fear. Then she quickly reminded herself that this was Michael McLain, and not some trucker on a back road in Texas.

"Jackson? Not *Michael* Jackson? We're going to his place for coffee?"

Michael laughed, not unkindly, she noticed. "Well, no, it's just a café. But it's a nice one. And they know me there."

Sharleen laughed out loud. "People know you *anywhere.*"

Michael greeted the hostess by name as they made their way from the main entrance to the corner table in the rear of the restaurant. Once seated, Michael ordered cappuccino for them both, then looked directly at Sharleen. She didn't know what the stuff was, but she'd drink it. Embarrassed, she looked around the glittering café. "Everyone in here is staring at you," she said.

"No, Sharleen. I'm old news. They're staring at *you,*" Michael told her.

Sharleen shifted in her chair slightly, and was grateful for the arrival of the waitress with the coffee. "Excuse me just a minute," he said, as the coffee was being served, and walked out of the restaurant. Oh, Lord, had she been so dull that he was going to leave without her? What would she do? Well, she could call a taxi, or if she had to she could call Dean. But then, in only a few moments, he returned to their table. "I'm sorry, I had to take care of something."

"I just can't get over you calling me up," Sharleen said after he sat down. "Did Mr. Ortis ask you to? He's afraid I don't get out enough, but, between work, and my new place, and memorizing scripts, I just don't . . ." She realized she was talking too much, and took a sip of cappuccino. "I sure do love this coffee. I never knew coffee could taste so good."

Michael smiled, reached into his jacket pocket, and pulled out a little box, all wrapped in pretty blue paper with a white ribbon. He handed her the present, all dressed out so nice.

Sharleen was confused. "What is it?" she asked, not reaching for the box.

"It's a little present from me to you. To welcome you to town. Go ahead, open it."

Sharleen untied the bow and lifted the cover from the

box. She pushed the tissue paper aside, then cried, "Oh, Michael." It was a necklace. She took the delicate chain out. Three stars were suspended from it, and it looked like there was a diamond in the center one. Sharleen had never had a diamond. She held it up to her face, as if looking into the stone. "It's beautiful," she said softly, then looked up to Michael. "But I can't keep this!" Still, her heart cried out for it.

"You'll hurt me if you don't keep it. And I can't take it back. Keep it."

"Thank you," Sharleen said, her eyes moist. "I never had nothin' like it before."

Michael was smiling broadly. "Of course not. I had it made for you."

"You did? But why?" Sharleen asked as she cradled the necklace in her hand.

"Because you're a star. One of three, but from what I hear *you're* the only diamond."

"Really?" Sharleen asked. "Oh, no!" But she blushed with pleasure. She had so far felt she was the least of the three. But she was the one Michael McLain had called.

"Wear it for luck," he said. "I think you're a very lucky girl." He smiled and helped her clasp it around her neck. "Now, how about finishing your coffee? I want to show you something else."

"I'm ready," Sharleen said, and jumped up. She was having such a good time.

Michael paid the bill, and followed Sharleen to the door. As they walked around the tables, she saw that people *were* looking at her, too. But that was because she was with *him,* she was sure.

Then there were lights—two or maybe three flashes. She winced and jumped in surprise. "It's nothing," Michael told her. "Just reporters. You'll be in all the papers tomorrow."

When they got into the car and pulled out, Sharleen turned toward Michael and asked, "Why are you being so nice to me?"

Michael smiled. "Because you're new in town, and probably could use a friend to show you the ropes." Then he put his hand gently on her knee for a moment and looked at her. "And because you're very easy to be nice to."

This was *too* easy, Michael told himself, partly satisfied and partly bored. She's either real smart or real dumb, and he figured it was the latter. She wouldn't last in this town. Meanwhile, he already had pictures of the two of them together, the necklace round her neck. It would probably be enough for Sy, but Michael felt he might as well do the thing. After all, she *was* attractive.

He checked the ice bucket at the side of the console. The Moët was chilled. Jim knew his job and did it well. For six years now, he'd driven Michael around in this Rolls, kept it in immaculate condition, and discreetly assisted in the seduction of the moment. Without a word spoken, he knew to drive up to the hills, to the spot Michael had used so often before. It happened to be right where Monty Clift had cracked up his car and his face.

"It's so pretty in the moonlight. I've never been up in these hills before," Sharleen said. "Can we stop somewhere for a while?" she asked. "I want to see the lights."

"Good idea," Michael said. "I'll have Jim pull over to a little place at the top of this hill. Wait until you see the view."

It was spectacular. Even after all the years of bringing woman after woman up here, it still impressed him. His town. Tinseltown. All of it stretched out before them, little lights twinkling. "Oh. It's beautiful," the girl gasped, right on cue. Jim pulled over.

"Let's go out to that rock," Michael suggested. "That's the best view." He took out the bottle of Moët. Then he grabbed two champagne flutes off the hanging rack and led the way.

Sharleen followed. The night air, for once, was clear, and scented with the pungent smell of eucalyptus and brush. Below them lay the entire city of Los Angeles. She walked to the cliff side and stepped out onto the rock there, the lights of the city flickering beneath her like an inverted starry sky. "Oh my!" was all she said. "Oh my," she repeated, and hugged herself.

Behind her, Michael opened the bottle with a pop, then stood next to her and handed her one of the filled glasses. "It's champagne," he told her. "You said you don't drink, but this isn't like liquor. It's like drinking moonlight. It's always to celebrate something important. Like our friendship. Try it," he urged, and knew she could see his most winning smile.

Sharleen sipped the cool drink, then wrinkled her nose. "So this is champagne?" she asked. "I don't know what they make such a big fuss about it for. It just tastes like a real sour ginger ale."

Michael laughed. "It kind of grows on you," he said. "Come sit over here. This is the best spot."

Wordlessly, Jim had set out the rug and pillows from the Rolls, then returned to it. Sharleen sat down on the soft cushions and took another sip. She stared out at the glittering grid beneath them, and dreamily she said, "You know, you see this kind of thing in the movies, but you never believe that it really exists, or that *you* can ever be part of it. And here I am."

She really was lovely, he thought, warming to his work. "Here's to you, Sharleen," Michael said, raising his glass to click hers in a toast. "A part of Hollywood."

Sharleen clicked her glass back, and, following his lead, took another sip of wine. She stretched, leaned her back against the pillows, and said, "I feel very happy."

"That's why people like champagne," Michael told her. "It helps them feel happy." He poured more into his glass, then nodded to Sharleen's. "Have some more. I'll just top it off for you."

Sharleen took another quick two swallows, then coughed. Michael tapped her gently on the back. "Go down the wrong way, Sharleen?" he asked, smiling in the faint light.

"I'm okay. I just drank it too quickly."

"Better take another sip. It will help clear your throat."

"It doesn't make you drunk?" she murmured.

"Only if you drink lots of it. We're only sharing this one bottle," Michael reassured her, and he poured more into her glass. She had to take another big gulp to keep

351

the champagne from spilling. He himself had better lay off, he realized. He couldn't drink and perform the way he had a decade ago.

"Oooh. I feel so good. Like I can reach right up and pluck one of them stars right out of the sky." Her voice was blurred. Time for his move, he thought. "They all look like diamonds," she murmured.

Michael reached over and gently touched the one around her neck. She lifted her hand to it as well, and their fingers touched. He leaned across her, and brought his face very close to hers. "I've never known anyone like you," he said. Then, looking into her eyes, he kissed her, sweetly, lightly, on the lips. He saw her draw back, and he touched the back of her head with his free hand. Slowly, now, he told himself. Slowly.

"You're very beautiful," he said. "Much more beautiful than the other girls. And sweeter, too." Then he pulled back. Not too fast, he thought again. He drained his almost empty glass, and indicated for Sharleen to do the same with her full one. Then he refilled both their glasses, and touched his to hers once again. "Here's to your success. I *know* you're going to be a *very* big star."

"Thank you," she said, and he recognized the glazed look that Moët, gifts, and the Michael McLain charm induced. She looked a little like a blonde bunny trapped in the headlights of a car. But she was a very beautiful bunny. "I'll help you any way I can. Let me. I can teach you a lot of secrets." He leaned forward. This time, she didn't pull away. He took the glass from her hand, and held her in his arms. Slowly, ever so slowly, he stretched out next to her on the blanket. "Let me love you, Sharleen," he said, and rolled his body onto hers.

Sharleen looked up at Michael, unable to see anything in the dark except the starry sky. A star, he had said. A big star. How could that be? she thought. She didn't even want that, but that's what Michael McLain had said. Maybe she didn't have to be so afraid anymore. Afraid of losing her job; afraid of Lila, who was mean; afraid of Jahne, who was smart; afraid of the police, of her dreams of Lamson; afraid that she and Dean would be found out.

She felt Michael's warm hand touch her shirt, and stroke her through the soft fabric. It felt different, so different from Dean's touch. This must be what movie stars did, she thought fuzzily. She felt Michael's lips on hers again, and tasted the champagne as she opened her mouth to him. Michael slipped his hand under her loose blouse, and placed the palm of his hand on her skin. Then he pulled back from her slowly, and laid his face against her bare stomach, kissing her navel, and the spot right under it. Then right on her belly button again. She almost laughed! Then he kissed below it. She heard a zipper opening in the dark, and realized it was hers.

"No," she said, starting to struggle up from the cushions. She felt as if the noise had awakened her from a dream. She hadn't meant for this to be—well for them to go so far. It was like a dream. But this was real. Oh, God, how had this happened? She hadn't meant to give the wrong idea. "No," she said.

"Yes," he whispered, and one hand was on her head, the other pushing her shoulder back, back down into the cushion.

"Don't you like me, baby?" he asked her.

"Yes. Yes, but . . ." His mouth covered hers again.

"Just yes. Yes," he murmured. God, she didn't want to hurt his feelings. Had she led him on? She hadn't meant to. She didn't hardly know him. He moved his head down to her breast, his lips on her nipples, on her belly. She tried to stop him, but she was falling into the dream again. The stars spun over her head. She felt as if she were floating over the city.

Michael tugged at her pants, bringing them down over her buttocks. Oh, God, what was he doing? His head was still down there, his lips now moving lower, lower down, down. Sharleen felt her nipples harden, released from her shirt, exposed to the air. Michael reached up and pinched each slightly, so gently that the pleasure made her move her hips.

Sharleen closed her eyes briefly. She felt tears well up in them and spill onto her cheeks. What was she doing? What was he doing to her? Everything continued to spin. She opened her lids and saw Michael stand, silhouetted in the starlight. He dropped his pants, then pulled off his shirt in a slick, single movement. He didn't mean to do it —to do *that*—right out here? She had to tell him to stop.

"The driver. Jim. He can see us. Stop. Please."

Michael said quietly, "No one can see." Then he was on her again, moving her legs apart, already moving his hips rhythmically.

"No," she said, "please." But it was too late.

"No one can see anything," Michael told her, just as Jim silently pulled the infra-red camera from the glove box of the Rolls.

23

Parties may just be parties in other places, but in Hollywood—or Holmby Hills, to be exact—a party is never just a party. It's a place to see and be seen, a place to make contacts, make deals, and make out. And if Hollywood has always been famous for its parties, the choicest, the fanciest, the most exclusive, was Ara Sagarian's Emmy party, held on the night of the annual television awards. Originally, it had been a party where the most select movie actors and actresses hooted with derision at the doings on the small screen. But for years now, the small screen had been too important to hoot at. Still, this party was the place where Hollywood let its hair down, so exclusive that no journalists were ever allowed. It was the hot ticket, and no one who was anyone ever admitted to being in town and not invited. It was the only important party that I, Laura Richie, was never invited to.

Ara, despite his courtly manners and exquisite politesse, winnowed the guest list mercilessly. Joan Collins had been dropped long before Dynasty was. Burt Reynolds was no longer invited. After all, an A-list party only remained A-list if no one but the crème de la crème attended.

But like all rules, Ara broke this one for the singular exception of Theresa O'Donnell. For twenty-two years,

*as long as he had hosted Emmy parties, Theresa had been
invited. Because although her star had waxed, waned,
and then waxed and waned again, she had been Ara's
first big star. And despite the booze, the pills, and the
paranoia, she was still a legend. She was his talisman,
his good-luck charm, and she showed the world (and his
clients and potential clients) that Ara Sagarian was loyal
to his clients. But now that he was no longer representing
her and not inviting her he felt guilty—terribly, terribly
guilty. Ara based lots of his self-worth on knowing he
was both a gentleman and loyal in a land of locusts.*

*But he had, at last, been disloyal to Theresa. That was
undeniable. His only excuse was that, despite his age,
despite the stroke, despite the disability, Ara still wanted
to play—he still wanted to be not just in the pack but in
the lead. Still throwing the most exclusive parties, still
representing the biggest stars. And he knew he had been
slipping. His stable was aging. He felt he'd had to take
the chance with Lila Kyle.*

Neil Morelli lifted the last of the trays of canapés from
the caterer's van and brought them into the kitchen. The
fat guy in charge kept referring to a clipboard and barking
orders to the swarm of waiters and chefs. All the asshole
needed was a fucking whistle, Neil thought. Neil resented
having to take this job, not that he didn't need it. Since
the show had been canceled, he'd lived hand-to-mouth,
using up his last few dollars licking his wounds. Now,
totally broke, he had to take whatever he could get. Because Sy Ortis wasn't getting him anything else in the
Industry; Christ, Sy still wasn't even getting his fucking
calls, or at least he wasn't answering them. So Neil threw
himself back on the old survival jobs of all players who
are "at leisure": driving a cab, waiting tables, and trying
again.

This one, working for Table d'Hôte, wasn't the worst.
At least he wasn't slinging hash in some public place,
making himself a spectacle, humiliating himself in front of
everyone. These were private parties: rich orthodontists,
corporate lawyers, and the usual crowd of Orange
County Reaganites. Stiffs.

It wasn't until the caterer had pulled the van full of waiters into the driveway of this one that the honcho told them whose house they would be working tonight. Ara Sagarian's Emmy party. Jesus. Tears nearly filled Neil's eyes. He'd been reading about this party in the columns since he was a kid. He used to gobble down the pictures of celebrities around the pool—all laughing, all perfect. His dream was to join them. Join them as an equal. He— Neil Morelli—should be on the other side of the table. That's what he had come to this town for, to be waited on, not to be a waiter. He stood at the kitchen door, paralyzed, not sure he could force his legs to cross the back-door threshold.

"Hey. You with the nose. Move it. Grab a tray," the fat guy yelled.

When Sy Ortis called Jahne and invited her to Ara Sagarian's Emmy party, she'd been surprised. "Strictly business," he quickly explained. "You got to be out and about now." Jahne was being talked about, but she was still an unknown to everyone outside the Industry and many inside it, too. So she said yes, though she could barely stand Sy. Sy might be handy for introducing her around, but it was clear that he also had disadvantages as an escort. Ara had been polite but cool to him. Of course, who *could* like Sy Ortis?

She was nervous about this, her debut in the Hollywood social scene. But Sy insisted, and he promised they'd come late and leave early. Now, with butterflies in her stomach, she turned to him. "Who would you like to meet?" he asked her smoothly. "Cher? Keanu Reeves? Hey, Michael Keaton is over there by the bar. He hasn't come to a party since Batman returned." Jahne smiled. "No? How about Crystal Plenum?" Jahne's smile disappeared. Take it easy, she told herself.

"No thanks," she said.

"So who, then?" Sy asked. Jahne looked around. An enormous man, at least six and a half feet tall and well over three hundred pounds, stood at poolside. It must be Marvin Davis. Jeff Katzenberg stood at the bar, a circle of people around him. And was that tall, old man David Lean? No, wasn't David Lean dead? Jahne's head spun. Before Jahne had a chance to answer, Sy took her arm. "Oh, here's somebody you *must* get to know." Sy walked up to a tall back and tapped the man's elbow. "Michael, say hello."

The man turned, and Jahne found herself staring up into the blue, blue eyes of Michael McLain. He smiled at her, and she couldn't help smiling back. "Any friend of Sy's is someone I'd better watch out for," Michael said. Then he extended his hand to hers. "Hi. I'm Michael McLain," he said.

"This is Jahne Moore. She's doing the new Marty Di-Gennaro show that premieres this coming season."

"Oh? Is Marty doing a TV show? What is it about?" Michael asked her.

She began to explain, and found him surprisingly easy to talk to, after she got over the undeniable weirdness of standing beside a man-sized Michael McLain. Not that he was exactly tall. She had her highest heels on, and Michael McLain only reached to her ear. After years of seeing him only in ten-foot-high close-ups on the screen, it was a difficult adjustment. No wonder people always thought movie stars were shorter in "real life" than they were on the screen. Still, other than his height, Michael McLain stood up fairly well. He was still very handsome, and if his neck was a little crepey and his eyes set in a few lines, it didn't bother her one bit. They chatted pleasantly for a few minutes.

"I was sure the two of you would get along," Sy said as he drifted away. "But watch out for him, Jahne. He eats girls like you for breakfast."

"Only if they *want* to be eaten, Sy." Michael smiled, though this time the smile didn't move up to those incredible blue eyes.

Crystal Plenum adjusted the fall of her signature white wrap on her equally white shoulders and walked into the big room ahead of her husband. That was part of their understanding. Entrances were *always* made alone, just as exits *never* were. She heard the stir she made, the slight pause and then the increase in the ambient noise, and smiled as her husband came up behind her. "Wayne," she said softly as he approached, "don't leave my side for *one minute*. And make sure and say everybody's name. You know how I get." Crystal was terrible with names, but knew how important it was in this town to be able to put a name with a face. People liked to be recognized, no matter who they were—or weren't. And they really liked to be recognized by a star. Plus, it kept her from wasting time on the unimportant people at parties. Although, Crystal knew, there were *no* unimportant people at *this* party. Except, of course, for the spouses.

Last year, Ara had neglected to send her an invitation. She'd told everyone she was going to be in New York, and then holed up at the Hotel Bel-Air instead. But now *Jack and Jill* had been lauded by the critics and was doing good box office for a woman's picture. She was up for a New York Film Critics *and* a Golden Globe. There was definite Oscar talk. The gamble she'd taken—playing her age, looking like shit, and trying to act—had paid off. Everyone would be kissing her cellulite-free ass tonight! She was on top again.

And she'd have to keep Wayne a while longer. Right now, she had to focus on prolonging the roll and starting her next film before she cooled off. A divorce, especially from a husband who was also her business manager, would be costly and distracting. She wondered if she'd get a *People* cover the way Joan Lunden did, because Wayne would sure stick her for a pile of alimony. She should never have let him manage her in the first place. Well, if it came to that, she never should have married him. There would be time for a divorce later.

"Crystal," Ara said, limping toward them, dragging his stroke leg, his hand extended to her, "how kind of you to come."

"Ara Sagarian," Wayne said quickly in a whisper.

"Him I know, Wayne," she told her husband, annoyed. Maybe she *could* afford a divorce this year.

Turning to the approaching small man, she said,

"Thank you for having me. I'm honored to be here, Ara. I couldn't be more pleased if I were winning an award *myself* tonight. Except not a *television* award, of course." They both laughed.

Paul Grasso hunched in the dark in the back seat of the taxi. Across the way, the drive to Ara Sagarian's house was lit by tiny twinkling lights and peopled by parking valets and the beautiful invited guests. He looked down at his tux, wrinkling into a pathetic mess as he sat and sweated in the warm darkness.

"Pathetic" was definitely the word for him. Pathetic that, after thirty years in this town, twenty years as a *player,* he was passed over by an old, half-crippled queer. What was Ara saying? That Paul Grasso was no longer worthy of an invite?

Paul knew that if his access to the people that matter was cut off, he could fold his tents and go home. And he had no intention of folding anything. If any folding was going to go down, Ara could take his invitations, fold them five ways, and put them where the moon don't shine.

But now the moon *was* shining. Just one more thing against him. Because Paul knew he *had* to be at the party. He owed too much money and needed work too bad to risk letting the word get out that he had been overlooked.

He watched and waited for his opportunity. The underbrush at the Fred Wiseman house was thick—more a jungle than a garden. Well, he'd have to use it to his advantage. Because the Wisemans' property was next to Ara Sagarian's. He hoped it wasn't patrolled by dogs.

Cautiously, he got out of the taxi and dismissed the driver. He didn't know how he'd get home, but he'd cross that bridge when he came to it. Stealthily, he moved into the underbrush that ran along the dividing line of the two properties.

Paul Grasso was not the only bitter, excluded person left in the darkness that night. In Bel Aire Theresa O'Donnell sat in the musty bedroom that was reserved for Candy and Skinny. She didn't speak to them or for them, but merely sat, motionless as the two puppets, and as empty.

April Irons wordlessly handed her empty glass to Sam Shields, and looked around Ara's vast, crowded living room while her escort went to fetch her a fresh one. They were negotiating on the new film she was producing, the remake of *Birth of a Star*. Wait until Marty DiGennaro found out! She knew he loved the thing. Maybe she'd introduce Sam Shields, as the director of the remake, to Marty. He'd eat his liver! But Sam would probably ass-kiss. April didn't feel the need to give her protégé entrée to absolutely everyone.

Her eyes stopped when, across the crowded room, she spotted a handsome man with Kikki Mansard, the new girl in town, on his arm. When his own eyes met hers, she beckoned with an exaggerated motion of her index finger for him to come.

He pointed to himself and mouthed, "Me?" April nodded her head up and down, deliberately. The man began to walk toward her, his hand on Kikki's back, guiding her. April shook her head and watched the man whisper to his date, then continue toward her, alone.

"April, you flatter me," Michael McLain said, and raised the tips of his fingers to his lips. "But don't you want to meet Kikki? She's doing the Dino De Laurentiis thing."

"No thanks. I had dog meat for dinner. This is business. You were supposed to call me about that script," April said.

"That's not a pout, is it? On April Irons?" Michael asked, his eyes twinkling. Jesus, these actors, she thought. They never turn it off.

"I'm ten years past pouting, you big prick. You *begged* me to see the script, I sent it over. Then nothing. What am I supposed to do? Chase you around town to get you to take a part that every male star would give his left testicle for? I'm not one of your twenty-year-old chippies."

He leaned into her ear. "Oh, yes, you are," he whis-

pered, using the voice that makes America's women wet.
April shrugged, though actually she always enjoyed spar-
ring with Michael McLain.

"That does it," she said, but she smiled. "I've got to
move on. Beatty wants the part. And I have to work the
room. So either you call me—soon—or I'm going to pass
it around town that Michael McLain can't get it up."

Michael made a look of mock horror. "Please don't do
that! I won't be able to get a night's sleep for months.
Women all over this town would take that as their biggest
challenge."

Sam Shields stood by the bar, nervously swirling the
vodka in his highball glass. He had not been invited to
this party. When he got the call from April to come as
her escort, he had been surprised. He wasn't sure if this
was business or pleasure, and though he wanted to work
with April again, he wasn't so sure he wanted to sleep
with her. She was a demanding mistress, and there was
something more than intimidating about her. To be blunt,
he felt that she used men the same way most men use
women. It made him nervous.

So did gatherings like this one. Sam liked to think of
himself as a player, but when he was surrounded by these
heavy hitters, he felt damn insecure. Nobody had sought
him out, and he wasn't very good at "working the
room." He wished he could go home. To kill time, he
watched the guests milling about. He tried to identify
them. The stars, of course, were easy. It was the power
brokers and studio suits he worked on. Mike Eisner.
Mike Medavoy. Michael Ovitz. Was "Mike" a prerequi-
site for success out here?

Then he saw the redhead. She was with DiGennaro. In
fact, that was Marty DiGennaro surgically attached to
her arm. She might be good for *Birth of a Star*. She
looked young and hot.

He looked over at April. She had been talking to a
series of movers and shakers, the last being Michael
McLain. Now, seeing her "between engagements," he
crossed to her side. Perhaps she'd introduce him to Di-
Gennaro. Perhaps he'd get a shot at the redhead. . . .

"I have had about enough of this," April said to him. "Let me just talk to a few more of these guys, and then what do you say we go back to my place and fuck?"

Jahne stood at the side of the pool, the lights threaded through all the palms twinkling like tiny stars. Big stars and big movers and shakers stood around the pool. No one knew who she was, and in the shadows she had a moment of privacy.

At a party like this, just being beautiful was not enough to draw interest. You had to be beautiful, successful, *and* famous. Because this was a party of the most beautiful, successful, and famous people in the world. And she, Jahne Moore, was there.

Well, she reflected, I must have arrived. How else could I be here? She smiled. This unreal scene was her reality. But the reality she was living was becoming more and more unreal. She breathed in the fragrance of night-blooming jasmine, mixed with just the slightest scent of chlorine from the pool. Essence of Hollywood.

Then, as she watched, a man climbed out of the shrubbery in the darkness. He was short, and almost as dark as the shadows he had hidden in. He looked up at her. "Hi," he said nonchalantly, and brushed off his crumpled dinner jacket. "I was looking for my wallet," he explained, and strolled off into the crowd. She shook her head.

Behind her, two society women began to gossip. They were older matrons, clearly married to Industry heavies. One looked up. "Oh. Oh! Look!" she cried. "It's Mary Jane."

Jahne felt a tug in her stomach. She felt herself almost dissolve, and instantly a film of sweat broke out all over her. God! Were they from New York? How had they . . . Then another older woman walked up to the group. "Mary Jane Wick, meet my friend Esther Goodbody," the matron said. Her voice faded.

Jahne could only hear the buzzing in her ears. She tried to take a deep breath, one that moved all the way down to her solar plexus. She took another wobbling step forward on her very high heels and almost slipped but caught herself just in time. Get a grip, Jahne, she told herself sternly, and then she looked up. There, across the pool, she saw him. He was wearing black and white, like all the men. She could hardly believe her eyes. It had been such a long time since she'd last seen him in New York. "Oh, my God!" she said out loud.

No, she told herself. She was merely shaken by the women and the mention of her old name. She turned her eyes away, blinked, took a few more deep breaths, and told herself to be calm. Now I'll look, she said to herself. Now I'll look, and find I am mistaken. But as she raised her eyes and looked across the tiny lights floating like lotus blossoms in the pool, she knew it was he.

It was Neil, and he was dressed as a waiter, serving canapés to the party guests.

Paul Grasso stood with a drink in his hand, moved slightly back and forth from heel to toe, rocking where he stood, and shook his leg. Yahta, yahta, yahta. He hated these fuckin' Industry soirées. But it was his shot to get to Marty, and he'd managed to corner his prey at last. You would think it would be easier, since Marty was there with Lila Kyle, who looked gorgeous as ever but not one bit grateful. But Paul knew there was no gratitude in this town. Paul thought of the Italian proverb that asked, "Why does she hate me so? I never did anything for her." Because Lila clearly hated him. She'd gotten the part but never delivered on the casting job she promised him. The job he was desperate for. Anyway, she never took his calls. Now she stood beside Marty, obviously gorgeous and obviously bored.

"Nice tux," Marty DiGennaro commented, his sarcasm heavy. Paul ignored him. He needed to pick up some work, but nothing was lower than asking for it here, at a party like this. Still, it wasn't like he was begging. Hey, he was *owed* it.

"So what you been up to? Make it over to Vegas lately?"

"Nah," Marty said. "Too busy."

"How's the show going? I haven't heard." Paul felt sweat bead his upper lip.

"Real well."

Well, he'd have to do it. "Got any casting trouble? Maybe I could help?"

"You mean maybe *I* could help. You looking for work, Paulie?"

"I wouldn't mind the casting for this new project," he admitted, and held his breath. Marty paused. It wasn't the pause that refreshes. It was the one that ended a friendship and turned it strictly business.

"Call my office tomorrow," he said, and Paulie knew he'd cashed in his last chip but that he was back in the game.

Lila cleared her throat and shifted from one leg to the other. It made her boredom more than apparent. Ara had invited her, since she was his client, but Marty had an invitation for two in his own right. She had refused to come with him, however, and told him she would meet him at the party. Now she was regretting her decision. This was all so dull. And Paul Grasso looked like he wanted to play "I've Got a Secret" with her. She'd blow them both off. "I'm going inside," she told Marty, and without a goodbye or acknowledgment she walked across the deck and through the open French doors to the huge tiled living room. Near the center of the room, a mammoth chair stood, surrounded by a gaggle of morons. Lila did not want to look too interested, but she floated toward them. Lots of power there: Don Simpson and Joel Schumacher. *Days of Thunder* meets *Peter Pan*. When would *she* be the center of attention? she wondered. As she came up to the group, not one of them turned to look at her.

At the center a tall, dark woman was talking to an equally tall, dark man. He smiled at her. She smiled back. From the corner of her eye, she saw Marty approach.

"Miss Kyle?" the tall man asked. She nodded. "I'm Sam Shields. And this is April Irons."

Lila gave April a big smile. April Irons meant features. First-class features. Marty joined them.

"Hello, April," he said, and took Lila's arm. Lila felt her annoyance build. He didn't own her. She took her arm back.

"So, what are you up to, April?"

"Oh, a new little project. Sam here is directing. Just getting some pointers from Don."

"Really?" Marty smiled stiffly. "Got a working title?" he asked idly, obviously bored.

"It's called *Birth of a Star*," April cooed.

Neil stood on the back porch, sucking on a cigarette, his hands trembling. Sam Shields. Fucking Sam Shields! Neil had been passing a tray of caviar and had turned to offer some to a small group. He recognized Michael Douglas, Kevin Costner, Richard Gere, Marty DiGennaro, and Crystal Plenum. He served Michelle Pfeiffer, Phoebe Van Gelder, Kirk Kirkorian. And that producer bitch, April Irons. Then the guy in front of him had leaned into the bowl of Beluga, scarfing it up. Neil almost dropped the tray when he saw it was Sam Shields. His first instinct had been to push the fucking bowl of fish eggs into Sam Shields' face; then he realized he had to get away.

The humiliation was stinging. It was both a relief and an insult that Sam didn't even recognize him, hadn't even looked at who was serving him. All the bastard could see was free four-hundred-dollar fish eggs.

"I told you, Nose, there are no breaks." The fat guy again, now standing at the kitchen door, warned him.

"You're telling me!" Neil said, flicked his cigarette into the Beluga, and began to walk down the driveway, unclipping his stupid black bow tie.

"Where you going, Nose? You got a job to do."

"Yeah, fat boy, you got that right. But it's not *this* one."

Where the fuck did the caviar go? Sy Ortis thought, looking around the room. Another waiter passed at that moment, and he grabbed him before he got away. But he was only carrying skewered vegetable on a bed of kale. Even in Mexico, we threw that crap out. But he was hungry—nerves always made him eat—so he took four of them. These guys disappear so fast, Sy didn't want to take a chance on *this* one's getting away.

"I'd like to have ten percent of everyone in this room."

Sy looked up from the skewers to find Milton Glick at his elbow. "Yeah, well, you'd have to be a faggot to get it," he said, indicating with his head Ara standing with a group of young men. Then he looked Milton up and down. "*And* a hell of a lot prettier than *you* are."

"I've already gotten fucked up the ass in this town. I guess it won't hurt to suck some dick." Milton shrugged.

"Who did you come with?" Sy asked.

"My wife. She's over there, talking to Mary Jane Wick about some charity ball. Who are you with?"

Sy shrugged. "Jahne Moore. The client Marty had to find on his own. The client from hell. Because *you* didn't get me two Sharleen Smiths."

"Nobody is perfect, Sy. Except you, of course."

Neil stood at the bottom of the driveway. *Now* what the fuck do I do, he thought? I can't thumb a ride. Not in Holmby Hills. And no money for a cab. There once had been buses in this town, but they must have ended in the tar pits with the hairy mammoths. He turned at the sound of the beeping horn. A car was parked across the road from Ara's driveway, and a woman was leaning out its window, beckoning to him. He walked over slowly, blessing his luck. He had never been picked up in this town—in any town, for that matter. Maybe his luck *was* changing for the better.

The woman stepped out of the car as he approached. She was not pretty, he could see. Shit, she was ugly. And old—well, middle-aged. But what the fuck? He was no Miss America, and was stuck here without transportation.

"Hi," she called out as he approached. "Working the party?" she asked, nodding toward Ara's house.

"Yeah. I should say, was. I just quit."

"I'll give you a hundred bucks for your waiter's outfit," she said.

Neil didn't answer for a moment. I should have known. "A crasher, huh? I guess people would do anything to be seen at Ara's party. A hundred, huh?'' he asked. ''John Ritter would give me a thousand.''

I shrugged. Yes, it was me, Laura Richie. And Laura Richie has stooped to lower than this to get a hot flash. For you, gentle Reader. All for you. ''Maybe you should be talking to John Ritter, then.''

''And what am I supposed to wear home? Your dress?''

I opened the back door of the car and reached in. I came out with a pair of black trousers. ''I have the pants; all I need is your shirt and jacket. And tie. I'll let you have my leather bomber jacket along with the hundred. That should get you home.''

''Throw in twenty bucks more for a cab and it's all yours,'' *he said, unbuttoning his shirt and pulling it out of his pants.*

24

''Did you get that tape?'' Sam Shields asked as they sat down on the bed. He was exhausted from the strain of Ara's party, and the idea of athletic sex with April was not, at the moment, number one on his hit parade. He began to unbutton his shirt as April stripped her own blouse off. ''Could you get the *3/4* tape?'' he repeated.

''Of course. Why?'' she asked.

''I'd like to take a look at it,'' he said, and reached across the bed for the remote control and clicked on the TV.

He guessed they were celebrating the deal they had just made: he agreed to the drafting of a new script for *Birth of a Star* and to directing it. He'd get half a million bucks—twice what he'd gotten for *Jack and Jill*—if the picture actually went into Production. He could hardly believe it.

''Sam, what are you doing?'' April asked, making no attempt to mask the irritation in her voice. ''Turn the fucking television off. Now is *not* the time.''

"I know, I know," Sam said, trying to calm her. "But now that I've seen Lila Kyle, I just want to see the show for a minute. Everyone is talking about the thing. Where's the tape?"

"In my briefcase, over there." It hadn't been easy to smuggle out a copy of *Three for the Road,* not even for April Irons. Marty DiGennaro was running a closed set and didn't want a knockoff of his stuff to appear the same season his show debuted. But in the end she'd managed.

She watched as Sam crossed the room, naked except that his cute buns were encased in those cute blue boxer shorts. He crouched, retrieved the tape, and popped it into the VCR. His eyes were glued to the screen, watching the opening credits. "I just want to see what Marty DiGennaro can do."

After the great critical reception of *Jack and Jill,* April was ready to move ahead with Sam on another picture. And Sam was glad April had made the offer; since he hadn't written anything else in the last two years, it might be what he needed.

April was certainly what he needed. After all, she was powerful. She'd never mentioned Crystal and seemed not at all bitter over his affair with the actress. After all, Sam figured the performance he had gotten out of Crystal had sweetened April's bottom line. So now they were talking preproduction. Costs, casting, above the line, below the line, the whole ball of wax. This was a big one. April was going to trust him.

Now he looked up. April had left the room.

"Wait. Where did you go?" Sam called out to her. "Come on back. I want you to see something . . . a genius at work."

"That would be a nice change," she snapped from the doorway, but her curiosity was piqued. Know your enemies better than your friends, her father used to tell her. And she hated Marty DiGennaro. She hoped the show died like a dog. There'd already been so much buzz: new techniques, feuds on the set, enormous budgets. Maybe it would bring that self-important little prick down. Might as well see what all the talk is about, she decided. She sat down on a far corner of the bed.

He patted the place by his side. "Come on, it's business," he said in a coaxing voice.

April leaned back against Sam's chest and took a deep breath. She had taken out her contacts, expecting to get right into bed with Sam and now she couldn't see the screen too well. But that was all right, she thought. It's only TV. They watched in silence for a few minutes; then April sat up and leaned forward, squinting. This was *not* your usual Sunday-night television fare. But, then, she thought, how could it be, with Marty DiGennaro behind it? He was a prick, but he was a talented prick. This was *good*. More like the big screen than television. But different from both.

"Sam, hand me my glasses. They're in the drawer of the night table," she said, not taking her eyes off the monitor.

She watched carefully. He'd used every trick in the book, but all in new ways and to great effect. He had the wiggle and the jiggle, but the women were tough, liberated, almost androgynous. He had nostalgia, but his cuts and fades and smears, his matching shots, were startlingly different. Better, hotter, newer than MTV.

And maybe, just maybe, there was a lead here for *Birth of a Star*.

"What do you think of the redhead?" Sam asked, reading her mind. "We saw her at the party."

April watched the girl. There was the angle that her mother, Theresa O'Donnell, had starred in the last reincarnation of *Birth of a Star*. That would be good for some free publicity. She was gorgeous, and sly, but . . . Anyway, April didn't want this film to look like nothing more than a shlocky parlor trick, a shtick remake. No.

"Too obvious. And the blonde is doing a Vanna White impersonation."

Sam kept staring at the screen. "Yeah, but watch the other one. The dark one."

April did. The girl was undeniably beautiful, but she had something else. Her voice, her movements were so . . . natural. The girl could act.

"Not bad," she admitted.

"We need a new face for the part."

369

"Well, she's a possibility."

They fast-forwarded through much of it. It was fascinating. The show ended, credits rolled. She looked over at Sam, his hard-on obvious through the sheet. "Is that for her or for me?" she asked him.

"For you," he said, reaching out and cupping her left breast in his hand. "But let's audition *her*."

"Sam, it's unlikely we can afford to use a television star, even if we yoke her with Michael McLain the way I want to do. We need a *movie* person."

"Yeah, so get me Kikki Mansard. She's hot. Or how about Julia Roberts."

"Come on. The Hermit of Hollywood? Unavailable, *and* her people insist on a big position. I don't give six percent of the gross to *anyone*. Bear that in mind, Sam: I don't give head, I don't give percentage of gross, and I don't give final cut."

She had signed him for a hundred thousand for a first draft and one set of revisions against four hundred thousand if they went into principal photography with him directing. He'd come cheap—his pussy agent had folded when April threatened to walk away. Sam didn't know she'd had another quarter of a million she was willing to throw below the line for it. Well, she told herself, she'd use the money to fix up a nice trailer for Michael McLain. It would come in handy.

"Please can I have final cut?" he asked in a wheedling voice. They had been arguing about it for days.

"Since *Heaven's Gate, no* director gets final cut."

"Woody Allen gets final cut."

She raised an eyebrow and looked at him. "To paraphrase Lloyd Bentsen: 'You, Sam, are no Woody Allen.' "

"But I give better head."

"I wouldn't be so sure of that," she told him. "Now, what else? Or can we just call it a deal and go fuck?"

"I shouldn't mix business with pleasure," he said, grinning at her now.

"You shouldn't, but you do. Just don't right now." She reached out for his crotch with one hand and flicked off the TV with the other.

25

Since seeing Neil at Ara's party, Jahne had been searching for him. Discreetly, of course. She began by calling Directory Assistance, but they had no listing. Then she looked him up in the white pages. When they yielded no listing, she stopped at the L.A. Central Library and looked for Morellis in last year's L.A. phone book, and in Orange County and all the surrounding areas for the last two years. There was nothing. Could he have an unlisted number? Or, worse, did he have no number at all? An out-of-work actor without a phone number was an ex-actor. Had Neil given up?

Next Jahne began calling answering services, trying to leave a message for Neil Morelli. But each night, as she worked her way through a dozen or so of the hundreds listed, she felt her hopes fade. It was tiring, depressing, to come up empty again and again.

She missed Neil, and she worried about him. But what would she do if she found him, she wondered. Would she reveal herself? She didn't think she could. Not yet. But maybe she could help him indirectly: send him some money, or ask Marty to use him in a small role on *3/4*.

She wished she could have a friend like Neil. Pete had been kind, but they'd had so little in common. He was still friendly, but not a friend. Sharleen had been friendly, but Sharleen was too limited. Jahne realized she was lonely. Jahne missed the fun of Neil's sharp rants, of the heart-to-hearts she'd had with Molly, the deep conversations she and Sam had shared.

Of course, the thrill of the show's coming together was fun. But her life, aside from work, was nonexistent. Now that she was getting into the rhythm of it, putting out the show was becoming, if not easy, at least routine for Jahne. She looked good on the screen, even in close-ups. She'd tested her face for still photography back in New York, but stills and film were completely different; one was a cool medium, the other hot. She agonized over it. It was the lights that had scared her the most at first. She hadn't thought about it until she was under them. Television lighting was brighter than theater lighting. It shone on every pore, making them look cavernous if the skin were not made up properly. Onstage, lighting was more highlighting and spotlighting. And there were no close-ups, no dense light. On the television soundstage, however, its purpose seemed to be to bring the sun right onto the set. Jahne would sometimes walk under the lights and know, just *know,* that what were tiny, hairline scars in the lighting at home in her bedroom turned here into deep, red gashes. Hester's scarlet letter. But it wouldn't be an "A." Perhaps "F" for fake. Or "I" for impostor. She would hold her breath as the cameramen did run-throughs, waiting for the inevitable cry of discovery. That they never came didn't lessen Jahne's vigilance. Even if there was nothing she could do about the lighting except submit to it.

Makeup, however, was one area where she could exercise some control. Her concerns for her makeup went beyond a professional's concern for perfection. For Jahne, it had become an obsession. She had made a point of becoming friendly with the makeup guy. Both agreed that the Flanders stuff didn't hold up. He smuggled in MAC and some stuff of his own, despite the contract. And since he would stand back every day and look at her face as if he had created the Mona Lisa, Jahne was more relaxed with that part of her preparation for the camera.

But all in all, going before the camera on this show wasn't the exciting opportunity Jahne had at first believed it would be. Marty DiGennaro was directing. She had assumed that meant the show would be above average in every way—camera work, writing, costumes. Unfortunately for Jahne, she became too painfully aware how limited a director's control could be. The writing seemed to her atrocious. A team of writers created dialogue like a "David Mamet-does-Huey-Dewey-and-Louie." It was stunted, unbalanced, hard to develop timing with. She started a sentence and Sharleen interrupted, only to have Lila finish it. So much for art, Jahne had thought after their first script run-through. Well, maybe on the air, finished, it would work.

Meanwhile, the persona of the three characters on the show seemed to have flowed over to the set itself. Jahne was perceived as the smart one, Lila the sexy one, and Sharleen the dumb one. They were being forced to play their roles in real life. Jahne knew she was smart. Or, more accurately, experienced. Because of her perceived age, it came across as smart. And Lila was sexy. Not sexual, really, Jahne could tell. But sexy. And there was poor Sharleen. She wasn't dumb, exactly. Just never exposed to much. And the mistake that the jaded almost always made was that "ignorant" meant stupid. Jahne was sure that that was not the case with Sharleen.

But of the three of them, it was Lila who was smart enough to have ingratiated herself with Marty. Now that she'd seen the first six shows, Jahne could see that Lila had somehow managed to get more close-ups, better lines. And "smart" Jahne was looking less and less directly into the camera, and getting fewer and fewer lines. Of course, all the lines were crap, but still. She laughed to herself. She was reminded of the joke about the two old women who met in the lobby of a Catskills hotel after dinner. The first woman said, "The food is terrible." The second woman added, "Yes, and the portions are so small." So Jahne's portion of bad lines was decreasing. Silly as they were, she admitted she would have liked to have more.

None of it was what she had imagined. It was only when Jahne was with Mai Von Trilling that she was able to feel she was really in show business. During the long waits on the set, she spent hours talking to Mai, hearing the stories of her life. And her loves. Jahne never tired of listening, and Mai seemed to take as much pleasure in telling them. Mai was a survivor of the earliest days of Hollywood.

Now Jahne was in Wardrobe, working on next week's costumes, hanging on Mai's every word. She looked down at Mai, who was managing to tuck a seam, hold her beer glass, talk, and keep the spare pins in her mouth, all at the same time. "So I left him, my dear. Vat else vas I to do? He vould alvays be jealous of my success. It vas poisoning him. After a time, he vould no longer haff luffed me anyvay."

"But you loved him?" Jahne asked.

"Huff course. He vas the vun great luff I had. For he truly luffed *me*. Not the image on the scrin. Alvays I could see the others, later on, seeing not me, but my image from the scrin. Or, vat vas verse, comparing me to it. You know. You vill see it. 'Oh, she's not as tall as I thought. Her teeth are not as good. She is thinner, smaller. Not as *much* as I thought.' " Mai laughed, but there was no humor in it.

It seemed so cruel, watching this wrinkled old woman as she knelt at the hem, remembering her glory years, how she'd been one of the world's first screen idols and how even then she had not been beautiful enough. What was it like *now*, when no one looked at her, at least not as a woman? When she couldn't trade on her face, or her body? And she *had* been stunning. One of the most beautiful. What was it like for her now? Jahne had neither the courage nor cruelty to ask. She looked down again to see Mai staring up at her.

"You are a strange one," Mai said. "Your eyes are too old for your face." She took the last pin out of her mouth and thrust it hard through the tough denim fabric. Jahne felt the hairs on the back of her neck rise. Could this old woman see through her? "You are alvays thinkink," Mai said. "As if you are in danger. But vat does such a pretty girl have to think about? I never thought until I vas forty."

"Just a habit." Jahne smiled at her as she stepped off the little platform before the mirror.

"No. You are strange."

"How?" Jahne tried to sound casual. But she was frightened. Did she give herself away?

"Vell, you let me say somesink like that. This is un-usual. And you come here, not make *me* come to *you.* . . ."

374

"But this is a favor you're doing for me! It was the least I could do."

"Silly girl. A favor for the star is a pleasure. It is money in the bank, a paid insurance premium, my dear."

"What kind of insurance?" Jahne asked, confused.

"Unemployment insurance," Mai said, and laughed as she stood up, slowly and stiffly. "Now, vith luck, you von't let me get fired."

"Oh, Mai! No one would do that! Bob loves you. You're fabulous."

"Fabulous today, unemployed tomorrow." Mai shrugged. She looked into the three-way mirror before them at Jahne's reflection. "You like?" she asked.

Jahne looked. Mai *was* miraculous. She had taken apart the jeans that the costume designer had provided and restructured them completely. Before, despite all the diet and surgery, Jahne simply wasn't as slim as the other two girls. Well, she was shorter and older. Now her stomach was flat as a pancake. "Oh, Mai. They're fabulous. Really. How did you do it?"

"A few tricks. A Lycra panel in the front, behind the fly. And those side seams. Reinforced that vay, they von't vrinkle to show a bulge at the saddlebags. But no sittink in these. For these, standink scenes only. And use a slant board to rest in. I am vorking on a pair for the motorcycle shots. For sittink only. They'll have a bigger seat, but still make your legs longer, thinner-looking."

"A sitting pair of pants and a standing one? It's so unfair!" Jahne laughed. "Women at home don't have you."

"No, and they vill never understand vy their jeans don't fit like yours." Mai smiled. "The magic of Hollywood," she said, and shrugged as she began to pick up the shears, snippets of cloth, and stray pins from off the floor.

"No, here. Let me do that," Jahne said, and began to help the old woman. Mai looked at her again.

"You see? This is strange. To be pickink up. Not just for a new star. Many are polite at first. No, but for a natural beauty like you it is very odd. And you took it as a compliment before ven I said you vere pretty. Beautiful girls don't like to be called that. Just like pretty girls don't like to be called 'attractive.' It is beneath them.'' She looked at Jahne appraisingly. ''Maybe you vere blind as a child?'' she asked. Then she laughed. ''Ach, now you see how I could be fired. I think too much, too.'' She looked down at her empty glass. ''That vas good beer. For me, good beer is better than champagne. Vich is just as vell, since I hafn't got a champagne purse. You vould like another glass?'' she asked Jahne.

Jahne wanted to, but she couldn't afford the calories, not with tomorrow's shoot. ''I'd better not,'' she said reluctantly.

''Some vater, then?'' Mai said, as if reading her mind.

''Yes. I'd like that,'' Jahne said, and smiled.

''Then sit down. But first, first take off those pants.''

When Jahne got home that evening, exhausted by the ten hours of filming at the dusty San Clemente location, she was so tired she could barely lift her arms to the mailbox at the gate to her drive. There was never much waiting there anyway. No packages from home, no cards from friends. Every now and then, a letter from Dr. Moore or a drawing from Raoul. She hoped the boy liked the roller blades and paint set she'd sent. Well, that was why she stopped now, tired as she was. It might not be much, but it was all that she had for a private life.

That was by her choice, she reminded herself grimly. But she admitted to herself that she missed Neil, her New York friends, the quick meetings in Greek coffee shops, the cheap pasta dinners. Most of all, she still missed Sam. More than anything, she still missed beautiful, brilliant Sam. But she reminded herself, for the hundredth time, how badly all that had ended.

Would all this, too, end badly? she wondered. What if the series didn't do well? What if it faded quickly once this early fanfare died down? What if it faded *slowly*, and for three seasons she was stuck in television hell—a show that ranked sixty-seven in the Nielsens and was neither popular nor canceled? Would she then be an actress who wasn't ever going to get choice roles? A Meredith Baxter-Birney—a good actress who graduated from ingenue only to be Michael J. Fox's mom and, when she was lucky, to have the disease of the week in a minor TV movie? An Elinor Donahue, who outgrew *Father Knows Best* to grow into a brief stint on *The Andy Griffith Show*, then played Felix's girlfriend on *The Odd Couple*, and finally wound up as Chris Elliott's mom on *Get a Life*. Had Elinor Donahue wanted a serious acting career? Had she had great expectations?

Sometimes, with her new face, her new body, her new life, Jahne seemed to herself invincible—all this was a bold gamble she'd taken and won. And other times—times like now—it seemed as if it might only be another false promise. Just as *Jack and Jill* and Sam had been. Her stomach tightened with fear. She was too old and too tired to try again.

God, she was morbid! It came from the unknowns in her life right now, and from being so much alone and tired. Well, she couldn't control the unknowns, and she was too tired and frightened to make friends at the moment. Her work exhausted her, and "playing" Jahne Moore was a constant drain. She had a correspondence with her surgeon, was pleasantly friendly with the crew on the set, spoke to Mai, but other than that had to marshal her energy to manage to survive her long days.

With a sigh, she pulled out the little door of the mailbox and emptied its contents onto the seat of the newly leased racing-green Mazda Miata. It was the usual, she thought, disappointed. No letter from Dr. Moore. A couple of bills, two catalogues, and some circulars addressed to "Occupant." But there was also a large cream-colored pasteboard envelope. And it was addressed to her, written in black ink in an Italianate hand. Postmarked L.A. If it was advertising the opening of a new boutique, it was a very expensive one, she thought.

Once through the gates and into the bungalow, she dropped her script, the catalogues, and junk mail onto a chair and opened the big envelope.

April Irons
requests
the very great pleasure
of your company
Tuesday, sunset
Drinks and dinner

Above the address, scrawled in an unfamiliar handwriting, it said, "Love to see you. Bring a friend. April."

April? April *Irons*? The most powerful woman in Hollywood was sending *her* invitations and signing them herself? *Love* to see you? She, Jahne Moore, was invited by a complete stranger—albeit a famous one—and the stranger would "love to see her"?

Jahne shrugged. Well, this *was* Hollywood, after all, and she *was* living a fairy tale. Hadn't she just wished she weren't so alone? Her wish was granted: she had an invitation to the ball. But now that Cinderella knew about the party, where would she find a fairy godmother to supply the gown, the glass slippers, the carriage, and, most important, the prince?

The idea of appearing as Jahne Moore, up-and-coming, young, beautiful actress, in front of all of social Hollywood was more than daunting. She had hated the party at Ara Sagarian's. But didn't she need to get out, meet people, build a life? She felt herself break into a sweat. Who would talk to her? What would she talk about? Who would care? And what would she wear? She had to smile at that. Well, she could ask Mai how to dress—maybe even borrow something through Bob at Wardrobe. Or go shopping—shopping with Mai! That was it. And after all, it wouldn't be Loehmann's budget dresses, and she was no size sixteen anymore. It could, actually, be fun! But how to behave? And who to bring?

There was Pete, but they'd broken up, and anyway she couldn't imagine Pete talking to April Irons. How embarrassing. They'd both look stupid. God, she'd hate that.

Well, she'd call Sy Ortis. He'd probably know what to do about "a friend." And he'd be pleased that she had such an important event to go to. He was always pushing her to "be seen." Hell, for all she knew, maybe he had set it up.

Jahne ran a bath, poured herself a glass of Beaujolais, and turned down the rheostat (even in the bathroom!) so the lights were low. Ah, the warm water felt delicious! She set the pasteboard invitation on the tile surround propped against a bottle of shampoo, sipped her wine, and stared at it. This was, perhaps, the *real* beginning for her.

"First of all, what do you wanna go to April Irons' for anyway? She's a world-class bitch. "

"I want to go. Should I go alone?"

"*Madre di Dios!* Forget it. I'll set you up with someone *appropriate.*"

"A blind date? I hate blind dates."

"Jahne. This is Hollywood. Only Stevie Wonder has blind dates. Do you think Michael Jackson and Madonna went to the Oscars together because they were *dating?* I'll set you up with someone, for business, that can do your career some good. At least someone who won't humiliate you."

Jahne sighed. "All right," she agreed.

Getting the dress was easy. Mai brought three things over; they picked one, and it was a knockout: a long, blue-black silk taffeta that started at her cleavage and then fell in perfect, clinging waves to the floor.

"So, it is beginning for you," Mai said with satisfaction.

"I'm so frightened I could die," Jahne admitted. "What if no one talks to me, or if I say something stupid or . . ."

"Ccht! Cht!" Mai made a clicking noise with her tongue and teeth. "Men vill *always* talk to you—vell, for the next ten years or so, anyvay. Und you should vorry about findink somevun who doesn't talk stupid, not vorry about vat *you* say. You are doomed to be bored a lot more than you vill be borink. See if I am not right."

* * *

Sy sat at his desk, his feet up on the credenza. More trouble. Jahne Moore troubled him. And Jahne Moore and April Irons were double trouble. Sy would not say he hated women: not women like his mother or his wife, who knew their place. Sy only hated *pushy* women. Like Jahne. And April herself. So, what if *he* escorted Jahne Moore to April's dinner party? That would piss Miss Irons off. It would start any relationship between them on the wrong foot. And he could keep an eye on both of them—excellent plan. Sy smiled and put down his inhaler.

But perhaps he could go one better. He still had to get Michael McLain to agree to let Ricky's name be billed alone over the title. The bet he had made with Michael was stupid. He'd regretted it immediately. Then Michael had informed him he'd already bedded Sharleen. *Putana.* Clients were nothing but trouble. But now maybe he could kill two birds with one rock. He would let Michael McLain take Jahne. That woman was not so easy as Sharleen. And after Michael struck out, he, Sy, could negotiate the Ricky Dunn deal.

Sy lifted up the phone and smiled.

Jahne was nervous, but, even so, she couldn't help taking in the scene before her. "I'm here, and I'll never forget this," she told herself. She was on the threshold, looking in. Michael McLain stood beside her, his arm locked around hers. The house was perfect—totally elegant in its simplicity, a big English Tudor. The huge double front doors opened into a reception gallery that was big enough to hold an L.A. Rams game, Jahne thought to herself. The sunken living room was an expanse of ivory upholstery and dark wood antiques, and candles—hundreds of them—illuminated the room. Beyond it, the dining room was inviting, the table draped with gleaming ivory linen napery and tall candelabra. Ivory orchids in moss-covered pots were everywhere. Some plants were six feet high. There was enough room for a hundred people, Jahne thought. But this party was intimate, with only a dozen guests.

Two waiters, balancing silver trays that reflected the

candle glow onto the cut-crystal glasses, passed among them, delivering an astonishing array of hors d'oeuvres and drinks. Jahne stepped down the three steps into the living room and was greeted by a dark, painfully thin woman in an ivory satin dress—April Irons, Jahne was sure. "Jahne, I'm so glad you could come," April said, extending her hand. Jahne smiled, thanked her, and turned to introduce Michael McLain.

"Mike. Nice to see you. Didn't take you long to find new talent," April said. Michael smiled.

"If you don't mind, we're going to go in to dinner right away. I have a film to screen afterward that I think you'll like. Is that okay?" April asked.

"Of course," Michael said, and turned to Jahne. "All right?" he asked.

"Wonderful," Jahne agreed, and the three of them crossed the polished floor to the dining room. Michael helped her into her seat. April began to make introductions. Not that the guests needed them. All were world-famous. Jahne almost had to pinch herself to be sure she wasn't dreaming.

Then she saw him.

He had arrived late, took the three steps down to the living room in one bound of his long legs, and moved easily, graceful as ever, to the single empty seat.

Jahne didn't drop her glass, or her jaw. But she stared. She stared at Sam, *her* Sam, drinking him in. And it was as if there had been no time, no pain, no operations, no new name, no new career, no triumph at the Melrose, no Marty DiGennaro, no television show. It was as if time had stood still.

And she wanted him as badly as ever.

Fame

"Remember when Pinocchio goes to Stromboli, and Stromboli convinces him to be an actor? And Pinocchio performs a little bit, and Stromboli puts him in a cage? Well, that's a lot like what it's like. You want to do this, and you're completely fascinated by the dream. And you get there. And suddenly you're in a cage."

—BETTE MIDLER

"There are photographers who sit in their cars outside my house all day long who frighten me."

—JULIA ROBERTS

Fame

1

Haven't we all wondered what it would be like to take our place among the stars? Not just as an observer, the way I, Laura Richie, have, but actually as one of them. Not to be tolerated, as a reporter is, or condescended to as a fan, but to be welcomed as an equal.

What does it feel like to sit down to dinner with a dozen of the most famous and most beautiful and most talented people in the world? What is it like to have Elizabeth Taylor—never "Liz"—call you by your first name, to have Cher ask you to pass the butter, to have Warren Beatty smile at you and ask about your work as if he's really interested? Before, Jahne was on the fringe. Tonight she was at the epicenter.

Jahne experienced it all for the first time but she couldn't focus on any of it. Instead, she focused on trying not to make a fool of herself over Sam Shields. She kept her eyes away from his, she kept her head turned the other way, toward Michael McLain, and Elizabeth and Larry, and April Irons.

What if Sam recognized her? Of course, she was completely different now—not just her looks, but the mannerisms she'd adopted, the way she moved. She was certain that she played the part of Jahne Moore well. But no one had ever known her as well as Sam. Surely he could see through her performance, and what if he did? Would he give her away? Would he despise her?

Her heart was beating so hard, so fast, that she was sure Michael, at her left, could hear it. It was almost all that she could hear, the pounding of her heart in her ears. Her flesh had gone clammy, and she felt herself begin to sweat.

She tried to lift the crystal goblet of water by its stem, but her hands were shaking too hard. She glanced around the table to see if anyone had noticed, and clasped both of her hands in her lap. Only April was looking at her, but April just smiled and nodded her head. "Where are you living, Jahne?" she asked.

"Birdland," she explained. "Off Oriole."

"Have you bought that place?" Michael asked.

"No. I'm only renting," she managed to say.

"Is security good there?" Goldie asked.

They began to talk about security—and the relative benefits of Malibu versus Bel Air versus Holmby Hills. Jahne listened as they complained about costs; she wondered if any of them had bodyguards. "Well, I was always happy at the Beverly Wilshire," Michael said. "I let the hotel worry about security. Best in the world."

"That doesn't work with children," someone said dryly. "A hotel suite isn't a home."

"It was for me for ten years."

"You needed the revolving door," someone cracked, and they all laughed. For a moment, Jahne wondered if they were laughing also at her—she must look like Michael's latest conquest. Well, she supposed that was better than looking like the professional fix-up they actually were. She looked around and saw that Sam Shields had his eyes on her. She turned away.

"You need a gated community," April was saying. "To be safe, and especially if you have kids."

"Oh, isn't that a bit paranoid?" Sam asked. His voice sounded better than ever—rich and deep, with that New York sharpness. "I mean, after New York, this is child's play. I'm in the canyon, and I love it."

"Isn't that what Sharon Tate said?" Michael asked.

"It *isn't* paranoid," April said. "Now, Barry Diller had a twenty-four-hour security guard watching his parking space at Fox. *That* was paranoid."

The conversation went on around Jahne. She could barely manage a bite of her shrimp-mousse starter, and did little better over the Dover sole and asparagus. For once, she wouldn't have to worry about her diet: she'd choke on a crumb. The plates were beautifully, artfully arranged, the fish set in a frame of asparagus, the gold rim of the dish sparkling along with the gold rim of the crystal goblets, of the gold-chased sterling candelabra.

She stared at the plate, trying to listen to the conversation as it ebbed and flowed. They'll think I'm mute, she told herself. I must say *something*.

She lifted her head. The talk had gone from security to real estate and then back to security again.

"Since I moved out of the Beverly Wilshire, I use La Brecque," Michael was saying.

"He's expensive," one of the others murmured.

"Yeah, but he's the best. And we *are* talking about our lives," Michael said.

"Isn't that a bit melodramatic?" Jahne heard Sam say. She still didn't dare to look at him, only in his general direction.

"You want to talk melodrama?" Michael asked. "I've had a guy in prison writing me death threats for seven years. He blames me for breaking up his first marriage: his wife was a fan. Since he killed his wife and was sentenced to twenty years, he swears he's going to get me. Shouldn't I be nervous?"

All of the people at the table murmured sympathetically. Sam cleared his throat. "I guess as long as he's in prison you're fine."

"Well, he was almost paroled last year. La Brecque keeps stuff like that under control. He presented the letters to the parole board. He had other testimony, too. He neutralizes things. As much as he can. Anyway, writers and directors don't know about this stuff—it's only us actors on the front lines who know." Michael turned to Jahne. "*Is* your place secure?"

"I don't know," she admitted. "Nobody has ever bothered me."

"Well, I hope that never changes, but I wouldn't count on it. When does your show premiere?"

"Next Sunday."

"How exciting for you!" Elizabeth said kindly.

"How has it been going?" April asked.

"Well, I don't have anything to compare it to," Jahne admitted, "but I think it's going well." God, couldn't she say something clever? Couldn't she be witty, if not charming? Well, at least she *did* sound like an authentic twenty-four-year-old ingenue, she realized.

"I'm sure you'll be a big success." Kurt smiled, and Goldie nodded.

"All of the key indicators are there—after all, Michael is dating you," April added. There was another murmur of laughter, and Jahne felt confused again. Annette nudged Warren and they both giggled. But Jahne could see no malice on these faces. Though they were joking, it was not at her expense. They were complimenting her, including her. She smiled.

Dessert was a lemon-and-mint sorbet. The conversation turned to the next AIDS benefit, and then the guests stood to take coffee in the living room. But Jahne needed a moment to herself. She headed out to the terrace. As she walked through the living room toward the open arches, she felt her legs tremble. The dress, its raven-blue-and-black taffeta falling so beautifully to the ground, rustled.

"Masterful."

It was Sam's voice, a low murmur at her shoulder. Jahne felt herself pale. She turned to look at him. Was he talking about her new incarnation? Had he seen through her already?

"Masterful," he repeated. "The dress and your hair. A perfect match. Both so simple and exquisite."

He was close to her. She could smell the clove of his aftershave and that sweet, warm scent his breath always had when he drank wine. It was hard to believe that here, in this warm night air beside her, stood the man she'd last seen more than three years ago in the dank, gray winter of New York. Here he was, the man she'd thought of, dreamed of, longed for, and tried to forget. Here he was, and he had followed her, sought her out, was standing at her side. She felt herself tremble. Was it with rage, or desire, or fear? It was dark on the veranda, and he stood very close. How much of her could he see?

"So, you live in Birdland," he said. She remained silent. "I always thought of myself more as the Benedict type."

"Arnold or Canyon?" she asked sweetly.

Jahne heard laughter in the living room, and Michael's

voice protesting. "We better join them," she said, and took a step toward the light.

"Have you ever thought about films?" Sam asked her.

She stopped and turned to him. How could she tell him that she used to, before she spent all her time thinking about him? She looked away, across the terrace, to the exquisite espaliered fruit trees in the garden. The balcony railing had ivy tied to it with raffia training cords, as if it were playing some sort of vegetable bondage game.

"Someday, perhaps," she told him. A breeze began to rustle the trees. She felt it raise her flesh into goose pimples, and waken the whispers of Mai's wonderful dress.

"There's a part I'm casting in a movie that you might be right for."

She laughed out loud. She couldn't help it. Was that the line he'd used on Bethanie and all the others? Well, hadn't he cast Mary Jane before he bedded her?

"Yes, and I am Marie of Roumania," she said, quoting Dorothy Parker.

He laughed in turn. "I know it sounds like the oldest line in Hollywood, but it's true."

"I'm very involved with Marty DiGennaro right now," she said.

"*And* with Michael McLain?" he asked.

God, what was going on? He was flirting with her. And now what would she do? How many times would she let herself be hurt by this man? There was no way this was a good idea. She heard more laughter coming from the brightly lit room where the others had gathered. She could see the sparkle of crystal and the light of the chandelier reflected in the pool. Sam stood beside her, his own face obscured by the darkness.

Get away now, she told herself sternly. Get away and stay away. This time, don't let anything start; stop the damage before it begins.

"That's really none of your business," she told him, and she left him there in the dark.

Michael McLain helped her into his car, deftly sweeping her trailing hem into the sedan before he slammed the door. He'd obviously had lots of practice. Then he circled to his side and got in.

Now that the ordeal of the party was over, Jahne felt as if she were waking from a dream, the very best dream of her life. But now her beauty, her achievement, her future weren't going to dissolve with her awakening. She was desirable, she was successful, and she could control her destiny. What could be better than this—having blown off the man who hurt you, and now sitting beside this idol, this movie star, driving through the Hollywood Hills in a Rolls convertible? Jahne took a deep breath. She hadn't just survived. She'd triumphed. She felt intoxicated, higher than she had ever been on wine or grass.

"Thank you for taking me," she said to Michael. "It was kind of you."

He laughed. "My pleasure," he said. "But you must be new in town to be so polite."

"Well, I know Sy asked you to do this, and I . . ."

"I owe him. Which, by the way, is just how Sy likes it."

She smiled.

"So, how's it going for you. Are you exhausted?"

"Yes!"

"Typical. Marty will work you to death, he's such a perfectionist. And Sy will keep throwing supermarket openings at you if you'll do them."

Jahne laughed. "Well, I hate to say no right now. I mean, a year ago at this time, I couldn't get arrested."

"Oh, yeah. The good old days." He took his eyes off the road and smiled at her. He had a nice smile.

"It's really the Flanders Cosmetics stuff I hate," she admitted. "I'm an actress, not a model or a saleswoman. But I couldn't get the part without agreeing to the hookup." She sighed. "The sessions take hours. I pose till I hurt."

"I'm sure the money doesn't hurt," Michael said. "Don't be too hard on yourself. We all had to struggle to survive. Even Elizabeth sells perfume."

When they pulled up to the house, she found herself inviting him in. He shrugged, nodded, and took her hand as they walked to her door. She felt almost stunned by the feel of his hand in hers. She opened the door, then switched on lights.

"Sit down. I'll get a bottle of something," she said.

"Don't take too long. I like looking at you," he told her.

She felt attracted to him, undeniably. The cute smile wrinkles around his eyes, the long lines that made a parenthesis around his full, sensuous mouth. Well, he was a grown-up, not a boy like Pete. And certainly in Sam's league. Maybe way past it. He was age-appropriate. Despite her streamlined exterior, she was, after all, approaching forty. And he must be over fifty. He had been a movie star she'd always had a crush on, and now he was sitting on her sofa, desiring her. He was Hollywood royalty—he was accepted in the highest circles by everyone.

"I like you," Michael said simply, echoing her thought. "You're nice. I'll bet you could be very nice."

She felt the compliment. Michael McLain had had every beautiful woman in Hollywood for the last two decades. Hadn't they joked about that over dinner? And now he wanted her. In a way, it was almost like an invitation into a very exclusive sorority: the beautiful women's club.

She took out the chilled bottle of white wine she kept for guests, grabbed two glasses, and joined Michael on the sofa. Her ego was dancing the tango, but she was also aroused and curious. His hand had been so warm, and his skin looked as if it had more blood flowing under it than other people's did: it was a delicious flushed brown color. What did it feel like to make love with Michael McLain? Wouldn't it be the perfect antidote to Sam? Because she was determined not to fall under Sam's spell again. She had spent more than three years banishing thoughts of him, not allowing herself to daydream of him. She would not weaken now. She looked at Michael and imagined his lips on hers.

But then reason, or morality, or fear intervened. Are you going crazy? she asked herself. She didn't even *know* him. What about AIDS? There was no such thing as casual sex anymore. This was the nineties. And Michael had been far from discreet in the past. Did she want her private life smeared across the tabloids? Worst of all, what about her scars? Making love with Pete, in complete darkness, was one thing, but Michael wouldn't settle for that. What was she thinking of?

"What are you thinking of?" he asked her, and she found herself blushing.

"I was thinking how comfortable it feels to sit here with you," she lied, because she felt a lot of things—excited, sexy, nervous, titillated, flattered, unreal—but none of them were "comfortable."

"Women say that to me all the time," he laughed. "I think it's because they've seen me on the screen, so they're used to looking at me."

She laughed. "Is that true?"

"I'm not joking," he laughed back. "You'll see. Once *your* show comes out, people will feel that they know you personally. They'll come up to you on the street and call you by name. They'll get your private phone number. They'll write to you. They'll dream of you."

"That's a spooky idea," she agreed. She felt the hair on her arms raise with gooseflesh. "But I've always felt that, despite the disadvantages, fame is a valuable commodity—something you could use as a chip. Trade it for power and control over your life. Once I've risen out of obscurity, I hope I can use it to get some feature work. To get some really good parts."

"You've already got some good parts," he said, with a joking Groucho Marx leer. She laughed and felt another wave of gooseflesh. Surely this was an invitation. Oh, God! She felt like a schoolgirl.

She rose and walked to the window, looking down on the sparkling lights. "Isn't this view beautiful?" she asked, as she watched the lights of the city glow like a carpet of giant fireflies.

Michael came up behind her, but he didn't touch her, he didn't push. "You like it, it's yours," he joked.

"No, it's nobody's," Jahne said, still peering out at the lights. "This town is like water. You can hold on to it only so long; then it drips right through your fingers."

Michael turned her gently so that she faced him. "A

little cynical for someone so young, and so new to Hollywood. There was a time starlets trembled at this sight. Like it was a dream come true." He sipped some of her wine and made a face. It wasn't very good. "Are you a cynic, Jahne? Or are you very wise?"

Jahne thought about it for a moment. The air was electric between them, but they were talking like a bad movie script. "A little of both, probably," she said. "What about you? Do you still tremble? Or are you wise?"

He put his hand on her arm. It was warm, so warm, and she could feel him tremble. God, Michael McLain was trembling for her! For *her*. Surely he couldn't fake that. She didn't move away. "The trappings of stardom don't make me tremble anymore. No, what turns me on is talent. Raw, driven talent. Like yours."

"You know," Jahne said, looking into Michael's eyes, "I want to believe that Michael McLain thinks I'm talented. That here I am, of all the girls in town, and Michael McLain is telling *me* I'm talented. And that it turns him on." Jahne shrugged and took a step away, breaking the current between them. "It's nice to hear and all that, but, come on, I'm not the first starry-eyed new-girl-in-town you've said this to. And you've never even seen my work. So how would you know?"

"I never lie about talent," Michael said. "Why would I? To get a woman to sleep with me? I don't need to lie for that."

Jahne thought of Sam and his line about getting her a part in his movie. She shivered.

Michael kept looking into Jahne's eyes. "You're one of three truly talented women that I have met in twelve years. I won't name the other two—chivalry forbids it— but, trust me, Jahne, you have talent. I saw you at the Melrose Playhouse." He leaned forward and whispered in her ear, "A *unique* talent. And a very old soul."

"Michael," Jahne chided, moving her head away. "Next you'll be telling me we knew each other in a previous life." But she was touched that he'd actually seen her perform.

Michael laughed, his charming, deep, baritone laugh. "I guess I mean you're very mature. Special." There was a silence between them for a moment; then Michael leaned across and kissed her. Jahne didn't respond, except to run her tongue gently along her lips afterward at the sensation that lingered when he moved away. This was fun. Maybe dangerous, but fun! It had been so long since she could talk, really talk, to a man. Since Sam, she realized. Too long.

Jahne knew then that she had already made the decision to sleep with Michael. He seemed considerate, and gentle, and interesting. And he kissed nice. But what about the scars? Would he be repulsed? Just how sophisticated was he?

Jahne lifted her hand and placed it behind Michael's head, drawing him closer. This time, she kissed him, first gently, then more insistently. He responded, holding her hard against his chest. Slowly, his hand moved down her back, dipping into her dress.

She pushed him away, very gently. "Michael, wait. I've been in an accident. I have some . . . well, some scars."

He laughed. "Who doesn't have scars in this town?" he asked, and drew her back toward the sofa. "You're very beautiful. No scar can mar that beauty," he whispered as he began to undress her.

The dress, Mai's beautiful creation, fell to the floor in an inky black cloud. Jahne took a deep breath and then, in the gentle but frightening light of the living room, she began to peel off the bodysuit. She was ungraceful, she knew, but Michael was fumbling with his own clothes. Only then did he turn to her. What would he say?

He said nothing. He simply reached across the gulf between them and ran his fingers lightly over the scar at her groin, then to the two that ran up the center of her breasts. His touch was as light as a breeze. She wondered if he could yet see the scars under her arms, or what he would say about the ones under her buttocks and along her inner thighs. No one could mistake them for accident scars: they were too symmetrical, too perfect. She trembled, waiting for his reaction.

But he merely took her hand and drew her to the sofa. He paused and took out a condom, slipped it on, then

pulled her onto the couch, covering her with his own
warm body.

As she lay naked beneath him, she began to shiver.
"Please, this is the first time anyone has seen me
since . . ." she whispered, and paused. How could she
ever explain? She took a breath and it sounded like a sob.
"I'm afraid about how I look."

Michael raised himself on his elbows and looked down,
scanning her breasts again with his eyes, tracing the thin
scars, from nipple to chest wall, with the tip of one finger.
He finally looked in her eyes, after examining her.
"Beautiful," he said. "You look beautiful."

2

A television premiere is nothing like a movie premiere,
Jahne thought as she slipped into her old terry robe and
padded barefoot to the TV. For her network premiere
tonight, there was no dressing up, no theater with spot-
lights searching the sky, no arrival of stars, directors,
producers, agents. There was no live coverage by reporters. Just as well, Jahne thought. As it was she was nervous enough. Because this, tonight, would determine her
future just as surely as Dr. Moore's scalpels had.

Tonight, for the first time, all of America was going to
get a chance to tune in to *Three for the Road,* and all
the time and money, all the effort, imagination, sweat,
technical tricks, the hours of waiting, the moments of
acting, all the makeup, the lighting, the musical scoring,
all the stitches made by Mai, all the stunts—all the work
was going to be applauded or rejected by the public.

Some of the crew, she knew, were getting together to
watch. But she had not been invited. Was it because she
had broken up with Pete? Was there resentment that she
had dumped one of their own? Or was it simply that the
Hollywood caste system was taking hold? Had anyone
already heard she was dating Michael McLain? Did they
think she was acting like a starlet? Did they feel that she

thought of them as nothing more than techs? She felt—she hoped—that she had never been a snob, that she liked and respected the crew. But did they like and respect her? She couldn't be sure. All she knew was that, the closer the show came to its debut, the more distant the crew had become.

Except for Mai Von Trilling. Thank God for Mai. Jahne felt Mai was her only friend in Hollywood. Well, in the whole world right now, except perhaps for Dr. Moore and little Raoul. The old woman had a way about her that charmed Jahne. Tonight, Mai had suggested that she join Jahne to watch the show, and Jahne had gratefully accepted. Somehow, watching her television premiere all alone with ten or even twenty million people had seemed unbearably lonely.

There was a knock at the door, and Jahne jumped up to get it. Mai stood on the doorstep, a brown paper bag in her arms. She looked Jahne over, taking in the old robe and still-wet hair. "I didn't know ve vere goink formal," she said dryly, and walked past Jahne into the living room. As always, she wore the white sweatshirt and soft black cotton pants that seemed, with her immaculate white Keds, to be her trademark.

She set the bag down on a low table and pulled out a bottle of Veuve Cliquot. "Napoleon and Josephine liked this. Of course, I am only speakink from hearsay. Even I am not *that* old." She looked about the room. "I don't suppose you have champagne flutes?" she asked. Jahne shook her head. "Just as vell I brought these, then." Mai smiled and pulled out a pair of impossibly graceful blown-glass flutes. "But an ice bucket? This even you must have."

"*Even* me?" Jahne asked, smiling as she went to get the Lucite ice bucket and filled it with cubes. "Am I such a barbarian?"

"Everyvun under forty is a barbarian. I vas, too." Mai pulled a second bottle of the champagne out of the bag. "Do you think I grew up drinking vintage French vines? I, the daughter of a tailor? It vas my beauty that let me into the club, und then it took a decade or two to learn vat vas vat. Vell, at least *I* learned. Gloria Svanson vas *alvays* a barbarian.''

Jahne had to giggle at the disapproval. But "Two bottles, Mai?" she asked. "Very extravagant!" How much did vintage Veuve Cliquot cost? she wondered. Could Mai afford it? She knew she could not offer to pay for one: Mai was proud.

"Vell, how often do you make your national debut? Next time, ve'll be more conservative." Mai sat down stiffly while Jahne put one bottle into the refrigerator and the other into the ice bucket. Carefully, she peeled off the lead seal, exposing the cork.

"Shall I open it now?" she asked. Mai looked at her watch and nodded. "Ve haff six minutes before the show starts. Shall ve drink a toast?"

Shyly, Jahne nodded. She twisted the wire basket off the cork slowly. The cork released with a low pop, the bottle smoking from the top. Mai held the two glasses while Jahne filled them quickly, before a drop was spilled.

"Neatly done," Mai complimented her. "But I alvays think it is sad ven vimmen must open their own champagne. Don't you?"

Jahne nodded, and couldn't help thinking of Michael. It would have been nice if he could have come over, but since Wednesday he hadn't called. She felt both excited by and ashamed of her night with him. Had she just been another conquest? Or did he mean it when he said he'd call? He had seemed so warm, so sincere. She wasn't sure how she felt about *him*, but she knew she wanted him to like *her*.

She turned to Mai, who seemed settled and ready, watching a commercial for the new Buick Skylark, with a minute to go. If the show worked, if it was good, Jahne might yet get to have the career she dreamed of, a worthwhile career. If not . . . she shook her head.

"It starts!" Mai hissed, and the screen went dark. The music began: heavy bass back beat, and then Martha and the Vandellas beginning the first verse of "Dancing in the Street." A red thread snaked across the screen, moving to the music, followed by a dozen, and then a hundred more. Then a white thread joined, also pulsing to the driving beat. It, too, was followed by hundreds of other white threads. Superimposed over that came an image of a woman rider on a motorcycle. Then another joined her. Finally, there were three. Behind them, the threads now covered the screen, and it became clearer now: they made the alternating stripes of the flag, red and white, with a blue-black patch in the upper left-hand corner. Then the camera moved out, focusing first on Lila, then Jahne, and lastly Sharleen. Crimson, Cara, and Clover. Their names appeared under their faces. Now, though the flag remained in the background, it became clear that it was hair, the mingled hair of the three girls, blowing and twisting, incredibly long, dancing to the Motown music. Then the title appeared, THREE FOR THE ROAD, spelled in tiny white stars.

The program opened with noise, with quick cuts of chaos. It was the antiwar-demonstration sequence they had shot in Bakersfield. Marty had made sure everything was perfect, and it did look almost like documentary footage to Jahne, until she herself appeared on the screen. But Marty used the cuts, and then a sort of psychedelic smear where one cut bled into another, so that it looked like no documentary Jahne had ever seen. It was sixties content with a nineties edge. Jahne watched as her character, Cara, met Crimson for the first time, on the steps of the courthouse. Then they were confronted by the cops and dragged off to jail. Their dialogue came off well, she thought. Next there was a black-and-white montage, the fingerprinting, the I.D. photos. It reminded her a little of *A Hard Day's Night*, but, once again, with an updated edge. The show had its own style. It was unique.

"It's good," Mai said at the first commercial break.

"I think so," Jahne agreed. Was it good enough to be popular? Was it *too* good? Would it go over the heads of the audience? She could see how Marty was making a serious statement about a better, more hopeful era, and yet simultaneously exploiting their looks, youth, and sex appeal. She and Mai watched in silence.

Using a single camera to shoot, shooting film, not video, working mostly on location rather than in the studio, focusing on the stunts, the fabulous special effects, it all seemed right. Jahne knew that each episode cost over a million dollars. They already had the first eleven done.

Well, she had nothing to be ashamed of. The show had quality. But it did feel kind of sad, just she and Mai sitting there in the dark. She wondered if anyone she knew would watch the show; if people in New York, or even high school classmates from Scuderstown, would tune in.

The phone rang. She looked at Mai. "No one has my home number," she said. It wasn't exactly true: Michael McLain did, and so did Sy and Marty. Mai shrugged. The phone trilled again. Jahne reached for it.

"You are great. So is the show. But you are the best thing on it." It was Sam's voice. Jahne felt her hand, holding the receiver, begin to shake.

"Thank you," she managed to say.

"This is Sam Shields. I hope I'm the first to congratulate you, and also the first to offer you a new job."

Jahne looked over at Mai. Could Mai see how disturbed she was? She took a deep breath. Had he been serious, back on the terrace at April's? Or was this just another stupid come-on?

"Are you interested?" he asked. "It's for a remake of *Birth of a Star*. I think you'd be perfect for the female lead. Would you consider it?"

"Call my agent, Sy Ortis," Jahne managed to tell him. "Let me take a look at the script, and then we'll let you know."

"Spoken like a true star!" Sam laughed. "I'll have a treatment over to him in the morning. Bear in mind, it's only in first draft. I can do better. I always do better the second time out."

"I'll bear that in mind," she said, and dropped the receiver into the cradle.

Lila sat in the darkness of her beach house, in the empty room on the second floor that looked out over the Pacific. The room that had once been Nadia's bedroom. The room Nadia had died in. Nadia Negron, who had starred in the first *Birth of a Star*. Well, the room wasn't totally empty. All around its edges, Lila had ranged candles—black candles—of almost every size and thickness. All of them now were lit. Since Ara's party, Lila had a single obsession, a single desire, a single goal. This was how she'd reach it. An offering. A twofold offering. Because Lila wanted—needed—to get to play Nadia's part, Theresa's part, in *Birth of a Star*.

On the wall, a single shelf held a sort of altar that Lila had created in the otherwise empty space. On it was a picture of Nadia, two more candles in silver candlesticks, a dish of smoking incense, and the video cassette of Theresa's *Birth of a Star*. Since she had heard about the remake, she had had no other goal.

Lila stood up and bowed to the picture of Nadia. Then she lit a candle, lifted it off the altar, and went around the room lighting one taper after another. Tonight, she had a lot to ask of Nadia. She needed her mother, the Puppet Mistress, to watch *3/4* and feel envy. She needed the premiere of *3/4* to rack up great ratings. She needed April Irons to watch it. But most of all, she needed Sam Shields to cast her in *Birth of a Star*.

Lila lay flat on the floor, her face against the bare tile, her arms spread. She said aloud the only prayer she ever said: "Whatever it takes. Whatever it takes."

Sharleen switched off the set and turned to Dean, who sat beside her on the floor, finishing the last of the popcorn. "Well, what did you think?"

"You're good, Sharleen. Real good," he said.

"Really? You *really* think so?"

"Sure." She could see his hesitation.

"But . . ."

"Well . . ."

"Tell me."

"Well, the show sure isn't as good as *Andy Griffith*."

Flanders Fields was the largest single piece of property in Bel Air. Inside it, in the master suite, Monica Flanders sat beside her Pekingese in her satin-brocade upholstered canopy bed. And not just *any* canopy bed, mind you, but the one that once belonged to Josephine, back in the days when she was a simple island girl from the West Indies. Of course she, Monica, had had it completely redone, but the provenance still mattered to her. It was the bed of a woman of no special beauty, whose charm and brains had raised her to empress. A woman not unlike herself.

"Will there be anything else, Madame?" her maid asked. Her *Irish* maid, not a *schvartzer* as so many women her age had to put up with. No. Monica Flanders was called the Queen of Cosmetics, and she lived like a queen. All the other great ones were retired, gone, dead. Helena Rubinstein. Elizabeth Arden. Coco Chanel. Now the business was ruled by corporations; heartless, mindless entities that lived and sold by statistics, by studies, by market share and focus-group results. Men like her son, Hyram. A good boy, perhaps, and a good father to his children, but a bit soulless, no?

What could those men in control know about a woman's needs? For half a century Monica had been selling women a dream: the dream of beauty and perfectibility. Perhaps a new face cream, a different color eye shadow, would do the trick: make them beautiful, make them loved, make them happy. That it never worked seemed not to matter; hope was what she sold and it simply kept most of them restlessly looking for the right product—the one that *would* work.

She had started by listening to their laments in the little beauty parlor in lower Manhattan: a husband who cheated, an engagement that was broken off, an empty marriage, insecurity, unhappiness, discontent. And to each she had nodded, clicked her teeth in sympathy, let her eyes fill with a sheen of tears. She understood them. And then "Try this," she would say. "Try this and things will change. You'll feel younger, you'll glow. People will notice a new you. A better you. Softer. Dewy. New. Young."

Since then, little had changed but the size of her market. Tonight, Monica felt that she had perfected her pitch. Tonight a million, ten million, perhaps even fifty million women would watch the new show that she had caused to happen. And each one, no matter her age, no matter her appearance, would look at the screen and envy the images she had put there. It was like an hour-long commercial. Maybe better. And she had the products ready, the advertisements that would tell these yearning, envious woman what they could do to look like those three beautiful, perfect girls on their screens.

"Put on the television for me and bring me the remote and my glasses," she told her maid. "I have something to watch on television." Monica had bet millions that this show would succeed.

And, as always, she was right.

In Bakersfield, Jake's diner was closed on Sunday nights. It was the one night a week that he could spend alone, without Thelma, watching TV. First *911*, then *Rescue Squad*, followed by reruns on cable. He stretched his feet out on the footrest and pushed the recliner until he was almost supine. As his hands scrambled in the seat beneath him, he yelled out, "Thelma." After no response, he yelled it again. Ah, she'd left. He settled back, sighed, ready for a pleasant evening.

Then, out of the blue, Thelma waltzed into the family room, kicked off her floppy rubber sandals, and dropped her large form down onto the plaid Herculon-covered sofa.

"What's the matter, Jake?" she asked, like she didn't know, and she placed a bowl of microwaved popcorn between them on the table, along with two beers she snapped open. Then, most shocking of all, *she* picked up the remote control.

"Hey!" he said. "*911* is coming on."

Thelma reached into the pocket of her housedress, took out a Kleenex, wiped her nose, and then calmly looked at him. "Not tonight it ain't," she said, and clicked a button. The twenty-seven-inch RCA screen instantly burst into color.

"What are you talking about, Thelma? You don't watch television Sunday nights. I thought you go play bingo over to the Bakersfield Rotary?" He couldn't keep the disappointment from his voice.

"Bingo ain't on Sundays no more. Don't you remember? They changed it to Mondays now. 'Cause of the TV show."

What show? he thought. Not the one she tried to get him to watch *last* week. Jesus, now he thought of it, she'd come in then, too. He'd had to go back to the diner and watch his shows on the black-and-white he had in the kitchen. Oh, shit. "I thought that was only a made-for-TV movie, or something like that. You mean to tell me it's on *every* Sunday night now?"

"Where you been? This show's the most-watched TV show in America," she said. "Where's your patriotism?" The television went silent during the opening credits. "Anyway, I got something I want to show you. A surprise I figured out."

Jake sat back, his arms folded across his chest. He was mad. Another woman's piece of shit, some *Designing Women* garbage or something, with the actresses in frilly clothes and crazy hairstyles. He looked over at the screen: a desert in Utah or somewhere, with Eagle Rock or one of them tall buttes. As the camera got closer, he saw three motorcycles, a woman in full leather on each bike, jackets open revealing full breasts under tight T-shirts. Nice tits. Well, so what?

"I'm going over to the diner."

"No, you're not. You're stayin' right here. Look carefully. Look at them girls."

Thelma was letting him look at tits? This was a new one. On the screen, each of the girls pulled up in a sharp gravel-spattering stop for a close-up.

"Remember I said last week that I'd seen that blonde somewhere before?" Thelma asked. "Well, I have. And so have you. Look at her close, now."

Jake squinted at the screen. Thelma was right—there was something about her that was familiar. "Maybe. What of it?"

"Jake, I think we just got on the map." Thelma held up a piece of cardboard with hand-lettering. "Jake's Place. Home of *Three for the Road*'s Clover."

The camera moved closer, and Jake's face lit up. There she was, big as life. Sharleen! "You mean that blonde waitress we had working for us? That's her? Goddamn,

Thelma. You're right. Holy shit, we had us a real star at the diner! But you fired her."

"Good thing I did. Otherwise you'da made a fool a yourself and she wouldn't be on TV!"

In Manhattan's East Village, what was left of the St. Malachy rep company's Movable Feast had moved from Saturday night to Sunday night. The tiny living room of the tenement apartment had people sitting all over—on the secondhand sofa from the Salvation Army, the stacks of Woolworth's cushions, even on the bare linoleum floor. The actors used to eat at makeshift tables, but that was before *Three for the Road* had become the focus of their weekly meals together. Now the meal was buffet-style, set up on the cover of the bathtub in the kitchen that doubled on these nights as a sideboard. Everybody watched *Three for the Road*.

"Anyone need anything?" Molly called out from the kitchen. "I'm not getting up again after the show starts, so let me know now."

The television had been on for several minutes, but with the sound off. "Here it is," Chuck, Sam's replacement as director of the group, said, and turned up the volume. The teaser began. Molly wiped her hands on the dish towel. The dialogue had already started. "Clover! Wow, man! That's psychedelic!" Then another voice spoke. "Groovy! I can't take it."

Molly blinked. For a moment, the voice had sounded exactly like her old friend Mary Jane. Had Mary Jane gotten a bit part out on the coast? Molly rushed to the doorway. But it was only Jahne Moore, one of the three stars, speaking. Molly sighed. Since Mary Jane disappeared without a trace, Molly had "seen" her on subways, on buses, in museums, and once on the down escalator at Bloomingdale's. But, like this time, she'd been wrong. Mary Jane had disappeared.

A close-up of each of the three actresses flashed on the screen with the opening credits. "They *are* beautiful women," Molly sighed, "*really* beautiful." And young, she thought. Very, very young.

"That's all it takes out there," another woman, Sharon

Malone, said. "That's why I'm sticking with the stage. You can get by on just talent here," she said, the sarcasm heavy in her voice.

"Now, let's not be catty," Molly called out in a sing-song voice.

"That's right, sometimes they *can* act. Look at Jahne Moore. I read she was discovered in some Ibsen play at the Melrose Playhouse. Not *too* shabby," Chuck reminded them.

"Still reading those *People* magazines, eh, Chuck?" someone joshed.

"See her, the tallest one, Lila Kyle?" Sharon asked. "Well, *I* read in *TV Guide* that it was hard for her to get taken seriously as an actress, since both her parents were so famous and all."

"Wait a minute; can you believe this shit? Remember what Neil Morelli used to say? Poor little rich girl? Come off it. Lila Kyle wasn't discovered while working in some hash joint. She was 'discovered' by Marty DiGennaro himself—*while they were having dinner, for chrissakes*. When was the last time *you* had dinner with Marty?" Harvey Jewett asked sarcastically.

"Sounds like I'm not the only one scarfing up *People*," Chuck laughed. "Try not to sound *too* bitter, Harvey."

"Hey, I could do an hour of material on that, but Neil would do it better," Harvey said. "Where's Neil Morelli, now that we really need him?" Harvey shook his head, his eyes glued to the screen.

"Where *is* Neil Morelli?" Molly asked, not for the first time. "Anyone hear from him?"

"Speaking of the lost and deported, do you think Sam Shields has put the wood to any of those honeys?" Harvey asked. "Maybe he's gotten real lucky. You know how he was in New York."

"Harvey," Craig, another of the out-of-work actors, said, "even Sam would be out of his league. These girls are working with Marty DiGennaro; Sam doesn't have a chance."

Then the program started again, and they were silent, drinking up the fast cuts, the dissolves, the weird, innovative camera angles, the quirky dialogue. And the youth and beauty of the three girls. Too soon, the show ended. Sighs went round the circle. They would all have to go back to their day jobs tomorrow.

In Los Angeles, George Getz sat down in his easy chair and clicked on the TV he had recently bought. George, child of the sixties, hated television. He was a movie person. But then he found out, a little late, what all the students in his classes were talking about with such excitement. *Three for the Road* was on its way to becoming the phenomenon of the decade. It wasn't until he heard the names of the costars that he reacted. Lila Kyle, his former pupil, was in a Marty DiGennaro series.

That hadn't hurt business, either, he thought. Now his classes were doubled in size and had waiting lists, for chrissakes. And he was, at last, happy. It was the money, he told himself. No, it was the money and the recognition he had been robbed of for so long.

He watched tonight's show with intensity. It was, as they would have said in the sixties, psychedelic. And all style, no substance, if you asked his opinion. But on a medium that usually had neither, it was a major breakthrough. Tonight's show gave Lila more close-ups and lines than the other weeks, he noticed. Leave it to Lila, he thought. She always knew how to draw attention to herself! As the closing credits rolled across the screen, George rolled himself another joint and lifted it in a silent toast to the screen.

"Taught her everything she knows," he said out loud to the empty room, and pulled the sweet smoke deep into his lungs.

Theresa O'Donnell squinted at the screen in the sitting room adjoining her bedroom, trying to make the double images converge into one. She reached for the glass of lukewarm vodka, neat, that sat at her elbow on the low table next to her chaise longue. Kevin entered the room, looked at the clear liquid in the glass, and was about to say something. "Sit down and shut up," Theresa growled before he could open his mouth. Since Kevin had been dumped by Lila, Theresa had inherited him. He lived there, kept her glass full and kept her company, much to the disgust of both Robbie and Estrella. Well, Theresa had no choice about keeping Kevin on. After all, he knew her secrets. Fuck Estrella. It didn't matter even if Estrella left. She'd still have her two little girls.

She turned to the wooden figure beside her on the sofa. "Do we have to do this?" Candy asked.

"It's *so* boring!" Skinny chimed in.

"Oh, now, you sound jealous!" Theresa admonished, but she smiled. "After all, she *is* your sister."

"She's a coldhearted bitch!" muttered Skinny.

"Language, please! Unless you like the taste of soap." Still, Theresa smiled, until the show began and Lila's face appeared. Then the smile disappeared.

Theresa stared at Lila's image on the screen for the third week in a row. Lila, a star. This was not good news, not good news at all. It made her look old—it could make her look bad. *Now* what's going to happen to me? she wondered. Doesn't the little bitch think about anyone but herself? Who's going to hire me now, when it has become so public that I have a daughter Lila's age?

Jesus, and on television. Television was over, finished. Everyone knew that, except maybe Marty DiGennaro. And Lila. It would *never* be the same again, not like it was in the days of Theresa's show, and *Lucy* and *The Honeymooners* and Ed Sullivan. Theresa marked the death of the medium from the day she and Ed had left the tube. It was downhill from there—a vast wasteland of no-talent trash. Trash and PR.

The build on this show had been ridiculous. In a place famous for hype, they had outdone themselves. Mother of God, there wasn't a magazine or newspaper that wasn't running some story or other. And not wholesome pieces, either. Not ones like she used to do.

"She looks like a tramp," Skinny said.

"So do the other two," Theresa agreed.

"But they're famous tramps," Candy taunted.

"If I hear another nasty word like that from you, I'm calling in Mr. Woodpecker!" Theresa threatened. But what Candy said was true. Lila was famous. So were the other tramps, who costarred. And when the fame became so big that every little detail of their lives would become public, what was Lila going to do then?

"I told her to stay out of the business. I told her, but she didn't listen." Theresa looked over at Kevin, who returned her look, then shrugged, as if reading her mind. Theresa drained her glass and held it out to him. Wordlessly, Kevin stood up and took it, refilled it from the bottle on the dresser, and returned it to Theresa.

"They're calling her one of the three most beautiful women in the world," he said to Theresa.

"Sweet St. Joseph! She'll be America's sweetheart. They'll be saying that next. The loveliest girl in the world." Like mother, like daughter, Theresa thought, and laughed bitterly at her private joke, then almost choked on her drink. Perhaps she was being too harsh, too bitter. There must be a way she could use this to her advantage.

Maybe that's it, she thought. Ride her wave. Maybe a mother-daughter show. Perfect! This show can't last. There's nothing to it. No singing, no dancing. After she bombs in this, I'll help pull her back up on top, rescue her with *our* show.

"Don't worry, girls," she told Candy and Skinny. "This won't last. And I have a plan."

They could begin rehearsing tomorrow, brush up a few old routines, maybe develop some new ones. She could get Robbie to choreograph a dance routine or two.

"Forget about plans," said Kevin bitterly. "She don't need you no more."

"Shut the fuck up!" Theresa snapped. "She'll come crawling when she realizes she can't get through this without me."

"She will!" Candy shouted.

"Kevin, get out of here," Skinny added. "We want to watch this alone." Kevin rose and, shaking his head, slowly left the room.

Theresa settled back to observe the rest of the show. Maybe things would work out for the best after all.

Dobe sat in the television lounge of the Wayfarer Hotel in Edmund, Minnesota, watching the screen in silence.

Sitting next to him was a John Deere salesman from St. Paul. The front-desk clerk, leaning against the door jamb so he could hear the phones if they rang, was engrossed in the show unfolding on the TV.

Dobe put his fingers to his lips, afraid that his delight would cause him to smile, and cause people to ask what he was grinning at. When you were on the grift, it was best not to call attention to yourself. But it was hard not to grin back at the pretty blonde on the screen. Sharleen was radiant, lighting up the room, making him feel young again. He was as happy as a father could be for his daughter. Good girl, he said to himself. You done it. I'm proud of you, kid.

The salesman leaned toward Dobe and whispered, "Look at the tits on that blonde."

Dobe looked him straight in the face; his smile faded. "Watch out, mister. You're talking about a lady," he said. Then Dobe turned his eyes back to the screen.

Brewster Moore sat across from the television, its screen flickering in front of him. The three women were incredibly beautiful, picked for their looks more than for their talent. But Dr. Moore knew that Mary Jane had always had talent. Now, thanks to him, she had beauty as well.

He watched her image on the screen closely. Was it professional or personal? he wondered. Her letters to him seemed excited, but they also had an edge of sadness, telling not only of her success but also of her loneliness in her new life. And Brewster Moore, divorced now five years, knew something about the loneliness Mary Jane wrote about. Like her, he had his work, but, unlike her, he knew his work would never quite be enough.

He had to force himself not to write too often to Mary Jane. That would not be right. He had created her looks; now it was up to her to create her new life. And he could not play a part in both. People wanted to forget his work once it was done. She didn't owe him anything, and she wouldn't want to be reminded of his services. Patients rarely did. But at least he had her letters.

Now he couldn't take his eyes off Mary Jane Moran—

Jahne Moore, he corrected himself. My handiwork, he thought. My Galatea. *I* made her, not God. Of course, he could never say those words out loud to anyone. His triumph was a lonely pleasure. But delicious nonetheless.

After all the reconstructions of burn victims, of the children with nature's defects, of faces that, despite all his skill, would never even approximate the norm; after all the Park Avenue matrons insisting on premature face lifts, after the models with perfect noses who wanted them to be a bit *more* perfect—Jahne Moore was unique. An achievement of perfection, appropriate and complete. Beautiful. Rewarding. Brave.

A woman he could love.

Neil Morelli owned nothing except the clothes in the closet and the thirteen-inch color TV he had bought from a guy at the club who was selling hot Korean TVs for fifty bucks. Well, he hadn't actually bought it yet, since he still owed the guy twenty dollars.

He had no money, no car, no friends, and nowhere to go. He had a stinking job driving a cab. But he had his television, and while that was on, Neil could feel he was still connected to the world. It was Sunday night, but it could have been any night in the week. The calendar didn't mean much to him anymore. All he needed to know was when *Seinfeld, Evening at the Improv,* and that show with Paul Provenza were on. So he could envy and hate them. But tonight he was making a special effort to watch the show all the assholes at the club had been carrying on about for weeks. He would never admit it to anyone tomorrow, but tonight he was going to watch *Three for the Road* for the first time. Just to see what the fuck everyone was going nuts over, the guys at the taxi garage especially.

Not that it was a hard show to watch, Neil soon saw. Three gorgeous girls, all with great tits and legs, romping around right before his eyes. And all that sixties shit. Love beads. Bell bottoms. Moby Grape. He was lying on his open sofa-bed, and had the television on a chair next to him. For this show, he had pulled the set up real close to his face, so that he wouldn't miss anything. Actually, this was the closest thing to a date that Neil had had in a long time. He felt his dick get hard as the show progressed, and he tried to fantasize which one he would fuck, if he gave them the chance.

He still hadn't decided by the end of the show, although he had begun to stroke himself, and was close to climaxing. Then the credits began to roll. Neil always was on the lookout for newcomers. Three kids had managed, against the odds, to break into the business big time. Well, good for them. He watched their names roll. Sharleen Smith, Jahne Moore, Lila Kyle.

Wait a minute. Lila Kyle? Neil knew who she was; he had researched her for his routine. She was the double-dynasty kid, *both* parents stars. He felt his dick grow limp in his hand, his frustration now fueling his rage at another Nepotism Squad target. She must have got the job through connections. Her mother got it for her. She got a free ride; he, Neil Morelli, got nothing.

You fucking cunt, he thought. I could kill you.

3

If politics makes strange bedfellows, just think of the couplings Hollywood creates. Doris Day and Rock Hudson. Madonna and Michael Jackson. Michael Jackson and Brooke Shields. Madonna and Warren Beatty. Michael Jackson and Diana Ross. Madonna and everyone else.

On the surface, Marty DiGennaro and Lila Kyle would seem as unlikely and ridiculous. But given their backgrounds, there was a certain symmetry to it. Both were loners. Both had spent their childhoods in darkened rooms staring at movies. In fact, both had stared at some of the same movies. Both Lila and Marty loved Birth of a Star, *and if one had a mother who had been featured in it, it enhanced everything for the other.*

So despite Marty's plain face and unimpressive build

411

and Lila's glamour and leggy height, the two shared more than most odd couples in L.A.

And when did a beautiful woman on the arm of an ugly, shorter, older, but powerful man ever look out of place in Hollywood?

Marty DiGennaro sat back in his limousine, his feet up on the folded seat in front of him, savoring the moment. Everything was better than good. The reception of *3/4* was great. He'd just heard that the Network was renewing for the next thirteen episodes. Monica Flanders was ecstatic. Their new cosmetics line was already profitable. And, on top of it all, Lila Kyle had accepted his invitation to dinner. In fact, she had accepted so unexpectedly that he hadn't had time to really plan. Unusual for a control freak like Marty. How many times had he asked her out? It seemed like every day since they'd started shooting the series, and always the answer was the same. A frigid "No, thank you." Then, just like that, she accepts. Go know.

Maybe it had just sunk in that he had done what he said he'd do: he'd made her a star. In just a month, the show had captured an unprecedented audience. You couldn't go by a magazine stand or a variety store without seeing the girls' pictures everywhere. So why question his luck? Or her motivations? He was too excited. Excited like he used to be as a little kid waiting for the Joan Crawford movie to begin. Or Myrna Loy. Or Merle Oberon. The other kids watched TV on Saturday for the cartoons. Not Marty. He was into beauty. He couldn't wait for his star of the moment to light up the old Dumont television screen as the *Early Show* began.

His star of the moment was definitely Lila Kyle. Only she was *real*—flesh and blood—not some color emulsion on celluloid. From the moment he met her, he knew she was different, special. She was Hollywood royalty, after all. A combination of the grandeur of the old stars and something altogether new and contemporary. At the end of the day's shoot, he couldn't get her out of his mind: her smoldering red hair, her narrow waist, the long, long legs that seem to start at her neck. He would catch himself staring at her while he was setting up a shot of Jahne or Sharleen, when his attention should have been on them. And the craziest part of it all was, she didn't seem to care that he—Marty DiGennaro—was paying so much attention to her. In fact, she didn't even seem to notice. Not that he needed that, but, let's face it, when you offer an unknown a chance of a lifetime, you expect a little something, a little appreciation. Not a fuck, necessarily. He wasn't into power fucking. But gratitude, respect, friendship, warmth. Lila gave him zip.

And the most amazing part was, he didn't think it was an act. She wasn't playing coy, hard to get, as his first wife had. Lila was simply cool. Cool as they come.

She hadn't seen him, except on the set. Tonight, she had agreed to have dinner with him, just the two of them, but then she asked that they not go out. She had smiled warmly; she hated crowds she said. She just wanted to talk. Every other chick he knew, when he took her out, wanted not only the hottest spot in town, but also the hottest *table* in that hottest spot. Women wanted to be *seen* with Marty DiGennaro. One bitch had even brought her own photographer to the restaurant to record the momentous occasion. But not Lila. He couldn't figure her out. And that gave Marty DiGennaro a hard-on.

He had one now, as he finalized plans for the evening. He had his office on the phone. Staci, his secretary, had taken care of most of the details, in her usual unflappable way, but Marty wanted to do *something,* put his own imprint on the evening, as it were. This wasn't just another date with just another starlet. He gave Staci a few comments, then hung up, but he was too restless to do nothing. Instead, he picked up the car phone and began to dial numbers. The first was to his florist.

"This is Marty DiGennaro," he said into the phone, and waited while the salesperson at the other end went into the usual fawning tizzy. Tonight, he allowed it. Everyone should get what they need tonight. He finally had a dinner date with Lila Kyle, and could afford to be magnanimous. "Brian usually does my house every week, but tonight is special. I need crimson gladioli." He had read in some stupid interview that that was Lila's favorite flower. "Dozens of them. Tell Brian I want at least four dozen each in the bedroom, dining room, living room, and two or three dozen in baskets around the pool. And make sure they're crimson, not that red-orange shit. And I need them delivered and set up no later than seven-thirty." He paused. *"Of course* tonight."

He planned social events of importance the way he planned his movies. He wanted every detail perfect. Next the caterers. Again, he wanted to check, although Staci had already made the call. He went over the schedule in his mind.

Drinks and hors d'oeuvre at eight. Dinner at nine. Bed at ten? Marty wondered. After all, she'd *asked* not to go out. Marty thought about her smooth skin, her long, shining red hair. How would it feel to have that hair draped across his chest, his belly? He grunted.

"Sally," Marty said into the intercom to his driver.

"Yes, Mr. D.?"

"I want you to pick up Miss Kyle at seven-forty-five. Exactly."

"Got it, Mr. D. Seven-forty-five on the nose."

"And I want you to put on your white jacket and serve drinks, then disappear when dinner's served. But don't go anywhere tonight. I might need you later, so hang around the pool house. Watch some TV. No drinking, and no nose candy, *capisce?* You're on duty until I tell you different."

"Don't worry about me, boss. I'll be available for as long as you want, same as usual. You can depend on me, Mr. D."

And Marty knew he could. He had known Sally since his earliest days in L.A. Sally was a gift he had inherited, more or less, from a capo in New York, someone who wanted Marty "treated right." And Sally had been just the man. He seemed to have no life of his own, just vicariously enjoying the life Marty had made for himself. But, then, Marty always saw to it that Sally got taken care of, too. Always had women, a little coke—only the best—now and then, a comfortable apartment over the pool house. And Sally was justifiably grateful. The last job he'd had was for an ex–wise guy who had been on edge twenty-four hours a day, a guy who had been shot at more than once. Sally felt his life had been spared when the guy died in his sleep. No more sweats when he turned the guy's ignition key, praying there wasn't a bomb wired to it. Working for Marty was like living in Disneyland.

Lila knew how to make good out of bad. After all, growing up with Theresa O'Donnell had taught her *something*. So, when an old fart in love with himself like Michael McLain called her and asked her out for dinner, she turned him down. Not because he was an over-the-hill playboy—which he was, in her opinion—and not even because she didn't think she could get through the evening without dropping her pants, which she knew she could. She just didn't want to date anyone. And she certainly didn't want to date a man who had once fucked her mother. Theresa bragged about all the men in her life, and Michael McLain had been on the top of her list at one time, when he was younger and Theresa was only a little older. It gave Lila the creeps. Michael was one of those guys who dated older women when he was young and younger ones when he was old. He made her sick.

But he *was* important. He still knew everyone that counted. No sense getting him angry. So she had to think fast when he asked. "I'm sorry, I'm involved with my director. Maybe another time." She hadn't wanted to alienate Michael, just to get him the fuck off her back. Marty would be a good cover; plus, now that she thought about it, it might even be the time to lean on him a little to see if he could get her the part in *Birth of a Star*.

So now, after a long day on location, she was getting dressed and putting makeup on yet again. She leaned back from the vanity mirror in her dressing room at home, and blinked her eyes. Perfect, she thought, as she always did after expertly applying mascara. She'd been taught makeup by Theresa when she was nine, and sometimes she even thought of herself as one of those Kabuki dancers in Japan who develop all their feminine wiles before puberty. Now that she thought of it, weren't they all men? But perfect in their female role, with nothing to learn. There was very little left for Lila to learn, either. From now on, it was performance time. Her years of understudying Theresa would pay off. She would take over Theresa's role and outdo her at it.

But could she get to April Irons to give her the part in *Birth of a Star?* And could she get Marty to help her? It would kill Theresa, Lila knew, and she smiled. Marty's already so crazy for me, he would do backward somersaults. Lila was aware—very aware—of how he followed her with his eyes wherever she went on the set. She pretended not to notice, but she did. Every time. And that's just the way she wanted it.

Well, she had tried to avoid it, but perhaps dating him was inevitable. The idea of dating frightened her, since Kevin. But she was feeling a lot better now, even about spending the evening with a man. Marty was one man she could handle. And he had more influence in Hollywood than any other man she knew. Certainly more than Michael McLain. She stood at her three-sided mirror and did a series of poses, liking what she saw. Tonight is going to be very good for me, she told herself, and smiled at her image.

The doorbell rang, and Lila jumped. Who the fuck would come up to the door of her house and ring the bell? She lived in Malibu Colony just to be sure that didn't happen. Who had gotten past security, and how? She walked down the curving stairs, and peeked out the peephole. Marty's guy—what's his name, Sally—was standing there, holding his cap in his hand. Lila flung open the door. "What are you doing here, Sally?" she asked. "Got lost?"

"No, Miss Kyle. Mr. D., he said I should pick you up at seven-forty-five." He indicated his watch. "It's seven-forty-five," he added, and smiled.

"I drive myself, Sally. Take the night off." She slammed the door and went back up the stairs to her dressing room. What was that all about? She didn't like the idea of being trapped without a car at Marty's place. She ran the brush through her hair for the last time, straightened the seams in her stockings (she figured Marty would *love* seamed stockings), put a black lace

416

mantilla over her hair, and ran down the stairs, car keys in hand. She opened the door, and Sally was still there, practically in the same position she had left him in minutes ago. "What are *you* still doing here?" she snapped, as she walked toward her black Land Rover.

"Miss Kyle, I promised Mr. D. I'd see you to his house. Why not ride with me? I promise I'll drive slow, and bring you home anytime you want. Come on, Miss Kyle, Mr. D. made me promise."

"What you promise Mr. DiGennaro has nothing to do with me. I feel like driving myself, so that's what I'm going to do." She hiked her blue suede skirt up and got up into the driver's seat, pulling the mantilla around her head to keep her hair in place. She put the car in reverse, then first, and squealed out the drive, watching Sally, in her rearview mirror, scamper into the limousine to follow her. She paused at the entrance ramp to the coast highway, then squeezed into a spot that opened between two cars, making it impossible for Sally to follow. But when she checked the rearview, he was just one car behind her. She accelerated, weaving in and out of traffic lanes, and arrived at Marty's house breathless but with a smile on her face. Marty himself answered the door. Well, she could surprise him.

"Where's Sally? Where's my car? Whose jeep is that?" The questions came out one right after the other, without pauses for answers.

"And how nice to see you, too, Mr. DiGennaro. Thank you for the compliments. I paid particular attention to my hair this evening." Lila let her voice drip sarcasm. "And may I come in, or is this as far as I'm getting this evening?" Just then Marty's limousine sped up the driveway, and Sally was out of the car almost before the engine turned off. "I'm sorry, Mr. D. She wouldn't come in the car, Mr. D. She insisted on taking hers."

"Fine, Sally," Marty said. "Come in, Lila."

But Sally wouldn't quit.

"I tried to keep up with her, Mr. D., but she drove like a man. I mean, no woman drives that good. No offense, Miss Kyle. Jeez, I'm sorry, Mr. D." He had his hat in his hands in front of him.

Marty looked at Lila, who was smiling a broad, innocent smile. "Don't be a chauvinist, Sal. I should have known better. Thanks for trying. Come on in the house and make us a couple of drinks, then take the rest of the night off."

"What can I get you to drink?" Sal asked Lila.

"Chardonnay?" Lila asked sweetly, still standing on the steps outside.

Marty jumped. "Lila, I'm sorry. Where are my manners? Come on in. I thought we'd have drinks on the lanai first. Would that be all right with you?"

They walked in, crossed the vast marble foyer with the grand staircase, and stepped out onto the marble-paved lanai. Sally joined them, placed the wine cooler next to Marty's elbow after pouring two glasses of the white wine, and went inside.

"What should we drink to, Lila? I feel that this is such an important occasion, we should formalize it with a toast. Should we drink to the success of the show, or is that old news already?"

"How about, to everyone getting what he—and she—wants." She clicked his glass and took a long sip.

"Well, I feel like I already have everything I want. A hit TV show, a nice home, and the most beautiful woman in America sitting opposite me. What else is there?"

"For me? Stardom."

"You already have that. You'll be on every magazine cover in the country, and most of Europe. Even South Africa. What are you getting in fan mail already? Five to six thousand pieces every week? Shall I go on?"

"That's celebrity, Marty. Not real fame. Fame comes with doing something that lasts, something like your first picture, that made everything else possible for you. *Back Streets* made you famous. *Three for the Road* makes me a celebrity. Celebrities are just famous for being famous. See the difference?"

"You'll get your shot at fame, then. Just hang on. Don't be so impatient. You're very young. Enjoy this, and then move on. Something will come along, the perfect piece, the thing that cries out for you and only you."

Lila leaned forward, her elbow on her knee. "Something has. And I want your opinion about it. And your help in getting it."

She could see she had piqued Marty's curiosity. "What's that?" he asked, his brow furrowed.

"*Birth of a Star*," Lila said, and sat back to watch his expression.

There was no movie that Marty loved more than *Birth of a Star*. Years ago, he'd tried to get an option on a remake. He was bitter that now it had gone to someone else. And not just anyone, but his old *bête noire*. Well, she'd fuck it up for sure. Wasn't it she who'd done the remake of *The Front Page* with Burt Reynolds and Kathleen Turner? A sacrilege. God, he'd love to do *Birth of a Star*. How had April gotten a hold of it?

Still, he couldn't show this loss of face, this loss of control, to Lila. Lila, whose mother had starred in the film.

"*Birth of a Star?* Are you crazy? That's a remake of a movie that wasn't very good to begin with. The only thing that movie had going for it was Theresa O'Donnell, and at that point in her career, *anything* she did would have gotten raves."

"I want to do the same thing to the remake," Lila said, keeping her voice low and steady.

"Remakes suck, Lila. I know that, you know that, the public knows that, for chrissakes. They are worse than sequels. The only one who doesn't know it is April Irons, and she's got her head up her ass. *Birth* is going to bomb, trust me. Now I remember what I heard: it's a so-so script, and its timeliness is over. It's passé. You want to make a movie so bad, let *me* direct you."

"I'd love for you to direct me. But first I want to do *Birth*."

Marty stood up and began to pace the length of the veranda. This was not what he'd expected. Where was her excitement over *3/4*? Where was her gratitude? Where was her respect? "Lila, listen to me. You're the hottest property in the United States at the moment. For your first film, you can name your own price, pick any script you want. Why would you fuck up your career to do that piece of shit? It would be like tossing all your opportunity down the toilet.''

"So you won't help me get it?" she asked, allowing her anxiety to show for the first time this evening.

"Help you? I'll do everything I can to *stop* you. I won't let you throw away something you've worked so hard to achieve. Something *I've* worked so hard to achieve. I have approval of your movie roles while you're on *3/4*. That's in your contract. I won't let you do it, Lila." He swallowed the last of the wine from his glass, and walked over to refill it. "And that's that."

Lila stood up, shrugged the mantilla up from her shoulders to her head, and turned to Marty. "You can't stop me. No one can, Marty. I want that part, and I'm going to get it." She turned and began to walk the outside path toward her jeep. "And if I have the celebrity you say I have, I'm *going* to get it."

Lila wasn't exactly surprised when she got another call from Michael McLain. It was Robbie who danced around the room like a deranged, obese ballerina on skates.

"Michael McLain! Michael McLain!" he caroled. "He's *sooo-oo* cute."

"He's *sooo-oo* old," Lila said, reaching for the little slip with his number. She knew from her mom's life how this stuff worked. If things went well, soon *everyone* would be calling her.

"Billy over at Sy Ortis' office said he might star in something with Ricky Dunn."

Lila stopped in her walk to her bedroom. "Really?" she asked. Ricky was hot. "Well, maybe I'll call him back."

"Maybe? *Maybe?*"

God, she hated how Robbie was down on her all the time. He wanted a full description of each day at the studio, of each bit of gossip he could milk and retell to his friends. She sighed.

"I said *maybe.*"

"Call him now. Let me listen on the extension."

"Forget about it." Lila sighed again. God, she felt totally smothered. Now that she was living in Nadia's house, she'd hoped for some privacy, but Robbie was *always* there.

"You wouldn't be so quick to blow him off if *you* knew what *I* know."

"What's that?" she asked, her voice nasty. He was always pretending to have some inside scoop, but she could see now that Robbie was just a small-time guy who got his inside tips from gay waiters and faggot secretaries living at the edge of the Industry.

"Well, I guess you're not interested in *Birth of a Star* casting," he said, and began to waltz out of the room.

"What are you talking about?" she snapped.

"I heard that April Irons wants Michael McLain for *Birth of a Star*."

"Get out of here!" she cried. "He's ancient."

"Not too ancient for that. Or to star with Ricky Dunn," Robbie sneered. *"You* should be so lucky."

Lila tried not to react. She wouldn't give Robbie the satisfaction of showing any interest. "Who cares?" she sneered. But she knew that she did.

The next day, from her trailer at the studio, she called the number that Robbie had copied down. It must have been McLain's private line, because he answered the phone himself, his voice husky. Was it with sleep, or some stupid sex appeal he was trying? Well, it didn't hurt to be nice, and even if it did, she could take the pain if it would get her the lead in *Birth*.

"This is Lila Kyle. I think you called me."

"I couldn't help myself."

Give me a break, she thought. "I don't really know you," she said, and wondered if he remembered the last time they'd met.

"Would you like to?" he asked, his voice suggestive. "I hear you broke up with your director friend."

Christ, gossip traveled faster than the speed of light in this town. But how could she find out if Robbie's rumor was true? She couldn't just come out and ask McLain what his two next vehicles were and whether she could be in them. Well, she'd just have to see him.

"I wouldn't like to," she said, "I'd *love* to."

4

With the relentless *3/4* shooting schedule, the publicity work for Flanders Cosmetics, the brutal exercise and self-maintenance drills, and her occasional secretive dates with Michael McLain, Jahne had succeeded in keeping herself too busy to focus on Sam Shields. Until Sam had called her. Since then, it had been hard to keep him out of her mind. Somehow, somehow, always in the background was a thread of awareness, an almost animal instinct that Sam existed: since he'd called after her debut, she'd waited to hear whether a script had been submitted to her agent. Jahne was not completely surprised when she got the call from Sy Ortis.

"I got a ring from April Irons' office. They're interested in casting you for some remake they're about to do. You interested in going over there for a look-see?"

She felt her heart beat faster, but she knew how to play casual. "Why not?" she asked.

"I say it's beneath your dignity. A look-see. Like you're not the hottest kid in town." Sy snorted. "Anyway, she's someone to avoid. A real shark. And I hear they want to use that guy Shields as director. He's the one who made Crystal look like shit in her last film."

"But I heard it was an acting triumph for her. She got good reviews."

"Fuck reviews. He made her look like a hag. She hasn't gotten a decent script since."

"Well, it can't hurt if I go; I need the experience," Jahne told him.

"I got other deals I like better. And I hear they're having trouble with the script. They only sent a treatment."

"Well, what can it hurt?" she repeated. And, really, what could it hurt? she asked herself. She would see Sam, and if she got the part she could turn down his job offer. It was an ironic little joke she could play, after he had rejected her so completely. And the beauty of it was that he would never know. It was the reward, the gift, she could give to poor Mary Jane Moran. She'd had to play poor Miss Havisham, but now Jahne could play Estella. Yes! She'd have the chance to be both the disappointed, rejected lover and the coldhearted avenger.

But the truth was, she could not resist seeing Sam at least one more time. And if she was seeing him through new eyes, so much the better.

She stood at the maître d's desk at Chasen's, where the Hollywood establishment ate. Henri immediately approached her. Though she'd never been here before, he knew her by name. "Miss Moore, how nice to see you. Miss Irons is waiting for you. Please follow me." He led her to a center table that could seat six, and she carefully made eye contact first with April Irons, and only then with Sam. Once again, she wondered exactly what their relationship was.

"Thank you for meeting with us, Jahne," April said, after the pleasantries were exchanged and the drink orders taken. "I know how busy you must be with the series, and all the other demands on you. You seem to be holding up remarkably well. Are you?"

"I have my moments," she said, then bit the inside of her lip. I used to say that all the time in New York, she thought. Before leaving home today, she had talked to herself in the mirror, reminding herself that this was the supreme test. If Sam didn't figure anything out after today's lunch, he never would. Watch your speech patterns, she'd told herself. That's the only way Mary Jane Moran could be uncovered. Now she added quickly, "But, actually, overall, it's been fan-*tas*-tic." There, just enough L.A. And definitely *not* Mary Jane Moran.

Jahne scanned the oversized menu and realized she was very hungry. Nerves always did that to her. But she'd been dieting again for weeks. Of course, she couldn't eat. It was almost impossible to keep her weight at 109. She certainly wouldn't blow it for Sam. "I'm starving," she said. "So I think I'll have a large salad, with the house dressing on the side." April ordered a salad also, but Sam asked for very rare filet mignon with

Béarnaise sauce. Some things didn't change. Jahne smiled to herself at the memory of Sam's unfashionable love for beef. Her big splurge one year for his birthday had been at the Old Homestead back in New York, where the steaks were so large they flopped over the edges of the plates.

Sam had greeted her, but April did all the talking about the movie. Jahne knew all about *Birth of a Star*, of course. She'd seen the classic with Theresa O'Donnell. But she had only glanced at Sam's treatment. Apparently, there was no script yet. She asked why.

"Sam, tell Jahne—may I call you Jahne?—tell Jahne your ideas about the project." April sat erect, her hands steepled in front of her, looking intently at Sam as he spoke.

"Have you ever seen *Birth of a Star*, Jahne?" Sam asked.

"Yes, and I loved it." She had rented the video only last week and run it three or four times. Old-fashioned and melodramatic. She took the plunge. "But I don't know if I'm the right age for Theresa O'Donnell's part. She was about, what, thirty-five, thirty-six when she played the role?" Jahne felt a scar tighten on her inner thigh—it felt like a caterpillar moving on her flesh—and slowly crossed her legs under the table. It began to itch. "What age do *you* see the character as?" she asked.

Sam spoke quickly. "Your age, Jahne. Theresa was really too old at that point in her career to play the ingenue. But she had the drawing power, and good skin, so she got the part." He chewed a bit of his steak, and wiped the corner of his mouth with his napkin.

April agreed, and they talked some more about it. How to update the story, how to make it work. Jahne picked at her salad and tried to appear intelligent.

But in reality Jahne was there simply to look at Sam. She watched him throughout the meal, one part of her present for the conversation and involved with the details of the script. Well, she *was* very interested, despite what Sy had said. But there was another part of Jahne, the voyeur, who sat there all the while and peeked into Sam's private self without his knowing. It was like standing outside his house, peering at him through his window, watching him eat. He was, if anything, better-looking than she had remembered. California clearly agreed with him. He was wearing a pair of black linen pants, and when she peeked down to the end of one long, ever-so-long leg, she saw that his narrow feet were sockless and tanned, slipped into casual but obviously expensive loafers. He was tanned, and the white shirt he wore made his teeth and the whites of his eyes seem to glisten. That was new, Sam in white. The only other change she could see was that his hair, still sleeked back into a ponytail, had begun to go salt-and-pepper. Even the gray looked good on Sam.

Watching him like this made her feel odd—half hot, half a voyeur. But it also gave her a perspective on Sam she had never had before. She had always believed that Sam was his own person, that he didn't kowtow to anyone. Now, though, he deferred to April. Even the simple act of delicately wiping the corners of his mouth with the edge of his napkin was so telling. Jahne remembered Sam's movements as being big. He'd never dabbed at the corners of his mouth. It was such a studied movement for Sam.

Sam was self-conscious, she realized, and seemed concerned with making an impression. But on whom? On Jahne Moore? That made her almost giddy. On April Irons? Of course, he *was* playing to April as well as to Jahne. What *was* their relationship?

She shook herself, almost physically, and realized their coffee had arrived. "So, Jahne," Sam asked, looking directly into her eyes. "Will you audition? Can I hope that we might be working together?"

Jahne smiled, first at April, then at Sam. The meal had progressed so quickly, and it appeared that she'd been a success. Her most important role ever: Jahne Moore. "It's certainly a possibility," she said. "There's a first time for everything."

She looked down at her almost empty coffee cup and saw that Sam was leaning on the table. April was busying herself with a lipstick and a gold Dior mirror she was peering into. Jahne looked away and felt a tingle in her right hand. It was his hand—Sam's hand—touching hers. Just the edge of his pinkie against the side of hers, but she remembered—oh, she remembered *everything*—and she remembered how very tentative he'd always been, half teasing, half waiting for her response. To avoid rejection and ensure success.

Now, once again, his hand just brushed hers. And it felt as good as it had back then—maybe even better. Because it had been so long and she'd missed him so much. And because she knew what that hand could do to her.

The hairs on her arm lifted, and she told herself no. It was too much. What had happened to her resolve? She was already involved with Michael. Was she becoming a slut? Had she always been faithful simply out of lack of options? What a horrible thought! And what if she slept with Sam? Surely then he'd realize who she was. What if she slept with him and he didn't? Jahne didn't know which was more unthinkable. And then it came to her: that which was really unthinkable.

And that was not sleeping with him at all.

5

Sharleen sat with the phone pressed tightly against her ear, listening, trying not to get angry with Sy Ortis, who was breathing heavily on the other end. He was just trying to do right by her, she told herself. He was teaching her manners and all. But somehow it didn't seem right.

"Stars don't *go* to crew parties. It's just *not done*," she heard him say again.

Sharleen sighed. "But why not? I been goin' to 'em all along. And I always had a good time. What's changed?"

"Everything! Do the crew get their pictures on the cover of *TV Guide?* Are they going to make a million bucks this year? Sharleen, you need to see and be seen with people on your *level*. Stars. Say, did Michael McLain ever get together with you? He called for your number." Sharleen blushed. She was glad she was not seeing Mr. Ortis in person, because she thought she could remember that night, though she didn't like to. It confused her, shamed her. The fun of going out with a movie star, Mr. McLain's kindness, his gift, his prediction about her career. But then there had been the drinks, the dizziness, and that time on the hill, when he . . . when it had happened like it did.

She wasn't surprised that she had never heard from him again, that he had never called. She'd behaved like a tramp. He'd lost respect. Well, she was sorry and ashamed. She felt dirty, so she tried not to think of it at all. "He called once. But not since then," she told Mr. Ortis. Probably he was seeing some other, nicer girl by now. She put her hand up to her neck, the necklace still hanging there, just over her breastbone. It had hurt when she hadn't heard from Michael McLain, but she hadn't been surprised. "So, now I'm a star? And everything is changed?"

"Exactly. Now, honey, you're big. Too big to go to some West Hollywood stuntman's parties." Sy paused. "Sharleen? Think of security. Those parties are open, no security check as you go in. If word got out that you were showing up—and it would, believe me—the party would turn into a riot. And no one could protect you. Don't put the guy in that position. They're good folk, and they really like you. But, you know, you can't just call up and invite yourself along. *They* know what the deal is. And they wouldn't say no to you."

"I used to make the potato salad for those things, for crying out loud." And Sharleen did feel like crying out loud, although she wasn't going to on the phone with Mr. Ortis. "And the guys used to call me Shar. Now they call me Miss Smith. That don't feel so good, you know? I miss them."

Sy's voice lowered. "I know you do, honey. But you can make other friends. Maybe Michael. Or someone else. Want me to ask someone to call you?"

"No!" Sharleen said quickly. What had happened with Mr. McLain was too scary, too much. She didn't want *that* again.

"You like Jahne Moore, don't you?"

"Sure I do. I like her fine. But we're not friends." Sharleen sighed. "I'd jest like to go out to a party again. All I do is work and take lessons. Singin' and dancin' and all that other stuff you lined up. And the exercise classes! Mr. Ortis, I'm so sore and tired. I'd like some fun. I mean just a *party*. At someone's house. Someone normal, you know?"

"Well, don't worry, you will. Listen, Sharleen, what do you think about that recording idea?"

Not again! She was tired of all this. "Oh, Mr. Ortis, I can't really sing."

"Sure you can. And there's a lot of people who'll buy the album."

"I'd feel stupid. It's bad enough bein' an actress that can't act. But also being a singer who can't sing? I . . ."

She could sense the loneliness fill up her chest once again, but tried not to feel it. It only made her want to cry, and what did she have to cry about, after all? She had Dean, and her new house, and every room furnished just the way they wanted from the old Sears catalogue. Funny that now they had money to buy stuff, the catalogue goes out of business! But one of Mr. Ortis' people got everything for them, just like they picked it. It had been fun, going through the catalogue with Dean in the evenings, after work, choosing whatever they wanted, then having the lady in Mr. Ortis' office arrange for the delivery, and getting some decorator to come in and put it all in place, make it look just like the catalogue pictures. But then, after buying everything they needed— everything they *wanted*, she corrected herself—they were left with evenings to fill, with no place to go and no one to see.

It wasn't so bad for Dean. During the day, he at least could go out wherever *he* wanted without worrying about getting trampled by a mob of people at the supermarket who recognized him because of the show, or from the pictures spread all over those magazines they sell at supermarket lines. So Dean went to places like Tail O' the Pup and the pizza joint without her, and he did the shopping and always came home with twice as much as they needed.

Anyway, even if she wasn't recognized, she couldn't go out much, 'cause she was booked up with these lessons. And posing for Flanders Cosmetics ads and publicity pictures, *and* goin' to those appearances Mr. Ortis' office set up, *and* bein' interviewed. She looked at her watch. "I gotta go. I got my voice lesson in about six minutes. And Miss Cardoza is real strict."

"Good girl. So you'll do the album, and you won't bother the crew anymore. Right, Sharleen?"

"Well, we'll see. I don't want to go where I ain't welcome. I sure don't want to give none of them a hard time. It's just that I feel like . . . like a prisoner." She hated the whining sound in her voice, but couldn't stop herself, now that she was saying what needed to be said. "Mr. Ortis, I have to have my private telephone number changed every week. I never give my number out, just to you and Mr. DiGennaro. But the calls—you should hear some of them. I can't answer the phone no more. Things sure have changed." Sharleen began to laugh. "There was a time I couldn't afford to make a local call at a pay phone. Now I have phones in every room of the house—oh, Lord, including the bathroom—and I can't answer them. And who'm I gonna call? It's kind of funny, isn't it?"

"Yes and no, Sharleen," Mr. Ortis said. "It might not be so good for you right now, but wait. After you get used to it, you'll be able to handle it."

"Will I ever be able to shop in a supermarket again?"

She heard Mr. Ortis laugh. "I sure hope not, honey."

Sharleen hung up and looked around the large room of their new house. They had to get out of that really nice one-bedroom apartment in town—people would sit in the lobby all day waiting for her. Lenny from Mr. Ortis' office found this big house for them, way out, almost in the Valley, with lots of land and trees around. And a high fence with a big gate. Mr. Ortis had hired security guards to sit at the gate and patrol the grounds twenty-four hours a day. And even *they* would go out of their way to peek at her whenever she walked on the lawn, or sat in the sun. It gave her the creeps, but she had to agree with Mr. Ortis. What else was she going to do?

She knew what she'd *like* to do. She'd like to walk down the street somewhere, and look in store windows, try on some clothes, maybe buy some shoes, have a hamburger at McDonald's, sit in a movie show. All the things she *longed* to do back in Texas. All the things she *could* do, now that she was making all this money. More money than she could *think* about. More money in one week than Mr. Hardiman, the richest man in Lamson, would make in a *year*. In *ten* years.

But Sharleen couldn't go to McDonald's. Sure, she could get a twelve-dollar hamburger at one of them fancy restaurants that she'd been to since she made money. But make reservations to have a *hamburger?* And then the hassle of getting dressed up fancy and getting a limo and driver. Dean didn't like to put on a tie, and he didn't feel right in those places. And even there, in those fancy restaurants where they only have celebrities, even there she was ogled, and approached. And bothered. Mr. Ortis had said it was time to get a personal bodyguard, but Sharleen drew the line there. "I'm not the President, Mr. Ortis. No FBI," she had said.

But there was *nothing* like a Big Mac. So Dean would go for her, bring her one home with a vanilla shake, but it wasn't the same. It wasn't normal. She picked up another of them catalogues Mr. Ortis' secretary had sent over when Sharleen told her how she couldn't go out no more. Her money manager had told her to order whatever she wanted. *Everything* she wanted. He would tell her when she was spending over her budget. He hadn't said anything yet, and she still had stuff being delivered every day, some in boxes still unopened. Sharleen knew she had to leave for her voice lesson, but she still sat there and flipped through the glossy pages, the color photos blurring before her eyes. Shopping from catalogues instead of in stores. Ordering food from outside to be delivered to the security guard instead of going out to dinner. Watching movies on the VCR and the thirty-five-inch Japanese TV, instead of going out to a show. It all would have sounded like heaven to her, once. But that was before she knew what fame was *really* like. Well, she better get a move on. She'd already missed ten minutes of her class.

Sharleen heard the front door slam in the distance. Slowly, she forced herself to get up and go down the hall to Dean. "Howdy," she said. "What did you get for tonight?"

"Top Gun," he said, "and *Terminator 2*. It's about this guy . . ."

Sharleen sighed. "Dean, didn't we see them before?"

"Yeah, but they're real good," Dean said as he made his way into the TV room and opened the cabinet. "Oh, and, yeah. I got us a paper-oney pizza, just like you like it, Sharleen."

Sharleen groaned.

"What's the matter, Sharleen?"

Dean got that worried look on his face he got whenever he thought she was unhappy. "Nothing," she said, with a big sigh. "Except I'm tired. I wish I didn't have to go to voice. And then I got to go to exercise."

"Oh, why don't you cut?" Dean asked.

"Hey, we *pay* for them classes."

"So what?"

The idea of simply not showing up was so sweet, so irresistible to Sharleen that she smiled for the first time that day.

"I don't have to be at work until the day after tomorrow. But even if I cut, I can't go nowhere, do nothing. What could we do that's fun?" She flopped onto the long Early American sofa.

"I can show you something great," Dean said. He whistled, and the three dogs all sat down. "Say your prayers," he told them, and, one by one, the dogs stood on their hind legs, crossed their paws, and put their heads down.

Sharleen had to laugh. "How did you get 'em to do that?" she asked.

"Oh, I don't know. Jest practiced them. It's not a sin, is it?"

"Surely not. It's great, Dean." She hugged him.

"Hey, I got an idea," Dean said, suddenly eager.

"Want to play Parcheesi? This time I'll let *you* win," he said with a grin.

"Dean, honey," Sharleen said, very patiently. "I've read every magazine, seen every movie, played every game. I even went through all those new catalogues. There is nothing I want to do except get out and go for a walk. Nothing. And we both know I can't do that."

"We could get that nice guy with the long limousine. He could drive us around awhile. How 'bout that?" he asked, hopefully.

Sharleen didn't want to upset him, and she could see she was. She forced a smile. "No, honey, I'll be all right. Put on *Top Gun* first."

As he popped the cassette into the VCR, the phone rang, and Dean answered. "What?" she heard him say. Then, "You little piece of worm dirt. If I get my hands on you, I'll cut . . ." He slammed down the phone.

"Dean, don't go getting yourself all upset. I'll just unplug all the phones tonight. Now, let's relax and enjoy ourselves, okay?"

"Sure, Sharleen," he said, but his face was red, and his eyes had teared up. "How come people are just so mean and dirty? I can't believe what that guy just said about you. I tell you, Sharleen, something's wrong when you can't be left alone in your own home." He flicked the switch of the remote control, and the screen lit up. Sharleen sat down beside him and stroked his soft, white-blond hair. It was funny: she should be happy, because she had everything she'd dreamed of: a nice house, a new TV, lots of clothes, and good stuff to eat. The Lord had provided for them. She should be grateful.

Oh, Lord, Sharleen thought to herself. I should have been more careful about what I asked for. I guess I didn't really believe You'd give it to me.

6

The traffic slowed suddenly as it came around the bend of the freeway. Probably an accident, Jahne thought, as she settled into the new pace. The drivers in the cars on each side of her seemed to be straining to look ahead, but Jahne could see no obstruction. Up ahead, the four lanes of traffic were moving, no stalled or wrecked cars in any one. What the hell was the problem? She had a meeting with Sy Ortis in only half an hour, and she didn't want to be late.

Jahne followed the craning heads of the other drivers, and observed that the slowdown stretched across all eight lanes of the freeway. Then she saw it. The billboard was at least four stories high, and displayed the three women from the show, standing next to each other, elbow to elbow, hair flying, arms akimbo, legs parted in a defiant stance. Their black leather jackets were open, revealing deep cleavages; in fact, the jackets barely covered their nipples. The only words on the billboard were: "SUNDAY NIGHT."

Jahne pulled the Miata over to the shoulder of the road, stopping on the dry brown grass, and got out of the car. She stared at the giant figures, at the massive sign that at one time would have been considered one of the seven wonders of the world for its size alone. That's me, she thought to herself. That's Jahne Moore. Or me, Mary Jane Moran. Whoever I am. It's *me*. She wanted to say it out loud to someone, but no one was there. Just the faces in the slow-moving cars staring at the three beautiful women on the billboard. It was hard to take it in. It was hard to breathe. For a moment, she felt faint, and bent over a bit to bring the blood to her head.

She had done it. If she never did anything in her life before or after, she had, at least, accomplished this. She was there, fifty times bigger than life, over the freeway.

And once a week, she was being watched by fifty million people.

Her will, her pain, her work, her courage had brought her to this. Unlike the other two girls, she'd had no natural beauty or family ties to help her. And even though it wasn't Shakespeare, even though it was only television, she had risen up out of the swamp of grayness to this.

"Miss?" a voice said behind her. She nearly jumped, then turned and saw a California Highway Patrol officer standing next to his scooter. "Are you in trouble?"

Jahne shook her head, then began to laugh. Realizing that she must seem like a crazy person, she tried to stop. "No," she said. "I'm just looking at the picture."

"Lady," the cop said, walking cautiously toward her. "*Everyone's* looking at the goddamn picture. You better get back in your car and get on your way. It's a little too dangerous to be standing out here." Then he stopped, looked at her again, stared at her face, looked up at the billboard. The light dawned. "Hey, you're the smart one!"

Jahne giggled, and nodded her head. "I'll say," she told him, and got back into her car.

What's On . . .

SUNDAY

8:00 p.m.—**Star Search Famous Look-Alikes**. Tonight, Rhea Perlman.

9:00 p.m.—**Three for the Road**. Crimson finds herself in the middle of the Kent State campus just before the National Guard appears. Clover and Cara arrive in time to prevent her shooting.

Jesse Helms' Anti-"Three" Rally Complete Bust

Winston-Salem, North Carolina. The much-publicized rally organized by Jesse Helms and the Christian Family Network to protest the airing of "Three for the Road" was the biggest non-event of this senator's eventful public life of protestations against what he calls attacks on family values. The rally was scheduled for nine o'clock Sunday night, but, unfortunately for him and CFN, only a handful of his most ardent followers showed up. Helms, reached at his Washington, D.C., office today, was unable to explain the lack of numbers in support of what he calls massive resistance to the show. He wouldn't comment on this reporter's speculation that perhaps everyone stayed home to watch the show instead.

TOP TEN REASONS WHY MEN WATCH *"THREE FOR THE ROAD"*

—FROM *Late Night with David Letterman*

10. They're into motorcycles
9. They can't get on the set
8. They've heard that in one episode Crimson will mud-wrestle Clover
7. There's so little *really good* serious drama left on television
6. To get back at their wives for making them look at Prince's bare ass
5. For the plots
4. For the great location photography
3. To make their girlfriends try harder
2. Six are better than two
1. They're willing to take their chances at going blind

Harold from the mailroom knocked on Lila's dressing-room door, then entered when she answered. Lila was very clear about that: no one was to be in her dressing room without her, and it was kept locked at all times. "Miss Kyle, where do you want your mail?" he asked. He wanted to get away from her as fast as possible. Everyone at the studio knew she could be dangerous, even without provocation. He was the one in the mailroom who had lost the draw, so here he was.

Lila didn't turn around to look at him. "Where the fuck do you think I want my mail? On the desk!"

"But, Miss Kyle . . ."

Lila turned to him. "Don't make a major production out of it. Just put the fucking mail on the fucking desk down at the end, where I told you to. And get out."

He watched her go back to brushing her long hair, shrugged his shoulders, and stepped outside. He lifted a large mailbag from the cart, and walked back in. "And take it out of the bag," she yelled at him. Harold lifted the bag and dumped the contents on the desk. He went back outside, and brought the other two bags inside, emptying each on the now buried desk. Bitch wants it out of the bag, bitch goin' get it out of the bag.

He closed the door quietly after him, and had begun to push the empty mail cart back to the mailroom when he heard Lila shriek. Then the door to her dressing room slammed open, and she stood screaming at him. "You asshole, get back here. I didn't know there was so much. I can't even walk! Get back here and put all that mail back in bags. Every piece, do you hear?"

Harold sighed, moved back into Lila's trailer, then began scooping up the fan mail and stuffing it back into the sacks. The bitch looked up at him.

"How many sacks did it come to?" Lila asked him.

"Seven, Miss Kyle. There's four more I couldn't fit on the handtruck."

She paused for a moment. Then she frowned. "How many did Smith and Moore get?" she asked.

Paul Grasso leaned back in his swivel chair and stretched as he listened to the harangue coming out of the

436

What's On . . .

SUNDAY

8:00 p.m.—**Star Search Famous Look-Alikes.** Tonight, Ivana Trump.

9:00 p.m.—**Three for the Road.** In San Francisco Cara meets and becomes romantically involved with a Tim Leary follower. Crimson, Cara, and Clover try LSD. Cameo appearances by Leary and Donovan.

phone earpiece. Yahta, yahta, yahta. "Mel, listen, I'm sorry, but we're booked till February. Ya wanna talk about then, maybe we could . . ." More Australian-accented yahta yahta yahta. "Look, I understand you'll be on location then, but that's the slot we got. Everyone and their bookie wants a guest shot. No, no, Bob definitely couldn't reschedule. I mean it, man. Look, I'm sorry. Maybe first episode next year. Sure. I know it's perfect. The girl road warriors meet the original. Right. Listen, here's what I'll do: I'll talk to Marty tomorrow, and his people will call your people, all right? Maybe *they* can find a slot. Right. You, too, babe."

Grasso hung up the phone and rubbed his eyes. He felt the stubble on his upper cheeks. Shit. He'd been out late last night, at a poker game with a few buddies, and he'd woken up so late this morning he hadn't had time to shave. He reached into the side drawer of his desk and pulled out the Braun electric razor he stored there, switched it on, and began to run it over the left side of his jaw. He didn't even need to use the mirror, which was just as well, since he must look like death on a bender after nine hours at the card table. He felt the smooth side of his jaw. You had to hand it to those Nazis. They knew how to build the shit out of anything. He moved the razor to the other side of his face. Then the buzzer began again.

"Yeah?" Christ, this business would kill him. One day you can't cast a fuckin' jeans commercial, and the next day you're the gateway to the hottest show in the country. "Whataya want, Patty?"

"It's another one."

"I'm out," he told her. "You handle it."

"I don't think so."

"I'm *out*," he repeated. Patty was smart—shit, she could run the fuckin' place without him—but she was sometimes a pushy bitch.

"It's Brando," Patty said.

It was hard to hear her over the buzzing Braun. "Brandon Tartikoff?" he asked. "What the fuck does *he* want?"

"Not Bran*don*. Bran*do*," Patty yelled.

"Holy shit!" Paul Grasso said. "*He* wants a cameo?"

"Apparently."

Paul Grasso laughed and turned off the razor. "Hey, Patty. Ya think the wild one can still ride a motorcycle?"

Jahne clutched her hands nervously behind her. The two other people in the green room—her publicist and some nerdy stand-up—stared at the screen where Arsenio was busy rapping with some black dancer. Jahne wished she hadn't agreed to do this. She was an actress, not a personality. This was the kind of stuff Neil used to want to do. How would he handle it? The butterflies in her stomach were as large as barn swallows. Then the assistant producer was there, leading her through the dark hall and leaving her to enter into the glaring light. Arsenio, now in person, stood up and extended his hand. She took it, smiled, and sat down. The chat began.

"So, are you as political in life as you are on the show, Jahne?"

"Not really." She knew she should say more, sparkle, be funny or sexy or something, but she was only an actress, and she had no lines.

"So, you've got no position on stuff."

"Well, women's rights . . ."

"Like abortion?"

"Yeah. I feel strongly that no women should be given

438

> **What's On . . .**
>
> **SUNDAY**
> **8:00 p.m.—Star Search Famous
> Look-Alikes**. Tonight, Larry
> Fortensky.
> **9:00 p.m.—Three for the Road.**
> Crimson and Clover and Cara go
> to Woodstock, N.Y., for the
> concert. Bob Dylan and Neil
> Young guest star.

abortions." She felt Arsenio stiffen, and heard a hiss
from the audience. "Unless, of course, they're pregnant," she finished, and after a beat she got her big laugh.
Thank you, Neil Morelli, she thought, and the interview
continued, smooth as silk.

It was her day off, and Jahne was exhausted. Who'd
ever imagine that success could be so tiring? Already Sy
had let her know that movie offers were pouring in—they
were mostly jiggle-in-leather scripts, but better things
would surely follow. The Arsenio gig had gone surprisingly well; after her initial stage fright, she'd loosened up
and been tough and funny. Now Sy was pushing more
appearances. She stared at the pile of movie treatments,
her next week's scripts, memos and pictures to autograph, and sighed. No, today she would simply rest.
She'd bought an Anne Tyler book, and she'd stretch out
by the pool, ready to enjoy it. But first she picked up the
copy of *Vogue*. It opened to the two-page spread of the
three of them. Gorgeous black-and-white photos. They
all looked beautiful. Only the three of them knew the
hours and hours they'd spent under the hot lights to get
that perfection, with dozens of specialists huddling over
them constantly to create the illusion of perfection. But
my, she looked fabulous. She stared and stared.

Dr. Moore had warned her about the sun, so she was
prepared. "Sun is bad for everyone, but it would be murder on you," he had reminded her in his last letter. "I've

been able to get such good results because you never tanned, so your skin, despite aging, has retained a lot of its flexibility. But in the future, no sun—ever." She'd laughed, and written him back to say he made her sound like a vampire, and that the only reason she hadn't tanned before was that she could never afford to go away to a beach. Now she had her own private lap pool. But she'd rubbed SPF number fifteen all over herself half an hour ago, she'd poured half a jar of conditioner on her hair, swathed it in a towel, and was wearing huge sunglasses. To stay cool, she had a long, white cotton robe, a wonderful, fine Egyptian cotton, smoother than silk. And the houseman had fixed her a pitcher of iced tea. Now, for the very first time, she was going to spend the whole morning just quietly enjoying the warmth, the pool, the vista. Then, later, she'd do her laps, work out with her trainer and, at two, a masseuse that Mai had recommended was coming over to work on her back and legs. Jahne stretched out luxuriously, opened to the first page of *Saint Maybe,* and took a deep breath.

She heard it before she saw it. There was a grinding of gears out front that sounded as if an eighteen-wheeler was making it up the hill in front of the house, and then a loud radio or something. Did politicians drive around the Swish Alps making announcements? Then she heard it more clearly.

". . . ACTUAL PRIVATE HOME OF JAHNE MOORE, BETTER KNOWN AS 'CARA' IN *THREE FOR THE ROAD.* THE ACTRESS LIVES HERE ALONE IN A TWO-BEDROOM BUNGALOW COMPLETE WITH POOL AND POOL HOUSE. SHE MAY EVEN BE AT HOME RIGHT NOW."

Jahne jumped up, her heart pounding, and turned. She could glimpse the top of the smoked windows of the bus from where she stood. Did that mean they could see her? She scuttled closer to the fence and peeped through a crack in the weathered gray boards. "See the Stars" was painted in rainbow colors across the side of the bus. "Tours of the Hollywood Homes of Your Favorite TV and Movie Stars," it said on a raised panel along the roofline.

Not sure whether she wanted to laugh or cry, Jahne

turned and walked, quickly as she could, back into the house, leaving her book unread and the tea untouched beside it.

from *Advertising Age* . . .

Flanders Cosmetics Go Through the Roof

In perhaps the most successful launch in the industry, Flanders Cosmetics has pulled off a coup historic both in conception and implementation. Tying in their new integrated line of treatment and makeup products with the hot new *Three for the Road* TV show has been a masterful stroke of market savvy and just plain hard work.

"I envisioned it and I made it happen," says Monica Flanders. Banion O'Malley, the agency that handled the project, echoed her . . .

"T-shirts only, Phil. We're doing a separate deal on posters and the rest." Sy looked across at the man who had waited three weeks for an appointment with him.

"Sy, please, this is just the tip of the fuckin' iceberg. . . . Sorry, Miss Smith. But, listen, you give us the T-shirts *and* the posters, and we'll keep our profit to five percent an item. What do you say?" He was begging Sy, but looking at Sharleen.

Sy was shaking his head. "We got the posters lined up already, Phil. I could have the T-shirts done by the same guys, but I wanted to give you a break, you know, a piece of what's happening. I don't forget my friends, but don't go greedy on me. T-shirts, that's it. And you still keep your share of the net to five percent." Sy waited for Phil to respond; then, when he nodded his head yes, Sy signed the sheaf of papers and passed them to Sharleen. After she scrawled her signature, he handed them to Phil. "Have my girl make copies of these on your way out."

When the door closed behind Phil, Sharleen finally spoke. "Only five percent? How's the poor man going to make any money?"

Sy grinned. "At five percent, honey, the guy's going to be able to retire. Do you know how many of those

T-shirts we're going to sell? Over five million the first month on sale. *Five million T-shirts!* He'll make six figures the first month alone."

Sharleen shook her head, as if trying to understand. "And we get money on each shirt?"

Sy nodded, waiting to see if Sharleen would calculate her share.

But she didn't. Sy almost laughed. This hillbilly was a pleasure. It was such a nice change to meet a beautiful woman who didn't have a computer for a heart. It made running his bodega so much easier.

"That's right, honey. And we haven't even figured in the posters, stationery, line of clothes, endorsements, pens, leather jackets, shoulder bags, lunch boxes. . . . Honey, we're talking millions here. Millions."

"Millions? For just my picture on things? Mr. Ortis, are you *sure* you got this right?"

Sy laughed. "Sharleen, about this stuff I don't make a mistake. I said millions, and I mean millions."

What's On . . .

SUNDAY

8:00 p.m.—Star Search Famous Look-Alikes. Tonight, Milli Vanilli.

9:00 p.m.—Three for the Road. Clover meets the Merry Pranksters and she, Cara, and Crimson "get on the bus" and tour San Francisco. Michelle Pfeiffer and Marlon Brando guest star.

THE MEDIA . . .

A three-character nostalgic TV series is hardly a phenomenon in these times of imitation and reproduction.

But this season's *Three for the Road*—yes,

another three-character nostalgic TV show—is special. Directed by film great Marty DiGennaro (*A Woman Matters, Back Streets, Trouble in the Tower*), the heir-apparent to George Cukor as a woman's director, the show has captured the style and the angst of the nineties, while delving into the fun and psychic scars of the sixties at the same time. DiGennaro, the Sultan of Style, has given us more form than function, but what forms! The three co-stars—Sharleen Smith, Jahne Moore and Lila Kyle (SEE: PERSONALITIES, this issue)—popped up out of nowhere, and, under DiGennaro's aegis, have developed into the personification of all that was good *and* beautiful in America. Great? Far from it. But a phenomenon in the impact it has made on the psyche of the television viewing public (now greatly expanded because of this show) cannot be in doubt. Quirkier than *Northern Exposure*, more stylish than David Lynch at his weirdest, hotter than *Miami Vice* ever was, *Three for the Road* has got legs—six of them. At a cost of more than a million dollars an episode, the shows are a pastiche of actual archive clips, new footage, and special effects. Like a gripping miniseries, the show has garnered a weekly audience that few specials can boast—and it goes on, week after week. While some critics carp that it trivializes its time (one asked what it would do next—have Cara date Martin Luther King?) its popularity has revived the lagging Network. Without question, the repercussions of this program, not only on future programming but also on how television programming as it is conceived, will be felt at Studio City in the very highest echelons in the lofty aeries of Executiveville.

—*Time* magazine

OLIVIA GOLDSMITH

MEMORANDUM

TO:	Ara Sagarian
FROM:	Lila Kyle
SUBJECT:	See Attached

Ara, what the fuck is going on? I got this fan letter and, as you can see, Sharleen Smith and Jahne Moore fans are getting silk-screened T-shirts. All Sy Ortis' work, apparently. I thought you had it all worked out with the Network? Are the people in Publicity on the same planet?

I don't want to have to go directly to Selma Gold on this myself. So, Ara, get them shaped up! I'm busting my ass here day after day, and then I find out Publicity is playing favorites. I want this kid to get two dozen shirts, and four dozen signed pictures, color, eight-by-ten glossy . . . assorted poses. And pins, medals, membership kits—the whole works. Have Gold put this kid on the priority mailing list. She's as important to me as the fucking assholes at *Time* magazine.

Do I have to think of everything? Stay on top of this, Ara. Sy Ortis is fucking you over—and me. What's he got going with Gold? Get back to me.

L.K.

Jahne was standing on the express checkout line at Mrs. Gooches, where celebrities did their fancy grocery shopping. The place was fabulous: all the fruit and vegetables were displayed like jewels and cost almost as much. She had a wig pulled down low over her forehead, and a large straw hat sitting on top of it. She wore an old, thin trench coat, although it was hot out, and a pair of tattered Reeboks. She felt like an escapee from someplace, incognito, taking a chance on getting mobbed because it was better than hiding behind locked doors another minute. It would have made her smile, but she didn't want to attract any unnecessary attention to herself. Going to the supermarket had suddenly become a daring treat.

444

She placed her basket on the edge of the counter, waiting her turn at the cashier. The magazines were screaming her name and her face at her. She picked up the first one at hand. "Three Beauty Secrets from Three Beauties," read the blurb on the front cover. Jahne flipped through the pages until she came to the article. "Jahne Moore, the brunette star of 'Three for the Road,' uses only . . ." Yeah, she thought. She uses only the finest plastic surgeon. So much bullshit. She was replacing the magazine on the rack when the woman behind her spoke up.

"Can you believe those three?" she said, indicating the picture of the costars of *Three for the Road* on one of the magazine covers.

Jahne smiled and nodded.

"They really piss me off, you know? How are any of us supposed to get to look like them? I mean, what am I supposed to do? You think eating carrots and doing fifty thousand sit-ups will make a goddamn bit of difference? Look, I always say, if God didn't give it to you, you can't get it. So I make do."

Jahne's turn at the register came up just then. "I know what you mean," she said, as she picked up the brown bag and walked out the door.

Marty DiGennaro's secretary, Staci, opened the door and rolled her eyes. "Unbelievable!" she said. "If this shit keeps up, I quit!"

Marty looked up from his messy desk. "What? Come in. Sit down. I'll get you some coffee. What is it?"

"What is it? They're driving me nuts. Every asshole in Hollywood—no, in California—no, maybe in the whole *country*—is trying to bullshit me to get to you. The girls are going crazy. Just this morning, we had three calls from your 'brothers,' a call from your 'doctor' about the 'test results,' a hysterical call from 'Joanie' about your son. . . ."

"Is anything wrong with Sacha?"

"Yeah, he's got a madman for a daddy. They weren't your brother, your doctor, or Joanie. They were assholes. And gifts—how about a diamond-and-gold Rolex

445

that's already engraved 'To my friend Marty from his friend Larry'?''

"Who's Larry?"

"Another asshole. Some producer out in East Bum-fuck who wants to talk to you about a movie deal. He needs two of the three girls, but he writes, and I quote, 'I don't care which two, and if you prefer we can cut the lesbian scenes with the full frontal nudity.' He enclosed the screenplay from hell.''

Marty laughed. "Come on, Staci. This isn't the first hit you've been through with me. You sound like a kid out of Katie Gibbs. You've handled worse.''

"Yeah, but not for so long. I mean, *week* after *week* after *week*. A movie comes out, it hits, we react, then it's over. This is relentless. Marty, you never heard me complain before, right? Well, I'm exhausted. I don't

MEMORANDUM

TO:	Sharleen Smith and Jahne Moore
FROM:	Sy Ortis
SUBJECT:	*Sports Illustrated* write-up, attached

Have you seen this?

Just received a call from Bill Gottlieb from *Sports Illustrated*. How about doing their annual Bathing Suit issue? Have already discussed this with Marty and he's all for it.

Let's talk.

S. O.

LILA KYLE

YOU ARE MERELY A PRODUCT OF HOLLYWOOD NEPOTISM. I WOULDN'T FUCK YOU WITH SOMEONE ELSE'S DICK.

JUGHEAD
President
National Anti-Nepotism League

What's On . . .

SUNDAY
8:00 p.m.—**Star Search Famous
Look-Alikes.** Tonight, Shirley
MacLaine.
9:00 p.m.—**Three for the Road.**
Cara helps an old boyfriend avoid
the draft. Crimson and Clover
stage a diversion and he escapes to
Canada. Ricky Dunn guest stars.

**TOP TEN REASONS WHY WOMEN WATCH
*"THREE FOR THE ROAD"***

—FROM *Late Night with David Letterman*

10. So they can hate themselves in the morning
9. They're into motorcycles
8. Their boyfriends make them
7. If they just lost a little weight and got the right pair
   of jeans, they'd look *exactly* like Clover
6. So they can call their girlfriends afterward and get
   down
5. Their husbands make them
4. They've worn out their tape of *Thelma and Louise*
3. They're into self-hatred
2. Crimson, Cara, and Clover are a lot better-looking
   than Leona Helmsley, who steals billions; Tammy
   Bakker, who steals millions; and Bess Myerson,
   who steals from Woolworth's
1. For a feeling of solidarity with their sisters

---

know if I can keep up with you on this one." Staci sat
back, her fatigue showing in the dark shadows around
her eyes.

"Okay, get yourself a secretary."

"But *I'm* a secretary."

"Not anymore. You are now my executive assistant.

With a raise. So hire yourself a secretary—right away—give her a week's training, then take a week off at the Hotel del Mar in San Diego. My treat.'' Marty smiled at the surprise on Staci's face. "Then get back here rested up and get back to work.''

"Marty, thanks. Hey, I didn't mean it seriously. I just like to bitch. I don't know. . . . I wasn't coming in here to hold you up. . . . I just wanted to get this stuff off my . . . Thanks, Marty.'' She leaned over the desk and kissed him on the forehead. "But what about you? You need a rest, too. To get away.''

"Get away? I've worked all my life to get *here*. And I'm staying for as long as I can.''

"Sickos,'' "Beggars,'' "Negative,'' and "Real Fans.'' The signs were lettered over the empty boxes, and Lila was explaining how she wanted her fan mail stacked each day to the secretary and clerk she had hired for the job. Lila knew from her mother that fan mail was an important indicator of how marketable one was. "The sick shit I want delivered to the head of studio security every day. Keep a record of names, addresses, and phone numbers that are on any of them, but usually they write anonymously. Staple the envelope they came in to the letter, in case there's someone who's scary enough to have to track down.'' The secretary, Myra, an older black woman, nodded. She'd been through most of this bullshit before.

"Beggars are sent my picture, the standard sympathy bullshit letter, plus a list of charitable resources they can write to. I'm not the fucking Red Cross.'' Lila twisted a lipstick up out of the tube and smoothed it over her pouty lips. The secretary noticed it was MAC, not the Flanders brand.

Lila continued. "Now, never show me the negative mail, but keep it in case I might want to go through it one day. The positive stuff—the stuff that seems to be coming from real fans—I want to see every one of them. Every one. Do you have that, now?'' she asked the two women.

Myra nodded. Poor sick bitch didn't have much of a home life if she cared about this.

7

Jahne was still surprised by how much she liked L.A. Back on the East Coast, Sam and her New York friends had always spoken about it with derision, contempt, and bitterness. But it *was* pretty. And it was easy. So much easier than New York. What had Bertolucci called it? "The big nipple." Yes. In some ways, it was as easy as that.

Jahne loved the little house she'd rented in the Hollywood Hills; it was only two tiny bedrooms and a big living room, but it had a deck with a view and the small lap pool. It even came complete with a part-time houseboy, and oranges on the orange trees!

Of course, at first Jahne had had to adjust. Being alone in a house was so different from being stuck in a dark fourth-floor walk-up on Fifty-fourth Street. Not that she got to spend much time here: with work and the dozens of business appointments, her hairdressing, facials and manicures, costume fittings, and the Flanders Cosmetics photo sessions, she wasn't home much. But when she was, the hours felt lonely. So Jahne got a cat—a sweet black Persian. In a typical burst of perversity, she named him Snowball, in honor of the cat she'd had as a girl in Scuderstown, and thought also of poor Midnight, her white cat left back in New York.

She thought of Midnight, and a lot more from her past. In fact, since she'd seen Sam at the Chasen's look-see, she couldn't seem to stop thinking of all her friends back home. She hoped that they, like Midnight, would get what they needed. What would they say if they could see her now? A TV star, with a great place to live, money in the bank, and an affair with Michael McLain.

It still amazed her that a star as big as he was interested in her. He had been so kind about the scars. He listened to her problems on the set, gave good advice, and even ran lines with her. If his performance in bed seemed a little bit—well—like a performance, she guessed it was a small price to pay. He was good company, and a wonderful listener.

But she still missed her old friends. She had never thought it was a mistake back then simply to drop out of their lives: not when she was so miserably a failure. Even now, she could easily conjure up Molly's look of pity for her and feel almost physically sick. She'd gotten so tired of the role of fat, plain, goodhearted, and pitiable Mary Jane that she didn't, couldn't, have anything to do with those who'd known her and expected her to play that role.

And now, even if she wanted to, it would be more than a little awkward to call up Molly or Chuck or Neil or any of them and say, "Hi! Sorry I disappeared like that, but now I'm famous, beautiful, and rich. I got my own TV show. How *you* doing?"

With her cute house, her new face, her perfect body, her cute kitten, her new romance, and a career that was taking off, Jahne figured she had nothing to complain about. If it was a bit shallow, so be it. She had her weekly letters to Dr. Moore, working now in a plastic-surgery mobile camp in Honduras somewhere. It was ironic that her best friend, the only person who knew her, was in another world. But he had taken the time last week to write her a long letter.

Somehow, though, none of it was enough to banish thoughts of the past. Thoughts of Sam.

She knew that the answer was to make new friends. But it was harder than she'd expected. Perhaps she could build some sort of relationship with Sharleen. And she *was* becoming friends with Mai. The rest would just take time. Slowly, she knew, her world would expand, and as she met more people, tested their loyalty, she would build a new community. Transitions were hard, she reminded herself, and thought of nursing school, of her first auditions, of the New York cattle calls, her first summer-stock job. She'd been alone then, and it was only natural to be alone now.

But since she'd seen Sam, something had changed. The loneliness she'd tried to assuage first with Pete and now with Michael seemed to grow: it was palpable, a real feeling in her chest. During the day, the busy, frenzied workday, she was all right, but in the evenings she found herself reliving those moments with Sam at the party and the lunch at Chasen's, trying to read their meaning.

He had seen her but not known her. In a way, it was a graduation: her transformation was complete. She was the consummate actress. If no one knew it, it should be enough that she did. And now she should forget him. But the feeling of his hand against hers, or their brief conversation on April's terrace, came back to her again and again.

She was proud of her performances: *I* walked away from *him,* she told herself. I haven't called them back about the audition. But she thought of his aftershave, and the warm scent of his breath. "That way madness lies," she murmured, and tried not to remember how he had looked at her, the approval in his eyes as he had complimented her hair, her dress. Twice since then, she had slipped into it again and stared at herself in the mirror, looked at what he had looked at. He had flirted with her. He had been attracted to her, had singled her out. Could she work with him? What would she do if he ever called her about the film? What would she do if he asked her out?

Maybe I could see him, she thought. Maybe I could try to make him love me, and then leave him. The ultimate revenge. She almost smiled, then shook her head. She had schooled herself to play the *belle dame sans merci,* the *femme fatale,* but could she really do it? Could she be the victimizer, not the victim? What would it be like to make him want her, love her, and then reject him? Sam deserved it, but could she trust herself to stay uninvolved? Perhaps the worst part of all this was how guilty it made her feel about Michael. Here she was, thinking about Sam, and she had a date with Michael McLain tonight! He was kind to her, but she knew she was using him. I'm acting the way men do! she thought. They are the ones who sleep with a substitute when they can't get the real thing. Oh, she was confused, but she had to admit it was a heady, exciting confusion.

Right now, however, there was no time for it. She sat, her legs up on the low deck railing, and waited for Laura Richie. She was going to be interviewed! And not just for a silly squib in *TV Guide,* but for a *Vanity Fair* cover story. Me and Demi Moore, she grinned to herself. And I'm not pregnant or naked. Of course, it made her nervous, even though she had been interviewed alone before.

How the interview with Laura Richie would go was anyone's guess, but the one thing Jahne *did* know was that she was not going be so relaxed with Laura. Richie had a reputation for both looking for the dirt and then getting you to spill it. On her televised interviews, she pushed and probed for the soft white underbelly. It was said that she hated to air one if the subject didn't cry. Jahne knew it was a fine line she was going to have to walk today: to seem open and interesting enough to keep Richie interested, yet not so stupid as to let her catch wind of what the story *really* was.

Network Publicity had offered to have a representative present, to field those questions that interviewers had the habit of dropping like bombs. But Jahne had decided that one-to-one was better. She didn't want to have to divide her attention.

And Publicity did tell her a little about Laura Richie. Not enough for Jahne to feel completely comfortable, but enough for her to know that Laura could be a tricky interviewer. So ground rules were set. The focus of the interview was *Three for the Road,* not just Jahne Moore, so that would keep some of the pressure off Jahne.

She'd decided that limited truth was the best approach. Small-town life. Upstate New York. Keep the dates blurry. Year of the Dog. If pushed, she'd tell about the car accident, though she could barely remember it. And she'd say both parents had died. She'd play the orphan; God knows she had always felt like one. She closed her eyes for a moment, visualizing the role she was about to play, as she often did before going out onstage or before the camera. "Hi, I'm Jahne Moore," she said to herself, and waited while the words sunk in.

When she opened her eyes, a car was pulling into her

driveway. Jahne got up and walked through the house to the front door, and had it open before Laura Richie reached the top step. "Hi," she said. "I'm Jahne Moore."

That was the first time I met Jahne Moore. I stood outside the door of that little tarted-up bungalow in Bird-land and I wondered how long it would take her to move to Laurel Canyon. She opened the door herself, dressed in white slacks and a deep-blue silk T-shirt. She invited me in, took me through to the kitchen, and indicated a stool at the breakfast counter. She poured the coffee and took out a tray of finger sandwiches the Network caterer had probably dropped off that morning, along with a small selection of petits fours. Of course, now I'd like to say that somehow I knew I was on the edge of the show-biz scoop of the decade, but it wouldn't be true. To me, this was just a routine profile, and I hoped it wouldn't take too long. I mean, how interesting can a twenty-four-year-old TV star be?

As Marty DiGennaro might have said: "Go know."

"So you cook," I commented, watching Jahne move gracefully around the kitchen. If she lied straight off about making the sandwiches, I would know where I stood.

Jahne paused, and tried to figure out if I was making a joke or not. She laughed. "No, I just heat, or reheat. I used to cook a lot, but now, with my schedule . . ." She let her explanation trail off.

Well, she passed the first test. "What a lovely little house, Miss Moore." I like to start off formal, see if they want the "Miss" stuff, see what they call me. Hollywood is an informal town, but it's best to know your place before someone puts you in it.

"Please, just 'Jahne.' If I can call you 'Laura.' " Well, she passed the second test. She seemed like a nice kid. "I like the house a lot," she agreed. "It's just the right size, too. Manageable." Jahne picked up the tray of coffee and snacks and started to walk to the living room. "Would inside be okay?" she asked. "I'm still not used to so much sun all the time." That was certainly true.

Her skin was pale. She took me into the living room. It was furnished charmingly—big Mickey Mouse armchairs in old faded florals, a few cute chotchkes here and there. Jahne had the white drapes drawn, softening the light. Maybe so I couldn't examine her too closely? But I didn't note it at the time.

I sat on the sofa and peered around the room. "You've done quite a lot in such a short time. I take it you did it yourself?"

"Well, it's only a furnished rental. But some things I already had. And I've picked up some others since I came here. Somehow, it all feels like home to me."

I shook my head. "I don't know. I see something in the store, I think it's pretty, I bring it home. I stare at it for a few days, then wonder where I got my taste. It always looks like shit, and never feels comfortable. I've got to get some professional help. You're very lucky. You have a wonderful touch."

Jahne looked over at me and shrugged. I liked her. She looked like she didn't bullshit anyone, herself included. Go know.

"That's a gorgeous suit, Laura. At least you have good taste in clothes. I hate to shop, and I never shop for clothes alone."

I sat forward, ignoring the compliment. After all, we weren't there to talk about me, and the suit ought to be nice—twenty-six hundred bucks at Escada bought nice. "Can we consider this the beginning of the interview?" I asked. "That's something I know readers are interested in. How you choose your clothes, how your house is decorated. All that good stuff. Have you ever been interviewed before?" *I took a small black cassette recorder out of my bag and set it on the table between us, clicking it on.*

"I'm going to consider this interview with you to be my first real interview. You certainly must have some clout if you were able to be the first person to interview all three of us."

"Nah, it's not clout, honey, it's persistence. Keep your finger on the doorbell, I always say. Like a vacuum-cleaner salesman. Pretty soon, someone will open the *door just to get you to go away.''* I put down my coffee cup on the table in front of her, picked up my notebook, and opened to a clean page. *''So just a little background. How did you get to where you are today?''* Sometimes that corny question is all I have to ask to keep them going for hours. All actors are narcissists.

But Jahne just shrugged. *''I've been asking myself the same question. At first I told myself it was talent—that always surfaces, like cream rising to the top. Then I thought, my looks didn't hurt. Then, well, I figured it was my time. Now''*—she shrugged again—*''all I can say is, it's a confluence of influences. Nothing more.''*

''That's very grounded of you, Jahne. But certainly your time practicing your craft paid off. You were discovered at the Melrose Playhouse, weren't you? Tell me how you got that part.''

Jahne laughed and started talking. The usual kid-comes-to-L.A.-scrabbles-around-for-work-and-gets-lucky saga.

I asked a little about her background. I've gone over the tape now a dozen times, but there really wasn't any clue that what she seemed was not what she was. Except perhaps for the momentary pause that stretched out when I asked her if she'd always been so pretty. Now it seems to me her voice was strained when she asked, *''What do you mean?''* but I didn't notice it then.

''Were you an ugly duckling? Did you go through a rough adolescence? Or were you always a prom queen?'' I asked. It's a funny thing. Almost every beauty I've ever interviewed likes to tell me how plain she was as a kid. Like they feel guilty about their looks. And a lot of them try to tell me how they're not really pretty now.

But Jahne just laughed. It was a bit more sustained than the question warranted. *''I guess I was always nice-looking''* was all she said.

''Any men in your life?'' I made sure that that came out of nowhere. Inevitable, but sudden. Sometimes it surprises them into honesty. And I'd heard a rumor about her and a certain much older Lothario-about-town. Plus, I'd seen her talking to Michael at Ara's party. But she was cool. *''Not at the moment, but in the past, and,*

*hopefully, in the future. Right now all I can do is work
and sleep. I'm in love with my job."*

Just before I got up to leave, I turned to her and said,
"You're remarkably mature for someone so young. I
wish I had been as smart as you at your age. Good luck,
Jahne." I leaned forward and kissed her lightly on the
cheek. "Don't take any wooden condoms," I told her,
and waved goodbye.

Out on the street, I threw my notebook onto the car
seat. A pretty girl who got lucky. A real dull but pleasant
enough interview. Nothing new there.

So much for Laura Richie's nose for news, right?

Jahne needed a little time to get herself together after
the interview. The woman had eyes like gimlets, she
thought. And that question had, unexpectedly, completely unnerved her. *Had she always been so pretty?*
Jahne didn't know if she should laugh or cry.

She bathed and laid out her clothes for the evening: her
first public Hollywood date. Her first date as a celebrity.

Celebrity was like a club, Jahne was finding out. And
if there was someone else in the club you wanted to meet,
you only had to ask another member. That's how Sam
Shields and Michael McLain got Jahne's telephone number. She was now a member of that club.

She'd probably agreed to go public out of guilt. At first
she and Michael had agreed to keep the thing private, but
what was there to hide? If Michael was going to use her
for publicity, she'd benefit, too. After all, wasn't she
using Michael to try and keep her growing obsession with
Sam under control? She liked Michael, but he was no
Einstein. Still, she enjoyed his company.

And she had to admit, tonight would be a kind of
threshold, another peak she had reached. There was a
certain thrill that she—plain Mary Jane Moran—was
now one of the starlets she used to read about. Michael
McLain, whose performances in movies had been lack-
luster for the last decade, seemed always able to sweep
down on the latest really hot starlet and score. It made
her a little uncomfortable that she'd once mocked those
starlets. Now it seemed different. Now she could empa-

thize with them. Because, for her, dating Michael McLain was really a rite of passage, an announcement that she, too, had arrived. If it helped her career, she couldn't afford to ignore that possibility.

Earlier that day, the doorbell had rung, and Jahne had found herself facing a tall bunch of flowers hiding a short delivery man. "For Ms. Jahne Moore," he said, and grinned at her in recognition as she handed him a twenty. When you were a celebrity, you had to tip generously, Sy had cautioned. The flowers were roses, three dozen of the palest-pink roses Jahne had ever seen. The card said, "Your beauty makes white roses blush. Michael." It was the corniest shit she had ever heard, but the roses *were* breathtaking. And it was sweet of him.

Now she lifted the flowers in their vase and held them in front of her like a Miss America Pageant winner, while watching herself in the full-length dressing mirror. She was wearing a simple A-line dress that Mai had sewn. The underlayer was black silk jersey, overlaid with sheer blue organza. Another Mai masterpiece of simplicity. Jahne pressed her face into the abundant blossoms and took a long, heady whiff of the bouquet. She now understood what the word "swoon" meant. It was hard to believe her life was real, and not some silly Danielle Steel novel being televised. There was only one person she could share her feelings about this moment with, who would understand. She *must* write to Dr. Moore, first thing in the morning.

Michael picked her up himself. No limo. That was nice. Just the two of them in that luxurious Rolls. The interior was like a leather-lined velvet jewel case. It made her feel pampered, as if she herself were a jewel. And when they arrived at the restaurant, Jahne was delighted Michael had been so original in his choice. She had assumed that they would be going to one of the big name spots, and had dressed accordingly. But this elegant little Thai restaurant was perfect for the occasion. It was furnished with rattan, and there must have been three hundred pots of orchids, all as purple as the walls. As if reading her mind, Michael spoke.

"Every Thai place I've ever been to is painted this

color. I think it's a patriotic thing," he said. "But I wouldn't have taken you here if your outfit clashed with the decor." Jahne smiled.

"It was nice of you to send me the flowers," she said. "I really appreciated it."

"My pleasure. Wasn't it nice of Sy to set us up? Sy rarely has such pleasant suggestions. Sy and a lot of people don't really get along."

"Really? Like who?"

"Oh, like April Irons. She doesn't like him."

"Neither do I."

Michael laughed. "A point in your favor," he said.

"I don't know what to order. It all sounds great. I'm torn between the red curry and the noodles in red nut sauce."

"Don't tell me you need a Thai breaker," he said, and she groaned at the pun.

The meal was excellent. And Michael couldn't have been more gentlemanly. After their arrival, Jahne had felt herself begin to relax. It was the first time she'd been out, doing something normal, in months. She began to talk to him about work, as she always did. In fact, he almost seemed more interested in her work and her career than in her body.

"What are you going to do when the season ends?" he asked her.

"I was thinking about taking a part in a movie during the hiatus."

"Good idea. Can you fit it in?"

She nodded. She felt too guilty to mention Sam or *Birth of a Star*. "Of course, I have the Flanders Cosmetics commitment. God, I hate doing that stuff. I never meant to be a model."

"Good exposure. I saw them in *Vogue* and *Harper's*. They're very classy."

"Oh, they're just ads. I hate them. It's degrading. Don't you think?"

"It is for an artist," Michael said.

Jahne smiled, pleased that he took her seriously, and as she did she realized she could sit here talking with

458

Michael for three more hours but there was nothing more she could manage to eat. And three cups of tea were more than enough to counter the effects of the champagne the very grateful owners presented to them with their meal. Jahne was impressed that Michael paid the bill, instead of pulling the bit that she had heard so many of the other actors did: "My presence alone pays for the meal. Here's an autographed photo, signed 'to my dear friends at Siam House.' " He paid in cash, she noticed. *And* left a huge tip for the waitress. Jahne was having such a good time that she didn't want the evening to end. So what if paparazzi photographed them leaving the place? She hoped they would make the papers. She was delighted when Michael suggested they go on to a club. "It's a real dive," he explained, "but lately it's become hip to be seen at the late show. Guaranteed to show in Army Archerd's column. We'll see some of my friends there."

There was a huge crowd outside the place, but after the paparazzi had again blinded them with strobes, the doorman waved Michael and Jahne through. Some of the women in the line started calling Michael's name, but Jahne was surprised to see that people also paid as much attention to her as to Michael. Once inside, she saw that the club was bigger than she'd expected, and it looked as if every table was taken. The maître d' led them to the front of the room, however, and a small table with chairs seemed to appear out of thin air, and was placed in front of the tiny stage for them.

"Kevin Lear's here," Michael said, after he waved to the handsome actor across the room. "He's with his latest fiancée, Phoebe Van Gelder."

"And Crystal Plenum is also right up front," Jahne said, nodding her head in the actress's direction. Her stomach did a little dance as she saw the woman who had played Jill.

"Do you know them? Want me to introduce you?"

Jahne shook her head no casually, making an effort not to show discomfort. She wouldn't mind meeting Kevin Lear, but she definitely *did not* want to meet Crystal Plenum. I have a successful career of my own, she reminded herself, but she still felt cheated.

459

"This club is the lowest rung on the comedy-club-circuit ladder," Michael was explaining to Jahne. "Only the really new kids work here. The ones without any following, no experience. After a while, they get to work other clubs, but here they have to be willing to work as waiters, too, and in return, they can get the mike two or three times during the night. I like to look in here a couple of times a month. Usually the routines aren't very good, and I've seen people booed right off the stage. But every now and then, you find a real comer. There's a crazy guy who does a real mean monologue. Mean, but funny."

Jahne had been through it all dozens of times, back in New York with Neil. She just smiled, and sat through two painfully unfunny routines, noticing that it was getting late. Talking with Michael had been fun, but just sitting through this was hardly bearable. The audience seemed to be there as much for the comics' humiliation as for entertainment. Perhaps that *was* the entertainment. But these guys were so bad, she ached for them.

Once again, Michael seemed perfectly attuned to her mood. "There's one more scheduled; then we can go. He's the one people are talking about, the one I brought you to see."

The emcee—one of the waiters, actually—came up to the stage to announce the next performer. Even though the emcee must have said his name, it wasn't until Jahne saw him bounding across the floor and jumping up on the stage that it hit her.

Neil. Neil Morelli! Jahne tried to make sense of it, but Neil was already beginning his routine. Oh, my God! Neil in a bottom-of-the-food-chain L.A. club like this! And as a waiter! A waiter who has to wait until the last spot to get up and perform. Yet, despite her horror, she began to tune in to his routine.

Neil was already talking, his delivery even faster, if possible, than it had been back in New York. "A couple of celebrities here tonight." Neil cupped his hand over his eyes and squinted out into the darkness. "Kevin Lear, ladies and gentlemen. I've had the pleasure of waiting on him this evening. Thanks for the buck, Kevin.

Now, if my mother lived in L.A., I could afford to call her."

The audience laughed, but Jahne felt frozen. Neil looked around the room, then stopped suddenly, as if overcome with surprise. "Oh, my God, it's Michael McLain. And—get this—he's with a starlet! That's right, who would ever believe it? He's here with the costar of *Three for the Road*, Jahne Moore." Jahne wasn't prepared, in her shock at finding Neil in this place, to be identified as Jahne Moore. It took her a couple of seconds and a tug from Michael to stand up; then she quickly sank back into her seat, her legs shaking. "Everyone knows about Michael's interest in riding. Motorcycles, that is." Mild titters from the audience. Jahne felt numb. Neil working the audience? Stupid smutty jokes? It wasn't his style.

"Okay, did I miss anyone?" Neil paused. "Any Fondas here? No? How about any Coppolas? *They're* everywhere. Are you sure? Look around you, folks. Be very sure, because I have something very important to say, but first I have to be certain these people are not here." He was almost whispering into the mike, his voice urgent.

"Any Carradines? Bridgeses? Arnazes? Okay, lastly, is Tori Spelling in the audience?" When no one responded, Neil began to speak in a different tone, slightly louder but more conspiratorial. "Someone watch the door and let me know if any of those people come in." Neil looked around the room for a few minutes, then let his eyes stop at Jahne. He looked thinner than ever—gaunt, almost—and his eyes had a paranoid gleam.

"Miss Moore, forgive me, but what did your father do?"

Jahne felt her skin turn to ice. "My father worked for the government."

"A diplomat?"

"No, he was in the army," she lied.

Neil laughed at that. "Just wanted to make sure. Not like your costar Lila Kyle, right? *Her* mother is Theresa O'Donnell, and *her* father was Kerry Kyle. Now, tell me, Miss Moore, exactly how hard did Lila Kyle have to work to get her part? Did she have to work as hard as you? Do you suppose the fact that your father was in the army, and Lila's father was a swashbuckling matinee idol, made any difference to the producers of your show? No, no, don't answer, I don't mean to put you on the spot." Neil started working the other side of the room. "Oh, coincidentally, Lila Kyle went to the Westlake School with Tori Spelling. About a hundred in the entire student body. Let's see," Neil said, pretending he was trying to figure something out. "In my high school, Evander Childs back in the Bronx, there were four hundred graduates my year, and not one, *not one*, got on a major television show. Isn't that hard to believe? What a bunch of losers, huh? And Westlake produces *two*. Must have a great curriculum, huh? Plus, it don't hurt that all the girls' mummies and daddies own the Industry," Neil said, and shook his head. There was some laughter. "You see, folks, it's becoming clearer every day that the only way to make it in this business is to be a member of a show-business family, a dynasty." He looked wild; nasty and bitter and intense. He went through the old New York routine Jahne had heard, but there was more. And it was all meaner.

Jahne couldn't take her eyes off him.

"I'm not talking about the brother-and-sister acts. Like Penny Marshall and Garry Marshall, and Randy and Dennis Quaid." By now Neil was talking louder and louder. Yelling, almost. "No, siblings helping siblings, that's okay. Hey, I help out my sister, Brenda. But what I resent," Neil began to scream, "what I resent is Tori fucking Spelling just fucking *happening* to get the lead on that TV show. The show that her father just *happens* to produce. And what's the show about, boys and girls? It's about a rich Beverly Hills brat in high school. Now, that's not really acting, is it, Tori?" The audience laughed. "She's going to be the next Sigourney Weaver. What, you don't know?" Neil asked, looking at the audience, surprised. "Yeah, Sigourney's father was a network heavy. You didn't know that? How the fuck did you think she got her jobs? Sigourney's what I call a Hidden. They're the ones whose family connections aren't easily known, the way the Sheens and the Fondas are. I just heard that Seymore LeVine, Bob LeVine's son —you know, the guy's the head of International Studios —was just made an associate producer. How many people here know what the fuck an associate producer *does?* I'll tell you what Fred Allen said: 'An associate producer is the only person in Hollywood who would *associate* with a producer.' "

The rest of Neil's routine was pretty much as Jahne remembered it from back in New York, except it had become sharper, harder, more nasty and desperate. Oh, Neil, she thought, what has happened to you? He'd always been extreme, but now he was scary.

"But blood is thicker than talent," he was saying. "I stole that line from someone else. But, what the fuck, these bastards are stealing my *parts.*" Neil was winding down. "You know the only people in this town who have made it on their own? The car thieves and the whores."

Finally, it was over, blessedly over. But before he walked off, Neil did his usual call for the formation of an antinepotism league, with the purpose of going out and killing all the Toris and Lilas in the business. Jahne felt sick. "Can we go home, Michael?" she asked, her voice small.

Back in the car, she felt sicker—almost dizzy. Neil seemed vicious and mad—like a dog that's been beaten. A terrible feeling of loneliness flooded her again. "I guess you didn't like it," Michael said as they drove down La Cienega. "I'm sorry. Maybe this will make it up to you."

He pulled the Rolls over to the side of the street and reached into the glove box, withdrawing a wrapped present. He extended his hand. "For you." Jahne took a moment to collect herself, then, looking up at Michael, took the present and unwrapped it. Michael sat still in his seat next to her while she did. She snapped open the black velvet box. She paused for a moment, then reached into the satin lining and took out the necklace. It was three gold stars, with a diamond in the center one, all hanging from a gossamer gold chain.

"It's very beautiful," she said. "How can I accept this, Michael?"

"Simple," he said, taking the necklace from her hand and fastening it around her throat. He looked at her face. "You just did."

Jahne was touched. At this moment, when she had felt so alone, so bereft, he had offered this gift of kindness, of generosity. She had never received an expensive present from a man before. Never owned a diamond, although now she could afford to buy one. All the emptiness she had been feeling earlier that day, all the horror at Neil's demise, seemed to loosen in her. Her eyes filled with tears, and the pain washed away in an instant. This man, how could he have touched me so? she thought.

But he had. Touched her, and made her happy.

"The star speaks for itself, Jahne. You're on your way, big-time. One day, when you're way up there, will you think of me, and this night, and touch the star around your neck? I hope so."

And all at once she was flooded with such gratitude, such pleasure in his warmth, his approval. They went back to his place. He ran a bath, helped bathe her as if she were a very young child. It was as if he knew how needy, how upset she had been. Then he wrapped her in a towel and carried her into his bedroom. Michael lifted her, lightly and easily, as if all her weight were nothing— she was, as the old clichéd song lyric went, "a feather in his arms."

And making love was such a release. She didn't think, she only responded. After the kissing and the back rub, after she felt hot and hungry for him, he held her by her shoulders above him, suspending her effortlessly. He teased her, lowering her face to kiss her and then pushing her away. Then, at last, he placed her on his dick, pushed her down, and lifted her, over and over, again making it effortless, making it fun.

He made her feel light, and small, and feminine. He moved her with grace and strength and skill. "Thank you," she murmured. "Thank you." She felt the necklace circling her throat. She moaned with pleasure. It didn't take long for her to come.

Afterward, as she lay beside him, she wondered at his stamina and asked, "How do you do that?"

"It takes a lot of push-ups, but it makes them all worthwhile," Michael said, grinning.

"It reminds me of that old biblical question: 'How many angels can dance on the head of a pin?' " She giggled.

"Hey—that's no pin!" he protested.

"Well, I'm no angel," she told him, and moved to cover his mouth with her own. Her blood hummed in her ears. Which was just as well, because it kept her from hearing the tiny whir of the concealed video camera.

While Neil Morelli was unwinding after his monologue and Jahne slept in Michael's arms, Sam Shields paced back and forth across the speckled tile floor of his office. Surrounding him were dozens of sheets of balled-up, discarded pages. He wasn't making any goddamned progress with the script. Maybe because it was a dated, hopeless melodrama, or maybe because he was a dated, hopeless melodramatic screenwriter, but, for whatever reason, it wasn't coming together. And while Hollywood had seduced him, there was still enough of the old Sam left to believe passionately that the story mattered, that the characters had to make sense, and that the unities should be followed.

He ran his fingers from his forehead down through his tangle of hair, which had come undone from the lacing that he used to pony-tail it. He caught a glimpse of himself in the mirror that hung on the back of his office door. He looked like a madman. Well, he *was* a madman. *Cinéma vérité*. He went back to the desk and peered at the screen of his laptop word processor. God, it was worse than he'd thought! Still, he printed it out to see it in black and white. Jesus! It was even worse on paper! He crushed the page and threw it down among the flotsam and jetsam already at his feet.

He was choking. Like Kareem Abdul-Jabbar, who could make any kind of action shot but could rarely sink a basket from the foul line when the crowd was watching. Too much pressure. But who was watching him? Sam had found it easier to be brave when he'd had almost nothing to lose. Now he was no longer a neophyte director with a low-budget first offer. Now he was Sam Shields, the successful director of *Jack and Jill,* and instead of it bolstering his confidence, he felt that he had something to risk.

How could it be that he had never noticed the number of danger points that stood in his path to continued success? If April didn't like the script, he was done for. If Bob LeVine didn't green light it, he'd be done for. If they went into production and he fell behind budget, or if April didn't like the dailies, he was done for. And if he managed to finish the script, cast the movie, get it shot on budget, and released, but the audience didn't come to it, he was done for. So many chances to fail, and such a slim hope for success—no wonder he wasn't sleeping.

He thought of his father's words of advice, "Don't fuck this up for yourself." Well, Dad, I'm trying not to. But you and Mom didn't seem to give me a base of confidence to work from. Couldn't you have picked some up for me on one of your trips to the liquor store?

Sam kicked viciously at the tide of discarded paper around him. He had better clean all this up, because, worst of all, he had to put a good face on everything. This was Hollywood. Never admit that you are hungry, angry, lonely, or tired. And never, ever, admit that you're afraid. On the evenings he saw April, he exhausted himself with fake passion and fake assurances to her that things were going well. If only he could level with her, talk through his problems and fears, he might be able to move forward, but April was no Mary Jane Moran.

Sam sighed, and thought of the days when Mary Jane would listen while he poured out all his insecurities and problems. She knew when to help with suggestions and when simply to listen and let him work things out on his own. Perhaps the work he did with her had come out so well because of her collaboration.

Collaboration? Well, that was going too far. His work belonged to him. She had merely been a good listener.

He knew what he needed. He needed the relaxation of a sexual relationship where he wasn't always on the line. He thought of the lunch with Jahne Moore. *That* was something he'd like to try on for size. She seemed to Sam to be more than just a pretty girl. He had thought about her a lot. She seemed to draw him to her, as if her warmth were a magnet and he a mere iron filing. She seemed so young, so fresh. And she had that hunger, that actor's need to perform, that so excited him. He felt that she would be a good listener. Well, he'd push April again to get the girl to audition.

Now he needed a good listener. He needed to throw his ideas at somebody who would neither belittle his suggestions nor cheapen them. Because Sam was saddled with a project that was, he saw now, a dog. How do you take a dated but revered classic film and update it to something relevant and real without turning off the old audience, while attracting the new?

He threw himself onto the lumpy sofa. There was a story line buried in the script that still made sense: the successful man who watches his woman surpass him as his sun sets. Themes of rivalry, jealousy, and love. But how the hell do you dramatize it?

Sam jumped up and began his pacing. There was a meeting to start on storyboards at the end of the week, and he was not going to hand in this piece of shit. With a sigh that seemed to come from somewhere deeper than his liver, Sam sat down at the desk. "Come on, get with it," he said aloud. "Don't fuck this up for yourself."

9

*They were running late tonight on the 3/4 location, and
no one was in a good humor. Oddly enough, the early
success of the show had not made the set more relaxed
and jovial, as success usually did. Instead, it seemed ever
more tense. I had heard about nothing but trouble, and I
had three crew people who fed me the dirt. I was there
just to get a bit of color for the* Vanity Fair *piece. Now
they were trying to get a complicated Steadicam shot in
the can. Some poor bastard cameraman was rigged up
with this ninety-pound monster, following the three costars down the stairs of the building that was doubling for
the scene of the Chicago convention center. It was, as
they say, a tough act to follow—the three costars had
such specific marks to hit that their progress down the
steps was almost choreographed, while the camera operator skipped backward in front of them.*

*This was the sixth take. The problem was that Lila
kept hogging the shot. It reminded me of the old rumor
that, during the filming of* Wizard of Oz, *both the Lion
and the Tin Man kept crowding Dorothy off the yellow
brick road. Poor little Judy. Now Sharleen kept blowing
her lines. In addition, they were losing the light. And if
that wasn't enough, everyone—from the crafts-services
staff to the Flanders Cosmetics representative—wanted
to leave and go home. But Marty had to get this shot—
this great, fluid shot—right.*

"Okay, let's take it from the top," Marty said, and
tried to smile as he indicated the top of the steps. The
Steadicam guy once again climbed up, slowly, with his
extra burden, uncomplaining. After all, he was a specialist, paid by the hour. What did he care? Marty had thirty-
five thousand dollars sunk into this sequence already—
he'd have their faces, their hair, their breasts floating
down the stairs, the violence of the convention behind

them. Soft against hard. Two minutes on the screen. Maybe only ninety seconds. And already thirty-five thousand bucks.

Now, before he started the action, he had to straighten Lila out. He walked wearily up the stairs to her. "I already have you in the center," he said to her. "I have you ahead of the other two. But I can't have you alone. You are the center of the wedge, but I need you to let them be in the frame. Please, Lila!"

Lila tossed her hair. Since their aborted dinner, she'd been particularly cool to him. "I'm not cutting them out," she huffed. "Can I help it if they can't keep up with me?"

He sighed. She was an enormous pain sometimes, but here—at the improbable setting of the Pasadena Library, at the end of the day during the time of special light they call "magic hour"—she was breathtakingly beautiful.

He looked over to Jahne and Sharleen, both being powdered by Makeup. "You ready?" he asked. Sharleen nodded, but he could see she was rattled. He sighed again. Marty needed to get the shot tonight—he was already over budget and couldn't afford the ungodly expensive Steadicam for another day.

"You look great, Sharleen. Now, just come down the stairs, and when you get to the bottom, turn to me and give the line. Okay?"

Sharleen nodded, silently.

Lila looked at the director with annoyance. What was he babying Sharleen for? Marty was one of *Lila's* assets, although sometimes Marty lost his focus, gave too much camera time to Jahne or Sharleen, or too much attention. Since their dinner, Lila knew she would have to put things into balance again. Give Marty a threat or a promise of something, a jerk on the leash. Marty had been too patient with Sharleen as she flubbed her lines through the multiple takes. Lila needed to let Marty know she was someone to be dealt with. Remind him what he just might get from her in return for his . . . devotion? Well, attention, at least.

"How many times does the hillbilly have to blow a line

469

before we're allowed to go home?'' Lila asked, loudly.
"I have a date." Let Marty chew on that for a while.

"Just hit your marks, okay?'' Marty asked wearily,
without admonishing Lila.

"Sharleen isn't just a dumb blonde,'' Lila said, em-
boldened. "If she dyed her hair brown, you know what
they'd call it?''

The rest of the crew had gotten tired of Lila's relentless
put-downs of her costar. But the Steadicam operator,
new to the set, fell for it. He looked at Lila questioningly.

"Artificial intelligence,'' Lila said, and laughed.

Now that the day's shooting was, at last, finished, Lila
flounced to her car. Sharleen had, predictably, blown her
line one last time; they'd lost the light and had to wrap
for the day. Lila smiled. She didn't look forward to her
long drive from Pasadena to Malibu, or her date tonight.
But she had to do it. She knew word of *who* she was
dating would get back to Marty. This was the way to treat
a man. At least, she thought it was.

Lila didn't really like to think about it, but when she
did she recognized that most of the men that she had
grown up around were homosexuals. Her father was, or
was bisexual—or probably omnisexual, if there was such
a thing. Apparently his rule was, if it moved, fuck it.
She knew about the famous statutory-rape case with the
thirteen-year-old. Of course, that had been before she
was born, but she'd seen Aunt Robbie's scrapbooks, and
the clippings were as complete as only a compulsive
Virgo queen could make them.

Not that she'd spent much time around her father. He
and the Puppet Mistress had divorced when she was a
newborn. He'd shown up every now and then, but the
PMS had custody, of course. Anyway, Lila hadn't really
known him, homo or not.

But she *had* known Robbie, and all those other gay
men who hung around the PMS. There was her hairdresser, Jerry, and for a long time there was Theresa's
business manager, Sammy Bradkin, and then Bobby
Meiser, her second business manager, and there was Ron
Woodrow, her *third* business manager (the PMS had

trouble with business), and Alain Something-or-Other, that totally hopeless, lisping cameraman, and the photographer whose name Lila couldn't remember but whose idea of a hot time was to sit up all night and watch the PMS cry. And of course there had been Kevin. Disgusting, lying Kevin. He was still hanging out at her mother's, Robbie said. Lila shuddered. Well, she was sick of them all.

But she had inherited one. Now it seemed that Robbie himself was switching his attention from Theresa to Lila. Where the action was. He was nothing but a fame junkie, totally beat, and Lila knew it. Almost as bad as Kevin, and always snooping. She could barely manage to keep him out of her shrine room. He had taken to saying "we" when talking about how Lila had gotten on the show. As if *he* had done something. Other than give her a bed, what had he done for her career? Sending her to George, for God's sake? Humiliating her at Ara's? What the fuck had he done? Nothing. Not a goddamn thing. She had done all her own work. Aunt Robbie was getting confused. *And* getting to be a pain in her ass. If Lila weren't sure that Robbie would go running back to the PMS the minute she sent him packing, she would have shut the door on him months ago. But she wouldn't give the PMS the satisfaction.

So, anyway, Lila admitted, she had grown up around a bunch of queers. And all of them were "Uncle" Jerry, or "Uncle" Bobby or "Uncle" Somebody-or-Other—except, of course, for "Aunt" Robbie, who was way too much of a queen to allow himself to be called "uncle." It wasn't surprising that those were the men that she was most comfortable with. She supposed that's why she said yes to Kevin: on some level, she *knew*.

Not that she approved. The thing about gays was that they were always thinking and talking about sex. It was so *boring,* for God's sake. Sex was something she didn't like to think about, much less talk about. Lila thought it was all mildly repulsive as well as ridiculous. Think about it: putting a flesh tube from one body into a flesh canal of another. She shuddered. Lila knew that *more* than almost anything she wanted to be sexy, but that *less* than almost anything she wanted to have sex. And with gays it seemed as if having sex was the main thing in life—like 90 percent—and they fit the rest into the 10 percent they had left over.

Of course, she realized, her perception could be a little, well, *skewed* or something, because of all the nutsiness with the PMS. And she'd been to shrinks since she was eleven, so it wasn't as if she were *stupid*. She had hoped everything would change, once she grew up and had a place of her own. But now being on the set, in real life around heterosexual men, didn't really seem that different from being with the gays. Well, they *acted* different, of course, but they all just wanted to fuck. It was only that now they wanted to fuck *her*.

She could see it in their eyes. Lila divided heterosexual men into two categories. One was the men like Marty and Michael McLain, who loved women so much, and wanted to be with them, and noticed everything about them. How they dressed, how they smelled, how they moved, even how they thought. That type might as well *be* homo, as far as Lila was concerned. They made her sick. Then there was the other type, the guys like Sy Ortis and that fat worm Paul Grasso, who talked about tits and beaver but really only liked making deals and hanging around with a bunch of guys. Come to think of it, that type was like homos, too. They were *all* homos.

The whole thing gave her a headache, one of those sick migraines, if she thought about it too much. So she didn't, because all she had to know was one basic fact: men were generally useless, and she hated them. She hated the gays and the straights, she hated how they talked, how they walked. She hated how they were hairy, how they thought they owned the whole fucking world, how they blotted her out, how, even when they wanted her, they made her feel like nothing. She didn't trust one of them. She feared them all. And she hated them all, even Robbie, even Marty. *Especially* Marty. There was no doubt in her mind: Lila hated men.

The thing was, no matter how much she hated men, Lila knew she hated women more.

Her mother most of all, of course. That went without

saying. But now, on the set, Lila's hatred had taken on a broader focus, you should excuse the pun. Working with Jahne and Sharleen had given her daily practice in woman-hating. Up until this show, Lila had never had much contact with women. Theresa wasn't exactly what you would call a *woman's* woman: she had no "girl-friends." Nor was she a *man's* woman, considering the males she surrounded herself with.

So, it wasn't difficult for Lila to understand how she'd gotten to be this way. Weird. A loner. It was realistic, really. Why have *anyone* close enough to compete? Only Candy and Skinny, and Lila *still* hated them. Estrella had been the only real female around when Lila was growing up and living in the Puppet Mistress's house, but she didn't count. A Mexican, *and* a servant.

Now Lila had two women, her own age, beautiful, very close: too close for comfort. She wasn't used to the smell of women, seeing their beauty every day, right there, in her face. It made her nervous. It made her angry. Because Jahne and Sharleen—while no competition—*were* a presence. A presence that others saw, considered, sought opinions of, fawned over. Not Marty so much—right now Marty was the only one who counted on the set, after Lila—but the others.

Thank God, Marty was giving Lila all kinds of special attention. Well, that was the way it *should* be. As far as she was concerned, the other two dummies could look out for themselves.

For most of Lila's solo scenes, she knew all eyes were on her. But for the group scenes, when all three women were in front of the camera, Lila felt—almost heard—the clicking of eyes and camera as they went back and forth from Lila to Skinny to Candy, back and forth, as if there weren't enough to look at. As if Lila weren't enough.

So Marty, as director, was the key. Lila couldn't control what people did with their eyes, but she could control what the camera lens focused on. She could control that by controlling Marty.

Lila had known, since the night she'd met him with Paul Grasso, what drove Marty. Beauty, of course. And talent, but not as much as beauty. What tipped the scales for Marty—*compelled* Marty—and what Lila traded on —was elusiveness: being always just a little out of reach, promising but unattainable. Wasn't that the essence of beauty? She had the mystery that Sharleen and Jahne lacked. It was the tantalizing that Marty—and so many men like him—relished. Merle Oberon, and all the other old-time actresses that Lila knew Marty worshipped. Jennifer Jones. Paulette Goddard. And Theresa O'Donnell. Lila knew what they all had in common.

They could not be possessed. They teased. As she would tease. For Lila, it was easy. She had no intention of delivering anything of herself, except on camera. And she had *every* intention of making Marty believe otherwise. Lila had perfected that talent, that magic. She'd watched her mother, and her mother's old films. She was smart enough to know that she should use every asset she was given. In that respect, she knew she was smarter than the other two. They were so middle-class, so open, giving too much. *They* didn't understand how to hold something back. She would be the one who succeeded, big-time.

Now she wondered if Robbie's stupid gossip was, for once, trustworthy. If it was true that Michael McLain was doing a Ricky Dunn film, and that he also was being considered for the lead in *Birth of a Star*. Well, she'd find out over dinner with him tonight. Her earlier refusals just made him try harder. And if seeing her name linked with Michael's made Marty try harder, all would be well.

Michael McLain sat across from Lila in the vast, high-ceilinged dining room of the Beverly Wilshire and smiled. Lila noticed the tiny wrinkles at the corners of his eyes, which spread, weblike, into his temples. His skin was still good—well, it *would* be, since she knew for a fact he has two facials a week from Gydia—but she wondered how much longer it could hold out. Jesus, how old was he, anyway? She imagined having to kiss him on camera and felt her stomach turn. But maybe the part was for *Ricky Dunn's* girlfriend. At least *he* was no wrinkle-bunny. Well, even if it wasn't, it wouldn't hurt her to costar with Michael. After all, she was savvy enough to appreciate the benefits of a slip yoke like this one. He had been a great star of the past, and she planned to be a great star in the future. If kissing him was a necessary rung on the ladder, she'd kiss him.

"My, my, my. You're a big girl now, Lila. How long has it been since I saw you last?"

Oh, Christ, was this going to be another one of those old Hollywood walks down memory lane? A remember-the-party-at-the-Nivens'-that-Christmas bullshit rap? She didn't mind pulling out the nostalgia for Marty, but with Michael she had expected something a little hipper. She reminded herself that he could help her cross over from TV to features, and flashed him her biggest smile. "Not since I was six, or maybe seven. It was my birthday party, I think."

"Really?" She could see him back off that. She had to hide her own smile. Like Theresa, he was one of those Hollywood mummies who wanted to exploit old times and connections while denying how very old they were. Well, Lila knew how *that* game was played. Just be positive about the connection, but hazy about the time. So she smiled at him. "You used to come over to our place a lot," she purred. "I really missed you when you stopped coming around."

"Your mom still live in Bel Air?"

Christ, everyone knew she did. The estate was still the hottest piece of property in town, even if the house was a tear-down. "Like she'd ever leave, except feet first. No, Theresa's still there, but *I'm* in Malibu. I live in Nadia Negron's house. She starred in the silent-film version of *Birth of a Star*." Let's get the subject back on track, she figured.

"Really? Where? I lived in Malibu for a while." And before she had a chance to get him onto the subject of *Birth*, he launched into some long story about the seventies, Steve McQueen, some grotty house party and mescaline on the beach. Real old-fashioned stuff. Mega-lame. She tried to nod at the right places. She knew that, if she blinked a lot, it kept her eyes wet and made them shine. That usually helped. Finally, it was over.

"I guess those were the days."

Michael cleared his throat. Shit! She'd made him feel old again. Well, Jesus, he *was*. She smiled, then ran her tongue over her teeth. She would have to do some makeup time here. Get Michael all comfy again. The waiter brought their blackened fish and twinkled confidentially at both of them, like he wouldn't be feeding any conversation he overheard to the columns tomorrow. Still, Lila smiled.

"So, you really knew Steve McQueen?" she asked, opening her eyes wide.

10

"You think I don't know people are laughin' at me? 'Cause I don't know how to talk and I don't know how to dress or anything like that?" Sharleen asked, teary-eyed. "I *know* they are, but I just try to ignore it. It's what my mother told me to do when the girls in school made fun of me."

Jahne nodded, handing Sharleen another tissue. Out of pity, she had followed her back to her trailer after the Steadicam sequence finally wrapped. It was the first time they'd spent any time together alone.

"You know, it might be easier for you if we could run lines together."

"Run lines? You mean practice? Just us two?"

Jahne smiled at the girl. "Not practice, Sharleen. *Rehearse*. Actors call it 'rehearsal,' but if you are only rehearsing the dialogue, then we call it 'running lines.' "

"Would you do that for me? But no. That would be too much trouble for you."

"I'd love to, Sharleen. I could use the rehearsal myself," Jahne lied. "Anyway, who else makes fun of you?" She was feeling guilty for her own private jokes about Sharleen.

"Well, Lila, of course. Look what she did back there. She gets me all flustered. I know she don't mean nothin', that she's just nervous herself, but I get upset over it. I try so hard. Every night, I read my lines over and over. I practice them out loud, too. Dean helps me. I know he's slow, but I guess I'm almost as dumb as he is. I know everyone on the crew hates to do it again and again, but I get so confused. And I'm so tired. It seems like I'm workin' or takin' lessons all the time I ain't sleeping. It don't help when Lila rags me.''

"Yes." Jahne nodded grimly. "She does make fun. But she hates both of us. Try not to take it personally. Who else bothers you?''

"Well, Mr. Tilden, the assistant director, he called me 'Elly May Clampett' the other day. Made all the crew laugh.''

"I don't get it.''

"From *The Beverly Hillbillies*. Remember her?''

Jahne nodded. Of course. Barry Tilden was a bitter, funny, middle-aged gay guy. But he shouldn't have mocked Sharleen before the crew. She *was* becoming the scapegoat.

"I know people think I'm ignorant, and I am. But I'm not deaf, dumb, and blind," she sniffed.

"No, you're not," Jahne agreed, handing her another Kleenex. "And you're not seven years old anymore, either. You've got some *power*. Do you know, if Barry Tilden insults you, you could get him fired?''

Sharleen lifted her head up, the long, lovely fringe of silvery blond hair falling away from her face like a white wimple. Despite her reddened eyes and her tears, Sharleen's face was still beautiful. Jesus, Jahne thought, she's even gorgeous when she cries. "Oh, I could never do that!" Sharleen said. "He's a wage earner. Why, he might have children to feed.''

"Two Shih Tzus, more likely," Jahne said dryly. "Anyway, the point is not that you *would* get him fired, but that you *could* if you wanted to. You're important to this production. All the cast and crew's jobs count on you and me and Lila. So no one should be making fun of you. You really *could* get them fired, just by telling Marty or Sy that you want them off the set.''

"Have *you* ever been fired?" Sharleen asked, her voice lower, calmer, and almost ominous.

Jahne, lying, shook her head.

"Well, *I* surely have. And nothin' feels worse than losing a job when you got rent to pay and groceries to buy."

Jahne smiled at Sharleen. "You're a very nice person," she said. "But, now, I'm not saying you *should* get Barry fired. Just let *him* know *you* know you *could* do it."

Sharleen seemed to let that sink in. "Well, what should I do?"

"Just look at him like this and say, 'Don't speak to me that way *ever again*.' He's a bitch, but he's not stupid. He'll stop on a dime."

"Well, maybe for you and Lila, but not for me."

Jahne stared at her. Boy, oh, boy, the nice-girl, modest-little-homespun act was wearing pretty thin. Then Jahne looked at Sharleen more closely. Was she kidding? This hillbilly bit was unbelievable, but could it possibly be true?

"Sharleen, don't you know?" Jahne asked her gently.

"Know what?"

"Know that you're the biggest sensation since talkies. You're *it!* Right this minute, there are girls cutting their hair like yours, trying to buy a jacket like yours. Women are naming their babies Sharleen after you. Don't you get it?"

"Oh, come on."

"Well, they are." Jahne took a breath. "Don't you read the newspapers? 'Sharleen's Three Beauty Tips for Teens.' 'Sharleen Smith models a dazzling new wardrobe!' 'How to be like Sharleen Smith.' Don't you see the magazines? Sharleen, you're about as hot as a star could get right now."

"Well, me and Dean don't get out much, and neither of us is much of a reader."

"Sharleen, I think you should know what's happening. We're a phenomenon. Like Garbo."

"Who's he?"

"*You don't know Garbo?*"

"Don't think I recollect him. Was he one of the Marx Brothers?"

Jahne laughed out loud. "How old *are* you?"

"Nineteen."

Jahne sighed. "Sharleen, you're very, very popular now. And people already want to know *everything* about you. Like the Laura Richie woman. All the columnists. The woman's magazines. *People. Entertainment Weekly.* They want to eat you up. What you have for breakfast, how much you weigh, where you shop, what your favorite color is."

"But why?"

"That, my dear, is the riddle. Maybe people are lonely, or bored, and we give them something to do. Or maybe we seem like their neighbors, their community, if they have none. Some people just need to look up to someone. Be interested in someone. Maybe they hope for our good luck. And other people just need to look down on someone. Maybe they feel superior when we have bad luck. So, for whatever reason, a lot of people are really interested in you. They see you on TV, they like how you look and what you say, and they want to know more."

Sharleen looked upset. "But what I say on TV ain't *my* words. The script says them."

"I know, but people who watch don't always make the distinction."

"But I don't want people messin' around trying to find out everything about me!" Sharleen cried.

"Well, you can't have everything. You got money and fame. You can't have privacy as well."

Jahne saw the color drain from Sharleen's perfect face, and something very much like terror welled up in her eyes. The poor kid really had no defenses. For a moment, Jahne felt enormous pity for the girl. After all, if this had happened to *you* fifteen years ago, she told herself, *you* wouldn't have known how to handle it, either; maybe you don't now.

"Sharleen, it's not so bad. You just have to be careful in interviews and be sure to be discreet in your private life."

"Like what do you mean?" Sharleen raised a hand to

her forehead for a moment, almost as if warding off a blow, and Jahne saw that the hand was shaking. Jesus, what could a simple kid her age have to hide?

"Well, be careful whom you trust. Be really careful with journalists like that Laura Richie. Don't tell your secrets to just anyone on the set. Be careful whom you sleep with. Don't pick someone who might sell his story to the press for a thousand dollars. Don't keep a diary, don't trust waiters or hairdressers or your cleaning person. Things like that. They could be reporters."

"What if I already haven't been so careful?" Sharleen asked.

That night, after her talk with Sharleen and the long drive home from Pasadena, Jahne had trouble sleeping. But it was a relief to be alone. Sleeping with Michael, like sleeping with Pete, wasn't really working. Despite his kindness to her, and his gift, she had to admit that she didn't feel deeply about him. Plus, she didn't really have time for a _sex_ life _and_ a career. The irony of it was not lost on her: now that she was at last desirable, she had no time for it. Between her evenings with Michael, her thoughts about Sam Shields, and her tension from the set, Jahne hadn't slept well for several nights. And she couldn't afford to miss sleep, to look haggard. But since seeing Neil Morelli waiting tables, waiting for his turn at the mike, she just hadn't been sleeping.

Seeing Neil had been awful. She wanted to run up to her old friend and put her arms around him, comfort him, and tell him how wonderful life had become for her—which, as Jahne Moore, she couldn't do. But she also wanted to run from the place, hide under a blanket, shut it all out, as if that would make it less humiliating for Neil. Of course, she had read about the cancellation of his pilot in the trades, and she'd seen him working Ara's party, but when she couldn't track him down she'd assumed he had returned to New York and picked up where he'd left off. To be honest, she'd _hoped_ he had gone back, so neither of them would have to be going through what she was going through now. Feeling helpless, and sad. And very worried about her old friend.

Neil was no good at handling adversity. And he had already had plenty in his life. But seeing him made her realize that, for Neil, there could be no going back. He had always been a bridge-burner, while she'd been conservative, an appeaser. Of course, she'd burned her bridges since then. Well, now, she thought, we have more in common.

She tossed and turned for several hours. She knew what she had to do—the idea had come to her sometime before dawn—and now that it was morning, she was dialing Sy Ortis' office. "It's Jahne Moore. Can I speak to him?" she asked politely.

She didn't have to wait. "Hi there. All set for your *Birth of a Star* screen test? They want to see you. But I still say it's a waste of time. I have at least three better scripts right here."

She felt her stomach flutter. So, April had given her a callback! She felt herself flush with pride, followed by nerves. Well, she'd have time to get herself together. "Yes, but . . ."

"I don't know why you're interested. It's a nothing. You know that?"

"Of course. But, Sy, right now I'm calling because I need a favor."

"Just name it," Sy Ortis said, as she knew he would. The show, she and Lila and Sharleen, all were hot right now. Now, when she didn't really need favors, she had only to ask.

"There's a guy in town, a stand-up comic. I saw him, and I think he's got a lot of talent. I'd like you to get him a guest shot on *Three for the Road*, Sy. He's *really* good."

"I'll give it my best shot, Jahne. What's his name?"

"Neil Morelli," she said, and listened to the silence at the other end of the phone. It was a long silence. "Sy, what's the matter? Ever hear of him?"

Sy found his voice. "Yeah, I've heard of him." Sy paused again. "In fact, my office represents him. Or we used to. And, to tell you the truth, Jahne, I don't know if getting him a job is the right thing to do. He's more trouble than he's worth. Temperamental, or maybe just mental, you know? A real Asshole. He made himself a few enemies from *Chakras*."

Jahne wasn't surprised. "Just do this for me, will you?"

"I don't know, Jahne. It's not like I'm the casting director. Grasso is in charge. Maybe they won't want him."

What bullshit! Jahne thought. As if Sy couldn't push his weight around. She hated to act like a pushy brat, but she'd obviously have to. "Sy, listen to me. I had a very bad night last night, and I need to be at my best for my screen test. Now, you represent two of the three costars on *3/4*. I say that gives you a little clout with Grasso. All I want is for Neil Morelli to get a spot on the show, maybe even a continuing. I'm not saying big. And as soon as possible. Make me happy, Sy." Jahne hated pushing people around almost as much as she hated being pushed, but it seemed to be the only way to get things done out here.

"Let me ask you, Jahne. Who's this guy to you anyway?"

Jahne had been afraid of this question, had even prepared an answer. "He's a friend of someone I used to know. I owe her."

"Like I said, I'll give it my . . ."

Jahne was losing patience. "Like the Nike ad says, Sy: Just *do it*. This is the only favor I've asked of you since you landed me in your stable. Remember you said representation was a two-way street? Well, now it's coming your way." She went to hang up the phone, then thought better of it and added, "Thank you."

Jahne leaned back in the armchair and took a deep breath. Why the fuck did everything have to be so difficult in this town? Such a big goddamned deal? Well, she'd done a favor for a friend. And she had her first screen test coming up. What did she have to bitch about? Things could be a lot worse.

* * *

The next afternoon, still on location in Pasadena, Sharleen was scheduled for shooting a small scene with Lila. Thank the Lord the Steadicam shot was in the can at last! Since Sharleen's talk with Jahne the night before, she was feeling a little better about herself and her work. Rehearsing with Jahne was just what she needed. Meanwhile, she only hoped that Lila was in a better mood than she had been in yesterday.

Sharleen was walking to her trailer to get dressed when she saw an assistant come running up to Lila with one of the ubiquitous mobile phones that everyone used on location. "Miss Kyle," he shouted breathlessly, "it's Michael McLain!"

Lila turned and grabbed the phone out of his hand, motioning the kid away.

Sharleen froze in her steps. Michael McLain calling *Lila?* What could he possibly want with *her?* Sharleen walked up to Lila, who was hunched over a slant board, restlessly playing with a long twist of her hair. She heard Lila say something about taking a ride to a canyon. Sharleen gasped. He wouldn't be mentioning how he took *me* to the canyon, would he? Sharleen's mind was whirling. Or is he planning to do the same thing to Lila that he did to me?

She felt sick. Lila had been unkind to her, but not even Lila deserved this. As a Christian, what should Sharleen do? Sharleen moved in front of Lila. Lila looked up, then turned around, surprised to see Sharleen standing there. Everyone knew Lila was a nut about privacy, and no one went near her or her trailer without an invitation. "Excuse me for a minute, Michael," Lila said with exaggerated patience.

Lila glared at Sharleen. "Just who do you think you are, standing there, listening to my telephone conversation?"

"Lila, I have to tell you . . ."

"You don't have to tell me anything. Just get out of here and mind your own business. Go get ready for the shoot, and don't screw up your lines like you did yesterday."

Sharleen tried to speak again, but Lila turned away,

and with the telephone glued to her ear she walked to her own trailer. All Sharleen could hear as she disappeared inside of it was Lila's low-pitched laugh as she continued to talk to Michael.

Please, God, Sharleen prayed, don't let him mention me to Lila, and don't let him do anything to hurt her.

11

Hitchcock said it best: All actors are cattle. Ara Sagarian knew that, and over the fifty-one years of his career, it had helped him to deal with all of them, from a hysterical Claudette Colbert, to a raging Joan Crawford, to the tantrums of Sean Penn. The one thing he observed that all his clients had in common was that they all wanted what they couldn't have. *"Ahmon!"* Ara sighed, mouthing the Armenian equivalent of "Oy vey."

Look at Lila Kyle. Posters of her in every shop across the country, her face on half the women's magazines and on all of the men's. Truckloads of scripts, a whole department in Ara's agency devoted to handling Lila's endorsements alone, national *and* foreign interviews, even an invitation to the White House. Everything except a mention in Geraldo Rivera's book, which she could have had and did not want, and a shot at April Irons' remake of *Birth of a Star*. So of course it was the part in *Birth* that Lila wanted—and couldn't have. Never enough! Ara was tired of the demands, and the demanding. *Bagos*—crazy. They were all *bagos*.

He lowered himself onto the downy cushions of the sofa in his office, sat with effort, and punched the speakerphone on the coffee table. "Put her through, Miss Bradley," he said, and leaned back with a sigh, pulling his legs up to stretch out full-length. "Lila, my dear, how are you?"

"Did you get her?" Lila snapped. Lila had eliminated the courtesy of a greeting dozens of phone calls ago. For the past week, Lila had been relentless. All her calls to

Ara—and there had been many, every day—were about one thing, and one thing only: her desperation for the part in the remake of *Birth*.

"She's been in New York, Lila. I told you. When she comes back, she *will* call me. Rest assured, child."

"I'm not your child!" the girl snapped. "Call *her* in New York, then. I mean, I can't understand why she hasn't called *you*. It's not like there are no *phones* there, Ara. Doesn't she *know* who you *are?* Maybe she never got . . ."

What, now Lila was going to teach him how to play the phone tag game? Ara had *invented* it. He could hear no more today. "Lila, darling, April is due into the office this afternoon. If I don't hear from her by three, I *will* call her back. Now, be a good girl and keep yourself occupied till *I* call *you*. And think instead about the Ricky Dunn movie. *That* I like."

"You're not purposely fucking this up for me, are you, Ara? I don't give a fuck whether you think it's right for me or not. I want to see April Irons. I want that part." Ara could picture Lila saying those words through clenched teeth. Tsk, tsk. Amazing that her enamel had not melted. He shook his head.

Ara knew what Lila *really* wanted. She wanted to have everything her mother had. Including him. Ara thought maybe Lila wanted to *be* her mother. "We'll speak after three," he said as gently as possible, more gently than he felt, and punched the speakerphone off.

Despite Lila's desperation, or perhaps because of it, Ara had to stop himself from smiling. It reminded him of one of the oldest of Hollywood jokes—the starlet who begs and pleads and grovels for a part to no avail. At last, she promises the heartless agent that, if only she gets the audition, she'll take his cock in her mouth and suck on it for as long and as hard as she can. "Yeah, but what's in it for me?" he asks her. Ara had to laugh.

But it wasn't a laughing matter: this girl couldn't act. Surely she knew that. It wasn't a tragedy. It wasn't even necessary. Lila was beautiful, no doubt about it, and, more than that, she attracted attention. She had that undefinable something that made people want to watch her, to know more about her. She was like Elizabeth Taylor. All she had to do was pick the right vehicles and be there. It was enough.

But they never knew what was enough.

"It's Miss Irons, Mr. Sagarian," Miss Bradley's voice came through the intercom a few moments later. Ara was still lying on the sofa. *"Ench bede nem?"* he murmured in Armenian to himself. What to do?

He punched on the speakerphone. "April, how was the Big Apple?" Ara asked.

"Like the Marine who went AWOL, it was rotten to the core."

Ara chuckled. "I'll forgive you that, April, if we can have a meeting of minds today. You know why I've called you—I outlined it in my fax. *Birth of a Star*. Lila Kyle." Ara paused, and used the opportunity to wipe his mouth and mustache with his linen handkerchief. He'd had to use it less and less frequently now, thanks to the therapy he had been receiving at Cedars since his stroke.

"Oh, Ara. I hate to tell you this, but the part has just about been cast. We're about to test the girl, and she looks good. Sam Shields is sold on her." Ara could hear the regret in April's voice. And why not? He had helped her in small but important ways on her rise. And in a couple of big ways, too. He had no reason to disbelieve April. *Ench bede nem?* What to do?

Well, there was still hope. "Just about" left some room. "That does put me in a bit of a spot, April. It seems Miss Kyle believes that all she has to do is meet with you and you will jump to offer her the part. Seems to think it's such a natural for her . . . and you. I can't say I entirely disagree with her reasoning, since her mother *did* do the original." He wiped his mouth again out of habit, even though it didn't need it. "Who have you picked?"

"Funny enough, it's a co-worker, Ara. Jahne Moore. You know, her costar on *Three for the Road*."

Ara muffled his groan with the handkerchief. "And who for the James Mason part?"

"Michael McLain may sign."

"I see what you're doing. You're taking a star on the

decline, and someone on the way up. Nice yoking. So that it looks like you have *two* stars, right, April? But you only pay half for each."

"I *hope* it looks that way," she said with a chuckle.

"Then, my dear, why *not* consider Lila if you're going with an unknown? What possible difference could it make *who* the unknown is? I mean, the publicity angle *alone* of casting Lila, the last star's daughter, will be enough to ensure some box office."

"Ara, honey, listen to me. I want *seichel*, not kitsch. There's a rumor going around that Jahne Moore can actually act. We don't want a *personality*, Ara, we want an *actress*."

Ara sighed. "Of course, you're absolutely right. But, as a favor to me, would you at least meet with Lila as if you *were* considering her? She has become so obsessed with this that I can't get her to see how ill-suited for the role she may be. I need to get her focused in other directions, and she won't take no from me." Ara hated to do it, but he was tired. If he didn't get Lila before the producer, then it would be *his* failure. But if he got her before the producer and she was rejected, then it was *her* failure. Ara usually tried to protect his people from that very thing, but he couldn't protect Lila any longer. Maybe she needed a little rejection. Some humility. And maybe he was getting too old and too tired to keep up this charade.

April wasn't stupid. She knew the game. "Ara, please don't ask me to do this. Not that I mind being the bad guy, but I'm up to my eyeballs in shit right now."

"Let's go down memory lane, April. Remember how I bailed you out of that Stallone thing? I was the genius who suggested a way to get both Newman *and* Redford. Right? And that time . . ."

"I give up, you old bastard." April was laughing. "Give me her fucking number."

Ara Sagarian was not the only agent in Hollywood having a bad week. Sy Ortis was also miserable. Maybe he shouldn't have laughed when CAA used a Chinese feng-shui master to guarantee "good vibrations" before *they* built *their* new offices on Wilshire. Maybe Early Artists should have done that too. Because all Sy had was bad vibrations.

Michael McLain was a thorn in Sy Ortis' side. And a bug up his ass, a boil on his dick, a toothache, a blackhead, a pubic hair in his coffee, genital herpes, an ingrown toenail, hemorrhoids—every fucking little thing that could make your life miserable, minute by fucking minute. Michael was like Chinese water torture, peeling one cell off Sy's body at a time, until he got down to bone. Sy looked down at the veal on his plate. Delicately sliced piccata. Michael was having osso bucco, and having trouble cutting it.

But now Michael had finally reached bone.

"Don't tell me anything more about Ricky Dunn. Jesus, Sy, whose side are you on? *You* work for *me*, right? So forget Ricky Dunn, for Christ's sake, and listen. I am *not* doing the Ricky Dunn piece of turd. Understand? Unless I have top billing, and maybe not even then. Do you want me to say it in Spanish, too? *Mi non esta* making Ricky Dunn's *muy stupido* fucking movie-o. *Comprende, amigo?*"

Sy was past reacting. This wasn't the first time he had gone round and round with McLain about a part. It was the ritual, in fact. Sy would come up with an offer for Michael, review it, study it, sleep and eat the idea. If it stuck in his mind after a few days of chewing on it, if it began to feel right, then he would go to Michael with it.

And every time—*every fucking time*—Michael said no. Then Sy would tell Michael why he should do it. And Michael would still say no. And Sy would do the dance. About why it was right. About why Michael needed to do it. About why it was a great shot for Michael. And, finally, after the dance, and the ass-kissing, and the begging, Michael would reluctantly agree. And—this was the part that really pissed Sy off—after a while, it would be like Michael had come up with the part *himself*, and had to talk *Sy* into it.

Usually Sy didn't give a shit. "Just give me the fucking money" was the mantra he would recite when he felt he was getting too emotionally involved. But now Sy wasn't going for it.

And why should he? He was sitting on top of the world. His merchandising company was projecting a banner year. It was bringing in more net than his agenting did! Plus, there were all the undeclared cash "gifts" he received from manufacturers who wanted either movie placements of their product or permission to merchandise one of his stars. He had indeed kept the bodega. Gone were the days of nickel-and-diming. So what if Michael had been the first big star he'd coaxed away from CMI? Sy now had a stable, a fucking ranch of money-making talent. And the two girls from *Three for the Road* would make him another bonanza. Plus a hell of a lot more independent.

"Now that that's settled, let's get back to the good news. I am considering doing *Birth of a Star*," Michael said. "That might be the vehicle for me. Irons has the financing, lined up an amazing young director. It's a go, Sy."

What was it with this *Birth of a Star* thing? First Jahne Moore, then Michael. Was April doing this just to piss him off? Did Michael know Jahne was interested? Did he care? But, to keep everything to himself, Sy had been going around about this with Michael for weeks. "And that's your final decision?" Sy asked. "No matter what I think, you're going to do it? I must say, I'm surprised."

"Surprised about what?"

"Well, about you being a welcher."

"A welcher. Since when? What are you talking about?"

"About our little bet. That you could fuck all three of the *Road* girls."

"Yeah?"

"So?"

"What do you mean, 'so'?" It was a vamp for time. Michael knew he couldn't lie outright—it was too risky —and he certainly wasn't going to tell the truth. He hadn't been able to nail Lila. At least, not yet. When he had tried to kiss her, she'd laughed. The thought of Lila Kyle's beautiful face wrinkling into incredulity and disgust was too painful to remember, much less to discuss with Sy Ortis.

"So did you put the wood to all of them?"

"You want pictures?"

Sy nodded. Michael pulled out a Polaroid from his pocket. Sy picked it up.

"My God!" he said, staring at the shot of Sharleen. "She's a natural blonde!" Michael threw another few photos on the table. Sy shuffled through the pictures hungrily. Michael looked down at his meat. There was something gross about Sy's curiosity. I mean, how often did a lizard like him get laid? Michael wondered. Michael knew he had a Mexican wife stashed somewhere, but Sy never took her out in public. Now he grinned over the pictures of Sharleen. "What about Jahne Moore?" he asked greedily.

"You're getting me top billing, right?"

"Right." Sy felt breathless. He loved the idea of the snotty Jahne being taken down a peg or two.

"No photos. But I've got videotape."

"A video?" Sy laughed aloud. "I *gotta* see this."

"You know, Sy, I've been thinking. This has been like taking candy from babies, and I'm coming around to feeling that it's ungentlemanly to kiss and tell."

"Bullshit. Did you do Lila Kyle, too?"

Best to distract him with a joke. "Hey, Sy, what's the difference between a blimp and three hundred sixty-five blow jobs?"

Sy shrugged.

"It's the difference, Sy, between a Goodyear and a great year."

"Oh yeah? Well, you may have had a thousand blow jobs, but you haven't had a good year since *Akkbar*. Did you do Lila or not?"

"Forget it, Sy."

"So you couldn't nail her! Do you think Marty has?"

"I didn't say I couldn't, or that I didn't. I just said that I don't think I want to talk about it. I think we should drop the whole bet."

Sy stared at him for a moment. Michael tried to look morally superior, giving him the look he had used on Rod

Steiger in *Corruption,* after he discovered that Steiger
had stolen from the pension fund. He used the same concentration, the unblinking stare, the whole bit, but, after
a moment, Sy lifted up his pointy chin and just laughed.
His laugh had the bark of a hyena in it.

"Not bad, Mike. For a moment, I thought maybe you
had gone gaga on her, like Marty. But you haven't, and
you haven't fucked her, either. So don't pull your dying-
days-of-the-Actors-Studio routine with me. I'm not some
shmuck from William Morris." Sy stood up and walked
over to the restaurant railing. "What is it with that
bitch?" he murmured. "Is she a professional virgin or
something? Or a rug muncher, maybe? But when did *that*
stop an ambitious dyke from going down on a director?
Is she smart enough to play *that* hard to get? I could
understand if she didn't do him or you 'cause she was
boffing Brad Dillon or Ricky Dunn or some other young
piece of meat, but we checked it out. *Nada.* I swear to
god, she's Marty's obsession. He'll have to start going to
Al-Anon meetings if he doesn't straighten out soon." Sy
shook his head and sighed.

"Well, speaking of Ricky Dunn, it seems as if you owe
me a meeting with *that* gentleman."

"Sy, I said I wanted to drop the bet. It's . . ."

"You can't drop the bet, 'cause you *lost* the bet. You
told me you'd put it to all three for the road, or else you'd
do the Dunn movie without top billing. Don't bullshit a
bullshitter, Mike. You're starting to slip. Losing the
touch, huh? It's time to settle up."

Michael couldn't take it. "I've done all three!" he
snarled. "I'll send over the video and the other photos
this afternoon. Now *you* owe me a meeting. *And* top
billing, Sy. My name over the title. And if you can't
deliver, I'm going to call Mike Ovitz."

Sy went back to his office feeling both angry and out of
control. If what Michael said was true, he, Sy, would
have to try to convince Ricky Dunn to give Michael top
billing. Almost an impossibility! He reached for his inhaler. He would lose face if he couldn't deliver, and he
wasn't sure he could. He was Dunn's agent, but Dunn

was no fool. Why should he give up top and only? How could Sy convince him to?

As always when Sy was rattled, he began to think of ways to increase his take. After all, money was power. He needed some other means of making more money on these clients of his. He was sitting on two of the hottest new stars since Julia Roberts, and realizing *nada* on them, aside from the extra fees he'd created out of the Flanders Cosmetics deal. He couldn't count on Jahne Moore to do any other commercials, advertising for bathing suits, or practically any other publicity. Sure, she was going to screen-test for *Birth of a Star,* but he knew that it wasn't going to make any money for him: April was cheap and smart, and even if she gave points, remakes never make any profit.

So how about Sharleen Smith? At least *she* was easy. He'd have to force her into the recording contract. Yes. Hal King was pushing for the deal. Her face alone would sell half a million copies. She couldn't sing? So what? If the little redneck only showed up and barked like a dog, they could always overdub her. Now all that was needed was a little influence. Because Hal King had promised Sy seventy thousand dollars in cash, in a bag, if Sy could deliver the kid to the studio. If Hal King can push for a deal, Sy Ortis can push even harder, he thought as he reached for the receiver.

Sy had had this conversation twenty times with Sharleen. This time, he'd have to get her to do it. Sy tapped his fingers on his desk impatiently. "Come on and pick up the . . . Hello? Dean? May I speak to Sharleen, please?" The guy was even slower than Sharleen was. Who was he? Her boyfriend? Her husband? Thank God, she kept him out of sight. That they had found one another was proof there was a God.

"Hello, Sharleen, Sy Ortis here. Sorry to bother you, but I have to get your go-ahead on the recording."

"Well, I . . ."

"So what do you say I call a studio and we set it up in . . . oh, a couple of days?"

"A couple of days? I don't know if I can do this, Mr.

Ortis, I mean, I just haven't had enough lessons and . . ."

"Now, Sharleen, I just know you'll be fine. You're doing so well with the TV show that I know you can do just as well making a record."

"I just don't know," Sharleen muttered.

"Look," Sy said with a little growl in his voice, "just come to the recording studio and give it a try. If you don't like the way it sounds, we can drop the whole thing."

"Oh, I don't think . . ."

Sy was searching his desk. "Where the hell is my inhaler?" he muttered. He choked once, sputtered, and grabbed for it.

"Mr. Ortis, are you okay? I don't mean to make you upset, Mr. Ortis. If you really think it will work, I guess I can do it. It's just that I'm so tired all the time . . ."

Sy took a deep breath on his inhaler, and with a sigh of relief said, "Great, Sharleen. You'll be thanking me all the way to the bank."

"The bank? I can't go now, Mr. Ortis. It's after five."

Sy laughed. "Don't worry about it. I'll see you in a couple of days, Sharleen."

Sy hung up the phone, sat back in his leather-upholstered chair, and put his feet up on the corner of his desk. That was seventy big ones in the bag. He smiled, looking at his inhaler. *Madre de Dios,* if all he had to do was have an asthma attack to get a client to give in, he'd have to try it on Michael McLain—if, as he suspected, he couldn't get Ricky Dunn to give Mike top billing.

12

Jahne had kept her promise. Now, after running lines for more than an hour, Sharleen seemed better, and more confident. "This really helps," she said cheerfully. "Thanks so much, Jahne."

They were at Jahne's place. Jahne had noticed one thing the two seemed to have in common: like Jahne,

Sharleen didn't ask people home or seem ever to mention her past or her private life. But now that their rehearsal was over, Sharleen seemed to want to talk. She stood up, stretched out her arms, and shook out her incredible hair. Then she walked over to the fireplace.

"Remember what you said the other day, about bein' discreet?"

"Uh-huh."

"Well, I don't think I been discreet."

Jahne smiled. "Unless you were shoplifting or recently slept with a married man, I don't think you'll wind up on the front page of the *Enquirer* or the *Informer.*"

Sharleen picked up an ashtray off the mantel and fingered it absently. "Michael McLain isn't married, is he?" Sharleen asked.

Michael's name and the *non sequitur* hit Jahne almost as hard as a slap. How does Sharleen know about my affair with Michael? Had pictures of their single public date already hit the papers? She felt her own stomach tighten. Was he putting her name all around town? Was he talking about her? More important, was he talking about her scars?

Jahne, scared and shocked, looked across the room to see Sharleen watching her closely, her perfect mouth slightly open, her eyes wondering. "He fucked you, too?" Sharleen asked. "Oh, excuse me," she added, beginning to blush. "I don't usually use cuss words. I was just surprised, is all."

Jahne could hardly take it all in. *"You've* slept with Michael McLain?"

Sharleen nodded. Jahne couldn't even manage to be polite. "When?" was all she asked.

"Not so long ago. He called and asked me out. To dinner. At nine o'clock at night! We didn't eat, I just went out for coffee. And he was nice. Really nice. I shouldn't a done it, but he was so kind, like, and he was so interested in me. And he really listened to me. He gave some real good advice."

That sounded like Michael, Jahne admitted. She felt her stomach turn over. "So you've been dating?"

"No. Only that once. And then . . ." She paused and

took a deep breath. "He took me in his car up a canyon road and we had champagne and . . . well, like they say, he didn't call me the next mornin'!"

Jahne was reeling. Was he seeing Sharleen right about the time he took her, Jahne, to April's party? Well, she told herself fiercely, he never said he was a virgin. Or that he was seeing her, Jahne, exclusively. So, he saw Sharleen, and took her out once. So what?

"He gave me this," Sharleen said shyly, and Jahne saw the twin of her own necklace hanging beneath the turtleneck Sharleen wore. But all at once, Sharleen began to sob. "It wasn't nice, what we did. It wasn't right," she said. Then Sharleen told the muddled story of what actually happened.

Jahne could hardly believe it! Was this the same man who'd been so forgiving of her own imperfections? He'd gotten Sharleen drunk and taken her against her will? Jahne felt her stomach turn. "Sharleen, that's date rape."

"What?"

"Date rape, Sharleen. He forced himself on you when you didn't want him to." Jahne shivered. Hard to believe that the gentle lover Michael seemed to be was capable of that. But Jahne knew one thing: Sharleen was incapable of lying.

Sharleen shrugged, ruefully. "I got what I deserved, cheatin' on Dean. Made me feel small." She looked up at Jahne. "Guess I shoulda known I wasn't smart enough for him." She paused, and wiped her eyes. "He really likes you, huh? You like him, too?"

"Well, I did." Jahne sighed. "Sharleen, he doesn't like me, either. But he didn't rape me. And it wasn't your fault he did it to you."

Oh, how could she, Jahne, be so stupid? She'd actually fallen for his bullshit, the old hambone. He'd never mentioned Sharleen. But he must run the same routine all the time. The advice, the necklace. Yes, Jahne thought wryly, and *you* thought you were special. She looked at Sharleen. The kid is for real, she decided. And he suckered her. Poor thing. Jahne would admit the truth to Sharleen, but not the whole truth. Not that she was *still* involved. Well, she wouldn't be for long. "I slept with him," Jahne acknowledged. "Not that we did much sleeping," she added.

Sharleen paused and considered for a moment. "Did *you* like it?"

Jahne was surprised by the blunt question. "Well . . ." Jahne thought about it. "I liked the *idea* of it. I liked the idea that it was famous Michael McLain who was doing those things with me, but if I close my eyes I can't say it was much fun. I kept getting the feeling that the whole thing was choreographed."

"What's 'corey-oh-graft'?"

"Like he'd done it all a hundred times before—like all his moves were rehearsed."

"Yeah, I know what you mean. Like there was no one home."

"Well put. He did all the right moves, but I couldn't *feel* him."

"Yeah. Like that Yule log that they show, Christmastimes, burning on TV. It looks like a fire, but you can't get no heat."

Jahne laughed. "Exactly."

"I didn't want to do it with him, and I don't remember that much. Still, I really liked him," Sharleen admitted. "But then he didn't call. I guess he was like some of the boys in high school." Sharleen thought for a moment of Boyd, and of that terrible night, but pushed the thoughts from her mind. She looked at Jahne. "But he must have liked *you*."

Jahne laughed. "No, I don't think so." Jesus Christ, she told herself. Thirty-seven years old and still falling for an actor's bullshit. Wouldn't she ever learn? How soon would Michael drop her? Well, she decided, not quite as soon as *she'd* drop *him*. It was over. She leaned toward Sharleen. "But I didn't know that you were involved, or that you cared about him. I wouldn't have dated him if I'd known. I'm so sorry if it hurt you. I'd never do that to a friend. I've had it done to me, and I know it hurts."

"Oh, Jahne! What woman could take a man from you? You're so gorgeous and so talented and so smart."

Jahne just smiled. "I had my ugly-duckling phase," she said.

Sharleen nodded, serious. "You'd have had to, because if you'd always been so pretty you'd have no charity for plain girls. Did you have a dumb phase, too?"

Jahne laughed again. "No, I think I'm having that *now*," she told Sharleen.

"Jahne, it ain't none of my business, but I just want to tell you that Michael McLain called Lila yesterday."

"*Lila?*"

"Remember she told Marty she had a date? I think it was with him."

"How do you know?" Jahne asked sharply. She felt her stomach go queasy, her hands clammy.

Sharleen explained what she'd overheard. Jahne did not know what to think. What kind of game was Michael playing? And just how dumb had she been? "I can't believe I've been so stupid," Sharleen said.

"So, speaking of stupid, do you think you've ruined it with Dean?"

Sharleen shook her head. "He don't know. But I feel *so* bad. Maybe I should tell him. Oh, I don't know what to do. Dean ain't smart. Lord, Jahne, he's way loads dumber than *me*. But he's got totally good feelings, you know what I mean? He don't never do anything mean or bad out of orneriness. Kind of like a hound, you know?"

Jahne nodded.

"I'm afraid to tell him, but I hate to be lyin' to him."

"Want my advice?"

"Well, I most surely do."

"Don't tell, and don't dwell on it, Sharleen. It wasn't your fault. Meanwhile, something real weird and real big has happened to us. It's like Cinderella. One day we were sweeping up the hearth, and the next day we're princesses. And you don't always know who's the prince and who's the frog." She thought again of Michael. A real frog. "It's a lot for anyone to adjust to. So we both went a little crazy. Let's just forgive ourselves, and promise each other we won't let it happen again." She held her hand out to shake.

"You mean it?" Sharleen asked. Jahne nodded. Sharleen took her hand and shook it enthusiastically. "It's a deal," she said. They were both silent for a moment. "You know, Sy Ortis wants me to do a record album."

"I didn't know you could sing."

"I cain't. But he says it will make a lot of money. And he wants me to. Think I should?"

"Sharleen, I don't know. If you want to, maybe. Sy Ortis doesn't want me to take a screen test for a movie, but I'm going to do it tomorrow anyway."

"Good for you! You nervous?"

"A little. Well, a lot, really."

"Kin I ask you somethin' else?"

Jahne nodded again.

"Did you mean it when you said you wouldn't do somethin' bad to a friend?" She paused, shy. "Do you mean that *I* was your friend?" she asked.

"I most surely do," Jahne said in a perfect imitation of the girl. Sharleen laughed.

"Hey, we better go," she said, and gathered up her bag. "I got to go to the recording studio." She sighed.

Jahne walked with her to their cars. And then, both tentative, both shy, they hugged each other. But as Sharleen got into her car, Jahne thought of something. "How did Michael get your number?" she called.

"Mr. Ortis gave it to him."

Jahne stood very still. Sy had also set up the first date between her and Michael.

Sharleen and Dean pulled up into the circular driveway at the recording studio. Before the limousine came to a full stop, the rear door was pulled open by a young woman. "Miss Smith, I'm *so* happy to finally meet you," she said, extending her right hand. "It's *such* an honor." The girl was wearing a full cotton skirt, a Mexican blouse, and sandals, which Sharleen thought made her look like a poor Mexican, except this one was blonde and was wearing about ten thousand dollars' worth of jewelry. "My name is Sandra," the young girl said. "I'm your personal assistant while you're here at the recording studio, so, if there is anything I can do for you to make you comfortable, *anything*, why, you just let me know."

Sy Ortis moved between them then, coming out from a dark limo that had been parked beside the entrance. He shooed Sandra back, took Sharleen's arm, and led her up the steps to the entrance door. Dean bounded up the stairs ahead of them, his tight, faded jeans straining at his rounded buttocks with each step, his black silver-tipped boots making clicking sounds on the concrete steps.

The cowboy hat Sy Ortis had given Sharleen just this morning sat forward on her head like a hen on a fence post, casting a shadow across her eyes. It was uncomfortable, but Mr. Ortis had insisted she wear it.

Sharleen felt at home in her faded jeans and a man's unironed white shirt, tied in a knot beneath her breasts, but the cowboy hat felt awkward on her head, so now, thinking of what Jahne had said, she took it off and carried it in her hand by the string. Hell, she hadn't worn one back in Texas. Why start now. Her feet in the new boots felt as cramped as a muskrat in a rabbit's hole, but she tried not to let the discomfort show. The whole outfit had been Sy's idea. "These people are used to working with all the C&W greats. Hal King has personally produced Crystal Gayle, Roy Acuff, and all the hit albums of the New Ozark Boys. He'll be more confident if he sees you're for real, Sharleen. Let him see your Texan side. It'll help set the mood for the recording session." Even though Sharleen knew there was no other side to her *but* the Texan side, as Sy called it, she decided to go along with his idea. So far, he'd been right about the endorsements and the other business deals he had arranged. And she sure didn't know cactus juice from cattle piss when it came to business contracts. So she smiled gratefully at Sandra and followed Mr. Ortis.

Sharleen felt a little nervous about bringing Dean, but she couldn't always leave him back home alone. It wasn't right. But she hoped he'd be—as Jahne had cautioned her—"discreet."

The glass door swung open as they reached it. A short, barrel-chested man stepped out and spoke in a deep drawl. "Why, howdy, young lady. I been wanting to meet you since the first day I set eyes on you on my television set. My name's Hal King," he said, and extended a huge paw of a hand, which Sharleen took and released quickly.

"And you must be Dean, Sharleen's friend. Any friend of Sharleen's is a friend of mine," he said, and shook Dean's hand vigorously.

Sy Ortis didn't wait. "Is there someplace where she can freshen up? It's been a long trip."

Hal jumped back and reopened the doors. "Why, of course! What could I have been thinking of?" he said. He turned to Sandra, who had scampered in just as the doors were closing. "Sandra, you take Miss Smith to the star's suite, and see that she gets everything she needs. Curtis," he said to a young man who had been standing by, "why don't you show Dean around a bit. Make sure he sees the recording studio Miss Smith will be using, and show him around the electronics board."

As if Dean would know the difference between a mike and an amp! Not that Sharleen knew much more. She nervously watched as Dean walked away. Then she and Mr. Ortis followed Hal King down the corridor of offices, the doors open onto each, secretaries peeking out, trying to catch a glimpse of Sharleen as she passed by. They finally came to a thick steel door, over which a sign said "Recording Studio. Do not enter when red light is on." Hal pushed it forward, and beckoned for them to follow. He opened another door, on the right, and Sharleen was immediately transported to someone's living room. The only indication that it was a recording studio was the four huge audio speakers placed expertly around the room at ceiling level.

"I hope you like it, Miss Smith," Sandra said in a reverential whisper.

"Oh, of course I do. It's real cozy." Sharleen turned to Mr. Ortis. "I'd like a few minutes to rest and have a cola first; is that okay with you, Mr. King?"

"It would be more than all right. But you must do me the favor of calling me Hal. Everyone else does." He turned the door handle and said over his shoulder, "Just buzz me on the intercom on the phone when you're ready. Now, you just take your time. Sandra, anything Miss Smith wants," he added, and opened the door.

"Hal," Sharleen called out, "call me Sharleen, would you? And would you kindly send in Dean as soon as he's finished with his tour?"

When she and Mr. Ortis were alone, Sharleen sat down and struggled out of her cowboy boots. "I swear, my feet haven't hurt this bad since I walked home from school barefoot on the gravel road when I was a kid. Now, don't you ask me to put these on again, Mr. Ortis, 'cause I ain't going to do it." She massaged her feet in silence for a moment. Why had she ever agreed to do this? Despite the voice lessons, Sharleen knew she couldn't sing. Not one song through without flatting.

Sharleen sat back with her feet dangling over the padded arm of the sofa, swinging them so the breeze would cool them off. She laughed and slapped her thigh. "Why, if the kids back in high school heard I was going to record a country-and-western album, they would die laughing. I tried out for the glee club, but was hooted out of the room. I never *could* sing."

"All you got to do, Sharleen, is what you did on the set a couple of months ago. Remember the scene Marty was directing you in? You were repairing a broken motorcycle, and he suggested you sing something to yourself while you were making the repairs. Remember that?"

"Well, sure, but I wasn't really singing. I was just imitating Patsy Cline."

"That's what you think, kid, but that day the crew went crazy when they heard your voice. That's where I got the idea for you to record an album."

Sharleen looked at him doubtfully. No one had said a word about her singing that day. Was Mr. Ortis telling the truth? "Even though I'm just imitating somebody? It doesn't seem right to make money just by imitating other people."

"Let's not go through all that again, okay, Sharleen? *You* say you're just imitating Loretta and Patsy, but that's not what's coming out. Trust me, Sharleen. You got a great voice all its own. Wait until you hear the playbacks today. You'll know what I mean."

The door flung open, and Dean burst into the room, as excited as a kid at a state fair. "Sharleen, I swear, they have every kind of gizmo and gadget out there. I bet Nashville ain't got nothing better. Curtis showed me all them color-TV screens. He can write music on them, and they can play the music back without any instruments. And Sandra tole me about her job. You know, she's got to pick all the green M&M's out of the bowl because they upset Loretta Lynn. No, maybe it was Garth that hates 'em." He paused, confused.

Sy looked over at Dean. "Dean, can Sharleen here sing?"

"Sing? I guess so. Sometimes she sings."

"See, Sharleen? Even Dean thinks you can sing."

"Oh, but she don't sound too good," Dean said.

"See? Even Dean don't think I'm any good. Doesn't that prove anything?"

"It proves you have another way of making money, Sharleen," Sy answered. "And you keep saying that's what you're looking for."

"Right. Okay, I'm ready," she said, and ran her fingers through her hair.

When she and Dean got home that night, Sharleen was well and truly exhausted. She had tried all day to sing a few tunes and knew how awful she sounded. She was embarrassed and ashamed, and wished she'd never have to go back there again.

Then, just as she was about to collapse onto the sofa, the phone rang. She groaned. There was no one—not even Jahne—that she wanted to hear from now. She was just too tuckered out.

"Sharleen, can you get that? I need to take the dogs out," Dean shouted.

"Okay. But I just hope it's not a crank call." She reached for the receiver. "Hello," she said.

"Hello yourself, young lady. How's my girl?"

"Dobe?" Sharleen almost looked at the receiver for confirmation.

"The one and only, young lady. Dobe Samuels, alive and well. So how are you and Dean?" he asked, his voice sounding friendly and cheerful.

"Dobe! Dobe, I can hardly believe it." She struggled

to sit up. "Where are you? How did you know how to find me?" Sharleen was beside herself with joy. "We moved since I sent you our last address. And this is an unlisted number."

"I got my ways, you should know that by now, young lady."

"Can you come on by?"

She heard his warm laugh. "Not right now. I'm in Oregon."

"What are you doing there?" she asked. She wanted to ask him to come to L.A. Lord, it felt so good to hear his voice!

"I'm working on a deal, honey-chile, and I can't get away. But, Sharleen, I need to ask you for a favor."

Sharleen paused. As fast as it had come, that good feeling ebbed away. She should have known. That was the way it had been going since she started doing the TV shows. Everyone wanted her to do something for them. But very few thought about what *she* might need. She shrugged off her disappointment. Well, if there was anyone she *owed* a favor to, she and Dean sure owed one to Dobe Samuels. She'd be happy to do Dobe a favor, she told herself, but, before she could say so, Dobe said, "Now, honey, if you're too busy, why, old Dobe would understand. I don't want you taking on too much."

"Oh, no, Dobe. It wouldn't be too much. I'd be happy to do you a good turn."

"That's my girl," Dobe said, his voice friendly as usual again. "Now, this is what I need you to do. There's a United States Customs auction in three weeks, at the Federal Building in downtown L.A. I need you to go to the auction and place a bid on something for me. I need you to bid on—now, write this down—I need you to bid on Lot Number 604. Can you do that, Sharleen? It starts at nine in the morning, and it will take a while for Lot 604 to come up, but it's *real* important to me. Of course, I'll pay you whatever you spend, but the most you'll have to bid is fifty dollars. Tops, seventy-five."

Sharleen was busily writing on a scrap of paper. Why did Dobe want this? Was it some kind of scam? "Now, wait a minute. What is it I'm bidding on, Dobe? Exactly.

503

Is it them red pills? It's not drugs or anything like that, is it?"

"Sharleen, this is one-hundred-percent certified legal. It's doing business with the federal government, and I don't mess with them G-men in their mirror sunglasses."

"Okay. So, in three weeks, I go to the auction and bid on this lot number. Then what?"

Dobe outlined the registering and payment methods for buying from a U.S. Customs auction. Then he gave her a number to call him at when she got finished with the auction, so he could arrange for pickup. "Got all that, kid?"

"Sure, Dobe. You can count on me," she sighed. "Are we gonna see you again?"

"I'll be in town to see you next month, Sharleen. And we're going to go out for a nice sit-down, you and Dean and me, and you're going to tell me all about how it feels to be a rich Hollywood star."

"Dobe," she said, in a whisper, "it don't feel that good. In fact, it feels real lonely." To her horror, she began to cry.

"Ah, there, there. Poor little girl. I told you, Sharleen. It ain't easy being a beautiful woman, especially a rich beautiful woman. But, now, honey, you hold on to them tears for a little while. Dobe'll be there next month to take care of both of you."

"Dobe, I miss you," she whispered, and wasn't sure if he'd heard her say it before he'd hung up the phone.

13

Pity the poor exposé writer. That's me, Laura Richie. Because you're only as good as your last scandalous book. And there aren't that many scandals to go around. Well, that may not be true: there are plenty of medium-grade, medium-weight, middle-class scandals, but they are not enough to make a best seller. So we are left with the scandals of the legends or the legends of the scandals, and everyone has done those. Between me and Kitty Litter (oh, Reader, you know who I mean), we have covered the waterfront. After her books about Ol' Blue Eyes and Nancy and that poor English dysfunctional family, and mine about Christina Onassis and the Cher book, there wasn't much left on the grand opera scale. So I was casting about me at this time for a new subject.

Because, let's face it: in gossip, people want the best. Sodomy and embezzlement barely raise an eyebrow unless the organs and amounts are the largest ever. And even then, the scandal palls quickly unless it's someone famous or who is attached to them. A story about a secret transvestite is only kind of sordid and pathetic, unless the guy is dressing up in famous underpants. And with all the stuff going on out there, there isn't much left that's shocking anymore. Look at poor Madonna. She has to stoop to photographing herself having sex with a dog to keep in the public eye.

My publisher was pressuring me. I was deciding between a Woody/Mia tell-all and a Michael McLain unauthorized but I was afraid that Woody was too New York Jewish for a broad appeal. And Michael had been around since the year of the flood. Plus, women were the ones who bought gossip books and they preferred gossip about women. My secretary was pushing for a triple biography of the 3/4 girls. But despite the absolutely massive wave of publicity they'd received, I felt they didn't have enough history to make more than a quick paperback out of. And I did only quality hardback gossip.

If only I'd known.

After Jahne heard Sharleen's revelation about Michael, and thought about the painful talk with Sharleen that had led up to it, Jahne rehearsed the ways in which she'd tell him off. At best he was a sexaholic who was out of control as well as a liar. At worst, well, it didn't bear thinking about. Jahne rehearsed in her mind what she would say to him when he called her. The accusations and names came easily. But each time she got rolling she remembered not only how kind he had been to her about her scars, but also how much he now knew. Was it safe to make him an enemy? she wondered.

505

It was a question she did not have to answer. Michael McLain never called her again.

It took more than a week for Jahne to realize Michael McLain had dropped her. It reminded her a bit of that old punch line: You can't fire me—I quit! But even if she didn't call him, she felt she had to do *something* to exorcise his memory. One afternoon, driving down Wilshire Boulevard, she passed Rancho La Brea and pulled over to the side of the road. One of the stranger juxtapositions of Hollywood was the La Brea Tar Pits, filled with prehistoric slime, sitting there next to the movie and television studios, business towers, and the Los Angeles County Museum of Art. There was symbolism there you didn't have to reach hard for. Jahne got out of her Miata and walked over to the cyclone fence that surrounded the pits. An appropriate resting place for Michael's gift, she thought, and took the diamond necklace on the thin gold chain out of her pocket. It was the first piece of jewelry a man had ever given her. She shook her head, and wondered if Michael got a quantity discount.

But, despite her joke, she was hurt. Not that she had loved Michael, or that they had been committed to one another. She had simply liked him, and she had believed that he had liked her, that he had understood her. Well, she'd been wrong. Now she looked down at the three stars in her palm. She hated the necklace, and, with all the force she could, she threw it into the air. The sun glinted on the diamond for a moment before it hit the viscous black of the pit. She only wished it was Michael, that old dinosaur himself, that she was flinging away. The necklace sank without a trace. Let the archaeologists of the future figure that one out, she thought, and turned back to her car. Then she drove home to prepare for her screen test.

If Jahne thought that TV had prepared her for movies, that the small screen was like the big one, she found out she was wrong. Makeup, for example, was a whole other reality. Bill Wougle the makeup artist seemed to paint another face over her own for the test. And the lights took more than an hour to adjust. Jahne nervously fondled the few sheets of script she'd been given. They didn't read like much. It was a fight scene between her and the male lead.

She was ushered onto the soundstage and was surprised—no, shocked—to see nothing but a fully made-up bed there, under the spotlight. She scanned the space, looking for Sam, and cleared her throat nervously. Was she expected to do this scene in bed? Then, from the corner of her eye, she saw him. Dressed in black, as usual, and striding toward her from behind the cyclorama. He tossed his head, swinging the pony tail from off his shoulder, a movement she remembered as habitual. "Jahne!" he called, in what seemed a cheery voice. She felt anything but. He approached her. She felt his presence moving toward her almost as if a wall of energy were coming at her. She tingled.

"What's this?" she asked, nodding at the bed, trying to keep the question casual.

He smiled. "Jahne, would you mind if I pulled the rug out from under you? You have every right to say no. But I'm not happy with the script I sent you. Not yet, anyway. Instead of lumbering you with it, I thought it might be better if we worked with something that wouldn't distract me. Something I'm familiar with." He handed her a script.

She looked down at the cover. *Jack and Jill and Compromise,* it read. Despite the incredible brightness of the lights, Jahne felt her vision darken for a moment. "I'm not prepared," she said, and she felt that it might be the understatement of the nineties.

"I know. It's a lot to ask. Will you be a trouper?"

Quickly, she ran through her options. She could turn him down, but then he would believe her to be afraid of cold readings. And he might just ask her to prepare this for later, or he might decide not to work with her at all. If she said yes, she certainly would know this material better than anyone else. She could probably blow him away with it. But wouldn't he recognize her, and could she stand to tear her heart out in front of him this way? Could she bear being filmed in the role she'd lost forever? "Give me a minute," she told him.

"Of course," he agreed, and walked her over to a chair in the corner. "Take your time," he said. "I've marked the monologue I would like you to try."

She waited until he left, joining the cameraman and boom operator. But she already knew. Of course. It was the "I've never been loved" aria. She'd recited it every night and twice on Wednesdays and Sundays for 426 performances. Back then she had thought that she was loved. She had thought that she was loved, at last, by Sam. She had had the strength to deliver it as a wounded bird, but what would she do now? She opened the script. She felt sweat trickle down her scalp and run to the back of her neck. The scars on her breasts began to itch. Her armpits were clammy; Bill's makeup must be running down her face; what could she do? What would she do?

Her eyes swept the script, and then the inspiration came. Not pathetic. Angry. Not sad and vulnerable because she'd never been loved, but enraged over it. She scanned the text. It would work. It would work *better*. She went through it, the whole thing, in her mind. She stood up and strode over to Sam. "I can do this," she said.

Jahne pulled the Miata onto the freeway, and released a long, noisy breath. I got it, she thought! I took my first screen test and I blew him away.

Of course, she couldn't be sure of anything. But she had taken his monologue, *her* monologue, and put a whole new spin on it. Instead of the pathetic cry "I've never been loved," it became one of rage. She delivered the whole thing with the passion of anger, of rage at the waste, the unfairness. And when she cried over the last words, they'd been tears of rage.

The crew had applauded. Jahne knew enough to know how rare *that* was, and if Jahne still knew Sam at all, she knew when he was interested in working with someone. And Sam was *definitely* interested in working with *her*.

Jahne wanted to be out of the car, physically moving, walking. The waiting for the callback was going to be tough. In the old days, she would have bought herself a good meal, or, better yet, a really sinful cake and some

Ben & Jerry's ice cream. But now she couldn't afford to gain an ounce. Well, when the going gets tough, the tough go shopping, she thought, and groaned to herself at the silly expression.

Still, it would make a good release, a nice reward. She pulled her car into the underground parking at the huge shopping center on the west side of Century City. Riding up the escalator to the main floor in the mall, she became aware of the looks and the whispers of people as they were going down. Damn, she thought, I forgot my sunglasses. Well, she'd just have to keep her eyes down. But as she scanned the displays in a store window, a teenage girl and her mother rushed up to her. "Aren't you Jahne Moore?" the girl asked. "May I have your autograph?" She thrust a crumpled Kleenex and pen out at Jahne, who signed it quickly while eyeing the entrance to the store. She'd better move into it. But, faster than she could get away, another woman came up behind the first two, and said, "Mine, too, Miss Moore?" It took a moment for Jahne to realize, but suddenly a crowd had formed around her. And then, almost in an instant, the crowd grew. "Me next," someone yelled, and two women began pushing. "Jahne Moore!" someone yelled. "Cara!" yelled another. The crowd pushed. She was being pushed. The space around her disappeared. Then someone actually screamed.

Jahne fought the panic closing up her throat. Over the tops of the heads of the throng, Jahne noticed a tall, black security guard coming out of the store, and begin to push through the crowd. She felt elbows in her back, and the bodies pressed in around her. Then someone pulled at her hair. There were more screams, and her name was being shouted over and over. She felt as if she were drowning. "This way, Miss Moore," the guard said when he finally reached her, and extended his hand. Jahne took it, and let the man propel her through the crowd, blindly pushing aside arms holding paper and pens as he pulled her along.

"Miss Moore, please, for my little girl," one woman said. Jahne hurriedly took the paper, signed it while she moved, and handed it back in the general direction of the woman. Another hand grabbed at it, but a new voice started screaming, "That's mine, give that to me." Jahne caught a glimpse of two women struggling, and, for the first time, she actually began to fear for her safety.

"Give me one, Cara! You gave one to that bitch, why not me?" a woman was screeching at her, as the guard pulled on the shop door to open it against the mob.

"No more autographs today!" the guard shouted.

"Too good for us, Jahne?" a fat, middle-aged woman shouted. She kept her head down. "Fuck you! We made you, you bitch." That last remark would have frozen her to the floor if the guard hadn't given her arm a final tug, pulling her to safety on the other side of the doors, which he then locked behind them. He led her to the back of the store. Jahne, feeling dizzy and almost faint, heard the security guard calling the police on his walkie-talkie, leaving the crowd to swirl behind the glass like aquarium sharks in a feeding frenzy.

Jahne didn't have to look in the mirror as she slumped onto the little office sofa. She knew she was pale.

"Drink this," a woman in a security uniform said, handing her a cup of water.

She gulped it, just to do something. But it did make her feel better. "What happened?" she asked.

"What happened?" the guard repeated. *"You're* what happened."

"I . . . I had no idea. I mean, I've never seen this before."

Two policemen came hurrying into the office from the rear delivery door. "Follow me, Miss Moore," one of them snapped. "We'll go out through the trucking bay and drive you to your car. Then we'll follow you in the squad car until you're safely home."

"Thank you, I can't tell you how . . ."

"Don't thank me. Just don't do this again. Next time, bring your own security, like all the others."

It was surprisingly difficult for Jahne to get an appointment with Gerald La Brecque. She resented it. Perhaps she was simply getting used to the star treatment she thought she deplored, Jahne told herself grimly as she waited for the man to arrive. Both Michael McLain and someone at Marty's office had recommended him, but, despite her calls, it had taken almost two weeks to get this home visit. Two weeks during which she had not heard a word from Sam Shields.

At two-thirty—*exactly* two-thirty, Jahne noticed—her buzzer rang. Not bad-looking, she thought as she opened the door. Oh, fine, she told herself. How desperate are we? Next we'll be looking over UPS men and personal trainers as potential dates.

The audition, seeing Sam, and the mini-riot had unsettled her, no doubt about it. Funny how being mobbed had made her feel lonely. It took the riot to make her believe that she was different now. Special and alone. Then she hadn't heard from Sam. Could he have recognized her? Could he have simply rejected her performance? For two weeks, she'd been obsessed with the question. No wonder she was looking for love in all the wrong places. She smiled politely at the security consultant.

But La Brecque really wasn't bad-looking. Average height, dark, with a neat mustache that looked very soft, although the rest of him looked anything but. He eyed her very directly—his eyes were a strange, very light gray that made them seem almost colorless—and accepted her offer of a seat but not a drink.

"Sorry about the delay in setting this up, Miss Moore, but we've been swamped just now."

"That's all right," she found herself saying, and meaning it, though she'd resented him two minutes before. He seemed so, well, so very *real*. God, when was the last time she'd dealt with anyone outside the Industry? she wondered. No time during the last five months. Even her houseboy was an unemployed actor.

He looked across the coffee table at her. "So," he began. "Why don't you brief me on the current situation . . . ?" His sentence trailed off with such a slight inflection that she barely recognized it as a question. It was more of a directive.

"Well, it's really an issue of security. I mean, of course it would be or I wouldn't call you. Security here and when I'm out. I mean, I don't want a bodyguard or anything. Probably I'm overreacting, but there have been a few . . . incidents. And fan letters." It was the letters from prisoners that really bothered her the most. She'd read the first one with compassion and a vague sense of obligation. Then the next. She got so that she could pick them out in the piles, the number at the upper left-hand side, the prison franking instead of a stamp. Some were almost all right, others merely obscene, but the worst were the fifty-page dedications, complete with drawings and/or poetry. Lots of them were worse, but the letters from men in prison really frightened her. "They make me nervous. But it's probably nothing. Religious nuts, or teenage pranks. You know the sort of thing. . . ."

But instead of smiling at her reassuringly, he only put his hand to his cheek and rubbed, a sort of assessment movement. "Have you saved them?" he asked.

For the very briefest moment, she thought he was talking as Sharleen might, in the religious sense. Then, stupidly, she asked, "The letters? No. They're horrible. Why would I save them?"

"To save yourself."

"Save myself from what?" she asked, fright rising, and with it anger. Jesus! She had waited to see this guy and used up a precious free afternoon to be reassured. Now was he going to try to scare her out of her wits? Is that how he earned his living? By increasing the ever-growing paranoia of the Hollywood crowd? "Are you saying this is a matter for the police?"

La Brecque rubbed his cheek again. "I'm afraid not. They only intervene *after* something happens. Before that, it's up to you, me, and the courts."

"But they're just the usual crank letters. You know."

"Well, I don't, because I haven't seen them. And probably most of them are. But there are others that are more indicative of possible deranged behavior. And we keep a computerized file of the dangerous ones we know about, try to be aware of their whereabouts. We keep adding to our data base. It's important to save them."

"I get a lot of mail from prisoners. They scare me," she finally admitted.

"Well, those are the ones behind bars. It's the *others* I

worry about. Rebecca Schaeffer. And that sniper shooting of Genny Logan, for example. Right in her living room. That one hasn't been solved. She wasn't a client of mine." He looked around. "If you don't mind my saying so, Miss Moore, you are being very cavalier about your safety. Anyone could get in here if they wanted to. And you couldn't stop them if you didn't want them to." He paused. "Do you own this place?"

"No."

"Good. Because it can't be secured. Not here in Birdland, and on a public road. They call this part of the Hollywood Hills the Swish Alps. Lots of gays. Nothing wrong with them, but lots of possibility of street hustlers."

"So what can I do?"

"You can move. Buy a place. We'll move to seal your property tax records so no one can access your home address. And we'll check out any place that you consider buying to ensure its safety. But you've got to get out of here."

"But I just rented it!" She'd barely settled in here, was just starting to feel comfortable, *plus* she had a lease she couldn't break.

"Miss Moore, this is really a matter of life and death we're talking about."

Jahne looked at him, expecting a smile at the hyperbole. But there was none. "You ever hear of Robert Bardo?"

"No."

"He walked up to Rebecca Schaeffer's door. She was starring in a sitcom. Lived in a place a lot like this. Never met Bardo. Didn't know him. Opened the door. Gave him an autograph. She was nice, pleasant, to him. It wasn't enough. He came back. He killed her." Jahne shivered.

"I'll do whatever you say."

"We'd need quite a bit of information to start."

"Such as?"

"Names of friends, past lovers, any enemies. Professional jealousies, past and current employees, that sort of thing. Relatives, their addresses, current relationships."

Jahne felt a moment of panic. Should she disclose her

past, or pretend she had none? Tell him about Sam, about Michael, about Michael and Sharleen, about Michael and Lila? Oh, Jesus, her life was becoming unmanageable!

"Of course," he told her, "all of this will be totally confidential. There has never, ever been a leak from my organization."

"And how much will all this cost?"

"Quite a lot, I'm afraid. For the time being I'll put staff on per diem. Then what I'll do is put together a proposal along with a fee quote. There will be an initial fee, and then a monthly retainer. A year will run in the mid-five figures."

She sat there, stunned, and just looked at him. Mid-five figures. Like fifty thousand dollars? She could take care of a lot of Dr. Moore's patients for that! And buy a few Donna Karan outfits as well. She sighed.

"It might make it easier if you think of it as part of the cost of doing business," he said gently. It was the gentleness of his tone, combined with the glint of his wedding band as it rubbed his cheek, that brought tears to her eyes. Because, all at once, she wanted him to rub his hand across her own cheek, to tell her that it would be all right. To take care of her.

Jahne spent the evening throwing a few things in a bag and calling hotels. She didn't know what she would do. In the meantime, she called Mai and slept at her house.

The next day, back to pick up more of her stuff, Jahne was still reeling from La Brecque's security evaluation. How vulnerable he said she was, how she would have to move to another place, how much it would cost, how she would have to watch her movements in public. It was all so depressing, so limiting.

And lonely. She almost blushed at remembering how she had reacted to the sight of La Brecque, as if she hadn't been with a man in years. As if she were desperate. He didn't catch any of it, of course. Nor the expression on her face when she noticed his wedding ring. At least she hoped not.

Jahne walked over to her desk, which, now she knew, dangerously exposed her to the sights of possible snipers from outside. She sat at it nonetheless, took out a piece of her new stationery—with her address here, which would be useless now—and began to write to the only friend she felt she had in the world.

> Dear Brewster,
>
> Thanks for the picture from Raoul. He's getting good. I'm glad to hear about the speech improvement. Who cares if all he wants to say are swearwords, as long as they are well articulated. I guess his speech therapy is working. I miss him and I miss you.

Could she write that? Wasn't it too personal? She'd sound pathetic, and give him the wrong idea.

The phone rang, and Jahne put down her pen and walked over to answer it. Anything was a relief right now, though she couldn't imagine who had her number except Sy and some other Industry types she didn't want to hear from. She sighed. "Jahne, it's April Irons. Have I caught you at a bad time?"

"Not at all. In fact, I was just sitting here, staring out at my view, feeling how wonderful it was to be in California. How are you, April?"

"Couldn't be better. And neither will you be after I tell you why I'm calling. Sam and I *love* you. We've screened the test a dozen times already. We feel you're *perfect* for the part of Judy in *Birth of a Star.*"

Jahne felt her heart surge in her chest. She was right! She had blown Sam away! "You *have* made me happy, April. *Very* happy. Thank you." But what was flooding her? It wasn't joy or triumph or even relief that she had "passed" her screen test. It focused on the "we": April said "Sam and I." April referred to them as "we." And why hadn't Sam called her?

"Of course, we'll work out the details with your agent, but I wanted to be the one to tell you personally. By the way, is your agent *still* Sy Ortis?"

Still? Jahne caught the inflection. "Yes, he is."

April sighed. "Fine. We'll talk to him, then. But I *know* we'll work everything out. I *know* you're going to be just fabulous."

"Well, thank you. Really. Thank you," she mumbled. God! She'd done it. She'd be in a movie. No, she'd *star* in a movie. If she wanted to. But Sy would be furious. He'd told her over and over that it was a stupid concept. Well, it was her career, her decision, not Sy's. "April, send the contract to me first. I'd like to think it over. And I'd like to give it to Sy."

"Fine. And congratulations, Jahne."

Jahne put the phone down and threw her arms around herself. She couldn't believe it! Even though she'd thought she'd been good at the screen test, even though she'd been confident, she hadn't really believed this could happen: that she could be cast in an important feature, that she could be a star, a *movie* star, and that she could work again with Sam!

She waltzed herself around the room, and then she stopped again at the phone. My God, she'd have to tell someone! Who could she call? Mai! And she'd get Mai a job on the picture, doing her wardrobe! It would be good news for both of them!

"Hooray for Hollywood," she said out loud, and drew the curtains so the snipers might miss.

14

Lila felt as if there wasn't anyone in her life who didn't want something from her. Marty wanted her gratitude, Michael wanted her body, Robbie wanted her fame, and every asshole out there wanted her autograph. This afternoon, all she wanted was to spend some time alone, but no one would let her.

Aunt Robbie had called and asked to come over. This wasn't going to be just a friendly visit, Lila was sure of it. His tone told her something was up. But, whatever it was, Lila didn't give a shit.

Lila stretched out on the lounge, her body glistening under the sleek film of oil. Beyond her, Malibu Beach also stretched out, glaring white in the sun, while the waves rolled relentlessly. She felt the knots of stress begin to uncurl, and willed the muscles in her body to soften. She heard the clomping on the steps to the deck, then opened her eyes to see Aunt Robbie's huge form lurching around the corner of the house. "Where're your skates?" she called out to him as she settled back and closed her eyes again. "Let me guess. José?"

Lila heard Rob waddle over to the other chaise and flop down with a grunt. "That queen Krazy-Glued the fucking wheels. Tight as a frog's ass."

Lila opened her eyes and sat up, pulling the backrest of the chaise into a sitting position. She picked up the towel at her feet and dabbed at the perspiration on her forehead. "If you want something to drink, you'll have to get it yourself," she said. "*And* bring me a Diet Coke," she added, as if she'd just thought of it.

"Where's Yolanda?"

"Catch up, Robbie. Yolanda was three or four wetbacks ago. I fired the latest lazy bitch this morning. Carmen or Carmela, or whatever."

"Why? Caught her trying on your crown or something?" Robbie snapped as he went in to pour their drinks.

That had a little too much edge to it to suit Lila. She felt her muscles tensing up again. She'd just have to get rid of him. She waited until Robbie returned. "I just like my privacy. If I tell them not to go into a room, they go into it. If I lock a drawer, they want to find out why." Lila sighed. "So, Robbie, if you have something on your mind, just spit it out, for chrissakes. I hate those sideways jabs you give. It reminds me too much of someone I used to know." She watched Robbie's expression change from feigned surprise to resignation.

"Okay," he said, and took a sip of his vodka Collins, as if to lubricate his vocal cords. Lila waited.

"I saw your mother," he said, and paused, as if Lila gave a shit.

"She's not dead yet?" Lila asked.

"She's in a bad way, Lila. She's fallen apart."

"So's the Soviet Union. I could not care less about either of them."

Robbie got up and came and sat at the foot of Lila's chair. "Lila, I need your help in pulling her together. She's killing herself, and Kevin is helping. Please, Lila. It's not like you didn't have something to do with the fall." He took another sip of his drink, then held the frosty glass out in front of him, looking at it. "And, after all, you *are* her *daughter*."

Lila didn't have to stop to think about it. She raised both feet and kicked Robbie hard enough to knock him off the lounge chair, right on his fat ass on the wooden deck. She couldn't see the shock in his face; she could only feel her own rage. "You fucking hypocrite," she screamed, now standing over him. "You are just jealous that she spends more time with Kevin than with you, and then you have the balls to pull the oldest guilt trip on the planet on me? Like your own fucking mother isn't living on welfare somewhere in Minnesota—you don't even *know* where—and you have the nerve to tell *me* what *my* responsibility is? Well, I'm *not* her daughter. You get that? I'm not and I never was!"

Robbie struggled to his feet while Lila strode over to the gate. But he still whined. "I can't take it alone, Lila. She needs help, and there's no one to help her except you and me. Ken won't go near her, won't have her in the house anymore. You've got to . . . ."

"I don't got to do shit, Robbie. Do you hear me? Not *shit*. She's *your* friend, not mine." Lila whirled around and through the door into the house, Robbie on her heels. "If you don't do something . . . ."

"What? If I don't do something, *what*, Robbie? What could possibly happen to Lila Kyle if I don't do something for Theresa O'Donnell?"

Robbie was rubbing his ass where he had fallen. "See her, Lila. Make contact with her. She loves you, Lila, in her own way. And she misses you."

Lila was suddenly very calm. She had thought Robbie understood, but she could see now he didn't, never had. He'd been on Theresa's side all along. He was nice to Lila, just to be close to the action, to be able to do what he was trying to do today: get Lila back under Theresa's talons. "She doesn't love me or anyone. She just wants a piece of the action. She just wants back into Hollywood. She misses an audience, not a daughter. Go back to the cunt and tell her I said she should die. And while you're at it, die with her, you traitor."

Lila walked calmly to the staircase to her bedroom, then turned. "Now get out, Robbie, and don't come near me again. I don't want to see you here again, ever. You're toxic, just like she is." Lila walked up the stairs, knowing, even before she reached the top, that she was alone in the house.

15

There may be one thing worse than having a TV show that bombs as big as Neil Morelli's did: having a hit. If Hollywood hates a loser—and trust me, it does—it hates and envies a winner even more.

Marty DiGennaro had been big and commercial before, but now he was big, commercial, and had to produce a constant string of toppers. Whereas he was used to producing one movie every two years, TV was forcing him to produce the equivalent of a movie every two weeks.

There were problems with the writers, problems with the locations, problems with the setups, problems with the sponsor, and problems with the suits from the Network.

Marty was used to dealing with problems, but he had never dealt with such a fast, massive buildup of interest in a project that he was still working on. Usually the media, the publicists, the critics, the money men started in on his work when it was done. Now they were all over him *while he still had a goddamn hour to film every goddamn week!* No wonder David had given up on *Twin Peaks.*

There was so much goddamn interest in the show, he knew he couldn't top it. And now he'd managed to script an end-of-season cliff-hanger that would have them screaming for more. But so what? Then he was going to have to follow it up with next season's opening show.

He'd hoped for a hit. He'd gotten it. He'd hoped to change the look of TV, to revolutionize it. He had. He wanted carte blanche, to write his own ticket. He had that. And the pressure was killing him.

Go know.

Worst of all was the situation with Lila. He, Marty DiGennaro, had leverage. He'd already had a string of Oscars, and now, after taking a risk, he's actually created a *succès d'estime* and an incredible money-spinner for TV, yet he had abso-fucking-lutely *no* leverage with Lila Kyle, the star he'd made, the woman he'd not only cast out of nowhere but given all the best lines, the best shots. Since their first and last date, nothing.

When she raised an objection, he folded. When she asked, he gave. Her picture on every goddamn magazine in the country, more film and public-appearance offers than she and a twin could handle, and she had Marty to thank for that. But she didn't.

She wouldn't sleep with him. No, it was worse than that! She wouldn't even date him!

It's not like there was anyone else. Sally had checked that out for him. Marty could at least understand if there were. Not *like* it, but understand. A date with Michael McLain. It ended early. Nothing else. Sally followed her everywhere for more than two weeks. *Nada*. Then, relieved at first, Marty thought, Maybe she's gay? But she didn't even have any girlfriends. Sally had told him that Lila had *no* friends, at least none who visited her at her house in Malibu. *Marty* had never even been in her goddamn house. Just that crazy old swish, Robbie What's-His-Name. He was the only one, came and went as if he lived there. But, then, there wasn't a starlet in the Valley who didn't have a pet queer.

Maybe Lila was just single-minded, put all her energy into her career, had none left over for anything or anyone. Marty tried to remember some of the other actresses he had worked with. *All* of them had one-track minds, for chrissakes, but he had slept with most of them, at least the ones he wanted. Actually, the ambitious ones were the easiest to lay. So why not Lila?

A religious nut? No way. Lila didn't have a spiritual bone in her body. Marty knew that much. What, then—celibacy? Fear of AIDS? Coldness? What the fuck *was* it? I'm not *that* ugly, he thought. I have money, I keep my body in fairly good condition, I'm sensitive, unselfish in bed—generous, even. Hey, I'm a fucking Boy Scout.

Once, long ago, Marty had been a nerd kid from Queens, a kid who couldn't get laid. But that was very long ago. And Marty didn't like, even now, to remember how it felt to be an awkward, lame outsider with fantasies that would never be fulfilled. Lila made him remember, though. Doesn't the bitch know I could still make or break her?

But, of course, Lila did. And it was almost like she didn't care. She even had told him that she was going all out for that April Irons *Birth* remake. And then she had the nerve to ask him to coach her. No other actress had ever treated him like this. They all had responded to his overtures; it was expected in the business. Actresses slept with directors, that was the Hollywood Law. Long ago, Marty had decided not to question actresses' motives, but to happily accept their attentions. And he got plenty of attention.

But not from Lila. And *that* only made Marty want her even more.

16

The pressure of a weekly TV taping schedule is beyond the imagination of the everyday TV viewer (what Sy Ortis would call "The Regulars"). The stars and crew spend a lot more time with each other than they do with their own families. Most of their waking hours are spent in each other's presence. And all the fear and competition, jealousy, insecurity, pettiness—all the ugliness of people under pressure—gets magnified and exaggerated.

The behavior on the set almost makes the U.S. Senate look mature.

Of course, feuds break out despite the work of publicists, and word often leaks to civilians about the bad behavior of the stars on the set. And there's plenty of it. The women act like children and the men act like babies. But in my experience, when there's fighting between women, it gets a lot more media attention. Catfights make better news. Hey, who said life was fair? My readers keep reading me, and that's what counts.

Sometimes, keeping the peace is easy: Just meet the star's demands. When there is only one big star, cave in or dump 'em to keep the peace. On Dallas, Larry Hagman had the biggest stick. On Dynasty, only Joan Collins played prima donna. And on Designing Women, Delta Burke was, in the end, expendable. But on Three for the Road, all the girls were necessary, and each, in her way, was difficult.

Never did bad blood run thicker, never did the competition get sharper, never were the stakes as high as on Three for the Road. Back in the days of Charlie's Angels, cast and crew alike were calling one of those stars Hate Jackson. But the nicknames on the 3/4 set were unprintable. And by the closing episode of the season, the bile flowed like wine. That was the scene a disintegrating Neil Morelli was so cheerfully walking into.

Neil stepped off the bus and walked the two blocks to the studio entrance. If he'd still had a car, the trip would have taken only twenty minutes. But by bus, transferring, stopping, and starting, it took almost an hour. The geriatric local. Where do all these old ladies come from? Neil wondered. Are they sent to California by the government when they reach a certain age? There ought to be a law. If it takes more than five minutes to climb onto a bus, you don't ride.

"Neil Morelli," he said to the guard, who looked him up and down before peering at his clipboard. "My car's been seized by DEA agents," he explained with a smile, while standing in the driveway next to the security booth.

The guard looked up and, now also smiling, said, "Oh,

yes, Mr. Morelli. You're expected. Lot Five. Take a left at the main building." He tipped his hat as Neil mimed starting a car engine, shifting gears, and, making motor noises with his mouth, driving away, turning an imaginary steering wheel.

This is more like it, he thought as he approached the lot. Back where I belong. Neil had been surprised—no, stunned—when Sy Ortis' office tracked him down and told him about this gig. He didn't speak to Sy himself, but maybe the guy *wasn't* a complete piece of shit. Maybe he was all right. I gotta call him later and let him know all is forgiven, Neil reminded himself. Some of those notes I sent him were pretty rough. But it just goes to show you, you gotta stay on these bastards' asses to get what you want. Perseverance pays off, especially when you don't have connections.

The large steel door was open, so Neil walked into the hangar-like building and looked around. The buzz of activity sent adrenaline shooting through his body, almost causing him to walk on tiptoe, he felt so high. "Where's the second-unit AD?" he asked a technician who was walking past, carrying a roll of cable. The guy motioned with his head and kept walking.

Neil approached the second-unit assistant director, who was wearing a sweatshirt and jeans, and holding a clipboard. She was in charge of shooting pickup shots, backgrounds, and some of the extras' scenes, but she reminded him of a camp counselor. All she needed was a whistle on a cord around her neck. She was standing in a semicircle of what appeared to be Hell's Angels, but were readily identifiable to Neil as actors in costume. Except for one guy who was more interested in his nails than what the AD was saying, everyone stared passively at the woman as she ran off a list of instructions.

When she dismissed the actors, Neil turned on his best smile. "Hi, I'm Neil Morelli."

"Yes," she said, as she continued to walk away, absorbed in whatever was written on her yellow pad. Probably the list of those who were to be shot at dawn.

"I'm in the show. There was some mix-up, and I haven't gotten a script. But I'm a quick study."

She stopped and looked at him, consulted her list, nodded, then made a checkmark on the pad. "I'm Ronnie Wagner, AD. Pick up your script at that table over there," she said, pointing with a gold Cross pen, "and read your part through; we'll start blocking in an hour." She started to walk away.

"What *is* my part?" he asked, hoping she would stand still long enough to answer.

She did, but impatiently. "I don't know. A waiter or something."

"Not a continuing character?" he asked, trying to keep the panic from sounding in his voice.

Ronnie looked at him and began to rattle off the specs of the job. "You're a bit, not a character. Four lines or under, used on an as-needed basis, no contract. Didn't whoever got you the job explain all this to you?"

He didn't like her tone, or her attitude. Whoever got me the job? He felt his anger boil up in him. "Hey, bitch," he said, "my *talent* gets me jobs. My *agent* arranges details. My *agent* is Sy Ortis. And I haven't gotten all the details from him yet. We'll be having a meeting after the shoot today. And I'll mention your name. So thanks," he said, and walked away.

He grabbed his script from the table, and began to look for his part. Whale shit. Once again he was playing a part as low as whale shit was on the bottom of the ocean. "FIRST WAITER" was yellow-highlighted. Jesus, who the fuck is *Second* Waiter? he asked himself. Whoever is is lower than whale shit, he answered. Not that that made him feel any better. The bitch was right, he thought as he finished looking over his lines. Under four. Well, at least that means no agent's commission. But if Sy doesn't even get a piece of this, why did he bother? What the fuck is going on? He looked over the part. The lines aren't even *funny*.

"How're you doing?" a voice said from behind him. "I'm Todd Shanley, Second Waiter." A big smile on his too-broad, too-tanned face. "I'm a friend of Ronnie's from school. Northwestern."

For Chrissakes, doesn't *anyone* in this town fill out an application for a job and take a test? No, he told himself, nobody does. Not even secretaries. "Nice to have pull," Neil said to the kid. "Who do you have to blow to get *five* lines?"

"Who do *you* blow?" Todd tossed back, still smiling.

Neil felt his scalp tingle, constricting under the mounting anger. "I been fucking Ronnie Wagner three, four times a week for a couple of years now. If I get real good at it, she said she's gonna get me an even *bigger* part *next* season." Neil pushed away from the wall, and began to walk toward the public phone, ignoring Todd's dropped jaw.

He dialed the now unfamiliar number of Sy's office. But the still-familiar secretary-from-hell spoke first. "Hey, Laura, let me speak to him. I want to thank him for getting me this job." Neil forced himself to smile. Amazingly, without a wait, he was put through. He spoke into the phone again. "Sy, hey, thanks for the gig, man. I really appreciate it. No, really, I know I've been a ball-buster . . . okay, a prick . . . but I just wanted to tell you, I really appreciate this chance." Neil paused. "Especially since you don't get a piece of it, since it's a four-and-under."

Neil waited for Sy to say something, but he didn't. "I'll make it up to you, Sy. Just wait. I promise. I'll turn this bit into a continuing character in three episodes, mark my words. But, Sy, tell me, is there anyone else I should thank? I mean, how did you get the spot for me? I don't want to appear ungrateful to anyone, you know, so how did it come about?" He paused, and listened while Sy both wheezed asthmatically and sucked on his medicine. What was he mumbling?

"Marty DiGennaro? Shit, if I had known *he* was in the audience, I would have been *good*. But that's great to hear. The director liked my bit at the club. Except, if I was so good, I mean . . ." He paused again. ". . . how come he didn't give me any funny lines?" Sy mumbled something else, warning him to take it slow, to behave. The usual bullshit.

"Sure, sure. You're right. I can be as patient as the next guy. And thanks again, Sy."

Ronnie, the AD with attitude, called everyone together

on the set, the interior of a hippie restaurant. Neil's heart started pounding as he saw the three stars of the show cross the floor from their dressing rooms to the set. He wasn't a fan type, but they really were spectacular. Neil hadn't been prepared for this reaction. He had made it a point *not* to watch the most-watched show in America, just because it was, and also because the dynasty-kid was on it, Lila Kyle. But when he got the gig, one of the guys he worked with had provided Neil with the tapes of every show since day one, and Neil had spent a brain-numbing twenty-four hours watching them on a borrowed VCR. He would have assumed that he had been desensitized to the three beauties, but instead he found himself gaping. He hated to admit it, but Lila was even more beautiful in person than on-screen. And the other two weren't chopped liver.

Marty DiGennaro joined them, and immediately got down to work. Neil hardly had time to be impressed by the guy, who was almost as short and skinny as he was. Neil started to relax. When there was a moment's silence, he even filled it with a little joke. The blocking was going well until Lila finally looked at his face. "Wait a minute," she said, stopping rehearsal. "Don't I know you?"

"I've never had the pleasure, Ms. Kyle. I'm Neil Morelli," he said, smiling, holding out his hand, then dropping it to his side. His face colored. Everyone on the set was looking. But, hey, she *was* gorgeous.

"That's what I thought. I heard about you. You're the guy that has a lot to say about families in the business. It's nice to see you're not too righteous to make money off them, though."

Neil noticed Sharleen Smith wince and avert her eyes and fold her arms across her chest, and Jahne Moore take a tentative step forward, then stop. "I work when I can, Ms. Kyle."

Sharleen came over and introduced herself. "Glad to have you on board, Neil. I heard you're very funny." Jahne Moore was right behind her. She patted him quickly on the shoulder, then moved away.

The tension on the set was real. And Neil became more

and more agitated the closer he got to doing his bit. In the first take, Lila stepped on his lines, then glared at him like *he* made the mistake. Then, for the second take, she jostled him with her elbow, and accused him of being off *his* mark. Neil wanted to strangle the bitch. He was so on edge, he was sure he was going to make a real mistake now. This witch was working on him.

They tried a third take, then a fourth—too many tries for a simple line. Neil started sweating, certain this was going to do him in. Sure enough, "I want a conference, Marty," she said, as she walked over to him. Neil heard Lila say, as he was meant to, "Get this guy off the set." But, this time, Marty shook his head, and walked away. Jesus, what do I do now? Neil knew that everyone's eyes would be on him, his every move scrutinized. And right there he made a vow to himself. Someday, he'd kill Lila Kyle. But in the meantime, he'd save face.

He tried to lighten the tension, and leaned over to Sharleen. "Was Lila ever a nun? She reminds me of my third-grade teacher."

"Oh, no," Sharleen said without the slightest glimmer of a smile. "She's been in show business all her life."

"It's not enough I have the *Birth of a Star* audition today, but now I have to put up with that asshole? Marty, I'm a nervous wreck. I can't work with him here. I'm too upset." She held her forehead in one hand, as if she had a bad headache.

"Fine. Let's finish the take so you can prepare yourself for your audition. Forget about the guy, Lila."

"I *can't* forget about him, for Christ's sake, Marty. He's the bastard who puts me down, compares me to Tori Spelling! He's upsetting everyone. Look at the expression on Jahne's face."

She saw Marty turn to Jahne, then back to her. "You're right, Lila. Okay? Now, go along with me on this one. Then I'll even help you with your script for the audition."

"Get him off the set," she said, making sure her voice was loud enough to carry. She wanted the worm to know, when he got canned, who was responsible.

Marty shook his head. "I can't, Lila. I owe someone. I have to keep him for one episode, at least." Then he turned from her and rejoined the cast.

Lila felt humiliated. Everyone had heard her demand the guy be kicked off. And now everyone knew Marty had said no to her. He didn't usually do that, but this time was more than she could tolerate. To take this guy's side over her! This little weasel, this ferret! Everyone knew what his comedy routine was. Lila had heard the crew snicker over some of the lines from Neil's act. She cursed Neil, and cursed Marty.

She pushed it from her mind. I've got other things I have to handle today, she thought. The big part, my chance of a lifetime. A part in *Birth of a Star*. Time enough to deal with the Neil Morellis of the world. After today, when she got the part. After today, when she would be more famous than her mother. Wait until April Irons sees me. Marty says I can be good. But *I* know I will be *great*. Then, *then* I'll step on the cockroaches. Lila flounced off to her trailer and jerked open the door.

It was comparatively dark inside, and she didn't bother to turn on the light. The darkness and the coolness were a relief after the hot lights. She began to tear off her sweaty blouse and underwire brassiere. The goddamn thing felt as if it was cutting holes in her rib cage. Then she unzipped the buckskin jeans that she wore and let them drop to the floor.

"Excuse me . . ." a heavily accented voice said out of the darkness. "I vas just leaving your new costume. . . ."

Lila clutched at herself, bending over and trying to hide her body. She scrabbled in the dim light for a towel, a robe, anything to cover herself with. What the fuck was anyone doing in her trailer?

Mai Von Trilling handed her a cotton cover-up from the hook next to her dressing table. Lila snatched it from her hand and struggled into it, tearing a sleeve as she viciously pushed her arm through the armhole. "What the fuck are you doing here?" she screamed. "Who gave you permission to spy on me?"

"I'm very sorry, I vas only . . ."

"You were only snooping. Did Jahne tell you to look through my things? Have you taken anything?" The skinny old bitch was backing out the door. Did she think that was it? Did she think she was going to get away with this? Did *everybody* think they could treat Lila Kyle like shit and get away with it? Lila followed her to the door and began calling for Marty.

"That's it! THAT'S IT! I want this bitch fired! I mean it, Marty."

The crew all turned to see the commotion. Jahne, Marty, and a few others ran toward the door. By now, Jahne could see that Lila was out of control. She was raving. "Goddamn it! How many times do I have to tell the old cunt that I want some fucking privacy?" Lila was screaming. "Tell the wrinkled bitch to keep her fucking nose out of my ass!"

Mai's face was pale, and Jahne could see tiny beads of sweat on her forehead and under her nose. "My God, and she eats vith that mouth!" Mai said, and, for a moment, Jahne had to smile.

17

Michael McLain had already given the photos of Sharleen to Sy. Next he sent over the video of Jahne Moore and himself. But either he had to bed Lila or fake a photo of it to save face and get top billing from Ricky Dunn.

Well, he figured, the other two proofs were legit; so what if he had to fabricate the third? Any tall, young hooker with a long red wig and a fuzzy focus ought to be enough. After all, how much could Sy expect? Close-ups?

But, somehow, this whole adventure left a bad taste in his mouth. It wasn't that he cared about that bitch Lila, or Sharleen. He had actually liked Jahne—she was smart and funny—but had sensed that she wasn't either smitten with him or overeager to please. And Michael liked his women to be both. Plus, there were those scars. Unsightly, almost ghoulish, but so secretive as to be almost erotic. And Michael didn't believe for a moment that they were from an accident. For one thing, they were too symmetrical. For another, what kind of accident causes incisions on the *inside* of thighs, or across the pelvic girdle, or under each buttock? Clearly, she had had plastic surgery, but how much could she have had? After all, a girl her age is too young for most of those operations.

He wrinkled his brow, then reminded himself to stop. After all, it wasn't worth a collagen treatment to him. Well, he could give up Jahne Moore. No problem. And, despite her bitchiness, he'd concentrate on Lila. Let word get back to Sy that they were an item. He smoothed his forehead and then dialed Lila's number.

She was weird. She certainly didn't seem to desire him. But she did seem, in some ways, eager to please. Michael knew her type: she wanted his help, his influence, but she didn't seem willing to come across with the standard *quid pro quo*. Michael was tempting her with two apples: a part in *Birth,* or in the Ricky Dunn thing. She seemed eager for either. And if he got her in on the Dunn thing, it would be one more person on his side. Then she'd have to come across.

Occasionally, just for a change of pace, Michael enjoyed fucking a woman who didn't want to fuck him. It added spice to a sex life that could otherwise be compared to shooting ducks in a barrel. Having a young and reluctant woman go down on him had a distinctive pleasure all its own. The last time he had done it—aside from the little dust-up with Sharleen Smith—had been when he promised a small part in a film to his friend Bob's fiancée in return for a blow job on the morning of her wedding. She didn't want to, but he knew how much she wanted the part. After she'd serviced him, he'd stood over her and asked if she'd liked it.

"No," she said, wiping her mouth, tears filling her eyes.

"Well. You weren't supposed to," he told her and, shrugging, zippered his fly.

So perhaps Lila would, in the end, reluctantly, coldly,

come across. And maybe Michael would really enjoy that most of all. He'd promise her a part in the Ricky Dunn movie and make it clear how the deal stood.

Jahne sat in the big, overstuffed chair in her suite at the Regent Beverly Wilshire Hotel. She was camped there temporarily until she found a new place to live and had it vetted by La Brecque. It was very luxurious camping. The phone that rang at her elbow was one of six in the two vast rooms: there was another on the desk, one on each of the two bedside tables, and extensions beside the bathtub shower and toilet. Jahne wondered who actually talked to friends or business associates as they washed their armpits or relieved themselves. The bathroom itself was splendid, and larger than her whole New York apartment had been. It was white marble, and in addition to two sinks, the loo, and the deep, almost pool-sized tub, there was a separate steam-and-shower stall with more jets than she could count, a makeup table that looked like something out of a Jean Harlow movie, and a dressing area complete with walk-in closets, three-way mirrors, and a white chaise longue.

"The nominations are in," Sy announced over the phone, a trace of triumph in his voice.

Jahne remembered that the Emmy nominations, formally known as the awards of the Academy of Television Arts and Sciences, were being announced this week. "So, how did we do?" she asked. Although by now she had little regard for Industry awards, the cast and crew of *Three for the Road* had worked so hard. It wasn't what she had hoped it would be, but the show deserved *something*.

"You mean you haven't heard yet? You got it."

"*I* got it? Well, I'll be damned." Jahne thought back to her days off-Broadway, to *Jack and Jill* and the Obie award she had received for her performance. Her friends at St. Malachy's had rejoiced, and she had, too. And Sam. Back then, everyone was forecasting a rosy future for her.

"But what about the show? What about the rest of the cast?" she asked again.

"Forget about the show for a minute, Jahne. Forget about the others. *You* have been nominated for an award —an *Emmy* Award. What, six months in television? Do you realize what that does for your career? With your talent *and* an Emmy nomination? Maybe even the award itself? Vaboom, kid. We'll be flooded with offers." Jahne winced. She had told Sy about the audition for *Birth*. And the offer. But not that she was determined to do it. He would only try to talk her out of it.

"Sy, I'm grateful for the recognition, I really am. But, you know, 'you're only as good as your last, et cetera.' " She laughed. "In a year or two, if I come begging you to get me a part somewhere—and I *might* be begging, you know that, too—I want you to remember this conversation. And when I say, 'After all, I've had an Emmy nomination,' I don't want you to tell me, 'Yeah, but what have you done lately?' Okay, Sy?"

Now it was Sy's turn to laugh. "You're very cynical for such a young woman."

"I prefer to think that I keep things in perspective."

"Well, I hope Sharleen keeps it in perspective. She's been nominated, too."

"Both of us? No kidding."

"No kidding. And Lila, too."

"All *three* of us have been nominated?" Typical. Just in case there weren't already enough stories about the competition between the three of them. Jesus! Hollywood! This would not lessen tensions on the set.

"Listen, Sy, did you go over the contract for *Birth of a Star?*"

"Listen, yourself: I have three better offers for you."

"Forget it, Sy. Do you have the contract?"

"Yes."

"Great. That's all I care about. Because I'm going to do the film. Don't say one more word about it. So, are you going to call Sharleen with the good news?"

"Yes." She could hear his silent fuming.

"Great. I'll call to congratulate her, too." But before she could, the phone shrilled again. She lifted it to her ear, and almost dropped it when she heard Sam Shields' voice.

"Congratulations."

"Good news travels fast!" She laughed.

"How are you going to celebrate?"

"I'm not sure."

"How about lunch with your director on Friday?"

"No," she teased. "I hate eating with Marty."

He laughed. "Your *film* director. Have you signed the contract?"

"I will by then," she promised.

"Great! Then we have two things to celebrate! Friday at the Getty Museum? One o'clock?"

Back in New York, Sam often made dates to meet in the museum cafeterias. Inexpensive and usually beautiful, although the food was rarely artful. The more things change, the more they remain the same, she thought. "One o'clock," she agreed, and held the phone to her ear long after he had hung up.

Sharleen hung up her phone and turned to Dean.

"What's the matter, Sharleen? You look like something's wrong."

Dean was watching *The Andy Griffith Show*, the episode where Aunt Bee enters her pickles in the contest. Sharleen knew he'd seen it a thousand times, that he knew that Andy and Opie hated her pickles and had replaced them with store-bought, and that, when Aunt Bee won the contest, they'd have to tell her. Dean knew all that, too, but he was watching as if for the first time. Sharleen sighed.

She sat in the armchair across from Dean and flicked her fingers in a motion for him to switch off the VCR. The room became suddenly quiet. "No, nothing's wrong, Dean. In fact, everything's right. I just got an acting nomination. An Emmy nomination."

"Uh-huh," he said, waiting for her to continue.

"I wish Momma could know about this," Sharleen said. "She'd be real pleased, I think."

Dean nodded, then whistled, and Cara, Crimson, and Clover came over and sat down. "Sharleen won a prize," he said, and made a clapping noise. The three dogs began to tap their front paws together, like applause. A new trick. Sharleen smiled. Dean always had a way to cheer her up.

"It's not a prize yet. But Sy says this could help me get my next job."

"Your *next* job? I thought you said we have so much money now that you'll never have to work again?"

Sharleen thought for a moment. "Not how Mr. Ortis explains it. There's taxes and fees and all kinds of stuff. Anyway, let's say I *did* want another job after this, Sy says the nomination would help."

"What's a nomination?"

Sharleen tried to sort it out for herself while she explained it to Dean. "All the people in the television business write in to say who they think is the best actress on TV. From those, some people are picked to be nominated for the award. 'Nominated' means 'considered.' Then they take another vote for only those people, and the one that wins that vote gets the award."

"So you got an award, Sharleen?" She could see Dean struggling to understand. How could he, when *she* didn't understand so well?

"No, I'm one of the people that got picked for the semifinals, like . . . you know, like in football."

"Does that mean that you got to go to playoffs?"

"No, honey. There's nothing more I can do to get the award. The committee is going to vote on past performance."

"Seems silly to judge people like they're judging Aunt Bee's pickles," Dean said. "People ain't pickles. But, hey, if there's nothing more you can do, why do you look so worried?"

And Sharleen agreed, and didn't know why.

"Who am I up against?" Lila snapped into the phone to Ara. When he didn't answer right away, she asked again, "Who, Ara? Tell me."

"Lila, that's not really important right now, is it? After all, *you've* been nominated for an Emmy," Ara said.

"It's only a nomination, Ara." What was it her mother used to say about nominations? They were like the last ten seconds in a game, the score tied. But only the final score mattered.

Ara didn't try to stifle the sigh that he now released. "Sharleen Smith and Jahne Moore."

"You've got to be fucking kidding me, Ara. Those two bimbos? Those nobodies? They're just supporting players. Dummies. Candy and Skinny. I'm competing with them?" Lila was screaming now.

"Don't be what we Armenians would call an 'ashek.' A jackass. There is no competition, Lila," Ara said gently. "You can see how it would be a very difficult decision for the Academy to pick one of you out of the three, considering the distribution of the three characters throughout the script."

"I can see no such fucking thing, Ara. I've busted my ass to be an actress. It hasn't been easy getting work, being the daughter of a star. I've had to work twice as hard as anyone else to get where I got. Those two bitches pop up out of nowhere and get made overnight. It just isn't fair, Ara. And what about *Birth of a Star*? Still no word?"

"I hear that it's deep in development hell, Lila. New trouble with the script. You gave a good audition. Now there is nothing more about the Emmys or *Birth* that you can do."

Lila slammed down the phone.

She bit the skin on her knuckle. There's got to be something I can do. *Something.* For the first time in her new house, Lila felt lonely. She had no one to tell about the nomination, no one to plot with, no one to praise her or admire her.

Lila let her gaze move beyond the glass doors of her house to the ocean beyond. What had she said the day she decided to buy this house? When she'd found it was Nadia Negron's house. It's going to bring me luck? Where's my luck now, Nadia?

Nadia had won one of the first Oscars for her performance in *Birth of a Star*. Lila had read up on her since she bought this house. But there was something about the award. The other nominees died? No, there was scandal.

Gigantic, humongous scandal. It destroyed the other nominees, and ensured Nadia her Oscar.

Now Lila remembered. Nadia Negron had been behind the scandal-mongering, it had been rumored for years. And Lila believed it. Nadia Negron had been powerful. She didn't just sit and wait. Maybe Nadia could help me. Maybe she would help me.

"I'm going to try to contact Nadia," she said aloud, as she walked upstairs.

18

Michael McLain literally dragged his feet down the hallway of the Château Martine, doing no good to the seventeen-hundred-dollar Tony Lama hand-painted snakeskin boots he was wearing, for this preliminary meeting with Sy, Lila Kyle, and that little prick Ricky Dunn. No other agent, no lawyers. A family get-together.

He was late, and he didn't give a fuck. After all, *he* was the one who had already paid his dues. When this little twenty-three-year-old dickhead manages to stay on top of the slippery pile called Hollywood for twenty years, then he'll deserve respect. Michael had decided to do the fuckin' movie—after all, he hadn't stayed on top this long by being stupid—but the kid would simply have to give him top billing. Like Newman and Cruise in *The Color of Money.* It was a sign of deference, of respect, and it had done good box office. So he'd do the movie, and Sy would get him top billing. And if playing the mentor instead of the hero made him look old, he'd fix that by having the character he played get the girl. Lila Kyle was wild for the part.

Sy had seen the video of Jahne and the faked Lila photo, and he had been forced to set this meeting up to go over the deal, to allow them all to meet face to face. But already Michael was annoyed. Why the fuck was it held here, instead of Sy's office, or the production company? The Martine gave him the willies. It was the West

Coast equivalent of New York's Hotel Chelsea: where the hip went to die of overdoses. It was expensive, exclusive, and seedy, and it made Michael very uncomfortable.

He had driven over himself, left the Testarossa with the valet, who looked as if he would immediately fence it off to some East Hollywood chop shop, and now Michael stood outside of Room 711. A lucky number. He straightened himself to his full height, sucked in his gut, and knocked.

Sy opened the door. Weird, but if Sy wanted to play hostess that was up to him.

"Michael!" Sy said, as if he were surprised and deeply pleased to see him. Michael didn't answer, just kept his gut in and entered.

The room was as shabby as the valet and hallway had been. Limp blue drapes hung a good four inches above the floor; the carpet was blue tweed, one of those speckled jobs erroneously touted not to show the dirt. It did, along with the cigarette burns on the side of the bureaus, the cheap glass ashtrays on the coffee table, and the sofa that looked as if it were covered in Herculon. Other than the sordid furnishings, the room was empty.

"Where the fuck is the little son-of-a-bitch? And where's Lila?"

"Michael, he called. There was a problem. Something about some looping that wasn't on target. He'll be here any minute."

"He's late? *He's* late for the meeting *he* set up?" Michael knew he himself was late by almost twenty minutes. That meant the little fuck was going to be half an hour late, or more. "Did he think I was sitting here with my dick in my hands, just praying for his arrival? Did you tell him *I* was late, too?"

Just then Lila Kyle walked out of the bathroom. Oh, great, now she was witness to his humiliation. Fuck! Michael grimaced. Ortis sighed. "Michael, please. This is no way to begin a picture. He'll be here any minute. Just . . ."

Lila smiled at him. "Don't you want to talk to *me?*" she asked.

"Not unless you're looking for top billing," Michael cooed.

"Top billing? I'd be happy to be in *anything* with you," she said. Christ, he didn't know when she was worse: when she was doing her fake worship act or exposing her real piranha personality. Well, he wasn't there to get her a part *or* make more points for Sy Ortis.

"Michael, this meeting is very important," Sy said. "Lila wants to meet Ricky, he wants to meet you, and all of us need to talk about a few things. We still have to straighten out the billing. . . ."

"Sy, this is starting to make a deal with Scott Rudin look good," Michael sneered.

"You know, maybe I should have brought Ara," Lila said.

"No. No. Not at all. He's an old man. A sick man. We'll wait until we have some of this ironed out."

Michael snorted. Yeah, like when Sy has ironed out a contract to represent Lila. Jesus. Anyway, what needed to be straightened out?

"Straighten it out? I thought you straightened it out already?"

"Well, partly. But there are some issues, valid issues, and this meeting . . ."

"Just shove this meeting up your ass!" Michael cried, and had begun to walk to the door when it swung open. A tall, cadaverous man, the palest, thinnest guy Michael had ever seen, walked into the room. He was dressed all in black. If Morticia Addams has an anorectic younger brother, this was the guy. Behind him was the little prick, Ricky Dunn, who, Michael noticed immediately, was not so little. The kid was taller than Michael by a good two inches.

Dunn was dressed in a pair of torn and filthy jeans, some kind of T-shirt that looked like camouflage or something, and an oiled canvas duster that must have been out of Wardrobe, used for some stupid Australian-outback movie. The Mickey Rourke look, but clean. He also had on a pair of wraparound sunglasses with mirrored lenses. He didn't take them off, though the room was dim.

"I'm Shay Wright," the cadaver said, holding out his

hand to Sy, who obviously already knew him but shook it. Michael didn't make a move, and Shay dropped his skeletal arm. "And this," he added, "is Ricky Dunn."

Shay nodded to Ortis and Lila, but Ricky acknowledged none of them. The two of them moved to the sofa and sat down so close together that they looked as if they were joined at the hip. Sy moved an armchair out for Michael and, unwillingly, Michael sat down. Lila smiled at Ricky. Michael noticed that she both licked her lips *and* tossed her head before crossing her long legs in front of them all. Christ, why didn't she just spread-eagle?

"We're sorry we're late," Shay said.

"No problem," Lila purred.

"I just got here myself," Michael told them. Fuckers.

"Fine, fine," Sy said. "So, Ricky, everything just about wrapped on *Zoom?*"

Ricky turned to Shay, bent even closer, and whispered something into his ear. "Mr. Dunn says he's very pleased with the rough cut."

Michael couldn't believe his eyes—or his ears, for that matter. Before he could say anything, Sy continued. "Did you enjoy working with Carpenter? I hear he's a hell of a director."

Again, Ricky leaned over and murmured something inaudible into Shay's ear. Shay nodded. "With all due respect, Mr. Dunn says that Bill Carpenter is a fucking bag of shit who couldn't direct traffic with a stoplight to help him."

Sy blinked. Michael definitely saw him blink, but he recovered without a whimper. What a reptile! "Have they picked a release date?"

This time, Shay answered without any tutelage. "Christmas Day."

Sy nodded. "So, we just love the script for *Scraper;* don't we, Michael?"

Michael hunched over to Sy and whispered, "What the fuck is going on?" Lila, still smiling, was following all this with eyes that looked as old as those of the Sphinx.

Sy only shrugged. "We did have a few questions about Buck, the character Michael will play."

"*Might* play," Michael corrected. He was sick of this

charade. Why not get to the point? "But, more important than that, we need to talk about the billing."

"That might be premature," Sy said, and cleared his throat. What the fuck was *that* supposed to mean? Michael flipped Sy a look.

"I'd expect top billing," Michael said.

Ricky remained expressionless, as did Shay, but Ricky, once again, began his inaudible murmuring. When he was done, it was Shay's turn to clear his throat. "Meaning no offense, Mr. Dunn says he would rather fuck Michael Jackson up the ass than take second billing to Mr. McLain. Understand that I'm only speaking for Mr. Dunn when I say that. . . ."

Michael scrambled to his feet, knocking over the coffee table. "Hold it! Hold it. If Mr. Dunn wants to say something, he can fucking well say it for himself. If I hear one more word out of you, you fucking bloodless cadaver, I'll break you into pieces. . . ."

"No need for that kind of talk," Sy began. "We're reasonable people and . . ."

Without a word from Ricky Dunn, Shay bent forward. "With all due respect, Mr. Dunn says he'll let you have top billing when you grow tits and fly away."

"That's it!" Michael McLain yelled. "I'm fuckin' out-of-here." He kicked the table out of his way and walked to the door.

"And fuck you, too," Shay said sweetly.

Lila ran down out the door of the Martine after Michael. "I guess this means no part for me," she said, almost breathless when she caught up with him. "Look, I never thought Ricky Dunn was worth shit. But you and me in *Birth of a Star* . . ."

Michael handed his claim check to the valet and only then turned to look at her.

"Forget about it," he said.

She stood, silent for a moment. Then she tossed her long red hair. Like that would help her. Michael snorted.

"Look," she said, "I thought we had an understanding. We had a deal."

The Testarossa pulled up, and Michael nearly dragged

the valet out of it in his hurry to get in. Only then did he look up at Lila, looming over the low-slung car. "Hey, babe, it was only a verbal. It's not like I balled you," he said, and, putting his foot on the gas, he peeled out.

Sy Ortis raised his head and stared at Jahne. "Are you crazy?" he asked, his voice low. "Are you?" he repeated.

He had already tried every rational reason he could think of to dissuade her. Faxed her half a dozen times, both on the set and at the hotel. Harangued her on the phone. Called her into his office for this special meeting. But she wouldn't listen, wouldn't cooperate. First Michael blows the meeting with Ricky. Then, in desperation, he wants to do this retread piece of shit for—of all people—April Irons, and now, *now,* this one, this one he made himself, waltzes in, cool as a frozen daiquiri, and tells him—*tells* him, mind you, not asks—that *she's* going to costar in *Birth.* Without a preliminary goddamned word to him. He gets the contracts from April, and the whole thing is a *fait accompli.* Only he looks like an asshole. Well, he'd eat Michael's shit and Ricky's, too, if he had to, but he wasn't going to eat Jahne's and April's for dessert.

He reached for his empty inhaler and fondled it as if it were some magic amulet that would make Jahne Moore disappear. "So, are you crazy, or what?" There was only one thing to do. He'd have to scare her. Then, maybe, she'd behave.

She stared back at him, insolently. She *was* an insolent bitch. Had been from the very beginning. "I don't think so," she said.

Sy laughed. "No, I guess you don't. I guess you think you're smart, or talented, or some other grandiose, self-inflated horseshit. The next Sarah Bernhardt. Better watch out you don't become the next *Sandra* Bernhard." Sy was so angry, so outraged, that he even slipped, his accent showing. "Well, let me esplain something to you. You aren't here because you're talented, or smart, or hardworking, or any of that crap. That doesn't esplain why you're here. What you are is *lucky.* Right now you might be one of the three luckiest bitches on the face of the planet. And you're too fucking stupid to realize it.''

"I guess that means that you don't think *Birth of a Star* is a good idea," she said coolly.

"Very good. Nice use of sarcasm. Maybe you're not so stupid." Sy felt his chest tightening. Hold on there, he told himself. You're losing control. You got to scare them, but not scare them *away*. Still, this was outrageous. Sy Ortis, the ultimate deal-maker, cut out of the negotiations, not even consulted. Left out of the deal. By not one but *two* of his clients. April must be laughing like a hyena in a fun house. Which just about described both her *and* International Studios. The thought of April Irons was like a band tightening around his chest. When would his secretary get back with his inhaler? Jesus, these bitches!

"Sy, it's a good deal. They've offered me points. Five points is very good."

"Five points of the *net*. There's never any *net!* Those are monkey points. Even *Batman* never made a *net* profit. You want gross points, and on this deal you want *nada*. You want out."

"Why?"

"It will stay in development hell forever. There still isn't a shooting script. And you have only ten weeks' hiatus. This will take twice as long to film, if it ever gets made. Plus, it's just not right for you."

He tried to calm himself. "Listen, Jahne," he said with a wheeze. "I'm talking to you the way I would to my own daughter. You can't have your cake and eat it, too. And the show is the biggest thing on TV. It's the biggest thing that's *ever* been on TV. It may save a fucking network. You're at the very best place you could possibly be. So why risk *Birth?* There isn't even a decent script!" he repeated. "How could you commit to something without even seeing a finished script? Has everyone gone crazy? What if it's *muy malo*—big-time bad? Why give up a gold mine for a bird in the bushes?"

The bitch smiled. Good, he'd won her over. But, *Madre de Jesus,* these women would kill him!

"I don't see it that way."

He couldn't believe it. "What?" he asked, his voice reduced to a rasp. When she had called him and told him she wanted to talk, he hadn't been prepared for this. Who would be? But she sprung the idea of doing the April Irons film on her hiatus from *Three for the Road*—and then added she'd need four *extra* weeks off from *3/4*. Like the show could wait. Like Marty wouldn't mind. Like the network wouldn't go loco. Like it was nothing. She was sitting on top of the world, and now, behind his back, she wants to go film some stinking remake with a pup director instead of keeping her sure thing.

"The reality is, Sy, I get the time off or I quit."

"What?" he whispered.

"Listen, the way I see it, it's all got to be downhill from here. What the show has going for it is novelty. That will wear off next season. And the imitations will start. If I leave now, it will be big news. Leave at the peak. Anyway, this show was *not* what I want to do. It was only a stepping-stone. And the Huey, Dewey, and Louey dialogue is really getting me down. I want to do some serious work."

"Since when is a potboiler like *Birth of a Star* considered serious? It's not *Hedda Gabler,* for chrissakes."

"It's better than the crap I'm doing now. And it's a *film*. I hate TV. Wasn't it Galbraith who said nobody could compete with us in producing morally depraved TV programs? I want out of the Flanders Cosmetics deal, and I don't want to do the show at all."

It was unbelievable. Women all over the country would give their left tit to be in those ads, and she wanted out? And out of the *show?*

"Wait a minute. Now you're not talking about an extension of the hiatus, you're actually talking about leaving the show altogether?"

"Well, why not? I only signed the one-year contract."

"Why not? Why not? *Sangra de Cristos!* Because they'll replace your ass so fast that no one will remember your name one year from now. You'll become an answer in trivia games."

"Maybe. But I could use a lot less fame than I've got

now. And if you don't agree, perhaps I ought to leave the agency.''

Sy got up from his desk, walked over to the window, and looked out on the glare and dust of the L.A. freeway. Holy jumping Jesus. It wasn't the Assholes or the Regulars. It was the Talent that would kill him in the end. He began to truly fight for breath. How many times would one of them crucify him, castrate him? Crystal Plenum insisted on doing that *Jack and Jill* bullshit that ruined her career. She was becoming the Zsa Zsa of her generation. Michael makes an ass out of himself and Sy in front of Ricky and Lila Kyle. And now this! Marty would kill him if he lost Jahne. Jahne would leave the agency if she couldn't do April Irons' movie. And April would bust his chops over Jahne's stupid contract.

He was one of the most powerful men in the goddamn Industry, and these empty-headed, loco *putas* tried to tell him that they were smarter. They were always smarter. Until they became yesterday's news. He turned to Jahne.

"Now, you listen to me. You want to become the Art Garfunkel of the television industry? Never quit a winner. This town eats up pretty girls faster than reporters chew up free lunches. You get your shot, you're hot, you can make any deal for any money; then along comes someone younger, a different type, and you're history. You can't get a fuckin' guest shot on *L.A. Law*. You'll be happy to make an appearance on *Hollywood Squares*. And you won't even get called on by the contestants.''

"Oh, come on. The first film I do is important, but it *is* just one film. I mean, it doesn't make or break a career. Who was ever ruined by one bad choice?''

"The list is long and distinguished. Suzanne Somers. Sexpot. Beautiful. Quit TV. Couldn't get a supermarket opening for a decade. Shelley Long. Walked off *Cheers*. Name one of her films. Or Farrah Fawcett. Hottest girl of her decade. One season, leaves TV. *No one* pays to see one of her movies, *ever,* except maybe Ryan O'Neal. Movies are riskier. People pay cash to see movies. Not like a TV series, where people get it free and want to see you every week. Even for a features actress, it's risky. One bad movie, two the most, and . . . Look at Michelle

Pfeiffer. Ellen Barkin. Or Melanie Griffith, Kathleen Turner. Holly Hunter. They each got to be the hot girl. For a year. Where are they now?''

"They work, Sy. They all work."

He looked at her, disgust plainly written on his simian face. "You don't get it, do you? You just don't get it. Right now you got *heat*. They want you. *Everybody* wants you. You can go anywhere. You can meet anyone. It doesn't last long, not without good management and luck. And once it's gone, baby, it's gone."

"I'm not your baby," Jahne said coldly.

Sy stopped. He looked at her directly. And in that moment of silence, Jahne knew how much he disliked, even hated her. She shivered.

Is it because I'm a client or because I'm a woman that he condescends so? she wondered. Would it be any better with another agent? "Sy, I know this won't really mean much to you, but I'm not doing what I don't want to do. The show is crap. Stylish, sometimes even funny, but it's crap. I want some work that's important. Work that I can respect. That *others* will respect."

Sy let out a small noise, a kind of sigh, as if this was childish and he'd heard it all before. Well, he probably has, Jahne acknowledged. His job is to turn people into deals and money machines; mine is to control that. Sy licked his lips, picked up what was left of his asthma spray, and began talking very slowly. "Listen to me. Things are different now: The networks are desperate. Television is still lucrative, but more competitive; they have to have hits or they'll go the way of the old studio system. With a hit show, even a small hit, a network can schedule something before and after you, they can spin you off. They can build a lineup. They can attract new viewers. And hold them. And they can attract sponsors. A show like yours is a godsend to Les Merchant. They'll put *everything* into getting you the Emmy. You'll probably win. You can propose a television movie. They'll back it. You'll *have* respect. They'll respect the *shit* out of you."

"Thanks, Sy. But shit is not what I want."

"Look, just tell me what is so respectable about a tired

old melodrama, a *puta* that's going to be directed by a newcomer and produced by a shark. Why, why would you want to do this to yourself?"

Jahne paused. She had known, clearly, before she walked in, what she wanted to do, but now she was uncertain, even a little scared. Could he be right? Could she wind up another out-of-work actress? "All right," she said at last. "All right. I'm doing the film, but I won't quit the show. I'll do one more season. And I'll make a deal with you: you arrange to get me enough shooting time with Marty. If *Birth of a Star* flops, then I'll stay. But if it's a hit, I quit the show."

19

Sharleen was stretched out on the couch in her *3/4* dressing room, trying to rest before her next camera call. Sy Ortis was on the chair next to her, handing her documents to sign as they talked.

"Listen, it's the end of the season, and with the Emmy nomination you're hot. I got a great job for your hiatus. A movie deal," Sy said, as he reached over and took a bunch of signed papers from her. "It's light. Fun. It's called *Buffy the Cowgirl*."

"*Another* job? Mr. Ortis, I'm tired. I don't *want* another job." She wasn't sure she could finish this one, even though there were only two more episodes to go before the season ended. Thank the Lord. "What happened to what you told me when I took *this* job—that this one would make me so rich, I'd never have to work again?"

Sy laughed. "Well, it might take a little longer, what with taxes and agent's fees and lawyers and all. And, to tell the truth, I never figured you'd get so famous, Sharleen. You gotta strike while the iron is hot. You're in demand, and this movie would be great for your career."

"I don't want no *career*, Mr. Ortis. I just have a *job*. And I think what you told me back then was right. With what I've made on this show, I'll never have to work again."

"Only if you don't want to live like a queen," Sy added quickly. "This picture deal could do that for you, you know. Make you richer than your wildest dreams."

"I'm *already* richer than my wildest dreams." She finished signing the last paper and, with a sigh, thrust the stack of them toward Sy. "No more today, Mr. Ortis. I'm tired. I'm *really* tired."

Sy stood up. "That's okay, Sharleen. It'll cost me money, and you might regret it later, but you do what you think is best. I'll send your lawyer over tomorrow with the rest of this stuff. You just take it easy for a while before they call you."

Sharleen closed her eyes and let her hand touch Sy's arm as he moved away. "Thanks, Mr. Ortis. You've been good to me."

The door clicked closed behind him, leaving her alone with the hum of the air conditioning in the darkness. She didn't want to think about how disappointed Mr. Ortis was that she wasn't going to work during her vacation. And she knew he was. But there was no way she *could* work. Sharleen had been working six days a week, twelve hours a day for months. Always nervous, always messing up. It was a little easier now that Jahne was helping her run lines, but still a strain. And I used to say *waitressing* was hard, she thought, as she slipped into a light sleep.

The hands felt real, but Sharleen knew she was dreaming. All those hands, pulling, grabbing, palms up. But this hand . . .

"Miss Smith, you're wanted on the set in twenty minutes."

Sharleen opened her eyes and saw Ronnie Wagner, the new second-unit AD, shaking her gently. "Boy, I must have been dreaming."

"Is there anything I can get for you? Cappuccino?" Ronnie asked. Sharleen liked Ronnie. Ronnie made a point of having fresh cappuccino available on the set when she heard Sharleen liked it.

"Yes, that would be nice." Sharleen sat up and put her

feet on the floor, then pushed herself off the couch with a low groan.

"You okay, Miss Smith?"

"Oh, yeah. I'm fine. Just a little tired."

Ronnie was about to say something else, then hesitated.

"What is it?"

"Well, the president of one of your fan clubs is out there to see you. And this one's a beaut. Ordinarily, I'd suggest you meet with her, but since you're so tired, maybe . . ."

Sharleen shook her head. From the beginning, she had decided that this went with the territory. She could never get used to the concept of fan clubs—as Dean said, "It ain't like you're Lucy Ball"—but she was overpowered by the sheer numbers in the groups that came from time to time. Mostly teenagers and young women, they all treated Sharleen both like a goddess and like they had known her all their lives. But to Sharleen they were still strangers. Strangers she tried to be sweet to. "Oh, no, Ronnie. I'll talk to her on my way out to the shoot. Maybe I could ask her to stay and watch. Would that be okay?"

"Sure, whatever you want, Miss Smith."

Ronnie let the man from Makeup in as she was leaving. While he retouched her face, Sharleen thought about the fan-club president again. She felt even less like seeing this one after Ronnie's comment. She hoped she was at least young, like most of the others. The older women frightened her. They all seemed so poor, so desperate. Somehow they reminded her of the desperation of Lamson. Sharleen could understand a young girl getting all excited at television people. She knew that for most of them it was a phase they'd outgrow. Jahne had explained all this to Sharleen. But the older ones, the ones in the pants suits and the high-piled hair, they upset Sharleen. The crew made jokes about these women. "Get a life," they would mutter under their breaths. But Sharleen knew how impossible it was for most of them ever to have anything of their own. She remembered herself back in Lamson, and shuddered. For most of her fans, this was all the life they were ever going to have, and that made Sharleen sad. She thought of Proverbs 6:25— "Lust not after her beauty in thine heart." But the poor women did.

Sharleen never had to be called to the set a second time; she knew what was expected of her. She let the door to her dressing trailer clink shut as she scanned the set for her visitor. She caught the eye of Ronnie, who pointed toward the waiting woman. Then she noticed Ronnie raise her eyes to heaven. Sharleen nodded a thanks as she followed Ronnie's gaze.

Oh, Lord, she thought. The woman was not only one of the older ones, but also loudly, though shabbily, dressed. She waved to Sharleen as Sharleen walked across the floor, and seemed to be standing on tiptoe in anticipation. Looking at her more closely, Sharleen could see that the woman was very different from the others. Down and out. Drawing nearer, Sharleen was surprised to see that the woman also looked worse than loud. She looked, well, cheap. She had dyed yellow hair which fell in tight greasy curls to her shoulders. She wore a pink sleeveless blouse, too tight across her sagging chest. One of the buttons had popped open. Her too-small yellow skirt had a tear along one seam, and her large belly strained against the fabric. She had no eyebrows, just half-circles of dark pencil lines in their place. A smear of red rouge on her cheeks was exaggerated by the thick gash of red-orange lipstick. Tangee for sure. Sharleen stopped in front of the woman, who was gripping a tattered Mexican straw bag in both hands in front of her, her eyes wide in anticipation, a hint of panic suddenly sweeping across her face.

Sharleen blinked once or twice and stared. The woman took a step forward. "Hello, baby," the woman called out. After a moment, Sharleen answered.

"Hello, Momma," she said.

Sharleen sat with the Bible opened on her lap, reading the psalms of praise. Who would have dreamed two years ago that she would be on TV, that Dean and she would get a wonderful home, and that they would find their momma? God was good!

She had begged her momma to come home with her, but Flora Lee had refused. "In these rags? Why, girl, I know how I look. Like hell in a nightie. Before I see my boy, I want to look right." So instead, they had agreed that Momma would freshen up in the trailer for now, and just the two of them would go out for dinner.

Sharleen had ached to call Dean with the great news, but perhaps this was best. Sharleen would have a chance to get reacquainted with Flora Lee, then tell her about Dean being . . . well, the way he was. Lovable and all, but maybe not so smart. But should she tell Flora Lee about what had happened back in Lamson? What if Momma felt it was their duty to go to the police? Sharleen never talked about it to anyone, and had cautioned Dean over and over not to. But would he talk to Momma about it?

Sharleen sighed, some of the happiness draining out. It was taking Momma a long time. She looked down again at the Bible. She was sure that God would forgive Dean. She thought about Flora Lee. Surely she was kind, and generous, and understanding. She saw the next line below her fingers: "The ungodly are not so but are like the chaff which the wind driveth away." What did that mean? she wondered.

When Momma came unsteadily out of the trailer, they drove to the Sheraton. It was a big hotel but not too fancy. Sharleen wore a baggy old dress she had borrowed from Mai, and a big hat, along with sunglasses. She had her hair tucked up, covered with a scarf. She hoped no one would recognize her.

"Where should we go to sit down?"

"Here's as good as anywhere, honey," Momma said, ready to dump herself down in the lobby.

"Well, maybe not here." Sharleen looked around. "Let's go somewhere quieter."

"Why, how about the bar?"

"The bar?" Sharleen never went to bars. Did her momma?

"It's dark and quiet," Flora Lee reminded her.

So they went to the bar. And Sharleen began with all the questions she wanted to ask. "What happened to you right after you left, Momma?"

"I got as far as El Paso. Thought I might settle there. Heal up a bit. Nice town, El Paso. Got a job at a truck stop. Got a place. But then I met a trucker. Should have known better, but after your daddy, well, any man looked good. He left me in Salem, Oregon. Stranded without a penny." Flora Lee emptied the nut dish out and called out to the waitress. "Honey, could we get some almonds and some service over here?" she called.

The waitress came to them and forced a smile. "What will you be having?" she asked.

"Ginger ale," Sharleen said.

"A beer, please. A Bud." Flora Lee turned to Sharleen. "Those nuts can make you powerfully thirsty."

Sharleen smiled at her mother, and now she felt her own smile was forced. Did Momma drink? She never used to. Well, she'd be entitled to a beer at the end of a day like this one. "What did you do then?" Sharleen asked.

"Oh, I spent a long time getting out of Oregon. Wanted to go to hairdressin' school, and the Department of Welfare was going to pay for it. But then I met a feller who worked for Chrysler—he traveled through the whole Northwest training their service mechanics. Took me down as far as Sacramento. We set up house there. Right nice, too. Till I found out he had a wife and four kids up in Olympia, Washington."

"Oh, Momma!" Sharleen said, and pulled the hat farther down on her head. The waitress brought over the soda pop and the beer. Flora Lee drank hers down in two or three gulps while Sharleen toyed with her own glass. Somehow, her happy feeling from earlier in the day was disappearing just like the bubbles that were leaving the glass.

Don't you be judging your momma, she told herself harshly. She wasn't even kin, and she raised you. And who are you to judge? You remember what you done with Boyd, and what that led to. And how Mr. McLain got you drunk. Momma was beaten and alone, without her children, and she must have been powerfully lonely.

Flora Lee rambled on, about more men and more towns. She beckoned again to the waitress. "You want to freshen that up?" she asked Sharleen. Sharleen shook her head.

"Well, I'll have another beer." Flora Lee paused. "Make that a beer and a ball," she said. The waitress nodded. Sharleen wondered what that was, but it wasn't until the waitress returned and put the beer and shot glass side by side that she opened her eyes wide. If Flora Lee noticed, she pretended not to. She picked up the shot glass and threw the whiskey back down her throat.

Well, Sharleen told herself, if she takes a drink, it don't mean she's evil. Tears filled her eyes. Poor Momma, all alone and turning to whiskey.

Flora Lee told a lot more of her story, but after another beer and whiskey, it, or Sharleen, or Flora Lee, or maybe all three became real confused.

"So you see," Flora Lee finally said, "so you see why, if I just had a little money for beauty school, and could set me up a shop, I know I could make a real killing. Why, Mrs. Ramirez, the woman who lives down my hallway, she asked me to do her hair just the other day. I didn't charge her or nothin'. I don't have my license, and I wouldn't want to get reported to the state, but that's just an example." She looked at Sharleen, expectant. Sharleen nodded, helpful. Then Flora Lee turned her head. "Where's that waitress got to?" she asked.

20

After weeks of Lila's calling Ara to nag him about the *Birth of a Star* audition, he had at last suggested to her that she come in, and she knew—she just knew—that her time had come. All the candles and other offerings to Nadia had paid off. Lila knew she was born to play this part.

Lila dressed carefully for her meeting with Ara. You never knew who you might run into at his office. She slipped her legs into tall, electric-blue pantyhose. Naked now, except for the smooth blue legs, she looked into the full-length mirror that covered the wall of her dressing room. She had legs that just wouldn't quit. At five foot twelve, as she had told the reporters coyly, at least half of her height was legs. She smiled at her reflection and undid the towel that turbaned her hair. Still damp, it fell in a flaming cascade, the red more vivid against the blue of her stockings. Her white skin accentuated the strawberry of her tiny nipples. She looked at her breasts appraisingly. Her breasts were perfect, but not really large. Big, really big breasts were the style. But there were far too many complications to having surgery now that she was famous. She'd surely find herself on the cover of all the tabloids if she tried to. She put a hand over each breast and pinched her nipples to redden them. Yes, she looked like a perfect female, she thought. This would have to do. She sighed and turned away.

Surveying the room full of clothes, she picked out a simple white silk T-shirt and a butter-soft bright-yellow leather miniskirt. She surveyed row upon row of shoes, each pair nestled into a specially built compartment that housed them. Smiling, she chose the electric-blue spike heels made of dyed snakeskin. They added three and a half inches to her height and cantilevered her forward in such a way that her tits jutted out and her calves were emphasized. She slipped them on. They were a bitch to walk in, but so was the skirt. Well, she wasn't running any marathon, so let's give the men what they want, she thought, and smiled. If I don't know, who does? she told herself.

She went into the bathroom to comb out her still-damp hair. Never brush it wet, Theresa had taught her, because brushing breaks wet hair. Carefully, Lila pulled the comb through, stopped for a moment or two under the amber heat lamps that dried the last bit of moisture without damaging the long strands. She tossed her head and approved. This was definitely a good hair day. Finally, she snapped open her jewelry case. She took out the lapislazuli cross that Aunt Robbie had given her, and fastened it around her neck. Just a touch of Madonna trash. She looked up at the picture of Nadia and smiled.

"You're going to be a big star," Ara smiled. He was seated at his desk as Lila was escorted into his office. "You are already a big name. But you'll be more. A star."

Lila grunted a laugh. "You'll excuse me, but I already know *that*, Ara. I hope that's not news to you. I thought you said you have good *news*. Now, tell me."

"Lila, where is your sense of values? You come in here, sit down, and start with the questions, always the questions. Why can't you be a little sociable? Have a cup of coffee with me, a glass of wine, talk a little?"

"Ara, this is show business. Like something could be more important than that? Your health? The weather? Give me a break, Ara. Now, do you have good news for me or not?" Lila couldn't stand waiting another minute. Ara was totally lame.

"I do have good news. I've gotten you *the* lead in *the* movie of the year."

She knew it! She knew it! Oh thank you, Nadia! She smiled at Ara. "That *is* good news. Now, isn't that more important than the weather? The lead, right, Ara?" Lila could hardly contain her delight.

"The lead. And the movie is going to be the biggest hit. *Princess of Thyme*."

Lila suddenly sat up very straight in her chair, but it seemed the whole room had tilted. "*Princess of Thyme*? I thought you were talking about *Birth of a Star*?"

"Lila, how many times in the last months have I told you, forget about that remake. It wouldn't have been right for you. Just as well you didn't get it. Now you can do *Princess of Thyme*. It'll make you bigger than big."

"I didn't get it?" For a moment she didn't recognize her own voice: it sounded like a very young child's. "I didn't get it?" she asked again.

"No, Lila," Ara said gently. "But I promise you this is a better movie. A more important one."

"Who got the part, Ara?" Lila asked, her voice very low.

"Don't do this to yourself, Lila. You're not the girl for the part, believe me."

"Ara, I was *never* a girl. Don't call me that again. Now, who got the part?"

"If it matters, I think it went to Jahne Moore. And let her have it. You're meant for greater things."

"Jahne Moore! Jahne Moore!" Lila could hardly believe it. "You useless old bastard!" Lila whispered, the rage rising in her and almost strangling her with its intensity. "Robbie was right. You're over the hill. You've lost it. I should have signed with Ortis. I could have that part now; instead, that insufferable, condescending bitch walks off with it!"

"There is the lead in *Princess of Thyme*, Lila. The title role. It will be bigger than *Star Wars*. And Lucas wants you. It's all lined up."

"A cartoon? With spaceships and Ewoks and crap! Are you nuts? I wanted to do the remake of *Birth of a Star*. I wanted *that* part." How long had he been keeping this news from her? How long? She'd like to pull his old, bald, drooling face apart, pull off his stupid mustache, kick his leathery football head into pieces. He wasn't taking care of her. He was killing her, suffocating her, using her. The prick. The goddamn cocksucking prick. It was him and her mother. Lila caught her breath.

"*When* did Jahne get the part, Ara?" She already knew, suddenly and clearly. She watched carefully, noticed Ara's mouth twitch. He paused, looking at her for a long time. Lila didn't drop her eyes, just sat there waiting.

"I'm not sure," he finally mumbled.

"Guess!" Lila demanded.

"Look, Lila, I got you the audition. And it didn't work out. What difference does it make when they made their decision? Decisions are made and unmade. I was hoping that, once they saw you, they might rethink . . ."

"They'd already picked Jahne when I auditioned! She already had it, didn't she? It was bullshit about script troubles. I see her on the set, she knows, everyone knows except me! This was just a plot to humiliate me. You did it just to shut me up, placate me like I was a little girl. Theresa made you do this, didn't she? You and Theresa worked this out. What do you think I am, a dummy?''

"No, Lila. Not at all . . ."

"Balls! She was jealous. She couldn't let me have the part that she once had. She couldn't stand to see me in the spotlight. So she gave the part to Candy. Candy gets the part, and I get nothing.''

"Not Candy, Lila. Jahne Moore.''

For a moment Lila stopped. "That's what I said. Jahne Moore.'' But that wasn't what she'd said. She'd said "Candy,'' hadn't she? Jesus Christ, she was losing it, and she was losing it here, in front of Ara Sagarian. Christ, now both of us are senile!

He was picking up a handkerchief to wipe his wet mouth. She turned away, suddenly nauseous. He was disgusting, a nasty, slimy, drooling, leather lizard of a man.

"Lila, I can see you're very upset, but you have to understand that was not the only part for you. It's not even the best one. The director is untried, and I think the thing is too big for him. Remakes are always dicey, at best, and remakes of classics are even more risky. *Old Acquaintance*. Bette Davis and Miriam Hopkins. Remade into that dreck with Jackie Bisset and Candice Bergen. Into the toilet. Then *Robin Hood*. Look what happened even to Costner when he tried to replace Errol Flynn.''

"Yeah. He made fifty million dollars.'' She began to tremble, and couldn't stop. Nadia has been wrong. Jesus! She turned back to look at Ara. The spittle-face. She was born to have her triumph over Theresa, her freedom from Ara, from Robbie, from all of them. But Ara and her mother had conspired. *That* she was sure of. And maybe with Robbie's help. He'd do anything Theresa wanted, even befriend Lila in the pretense of helping her, but all the while plotting with the Puppet Mistress against her. They had lost her the part.

556

"What did my mother tell you about me?" she asked. "What did you tell April about me?"

"Nothing, Lila. Please, you must . . ."

"What did she tell you?" Lila asked again, her voice rising.

"Lila, it had nothing to do with Theresa or me. It was your audition. They hated it. It was your audition, not anything I did. . . ."

Lila was across the desk in a moment, her hands around his throat. Her long legs scrabbled for purchase on the shiny desk surface, her skirt rucked up, her feet pushed off papers and mementos. Lila began to squeeze, her big hands reaching deep into the folds of Ara's leathery turkey wattles. "What did she tell you about me?" she screamed, as she cut off the air in Ara's windpipe. "What did she tell you?"

Ara spent the rest of the morning trying to recover. After his secretary and two agents had pulled Lila off him, after the security men had escorted her off the premises, after Ara had taken a few pills and managed to coax a glass of sweet tea down his bruised throat, he had asked not to be disturbed. He lay down on the big blue sofa in his office and found he was trembling. God, the woman was *bagos*. Worse than a Turk! He lifted one hand to his throat and shook his head. She was strong as an ox, too, and dangerous. He shook his head again. *Ench bede nem?* he asked himself. What to do?

Ara was no longer young, and just now he felt every one of his eighty-four years. Maybe his doctor was right. Maybe it was time to retire, to move down to his place in Palm Springs. He was too old, too tired to deal with the craziness anymore. He had, perhaps, another decade left. He could sit in the sun, a survivor of the Armenian holocaust, a survivor of Hollywood, and enjoy life. Play a few rounds of golf. See Frank, and Johnny, and all his cronies.

Just the thought of giving it all up, of stepping out of the action, made him almost dizzy with dismay. For over fifty years, he had lived to make deals. He had survived while the studios died. He had managed not to dwindle but to gain power. Lately, he had lost a few clients, perhaps, to the sharks like Ortis, but he was still respected, still a *player*, and he still reveled in the action.

But this scene with Lila Kyle had been too much. He had made a mistake with the girl. She was crazy. Worse than Crawford had been. And he'd betrayed Theresa, an old client, for this one. Worse yet, once he signed Lila, he hadn't been able to manage her. He shouldn't have gotten her the fake audition for *Birth*. He shouldn't have tried to soothe her into forgetting about it. She, like so many of their new stars, was empty of everything but ego and ambition. And now, without the studios, without any real control, chaos reigned.

He thought of Louis B. Mayer's reaction when he'd heard that Chaplin and Pickford had formed their own movie company—"The lunatics have taken over the asylum," he'd said. And United Artists *had* been a madhouse. Artists needed businessmen to help them, and businessmen needed artists to create a product. Ara had spent more than five decades trying to make that marriage work, but things were worse than ever.

Well, it was time. The party was over. In a way, he should thank the child for showing him the light. He would retire. He would enjoy life. He would rest. Not without regret, but with relief.

The telephone buzzed. He lifted it. Who would Helen put through now? he wondered. "Ara, I'm sorry to bother you. But it seems very important. It's Michael McLain. He's very upset. He says he must see you as soon as you can. About a possible change in his representation."

Ara blinked, and wiped his mouth. Michael had been his star, his protégé, his success story. But Michael had left him nine years ago, at the height of his success, to go to Sy Ortis. Lately, Ara had heard rumors that all was not well between them. Could it be that the prodigal son was returning to the fold? Signing Michael McLain! Stealing him back from Sy Ortis! That would show everyone that Ara Sagarian was still a player. Ara sighed. *Ashek*—jackass—he told himself. You would be better off in Palm Springs. Can't you give this up? It will kill you, he told himself.

He stared for a moment, unseeing. *Ench bede nem?*

Then he smiled into the phone. "Tell him to come around," he told his secretary. "It would be a pleasure to see him."

21

"I'm as tired as a duck in a hailstorm," Sharleen complained as they walked off the set together.

Jahne laughed. "Me, too." She shrugged off the makeup man and picked up her jacket, putting it on herself.

"Jahne, kin I talk to you for a minute?" Sharleen asked. It was the end of the day's shooting, and Jahne was bone tired. Well, Sharleen looked even more tired than she was. This wasn't like Sharleen. Something was obviously bothering her.

"Sure. Let's go to my trailer." They walked to it and sat in the cramped "lounge area."

"Is some of all this startin' to git you down?" Sharleen asked, waving her hand around them.

"You mean the show?"

Sharleen nodded. "The show, the crowds, fans, bein' like a prisoner in my own home. All of it."

Jahne knew what Sharleen meant. "Sure. A few weeks ago, before I moved into the hotel, I was sitting at my pool when I heard a voice over a loudspeaker. A tour bus, for God's sake. With a tour guide showing them where I live. I had to run inside, I became so paranoid. I didn't know if those ladies with blue hair were going to come over the hedge or not." Jahne looked at Sharleen. "Is that the kind of stuff you mean?"

Sharleen paused. "Kinda. People you don't know wanting to know you. Relatives you ain't seen in years showing up. Friends askin' for favors. And about not being able to have any friends. I mean, I have you and all, and Mr. Ortis. He's good to me. But the crew all act all different, like I became queen of England overnight. I did like you said with Barry, and it worked. But I'm not comfortable. I mean, they worked all their lives in television. Don't they know this is all make-believe? Lordy, if *they* don't know, sometimes I'm afraid I'll get to believin' maybe I *am* queen of England or somethin'."

Jahne laughed at Sharleen's observation. She was right. If the people in the Industry took it all so seriously, then why was everyone surprised that the public did? But Jahne wasn't upset. She had lunch Friday with Sam. She had something to look forward to.

" 'Member the impersonations Phil Straub used to do? He was so funny. He used to do Marty DiGennaro perfect—better than Marty hisself." Sharleen laughed at the memory. "Now Phil calls me 'Miss Smith.' All the fun's gone." She shrugged her shoulders. "Well, anyhow, I got you, and Dean. And the dogs. So, it can't be all that bad. 'Cept we can't go to malls and stuff. 'Member what happened to you?"

Jahne shuddered at the memory. Sharleen seemed really sad. Was something else bothering her? "But maybe, Sharleen, we could go shopping together. We both have security staff now. But no malls," Jahne laughed.

"Right. 'Cept we'd both have to take them FBI men with us," Sharleen reminded her. She sighed. "I got all the trouble of bein' a star but none of the fun." She thought about her momma showing up, and how it didn't seem as good as she had dreamed. How could she tell Jahne about that? She couldn't, she realized.

For a moment, Jahne was filled with sympathy for the girl. "Why don't we just have fun like stars tomorrow?" Jahne asked. "With bodyguards, in an expensive restaurant, after we shop in expensive stores? Like good little stars should."

They sat down in the back, though Jahne would have preferred one of the charming window tables that looked onto Melrose. But by now, after the briefings that Gerald La Brecque had put her through, she knew that was only asking for trouble. So the two of them parked their shopping loot on the banquettes and took seats that discreetly faced away from the rest of the restaurant.

Jahne was tired, and hungry, and thirsty. She'd have a beer, despite the calories. "I'll have a Beck's," she told the waiter, a gorgeous blond Adonis. His eyes registered recognition, but then he pulled down the shade of discretion necessary to be cool in L.A.

"Yes, ma'am," he drawled, and turned to Sharleen. "And for you, Miss Smith?" he asked.

"I'll have what she has," Sharleen told him. She was thrilled with their shopping, and glowed with excitement. "Oh, Jahne, I don't believe I ever saw such things. How did you find these places? Wasn't that pink outfit cute? And the leather shop! I loved that purple fringed-leather bikini. And Planet Alice. Wasn't that stuff wild? I never saw elephant bell bottoms before."

Jahne, who remembered the seventies disco scene, and had almost been old enough to be part of it, smiled. "Yeah, it's all updated L.A. versions of Carnaby Street, as if Carnaby Street the first time wasn't enough. Well, they didn't have Lycra then. It makes all the difference."

"But you didn't buy hardly anything." Jahne had seen lots of things, but she felt most comfortable when Mai dressed her. In fact, she had an appointment with Mai this afternoon for a fitting.

"Well, mostly I like Donna Karan. Anyway, there's nothing I need."

"Jahne Moore, when did shoppin' have to do with what you *need*? Even when I was dirt poor, I knew *that*. We just used to look over the Sears catalogue and dream on what we *wanted*."

"Well, I don't want much. And I feel like all this clothing and makeup is so confusing. It seems like I never have the right things. You need the right dress shoes, the right casual shoes, the right sports shoes. And they have to be the right color for the dress or the skirt or the slacks or the shorts or the gown. And then you need the right sweater or wrap or jacket. And the belt and the purse, and that's not mentioning jewelry or makeup. Don't wear salmon lipstick with pink earrings. I don't know what I'd do without Mai. She's a pro. God, it gets me confused."

"You, too?" Sharleen sounded shocked. "But you always look so great."

"Do I?" Jahne asked, surprised. She knew she owed it to Mai. "I just keep it real simple," she told Sharleen.

"Well, Lila isn't simple. She does it every day, and she does it perfectly. How do you think *she* does it?"

"Maybe it's in her genes."

"But she don't hardly wear jeans."

"No. I mean genetics. Maybe she gets it from her mother. After all, her mom was a movie star, so maybe Theresa O'Donnell taught her some tricks."

"Did your mom teach you any?"

Jahne winced. "No. She died in a car accident when I was very young."

"Oh, I'm so sorry. My mom left home when I was nine, but I'm so happy for those years and all she taught me." For a moment, Sharleen paused, and Jahne thought again that Sharleen was upset about something. Well, it must be hard to have a mother run out on you, Jahne thought. Maybe worse than having a mother die.

"My mom taught me a little poem. 'I desire to leave Elmira!' " Jahne smiled at the vague memory.

"What's Elmira?"

"A really dreary town in upstate New York. I grew up there with my grandmother."

"Well, I guess you listened to your momma, though." Sharleen turned and surveyed the glitzy restaurant, which was decorated as an Italian spa, complete with *trompe l'oeil* pool on the ceiling and crumbling pillars along one wall. The gaily striped chairs and awnings indoors sparkled, as did all the cerulean-blue china and glassware on the marble table. "This," Sharleen said, "sure ain't Elmira." They both laughed.

When the waiter returned with their drinks, they both ordered salads. After he nodded conspiratorially and left, Sharleen turned to Jahne.

"Kin I ask you a question?"

"You surely can," Jahne said, and Sharleen giggled.

"Do you worry about how you look? I mean, Lila is so beautiful and all, but seems as like she worries a heap about it."

562

Jahne almost laughed out loud.

"Sure, I worry."

"You do, too?"

Jahne took a deep breath. "Wait a minute? You mean *you* worry, Sharleen? But you're gorgeous. I mean, I can understand worrying about what you wear, or makeup, or something, but you're perfect—your skin, your hair, your eyes. Everything. Sharleen, you're absolutely gorgeous."

The color rose in Sharleen's perfect face. "Oh, no. I ain't—I mean I'm not—nowhere as pretty as you or Lila. I mean, the two of you is about as beautiful as movie stars. I just look nice."

Jahne stared. Then a wave of a kind of sick horror hit her. Here they were, by luck, by genetics, and by surgery, maybe the three loveliest and most desirable women in the country, perhaps the world, and two of the three, at least, didn't even believe in their own beauty. For her, of course, there was the contrived nature of her looks. But Sharleen was clearly a natural beauty and had always been, yet she, too, felt imperfect. And, in a moment of almost frightening clarity, Jahne bet that Lila, perhaps the most beautiful of all, was the most insecure. Out of nowhere, tears flooded her eyes.

"What is it?" Sharleen asked, her voice full of concern.

Jahne made a noise, nearly a groan. "Oh, it's just so very sad. If *you* don't think *you're* pretty, and if *I* don't think *I'm* pretty, how do those poor women in America watching us feel?"

"Pretty bad, I guess. If they care."

"Oh, Sharleen, every woman cares. They make us care."

"Jahne, do you feel bad about them makeup ads? All them tricks and mirrors and lights?"

Jahne nodded. She thought of poor Mary Jane Moran. "It doesn't do what it promises, does it? It doesn't make any of us beautiful, unless we already are."

They were silent for a while. Jahne looked over at her companion. She realized how much she really liked her.

She'd miss her over the hiatus. "How is the album coming?" she asked kindly.

"Well, everyone thinks I kin sing 'ceptin' me. I guess it's okay. At least it's almost done, and then I'm takin' a long rest. Me an' Dean is going to get us a truck and go up to Yellowstone, or maybe Montana. Take the dogs, and the FBI, too, I guess. What about you?"

"I'm thinking of doing that movie."

"Workin' on your vacation?" Sharleen could hardly believe it. "Mr. Ortis wanted me to do a movie, but I said, 'Heck no!' Ain't you dog tired?"

"Yes, but I really want to do this movie."

"Boy, with a movie and a TV show, then you'll *really* be famous."

Jahne laughed. "I don't think we could get more famous than this. But if the movie works, maybe I won't come back to *Three for the Road.*"

Sharleen's face dropped. "Not really! Oh, Jahne, you wouldn't just leave me alone with Lila? She'd eat me up."

"Oh, come on. You've got to get tougher than that. Just tell her to fuck off."

Sharleen blushed and giggled. "Oh, I could *never* do that."

"Sure you could. Try it now. Practice on me."

"But it's not religious."

"Sharleen, where in the Bible does it say, 'Thou shalt not use the word "fuck" '?"

Sharleen giggled again. "I don't know. Nowheres, I guess. It's just that nice girls didn't . . ."

"Sharleen, nice girls were all *doing* it but not *saying* it. So just stop being a girl altogether. Practice now. You're a woman. Tell Lila to fuck off."

Sharleen looked at Jahne, thought for a moment, then nodded. "Okay, I'll try, but I don't know if I can."

"Try it."

Sharleen pursed her lovely, soft pink lips. She took a deep breath through her perfect nose. "Okay." She paused. "Eff you."

"Oh, come on! That was pathetic. Tell the nasty piece of work to fuck off."

564

"All right," she paused. "Lila, you just . . ." Her voice was sweet as ever.

"Come *on*. Be angry. She's so awful to you. And to me. And the crew. And she makes Marty be mean, too. Come *on*, Sharleen. Don't be such a little wimp!"

"Oh, fuck off!" Sharleen burst out.

The people at the next table turned to look at them. Sharleen's face grew rosy, and she covered her cheeks with her hands.

"Bravo!" Jahne told her. "You've broken the 'eff' barrier. Now you can live in Hollywood."

After lunch with Sharleen, Jahne dismissed La Brecque's guard and drove over to Mai's apartment on Cahuenga to discuss an outfit for tomorrow. It was easy to slip in—there was no gated security, just a pleasant but shabby U-shaped two-story stucco apartment building with dark-green shutters. She knocked at Mai's door.

Mai was wearing all white—as she almost always did. White, or the same silver-gray as her hair. Today she had on a sweatshirt made of some kind of stretch terrycloth, with a strip of it wrapping up her head in an impromptu turban. Her face lit as she greeted Jahne.

"So, you are vell? You look so."

"Yes," Jahne said, and realized she was. It seemed that, perhaps, at last, the loneliness was lifting. She'd enjoyed her lunch with Sharleen, and she had a feeling that she'd enjoy this time with Mai. She was making friends. And she had her lunch with Sam to look forward to.

"Sit down," Mai said, indicating a chair. Jahne, who'd been here before, wondered at the apartment. It was only three big rooms, but all three were immaculate, and painted white from floor to ceiling. All the furniture—not that there was much—was slipcovered in white cotton. There was a lot of sunlight filtered through the green-black shutters, and, other than one large fern in a white tub, no decor at all: nothing hung on the walls, no knick-knacks on the table. But somehow, with the sunshine and shadow, with the cleanliness and the whiteness, the rooms seemed filled, not empty.

"This place is so . . . original, Mai. Like you."

Mai shrugged, and took two glasses out of a cabinet. "Ven you are young, you are original. Ven old, you are only veird. But this suits me. I love color and paintings and *objects*. But now I look at them in museums. It is a relief to have so little to care for." She poured half a beer into one glass and was about to fill the second.

"None for me," Jahne reminded her. "I have to lose weight, not gain it."

Mai sighed and brought out a bottle of spring water. "For tvelve years, I ate the same dinner every night: a small steak and a salad vith no dressing. Think of all those meals I missed! If you vant diet help, call Nikki Haskell. She is Liz Taylor's guru." She looked up at Jahne. "So, is it vorth it, being famous?"

Jahne sat on the sofa and put down the glass of water. "Not if this is all there is," she told Mai.

"Vat more do you vant? You are famous und vill be very rich, und you are young and healthy."

"I never wanted fame, and the money wasn't the main thing. I wanted, I still want, to make films—to be in good films and do good work in them. To build up a body of work, something I can be proud of."

Mai shrugged. "You may be too famous for that now," she said.

"What do you mean?" Jahne asked. She felt a moment of panic, a flutter against her rib cage.

"A famous and beautiful voman becomes a . . . a special kind of force. You cannot do normal things. You do not have normal friends. You are a target of many. You are loved by strangers, but you sometimes have no friends. And often, just as you adjust to being a goddess, you are finished, or they are finished with you. Think of how many are chosen and burn bright, but only burn out: so many new girls, so many girls of the moment, so many. But think of how few *vimmen* have lasting careers. Can you name five, even? Five who have built up a body of vork?"

"Yes. Of course. Susan Sarandon."

Mai nodded. "Who else?"

"Meryl Streep."

"Of course. But vat has she done lately? Und who else?"

"There *are* women who have done it."

"Yes. But, as hard as it is to become famous, it is a hundred times harder to stay so. To stay 'hot.' Use this time vell, Jahne. It may not last for long."

22

Jahne had asked Mai for help in dressing for her lunch date with Sam. "I want to be casual, but also look really good." She giggled. She'd finally signed the contract for *Birth* and, despite Sy Ortis, she felt as if she were five years old and on her way to a birthday party. "You understand, Mai. Understated devastation."

"Of course." Mai had smiled. "Like you just threw on your clothes and took no trouble, when you have really vorked on yourself for hours. That is the trick. The study of naturalness. But, my dear, haven't you already gotten this part?"

"Yes, but . . ."

"But maybe there is another part you are auditioning for? Is that it?"

Jahne just laughed. "What do you think? Slacks or a skirt? Slacks look more casual, but I can show more leg with a skirt."

"Vere are you lunching?"

"Over at the Getty Museum."

Mai made a face. "Vell, he is maybe cultured, but has bad taste in food." She regarded Jahne for a moment. "I think maybe a low-cut tank top vith a matching long jacket. Quvilted silk for the jacket. Lined. Blue lining. Black jacket, and the blouse in the blue of the linink."

"Really? But I'd feel too dressed up in a jacket."

"Not if you vore it vith jeans," Mai told her. "Perfect, no?"

"Perfect, yes. But could you get it done in time?"

"Ven is this lunch?"

"Tomorrow," Jahne admitted guiltily.

Mai had laughed. "Who am I to hold up progress? But I'll have to leave right now to shop for fabric."

"Yes, of course."

Sometimes Jahne wondered if Mai tried so hard to please her because she had saved Mai's job when Lila had gone ballistic and tried to fire her. Or because Mai needed the extra income. Or because Jahne had secured her a job on the *Birth of a Star* project. Or because Jahne was the star. Would Mai pretend to like me if she didn't really? Jahne wondered. But Mai never seemed to show any special fondness for Sharleen, or, of course, for Lila. Yet they could be helpful to her career.

I have to believe she really does like me, and if it means another movie job for her, or some money on the side, or someone to stand up for her when Lila goes nuts or Bob is abusive, so what? Isn't that what friends are for? Jahne asked herself. I have to be sure not to ask for too much, and not to take her for granted or underpay her.

Still, it made Jahne a little uncomfortable to think that the woman she was closest to was paid to be with her. She pushed the thought from her mind. Instead, she tried to imagine the quilted silk jacket. She'd be gorgeous in it. Sam, always sensitive to such things, would be impressed.

Everything in Los Angeles was different from New York. Even the museums, Jahne thought with a laugh.

The Getty was located just off the Pacific Coast Highway. And, believe it or not, you had to call ahead to make a reservation. Not to see the collection, but to park your car! So-o-o L.A.! She laughed to herself.

Of course, she hadn't known that until the parking-garage attendant asked her for her reservation number. She thought he was joking. But then he explained how the museum had been built by J. Paul Getty in a residential neighborhood, and the neighbors in Brentwood, Pacific Palisades, Los Flores, and Topanga had enough muscle to ensure that no one would park on *their* streets.

Luckily, the guard recognized her and made an exception. "We always keep a few spots for celebrities, Miss

Moore," he told her confidentially. She hated to take advantage, but she was so pumped up for her lunch with Sam that she simply thanked the guard and parked.

A narrow staircase led up to a wide garden carved out of the cliff face. And there, in a perfect Hollywood style, was a *faux* Pompeian villa, complete with not only Doric but Ionic *and* Corinthian columns. Typical Hollywood: If one was good, why not have all three? Authenticity be damned. Blazing bright wall murals, complete with more columns, this time *trompe l'oeil,* lined the porches of the two colonnades which enclosed the Peristyle Garden, the center of which sported a gigantic turquoise pool. Jahne put on her sunglasses to avoid squinting at the bright reflection. She wandered down the South Porch, gliding over the inlaid-marble floor. The Tea House was in the West Garden, and before she went to it she stopped in the ladies' to check herself out and calm herself down.

She was alone there. She smiled at her reflection. Mai's jacket fit like a supple skin, and the blouse showed just the right amount of cleavage. She took out the pink Flanders Cosmetics lipstick that she wore and carefully reapplied it. She had spent fifty minutes on her eye makeup: carefully lining her lids with a subtle blue-black and then building layer upon layer of matching mascara. She wore matching contact lenses and only a smudge of eye shadow, buried in the crease at the outer edges of her eyes. But it did the job. When she took off her sunglasses, her eyes looked enormous. She knew she was beautiful, and, smiling at herself, she felt confident. If Sam came on to her at lunch, she could handle it. And she was certain that he would be mesmerized.

He rose as he saw her crossing the formal garden. The Tea House itself was casual. She took the chair opposite his, pleased that it was in the shade.

"Quite a venue," she said.

"Do you know much about art?" he asked.

"Oh, I know my Jan van Huysums from my Jan Vermeers," she said airily.

"Speaking of van Huysums, they have *two* here."

"I'll look forward to seeing them." She smiled sweetly.

They ordered iced teas and salads. Sam congratulated her again on the Emmy nomination, and they talked desultorily. She had a chance to really look at him.

He hadn't changed much. If anything, he was a little thinner. His dark hair was pulled back, but the pony tail had been trimmed to a discreet George Washington. He was tanned, though, and his brown hand, lying beside hers on the table, looked beautiful, lean and long and sensitive as ever.

He caught her eye and looked down to the table, too. But he noticed her hand, and picked it up in his own.

"You're so cold!" he exclaimed.

"So many men have said that," Jahne intoned, "but I thought with you, with you it would be different."

He stared at her for a moment, recognizing the dialogue from *Jack and Jill,* and then she laughed, and then he did, too. His teeth, always good, white and strong, looked better than ever against his tan. The sinews in his throat moved as he swallowed the last of his laughter.

"I was blown away by your screen test," he said. "It was . . . novel. But more. It was intelligent. And heartfelt." She felt herself start to blush. She murmured her thanks. "I must have watched it a hundred times. And it was uncanny. You reminded me of someone. I'm not sure. It was so evocative."

She had to change the subject. "I look forward to playing Judy. So, how's the script coming?" she asked. She wondered again, for a moment, if Sy could be right. He might be a chauvinist pig, but he did know the business.

Sam stopped smiling, then recovered himself. "Well, it's coming. It's a great theme: Does a woman love a man for his success or for who he is? And can a man love himself if he fails?"

"Funny, but I always thought the movie was about envy—Judy loved James and never envied his success. But when *she* succeeds, he envies hers so much that he ceases to love her, if he ever really did."

"Interesting view," he said, and he looked at her, this time with a deeper, more quizzical look. "Are you an envious person?" he asked.

"No. Not really." She was surprised by the question,

and by her answer, but she was aware it was the truth. She wondered why. "Maybe it was because I had such low expectations. I never imagined myself a candidate for other people's success."

"Really?" he asked. "I'm the opposite. If I read about *any* director's triumph, my first thought is why *I* didn't do that or get that or present that."

"It must make life very uncomfortable for you." Jahne took a sip of her iced tea, watching him over the rim of her glass. This was going well, very well. She was succeeding in being both seductive and distant—a deadly combination. She smiled. What if he fell in love with her? What if he did, and she could spurn him? She almost giggled.

"You are so incredibly beautiful," he said. "That's the smile that played so well in your screen test."

Jahne blinked. Was he being personal or professional?

"I was nervous," she told him.

"Didn't show," he said. "April and I were both fascinated. She said . . ."

Jahne felt her smile slip. There it was again. Was it her imagination, that he and April had more than a working relationship? He went on talking while she wondered. Why had he invited her out? Was it a professional courtesy, a business lunch, or was it more? She tried to focus on what he was saying.

"They're talking about this as this year's *Pretty Woman*."

"Well, I hope not. I mean, that was a film about a prostitute who got lucky. I hope there will be more content than that."

Sam looked uncomfortable. "You do take yourself seriously."

"So who are you going to cast opposite me?" she asked him.

"We were thinking of Michael Douglas, but he's not quite old enough."

"But he's such a great actor! I'd love to work with him!"

"What do you think of Newman?"

"*Paul Newman?*" She could hardly believe it.

"April thinks he's maybe too old, but she thinks she can get him interested."

"Oh, God, that would be wonderful!"

"You think you could play a convincing love scene with him?"

She laughed. "Just try me."

"I'd like to!" he said, and smiled. Jahne felt the heat. He *was* interested in her. "I tell you the one reservation I have," he confided. "I don't see Judy as a beautiful woman. I felt maybe you couldn't be convincing as a plain girl."

She began to laugh. And, for a frightening moment, it seemed as if she might not be able to stop. "I'll research it," she said at last.

"Great. Glad I entertained you." Then he looked down at his watch, which, she noticed, was a gold Rolex. "This has all been great," he told her, "but I've got a script to write. Can I walk you to your car?"

She declined. She needed a few moments alone. "No, I'd like to take a look at the collection."

"Oh, yeah. The van Huysums." He grinned at her. "Maybe you want to drop by my office this evening. Run a few lines." He looked at her.

"No." She smiled. "I think there's been enough lines thrown out already."

He laughed, leaned over to her, and gave her hand a squeeze. "Forgive me," he said. "I can't help myself." Then he picked up her hand, kissed the palm, and strode away.

It took her a moment to control her voice. "Good luck with the script," she called.

After he'd left her, she sat for a few moments alone. The lunch had been interesting, to say the least. But was Sam simply being a professional flirt? Could she keep her cool if only this much attention from him excited her so?

She freshened her lipstick, then wandered over to the galleries. She picked up a brochure and found there were indeed two van Huysums. "What the hell," she murmured to herself, and went in search of them.

They were magnificent: one a floral still life and the other a bounty of fruit. Both were in the jewel colors of a thousand Persian carpets. She knew it had taken years for the artist to paint each one, applying layer after layer of transparent pigment, building the depth of color and shading before her. Years and years to create beauty almost everlasting. And for close to four hundred years, art lovers had admired the flowers and fruit at their ripest moment of perfection. She stared at the visual feast, but her mind was on other things.

After the hard years in New York, after the surgery, after the fiasco with Pete and the nasty affair with Michael McLain, after taking this job more than anything to get to work with Sam, it seemed that Sam and April were still a "we." And that Sam was as flirtatious as ever. But he probably had no interest in her, except as a co-worker. Well, she told herself, it's just as well.

Her life was no longer empty and gray, she reminded herself. It was a colorful abundance, like the van Huysum paintings. But, like them, it was unrealistic, chaotic, and perhaps even wasteful. All that fruit, about to rot, all those out-of-season cut flowers, about to wilt. Wasn't she like that? A perfect bloom that would go unsavored until she wilted?

Hooray for Hollywood, she murmured again, and walked down to the garage to get her car.

23

Nothing was easy, Sharleen told herself. She had to get up, out from their warm bed, while it was still dark, so she forced herself up and began to gather her clothes to creep into the bathroom to get ready. She was so tired, it was hard not to resent Dean, lying there asleep, looking so angelic and so at peace.

Well, I'm not at peace, and that's for danged sure, Sharleen told herself, and patted Clover, who raised her head off the bed, but then snorted and turned over. All the dogs slept on the bed. So did the cat, and Dean. It was only she, Sharleen, who couldn't sleep. She had too many worries—worries that started up just as she closed her eyes for sleep and then continued all night.

She was still afraid, still dreaming about her daddy's death, and about the police comin' to look for her and Dean. She was worried about rememberin' her lines, about not makin' a fool of herself or gettin' fired. She was worried about the stupid record album, lookin' like a fool when it came out. She was worried most, maybe, about her momma. She hadn't yet told Dean a word about her. The funny thing was, she'd prayed and prayed to get to be with her stepmomma again, to help share the good luck and part of the burden of Dean, to be reunited, protected, comforted.

Well, be careful what you pray for, or you just might git it, she told herself again, and looked grimly into the mirror. She looked awful. The sleepless nights sure were showing in her face, and she already knew that the camera was merciless. Talking to Jahne would have been a comfort, and she was tempted to tell her everything, but she was too ashamed. Sharleen almost cried, but that would make her face worse. Instead, she filled the sink with icy water and, taking a deep breath, submerged her face in it.

It was terrible. Like dying by drowning in a freezing lake. But it would bring down the swelling under her eyes, reduce the puffiness, restore a little natural color to her paleness. She counted—fast—to fifty, then came up for air.

It wasn't good enough, so she got two trays of ice, threw the cubes into the sink, and swished it around with her hand. Lord, it was cold! But, though she hated to do it, another look at her face forced her to. Lord, she looked old—maybe thirty!

Her face pushed again into the ice water, she tried to distract herself from the thought of Flora Lee. Why did she have to be a drunk? Because she was one, and Sharleen knew it. If there was a single thing her daddy had learned her, it was all about drunks. Flora Lee had left them with her daddy, and she didn't get no job to help them or try to find them. She just got herself drunk.

It hurt Sharleen right in her heart. And not only for

herself but for Dean. Dean was Flora Lee's baby, and sweet as sugar. How could she just up and leave him and never try to help him at all? And though he wasn't so smart, Sharleen knew that Dean would wonder, too.

She pulled her face up out of the ice water. Then she remembered. For Lord's sake, today she wasn't shooting! Today was one of the few days she had off, but it was also the day she had to do that business for Dobe! Her face burned and tingled. All that ice water wasted!

With all the worries Sharleen had about her momma, the police, and the show, she had nearly forgotten about Dobe's date for the Customs auction. It wasn't easy to get time off when you were a TV star. Lucky it had come out this way. Sharleen told Dean not to tell anyone who called where she was going, just that she was going out.

She dressed quickly now. Her car and driver were right on time; it was only a green Plymouth sedan, not a limousine, and she'd ordered it not from the studio but from the car service that drove her cleaning ladies home. She looked at herself in the hall mirror before going out the kitchen door. Everything was right, she thought. The long black wig under the floral-print kerchief tied under her chin, the oversized Jackie O. sunglasses, the plain, tattered trench coat she had borrowed from Mai in Wardrobe covering the two bulky sweaters to make her look fat, along with a pair of baggy slacks of Dean's. Just right. Not even he would recognize her.

"Federal Building," she said to the driver when she got in. She noticed him glancing in the rearview mirror. She read the address off the paper Dobe had sent her.

"Do you work for her?" the driver asked as they drove away.

"Who?" His question had taken Sharleen by surprise.

"Sharleen Smith. That's her house you came out of, right? What's she like?"

Sharleen relaxed a little, then smiled to herself. "Yes, I do. She's a right nice person." Well, that was all true, Lord, she told God. I do work for myself—and Dean, and now maybe Momma—and I am right nice. But, she realized, she hadn't disguised her voice, so she'd better shut up. She didn't know who might be watchin' her or followin'. She just prayed Dobe wasn't sending her into trouble.

Because now it wasn't just Dean, it was her momma who needed her, too, at least for a while. Sharleen had already given her money to move, and money to register in hairdressers' school, and some more money for some nice clothes. She couldn't afford to get in trouble over this Dobe business.

At the Federal Building, Sharleen followed the directions to the auction room the man at the front desk had mumbled to her without giving her a second glance. A quick look around the spacious lobby told her there were no reporters, something she had come to expect whenever she left the house. Her disguise had worked.

She walked into the crowded auction room, and was suddenly caught up in the commotion and din. She registered under a fake name at the desk, just as Dobe had told her to, although Sharleen wasn't sure if that was legal or not. The woman handed her a sheet of paper with instructions on how to bid, and a catalogue with descriptions of the lots. "Lots," Sharleen thought, confusedly, were property. Dobe had wanted her to buy him property, hadn't he? Sharleen found a seat in the last row and waited for the right number to be called, then flipped through the booklet, looking for Lot 604. She had to know what she was getting into.

As she skimmed through the pages of the inch-thick catalogue, she felt her heart racing. What was she bidding on? It wasn't land. They called everything "lots." But here was all kinds of stuff being sold.

Maybe she was bidding on something illegal. She liked Dobe, but she knew he wasn't completely honest in business. Still, Sharleen trusted Dobe, she really did. If he said there was nothing for her to worry about, she believed him. But Dobe was nervy, she knew that.

Drugs? No, not Dobe. He was a good Christian, he'd never do that. But what? And was it illegal? Oh, Lord, she prayed, I hope not. Sweat broke out on her forehead and upper lip. She hadn't really stopped to think this all out before she left the house.

Could I be arrested? Sharleen thought, glancing at the

uniformed security guards stationed around the auditorium. That would be terrible. They'd find out about Texas, about Dean and her. About their daddy. Panic began to well up in her throat, so she said the Lord's Prayer, as she did whenever she was frightened. Then Psalm 23 for good measure, and, with a deep sigh of resignation, she returned to the catalogue.

She hadn't yet found the lot description in the booklet when she heard the auctioneer call out "Lot Number 604," and ask for an opening bid of one hundred dollars. Sharleen froze in her seat. She didn't know what to do, so did nothing, since Dobe had said she probably wouldn't have to pay more than seventy-five dollars.

When there were no bids from the floor, Sharleen heard the auctioneer drop the opening bid to fifty dollars. Well, she'd done the right thing. She felt her palm wet and hot on the handle of the paddle. This was when she was supposed to raise it, she knew, but the pounding of her heart was making her breathe too fast. She felt dizzy. The security men around the room scanned the seats. Sharleen pulled the kerchief forward on her face and raised the paddle in the air, then quickly pulled it back down.

The auctioneer nodded in her direction and took her bid, but then he didn't seem to stop talking. He kept droning on, and Sharleen grew panicky. Torn between the fear of being pounced on by the guards or the police, and the need to get the bid in for Dobe, Sharleen felt her shakes increasing. If there's dope in them packages, Dobe Samuels, and I go to prison, I'm goin' be mighty mad. Here goes, she thought. Sharleen raised her paddle again.

"Sold! Lot Number 604 for sixty dollars to Bidder 123."

Sharleen looked at her paddle number, just to be sure, then looked cautiously around the room. That was her number, all right. But no one was paying her any attention. The auctioneer was already going on to another lot. She took a few minutes to calm down, then stood up gingerly and walked back to the payment desk. She handed the bored-looking woman the money, got the receipt and instructions on when to pick up the lot, and where.

As she walked away from the desk, she tensed, waiting for a voice to scream out behind her, but none did. She got into a waiting elevator, and as the doors closed after her, she took her first breath in what felt like hours. She looked at the receipt for her purchase, which she still grasped in her hand, read the description of what she had just bought for Dobe, and gasped.

Why would anyone in their right mind buy 837 shoes—all for left feet only?

24

Neil Morelli dropped his fare in the box and walked down the aisle of the bus as it lurched into the traffic. He took the only single seat available, relieved that he didn't have to stand all the way to the garage. Either a seat alone or stand—that's the way it had to be for Neil. The thought of touching elbows or shoulders with these other people could make him gag right now. He screwed up his long, long nose at the odor. Neil had forgotten that people who rode buses and subways smelled. When he'd left New York, he'd thought he would never be riding public transportation again.

But that was then. Now, since the dynasty-bitch got him kicked off his gig on *Three for the Road*—his last hope—Neil was back riding buses. And *driving* cabs, not taking them.

It wasn't even limos, with maybe some hotshot sitting back there, waiting to discover talent, someone who could give him a boost, someone who would take Neil's résumé and head shot and maybe—just *maybe*—give him another chance. No, Neil was reduced to pushing cabs around the streets of Los Angeles. Okay, at least it was dispatch cabs, not cruising for fares. But, still, most of his work was hustling Vietnamese home after their office-cleaning jobs were finished for the night. The companies paid the tab. Or picking up a guy too drunk to drive himself.

And lots of runs to East Los Angeles, where Neil had to keep his eyes open, be on the lookout every minute he was on those streets. He never knew where it was going to come from. He hadn't been held up yet, but the other guys in the garage—mostly Mexicans and Iranians—had warned him to be careful. Told him horror stories of how they had been ripped off for a couple of bucks and a pack of cigarettes. How a couple of the guys had resisted and were shot—in the head.

Neil took those stories seriously. He knew how dangerous the town could be. Even where he had spent most of his time since coming to the city, he knew how you could be robbed and no one would come to help. Robbed of your dignity, have your job stolen from you. Your livelihood. These wetbacks weren't telling Neil something he didn't know.

He thought again of how Sy Ortis had betrayed him, of how Lila Kyle had ruined his last shot, a good shot, at getting a continuing part on 3/4. No, the cabbies couldn't tell him anything about getting ripped off that he didn't already know about.

But they did tell him something he hadn't thought of. Since the riots, all those guys had access to guns—handguns, rifles, whatever. And some of them carried while driving. Neil didn't like the idea of carrying a gun, but he had begun to think about it.

And the more Neil thought about guns, the safer he began to feel. He reminded himself to ask Roger about that tonight. If Roger got in contact with him.

The trip to the garage was only a little more than ten miles, but with waiting time it took almost an hour, on the slowest bus system in the country. Why should it be efficient? It was only for the illegals, and the other poor. The people who worked for hourly wages if they were lucky to work at all. Neil looked around at the fat women and shifty-eyed men. No one was happy to be here, Neil could see. So how bad must it have been where they came from?

Living hell, he thought. He felt for them, but he had

his own problems. And one of them was now approaching. His stop came, and he got out of the bus to walk the three long blocks to the garage, where he had a twelve-hour shift coming up. He'd worked for the last three nights without one word from Roger. After his initial contact, Roger had stopped calling. Neil wasn't sure why. He knew why Roger had started to call him, but now he couldn't understand why he had stopped. Two nights in a row, he'd gotten Roger's messages, coming in over the dispatch radio in Roger's best newscaster voice.

Of course, at first Neil had been surprised. He didn't think Roger Mudd even knew who he was. But Neil guessed Roger had heard how Neil had respected the man, how he'd handled his career and all. And when Roger had radioed him privately, coming through on Neil's own radio that night, and told Neil not to get down on himself, that he, Roger Mudd, was going to contact Neil again, and tell him how to handle this mess, how to get out of it, Neil began to feel better.

So Neil waited. He *knew* Roger was going to call again. He just knew it. But he was afraid. Because, without Roger, he didn't know how he'd get along. Then it hit him. Maybe, Neil thought, maybe Roger meant *I* should radio *him*. Neil stopped on the sidewalk. He thought about that for a minute, then continued to walk toward the garage, now looming in the darkness at the corner.

But how do I get him? I don't know how. Neil decided that he could figure it out. There had to be a way. After all, Roger Mudd had found *him*.

The cab smelled of some goddamn foreign food, not Mexican or anything from the Western Hemisphere. This smell came from like out of a desert tent, like rancid cabbage cooked over camel dung. Neil wondered how these fucking Arabs were able to get camel dung in this country. Maybe way down in the San Diego Zoo? I'd walk a mile for a camel turd.

He rolled down the window, trying to get some air circulating in the car, but he knew from other nights that the smell was here to stay. It gets in the fucking vinyl and wraps itself around the vinyl molecules, and combines with them, becomes a new substance, a new chemical.

One that would never go away. Like the smell of dog shit on the bottom of a shoe. Once you know you've stepped in dog shit, you always smell it whenever you wear those shoes again, no matter how you cleaned them.

Fucking Iranians. They should stick to international terrorism. They're better at that than cooking, for chrissakes.

His dispatch radio scratched into voice, startling Neil. He reached for the volume button as he rolled along Santa Monica Boulevard, adjusting it to a bearable level. The guy that was driving the car just before Neil must have been deaf. Or had his burnoose tied too tight.

Neil radioed in his position, then pulled into Century City, where he was supposed to sit and wait for his first call. He waited and waited. He turned off the engine, then put his head back. It was going to be a long, slow night, Neil decided. There hadn't been one call since he got in, except for the location call. And Neil was tenth on line. He would have been twenty-second, but he had figured out the scam. If he paid off the dispatcher, he got moved up. So he had, but, still, he only had number ten. The fucking Iranians must have dropped a lot of rials tonight, to get so far ahead of Neil. Dollars aren't what they used to be.

He wasn't sleeping, Neil knew that. He had his eyes closed, and his chin had dropped to his chest. There was a short rivulet of drool out of the corner of his mouth. But he hadn't fallen asleep. The voice from the radio was familiar.

"Roger, I hear you, go ahead," Neil said into the air instead of the hand-held mike. Neil listened, while Roger told him the whole story. How he had been passed over and didn't get the national anchor spot, just because he had the wrong family tree. His great-great-granduncle had been the doctor who treated John Wilkes Booth. How Roger didn't have the right connections. Neil had read a little bit about it in the newspapers when it happened, he was sure, but now Roger was giving him the inside dope. Why he understood what Neil was going through. How the assholes of the world have a private club that gives them special membership discounts on bullshit. How the rich and connected were going to do away with all the little guys that wouldn't allow themselves to be pushed around. Roger talked about Lila Kyle, and the other two. All the pretty women who had laughed at Neil, rejected him.

Neil listened, not opening his eyes. Then Roger explained everything. About how unless your father owned the network, how unless you had connections or were very good-looking, you got fucked over. But Roger was now going to be Neil's connection. Roger would take care of everything.

It wasn't till Roger told him what to do—*exactly*—that Neil opened his eyes. He jumped for the mike. He *had* to talk to Roger. Just to be sure he'd gotten the instructions right. He blurted into the mike, calling Roger's name, but got no response. He began to play with the dials of the two-way radio, all the time screaming into the mike. *He had to get back to Roger.* "What's the frequency, Roger?" he kept screaming over and over.

"Hey, Car Forty, leave the radio alone. What you doin' to it, man? You screaming over there. Leave it alone!"

Neil put back the microphone on the stand, his hand trembling. Could Roger really have meant it? Neil thought for a moment. Yeah, Roger meant exactly what he said. No two ways about it. Neil made a mental note to talk to the guy in the garage that could get things. Neil needed something. Real bad.

And now Neil didn't feel alone anymore.

25

When the phone rang, Lila wasn't surprised to hear Aunt Robbie's voice at the other end. She just hadn't thought it would be so soon. "Don't hang up," he said when she answered. Lila had no intention of doing that. To tell the truth, she was bored and needed some diversion. And if *she* was bored, think how bored Robbie had to be—he who'd put up with years of abuse from Theresa just so he could be the lackey of a star, so that he could be a witness to the action.

"Are you there, Lila?" Robbie asked sheepishly.

"Where the fuck did you think I was?" But the fact was that, just as Robbie needed to be a party to the fame and the action and the success, Lila needed him—or someone—to witness it. All the interviews, all the fan mail, all the offers, the invitations, the publicity—none of it seemed to be really happening to her if someone else wasn't there to be excited and impressed by it. She would not hang up. Keep the line open, but don't make it too easy for him. After all, she had to get him to agree to her plan. Her new perfect plan.

"I was thinking, Lila . . ."

"Uh-huh," she said, examining her manicure.

"I was thinking . . . I mean, we've been friends for years, since you were what? A baby? It's silly for us to quarrel, Lila. I'm not mad at you."

"What does that have to do with anything, whether *you're* mad at me or not?"

"Well, I mean, after our fight and all. I mean, I have no hard feelings."

"Why should you?" she asked, letting the wonder roll over the telephone lines.

"Well, you kicked me, but . . ."

"You asked for that, Robbie."

He didn't say anything for a minute. "Well, I admit I shouldn't have brought up the subject of your mother, but, well, your reaction was a little extreme."

"I'm confused. Why are you calling me? To tell me I was wrong? That doesn't seem very sensible, does it? I mean, Robbie, come on. It wasn't *me* that was in the wrong." Either he was going to crawl or he wasn't. Lila wasn't going to play this game much longer, so she decided to listen to one more sentence from Robbie. If he didn't know how to do it, she was going to hang up on him. Not a loud crash, like he was important to her or anything. Just that low click that would make him think —but only for a minute—that they had been disconnected by accident.

Robbie was getting it. "Look, I'm sorry, Lila," he said.

"For what, Robbie?" Like Theresa used to make Lila do when she was a kid and had been naughty. Make her apologize to the two dummies. Rub her face in it.

"Lila, this is very difficult."

"Then maybe you should send a candygram or something, Robbie. If you're having trouble finding the words."

She waited while Robbie took a deep breath; then the words began tumbling out. "I'm sorry I overstepped my bounds, Lila. I shouldn't have tried to manipulate you like that. You're right. Theresa did it to herself, I see that now." Then he paused. "Forgive your old auntie?" he asked, in that fucking baby-talk voice that put her teeth on edge.

Now Lila imitated it. "But Auntie's been a naughty auntie. She should be punished, shouldn't she, Robbie? She's been a naughty, naughty girl."

"Aunt Robbie should be punished, Lila. What can she do?"

There was a pause, and when he spoke again Robbie's voice had an edge of panic in it, as he realized they weren't just playing games. "What, then? What do you want, Lila?"

"Candy," she said.

Robbie laughed, relieved, "Oh, sure, I'll get a box of Godivas—a five-pound box. We can sit up all night and eat chocolates."

"No, Robbie. I mean Candy . . . and Skinny." Lila paused, feeling her breath quicken. "A kidnapping. You know where they are, Robbie. This is something only you can do."

"No, Lila. Your mother would . . ."

"Fuck her!"

"Lila, please."

"I mean it, Robbie."

"But why, Lila?" Robbie's voice had tears in it. "What do you want *them* for? You know what that will do to . . ." He stopped himself from saying Theresa's

name. She heard the realization hit, and the acceptance.
"Okay. I'll do it."

"That's the good auntie," Lila said, in her baby voice
once again.

"Lila, now I need a favor," Robbie said.

Jesus. He simply didn't get it, did he? *No, no, no.
That's not the way it's done, Aunt Robbie. First the tribute, then maybe a favor. Ta-ta,"* she said, and hung up.

It would be a good punishment, and would keep him in
his place. It would also be certain to put him on Theresa's
permanent shit list. There's only one way to deal with
traitors, Lila thought to herself sternly. And she realized
she was smiling for the first time that day.

26

Bouncing back from the shit meeting with Ricky Dunn,
Michael McLain had decided he had to take an action
and take it fast. So he'd signed the contract with April
Irons for *Birth of a Star*. He signed it, and *then* he sent it
over to Sy's office. Sy would be furious, but fuck him.
Michael would leave him for CAA or William Morris or
even for Ara if Sy gave him any more shit. April knew
her stuff, the old film had been a classic, she was willing
to pay top dollar, *and* she was getting Julia Roberts for
the female lead. Michael signed, despite not having a
finished script, despite Sy's warnings.

Now he was feeling actor's remorse. He threw the
script that had just been messengered over across the
room, its pages fluttering like the feathers of a dirty pi-
geon. He'd read crap. He'd watched crap. Hell, he'd
even *been* in crap. But he'd never had anything to do
with crap as bad as this. *Birth of a Star* should be called
Death of a Star, he thought angrily. *This* star. Me. It will
pull me lower than Redford after *Havana*. Christ, it's
worse than *Akkbar*. And nobody, not any star in Hollywood, could afford *two Akkbars*. In his heart, he knew
he should have followed Sy's advice on the fucking Ricky

Dunn movie. Eaten crow, given up on the billing issue. But screw it. He wasn't ready to play sidekicks yet.

Still, after this dreck, he might not get the option to.

He almost shivered, then pulled himself together. All right, so the screenplay is shit. That's a definite. He didn't have to think anymore about that right now. If that was all that was wrong with this movie, then he wasn't going to worry. Not just yet, anyhow. Scripts could be fixed.

Michael always did this final analysis of a project perhaps a bit too late: after the contracts were signed, the dates set. Then, because there was no way out, his denial would break, and in fear and loathing he would let himself see the negative side. Up till now, when he was still pushing for the job, he would only consider the good aspects. In this case, one was the money, *lots* of money. And work, for the first time in over a year and a half. With the Dunn project blown, he needed a movie right away.

Point two: the director. April had told him about Sam Shields, praising him to the skies, but Michael was definitely not impressed when they met. The guy had been an off-Broadway director in New York, not exactly an exclusive club. Then, somehow, he got himself hooked up with April and did *Jack and Jill* with her. Got good reviews, made some money, and even got Sam mentioned seriously in some Hollywood circles. But let's face it, the guy had only busted his cherry: that didn't make him a director. *Jack and Jill* had been a small movie. This was a big one. A *real* big one.

Lousy script, half-assed director. Now he was down to one out of three. At least the stars would be top drawer —him and Julia Roberts. Her comeback and his. And if this May–September romance was a bit too much like *Pretty Woman*—well, the public had loved *Pretty Woman*. And it wasn't as if she—or Michael—needed a lot of directing. All Julia ever had to do was walk in front of a camera and people fell in love with her. Luckily for her and everyone else, she could act and carry a project. So, while Sam Shields was no hotshot director, Michael was certain that he and Julia would be able to pull off *Birth of a Star*, given a few changes in the script. With his talent, and Julia's star quality and likability, and considering that April, who was no fool, seemed to be able to lead Shields around by the gonads, this might not be so bad.

Michael started feeling better. He went over and picked up the script again, flipping through the pages where he had earlier made margin notations in red. He picked up the phone and called April at home. He knew how to work as a team player. He'd call the coach and give *her* a pep talk.

April answered her private line. Michael dropped his voice to his deepest baritone. He took an audible breath, then said teasingly to April, "Talk down and dirty to me. Say something that will make my blood froth over."

"You're a lousy actor, Michael," she said. "Is that down and dirty enough for you?" Without waiting for an answer, she continued, "Come on, what do you want, Michael? I was just about to brush my teeth."

"I thought you had them sent out. *Both* of them."

"I know you have something on your mind when you call all cutesy, Michael. What's up?"

"Julia Roberts. She's signed for *Birth*, too, right?"

"I never said she was *signed*, Michael. I only said we were talking."

"Talking? Listen, principal photography is supposed to start in two weeks, and you haven't signed her?"

"Actually, Michael, we decided you're such a strong presence that Julia would be overkill. We needed someone newer, someone who would be a perfect counterweight to you."

He knew it. Goddamn it, he knew it! After over twenty years in the business, Michael McLain had a built-in shit detector. And he was waist-deep now, and sinking. "Uh-huh. Like who?" Michael said.

"You're going to love this, Michael. Jahne Moore."

Michael didn't say anything for a long moment. It was too fucking much. Starring him with that TV tramp! "You're wrong, April. I don't love it." In fact, he hated it. And he hated the bait and switch. He was too old to fall for it, but he had. "Jahne Moore is a nothing," he said.

"A nothing? I was sure you would be ecstatic. She's the flavor of the fucking month! She's beautiful, relatively unknown—in the movies, I mean—and you two have . . ."

"She's a lightweight, April. Television. It'll all be on my shoulders. New director . . ."

"Hardly new, Michael. He's made me a lot of money on *Jack and Jill*."

"You made a lot of money on that because you had a nothing budget. *Shields* didn't make it for you, the *accountants* did. And now you're giving him—what?—a forty-million-dollar budget? And a dumb bitch from the Melrose Playhouse as my costar?"

Michael couldn't hold it in any longer. He was screaming now. "I see the plot. A real-life drama. Fading movie star. Young TV nothing. A slip yoke. Perfect for you, April. But I'm not carrying the weight for the whole fucking movie, April. I'm not fucking doing it!"

"You don't have to, Michael. All you have to do is show up every day and take direction. This movie is my responsibility; let's be very clear about it. *I'm* the producer, and *you're* the actor. And your contract is airtight. No costar approval. So you show up next Friday or prepare to meet with our lawyers. Okay?"

April hung up before he could say another word.

Sy Ortis and Michael McLain sat at the best table at Via Veneto. Michael was getting loud. A lot too loud for this place, where the big money, the real heavy hitters, ate.

Michael had been ranting for the last twenty minutes about his *Birth* deal. How April had baited him with Julia Roberts and switched him to Jahne Moore, how the script sucked, how he hated the director already, how he—Sy —had to find a way to get Michael out of the contract.

Sy simply listened. He had known for over a month about Jahne's role. If only Michael had not kept his talks with April secret from Sy. This served him right.

"So, you got to get me out of it. Just get me out of it. I can't do this piece of shit. I won't."

Typical. Like a child. "I'm afraid you'll have to. A lot

of money is tied up in this, and if you back out now, it will cost."

"Tell them I'm sick."

"*If* they believe it, it will be around the Industry in an hour. Remember what those rumors did to Burt Reynolds' career? What did Sydney Pollack say in *The Player?* How rumors were always true? And it won't be so easy to get insured on the next one. If there *is* a next one."

"What's that supposed to mean?"

"Michael, you made your bed. You'll have to lie in it. I told you not to do this movie. I begged you. Just like I told you not to insist on top billing with Ricky Dunn."

"Okay. Get me out of this piece of shit and I'll do the Dunn thing."

"Too late. Eastwood signed on."

"Goddamn it, Sy! You better take care of this. Find a solution. I mean it."

"Is that a threat, Michael? A threat that you'll leave the agency? That you'll fire me?"

"You got that right. And if you don't like it, Sy, you know where the door is."

Sy had been waiting for Michael to say this. Michael always said it at the end of one of his tirades. Usually Sy would just switch to another tack, wait for another time. But not today.

Sy put down his fork, swallowed the last of the veal piccata, wiped his mouth with the oversized linen napkin, and looked across the restaurant table at Michael. "It's been a pleasure, Michael. Sorry it couldn't have worked out between us, but I respect your judgment." Sy pushed back his chair and stood up.

Michael looked up at Sy, his eyes wide. "What? Where are you going?" Michael still had a forkful of food dangling in the air, halfway toward his mouth.

"The door. I finally figured out how to get there, after all these years of you telling me I knew where it was." Sy motioned with his hand. "So, *muchas gracias* for firing me, Michael. It saves my having to quit. And *adios, amigo!*"

27

When Jahne received the revised *Birth of a Star* script, messengered to her at the Beverly Wilshire Hotel, she was disappointed to find no note from Sam included. What did you expect? she asked herself crankily. A marriage proposal?

She *was* cranky. She'd spent the day in the seemingly endless round of upkeep and grooming appointments that filled so much of her spare time: first a facial, then three hours at Antonio's, having the gray covered and streaking the black and blue and other shaded highlights into her hair. That was always a trial, because of the face-lift scars buried in her hair. Viendra looked at them, looked at her, and winked. She tipped him a hundred bucks and hoped he'd keep his mouth shut. Every time. Then two grueling hours with Arna, her trainer, who didn't believe he'd really worked you unless you were doing dry heaves by the end of it. Even now her legs were shaking. And she still had to change, do a quick interview with Melinda Bargreen, a journalist from Seattle, and then look for a place to live: at $480 a day, the hotel was a high price to pay for security.

She got through the interview, and then spent three exhausting hours touring with Roxanne Greely, house broker to the stars. She came back to the hotel exhausted and depressed. Roxanne had explained that she might be able to find something for $750,000, but that anything nice was over two million! Jahne knew that the world out here was nuts, but this proved it.

It wasn't until that evening, back at the Beverly Wilshire, that she got to relax. She ran a bath, a rare luxury. Brewster Moore had cautioned her that more than three minutes of immersion in water was injurious to the dermal layers, but tonight she didn't care. She threw in a generous handful of Flanders bath salts (another Brewster no-no) and slipped, with a sigh, into the huge, deep, sparkling tub. Then she opened the *Birth of a Star* script and started to read.

She was on page 37 when the tub-side phone trilled. She reached for it, wondering if she could be electrocuted by a phone call. She could just see the headlines: "CARA DIES IN BATHTUB TRAGEDY." The *National Enquirer* would have a field day.

She picked up the phone.

"What do you think?" Sam's voice asked.

As if it were the most natural thing in the world, she answered, "I'm only up to page thirty-seven, but I like what I've read so far. That opening is visually brilliant."

"Goes along with the rest of me," he said. "How about a drink?"

"Tonight? Sorry, I'm bushed. I've spent the whole evening looking for a place to live. I'm looking forward to crawling into bed with your script."

"Lucky script. So, did you find a place?"

"I saw something I could maybe lease in Bel Air. Expensive, and it's a bit pretentious, but La Brecque tells me it's secure as Fort Knox."

"So, how 'bout dinner tomorrow night?"

Dinner instead of lunch. This was an upgrade.

"I can't make it until Thursday," she purred. "And not until about nine," she told him. Then she regretted it. She was still playing too easy, making the same mistake Mary Jane used to make. She should have just told him no.

"Fine. I'll pick you up at the hotel." Why was she doing this? she wondered. It was ridiculous. If you wanted to work with Sam, you are, she told herself fiercely. That does not include visits to art museums and dinners alone.

Or would they be alone? It hadn't occurred to her to ask. But maybe this was to be a working dinner. She and April and Sam and God knows who else. Michael Douglas? Paul Newman?

Jahne was up to the second act of the new *Birth of a Star* script when she got to the love scene.

FADE UP with a POP DISSOLVE
              [James]
PULL BACK to reveal James, his face a mask of desire
    Judy, you know how I feel, don't you?
              [Judy]
PULL BACK. Judy in bed, holding sheet.
    Yes. I think I do.
              [James]
WIDER
    But show me how you feel.
              [Judy]
    I feel bared before you. Like this . . .
**[Slowly, she slips out of her robe. She is awkward with
love. Under it, she has on only a plain man's pajama
top. She slips it off and stands revealed before him,
naked and in a state of grace.]**
              [James]
FOLLOW his eyes
    You're so beautiful!

A nude scene! And from there, on pages 50 and 51,
they make love. Well, of course Judy and James were
lovers, but in the first version she'd read it was not as
explicit as it was now. Jahne read now and groaned.
*"Close-up. He cups her breast. Long shot—his hand
moving from her ankle to her knee, from there to her
thigh."*

Oh, God! She should have known! She felt herself
break into a sweat. She was too upset to judge whether
or not it was a good scene, or justified. All she knew was
that she couldn't do it. Not with her body. Not with her
scars.

Well, she'd talk to Sam. She'd get him to change it.
He'd have to. She'd insist.

Certainly she wasn't the first actress to resist nudity.
Many actresses did. They were embarrassed by nudity,
or felt exploited. No women wanted to do it, except for
the few exhibitionists. Well, it was not in her contract,
and she wouldn't do it.

She read the rest of the script numbly. She couldn't

judge it, couldn't be intelligent. She just prepared for her battle Thursday night.

Thursday came quickly. The restaurant was a hip L.A. version of a sushi bar—very white walls, black tables and chairs, and a long black counter with the sushi chefs on one side, diners on the other. As if in unspoken agreement, most of the patrons wore either black or white clothes. They were a mixed bag: some young, dressed almost sloppy-casual, and others, older, who looked like Industry suits in their linen Armanis. The place was crowded, and the tables were close together, the noise level high. Along the walls, shadow silhouettes were painted: a ponytailed man holding chopsticks, a woman with a hat on. They were clever and disconcerting: at one table a small, birdlike woman appeared to be casting the painted shadow of a big man with an Afro.

In case Jahne had any question of the hipness of the place, Sam pointed out Barry Diller, a small bald guy who sat with an entourage of young men. "Past chairman of Fox," Sam told her. "Just up and quit one day. People say he got tired of the game. Now he's into home shopping."

They were taken to a table by Yoshi, the owner, who welcomed Sam by name. There was a stir, the usual moment when the conversation silenced as she entered a room; then the buzz continued, a little louder than before. Fame. She wondered if she would ever get used to it.

Sam ordered saki, but she only tasted from the tiny black pottery cup she was offered. She played with the cup nervously. She didn't care for saki, but she loved Japanese beer. And a beer would calm her down right now. Too bad it was as fattening as American beer. Well, she'd call Nikki in the morning.

She looked up from the menu to see Sam staring at her. "Is something wrong?" she asked.

"You remind me of someone," he said, and continued staring.

She stopped breathing, and then reminded herself that she had to take another breath. "Really?" she managed to ask, and lowered her head, letting a black wing of hair fall forward.

"No," he said. "Don't do that." He reached across the table and brushed back the hair. "Let me look at you." She surveyed him from under her eyelashes, everything stilled for what might have been half a minute but felt like hours. Now he sees, she thought. At last, he'll know me. And what will happen?

"I know!" he said triumphantly. "The young Vivien Leigh!"

She breathed again. But her body felt loose, as if she'd been working out too hard all day. She was frightened. Frightened and weak and fascinated.

"So, what did you think of the script? I'm dying to know."

"Well . . ." She'd have to talk about the nude scenes.

"You hate it. God, you hate it!"

"No. No. I just . . . I have some reservations."

"Look. It hasn't been easy, updating this. I mean, essentially it's the story of a sadistic man and a masochistic woman—old-fashioned melodrama."

"Is that old-fashioned? I think it's pretty current."

"Oh. The old 'Women Who Love Too Much' and 'Men Who Make Hitler Look Good' scenario. Well, I didn't want to write some codependency screenplay."

"Look, I don't think that's the problem. It's . . ." she paused.

"You're killing me. First Michael McLain, then you."

"Michael McLain? What about him?"

"He complained, too. Says he doesn't want to be typecast as a degenerate fucked-out star. So why did he take the part?"

"Michael?" Jahne asked. What was Sam talking about?

"Well, yes, Michael McLain. He's costarring with you. Didn't April tell you?"

"Tell me? Last I heard, you were considering Paul Newman for the part."

"Oh, no, not really." Sam lowered his voice to a throaty whisper. "April wanted Michael, I wanted Newman. So she gave me you, and I gave her McLain." Sam paused, then asked, "You *are* excited about working with Michael, aren't you? He's perfect for the part of James. It seems that the two of you are already close. I thought you'd be jumping with joy."

Well, of course. He had seen her with Michael. He thought they were still an item. Maybe that was why he wasn't being more aggressive with her personally. One thing she knew about Sam was that he didn't like to compete with another man to get a woman.

Should she tell him that she and Michael were—well, estranged? That the way was open for him? And that she didn't want to work with Michael—didn't even want to see him?

But it was none of his business, or if it was, he'd find out for himself. This time, she wasn't going to grovel or pave the way.

But, God, what would it be like if she had to work with Michael? And if she had to watch Sam nuzzle April Irons right in front of her? She wasn't sure she could take it. Jahne caught herself. Well, if it wasn't definite, there was a chance it wouldn't happen. She would have to hope not. "I'm just so surprised, so . . . overcome. Me working with you *and* with Michael McLain! It's like a dream come true. I'm delighted, Sam, and really very honored."

He seemed not to notice how shaken she really was. Well, she reminded herself, when he was wrapped up in a project, he never did notice anything else.

"But listen. We do have a problem. I can't do the sex scenes," she blurted. "I can't."

He stopped, smiled, and looked at her. Then he laughed. "Is that all this is about?" he asked. "The nude scenes?"

"I don't consider that 'all,'" she said stiffly.

"Oh, look, if you don't want to strip, we get you a body double. No problem. I can fake the frontal shot. Cut from your face to her body. No problem."

"Why have it at all? Why *show* it?"

"It's a love story."

"But it's not a sex story."

"Oh, come on. *Basic Instinct. Damage.* Modern times. A necessity."

"But it isn't necessary to show a nude Michael McLain. Isn't *that* modern?"

"I'd guess it was late-middle-aged," Sam smirked. "But *you* ought to know."

"You *know* what I mean. Why is it necessary?"

"Oh, you know the answers as well as I do. Because men like to see it. Because women don't mind. Because men *don't* like to see nude males. . . ."

"Why not?"

Sam shrugged. "I don't know. Ask Neil Jordan. Don't want themselves compared to someone else. Are afraid of their own homosexual feelings. Or feel degraded by the sight . . ."

"What if women feel degraded by all the female nudity? And no matching male?"

"Oh, come *on*. I didn't invent the world. This is the way it is. A naked female is beautiful. A naked male is offensive."

"I think it goes deeper than that," she said. "I think it's a way to control women. To show them how perfect they are supposed to be. To use their bodies to sell something—a product, a film, an idea. And to teach them to sell themselves, the way you want me to."

He reached his hand out to her and covered hers with his. She pulled away.

"I can see you like me, Jahnie. You don't want to, but you do."

"Of course I like you. You're my director."

"No, I don't mean that you like me professionally. I mean you like *me*. And I'm very impressed with you. You have integrity. You're a very unusual woman. Not just beautiful, but really focused, really intelligent. And we can work this out. I understand your concerns. But like me. Work with me. Trust me."

She looked into his long, tanned, and handsome face. He was still the best-looking man she'd ever known. And the blend of his intelligence, his drive, and his "Hey, I'm one of the good guys" attitude was as seductive as ever. She felt herself blush, and glanced down at the tabletop.

She couldn't help noticing his lap. Was that sashimi in his pocket, or was he really glad to see her? She looked away. Despite the restaurant noise, she could hear him breathing, and she could hear her own breathing as well. God, if just for an hour they could lie down together and comfort one another, be truly together even if only for a little while.

He reached for her hand again, and this time she let him hold it. "I'll protect you," he said. "Just let me in. Let me try. I'm a good director. I love my actors, Jahne. Trust me."

"I'll try," she promised.

28

Sharleen had the maid service make a special trip to clean the house for Momma's arrival. Now it was spotless, except for the boxes that Sharleen had bid on for Dobe. Just what is he going to do with all of these left shoes? she wondered for about the thousandth time. Could he be coming up with another scam like he did with the gas tablets? Dobe, you better not be makin' me store somethin' that's against the law, Sharleen thought to herself. Just what would she say to Momma when she got here and saw all these cartons? If Momma ever did get here.

Sharleen sat in the big living room, flipping through a catalogue and out of the corner of her eye watching Dean playing with the dogs. Then her eyes flicked to her watch once again. Sharleen had arranged for a car to pick up Momma and bring her here at seven. It was almost eight o'clock. The food had already arrived and was getting cold. An hour late; Sharleen was worried. Tonight, Dean was going to see Momma for the first time. Sharleen didn't want anything to go wrong.

But so much had already gone wrong: Flora Lee had taken the money to move, but she hadn't moved—she was still in the bad place in East Los Angeles. And they'd made two dates for her to come over, and both times she hadn't come at all. Then, the next day, she'd called Sharleen and cried, telling her she was too ashamed to see her baby.

Dean had been upset.

Now Dean broke into her thoughts. "Do you think Momma will know me?"

Before Sharleen could answer, the security guard at the gate buzzed and admitted Flora Lee's car. Thank the Lord! "Of course she will," Sharleen reassured him. Together, they opened the front door and stepped outside, standing on the top step as the car pulled into the driveway. Flora Lee got out and, with the driver's help, was able to steady herself on her feet. Flora Lee looked up and saw Sharleen and squealed, then began to run up the stairs to her, her arms open. "My little girl," she said, as if she hadn't seen Sharleen since Lamson. Then she slipped. Sharleen reached out and broke her fall. Flora Lee righted herself as if nothing had happened. Sharleen's heart dropped to the pit of her stomach. Flora Lee had been drinking. That's why she was late.

"Now, where's my little baby boy?" she yelled, as she walked unsteadily into the house, straight past Dean. He followed her. "I'm right here, Momma," he said to the woman who was moving around the living room in a crooked line. She turned to him and flung her arms out.

Dean took an involuntary step backward.

Sharleen watched Dean as he looked his momma up and down. Then she took a look at Flora Lee's attempts to make herself look special for this reunion. They had made her look ridiculous. Especially ridiculous to Dean, a boy who was only six when he'd last seen his momma. Flora Lee's hair was fairly neat, but way too yellow. The lime-green dress had too many flounces at the neck and shoulders. There was way too much jewelry, and Sharleen could smell the perfume all the way over on this side of the room. And the shiny yellow high-heel shoes didn't help her studied attempts to walk normally.

Flora Lee was all over Dean before Sharleen could say anything. "My little boy, my baby." Flora Lee had her arms around Dean's shoulders, and her face on his neck, crying. "You got so big I didn't know you! Momma's home, baby. Momma's home."

Dean didn't move, but his eyes found Sharleen's and locked on them. Sharleen met his gaze, for a moment. "Momma, why don't you come sit over here?" She guided Flora Lee to the end of the sofa, and eased her gently onto the cushions. "Now, if you just sit a bit, Dean and I will get things ready in the kitchen. We'll be right back, okay?"

"Don't you think this calls for a drink? It's a celebration, ain't it?" Flora Lee suggested.

"Okay, Momma," Sharleen said, guiding Dean through the kitchen door before her.

"That ain't Momma," Dean said, the moment the kitchen door closed behind them.

"What do you mean, Dean? Course it is." But Sharleen felt her stomach sink.

Dean shook his head. "No, it ain't. I remember how Momma smells, and she don't smell like Momma."

"Well, people change. She ain't so young as she was. Remember when you were a little boy, and Momma took you to school your first day? Remember? You told me the other day you did."

"Yeah, I remember that. Momma was pretty and not fat, and had brown hair. And she didn't wear no makeup, or smell like Daddy."

"You kids comin' out?" Flora Lee yelled from the living room. "We got to have a drink together, remember?"

"Dean, just give her a chance. You'll remember more in a little while."

When they got back to her, Flora Lee was sitting on the sofa, the Bible open on her lap. She looked up at them, her painted face crumpled in surprise. "Why, you kept my Bible the whole time since I saw you."

"We try to live by the Good Book, just like our momma taught us," Dean said, and he took the Bible out of her hands before he handed Flora Lee a glass of vodka and ginger ale. "Ain't that right, Sharleen?"

"Yes," she said. "Just like *you* taught us, Momma."

Holding up her glass, Flora Lee said, "Now, what should we drink to?"

Dean stared at Flora Lee for a long moment. Flora Lee saw the scrutiny, and reluctantly lowered her glass. "Well," she said. "Maybe I'm jumpin' the gun. Maybe you all aren't as happy to see me as I am to see you."

"Of course we're glad to see you," Sharleen said, and hugged the woman. "Aren't we, Dean?"

Dean stood there, still holding the battered white Bible in one hand. He didn't say anything.

"I've got a nice supper for us," Sharleen said. "Why don't we eat it?"

Over fried chicken and slaw and biscuits, Flora Lee did most of the talking. She wanted to know all the details about TV, about how Sharleen got the job, about what her costars were like. She complimented Sharleen on her dress, on the cooking, on the house, and she complimented Dean on his suit and the behavior of the dogs. Then she pushed away her plate and asked for another "teeny-tiny drink" and a tour of the house.

Reluctantly, Sharleen led her around, through the big dining room to the even bigger kitchen and den, then upstairs to the three empty spare bedrooms and the room she and Dean shared. Flora Lee stopped on the threshold. "You *both* sleep here?" she asked. She looked over at Sharleen, who felt herself blushing.

"Dean's still afraid of the dark," she told her momma.

Flora Lee raised her eyebrows. "Ain't we all?" she asked.

"You got plenty of room here," Flora Lee remarked as they trooped back downstairs. "Empty rooms. Why, you should see my teeny-tiny place. You could put it in a corner of your bedroom."

"Maybe you want to live here, Momma," Sharleen offered. She felt Dean stiffen beside her.

"Well, that's a right nice offer, dear," Flora Lee said. "But I might bother you with my guests." They had walked into the living room. "But do *you* want me to, Dean? Do *you* want your momma back?"

"Why did you leave us, Momma?" Dean asked.

Sharleen watched as the expression on Flora Lee's

face changed. The smile, along with the rest of her face, seemed to disintegrate. For a moment, Sharleen thought she glimpsed the other face of Momma, the face she had back in Lamson. "Honey, I had to. If I had stayed, your daddy would have killed me. I needed to get away . . . to find us a safe place, get a job and all. *Then* I was going to get you both." Flora Lee eyed the almost empty drink in her hand.

Dean lowered his head. "Then why didn't you come back for us?"

Sharleen was aware of the silence that fell over the room. She, too, waited for the answer to that question, although, to be honest, she could never have brought herself to ask it. Finally, Flora Lee spoke.

"Honey, things were very bad out there. A lot worse than I thought they was going to be. I couldn't keep a job long enough to settle down. I was laid off so many times, I finally lost count. And when I was working, I couldn't hardly make enough to live on myself, never mind support two children. And, after all, only one of you was mine." Flora Lee paused, then forced a small smile. "Honestly, you was better off with your daddy. At least he could give you a place to live."

"But you said you was coming back for us. We waited for you. Waited and waited."

"I know, baby." Now her smile was back, broader than ever, but her face still had the collapsed look of an empty paper sack. "But Momma's back now, so let's drink to our all being together finally. Like I promised."

Sharleen felt stung, but also sorry for Flora Lee. "Sure. And soon Momma's going to have a job as a hairdresser, just like she always wanted. She's going to school and everything. Right, Momma?"

"Well, I don't really think that place was for me, Sharleen," Flora Lee said. "They started at eight A.M. Now, who comes in at that time for beauty appointments? Got angry if I wasn't there. Chewed my ass in front of those little snot girls. I don't want to waste my time on an amateurish place like that."

"Oh," was all Sharleen could say.

"But let's have a drink"—Flora Lee raised her glass —"to a happy reunion."

"We don't drink," Dean said, and walked out of the room, calling his dogs after him.

Sharleen had sent Flora Lee home, and it had taken the better part of two days to stop Dean from cryin' and mopin' around the house. And it was real hard to do, because Sharleen felt like mopin' and cryin' herself.

And then, in the mail, she'd gotten a package that she thought might help. She coaxed Dean out of the bedroom and sat him on the sofa. "I got a real nice surprise for you," she said, and slipped the CD out.

At the studio, Sharleen had been amazed at the sound of her voice they had recorded. In fact, she couldn't believe it *was* her voice, but Mr. Ortis and the others insisted it was, that with modern electronics they could do anything. Well, they'd done a good job of making her sound like a real singer. Sharleen was impressed. Still found it hard to believe, but impressive. She guessed that all those exhausting lessons had paid off.

"Dean, listen to this." Sharleen inserted the new CD and pushed "play." She sat back, and watched Dean's face as the music began to fill the room. "What do you think?" she asked him.

"That sure is pretty, Sharleen. I like it."

"See, you said I could sing and you were right," Sharleen chided, smiling.

"Sure you can. But who is *that* singing?"

Sharleen grew serious. "Dean, that's me. That's my new album. Mr. Ortis sent it over. Remember, I made a record?"

"Sure I remember, but that ain't it." He paused for a moment more, listening to the voice more closely. "Sharleen, that ain't you. I don't care what you say, or what Mr. Ortis says. I know how you sound, and you don't sound like that. You can sing all right. But, Sharleen, don't let anyone tell you that that there is your voice, 'cause it ain't."

Sharleen stared at Dean, the chill of the truth creeping

up her spine. "What makes you so sure, Dean? I mean, I trust you and all, but why are you so sure?"

"Why? Sharleen, you could *never* sing that high. Remember how we used to laugh when you tried to sing the 'Star Spangling' song before baseball games? You could only go so high, and no higher. This gal can go way up there, and more. Nope, it ain't you." Dean paused, and continued to listen to the music. "But, hey, it sure is pretty," he said.

29

Sam Shields was working feverishly on *Birth*, both the script and preproduction work. He was also sleeping with April. And he was thinking more and more about Jahne Moore. Surely these were four full-time jobs. No wonder he was tired.

Principal photography began in only a week, and there were still several smaller parts to cast, a body double to locate, a Northern California location to finalize, and lots of rewrites to be done. Sam sighed and looked over at April. If he had to cut something or someone from his overcrowded life, it would be his affair with her, but he knew that wasn't possible. She had allowed and forgiven the dalliance with Crystal Plenum, but she'd made it clear that Sam was not to stray like that again or she'd take it personally. The specter of a vengeful April Irons was not a pretty thought.

Now he needed help, and was casting about for an assistant. Sam knew that an assistant director was a necessary evil, although he wasn't completely convinced, even after *Jack and Jill*. He had barely consulted the AD on that one, and wouldn't hire the same guy again. But that, April kept reminding him, was a *small* movie.

On the stage, there was no AD. Only in the movies, where many sets, and location and studio shots were called for, was it necessary. The AD could save time and money by shooting exteriors, location shots without the actors, or establishing shots—those quick cuts to street signs or skylines that told the audience where you were.

Casting for AD was going to be easy. Since Sam wasn't looking for someone with creative ability, just a gofer mentality, the field was wide open. He supposed that A. Joel Grossman was as good as anyone. But he didn't say that right away.

"What do you think?" April asked, after the interview was done and Joel walked out of the room.

"He hasn't had very much experience," Sam said.

"But he comes well recommended."

"He's your boss's secretary's son. What kind of a recommendation is that?"

April dismissed Sam's question with a shake of her head. "He's done those jeans ads. They were hot. And about a thousand other commercials. And he's been on enough sets to know how to handle himself. He's dependable. And I think he can be inventive, if not creative. You'll get your money's worth, Sam. Trust me on this."

That was the whole point: Sam trusted no one. But he did think A. Joel would work out, just because he had little experience, and had artistic pretensions. If he could shoot those jeans ads, he could walk around behind Sam carrying a clipboard. This guy wanted a job in features, any job. "Okay," Sam finally said. "But I hope it doesn't come back to bite me on the ass. And you owe me." Sam looked down at his list of actresses scheduled for readings today. "Who's next?" he asked.

April raised her empty coffee cup in the air without looking up from the script notes in front of her, and the cup was immediately taken by an unobtrusive hand. When a refill was placed in front of her, she took a sip, then suddenly spit it out on the floor. "Who the fuck did this? Goddamn it, Melanie, this has Equal in it."

The young woman came running up to her. "I'm so sorry, Miss Irons. . . ."

"Sweet 'n' Low—how many times do I have to tell you?" Melanie ran off to get a fresh cup. "Christ!" April said to Sam on her right at the table. "Where do these people *come* from? Can't even remember how I take my coffee." April pushed the script aside, along with a stack of rejected résumés. "And I can't get an actress to read a few lousy lines through without a flub. *Read* them, for chrissakes. Not memorize and *act* them, just fucking *read* them."

Sam thought of Jahne Moore and how she'd blown him away with her audition monologue. At night, alone, he ran the film of it over and over. Sam brushed his dark hair back on his head, then let his forehead rest on his palm. He was tired. They'd been at the casting table since eight this morning. It was now almost four. Seventeen readings, and not one even adequate, let alone good enough for a screen test. It was going to be a long night. "I got better reads from the kids trying out for my group in New York. At least they could read. Hollywood," he said, shaking his head. He'd better stop there. Sam knew April didn't want to hear another attack on Hollywood by "Mr. Off-Broadway," her derisive nickname for him. But now, apropos of nothing, Sam remembered Mary Jane Moran, and the time she had come for that first cold reading of *Jack and Jill*. She had been one of a slew of actresses, all good. Except she was the best. By far the best. Why couldn't there be another Mary Jane in this town?

He realized that lately what he missed the most was playing mentor. Mary Jane had been a wounded bird who had blossomed under his direction. And she had also bloomed in their personal relationship. Why did he so like the role of director, of Pygmalion to Galatea? He enjoyed being needed, being wiser, being more experienced, more in control. Was it a power trip? Yes. Was it because he was insecure? He didn't think so. What was so wrong about wanting to teach someone, wanting to help someone? How would he find that fulfillment? Where was another pupil for him?

Well, perhaps, in a way, there was. Jahne Moore, Sam knew, had already memorized the entire new script, and they weren't even in rehearsal yet. She was intelligent, hard working, and she was good. He was sure of it. But she was young, and needed direction. He had been working with her for a little over two weeks, every day, and was amazed at what a quick study she was. He knew filming *Birth of a Star* was going to be a breeze with her. He'd calmed her down about the nudity, and he enjoyed their give-and-take. Jahne was professional, refreshing, beautiful, and funny. Yet not hardened, the way April was. A dynamic woman, he thought. Yet still vulnerable.

Sam had been impressed first with Jahne's looks, then her talent, and now by her brains and professionalism. He found that, more than any other part of his job, directing Jahne was what he most looked forward to. It would be . . . satisfying. There was something special about Jahne Moore.

But now April was talking. "You're wasting our time, here, Sam. And time is money. You have to change the way you motivate actors, Sam. Movies are different than plays. I've been telling you that. You've got to approach movie actors in a different way. They're used to a scene-by-scene prep. You're giving them the script overview. Just do the moment. Don't waste your time. Or mine."

"Look, that's just not the way I work."

April looked at him coolly. "Well, this isn't working. We haven't cast one more part." She paused. "Maybe it's not the direction, Sam. Maybe it's the script. Try using the word 'abandonment' in a sentence. It can't be done. But this character has to say the word *three times* in a page and a half of dialogue."

Of course she was right. No one had ever accused April of being stupid. His script was rough—very rough. And Sam was, he had to admit to himself, scared. And he didn't like the feeling. Always before, he'd been the most powerful person in any group. Back on off-Broadway, at St. Malachy's, even on *Jack and Jill.* He hadn't just been the shmuck writer, he'd also been the director; it was *his* movie. The line producer Seymore LeVine was a nothing, the son of Bob (International Studios) LeVine, and Sam had bedded Crystal Plenum right away. Although *she'd* been the real star of the movie, once he'd slept with her, *he* had the power.

Of course, he told himself, he hadn't slept with her for the power. Who wouldn't sleep with her, if they could? An entire nation of men wanted to sleep with her. And they'd had a good time, until the end of the picture. Then he had started up again with April. . . . Well, being with April was a whole other scene.

Sam knew the world of acting, of directing. Hell, he'd been at it all his life. But April seemed to know *everything*. Including that grown-up world of money, deals, and percentages of the gross. She was as smart and as tough as any of the men, and as sexy as any of the women. And he liked that. With April, he felt like he was with the very best, the Rolls-Royce of women.

It was only that with April he sometimes felt different about himself, almost, well, inadequate. It wasn't the way it had been with the other women. When he slept with April, instead of gaining her power, it was as if *she'd* stolen *his*. Not sexually. She was a tigress, but he could keep up with her. And it wasn't anything she said or did. It was just that he didn't feel any submission from her. Not that he asked for any. Certainly not. And he knew she liked him. But with other women he had felt his leaving them would matter. With April, he knew she would continue, as seamlessly as before.

It unnerved him, and on top of that there was the problem of Michael McLain. Let's face it, I hate the prick and he hates me, Sam told himself. The guy was a coaster—he'd coasted through on his good looks and his reputation as a womanizer, not as an actor. Perhaps April was right. That as a guy on the slippery slope down, he'd be perfect.

But the problem was that the prick had accepted the role and now didn't want to play it. Christ, the guy couldn't act, but if he simply *read* these lines he'd get an Oscar on this one. This part *was* Michael McLain. All he had to do was show up. But now he wanted to "improve" on it, to sweeten it. He wanted the character to have an upbeat, charming slide, not a desperate one. He'd actually suggested that, instead of a suicide in the sea, James should die saving Judy from drowning! What bullshit!

So the son-of-a-bitch was taking every cheap shot he could at the script to try to get his way. His way, which would weaken or kill the goddamn thing.

Sam didn't have to tell April there were problems with the script. Act Two was weak as hell. She knew it, and had said as much this morning, both to him and to Michael. But she'd stuck up for me, Sam thought. "James is a suicide," she told Michael. "He has to be." But what, Sam thought with a little chill, what if she hadn't sided with me? Because that was the least of Michael's script suggestions. The script had already gone through five revisions even before this casting call. Sam looked over at April. How long would she side with him, and what would happen when she didn't? She looked at him now, with that unnerving look, as if she were reading his mind and found it amusing.

"Get them to *act*, Sam. We can always fix the script later. Okay? Ready?"

Sam nodded.

"Send in the next bimbo, Melanie," April called out, and leaned back in her chair, her arms securely folded.

30

After Lila had been pulled off Ara, she managed to get herself home. Then she spent three days licking her wounds and regrouping.

She'd lost *Birth*, and there was nothing she could do about it. All she could do was focus on her future, a future that had to be bigger and better than Jahne Moore's. There were three things she could do: First, get Marty to direct her in a film, a major feature. Second, be sure that it was her, not Sharleen, and certainly not Jahne, who won the Emmy. Lastly, get Sy Ortis to represent her.

She handled the first part of her campaign with a phone call to Marty, setting up dinner. If he was surprised by her invitation, he didn't show it. Then she called Sy Ortis' office for an appointment at the end of the week. Only then did she get dressed and leave the house.

Lila drove to the right address and stood looking at the facade of the two-story building in front of her. It was far from the typical excessive Malibu and Beverly Hills real estate she was used to, in one of the seedier sections of

Los Angeles, an area not well known to the Hollywood crowd, unless their business was of the nature of Lila's.

Lila figured this was one way she could help herself win the Emmy. And Nadia had shown her how. Not with the stupid candles and incenses. That was beat. But Nadia had won an award. And, by thinking it out carefully, Lila realized what she needed. Lila Kyle needed a private detective.

The requirements for the job were basic enough: a nose for digging up dirt and a love for money, whatever its source. Lila looked down at the card in her hand, the one Aunt Robbie had once given her. "Minos Paige, Private Investigator." Lila had learned from Aunt Robbie that Minos Paige's expertise was used from time to time by the national tabloids. This was the guy who got the picture of Jimmy Swaggart coming out of a motel room with a prostitute. And she'd heard from Robbie that Minos was the one who tipped Mia about Woody's affair. Lila wanted no less from Minos Paige. It was time to get the upper hand again.

Since the word had got out that she hadn't got the part in *Birth of a Star*, Lila had felt her upper hand lowering. And now that they were in hiatus, she felt she was losing the publicity edge she had on the show. *TV Views* had run a story about trouble on the set, blaming her. Suddenly Jahne Moore was getting the professional respect Lila had been demanding, and Sharleen Smith had become everyone's darling, thanks to the album publicity and the poor-little-Texan act she was able to pull off. It was clearly time for action.

Lila pushed through the glass door at the entrance to the building and walked up the flight of stairs to the second floor. Paige's office was one of four on the floor, the last one at the end of the corridor. She knocked loudly, then opened the door without waiting for a reply. Instead of the reception area she anticipated, Lila found herself in a room hardly bigger than a closet, facing a large desk, behind which sat a small man in a gray polyester suit. He had on a dull-white shirt and a god-awful orange rayon tie. She could see the pilling along the suit sleeves from here. His shirt collar was a size too big, making him look even smaller.

"Minos Paige?" she asked.

"What does Lila Kyle want with Minos Paige?" the figure asked, not having moved a muscle since she opened the door.

"That's only your business if *you're* Minos Paige," she snapped, staring down at the pale-faced man. He blinked, nodded, then indicated a seat in the corner of the room.

"What can I do for you?" he asked, now leaning back in his creaking chair.

"I need someone investigated. Two people, actually. I understand that's your line of work."

He nodded his head imperceptibly, almost without moving. "Who?" he asked.

Lila took in a breath. "Jahne Moore and Sharleen Smith."

Minos didn't react. That was something he knew: don't react no matter what you hear. He, like Lila, also knew that most people had more to hide than they would like to admit.

Lila reached into her bag, then handed Minos two sheets of yellow legal paper. "These are the details of their present lives—addresses, where they eat, where they shop recording dates, and their shooting schedules." Lila placed the sheets on the desk in front of Minos when he didn't reach out to take them. "I've also included some of the facts about their pasts that I've dug up on my own. Not the publicity stuff—facts. Things I got directly from them, in casual conversations."

Minos didn't say anything, just peered down at the notes in Lila's plain block print. "Those details would be the starting point. Like"—she leaned over and pointed to a line on the page—"what did Jahne Moore do before the Melrose Playhouse? How did she get that part? Not much is known about that."

Paige continued to look at her.

"And Sharleen Smith. Supposedly, she came from some town in Texas. What about her family? High school?"

Minos Paige finally spoke. "What do you want this information for, Miss Kyle?"

Lila thought of telling him it was none of his business, but could see that that was not the way to get this guy motivated. "I like to know who I'm working with. I don't like secrets, and I think both of these bitches have secrets."

"And what's *your* secret?"

Lila didn't flinch. "I have no secrets, Mr. Paige. That's the point. *My* life is an open book, the legacy of being the child of two celebrities. What you see is what you get. So you can understand when I say I'm at a disadvantage. They know everything about me, but I know next to nothing about them. And, frankly, that makes me nervous." She thought she saw the slightest hint of a curl to his lip, but chose to ignore it. "Are you interested in the job?"

"Let me make sure I understand exactly what the job is." Minos tucked a finger in his loose collar and tugged at it slightly, as if it were too tight. "You want all the dirty little secrets of their lives, like who they slept with, and if they did it for money. Any porno movies, scandal. Family background, legitimacy, money problems, prison records, sexual tastes, any illegitimate children, abortions, drug history, shoplifting, felonies, homosexuality, bestiality, necrophilia . . ."

Lila smiled for the first time since meeting Minos Paige. "I think you got the general drift, Mr. Paige. What will it cost?"

"A ten-thousand-dollar retainer. To start. Expenses billed separately. There will, no doubt, be some travel involved. I'll keep you posted on that."

"Fine. When can you start?"

He cleared his throat. "The minute your check clears." He shrugged apologetically. "It's company policy."

Lila opened her bag, took out her checkbook, and began writing the check. "By the way," she said as she scribbled in the little details on the check, "I have one other minor situation. It's not a problem really." She handed Minos the check. "It—I think it can be covered by the extra amount I've included in your retainer."

Lila opened her bag again, replaced the checkbook, and took out a small packet of letters, held together with a rubber band. "I've received these lately. I get a lot of crazy stuff in the mail, you must know that. But these are a little over-the-top. They're written by a member of some league or something. A guy named Jughead signs them. Could you look into these for me also?" Lila stood and handed Minos the bundle.

Minos opened the first of the envelopes and took out one sheet of paper. "LATEST BULLETIN FROM THE ANTI-NEPOTISM LEAGUE," he read. "DEATH TO LILA KYLE. Guess which famous Hollywood star's daughter got a part on *Three for the Road?* Lila Kyle, of course. And she claims, in a recent interview in *People* magazine, that it was really harder for her to get seen as an individual in her own right, that she had to work harder. . . ."

Minos refolded the paper and put it back into its envelope. "Surely you get a lot of these. Hate mail. Goes with the territory."

"There are a lot like that. Crazy. But I just don't like the idea of any *league* of crazies. And this is delivered to my door. Not by mail. It just shows up. Individual nuts I can deal with. This bothers me."

Minos Paige nodded. "Don't worry about a thing. I'll look into it. Like I say, the minute the check clears."

Sy Ortis laughed with true delight. He'd done it! He hung up the phone and for a moment he thought he might dance around the room like a demented, loco little His-panic leprechaun. And why not? He'd won the biggest poker game of his career so far! He was signing Lila Kyle, and what sweetened it all was that she was leaving Ara Sagarian to come to him—Sy Ortis, the wetback, the spic, the Johnny-come-lately. He held three queens against Ara's empty hand! Ha! The courtly old *maricón* would have a stroke on his right side to match the one on his left after this. Then he'd have to carry *two* fuckin' handkerchiefs!

Of course, he had reservations: his film clients didn't

like him to represent TV. And Lila would be a handful
—a true bitch. But she was a thoroughbred, an AKC-
registered bitch with the right bloodlines, not some little
mutt from nowhere. Lila's grandeur was born, not delu-
sionary, like most of the *nouveaux* Sy dealt with. And if
he could handle Crystal Plenum and that *puta de diablo*
Jahne Moore, then he could handle Lila, too. Because
Lila had it—the star quality that most of these girls
lacked, that secret magic *something* that went beyond
looks or talent, that power that compelled you to watch
her.

Sy walked to his office window and laughed. Wait until
all the agents in town heard about this!

31

Birth of a Star would be filming in Northern California
for nine weeks. Jahne was flown up in the International
Studios corporate 727, and when they landed at Oakland
Airport a limo was waiting to take her to the Cupertino
hotel the crew and cast were put up in for the duration.
The next morning, she was whisked down to the first
location and shown her dressing room, where Mai was
already waiting.

Jahne stared into the mirror in the plush trailer. It was
far more luxurious than the utilitarian tin box she was
assigned for *Three for the Road*. Everything about an
April Irons production was first class. The trailer had
a beveled and highlighted mirror, a built-in mahogany
makeup table beneath it, a tiled bathroom, a tastefully
furnished flowered-chintz sitting area, complete with
crystal-and-brass lamps, and a separate bedroom—with
a four-poster bed! Not for her to spend the night in, of
course. Just in case she wanted a nap! Jahne felt like a
star. Flowers splayed from a Baccarat crystal vase—a
gift from April Irons.

But did she look like a star? Anxiously, she began,
once again, to search the flawless face before her in the

mirror. Even the return of Mai, lugging another huge garment bag, didn't break her concentration, or her fear. But she was too self-conscious to study herself that way for long in front of another person, even someone she felt as comfortable with as Mai.

The night before, she had had a terrifying dream: she was onstage, doing a nude scene before a full theater. The scene was serious, moving; and then she felt first one thigh, then the other bulge out. There was a titter in the audience. Then her stomach bulged. Next a breast expanded, and hung to her waist. The audience began to laugh. She threw her hands up to her face, only to find her old nose, her old weak chin. The audience roared. She woke up in a sweat.

She was sweating now as she turned back to the huge mirror, catching Mai's eye. "Did you *always* think you were beautiful?"

"Neffer."

"Never?" Jahne spun around. "*Never?* Mai, you were the most beautiful woman of your time. You *never* thought you were?"

"Now I know I vas. *Now* I can see it—in the old movies, in the stills from that time. But then—no. I vas alvays vorried dat someting, some imperfection, vould show. My mouth—too big. My eyes, too round. I vas alvays comparing myself—first to other girls, then to other vimmen. And ven I came here! Hollyvood! Theda Bara! You can't imagine! And Nadia Negron. And, of course, Garbo. The Face of All Faces. I vas never goot enough. Not goot enough for me, or for the camera. Or for the men. All of the time I vas beautiful, vasted."

Jahne watched Mai in the mirror, then flashed her eyes back to her own face. Still retaining its elegant bone structure, Mai's face was a ruin of wrinkles, sags, and age spots. Jahne's was young, fresh. How long would it stay that way? And was it beautiful enough? Beautiful enough to fill a thirty-by-fifteen-foot screen at the Triplex Odeon? She certainly was not as lovely as Mai had been. And she had thought she focused on her imperfections because of her past—because of the face she once had had. But Mai had done it, too. And Sharleen had told her she didn't feel as pretty as Lila or Jahne herself. And Lila . . . well, Lila was a freak. No one was ever allowed to photograph her without her approval of the prints.

Now, faced with the terror of the big screen, Jahne found herself afraid and almost obsessed with her looks. And it wasn't only her: Jerry, the makeup guy; Laslo, the principal cinematographer; Bob the cameraman—all of them were fixated, it seemed, on how she would look. Jahne bit her lips and looked over at Mai, who, once, long ago, had been through all this.

"Oh, darlink, are you vorried about photography? You vill be lufly. Listen, ve vill do some tests and find all your best angles. Ve vill make you perfect."

"I was hoping I already was."

Mai laughed. "My dear, so silly! Vy, Jean Arthur— she had only vun side. *Alvays* her left. Whole sets built so she could enter from the right and never show her right profile. Everyone knew it. Capra never minded. And Claudette Colbert also. Very French, very chic, but a face like a—vat you call dem—pumpkin. Special lighting to give her cheeks. Even Elizabeth Taylor. Shadow on her upper lip. *Alvays* must be covered. So vat, darlink, is your problem?" Mai laughed.

Her problem, Jahne decided, was threefold: One, she was scared of how she'd look on screen. Two, she was scared of what was going to happen with Sam, and, three, she realized with surprise, she was angry.

"Why all the tricks?" she asked Mai, though she didn't really expect an answer. "Knowing our good side, lighting, retouching. Why aren't we good enough as we are?"

"Because, my darlink, as ve are is not the vay men dream of us. You know the story of John Ruskin?" Jahne knew of the English Victorian art critic, but when Mai said the name she made it sound like some Russian count. Jahne shook her head.

"He vas London art critic. No: even more. He vas journalist who made the taste of that time. He told people vat to like, vat vas beautiful, vat vas ugly. Very important man in arts in London. Maybe most important."

"Yes," Jahne said. "Now I remember his name."

"Vell, he married. Beautiful young girl. He vorshipped

her. Until after ceremony. Und ven she undressed on vedding night, he vas sicken. You know vy?''

Jahne shook her head.

''He saw her pubic hair! It made him sick. Alvays he had been looking at statues of vimmen. Alvays they had been hairless. His real, beautiful vife disgusted him!'' Mai laughed. ''This is how it is for vimmen, alvays. This is the joke the gods play on us. Ve are of the stars but also of the earth. Ve are closest to perfection, but neffer perfect enough.'' She paused. ''Is a funny thing, really. All the aesthetics in America are on the decline: only think of art and architecture. Only female beauty obsesses us. And always more perfect. Ah, the tyranny of beauty.''

''That's so sad. Is it all true?''

''About Ruskin or life?''

''Both.''

''Vell, it is true for both. Marilyn Monroe, I worked on her costume alterations for *Misfits*—that is vere I learn about jeans. She throws up before every take, afraid she is not pretty enough. Vell, and again; Garbo *is* perfect voman. At thirty-five, sees a few lines on her face on the screen, she cries for three days, they must stop filming. People say she didn't care about her looks! She cared so much she spent the rest of her life hiding! Can you imagine? If ve are imperfect, ve are scorned and hate ourselves. If ve are perfect, ve age und *then* are scorned and hate ourselves. You know, ven Greer Garson vas big star, they alvays used her favorite cameraman, Joe Ruttenberg. He vas genius. But after a long vile, she vas unhappy. She called him in for talk. 'You know, Joe,' she said, 'you're not photographing me as vell as you used to.' He said, 'I'm sorry, Greer, but I'm ten years older.' Poor Greer. Dead now.'' Mai sighed.

''Men make these dreams, men run the studios. Alvays the studio says, 'Somethink is wrong. You are not perfect enough for our dreams,' and alvays ve believe them.''

''But why do they do it?'' Jahne cried.

Mai shrugged. ''To control us. Because they are afraid of our power. So they make *us* afraid.''

Jahne sat, feeling very small suddenly, her knees

tucked under her. "What happened to Ruskin's wife?" Jahne asked.

"She stayed virgin for long time. Then, finally, she ran off vith artist. A real man. First he used her as a model. To him, at least, she vas perfection. Hunt, I think, vas the artist, but maybe Millais. She had his baby in the end. You know vat is moral of story?"

Jahne shook her head.

"Stick vith the artists, not the critics," Mai smiled.

Mai helped Jahne prepare for all the wardrobe tests—preliminary filming of her in costume to see how they, and she, looked on the screen. Usually these were done before principal photography began, but everything seemed to be running late on this film, and the tests had just started. Sam had been remote, distracted, and—thank God—Michael wasn't due to show up for another three days.

It was late, past seven, when Mai helped her change and waited while she took off her makeup. And Jahne was bone weary. "I vill go back vith you to the hotel, if you like," Mai offered.

"Yes. Let's have a late dinner together," Jahne suggested.

"A beer. All I vant is a beer," Mai sighed.

They were driven back to Cupertino in silence. Even Danny, the driver who would actually get a screen credit for this job, was tired. And in the darkness of the back seat of the limo, Jahne wondered at who she had become and what she was doing here, in a town she'd never seen, working on a film she didn't really like from a script that wasn't finished. Beside her was the latest draft, the new version photocopied on pink pages. Each version was on a new color, to prevent confusion. How many colors had she already seen? Light-yellow, dark-yellow, green, lavender, blue. Had there been a white version? A gray? She couldn't remember anymore. What happened when they ran out of colors? Well, she reminded herself, Michael Curtiz filmed *Casablanca* without a finished script. The actors didn't know the end until the day they shot it.

She wondered again if she was making a mistake. With the choices she had, why this film?

It was Sam, of course. Like a moth to a flame. She sighed. And, like a moth, would she wind up burned? Hadn't she gone through her transformation so that *she* could be the flame, the center of attraction? Well, her flesh had changed, but her center had not been altered.

Suddenly, there in the back seat of the lush limo, a wave of terrible loneliness and despair rolled over her. She felt overcome, a million miles away from Mai, sitting there beside her in the dark. If I died right now, she thought, who would know me? Who would really know me? What am I doing in this place? She shivered, though it wasn't cold. She felt so truly miserable that only a groan or a wail could relieve her. What would Danny and Mai think of that? For a few more exquisitely painful moments, she restrained herself as they rode along in silence, Jahne crushed by the immense burden of her loneliness. Then they arrived at the hotel.

She was so tired when she got upstairs that she suggested room service to Mai, who cheerfully agreed. Then Jahne showered and got into a robe. Under the hot water, she felt a little bit better, but she also knew she could not go on this way: having more nightmares, sitting through other panic attacks. So, there in the shower stall in that Cupertino hotel, Jahne came to a decision.

When she emerged from the steaming bathroom, Mai had already dismissed the room-service waiter, and dinner was set, waiting, on a rolling table pulled over to the window. They sat down together, the white linen and sparkling silver between them. Jahne sipped at the hot consommé, and then they began on the mesquite-grilled chicken paillard.

"Mai, I want to tell you something."

Mai put down her pilsner glass and looked up, expectant.

"I feel as if I have to tell someone or I'll die," Jahne said, and then she began.

Mai was a good listener. She let Jahne cry, and she waited, silent, during the long pauses while Jahne fought for the words and the courage to continue her story. Mai didn't interrupt, and asked only one question—exactly how Jahne had found Brewster Moore—but she responded through the long tale with little nods and sympathetic sounds. Jahne finally finished, and the two of them sat beside the window, the suburban lights of Cupertino twinkling beneath them. Then Mai sighed, and pushed her chair away from the table. She stood up, walked to the window.

"Vat ve do to ourselves! Vat they do to us!" she whispered. Then she turned and looked at Jahne. Her face showed no shock, no disgust, but only love and sympathy. "My dear, I am so sorry," was all she said.

Jahne actually slept through the night, better than she had slept for a long while. The next morning, Mai was already in the living room of the suite, waiting for her.

"My dear, I vould like very much to talk to you," she said. Jahne nodded. "I haff been up all night thinking of this, of your story. And I must tell you, I think you are in grave danger."

Jahne sat down on the sofa, her heart beating fast. "What do you mean?" she asked.

"When God gives great beauty, he also gives us time to learn what it is useful for. For beauty is power in this vorld. Men haff made it so. And it can be a veapon or a tool. Most of us haff the luxury of time, first to see our power grow, then to test our powers, and at last to see them decline slowly. A few unlucky vimmen vere given great beauty vithout the knowledge that they had it. It kills them. Alvays. Jean Harlow. Marilyn Monroe. Jean Seberg. You know the list."

Mai paused. "I am speaking to you as one who knows. I vas vonce beautiful. But you, my dear. . . You are beautiful outside, but you haff not come to terms vith your power. I have noticed all the strange lapses. You are shy to look at yourself in front of others. Beauties never are. You are pleased ven someone calls you 'pretty.' That is an insult to a beautiful voman. There are many small signs I vondered at." She sighed.

"But you need your power. You need to use it, to

acknowledge it deeply. Because, if you don't, the veapon vill turn against you.''

"Oh, Mai! You're scaring me. What can I do?''

"I don't know. This is indeed a new vonder of science. But I vill help you any vay I can. Maybe I can teach you. If you vant.''

Jahne felt her eyes fill with tears. "Thank you," she said.

32

Marty watched Lila as she talked, her hands moving like Japanese fans, her elegant red nails punctuating the air. They were sitting together on the sofa in Marty's living room, and Lila had just finished telling him about the role she had turned down in the movie *Princess of Thyme*. Then she began to talk about Ara Sagarian, what a disappointment he was. Her eyes, he saw, were wide with excitement; her skin had a rosy cast under her golden tan. All this about a part in a movie. How much more passionate would she be in bed?

Marty had almost given up on Lila. And then, once again, she had called him. This time, Marty was determined that nothing would go wrong. He had sent Sally into town, he'd underplayed everything. No gladioli, no catered dinner. And things were going well. This was simply going to take patience. There was going to come a time when he would have her. Somehow, some way, Marty was going to make love to Lila Kyle. Up to now he had accepted her distance as a temporary thing. But till now it never seemed to waver. Still, *she* had called *him* and she now seemed ready for a friendship, at least. Why now? Go know.

Marty was a lot of things—short, skinny, stoop-shouldered, pockmarked, maybe even ugly—but one thing he wasn't was a shmuck. Lila had almost made a shmuck out of him. Yet now, tonight, he wanted her more than ever. He would have to get the upper hand. Perhaps advice and avuncular patience were the answer.

"Ara is just too old, Lila. Family loyalty is nice and all; you need someone like Sy Ortis to manage you."

"Really, Marty?" she asked. Marty felt a small thrill. He liked it when she listened to his opinions.

"Would you like me to call him and set something up? I'm sure he'd love to talk with you."

"Sure. Great idea." Lila wondered if he'd find out she'd *already* called. Well, she'd tell Ortis' secretary that Marty had told her to.

So, what else could he do to help her, to move the friendship forward? Marty wondered. "Do you want to hear my idea for next year's first episode?" Marty asked. May as well dangle the bait now, he figured.

Lila curled her feet up under her. "Sure. What's your idea?"

"I thought I might have the opening episode with only one girl. Let the other two be flashbacks, or sidebars, maybe not even refer to them. I don't know yet." He didn't have to look at Lila's face to know what she was thinking.

"It might be interesting," she said cautiously. "It might work, depending."

"Depending on what?" he asked, egging her on, getting her into position.

"Well, to be very honest, Marty, its success or failure would depend completely on which girl was being spotlighted. Like, she'd have to be strong enough to carry that kind of weight, but also . . . ."

"I've already decided."

He watched Lila, sensing, almost hearing, her brain whirring. "Yes?" was all she said.

"Uh-huh. You."

Lila shrieked and threw her arms around his neck and hugged him. Touched him for the first time. Marty felt himself tremble. He hoped Lila didn't notice. "Me? Oh, Marty, that's wonderful. You're brilliant. A genius." She sat back. "Tell me more. What's the story line? What's the setting?"

She settled back in the sofa, curled up like a cat on a fireplace cushion, ready to listen to every word, to soak up every gesture.

"It's you leaving home, showing why you've taken to the road."

"Great idea. I love it."

"You'll be walking out on a privileged life: wealth, huge house, cars, servants, absent father, domineering mother . . . everything. Use the Beatles as background. You know, 'She's leaving home after living alone for so many years.' It's been a living hell, and now you're leaving. Sort of a sixties thing, but relevant to the nineties, turning against the eighties."

"I like it, Marty. It's perfect."

"You walk out, leaving all this behind you, to get away from your mother. . . ."

Lila was nodding, her face lit up with anticipation and maybe something else.

It may have been hiatus for Lila, Sharleen, and Jahne, but not for Marty and the production crew of *3/4*. Things were going well with Lila, but Marty had to top last year's ratings. And deal with the problem of Jahne Moore's schedule. Today the production meeting would be brief, and to the point.

"Just keep on doing what you're doing, folks," George Young, the producer, said as he said at every production meeting. "I'm not going to fuck with a winning formula." Not that he could. Sy's contract was ironclad. They couldn't change a hair in the girls' coiffures, even if the show took a nosedive. It was all in Marty's control.

"But there is one thing we hadn't considered, George." Now the guy from publicity was about to come up with another lamebrain idea. Marty sighed. So much for not fucking with a winning formula. Still, he'd sit through the meeting and then try to brainstorm a few more ideas for next season.

"I'm getting calls, lots of calls. Everyone and her sister wants an appearance or a continuing part on this show. Even Katharine Hepburn, can you believe that? Her agent says Kate sees this as *the* woman's TV format for the nineties."

Marty spoke softly. "Fine for a cameo, but not a continuing character. From the beginning, I told you I want unknowns on the show. Only unknowns. And aside from cameos, that's what we got, and that's what's working. Now, with what I've achieved with them, you want to undermine it with Katharine Hepburn, for chrissakes? There's no justification for Hepburn on the show. We look like a documentary. She'll look like an actress, for chrissakes. It's an obvious manipulation." Marty kept his voice from raising. "No way." He looked directly at George Young.

George shook his head. "Except, the opening episode this season has got to really make a statement. It has to say the second season will be better than the first, no matter how good the first was. And we don't want to lose even a tenth of a point, even if *every* other show does that week. In fact, we want to *gain* points. That *hasn't* been done before, and I think this show, of any show, can do it. We need a gimmick, and—quite frankly, Marty —I think a superstar might be just the thing."

Marty made it a point to appear to consider every suggestion a producer made before commenting on it. Even though they were almost always empty, stupid windbags, as George certainly was, he pretended to consider. He did that now. But the silence of the room was broken by George's production assistant, a young girl too young and too pretty to have been hired for her knowledge of the business.

"How about Theresa O'Donnell instead of Hepburn?" the girl asked. "I mean, she's both. She was a superstar and she's Lila's real mother. Documentary. You know?"

No one said anything. Finally, George said, "Lila Kyle's mother?"

"Yeah, sure. Have Lila's mother play her mother."

Marty smiled at the young woman. Theresa O'Donnell! What Marty wouldn't give to work with Theresa O'Donnell! The kid was right. The tie-in was perfect—real, commercial but not overpowering. But would she do it? Theresa O'Donnell hadn't done anything in years. But now, with her daughter on the show . . . Marty was sure Theresa would see both the artistic and the commercial value in it. "What's your name?"

"Leslie Snow," she said.

"I'll consider it, Leslie. Okay, boys and girls. Let's strap on our steel jockstraps and fight the good fight."

33

Sharleen had been calling the telephone number Dobe had given her for two weeks, but hadn't been able to reach him. She was more than a little concerned: she still had his cartons all over the house, and she wasn't sure what she should do if she didn't hear from him. Should I have it picked up and stored somewhere? What might be in those shoes? Well, with all her other worries, she didn't have to think about that now, she decided. She'd give him two more weeks. But still, she'd keep trying.

Sharleen picked up the phone once again and dialed Dobe's number, as she'd done every day since the auction.

This time, though, after two rings, Sharleen heard Dobe at the other end. "Hello." His voice was cheery.

"Dobe Samuels, you got some explaining to do! I've been calling you every day. Where have you been? And what in Sam Hill are you going to do with a hundred dozen women's left shoes?" she asked.

"Sharleen, honey. You did it! How much?" he asked.

"Sixty dollars. Now, you goin' to answer my questions?"

Dobe's voice got serious. "I'm sorry, Sharleen. I had to go out of town on business. I should have called you before."

"What kind of business? Dobe, what do you need those sneakers for?" She tried to sound strict. But Sharleen couldn't stay mad with Dobe. She was just so glad to hear his voice again.

"Not sneakers, honey. The best aerobic shoes money

can buy. See, I'm in the import-export business now, Sharleen," Dobe began. "And I needed to get those 'sneakers' for a customer of mine. But the import duty on *pairs* of shoes is so high, I'd never make any money, so I had the shoes shipped in two separate shipments, one shipment of left feet to Los Angeles, one shipment of right feet to Portland." Dobe paused to chuckle to himself. Sharleen joined him—the idea sounded so silly. "And when no one came forward to claim them and pay the duty, I knew they would go on auction, and that no one would want *left* shoes only, or *right* shoes only. So I get the whole shipment without paying duty, and saved a lot of thousands of dollars. Sweet, ain't it?"

Sharleen didn't say anything for a minute. He was slicker than a greased goose. "Dobe, now you tell me. Was there anythin' in the heels of them shoes? You know, like dope or somethin' like that? Now, tell me true, Dobe Samuels."

Dobe's voice got very serious. "Sharleen, I told you once I would never hurt you. And I won't. I would never —*never*, young lady—do anything to harm *you* or *Dean* in *any* way. It's like . . . it's like you're family, Sharleen. Okay? I need you to trust me."

"Dobe, I do. I honestly do. It's just that I read the other day a guy got off a plane in Miami and got arrested for smugglin' dope. He had it in the heels of his shoes! So I guess I just got a little scared." Now she laughed. "Dobe, you still making them water-into-gas pills?"

Dobe's laugh came back to her over the miles. "I'll tell you all about it when I see you tonight."

"Tonight?" Sharleen asked. "You're going to be here *tonight?*" Lord, her momma was coming over tonight, too! But Dobe would be welcome. Maybe he could even give her advice about Momma. "How long are you going to stay? You're coming to stay for a while, right? Dobe, we got a big house. Wait until you see it. And wait till I tell Dean." She gave him directions to the house, and told him about the security guard outside.

"Sounds like you're in a safe neighborhood, girl. Makes me feel a lot better about you being in that city."

"Dobe, it's more like a prison." She didn't stop to

explain. She wanted to get home and get everything ready. And tell Dean. "Dinner'll be ready, Dobe. And we'll be waitin' for you."

Sharleen hadn't felt this happy since . . . Funny, she couldn't remember feeling this happy—ever.

Filled with new energy, Sharleen went to look for Dean. She walked through the living room, past the dining room and pantry, then into the huge kitchen she was usually too tired to use. "Dean," she called out again, as she walked past the gleaming, untouched stove to the back door, where she peered out the window to the hedge-and-brick-enclosed garden. She knew she would find Dean out there, either working on the flower beds or playing with the dogs. Or both.

Dean had taken the overgrown back yard and transformed it into a garden like you would see in the garden magazines he would look at over and over. Here, in what Sharleen was told was the most expensive four acres of property in America, Dean had created the equivalent of a perfect tiny farm.

Dean knew the name of every single thing he had growing, could even identify the occasional weed that had somehow missed his eye. He had talked to her so often about them, *she* now knew them all by heart. There was a small stand of fruit trees—a mini-orchard, really. Two peaches, four apples, and three pears. And a vegetable garden filled with beefsteak and plum tomatoes, three kinds of lettuce, scallions and onions, cabbage, broccoli, cauliflower, green and yellow beans, carrots, and okra. He even had peas growing up some teepee he'd built of sticks. Beyond the vegetables, there was a small pond stocked with fish—carp, she thought—that Dean fed by hand from the little wooden bridge he'd built across the pond.

Prettiest of all to Sharleen were the flowers. Alongside one brick wall, extending maybe thirty, forty feet, was a perennial bed. He had planted all the old-fashioned flowers that he loved so much, and, in less than a year, he had made them bloom. There were peonies especially for Sharleen, because she favored them, and also larkspur, hollyhocks, and foxglove. There was a stand of delphiniums almost as tall as she was, but Dean considered them a cheat, since he'd bought them potted and blooming and only transplanted them. Still, they were gorgeous.

Beyond the perennials, around the lawn, he had annuals bedded out—pansies, johnny-jump-ups, lots of zinnias, their colors sweeping the rainbow, strong-smelling marigolds, and nasturtiums. The grass was trimmed perfectly; he did it himself. And a rose garden, his pride and joy, had center place. But despite his garden, Dean was glum. Sharleen could tell.

Well, she knew what they'd do to cheer him up. They'd have a barbecue for Dobe and Momma. She saw him romping with the three pups on the emerald lawn. "Howdy," she called to him as she walked across the grass toward him. "Whatcha doin'? Teaching the girls new tricks?"

"Yeah, and watch this, Sharleen." He was like a little boy. Whenever he got the three dogs to do somethin' new, he always presented the trick to her like a bouquet of flowers. Just as well, because Dean hated to cut the flowers out of the beds. "They're dead once you do that," he'd explained. And to Sharleen, the dog tricks were just as good, if not better than a bouquet. She liked to see him happy, and she knew she had news for him that would really get him goin'. But she decided to wait a little bit before she told him who was comin' tonight. He'd be pesterin' her the rest of the day if she told him now.

Dean called the three dogs and made them sit in a row. It took some coordinatin', but they finally were all sittin' at the same time, their eyes turned up adoringly at Dean. He stood back and took a ball from his pocket and called out, "Cara, go git it, girl," and Cara ran and jumped into the air and grabbed the ball in her teeth. "Now, give it to Clover; good girl." And Cara walked over to Clover and dropped the ball in front of the other puppy.

"Clover, give the ball to Crimson," he instructed, and Clover picked up the ball in her mouth and walked to Crimson and dropped the ball, then walked back to her place. After their performance, he was beaming, and gave each of them treats from his pocket.

"That sure is something, Dean. How long did it take you to teach them that?"

Dean was stroking the dogs. "Just a few days. Ain't they smart, Sharleen? Now they know eight tricks. Smart dogs," he said to them, then stood up and looked at Sharleen. "You tired, Sharleen? Let's go inside, I'll get you a pop."

Sharleen sat at the kitchen table sipping the cold soda from the can. She could see something was botherin' Dean, and considered telling Dean the surprise she had for him. But first she wanted to know what was wrong.

"Momma was here yesterday, while you were out," he said, as if answering her unasked question.

"I forgot to tell you she was comin'. I left an envelope for her on the table. She run short," Sharleen explained. "Was she . . . okay?"

"Yeah, she was, but not for long, I could tell. All she wanted was to get the envelope and leave. And she asked a lot of questions about . . ." He paused. "Well—about stuff. Like how we slept together." Dean paused, then looked directly at Sharleen. "Sharleen, it ain't like I thought it was goin' be, having Momma back. Like bein' a family. It's like she's someone different. I don't remember her like this. She's old, and smells like whiskey all the time. It's like she ain't *our* momma, you know?"

Sharleen did know. She *wasn't* like their momma. Not the momma she had known when she was a kid. *Before* she left them. All these years, Sharleen and Dean had believed that their momma was going to get them some help or something, and even when she didn't come back, they kept believing.

Now it was hard to believe anything good about Momma. She was a drunk, and only thought about herself. She'd quit beauty school, and it looked like she was planning to live off of them. Sharleen remembered what Jahne had told her about not trusting *anybody*. Would Momma talk to newspapers about Dean and her? What a terrible thought! Well, Sharleen wasn't exactly sure why, but she didn't trust her momma. She did trust Dean. And Dobe.

"Dean, honey, have I got good news for you," Shar-

leen suddenly said, then sat back and crossed her arms,
a teasing smile on her face.

Dean opened his eyes wider. "What, Sharleen?"

Sharleen stood up and started to leave the kitchen.
"Oh, I think I changed my mind. I don't think I'll tell you
about the surprise. About who's coming tonight."

"Momma?" Dean asked, his face dark.

"Momma and someone else," Sharleen sang out, teasing, "Me to know, you to find out."

Dean smiled and jumped up and ran after her, and
grabbed her around the waist as she got to the stairs.
Sharleen shrieked and squirmed her way out of Dean's
grasp and ran up the steps. "No, Dean, I ain't telling
you," she yelled, and continued to run. Dean grabbed
her by one foot and got her down.

"Oh, yes, you are," he said, now straddling Sharleen,
"or I'm goin' tickle you to death." He held one hand up,
squiggling his fingers threateningly.

Sharleen shrieked again, and begged Dean not to do it
to her. "Okay, then, you gotta tell me the surprise." He
loosened his grip, but didn't let Sharleen stand.

She gave up. "But first take one guess. And it ain't
only one person. It's two." Dean looked perplexed.
"What two people would you want to see more than
anyone else in the whole world if you had your wish?"

Dean's eyes squinted as he tried to think. "Oprah and
Dobe?" he finally asked, his question spoken softly.

"Right, honey. Oprah and Dobe are coming here to
visit. Tonight!"

Dean scooped Sharleen up in his big arms, and ran up
the stairs with her, two at a time. He was yelling like a
hound dog in the bayou. "Sharleen, wait till I show Dobe
the dogs! And all the tricks they know. Oprah, she's
going to love them, even if they're only babies." He
kicked open their bedroom door and dropped her on the
huge bed. "Yippee!" he screeched.

That night, the four of them sat around the dining-room
table, the first time since Momma's dinner that they had
laid out a spread like this. Left on the table were remains
of the fried chicken, ribs, and fixings Sharleen had had

prepared, along with the fresh vegetables from Dean's garden. Dobe was sitting back, wiping his fingers on a wet towel Sharleen had given him. Momma seemed to be staring at Dobe, a big smile on her face. Sharleen wondered how much she'd had to drink. "You are one hell of a man, Mr. Dobe Samuels. I bet you've put a smile on a lot of ladies' faces." Flora Lee smirked. All through dinner, she kept laughin' at his jokes and sayin' how smart he was. Dean hadn't noticed, thank the Lord, because he had Oprah's head on his lap the entire meal, and was feeding her a piece of food for every bite he took.

"Did you get enough for the guys at the gate?" Dean asked Sharleen. Usually he made sure before he started eating that the security guards got food also, but tonight, with Momma and Oprah and Dobe here, he'd been so excited, he forgot until now.

"Sure did, Dean. I got something for them, too. Just like you told me." Sharleen looked over at Dobe and saw him smiling.

"Well, I've got to go to the little girls' room," Flora Lee declared, and left the table, her walk affected by all that she had drunk.

Dean got up and began to gather the rib bones. Oprah began dancing around him, and the three pups joined her. "Let's go, girls. Let's go out," he coaxed. "When I come back after taking them for a walk, you all want to watch *The Andy Griffith Show* with me, Dobe? I got practically all of them on tape, if you want to start from the beginning."

"Sure. I love that show. I love what's-his-name—the barber. Floyd." Dean was rushed out the door by the pack of dogs, who knew they were going to have fun. "He's one sweet boy," Dobe said. "And it looks like you got one sweet life, from what I see and read."

Sharleen looked at Dobe. "Dobe, it ain't how it looks." She had to tell him, had to tell *someone,* what it was really like. She didn't want to complain. But Dobe was the only person who would understand that just because things got better didn't mean that things got good.

Sharleen told him the whole story. How she got the job

as an actress on TV, and what it had been like since. Not all the good stuff—that he already knew—but what she had lost when she gained so much. She never thought that the success, the money, would be a trade-off, a phrase Jahne had once used that Sharleen now understood all too well. If she had been asked back then, when she was offered the job, she would have said that she had nothing to give up in return for great fame and wealth.

Now she knew different. She had lost her freedom. "I can't go out by myself. I can't go to a movie like other people. I can't go into a supermarket, even though I can afford to buy the whole store. I have to go everywhere in a car with a driver and a security guy. A *bodyguard*, for goodness' sakes, Dobe. *I* need a *bodyguard!*" Sharleen wasn't concerned whether she was sounding ungrateful or not, or whining. Dobe understood. "When I'm workin', I'm tired all the time. Men are always hittin' on me. Worse than ever. And I have no one to talk to."

"What about your momma, Sharleen? Now that you found her. Can't you talk to her?"

Sharleen wiped tears from her eyes on the linen napkin and grunted a laugh. "*We* didn't find *her*. *She* found *us*. I never thought we was goin' see her again, although we wanted to. Then, one day, she shows up at the studio. At first, I was real happy. Now? Now she's never sober long enough to hold a conversation with. She just comes by for her money, then goes back to the bars, where she throws it all around. Dean don't like her. I know it's a sin, Dobe, but I can't blame him. 'Cause she don't want to be nice. She don't, Dobe. I give her lots of money. But it seems there's never enough. She keeps coming back for more and more. And she's started askin' questions. Nosy, like. And it upsets Dean. He still remembers her as our momma, but now . . . well, he don't like her. Momma ain't Momma no more." A tear rolled down Sharleen's cheek. "I wish she'd never found us."

Dobe stood up and went over to Sharleen. He pulled her out of her chair, put her head on his shoulder and his arms around her. Sharleen felt herself grow limp in Dobe's arms, and she cried like she hadn't cried since she was a little girl. Since then, she'd always had to be strong, to take care of herself and of Dean.

"Your momma's had a little too much to drink. Why don't I just take her home and make sure she don't get into any trouble."

Mutely, Sharleen nodded. Somehow, she already felt much better.

34

I have never had the advantage of beauty. Somehow, you're not surprised, right? Who ever heard of a beautiful writer? Writing—even the kind I do—is hard and lonely work. Who'd do it when they could be out getting laid? Not that I haven't had my share of men. A bad first marriage (that's where I got Richie as a last name) and then several bad affairs. But beauty wouldn't have ensured any better men. Just different ones. I figure it like this: Beautiful women have a better early life. Then they have to suffer more later. Us plain ones have a tougher beginning—you know, no date for the prom, and the usual heartbreak—but if we work at it, life does get better. Maybe.

Hollywood has made it worse for all of us women: the expectations are higher and more unrealistic than ever while the "life expectancy" of an actress is shorter. Female stars used to reign for a long time. A decade was a short career. Now a year is. Men want novelty. Younger, fresher, newer. And there is always some kid ready to fill the void.

There aren't any women—with the notable exception of Barbra—who can open a movie. The days of the Crawfords, the Hayworths, the Grables and Hepburns and the like are not just over, they are almost forgotten. And the women on our screens today most often play whores or victims or sluts or long-suffering secondary roles. Dehumanized, turned into a body or a stereotype, a simpleton or a cliché, the actresses are angry and sad. And none of them are bankable.

But the saddest ones are not the ever-more-quickly fading stars. The saddest are the body doubles. The girls who are not quite good enough all over for a part, but whose breasts or stomachs or asses or legs get to star in a feature. Each time they get called in by the director for the close-up of their navel, there are a hundred technicians and movie people glorifying a piece of them and insulting their face and talent. Think about it. Would you like to play Julia Roberts' belly in Pretty Woman or Jane Fonda's breasts in Klute?

Most body doubles are paid very little and have to sign an agreement swearing them to secrecy. After all, none of the stars want to publicly admit their bellies and breasts aren't good enough. Spoils the illusion. The illusion that you, dear Reader, buy.

Anyway, there's an old adage in Hollywood: the director gets to fuck the star; the AD only gets the body double. And Birth of a Star would be no exception to that rule.

A. Joel Grossman was more than eager to do what he could for Sam. But it wasn't as easy as he had expected to curry favor on the Birth shoot. He'd been lucky to get the job, which so often went to the director's sidekick or his longtime bag man. Walking into an assistant directorship on an important film like this one was sheer luck, made possible only because Sam was such a loner and had no sidekicks or pals. That was the problem now. Sam gave him little to do, barely talked to him, didn't seem to trust him. Oh, Christ, let's face it, Sam didn't trust anyone.

And things weren't going so well. In his opinion, Michael McLain was a putz, and a washed-up old has-been. Plus, the rumor was that he had been shtupping Jahne Moore, but now it looked like Sam was interested. Although the rumor was that Sam had been shtupping April Irons as well. Or perhaps that was before he was shtupping Jahne Moore. Joel sighed and shook his head. How did these men let a little thing like sex get in the way of their careers? He couldn't understand it. Anyway, something was making the shoot go particularly slowly and be as difficult as hell. There wasn't one take in ten with any warmth or feeling. But Sam, of course, wasn't asking for his help, though Joel would have been happy to give it.

So, when the call came, Sam sounding so urgent about the need for a body double, Joel felt it was a godsend, his chance to do something, anything, that would give him a shot at the next job, through either Sam or the studio. Sam had asked for his help in casting the body double, something he could do. "Total security on this," Sam had insisted. "No middlemen, no publicity. I mean it. Can you do it?" "A mere bagatelle," he'd answered. Now he was desperately going through his messy pile of cards and torn bits of paper, looking for the girl's name. The one that Paul Grasso had brought over that time. The one with the so-so face and the body that would melt molybdenum. He hadn't used her, but he knew that in Hollywood she couldn't afford to hold that against him.

There it was! Adrienne Godowski. Jesus, what a name! He picked up the telephone and stepped out onto the veranda overlooking the little sapphire-blue pool. He punched Adrienne's number into the receiver.

"Hullo?" a voice said. Christ, it sounded like she'd just woken up. What time was it? He looked at his Oyster Rolex.

"This is Joel Grossman. Adrienne Godowski, please."

"Who's this?" It was a woman, but the voice was so gravelly, it was hard to tell at first. Christ, was she drunk? Or dying?

"Joel Grossman. I interviewed Adrienne once, through Paul Grasso. Is this Mrs. Godowski?"

There was a pause, then a deep cough. "Oh, yes, Mr. Grossman." The woman's voice sounded like it was an effort to speak. "What can I do for you?"

"I have a part in a movie, small part, no lines, and I wanted to see Adrienne for it. Can she come over right away?" He gave her the address.

"I'll put her in a cab. I got a very bad virus or I'd bring her myself." The woman coughed again, as if to prove the fact. "She'll be there in twenty minutes," she slurred.

Fifteen minutes was more like it. "My mother said you would pay the cab. She didn't have any change," Adrienne announced, as she stood on the front steps looking at him. Joel went out and paid the driver in the beat-up Chevy.

Adrienne was still standing outside the door when he returned. "Let's go inside," he said. "Got your résumé with you?"

Adrienne dug into the large, beaten-up leather bag, pulled a dog-eared sheet of paper out, and handed it to him. He looked at her résumé. Jesus. L.A. was the kind of place where an actress would put a CAT scan down as a film credit, but this was ridiculous. What the hell was "lead . . . *Girls in White Satin*" supposed to mean? If it was a lead role, why didn't it have a name? He looked at the misspellings and the ragged margin.

"You need a manager," he said.

"I got one. My mother." Her tone was flat, affectless.

"No, I mean a professional," he told her, though he knew it was useless.

"No one could be more loyal than a girl's mother," Adrienne said, but she said it in the same dead tone, as if she were merely parroting something repeated to her a million times. Was she all right in the head? She gave him the impression of being hypnotized, or mildly retarded, or both. And it gave him the oddest reaction: he could feel the boner growing against his pants.

He decided it was best to ignore both her answer and his hard-on and just get on with it. "So, we need a body double for Jahne Moore, and when the director asked me, I said you'd be perfect for it." What the hell, build it up a little. "He had someone else in mind, but I'm pretty sure I can get it for you. I need some pictures, though." He stopped.

"I got these," she said, and handed over a messy pile. He rifled through them.

"No, no. I mean some special pictures. Ones where we'll have to show all of your body. Because you'll be a body double. You'll do all the love scenes. And some other stuff.'' He stopped, waiting for a reaction, but there was none. ''So is it okay?'' he asked.

''I have to ask my mother,'' Adrienne told him, and walked across the room to the phone. Her legs moved so smoothly that, from behind, it was almost like watching the ocean recede. If her face and brain left something to be desired, that perfect ass, those lean, coltish legs, those incredibly slender ankles left him with nothing but desire. He licked his lips nervously. When the dick stands up, the brains go into the ground, he told himself, but his dick didn't seem to be listening.

She was only on the phone briefly, then turned back to him. ''Okay,'' she said. ''My mom says it's okay.'' And then she reached up and began to unbutton her shirt.

''Uh, listen. Let's do it out on the deck,'' he said. ''I need the light. '' And some air. And the *camera*, he reminded himself, and went into the hall closet to get it.

When he returned, she was standing in the middle of the living room, her clothes in a pile on the chair beside her. The only thing she was wearing was those cheap, scuffed white shoes, the pointed toes curling up, showing a bit of the sole. Her body was perfect, and its whiteness glowed in the center of the almost empty room. ''Where do you want me?'' she asked him.

''Outside,'' he answered, not surprised to hear the hoarseness in his voice. She turned, and he followed that perfect ass out onto the deck. It was the contradictions of her body that created the tension he felt when he looked at her: she was lean yet curved, toned yet soft, long yet round.

He posed her on a wooden chaise longue. He had no cushions for it, but her white body against the rough wood stirred him deeply, and he figured it had to work on Sam, unless the guy was made of concrete. He shot a roll, thirty-six exposures. He had her stretch out with her arms over her head; then he asked her to hold a breast in each hand, then to sit up. He tried to keep her face out of most of the shots. ''Sit at the edge of the chaise now,'' he suggested. ''Put both arms behind you.''

She did as she was told. He wondered how far her docility would go. She looked at him mildly, her face

636

registering neither disapproval nor pleasure. "Hook your legs under each leg of the chaise," he told her.

"Like this?" she asked, as she spread her knees.

"Yes," he said, and squatted down, angling the camera up. A beaver shot. What was possessing him? He could never show *this* to Sam.

He felt as if he had been privy to a secret, a great mystery, and by exposing it to the sun, to his eyes, to his lens, he was desecrating it at the same time as he worshipped it.

"Look, I want to splash some water on you? Okay? There is a scene in the water."

"Okay," she agreed, "but it's kinda cool. I don't want to get sick, like my ma."

"Don't worry. We're almost done." He went to the hose beside the house, shut the nozzle, but turned on the faucet. He approached her, the hose dragging behind him, a long tail. He pointed the nozzle at her belly and pressed the trigger down hard.

The jet of cold water arched up into the sun and gushed down onto her flat white belly. It contracted, and the water splashed up to her perfect pointy tits, the doll-pink nipples immediately hardening, one pointing to downtown L.A., the other directly at Joel. "Oh!" she gasped, and he released his grip on the nozzle and threw it aside. He watched as the water ran down her belly, glistening on the soft brown patch of hair, wetting her between her legs. His penis pressed so hard against his zipper that he felt dizzy.

You are taking your life in your hands, he told himself, sounding like his own grandma. You French-kiss her and you may wind up with French foreign lesions. Before you put that in your mouth, do you know where it's been?

"Come inside," he said, against all his better instincts. "Come inside. I want to fuck you," he groaned. As he knew she would, she stood up and began to follow him. He stumbled through the open door, through the living room into the bedroom. He walked around the unmade bed to the side table, opened the drawer. Thank God. Four condoms. He grasped at one, turned, but she wasn't behind him. Had he misunderstood? Wasn't she coming?

He walked back out to the living room just in time to see her hanging up the phone. Christ! Had she called for a cab? Had she called the cops?

She was just hanging up the phone. She looked up at him. "My mother says as long as I got the job it's okay," Adrienne said, and began to walk toward him.

35

Jahne sat, protected from the lights both by a creme block and the white canvas umbrella, staring at the script. Her heart was pounding in her chest. Today was the first day of shooting with Michael McLain, and she was nervous. Nervous about seeing him, about April Irons' visit today, about the script that still wasn't working. Sy Ortis had been at least partly right. The working script for *Birth of a Star* wasn't awful, only pedestrian, but Jahne hadn't been prepared for the rewrites. Each day, new versions were distributed, and each one worse.

While the story hadn't changed, the settings and style had. And now there were three—count 'em, *three*— scenes with nudity. She put her hand to her chest, as if it would do any good to cover her breasts now. Well, at least she wouldn't be the one who had to expose herself in front of a couple of hundred strangers. Sy and her contract had seen to that. But she felt sorry for the poor, anonymous girl who would.

The San Francisco soundstage, large as an airplane hangar, was chaotic. Cables crossed the floor in a demented roadmap. Equipment of every conceivable sort was heaped about. Grips called out to one another, barely audible over the noise of hammering and rendered invisible by the shower of sparks from arc welding that fell in a bright cascade from somewhere on a catwalk overhead.

Mai had told Jahne how different movies were from television, but she couldn't have imagined the scale without seeing it. From the lushness of her trailer to the vastness of the soundstage to the numbers of crew, the enterprise was intimidating. Jahne thought of the little band of players in St. Malachy's basement, and of the cast of two in the original production of *Jack and Jill*. How had Sam learned to handle so much so soon? And could he handle it? Jahne had always admired him as a director, but this was too much for anyone to manage.

She made her way through the maze of workers and crates and props and lights, the little AD at her side. Jahne, always polite, remembered that his name was Joel Something. She turned to him. "Joel, who will attend this meeting?"

"Oh, Sam, April, Michael, Bob, and Samantha Reiger."

"April Irons will be there?"

"Yeah. It's unusual, but this is such a big-budget baby that I guess she wants to see it off on the right foot." He flashed an ingratiating grin at her. "Not that it won't be a huge success with you in it," he told her. "I really admire your work."

Jahne nearly laughed. After almost a year, she still couldn't get used to the L.A. crowd's talking seriously about dreck like *Three for the Road*. And sometimes it was hard to figure if they, too, knew it was dreck, in which case they were toadies, or if they actually did admire it, in which case they were subliterate. Joel, she could see, was a toady. That made it easy for her. She didn't have to feel sorry for him or like him.

She sighed. "Tired?" he asked. Christ, the little worm was right in her face! Jahne knew the biggest job of an AD was babysitting the stars. Well, she didn't need a sitter. What she did need was a little more confidence in her judgment and fewer butterflies in her stomach. Her fear was that Sy might—just possibly—be right: that *Birth of a Star* was nothing but a potboiler. And Sy called her every other day to remind her over and over how important her first picture was. "If this goes down the toilet, you'll be a TV queen forever," he had said. "Totally ABC's *Movie of the Week*. Coming down with the newest disease or vamping through some stupid romance. Strictly Jane Seymour territory." Involuntarily, Jahne put her hand to her stomach.

"You okay?" Joel asked.

"Fine," she told him, and her annoyance showed in her tone of voice.

But she wasn't fine. Because she had worked so hard, had suffered such pain, had been so brave, all so that she could get here. Here. On this set. And, if she was really honest with herself, she knew she hadn't made the best choice. If this movie bombed, she'd gone through the surgery, the humiliation, the loneliness, the fear. . . . for nothing. She'd never get to play any of the great roles. She'd wind up nothing more than a TV whore, which, in her cosmology, was several steps lower than a Broadway gypsy. And she'd picked this role, against the advice of her TV director and her agent, for one reason.

So she could be with Sam, the man who had betrayed her once already.

She felt the butterflies dance in her stomach. Why should she be nervous, seeing Michael? *He* was the one who had behaved like a dog, not her. And if he had never called her, she certainly hadn't wanted to be called. So why, now, did *she* feel almost—well—ashamed?

Ridiculous! she told herself, but the butterflies didn't go away. Nor did the curiosity about April Irons and Sam. What *was* their relationship? If she watched them, wouldn't she know? Couldn't she tell who Sam slept with, after all this time?

Sam looked good on the set. Even leaner, his mouth more deeply parenthesized by the long dimples on either side, his jaw sharper. He was still tanned, and it still suited him, but it didn't cover the darkness under his eyes.

Jahne wondered if he actually sat beside some pool, his face turned to the sun, Bain de Soleil with an SPF of 8 slathered on his face. Somehow, it put her off, thinking of him indulging in the most ordinary of Hollywood cosmetic improvements. As if *she* were in a position to judge anyone else's vanity. She almost sighed again but caught herself before Joel had a chance to inquire about her health, digestion, bowel movements, or the state of her spiritual life.

Sam looked up from the conversation he was having with the best boy and a grip. He didn't smile. Instead, he did that thing where his mouth stayed still but his eyes warmed. Jahne felt as if she could be tanned by the warmth. Oh, Christ! she told herself. Don't be a fool.

She walked up to the group that sat under one of the location tents, slightly removed from the hive of activity. There was April, looking cool and elegant as ever, plus two other actors, and Michael. As she approached, Michael turned and looked up at her.

"Jahne!" he said, and stood up. "Jahne!" And before she could move, before she could react, he had his arms around her, and his mouth on her mouth! She was so surprised that she was speechless. Michael kept one arm on her back and walked her over to the group. She joined them and couldn't help noticing April's satisfied smile and Sam's eyes on her. She couldn't help it—under his scrutiny she blushed like a schoolgirl.

"Sit here, next to me," Michael cooed, and laid his arm proprietarily across the back of her chair. Jahne sat down, conscious of all of them watching her.

Blessedly, the AD came over with a question for Sam. In that moment, Bob Grantly and Samantha Reiger, two supporting cast members, introduced themselves and said hello. Then the meeting began.

Jahne could barely keep her eyes on the script. Michael seemed to think that nothing had changed between them, or that, if she was upset by his disappearance, she would completely forget it now that he was back! Of course, he didn't know that she knew about Sharleen, the matching necklaces, the calls to Lila—and perhaps a necklace for Lila as well. Well, Jahne didn't care who Michael fucked as long as he kept his hands off her and didn't rape her friends. She sat there, longing to wipe the feeling of his lips off of hers, so angry that the script in her hands trembled. The meeting seemed interminable.

At last, they were through. April wished them luck and left to fly back to L.A. It was then that Michael turned to her.

"How have you been?"

"Just fine. How about you? And Sharleen? And Lila?"

she asked, her voice as cold and hard as she knew how to make it.

He had the grace to pause, at least for a moment, the smile gone from his face. Then he sighed and shook his head. "What's that line?" he asked. "Hell hath no fury . . ." he murmured, and his smile turned to a smirk.

" 'Hell hath no fury like a woman raped,' Michael? Is that the quote you're looking for?"

His world-famous blue eyes grew cold as the north Pacific. "What are you talking about?"

"Sharleen Smith. Drunk and struggling."

Michael barked out a laugh. "Come off it, Jahne. I dated her once. The little Okie *begged* me for it."

Jahne blinked. For a moment—half a moment—she wondered if perhaps Sharleen had exaggerated or misunderstood. Then, disgusted with him and herself, she looked him in the eye. "You're a pig!" she said.

"You're a slut," he answered, and began to turn away.

All at once, her fury at him, at all men who did what they wanted with women and then walked away, seemed to rise up in her. Before he'd taken three steps, she was beside him and had grabbed at his shoulder. He turned, surprised, and she lifted her right arm, swung it back, and then slapped him, as hard as she could, across his world-famous left profile. The sound her hand made as it connected was loud and frightening. All of the crew stopped what they were doing. Silence fell over the place. Michael, stunned, lifted both hands to his face and stifled a groan.

Without a word, Jahne turned and walked off to her trailer.

"Jesus Christ!" Sam cried. And ran over to Michael's side.

The pandemonium had calmed down. Sam had run back and forth, between a raging Michael and a frigid Jahne, until one had been soothed with both an ice pack and an apology, and the other bribed with a promise that she didn't have to see Michael anywhere except on the set. And an invitation to dinner with her director.

The crew had been buzzing all afternoon, but now, as

evening came on, the scandal was calming down. Sam sighed, flipped the visor on the car to block the rays of the setting sun, and turned to Jahne.

"Couldn't you wait until after the wrap to hit him?" Sam asked plaintively, but then he had to laugh. "Not that he doesn't deserve it, but it could make filming rather —how you say—*difficile?*"

Jahne shrugged. For once, she'd behaved badly, and this trip was her reward. She had actually seen nothing of California in the year since she had relocated. She'd arrived in L.A., got the Melrose job and then *Three for the Road*. She'd been on back lots and gritty locations like Louisiana and Idaho for *3/4*, but had seen nothing of the Golden State. Now she would see something, if she could keep her eyes off Sam. He was taking her out, going to show her around, he said, before dinner. It was supposed to be a meeting to calm her down, to discuss the script, he said. Now that Michael's face had been packed in ice and Sam had spoken to him, it was her turn. She smiled. She actually felt good. She'd never in her life acted like a prima donna, she'd never caused a scandal. And now she wasn't being punished for it, she was being "handled." She smiled and looked at Sam again. It's probably just business, she told herself, but he *had* asked her out. He had. And, like a teenager waiting for her first date, she wondered if he liked her. But that's the old Mary Jane. I should only be worrying about whether *I* like *him*.

Sam had picked her up a few minutes early, as if he couldn't wait to be with her. Stop reading into things, she'd told herself sternly. Just stop. But she couldn't. She slid into the low seat of his rented Nissan 300ZX Turbo and breathed the same air he had been breathing. Her lungs hurt. *Eine kleine Nachtmusik* was playing on the sound system, filling the car. Sam had stepped around to the driver's side and folded his lanky frame into the black leather seat. As he accelerated away from the hotel, she felt herself pushed back into the seat, almost as if his weight were already on her.

"I'd thought we'd go to Santa Cruz for dinner," he said now. "Have you ever been?"

"No," she told him. "I don't know Northern California at all."

"Never been to Muir Woods? Never been to the wine country? No? I'll have to take you. It's wonderful."

She tried to remember if he used to say "wonderful," back in New York. She didn't think so. But then, not much had been wonderful. Except maybe *Jack and Jill.* Except maybe their time together. And, then, she thought, maybe it had only been wonderful for *her.* Hadn't he just said something about taking her someplace? He meant to see her again. He *assumed* he would. And she felt both angry and breathless.

Well, of course he'll see me. Why shouldn't he? I'm the star of his latest production. He's a star fucker. And I'm pretty. I'm sixty-seven thousand dollars' worth of pretty. Why shouldn't he expect to see me again? And why should it make me happy that he does? I ought to learn to take this stuff for granted, as Mai told me to. She sighed.

"Well, that doesn't sound like a delighted response," Sam said dryly.

"No, I guess not. But I *am* delighted. I'd love to see Napasonomamendocino, or whatever the place is."

Sam laughed. "Those are *three* places, and the third one is the prettiest. I know a little inn at a small winery there. It's just great. A sort of merging of all that's best in Europe and California."

Jahne wondered if April Irons had introduced him to it. And if it was before or after he had agreed to cast Crystal Plenum in the role of Jill.

"You know, Jahne, your conduct on the set today won't make this production any easier to get off the ground."

"He's an animal."

"It wasn't very professional," he admonished.

"It wasn't very professional for him to grab me and tongue-kiss me. We broke it off months ago. He's a pig. And I don't want to talk about it anymore."

The car took a sharp curve, and Jahne felt Sam's shoulder brush against hers. The soft leather of his jacket was warm against her bare skin. She felt a chill run up her back.

Something had changed in the air between them. Somehow, she *knew* that he was interested in her—that he wanted her. Was it her slap at Michael that had done it? Was it because she'd acted like a brat? Or like a woman? She didn't know. But something *had* changed.

Well, this time, she swore, whatever happened, it would be different. As the French put it, this time she would be the one who was kissed, not the one who did the kissing. This time, Sam would love her more than she'd ever let herself love him. She'd no longer play Miss Havisham. It was Estella all the way.

They broke free of the traffic and moved onto the coast road. Jahne marveled at the dry brown hills—austere but beautiful in their way. The wind from the Pacific rippled the long grasses as Jahne had always imagined wheat fields to ripple, a beautiful undulation, a sexual wave that fascinated her.

"Where exactly are we going?" she forced herself to ask, but she didn't really care. Cupped in the comfort of the car, the Mozart rippling around her, Sam beside her at last, she only wanted this moment, this final reward, to continue forever. Her great expectations were at last coming true. Let me remember this, she told herself. Let me remember it and know that once I was perfectly content.

"I'm taking you to a restaurant in Santa Cruz," he said as the sports car effortlessly crested each hill. "It's sort of the end of the line, the last stop on the train for all the wanderers and frontiersmen and westward-ho–ers. When they got to Santa Cruz, there was nowhere farther west to go but into the ocean."

"Did some of them drop into it like lemmings?" she asked.

"Probably the better genetic stock started swimming for Asia. The chickens stayed behind."

"So Santa Cruz is based on chicken stock, like a good cassoulet?" she asked.

He laughed. "You're a little too clever, aren't you?

Santa Cruz is the end of the road, kind of like Key West. Ever been there?''

She'd been there with Sam, on the one and only vacation they'd ever taken together. All at once, she was flooded with the memory of their walk down Duval Street, the beer in Sloppy Joe's, their visit to Hemingway's house. That was a time when she thought he'd loved her. For no reason, tears filled her eyes. She'd been through a lot today. She was not handling this as easily as she had planned. She turned her head toward the sere hills and blinked the tears away.

"Yes. Route One ends there," she managed.

"Well, so do a lot of people's dreams. Santa Cruz is like that. And it's been the location of a lot of films—they did the last *Dirty Harry* here, and then *The Lost Boys*."

"It sounds kind of gruesome."

"No. It's got a real down-at-the-heels charm. Rather like my own." He smiled.

She could almost feel his warmth, his seductive "like-me-even-though-I'm-trouble" come-on envelop her. His profile, hawk-nosed and as clean as a paper silhouette, was dark against the sunset behind him. In the ruddy light, his skin glowed. She wondered how it felt. She'd have loved to reach out and stroke his face, feel his cheek under her palm, run a finger across his wide mouth. She clutched her hands together in her lap and looked away from him.

The Mozart CD ended, and Sam slid in a new disk. Tom Waits' raspy voice filled the car. Sam had introduced her to Waits' clever lyrics and almost unbearable vocals years ago.

"Ever heard Tom Waits?" he asked now.

How many women had he asked that question of? she wondered. Had Crystal Plenum liked Tom Waits? Had April Irons? Oh, God, she thought. I'm going to drive myself crazy if I keep this up. Just let it alone, Jahne. Tell him no.

But she couldn't stop herself. "Yes," she said. "And the piano sounds drunk," she added, misquoting a lyric.

Sam smiled in delight. Her friend Molly used to call

this "the Seiko phenomenon"—when two people met and discovered the mundane things they had in common, they all seemed to be preordained and of earthshaking significance. "You use Paul Mitchell shampoo? I do, too! *You* wear a Seiko? *I* wear a Seiko!" She laughed at the thought.

"What's so funny?" he asked.

"Nothing."

He looked at her. "Mysteries, mysteries," he muttered, a line from *Jack and Jill*.

"I liked your play," she told him.

"You saw it?" he asked. "The play, not the film?"

"I never saw the film, only the play. I loved it."

"I'll get you the tape of the movie. Maybe we could . . ."

"I'd rather not," she said quickly. *That* would be more than she could bear. She moved on to another subject, any subject. "Is this Santa Cruz?" she asked, as they finally topped the last of the seemingly innumerable hills and looked down on a collection of brightly colored lights, like the contents of a little girl's jewelry box spilled along the coastline. Sam nodded.

"I remember the opening of *Lost Boys* now. I think they used a long shot like this," she said.

"Great opening," Sam agreed. "It was shot from the ocean side, though. Too bad the rest of the movie didn't live up to it."

She nodded. "What other openings did you think were great?" she asked.

"*Once Upon a Time in America*. It had that opium dream. . . ."

"With the phone ringing!" she continued.

"Yeah, that was masterful. What ones did you like?"

"*The Pope of Greenwich Village*," she told him.

" 'Summer Wind'! Frank Sinatra singing and Mickey Rourke shooting his cuffs. Great opening!" he agreed approvingly. "So, what movies did you hate?"

"*Internal Affairs*. Every man was brutal, and every woman was a whore. Richard Gere hit seven actresses, and Andy Garcia, playing the good guy, beat up his wife."

Sam nodded. "Realistic, though," he said.

"Oh, come on. All the cops' wives were a size six. Tell me *that's* realistic."

Sam laughed. "Okay, okay." He looked at her, his eyes warm. "You've got good instincts," he smiled, and she was angry to find how much his approval pleased her.

He pulled the car into a parking spot, and stilled the engine. Then he turned to look at her again, deeply and carefully, with his director's eye. She remembered him looking at her this way, so very deeply, almost *through* her, just before he cast her as Jill. She tried not to cringe, but now surely, *surely* he'd recognize her. Now he'd know, and it would all come tumbling out; for good or ill, it would all be told.

"You're a deep one, Jahne," was all he said, and he slid out of the car, coming around to help her out.

Santa Cruz was diverting, a sort of decadent playland, a scenic boardwalk nestled on the ocean, with just that undercurrent of carny danger. Sam took her to an indifferent Italian restaurant where they split a bottle of indifferent wine, ate pasta, and shared the breathtaking view of the white-frothed combers pounding in from the night-black sea and sky. Then they walked the boardwalk and tried a few games of chance, where chance seemed to have little to do with the inevitable outcome. Sam seemed undismayed that he didn't win her even a tiny stuffed snake, the lowest possible prize. The snakes were made of ugly plush, with eyes of glued felt, bedraggled ribbons around their necks, if snakes had necks.

"You don't want one of those, do you?" he asked. "Obvious phallic displacement."

"No," she told him, and laughed, but she found she did. She desperately wanted something he would give to her, win for her, that would remind her of this night.

"Athletics are not my strongest suit."

"And what is?" she heard herself ask in a smoky voice. She couldn't believe she'd thrown out a *double entendre,* especially when she was determined *not* to sleep with him.

"Would you like to find out?" he asked, looking at her

648

directly. Then he placed his hand, his long, lean, tanned hand, under her chin, and tipped her head up to his face. He bent his head down to hers, and then his lips were on her lips, his tongue in her mouth, his delicious breath mingling with hers. She had never been kissed like this. It was Sam, and he wanted her, he was kissing her, and she could feel his heat, she could feel his desire. Her whole body felt alive, vibrating. He wants me, she thought. He really does!

He lifted his mouth off of hers. "Would you like to find out?" he asked again.

She caught her breath. "If I do, I'll ask April," she told him. "Now I'd like to go home."

36

Marty hung up the phone and smiled. Normally he was too big-spirited to wish ill on anyone. But after April taunting him about her option on it, after all the trouble with Jahne Moore, with the concession of time off and the schedule for the taping of next season's show completely revamped because of her, and then the total shit storm that caused with Lila—both personally and professionally—well, he couldn't help but smile to hear the *Birth of a Star* shooting was in trouble. She'd need another two weeks, and he'd grant it. What the hell. He already had his season's first two shows scripted, and neither included her.

It wasn't just that she'd caused him trouble. Also, he admitted, he simply couldn't wish April Irons well. It was like that old showbiz saying—"Why does he hate me so? I never did anything for him"—but with a new twist. He had backed out of an agreement, an early one, with April, and it had hurt her badly. Marty knew himself—too many years of therapy to deny that—and he knew that he felt himself to be an inherently good guy. That's why he worked with Sy, for example. Sy was born to be the bad cop. But Marty had been bad to April, and it made him feel guilty, even now, years later. So he couldn't like her or wish her well. Then, when he heard she'd gotten the option on *Birth,* one of his favorite old films, well, he'd resented it. But, as much as he resented April, he knew she resented him more.

Anyway, she knew vendetta as well as any Sicilian, and played it better than most. Casting Jahne Moore had made nothing but headaches for him. But he'd endured to triumph. The first two shows of the new season would feature Lila. And her mother. Paulie Grasso was setting it up. Because Jahne wasn't available, and it could be done partly as backstory: why Lila had left home, and then the return of the prodigal son. Well, daughter. The scripts sang, and the visuals would be unbelievable. Because, Marty acknowledged, he was obsessed with Lila. And a season premiere that starred her and brought in her mama would also bring in the ratings. He owned the youth audience on Sunday night, but Theresa O'Donnell would bring in the heavy-furniture crowd, too. He'd kill them. The Network might even set up a St. Marty of the Road shrine and begin worshipping there. Not that they weren't already kissing his skinny Italian ass. But a killer rating for the first two shows of the season, which starred Lila, and which brought in the older audience, would give Marty leverage in about twenty-three directions at once. And if Lila had a few objections, that was just as well. But for once, he'd get his way. Because he knew there was no love lost between Lila and her mom.

So, it seemed he had all kinds of bases covered. And just to be safe, he'd throw in a few long shots of Sharleen and Jahne in the beginning and the end, when Lila rejoined them—Clover, Crimson, and Cara on the road again. It would be a blockbuster. It might even exceed that "Who shot J.R.?" episode. Then again, departing from the formula might bring down the wrath of God.

Go know.

Theresa O'Donnell hadn't been as excited about a job since she'd had her own show with Skinny and Candy. Paul Grasso had told her the part on *Three for the Road* was "significant, integral to the story," but she hadn't yet seen the script. In fact, she was supposed to have received it first thing this morning, and here it was almost three, and the assholes at Grasso's office hadn't followed through.

Theresa sighed and reached over to the white table by the pool, picked up her drink, and sipped. Well, she could wait. It wasn't like she ever needed more than a day to memorize her part. She was a quick study. Always had been. Had to be, to keep up with the younger tramps that were creeping up behind her.

Like Lila. Theresa laughed, picturing Lila's face when she was told her mother, Theresa O'Donnell, was going to play the part of her mother on *Three*. In fact, she threw her head back and laughed out loud. The bitch. It serves her right. Fuck with me. I'm *good*, she thought. *Real* good. And they couldn't ignore that fact. I have a strong following, and the powers that be know that. It was Lila who didn't.

Or maybe she did; that's why she hates me so much. She may be young, she may be pretty, but I still have drawing power, stamina, after all these years in the business. And Lila is afraid—deep down inside—that she wouldn't be able to maintain her edge. Not like I have.

Well, maybe I have slipped a little, Theresa admitted to herself. She hadn't done a movie or TV show in . . . well, a long time. But she didn't *like* the movies they were making now. And she'd done a guest shot, well, last year. No, the year before.

Paul Grasso, the guy Marty had given the casting job for *Three* to, had caught her off guard when he called to offer her the part. "I tried to reach you through Ara, your agent, but he tells me he doesn't represent you anymore."

"Mr. Grasso," she had almost stammered, "I no longer *need* representation." And, of course, Mr. Grasso had agreed. She'd put the word out that *she'd* dumped Ara, the old fairy.

Now she picked up the portable phone from the corner of the chaise while taking another sip of her drink. She looked down at her personal telephone book, lying open on her lap. Who's next? she wondered. She'd been on the phone all day, letting the right people know that she was going to be on television again.

Of course, she had to play the game a bit. She had implied rather than stated some out-and-out lies. Like that her part would be a permanent character on the series. That Lila was as excited as she at the thought of working together. That Theresa might have a picture deal with Marty DiGennaro. How absolutely thrilled Theresa was to be able to work with a director of Mr. DiGennaro's stature.

But, she thought to herself as she began to punch in yet another telephone number, this is the way the game is played.

Then a shadow fell across her. She looked up. It was Kevin, unshaved, drunk, and disheveled. "No script yet?" he asked, his voice nasty.

"It's on its way," she said, but the fear sounded in her voice. She was paying him over a thousand a week now, but he got worse and worse.

"So, you'll get to see our little girl," he sneered. "That is, if they do wheel you out for the part."

"I'll get the script."

"Yeah. And I'll get married."

37

Nothing is like a movie shooting on location. It is its own little world, where a group of highly trained, highly paid, and usually highly sexed professionals come together under enormous tension to try and create. Freed from their families, alternately bored and overworked, separated from the world of the Regulars and the Assholes, the "Talents" find themselves tired, lonely, and frustrated. Little wonder that such close friendships, so many intense affairs spring up on location. And both the friendships and the affairs generate lots of gossip.

The gossip takes on a life of its own. That's where I, Laura Richie, come in. I seek it out, publish it, and it affects both the people on location and the folks they've left at home. Sometimes the gossip lives on longer than the people gossiped about. But one of the secrets of Hollywood is that, after a movie has wrapped, none of the friendships and few of the affairs continue.

Of course, Jahne's slap was heard round the world. Michael's swollen face was fine by the following day, but his ego was more than bruised. If it hadn't been difficult to hit Michael, it was difficult to work with him, Jahne had to acknowledge. "Ach! He iss a child!" hissed Mai, and she was closest to right: Michael was behaving as only destructive, angry children do. He had temper tantrums when he had to wait for anything—and Jahne had already learned that the movie business was all about "hurry up and wait"—and he sulked when they had to do take after take, even if it was he who had blown a line.

They spoke, but only when necessary, and neither was civil. Jahne was afraid Michael made jokes to the crew at her expense.

He seemed to feel perfectly comfortable making the meanest personal comments, and they were always true, or true enough to cause alarm. If Jahne missed a mark and ruined a careful setup, he sneered and called her "the movie virgin." When the unfortunately rabbitlike continuity girl forgot to put his tie back on for a shot and the entire scene had to be done over the following day, he called her an "airhead with an overbite" and ripped her apart verbally in front of a dozen people.

"*Ach*, he is disgusting. And a bully. I can't understand such a man. He iss still so angry because you give him a little slap and von't sleep vis him? Ridiculous! Didn't any vimmen say no before?" Mai, who had been virtually remaking all of Jahne's costumes, looked up from her sewing and rubbed at her temples. "He even giffs *me* a headache. Surely ozzer vimmen haff told him that?"

Apparently very few had, but Jahne knew it was more than her rejection that rankled. Like a pig trained to hunt truffles, Michael McLain was a specialist in detecting the scent of sexual tension in the air. She watched him watch her and Sam. And since he wasn't the object of the passion, he was enraged.

Because it was, of course, she and Sam generating the heat.

She constantly thought about her hunger for him. To be honest, she thought about very little else. She remembered everything she could about what it used to be like, what he did, what he said, how it felt. But what she remembered, felt, most about their sex was shame. Shame over the size of her thighs, shame at the stretch marks on her breasts, shame at the way her belly hung down when he rolled her on top. It wasn't sexual shame, not a feeling that sex was dirty. It was personal shame, a shame that she didn't look good enough, perfect enough. A shame that he wouldn't desire her sagging breasts, her wide hips.

Was she the only woman who felt that way? She had not always been overweight, but she'd always been shamed. Now that she was transformed and saw what it took, even in Hollywood, to get the right images on the screen, perhaps she could blame it on Hollywood. Every love scene she had ever seen had beautiful people in it. Ugly ones, fat ones, short ones were objects of fun or of scorn. Older people, wrinkled people, unlovely people didn't have sex, or if they did it was dreary and always offscreen. How could she blame herself, when all the images she had ever seen had been so much more beautiful than she?

And now wasn't she a participant in this scam that robbed people of their sexual comfort? Because the love scenes they were shooting were anything but real. With a body double, makeup, lighting, special diffusing lenses, and every other trick in the book, she'd be up on the screen making every woman in the audience feel inadequate.

She hadn't slept with Sam. And even though she wanted to, wanted to so very badly that she found it hard to think of anything else, she wasn't sure that she would. What would he think of her scars? How would she explain? And, worse, once she had given herself to him, how would she control her feeling for him? How could she keep the upper hand? Continue the Estella role. Mai had given her advice—"Don't ever be liking heem more than he is liking you!" It was advice Jahne planned to follow, but it was becoming difficult to resist him.

He was certainly attentive. In fact, it seemed as if he tracked her all day long, that every comment he made, each joke, each order, was also a secret message to her. Each evening, after work, he came to her suite, or sent a car to bring her to the house he had rented for the duration. They discussed the day, the difficulties with Michael, the problems with the crew, the script. She thought about telling him who she really was, toyed with the idea each evening, but never acted on it. They laughed a lot, ate together, and drank some wine—though Jahne was careful of the calories as well as its effect on her face and libido. She never talked about herself. And she tried to be as seductive as possible. Yes, she was making him crazy! But since the one kiss in Santa Cruz, she hadn't let him touch her. Except once. Yesterday, as she was leaving, he took her hand and held it up, flat, against his hard chest.

"Can you feel my heartbeat?" he asked.

"Yes." She tried to keep the breathlessness out of her voice.

"You've kept my heart beating like that for weeks now. What is yours like?" He moved his hand, still on hers, to her own chest and pressed her hand against her own heart.

"It's quite steady," she lied to him.

"Liar!" he said, and for a moment she thought he had read her mind. "Liar!" he repeated and smiled. "You're heartless. Heartless or sexless. One or the other."

"Men's oldest incorrect assumption: that any woman who doesn't have sex with them doesn't have sex at all! I'm sexless? Just because I don't roll into bed with you?" she asked, trying to laugh.

"No," he said, serious, his voice low. "Because you don't love me back. Do you?"

She'd pulled away from him wordlessly and gone back to the hotel, to her empty bed, to another night of troubled sleep. When she awoke at 2:00 A.M., she felt so upset she almost called Mai. But Mai needed her rest. The old woman looked so drained and tired. Well, Jahne told herself, so will I if I don't get some shut-eye. Yet she was as nervous as a cat. She had never in her life played hard to get. But was it morality and strength that kept her from sleeping with Sam, from loving him? Or was it simply fear that he'd be turned off by her scars, that he'd stay involved with April and reject her once again? Or worse, she asked herself. Worse, that he'd make love to her and realize who she was. Or, worst of all, that he wouldn't.

She laid her head against her rumpled pillow again. Did Sam love her? she asked herself. And if he did, who was it that he loved? Did he love who she had been, or only who she was? Had he only left Mary Jane because of his weakness for beauty, and now that she was beautiful, would he not leave her again? Or was he simply . . .

There was a knock on the door. It was soft, but it was unmistakably a knock. Jahne lay absolutely still. La Brecque's security people were on the job, as well as the movie security staff, and the hotel's. But the knock came again, this time with a whispered "Jahne."

Her heart jumped within her, but not in fear. She got out of bed, took a minute to turn on a low light and run to the mirror. Then she went to the door.

"Yes?" she asked. "Who is it?" But she knew.

"Please," he said, and she opened the door. Sam made no move to come in. He simply stood there, his face wet with tears. "I've never felt like this," he whispered. "Never."

She looked at his long, lean face, the shadow of his dark beard on his cheeks, the wrinkles at the corners of his deep-set eyes, eyes wet with tears, tears shed for her. Surely this was proof. No man had ever cried for her before.

"What about April?" she asked.

"Forget her! I have. It will probably ruin my career, but I have. And you don't care."

"I care," she told him. Taking his hand, she drew him into her room and into her bed.

38

Sam's long body lay beside Jahne, his right arm over her shoulder and just barely touching her back. She was having trouble breathing, and she couldn't swallow. Her hip bone was pressed against him, her left foot just brushing his. And all those places where they touched—her back, her hip, her foot—felt as if they were burning.

She would have him at last! And have him on *her* terms. Have a man—not just *any* man, but Sam Shields—have him love her. Adore her. Have him lusting after her. Wild for her. Crying for her.

But the excitement, the thrill, was almost too painful. She wanted to tear off her bra, her panties, rip off his blue boxer shorts, and fuck him to death. She wanted to ride him, to swallow him inside her and rock away this unbearable tension. She could hardly control herself. And I must tell him, she reminded herself. I must tell him who I am, now, before it's too late.

His face was inches away from hers. In the semidarkness, she could see his eyes gleaming. He, too, was breathless with desire. Looking deeper into his eyes, she saw two tiny reflections of her own face. What was he seeing in *her* eyes? Surely the ghost of Mary Jane?

He began to move, only the slightest bit, and now her nipples were just brushing his bare chest and she could feel the head of his penis—through his shorts—pressing against her thigh. His shorts were wet there, and the wetness echoed her own. He lifted his hand from her back and gently, ever so gently, ran it all along her side, from her shoulder to her knee and back. She shivered.

"Cold?" he teased, and his voice was almost unrecognizable, it was so gritty with desire. She couldn't speak at all, she only shook her head. He reached over to her face then and held her head still, his long hand cupping her chin. His hand on her face felt so good—she could only think of Snowball and the way the cat pressed itself against her hand, pushing the caress. She, Jahne, wanted to rub every part of herself against him, like a cat pushing on a rubbing post. Then, still holding her face, Sam kissed her, and she stopped thinking of anything.

His lips against hers were so hot that they sent another shiver down her back. But his other hand was there to draw her closer against him. He held her face to his as if her mouth were a fruit that he was eating. His tongue moved slowly around her mouth, tasting each cheek and under her tongue and behind her upper lip. Then, gently, ever so gently, he took her full lower lip between his teeth and slowly—ever so slowly—bit her.

She groaned, and he let go just at the second the sensation moved from pleasure to pain.

"I want to eat every bit of you," he whispered. "You're delicious. I want to love you with my hands and my mouth and my dick." He unhooked her bra and effortlessly freed her from it. Oh! The heat of his chest on her breasts was exquisite, and she felt her nipples tingle. Yes! She had sensation there. They tingled. She took a deep breath, and it pushed them even harder up against him.

He took her hand, and moved it down, to his penis, still clothed in his boxers. It almost burned her hand. It was hard, and she let the head press against her palm. It was slick with his fluid. "That's for you," he told her. "All for you."

He moved his own hand and put it down the waistband of her panties. He pressed it against her flat stomach, the very tips of his fingers just touching her pubic hair. She groaned again, and he moved his fingers—not any lower —he simply drummed them gently for a moment there. She shuddered, and he laughed and kissed her again, this time only lip to lip. But she wanted his tongue, wanted his hand, wanted his cock. Still, he pulled back, and began to kiss her cheek, then her neck, then, slowly, her upper breast. His left hand remained on her mons, but he moved his other to cup her breast to his mouth. "Oh, God, yes!" she whispered, but instead of taking it in his mouth he only held it to his face, and then, gently, breathed on it. And her nipple felt every breath.

She was crazy with desire for him. And she felt his desire, but also his control. He isn't like Pete—all humping and no technique. And he's not like Michael, who was all technique and no passion. Sam had the control and subtlety to choreograph his lovemaking, but he also had the passion and energy to make it so much more than a horizontal dance.

Her body had never felt so alive. The slightest touch, the least change in pressure or position, made her tingle. Now, at last, he put both of his hands on her breasts, covering them completely. He put his mouth against her ear. "Hold me tighter," he told her, and he squeezed her breasts gently in his big hands. "Hold me like that," he said, and she felt his penis jerk in her hand. She closed her fingers around it and echoed his kneading. He moaned, and she felt a surge of power and lust that was electric. *She* had made him sound like that. She tightened her fingers around him again, and again he moaned.

She used her other hand and pulled down his shorts. Then she took him in her hand again and rubbed his cock slowly against her belly. "Oh, yes," he groaned. She felt the trail of wetness it left. She put both hands around it and squeezed hard. He had his tongue in her ear, and what he was doing felt so good, so wild, that she had to let go of him. She felt as if there were no time, no place, only the waves of feeling from her ear to her neck to her nipples to her pussy.

"Don't let go," he begged, and moved a hand down to hers, pulling it back to his penis and pushing himself against her palm. "Don't ever let go of me," he begged, and kissed her, deeply and hard. He rolled on top of her and his weight was perfect. Face to face, chest to chest, belly to belly, thigh to thigh, they lay for a moment.

"Let me come inside you," he whispered, and, when she nodded, he reached for a condom and slipped into it. It gave her a moment to breathe. What am I doing? she asked herself. This wasn't what I planned. Not to sleep with him. Not to keep in the dark about who I really am. I *have* to tell him now. It's my last chance.

But he moved his hand down, again to her panties, and

then, quick as a fish, slid his hand under them to the slickness between her legs. "Ah. Yes," he sighed.

She felt him slip a finger inside her. She arched her back and pushed against his hand. "Does that feel good?" he asked, his voice a thick whisper. He began to stroke her, and she thought she'd die from the pure pleasure. "Do you feel good?"

"Yes," she whispered back. "But I want more."

He pulled her panties down to her knees. She started to wiggle out of them, but he stopped her. "No, let me look at them there. Let me look at you exposed." He got up on one elbow, eyeing her. "Open your legs a little wider," he said. The panties pulled at her knees, but she spread them as far as she could, conscious of him staring. "Ah," he sighed. "That's how I've pictured you a hundred times. It's such a wanton look. Let me put on the light."

"No!" she cried. "No. Not now."

He shrugged. And reached over and put his hand back on her, opening her first with two fingers, then a third. She had to thrash her head back and forth on the pillow, her pleasure was so intense. "Oh, God," he groaned. "You're so beautiful. I don't know if I want to watch you or fuck you."

He pulled his hand away from her, and she opened her eyes. He was rubbing her wetness on his cock, covered as it was by the condom. Then he tore off her panties and spread her legs wider, positioning himself between her knees. He bent over, kissed her belly, and moved his mouth up to her breasts, her neck, and then covered her own mouth with his.

"Now?" he whispered. "Can I have you now?"

"Oh, yes!" she nearly screamed, as she felt him slip just the head of his penis inside her. He didn't move for a moment, but her urgency had her shivering and almost bucking underneath him. "Slow down," he whispered. "You've got me so nuts I'll come in a second if you move."

She stopped, trembling. Slowly, bit by bit, he slid the entire length of him into her until she felt so full that she almost clawed his back. "There. Is that what you wanted?" he asked, and she felt tears spring to her eyes.

"Yes. That's what I wanted," she confessed.

"Me too. Me too," he whispered.

He began then to move on her, slowly and smoothly, entering her over and over and over. "Oh, you're so good. It's so good," she wept.

"It's all for you, baby. All for you." She felt the waves of pleasure overtaking her then, and knew she was about to come. "Ah," he cried. "Give it up. Give it up, baby," he told her, and she did.

Jahne sat the next morning, smiling and humming, in front of the makeup vanity. "Are you likink him more than he iss likink you?" Mai asked.

"No. No. Not at all."

"I think this is qvite dangerous," Mai warned. "He is critic, not artist, don't you think? You give all to him. Vat does he give you?"

"His love," Jahne said, simply.

"How do you know?" Mai asked.

Jahne turned to her, serene. She had proof. She almost shivered as she remembered Sam's passion in the dark the night before. And the tears that had coursed down his face. "Because he cried over me," she told Mai, turning back to her own reflection in the mirror.

"Phaw! Men *alvays* cried over me. They cry over beautiful vimmen every day. Vat else?"

And Jahne watched the smile disappear off her own beautiful face. Because she didn't have an answer.

39

Lila was beginning to look forward to her time with Marty. At first, when his attention to her on the set became obvious, Lila had accepted it as both a tribute to her beauty, and a stroke of good luck. But beauty is an abstract, and an abstraction isn't human. Marty craved glamour, and glamour was remote. If she warmed to him, would he still worship at her shrine? No one in Lila's life had ever given so generously of his time to her. No one had ever really listened. At first, she was like a caged animal suddenly let loose in the jungle. She had pushed and criticized, obstructed Marty in every way. And Marty had hung on. Until she began to trust. Now he listened to her all the time, and she even occasionally listened to him. He knew stuff. He was really smart.

Trust was new to her. How could she ever really trust anyone? Not the PMS, that was for sure. Not Kevin. And not Aunt Robbie, she had gradually come to learn. Not that she believed that Aunt Robbie would deliberately hurt her, as she believed her mother had and would, but Robbie was a little too far out for anyone to consider dependable. Since Lila had laid out her terms of forgiveness, she hadn't seen Robbie, and she knew why: he was afraid to burn his bridges with Theresa by bringing Lila her "sisters." Fine. He'd made his choice.

She was spending all her free time with Marty, and she found that she didn't need anyone else. At first, being seen with Marty in public was enough of an incentive. The man had a presence, a persona, that seemed to appeal to everyone, men *and* women. It wasn't the allure of sexuality, nor the macho attitude that some men projected. Marty was different.

For one thing, when they were out in a restaurant, or at one of the A-list parties, Marty never took her elbow to steer her around. Lila appreciated that. She hated to be touched, and led around like a dog on a leash. Marty seemed intuitively to know that, and to respect her separateness. As a result, when she walked into a crowded room with him, she felt she walked in with him as an equal, not as a prized possession.

And the more Marty's attentions to her became known, the more everyone on the set treated Lila special, with a heightened awareness of her presence, of her unspoken needs. She knew that, of the three co-stars, she was the one that was feared. And the fear made Lila feel secure, because she knew that there had to be something to keep people in line, and fear was the basis for power.

Except Marty didn't use fear to project his strength. It puzzled her.

While Marty was single-minded in his work, he also knew how to spend his free time, the little he had. Marty loved opera, so they went up to San Francisco. And symphonies, ballets, art shows. And theater, although there was less of that in L.A. than one might imagine. Marty seemed to take pleasure in exposing Lila to those things that, despite her privileged background, she had not experienced before. Marty was knowledgeable. And very patient. He was making the down time of the hiatus fun for her. And the publicity of their dates wouldn't hurt her Emmy chance at all.

Meanwhile, he hadn't tried to touch her. They spent an evening at her place, sitting on the deck, overlooking the Pacific. Marty had been in production meetings all day, and now he was talking about the new opening for the season. Lila was staring at the water, mesmerized by the spectacle of the sunset over the waves. He droned on while she nodded.

"And we'll have Theresa play your mother," Marty said casually.

For a moment, Lila's expression didn't change, as if she hadn't heard what he had said. Then, suddenly, her face was ashen. "What?" she asked.

"Theresa has agreed to play your mother."

Lila couldn't believe what she was hearing. "No, Marty. Not my mother." Lila finally croaked out a hoarse whisper.

Marty didn't know very much about Lila's relationship with Theresa, but he knew that it wasn't very good, and that Lila had very little to do with her. Still, he hadn't thought she *hated* her mother. But the look on Lila's face was unmistakable. Lila *did* hate her mother. In that instant, Marty knew that he now had the upper hand.

"Why not? It's a natural, Lila. Think this through."

"I won't work with my mother." She folded her arms across her chest.

"Come on. Don't be so quick to make up your mind. Don't you realize what this could do for your career? This could give you an incredible boost, and it certainly would help the show's ratings. You'll need those rating points, don't forget, when it's Emmy time, and also when you negotiate your next contract.''

"Fuck the points. I said no!''

Marty wasn't Italian for nothing. And Machiavelli had nothing on him. At last! The worm has turned, he thought to himself. Marty smiled at Lila. "You have nothing to say about it, Lila. I'm only telling you this as a courtesy, as a director to an actress. I'm not asking your permission.''

She should have known! She should have known not to trust him, not to trust anybody! "Who the fuck are you? God? You're not God, Marty, you're just a director.''

"And you're just an actress, Lila. I *made* you an actress, remember that.'' Marty stood up, feeling in control for the first time since he had met Lila. He spoke more casually then he felt. Now he could practice diplomacy, and wind up getting them both what they wanted. "Anyhow,'' he said, walking to the edge of the deck, "I haven't made my final decision yet.''

"About casting my mother?'' she asked. Marty could see the hope rising in her eyes.

Marty turned to the sunset for a moment, then turned back and looked directly at Lila. "Listen, I've committed to *her,* but we could make a change.''

"Get rid of her?''

"No. We could feature Sharleen. Have Theresa play *her* mother.''

Lila sank onto a chaise, as if his implied threat had a physical impact on her.

"But you said *I* have the lead.'' Her wail of betrayal sounded almost childish.

Marty stood up and shrugged. "That was my scenario. But you don't seem to like it. And we have a play-or-pay contract with Theresa: she's paid if we use her or not.''

Lila, he could see, was near tears.

"I'm sorry, Lila. I didn't know you felt this way. You never told me.'' He finally had his advantage, and now he was going to push it home. She had had him spinning since they met. Now it was *her* turn. She wanted something from him? This time, *this* time, Lila was going to have to negotiate.

She remained seated. "Please, Marty, couldn't we talk this out? Why my mother? I mean, the idea of the rich girl leaving home is perfect. Sharleen can't play that. But you want an old bag like Theresa for the show? There must be a million others who'd jump at the chance. Let's think of someone else. How about Debbie Reynolds? Or Dina Merrill?" A forced smile strained Lila's face.

Marty almost felt uneasy at Lila's desperation; almost, but not quite. The taste of his own recent desperation was still fresh. Only last night, he had dreamt about her, had fantasized watching her undress in front of him, seeing her lying next to him, her long, slim body stretched out, waiting for him, her legs open, inviting, then accepting.

"You're a very beautiful woman, Lila." He looked directly into her eyes.

Lila stared up at him, then dropped her eyes. "I know you're attracted to me, Marty. But . . ." She stopped.

Marty didn't say anything. He knew his time had come. She spoke again. "It's not you." She paused. "I'm . . . I don't enjoy sex, Marty. I mean, I never had sex. I'm still a virgin."

Marty wasn't buying that virgin bullshit. Anyhow, he wasn't one of those men that worshipped at the altar of virginity. "You don't owe me anything, Lila. I don't want you to feel that you *have* to do anything. My decisions are based on artistic considerations."

Lila reached up and took Marty's hand, pulling him gently back down to the chaise. "But isn't there something I *can* do? I mean, Marty, I *can't* work with my mother. You have no idea what she's done. What it's like between us. I *hate* her, Marty. I *despise* her. Please, don't use her, Marty. Please, *please*."

He felt her free hand touch the zipper of his pants, and he immediately grew hard in reaction. He smiled. "Don't, Lila. You're a virgin, remember?"

But she didn't listen. Or didn't hear him. She had the zipper down, and his penis between her perfect lips before he even knew what she was doing. Right there, on the deck, in the fading pink light of the sunset. Oh, God, he thought, as the warmth of her mouth enveloped him. He looked down to see her beautiful head moving at his crotch. A beautiful head giving beautiful head. He swelled in her mouth. This wasn't exactly what he'd had in mind, what he had dreamed about, but it was a good place to start.

The phone beside Theresa rang. She turned to Kevin. "Be a dear and answer it for me, will you? I'm hoarse."

Reluctantly, Kevin did, then handed the phone to Theresa, knowing she would want to take this call. "It's Paul Grasso."

Theresa smiled brightly, as if it were a camera, not a phone, she was speaking into. "Paul, darling. How are you?"

"One minute for Mr. Grasso, please." Then Theresa was put on hold.

Christ, she hated that! Put on hold by a secretary! "Am I old-fashioned, or doesn't anyone dial their own phones in this town anymore?" she asked aloud as she held for Paul. Then he was on the other end.

"Yes, Paul. How nice to hear from you. Where's the script?"

As she listened to him, both the color and the smile drained from her face. No. It wasn't possible. No fuckin' way. Theresa tried not to let her feelings show in her voice, but the effort was too great. "What do you mean, *they've* gone with someone else? *Who's* gone with someone? You mean *you've* gone with someone else. *You're* the casting director, for chrissakes, aren't you? Why? I demand to know. I *wanted* that part. That's *my* part. I have the right to know."

Theresa was now sitting up on the edge of her chair. Grasso, the goddamn cocksucking dago prick. It was him. Him and Lila. "Lila made you do this, didn't she?"

Theresa understood now. He mumbled something. "Out of your hands!" she cried. "Out of your hands! And right up your ass. You and Lila! Both of you together! She was jealous. She couldn't let me be on the same show with her. She's afraid I'd walk away with the spotlight. She couldn't *stand* to see *me* in the spotlight. So she gets *her* way, and I get *nothing*."

At the other end of the phone, Grasso was yammering. Across the room, Kevin sneered. "Fuck the money. It's not the money I care about!"

Theresa stopped for a moment, trying to catch her breath. She felt like she was losing it—in front of Kevin, but, worse, in front of Paul Grasso. A nobody. A nothing. He disgusted her, a nasty wop toad of a man. She mustn't let him hear how desperate she was for the part. How desperate she was to prove to everyone—to Lila—that she was still on top. How desperate she was to work, to get before the public again.

She forced her voice to frigid normalcy. Icy calm. "Well, Mr. Paul Grasso, I can see we have nothing else to say to each other. Of course, you realize, you *will* be hearing from my attorney." She paused. "I don't care that I get paid anyway. I want that part!" She slammed the receiver down, then flung the phone across the pool, where it clanged against the stone garden wall.

She looked over at Kevin, who, up to this moment, had said nothing, hadn't even moved. "I guess you heard all that," Theresa said to her old friend.

Kevin leaned back on his hands and crossed his legs. "You were heard on Capistrano. Killed off a flock of swallows while you were at it." Theresa was not in the mood for Kevin's so-called humor right now. "Theresa, I am sorry. But perhaps it's for the best."

Theresa snapped her head up, her eyes almost bulging in unconcealed rage. Perhaps she had to show some control in front of Paul Grasso, but not before this blackmailing bastard. "For *whose* best? Lila's? Certainly not *mine*, Kevin."

"I just mean that maybe you and Lila shouldn't be around each other, especially in a work situation. Let things continue to calm down. Wait until you both have had more time apart. You can both use a rest from each other. And then bring us together again. Give Lila what she needs."

"How the fuck would you know what she needs? What

667

did she tell you?" Theresa shrieked at Kevin, now standing over him, her fists clenched by her side.

Kevin looked up into her face, the sun coming from behind Theresa causing him to squint. "Nothing, Theresa. Only the usual rebellious-teenager stuff. You *know* that." Kevin put his hand across his eyes to shade them from the glare.

"Listen to me, you little hustler. I know that you're gloating over this. And that you still hope to cash in bigtime with Lila some day. But you can forget it! I wouldn't wish you on Saddam Hussein, much less my daughter."

Kevin narrowed his eyes, turned abruptly, and began to walk away.

"Where do you think you're going?" she screamed in panic.

"I've heard enough for one day, Theresa. I'll be back when you calm down."

40

Flora Lee opened her eyes to the pounding at her front door, and, in the darkness that now surrounded her, she couldn't find the light switch. She heaved herself upright on the edge of the bed, and became aware of the weight in the bed next to her. Dobe. He was still asleep. What time is it? She made out the green figures on the clock on the table next to her bed. Four-thirty-three. A.M. She could remember flirting with him over dinner at Sharleen and Dean's, and then Dobe had offered to take her home. She just knew he'd be a wild man in bed, but they'd stopped at a bar, and then another, and—well, she often didn't remember the rest of her evenings.

The pounding took on a new intensity, so she struggled upright, and began to feel her way out of the room toward the front door. "Who is it?" she croaked to it.

"Police."

Holy Jesus! What were they doing here? "What do you mean, the police? How do I know you're the police?"

She peered through the peephole and saw the badge being held up in front of it. She looked down at her nakedness and said, "Just a minute till I get some clothes on." She snapped on the living-room light, and looked around at the empty glasses and bottles on the coffee table in front of the sofa. Flora Lee closed her eyes for a moment, trying to remember, then pushed open the door to the bedroom, the light from the living room coming in over her shoulder.

What she saw in the bed was so frightening, she couldn't scream, or even move. The pounding at the door was harder now. Flora Lee put her hands to her mouth to keep from shrieking. What had happened? Why was Dobe lying in her bed with her kitchen knife sticking out of his chest? What had she done? Jumping Jesus Christ!

She grabbed her coat and rushed to the door, grateful the police were here. Her hand was on the doorknob when it hit her. They're going to think *I* did it, she thought. She stifled a sob, but since the pounding continued, there was nothing to do but open the door to let them in.

There was only one cop, and he was in plainclothes. He flipped open his wallet and showed his badge and ID to her. He stepped into the room warily, and looked around. "We have a complaint of a fight, screaming coming from this apartment. Are you all right, ma'am?"

It wasn't the first time the neighbors had called the cops. Probably Mrs. Ramirez, the bitch. But she couldn't remember no yelling. Flora Lee slumped down on the sofa. The plainclothes cop looked at her, then moved over and put the coffee table right. "What's wrong, miss? What happened?" He sat down on the sofa next to her.

He seemed very nice. Flora Lee didn't know what to do, but she knew she had to tell the policeman about the dead man in her bed. "I been drinking. I didn't know nothing till I heard you at the door. . . ." Flora Lee began to cry. She wished she were sober enough to think.

"Go ahead, tell me," the cop said, very gently.

Flora Lee tried to stop sobbing, and pointed her finger toward the bedroom door. The cop stood up quickly and walked into the bedroom, was in there for what seemed like a long while. Maybe he's not dead, Flora Lee thought. Maybe Dobe's still alive. As she was about to get up to go in the bedroom, the policeman came back into the room, closing the door behind him. "Lady," he said, taking a small card from his pocket, "I got to read you your rights. I'm arresting you for murder. 'You have the right to remain silent. . . .' "

"Wait, wait," she wailed. "I didn't murder *nobody*. We were just having drinks, and, the next thing I know, I'm waking up next to him dead and you're pounding at the door."

"Let me finish reading you your rights. 'You have the right to an attorney. . . .' "

"*Listen to me*," she nearly screamed. "I didn't do it. It must have been a heart attack, or a burglar. It couldn't have been me."

"Why not?" the cop asked.

"Because I never hurt nobody in my life. And he was a real nice man, real nice to me. He's a friend of my kids. A gentleman." She began to sob. "I don't know how this could happen. Dear God, on my word as a Christian, I didn't hurt him."

"You're a Christian?" the cop asked. He sighed. He was a nice-looking guy, about fifty-five maybe, tanned, wrinkled face, brown hair. Maybe now he'd be a little more on her side. He sat back down on the sofa next to her. "Is there anyone you can call? Someone who can come to the jail right away? I'm not supposed to do this; I'm supposed to wait for you to make your call from jail, but, seeing's how you and I are both Christians, well, maybe, just this once . . ."

Flora Lee looked up; the first glimmer of hope passed over her since she had flipped on the light and looked at her bed—only moments ago, but it seemed like years. Would a blow job help, too? No, she figured, murder was more serious than that. "Oh, yes. I got a son and a daughter. Maybe you know her. Sharleen Smith? I could call her. She'd take care of everything. She's got lawyers, and money and . . ."

"Sharleen Smith? You don't mean that actress on television, do you? *That* Sharleen Smith? She's *your* daughter? *You're* Sharleen Smith's mother?"

Flora Lee nodded, animated. Maybe she could get out of this mess after all. Who would believe that the mother of a famous star would *kill* someone? "Yes," she said, as she reached for the framed picture on the end table and handed it to the cop. "See? That's my baby."

The cop studied the picture for a moment, then handed it back to Flora Lee. "Anyone can have a picture of a star. I have a picture of Sharleen Smith at home myself. A fine woman, and a good Christian."

"But, see, it says 'To Momma, Love from your daughter, Sharleen.' That's me. Momma." She waited while he mulled it over. Then he stood up, and began to pace back and forth. Flora Lee watched him, her eyes eager. Finally, he stopped pacing and stood in front of her. "If she's your daughter, you have her private number, right? Let me have it."

Flora Lee ran to her pocketbook and took out the card with the number on it. The number she was never supposed to share with *anyone*. "Here it is. I always carry it with me, 'cause I can't remember numbers."

The cop took the card and sat in a chair next to the phone. "Okay, lady, I'm going to give you a chance. Because, in this town, television is important and we don't want to mess up the Industry. But if you're lying, and this isn't Sharleen Smith, or she don't know you, you're in big trouble. Murder One gets the death sentence in this state. Now, what's your name?"

"Flora Lee. Smith." Well, maybe she better not lie. "Flora Lee Deluce." She began to explain. "See, I wasn't actually married to Sharleen's daddy. I'd been married, but Deluce ran off. Me and Dean Smith Sr. had been together, oh, seven, eight years. Dean Smith was her daddy. My husband. Well, let me explain." Flora Lee talked about those days back in Arkansas, and then the move to Texas, and desperation, and about Dean Sr., and Dean Jr., and all what happened. But then, after a few questions, the cop stopped her.

"Now, is this all the truth?" he asked. "You got birth certificates and all?"

"Well, I don't no more. But they have 'em at the hospital. See, I had another baby there, too." She was about to launch into the story.

"And what was your maiden name before Texas, back in Arkansas?" He was busy taking notes, which made her nervous. He stared at her now. "If you're lying now, Mrs. Deluce, you're going to fry."

"I'm not lying," she whispered.

"Okay, Mrs. Deluce. I want you to go into the bathroom and take yourself a hot bath. Wash off all that blood. And clean out the tub. Real thorough. Don't come out till I call you. Understand?" He picked up the phone and placed it on his lap.

"Could I . . . . ? I mean, I'm awful shook up. Look, I'm trembling. Could I take a drink before I go in? For my nerves?"

"Take the whole bottle in with you, I don't care. Wash up real good, but don't try to get away. I already checked the window."

Flora Lee closed the bathroom door behind her, turned on the taps, then quickly unscrewed the top of the vodka bottle, and took three long pulls on it before coming up for air. Then she took three more. She placed the bottle on the edge of the tub and sat on the commode, waiting for the alcohol to hit.

How in the name of a bad bull's balls did I get into this? she thought. What happened? Did someone come in and kill Dobe while I was passed out? Maybe he killed hisself. No, the knife was in the middle of his chest. Christ Almighty! Could I have done it? In a blackout? Flora Lee knew all about blackouts. She was used to drinking and then finding herself in dingy rooms with dirty men she didn't know. But she had never hurt nobody before while she was in a blackout.

But that she couldn't know for sure. Maybe she did and couldn't remember. Oh, sweet Jesus, get me out of this. I don't want to die. I'll stop drinking if You just help me. For the first time in almost a dozen years, Flora Lee dropped to her knees for something other than a blow job. Oh, please, sweet Lamb of God, please help me, she prayed.

Flora Lee stood up and turned off the water, then took a couple more pulls on the vodka bottle. She stepped into the tub and began to wash her body roughly with a washcloth. She was out of the bath and onto the bottle of vodka again when she heard the policeman call to her. He still held the phone to his ear.

Flora Lee opened the door to the bathroom and cautiously came back into the living room, her robe pulled tight around her. She was feeling a little better, but she still knew she had a problem. Still, he was such a nice man. He seemed to be on hold, only listening. "Would you like a drink, officer?" she asked quietly.

"Mrs. Deluce, I'm on duty. Just sit down."

She took a seat at the edge of the sofa.

"I just got finished talking to your daughter. You're who you say you are, all right. Now, let me tell you, I don't like this situation any better than you, but for Sharleen Smith I'd do anything. The Department and the studios don't like this kind of thing, either. Bad for everyone. The guy was just a drifter. No one will miss him. And I'm too close to retirement to have this ruin me now."

Flora Lee felt some of the tension leave her body, but she still remained perched on the edge of her seat. Had God listened to her prayer? "What is she going to do for me?"

"You're going to get dressed, pack a suitcase, get a cab to the airport, and be on the first flight to New Orleans this morning. In New Orleans, you're going to call this man," he handed her a piece of paper with a name and a phone number. "He'll set you up with a place to stay. Miss Smith was shocked, but she was kind enough to say that she would continue your allowance, but only through this man. He'll see you get a check each month."

Flora Lee started to cry. "I knew it. I just knew my baby girl would help me. And thank you, sir." The sobs started to rack her body again.

"Hold up, lady. There's more. If I let you go tonight, you're never to contact Sharleen or Dean again. You're *never* to mention your relationship with them, tell *anyone* you know about them. Nothing. This means you'll never

see your kids again. But that's the only way I'm going to
let you out of this without at least a life jail sentence, and
a short life it might be.''

Flora Lee didn't take a moment. ''Sharleen said she'd
keep sending the money?''

The cop nodded his head. ''Yeah, but you gotta watch
that mouth of yours. You tell anyone, and the FBI gets
involved. Then you're in the chair for sure.''

''Well, she got nothing to worry about from me. I'd
never hurt either one of them. It ain't like I raised them
or nothing.'' Flora Lee nodded her head. ''I'll go to New
Orleans, and you kin tell her, starting tomorrow, I'll
never drink again. I just promised the Lord that in the
bathtub.'' She dabbed at her eyes with the edge of her
robe, then stood up.

''I have to pack my bag . . . in there.'' She pointed to
the bedroom where the murdered man still lay.

''Make it fast. I got some more work to do tonight
before this whole mess is over. And two other cops are
coming. I want you outa here before they get here.''

She didn't have to be told twice to rush. Flora Lee
grabbed a couple of pants suits, some underwear, and as
much of her makeup as she could squeeze into the brand-
new suitcase Sharleen had given her. She was dressed
and back in the living room in less than five minutes, and
hadn't once looked at Dobe in the bed.

The cop had money in his open hand, which he was
thrusting toward Flora Lee. ''This will be enough to get
you to New Orleans. You'll get more when you arrive
and call the number I gave you.'' Flora Lee reached for
the money with one hand, grasping the handle of the
suitcase with the other. ''There's just one more thing you
got to do before you go.''

Flora Lee looked up at him with renewed alarm. Was
he going to make her sign a confession or something?
''You got to write this note in your own handwriting before you leave.'' He handed her a piece of paper.

''*Dear Sharleen and Dean*,'' she copied. ''*In case I
don't never see you again, thanks for everything. I feel
like a burden to you, nothing I aimed to be. I won't be*

coming back, so don't expect me." She signed it, *"Love, Momma."*

Flora Lee jumped up as she heard a horn blast. "That's your taxi. I called it for you. Here's your money."

Flora Lee grabbed it and stuffed it into her pocketbook. "I'm told they're bringing back death by hanging. It's a terrible way to die, Mrs. Deluce. Understand?"

Flora Lee nodded her head, grabbed her suitcase and the bottle of vodka and ran out the door.

The cop stood at the window and watched her scuttle away. He sat down and dialed the phone. While he was on the phone, the door to the bedroom opened slowly, and Dobe came through it, the blade of the knife still protruding from his chest. The cop turned to look at him and smiled.

"Goddamn it, Barney, it took you long enough. I've had to take a piss for the last hour," Dobe said, as he opened his shirt and removed the trick half-knife.

"You did an excellent job—for an amateur," Barney said with a nod of approval.

Dobe moved into the bathroom now, where he made sounds of relief. When he came back out to the living room, he slumped into a chair, and Barney handed him a double vodka from another bottle he'd found in the kitchen. "Well, Barney, that was probably the easiest thousand dollars you ever earned in all your years in acting." Dobe smiled. "Thanks for making the riff work."

"No problem. How'd you like it when I told her hanging was coming back?"

"Ad-libs were never your strongest suit, Barney. Now, give me all them notes on the birth certificates, and let's get out of here."

41

"Darling, wonderful lunch, but I simply have *got* to run," Crystal Plenum told Sy Ortis as she slid out of the booth, then bent to kiss him on both cheeks. "Being on time is my Hercules' heel."

"Achilles' heel, Crystal."

"Whatever!"

Her two camp followers, Crystal's constant companions—her "people," for chrissakes—hovered before and behind her, as they made tracks to the exit. Sy watched as Crystal stopped occasionally, air-kissed somebody while her "people" stood waiting, then, finally, made it to the door.

Sy let out a sigh of relief as the door shut behind Crystal. There were two kinds of lunches: the hard and the soft. Sy found the soft ones more difficult. This lunch, a soft, had no purpose—no immediate purpose, that is—except to keep Crystal warm, tell her how beautiful and talented she still was, and what great properties he was looking over for her. All lies, as it happened. A sort of aborted jerkoff: a lot of stroking but no climax. Ass-kissing, it would be called in any other line of business. The part Sy hated most about the way he made money. These stroking parties left him feeling more like the puppet than the puppeteer.

Crystal was sinking, and both she and Sy knew it. Since *Jack and Jill*, there had not been a decent lead offered her. Of course, there were never many leading parts for women approaching thirty-five, but she'd been big box office up till *Jack and Jill*. That film had changed the public's perception of her. Now she couldn't play young anymore.

Sy sipped the last of his coffee, and didn't have to beckon to a waiter for a refill. It appeared before him, before even *he* knew he wanted a second cup. But, then, this *is* the Polo Lounge, and I *am* known here, he thought. If I can't get it here, where would I get it?

He was startled for a moment by the presence of a small, impeccably dressed man, standing at his table. It took him a minute. "Ara Sagarian," Sy finally said, and just looked at him. Ara was obviously on his way to his own table. "Mind if I join you?" Ara asked. The waiter hovered, waiting for Sy's decision.

"Well, I'm on my way out. Just had lunch with Crystal. My last espresso," he added.

Ara sat down opposite Sy, not accepting the brush-off, and the waiter hurried to set his place. Sy grimaced, not giving a shit whether Ara noticed or not. Sy could see that Ara obviously had something on his mind, but at Ara's age, and with a stroke, it would probably take a little time for him to get it out. Sy wasn't in a very patient mood.

"I don't know if you've heard," Ara said, coming surprisingly quickly to the point, "but I wanted you to hear it from me." Sy watched Ara meticulously wipe the corner of his mouth. "I've signed Michael McLain. I didn't solicit him, I want you to know. He came to me."

So that was it. The old Armenian *maricón* wanted to lord it over him. Sy leaned over toward Ara. "*You* know who I got in my stable. And, the way I see it, three queens beat a pair. Michael McLain for Lila Kyle isn't exactly the trade of the century. I wouldn't brag about it if I were you."

"I'm not telling you to brag. I'm simply extending you the courtesy of hearing it from me."

"I think you confuse me with someone who gives a shit," Sy snapped. He stared into Ara's rheumy eyes.

"Let me tell you something, son," Ara began. "In this town, in this Industry, it's best to be nice to everyone. On your way up especially, because you might need them to be nice to *you* on the way down."

Sy watched Ara as he ministered to the drool on his mouth, then picked up a fork to begin to eat his salad. Sy's lunch was now grinding away at his intestines. How dare this old *maricón* give him advice! All the bile from his lunch with Crystal, from all the ass-kissing he'd had to do, rose into his throat. "You fucking old has-been. Who the fuck are you?"

Sy saw Ara blink. Then the old man struggled visibly for control. "Let me tell you a story, Sy."

Sy held up one hand to hold off Ara for a moment, beckoning for a waiter at the same time with his other. The waiter was at the table in a second. "Do something for me," Sy said to the waiter. "Listen to this pathetic old guy's story, will you? I have something more important to do."

Sy stood up, walked passed the maître d's desk, stopped to sign his tab, then went through the open door out to the parking valet.

With all his aggravation that afternoon, it was just as well that he didn't see Neil Morelli lurking near the entrance to the car park, his hand in his jacket pocket, holding an ominous bulge.

42

Marty DiGennaro, famous director, conqueror of the film world, recipient of four Oscars, winner of a contest of wills with Bob LeVine, television's new prince, the most powerful creative man in Hollywood, lay tied to the four corners of his bed, spread out as flat as a roadmap and naked as a newt. He strained at the silken tasseled cords that wrapped around the mahogany bedposts and doubled back over his wrists. The knots were neat half-hitches, he noticed and, absurdly, he wondered if Lila had been in the Girl Scouts. Back in Queens, he'd made it all the way to Eagle Scout. Classic nerd. He still knew how to tie clove hitches, square knots, and sheepshanks. In the dark, he pulled against the taut restraints and grinned. As an Eagle Scout back in New York, even in his wildest masturbatory fantasies, he'd never imagined this.

The first time Lila had tied him up, roping him to the bed, he'd been shocked, but not because he was a prude.

It was just that she was so, so, well, *reluctant* to have sex at all that he assumed her to be, if not the virgin she claimed, then at least inexperienced. Or perhaps damaged in some way.

So, when she raised a perfectly arched eyebrow and slowly began to pull the silk rope out of an Hermès bag, he had been nonplussed. And, to be honest, turned off by the idea. He had, of course, done a little role-playing—his ex-wife had liked spankings from time to time—and he'd had more than any man's fair share of kinky starlets who demanded everything from golden showers to letting their dogs participate.

But being tied up himself, being vulnerable, immobilized, pinned to the bed, didn't seem desirable. Still, for Lila to suggest anything, to allow anything, was such a surprise that he had agreed. Without a smile or a giggle, with utmost concentration, she had wrapped his wrists and ankles in businesslike knots. Then she'd lowered the lights and left him alone, tied down.

The strangest thing to Marty was that *that* was when his erection began. There, powerless and naked in the dark, he felt the anticipatory tingling, the excitement that he hadn't felt since the old days at the Flushing Loew's movie house. He smiled at the unlikely association. So much in life—well at least in *his* life—had been more exciting in the anticipation than the acquisition. The movies he ran in his head were almost invariably better than the ones he made. He sighed. He supposed that was what made him so successful as a director.

But, once tied to the bed, he was the director of nothing. Lila had re-emerged, her long hair loose and bright as a flame, even in the dimness. She wore a kind of corset or something—Marty didn't know exactly what to call it —a bronze-colored bustier without cups. Her breasts, so full, so perfect, rode over the top of the thing, her waist even more compressed by the lacing. And she wore a matching lace G-string, a sort of high-cut triangle in the front, but when she turned around, all there was in the back was a silken cord that slid up between her perfect ass cheeks to hook on the bottom of the corset. Marty tried to take a breath, but it was hard; his chest hurt him so. Aside from a few blow jobs, he hadn't had sex with her, and he'd never seen her naked. Her incredible long legs, her perfect ass, her tits, so swollen, so round, so perfect, all moved him. His penis strained toward her, but it was the only appendage he could move.

"Pretty?" Lila asked.

"Beautiful," he gasped.

"Want to touch?"

"Yes." His hands pulled against the rope. "Untie me," he said.

"Oh, no. Where's the fun in that?" she asked, her voice husky. She sashayed over to him and bent from the waist until her right breast, her perfect right breast, just barely brushed his outstretched left hand. He tried to close his fingers around her softness, but with a smile she pulled away. "Oh, no," she said again. Her voice was a throaty whisper. "First you have to kiss it."

He smiled back at her. "My pleasure," he whispered. "Untie me. Please."

"Oh, no," she demurred. Instead, she moved to the foot of the bed. Then, in a single graceful movement, she stood on the bed, over him, a foot planted on either side of his waist. He could feel her slim ankles against his hips. Looking up, he saw her breasts over him, her cool, perfect face, her hair hanging down like a velvety curtain. She straddled him, careful not to touch his swollen penis, and sat on his chest.

"Kiss it," she told him, and slowly, ever so slowly, she lowered her breast toward him. Hungrily he strained his head up toward her, but the ropes held him firmly, and she stopped just short of his mouth.

"Say 'please,' " she told him.

"Please," he begged.

"Please what?" she asked.

"Please . . . please, may I kiss your breast?" His voice was a croak. His testicles felt as tight and as hard as summer plums in their skin. He groaned.

Lila smiled. She bent lower, her tiny coppery nipple suspended a half-inch above his pursed and open mouth. "Here," she said, and let the nipple just brush against his lips. It was hot as a flame against his dry tongue. He groaned again, her weight heavy on his chest.

"More," he pleaded.

Then Lila slid off the bed and stood beside it. She lit a candle and in the flickering glow she stood, displaying her perfection. She was, he thought, the most exquisite woman ever created. Her flawless skin gleamed. Her hair, so thick, so glossy, so long, was like the tail of the most perfect thoroughbred. Her teeth, her eyes, her lips reflected back the light. Tears filled his eyes.

"Want to touch me?" she asked.

Marty could only nod.

Lila cupped both her long, slim hands under her full breasts. He could see the shapely nails of her perfect manicure sink into the milky flesh near her nipple. "Want to touch me here?" she asked, a little breathless. He nodded again. She smiled, and slowly, ever so slowly, squeezed her breasts harder, lifting them up like offerings. Then, with thumb and forefingers, she pinched each nipple, first the left, then the right. She closed her eyes. "Oooh," she moaned. "It feels so good. Do you want to do this?"

Marty couldn't even nod.

Lila ran her hands along her waist, down her thighs, up over her belly, touching, stroking, pinching her own flesh, while Marty lay there, powerless to do anything but watch, his penis engorged and throbbing, throbbing in a way he had never felt before. She turned her back toward him, and he felt a pang at losing sight of her wonderful tits, but Lila again began to run her own hands over her back and then down to her rounded, perfect ass, her fingers kneading her own flesh until he almost cried out that she must be bruising herself.

She turned to him. "Do you want me to touch you?" she asked.

"Oh, yes. Please," he said. She smiled, and slowly moved her lovely long hands toward him. Lightly as a butterfly, barely touching, she ran her fingers over his bony chest, then down to his flat belly. His penis twitched up at her. He could see a bead of clear liquid at its head. "Yes," he moaned, but her hands moved up, away, up to his chest, to his own nipples, then over his face, his eyes, across his mouth. He kissed her fingers then, and they stopped for a moment in their movement to explore his burning lips, his mouth, his tongue. Slowly, Lila inserted a finger into his mouth, and hungrily, eagerly, he sucked at it. Then another finger, and another, until his mouth was stuffed full of her hand. Gratefully, he held her in his mouth with his lips, his tongue, even his teeth. He held a part of her, but too soon, too soon, she withdrew and moved her hand again across his hairless chest, over to a nipple, which she idly tweaked with a fingernail, then drew her nails down, down, but once again past his loins, past his aching joint, not touching his straining testicles, down his thighs, raking his calves, not stopping until she was at the foot of the bed, holding his feet. Gently but firmly, she cupped his feet in her hands and then carefully, deliberately, she began to rub her breasts against them.

The heat shot through him like an electrical charge. His feet were connected, directly connected, to his penis. He'd never known that before. Through his bare soles he felt Lila's hard nipples moving back and forth. He strained again, uselessly, against the ropes that held him. He had never known such heights of sexual frenzy, of utter frustration. Hopelessly, he arched his feet against the heat and softness of her breast. And then he began to cry.

The sobs, small at first, began to rack him. He pulled against the cords and shook as the crying—deep, deep sobbing—welled up from somewhere in the very center of him. Tears ran down from the sides of his eyes, wetting the sheet. He turned his head to one side, his silent sobs continuing.

And then Lila was on him, her face beside his, her hair cascading over his eyes, his nose, his mouth. "Ooh, baby. Oooh, no. No, baby," she crooned. She wiped his face with her silken hair. "No, baby. No," she said, gently as a loving mother, and kissed his lips, his eyelids, his still-wet cheeks. "Here, here, baby," she said, and lifted her heavy breast into Marty's mouth. "Here. Here," she told him. He suckled, too crazed, too frenzied to be embarrassed. And then she crouched over him, her back to him, and bent over his cock, her soft, hot, perfect mouth kissing him there, her hands stroking him, her fingers loving his balls, his ass, his cock. Through his tears he could see her move her G-string to the side, watched her as she mounted him, feeling the head of his penis push against her, into her. At last. At last. He was surprised but he was beyond questioning, beyond judgment, beyond words, and she was in control; she pressed her perfect flesh down onto him, impaling herself slowly, so slowly, on his throbbing dick. Moving up and down, using her knees, in an atavistic crouch, she slid up and down on his cock, whimpering.

Marty made no sound. But it felt as if his whole being, the whole universe, was centered in his loins, an inferno of pressure that pushed and throbbed into Lila's silky flesh. It was agony, and yet it was the best, absolutely the best that Marty had ever had. He came at last, and he sobbed as he did, gasping with each endless spasm, filling her to overflowing, emptying and cleansing himself.

And so it went. The ritual changed slightly, and it was only once a week, or maybe less, but each time Lila brought out the silken ropes, Marty was more and more inclined, more hungry, more grateful.

And it was strange. Because it wasn't worrying him that he was drawn into this utterly powerless, passive sex. Instead, he found it a huge relief. He realized that all his life had been spent striving to please demanding, difficult women. First his mother, then his professor, then his wife, and a host of beautiful, spoiled Hollywood actresses. He was, he knew, simply a small, skinny, bright, hardworking, overcompensating kid who had been trying to satisfy the goddesses' demands. At thirty-seven, he was still the strike-out kid from Queens, desperate to score, to please his lovers, to perform and be liked.

Now, with Lila, he was relieved of all the burden. The director finally became the directed. And the relief was so enormous that each and every time it brought tears to his eyes. He was no longer responsible for the timing, for the choreography, for the sexual etiquette. Lila chose to perform for him, to be in charge, and if that made her more comfortable, if she needed to be in control so as not to be frightened, it was more than fine with Marty. In fact, Marty was pathetically grateful. For once in his clever, hardworking, overcompensating life, Marty didn't have to work to please a woman. Lila pleased herself, and he took his pleasure like a precious gift.

Once again, he lay in the darkness, one of the most powerful men in the Industry, tied to the bed, flat as a roadmap, naked as a newt. Who would imagine this? Who, in this morass of climbing, backbiting Hollywood serpents, could picture the sex life of one of their most powerful directors and one of their most popular stars? Marty smiled in the darkness. Go know, he thought, and pulled against the tightness of the cords at his wrists and ankles.

43

Jahne lay in the circle of Sam's arms, alternately watching his face while he slept and the face of her watch. These moments were so precious to her, but, no matter how much time they spent together, she was left hungry, ravenous, for more. And soon, too soon, they'd have to be up, preparing for the difficult shoot on the beach.

This was what she had always wanted! And now, at last, it was hers. Sam loved her. She knew it! By his touch, by his gaze, and by the way he made love to her. His passion was so strong that both of them were dizzy, even exhausted by it. All she wanted was him, more of him. And all he needed was her. If only they weren't forced to work on this stupid film together.

He had told her how unsure of it he was. She comforted him. And she told him how afraid she was as well. They gave one another comfort. In bed together, nothing else mattered. The world went away.

Jahne sighed. Neither she nor Sam had said so out loud, but the film was not going well. Michael was almost impossible to deal with. During her big breakdown scene, he'd left his fly undone—an accident, he claimed—and the whole thing had had to be reshot the next day. That wasn't all. Jahne had seen the dailies, and she looked wooden. Beautiful, but wooden. Her new face didn't react in the same way as her old, and on a big screen it looked lovely but almost . . . bland. She'd have to learn to exaggerate her reactions, but it was already too late for the half of the script that was in the can. And it was exhausting to hold the youthful posture she'd created. She projected her chest always forward, her shoulders back; she stood swaybacked to give the illusion of youth. But it was agony to hold. And day after day, it drained her. Of course, Michael and his hammy performance didn't help. Every day was a torture. It was only this time, the time in the dark with Sam, that mattered; it was all she cared about.

After making love that first time in the dark, in her hotel suite, she had had to tell him about the scars. She had been frightened of his disgust or censure or even mere distaste. But he had only looked at her and asked, "Don't you understand? I don't care about your looks. I don't care about that. I love *you*." Then they'd made love again, even more hungrily than before. And she seemed to be fed by his words. "I love *you*. Only *you*."

And it seemed that he did. Each evening, they lost themselves in one another's arms, in one another's bodies. She kissed him all over, tears in her eyes, so happy to have his flesh returned to her. And he caressed every part of her, made love to her so completely, his love burning like a fever under his skin.

"I love you," he murmured as he kissed her neck, her hair. "I love you. I love you." And she, Jahne, believed him as Mary Jane never had.

But what would happen if he found out the truth? She could never tell him now. Once, she'd planned all this as revenge. Now it seemed a punishment for her. She had everything she had ever wanted from him. Why was it, then, she wondered, as she watched his face and the clock's, why was it that she was so sad?

* * *

Michael McLain hated Northern California, he hated filming on location, he hated Sam, he hated April, he hated this script, and he hated this movie, which was a definite *pièce du merde*. Most of all, he hated Jahne Moore, and, he realized with a start of surprise, he hated acting. Not just acting in this dog-meat production, but in *any* production. Christ, it was foolish and wimpy and childish. It was boring. And if, at his level, it paid well, that had long become irrelevant, because he already had all the money he'd ever need.

Still, he couldn't give it up, because, aside from this, he couldn't think of anything else to do. What the fuck else was there? He'd always liked being a star and fucking beautiful women. But now both had become tiresome.

He was too young to retire, and business had never been interesting to him. Somehow, starting a popcorn or a spaghetti-sauce company, or, worse, opening a chain of restaurants, didn't seem attractive. Because, whatever his next venture would be, he knew two things about it: it would have to be on a grand scale, and he'd have to be number one.

Of course, one natural next step was directing and producing. Everyone wanted to direct. But Michael had tried it once, on *Cliffhanger*, and he didn't want to do it again. The pressure was crippling. You were number one, but only until the picture came out. Then they ate you alive.

He could try to pull off some kind of Sundance bullshit, but, let's face it: Redford had already done it, and Michael really didn't have that much interest in sitting around listening to asshole students from Chicago explain their views on "the cinema."

Politics was an option. But not if he had to do it on some local scale, like that putz Sonny Bono. National politics was far more intriguing. He'd done a lot of fund-raising, he was plugged into his party. But where was the niche? Senator? Could he beat the incumbent? And then wouldn't he just be one of all those senators?

"Ready for you, Mr. McLain!" one of the assistants called to him from outside the trailer. Michael clenched his fist, banging it down onto the table before him.

Christ, he thought. Sometimes life was so unfair! He was not only better-looking than Ronald Reagan had ever been, he was also a better actor. How come Ronnie had gotten the good part?

They were losing the light for the beach shot, and the crew was scrambling to beat the clouds. They could cheat, to a certain extent, with kliegs, but without that natural light the film came out looking like videotape. After trouble with a cable (don't mix electricity and water, something almost inevitable on a beach), and then trouble with a lens (don't mix sand and cameras, either), they were finally ready. It was a long panning shot, ending with a swooping close-up of an embrace and kiss. Jahne, jittery enough at the thought of the upcoming scene with Michael, felt just about crazy from the delays. Now, at last, they were ready.

She turned to Mai, to take her sweater and to replace it with the deceptively simple white shirt she would wear for the shot. Of course, the shirt was far from simple. It looked like a man's, was in fact supposed to be Michael's shirt that she'd put on for this walk after their love-making, but it was fashioned out of the finest cotton cambric, softer and more sheer than any man's shirt. And, to heighten its ability to reveal her, it was dampened, so that it turned semi-transparent, molded itself to her breasts, and clung.

Jahne had wanted them to use the body double for this shot, but Sam had begged her to do it. "It would be hard to fake convincingly, and your breasts *are* lovely," he'd murmured, burying his face against them as they lay in bed. Jahne had argued, but he had prevailed. "Trust me. The scars won't show."

Now she turned to Mai, both for the shirt and for the reassurance that the old woman gave her. When it came to Jahne's appearance, Mai was the only one Jahne trusted. God knows how she could have made it through the filming if it hadn't been for Mai.

"It is all in the skin, my dear," Mai told her. "Notice how disappointing stars look in person?"

Jahne nodded. They had looked unspectacular.

"It is the skin. Alvays it is uneven. Splotchy. Or else makeup is obvious. but on the screen, makeup disappears. On the screen, more than anything, it is the flawless skin that creates the illusion of beauty. We must make you up to create the illusion."

"Even my cleavage?"

"Especially your cleavage. We all like smooth. It is primal, infantile. The full breast. Not empty, withered dugs like these." Mai patted her own chest and laughed.

But now, as she turned to the old woman, it was Mai's appearance that startled Jahne. God, Mai looked old! Her face was paper-white, and it seemed to Jahne that every line, each wrinkle was etched deeper than ever before. Is making this movie as awful for Mai as it is for me? Jahne wondered. "Are you all right?" she asked.

"A headache," Mai said, and winced, but that was all Jahne had time for before Joel hustled her out. The wardrobe mistress began misting her shirt some more, while the hairdresser sprayed some artfully tousled strands across her face.

"Watch out for my makeup," Jerry Detria warned him. Jerry crossed his arms, his brush ready to correct any flaws. Jahne almost smiled. Jerry was so protective that, when he finished with her, he'd tell her to "be careful of my face." Now he looked her over minutely, nodding his approval, and Joel moved her to her place. Her stand-in, a nice woman named Dorothy, smiled and stepped out of the way. Jahne took her spot. Then she waited.

And waited. And waited. At last, after perspiration had begun to trickle down her side despite the cool wind whipping at her wet blouse, Michael stepped onto the set. Without a greeting, without even a look at her, he turned to the camera and the place where Sam was ensconced with the cinematographer and the best boy. "Ready," he told them, through tight lips.

There was another pause, and then: "All right, ready, action." There was a pause. "Rolling!" Michael took her in his arms, and the long shot began, the camera circling them from a distance as they embraced, beginning the long dolly ending with her close-up. Michael nuzzled her neck. He smelled good, a vague mixture of English soap and some mild spice.

"Like it?" he asked, holding her tighter. It wasn't scripted; there was no dialogue in the scene, so they weren't miked. "Like it?" he asked again.

To be polite, she made a "mmmm" sound.

"I know you like it, you little slut. But do you like it better from Sam or from me?" Michael said, still hugging her tight, the camera moving in for her close-up, only to catch her face frozen in a grimace of distaste.

"Okay. Cut!" Sam yelled. He stepped from behind the cameras and lights. "I know it's a lot to ask, Jahne," he said, "but can you *try* to act as if it's not disgusting to be held by that man?"

Jahne broke out of Michael's grasp. "*You* ruined that shot!" she yelled at him.

"What did I do?" Michael asked, an exaggerated innocence playing on his face.

"Oh, Jesus! Would the two of you stop bickering?" Sam asked. "We're losing the light! Jerry, could you fix her face? Laslo, we'll back it up and try once more. . . ." There was a loud murmur behind him, somewhere. It simply wasn't done when the director was issuing orders. "Could I have your attention?" Sam asked, annoyed. But the noise didn't stop. It grew.

"Get the nurse. Someone call an ambulance!" Joel yelled. Jahne moved, along with everyone else, toward the ruckus. A group was already huddled near her chair. Because she was the star, or for some other reason, it parted for her and she moved through them, as if in a dream. At the center of the group was a small clearing, where Dorothy, her stand-in, sat on the ground, Mai's head in her lap. Even from where she was standing, Jahne could see the thin stream of blood at the corner of Mai's mouth.

"Oh, God!" she cried, and crouched beside them. "Get a doctor!" she screamed.

"It's too late," Dorothy told her.

44

Sam entered the darkened bedroom quietly. Jahne lay, exhausted and sedated, asleep under the top sheet. Only her dark hair and one hand were exposed, her hand flung over her head and now lying limp and all but lifeless on the pillow, an abandoned leaf. The room had become too warm, almost stuffy, since he and the doctor had put her to bed and turned up the thermostat to help stop her shivering. Now he turned it down a bit and went to check on her. Jesus, he didn't need this! Another delay. April was already on his back. How soon could he expect Jahne to recuperate? And why was she taking the death of the old lady so hard? She was a very sensitive girl. Gently he lifted the sheet away from her face. Jahne was so pale she was almost luminous, dewed with a light film of perspiration. He carefully lowered the sheet. She was bare, and he pulled the cover down as far as her waist. Jahne murmured, moved her head to the left, but continued sleeping heavily.

Standing beside the bed, he watched her. She was so beautiful to look at. Her perfect face was partly obscured by her hair, but her neck, her arms, and her breasts were revealed to him. From this angle, he could not see the slight scars on the underside of them. She looked perfect, but, beautiful as she was, she reminded him of nothing so much as a wounded bird—his dove.

Sam felt a stirring in his chest and in his groin. He knew that he had never felt this before. There had been women—lots of women—that he had felt desire for, and he had felt a tenderness this strong for Mary Jane, back in New York. But now, for Jahne Moore he felt a welling up of tenderness that almost brought tears to his eyes, along with a desire so intense that even now he felt a tug at his crotch. Unlike April, Jahne was beautiful *and* vulnerable. Unlike Mary Jane, Jahne was vulnerable *and* beautiful. How had it happened that he was finally granted this woman?

And now, after the death of Mai, Jahne needed him.

He slipped out of his jeans and into the bed beside her. He would hold her until she woke up. What could be more comforting after a shock than that? He would hold her and comfort her for as long as she needed it. To hell with the shooting schedule.

Her body was voluptuously warm against his. He put his chest to her back and fitted his body to hers so that they curved against one another like two spoons in a drawer. She fit him perfectly, and he felt a wave of such tenderness, mixed with such passion, that he couldn't resist putting an arm around her and cupping her left breast in his hand. The heaviness of her flesh and her unconsciousness made the moment intensely erotic and private. He felt almost as if he could possess her more now than he ever had. He also felt his erection bump up against the soft curve of Jahne's buttocks.

Perhaps she felt it, too, for she stirred a little and murmured in her sleep. Oh, how he longed to enter her now, to lie beside her, inside her, until she woke. But was that for her or for him? Wasn't it selfish, even masturbatory, to consider it at a time like this? He wasn't the kind of man who had ever enjoyed taking advantage of a drunken date. He didn't like them passive. But, somehow, his feelings for Jahne were so strong, and at the same time so insecure, that the more often he had her the less he actually felt he possessed her. The public, the media, the Industry owned her. Would she leave him, in the end, the way the other beauties had left him? Was she gone when the picture wrapped?

He pulled her closer against him. This time, in this relationship, he felt her warmth, he felt her sincerity. Was it because he had gotten her while she was young and inexperienced? But what would time and fame do? She was hot, and this film would probably make her hotter. She could negotiate any deal she wanted. She could also take any man she wanted. Would she keep wanting him, or was this merely an adventure? And was she old enough to know?

He ran his hand along the sensuous curve of her side, letting it rest on her hip. His hand was trembling, so filled with desire that it seemed to have taken on a life of its own. It ran over the smooth skin of her behind, and then slipped between her legs. He buried his fingers in her pubic hair and cupped her sex in his hand. Holding her there, his palm at the mouth of her femaleness, both soothed and further aroused him.

Then he felt her wake. "Oh, Sam!" she breathed, her voice thick with sorrow, sleep, and drugs. He nuzzled into her neck and kissed her there. He felt her move her head. Was it toward his caress or away?

"Oh, Sam! Mai. She's dead, Sam. I'm all alone again."

His own voice seemed husky with his restrained lust. "You're not alone. I'm with you now. I'm with you, and I'll never leave you." He rose on his elbows and covered her mouth with his own. She tasted of tears, and the metallic tang of the sedative. He couldn't bear to take his mouth off hers, or to wait a minute more. He'd never felt this for a woman, any woman, ever. He could hardly stand it. He spread her legs and entered her swiftly, then held still, his body shielding hers.

"I'll never leave you," he promised.

45

"I can't believe she just disappeared!" Sharleen said to Dobe. "I mean, I just can't." Sharleen was seated at the redwood picnic table in her backyard. Flora Lee's letter was before her. She looked up. Dobe was preparing to barbecue ribs. Sharleen watched as he turned a slab of ribs over in the marinade with the long-handled fork. Then he sat down at the table opposite Sharleen.

"It's for the best, Sharleen," he told her, his voice serious and low. "We had a long talk. She was ashamed of what she was, and of being a burden on you. She thought this was best."

Sharleen shook her head, indicating that Dobe

shouldn't speak in front of her brother. "I don't know what he'll think," she said softly to Dobe. Dean was sitting on the grass, tossing balls to the dogs, who chased them across the lawn. Oprah sat upright at Dean's side, unmoving.

Sharleen smiled at the picture Dean and the little herd of dogs made, then looked at Dobe. "We're goin' to miss her, Dobe," she said.

"I ain't," Dean said, not looking at anyone. "Not Flora Lee. *She* wasn't my momma. I'd know Momma in a Texas minute, and that weren't her."

"What makes you say that, Dean?" Dobe asked.

" 'Cause of the way she smelled. Like my daddy used to. But Momma, she used to smell different than him. All sweet, like clean laundry."

Sharleen knew that in a way Dean was right. Their momma *had* always smelled good. She remembered it, too. Momma was always washing herself, her clothes, her hair. Sharleen remembered how she used to brush her momma's hair, after it was washed, for what seemed like hours, and her momma would nod off to sleep while Sharleen brushed.

"No," Dean said, "I'm glad Flora Lee's gone. Now I can go back to rememberin' my momma. That was better than having Flora Lee here." He stood up, and all four dogs jumped to follow him. "I'm goin' to do their tricks one more time with them, make sure they got it right, then I'm goin' to come back and show you all. All four of them. How much longer for the ribs, Dobe?" Dean grinned. "I could eat a calf and a half."

"You got time enough to play with the dogs. But the hot dogs is done. Help yourself. They'll hold you for a while."

They watched Dean walk away, the dogs bounding around him, each trying to get the hot-dog bits that Dean began tossing at them.

"I'm surprised he said that, Dobe. I guess most folks would say Dean is simple, but it seems to me he gets most things right. Still, I feel scared about Flora Lee. Should we do somethin'?"

"Sharleen, I'm here to tell you some home truths, unless you don't care to hear 'em."

Sharleen looked at him silently, then visibly took a breath, but said nothing.

"Sharleen," Dobe continued, "your momma, who *ain't* your momma anyhow, is—excuse my language now —nothin' but a whore, and maybe a little bit worse."

Sharleen winced, but she continued sitting, silent and still, except for a tear that flooded over her lower left eyelid and began a slow course down her cheek. "I don't say this to hurt you, girl. I say it to clean out an infected wound. I know it pains you, but you gotta know."

"Didn't you think I did?" Sharleen asked quietly.

Shamed, Dobe looked away. He had underestimated her. "I had to be sure you knew. 'Cause she's gone away and she won't be back. She's taken care of—least as well as she can be, till someone puts an end to her, or she puts an end to herself. And there ain't nothin' you can do to change that, Sharleen. Not one damn thing."

"I know that, too," Sharleen said. "I watched my daddy dyin' for years. But Momma—Flora Lee—well, maybe she wasn't my blood kin. But she was good to me. And she is my family."

"Family ain't what you inherit, girl, it's what you make with those you love who love you back."

Sharleen thought about that for a while as the ribs sizzled on the grill. "I wanted to be a good daughter," she said. "Maybe, if I'd done better, she could have . . ."

"Ain't no one can be a good daughter to a bad mother," Dobe interrupted. There was silence between them for a long while.

"I'll tell you what's funny," Sharleen said. "Seems like I lost my real mother early, but I was given Flora Lee. She *was* a good stepmomma, Dobe. Honest she was. She treated me good as her own child. Never made no difference between me and Dean. I never blamed her for leavin'. My daddy would have killed her. But I did sorely miss her, all them years. Then we found her. And here's the funny thing: I missed my momma most, right

694

here in L.A., after she came to us. It was like I'd lost not only her but her good memory, too."

"I know how that can be, Sharleen," Dobe said. "I was married once." He stepped away from the grill, wincing at the smoke. "Sharleen," he said, "I want to give you this." He handed her a key.

"What is it to?"

"A safety-deposit box at California Central Bank. It has important papers there. Papers from your momma. I want you to have the key for safe keeping. Go look at 'em someday."

The phone rang inside. "I'll get it," Dean said, and jumped up. He returned with a portable phone, and handed it to Sharleen. "It's Mr. Ortis," he said. Dean made it his job to answer the phone, to make sure Sharleen didn't get any of them dirty calls.

"Hey, Mr. Ortis. What're you doin' workin' on Sunday afternoon?" But Sharleen knew that Mr. Ortis always worked, and always called her with more work for her to do. Sharleen listened to his excited voice.

"I'm not doing it no more," she insisted. "No more albums. It ain't right. It ain't me singing, no matter what you say. No. No. I mean it." She hung up the phone.

Dobe raised his eyebrows as she'd raised her voice. "Another problem, Sharleen? Sounds as if you do got a lot of troubles." His eyes wrinkled in a smile. "It's 'cause you're such an important person."

"It's a good thing you know me, Dobe. 'Cause sometimes I begin to wonder about that. But then I look at you or Dean, and I know. I'm just regular folk."

"Well, it seems you're folk that can sing."

"Dobe, I ain't kiddin'. I *can't* sing."

"Well, you could have fooled me. I heard that record. They're playin' it on the radio night and day, and, Sharleen, you *can* sing, girl."

"That's just it, Dobe. That don't even sound like me. Sy says they can fix your voice with all that technology they got. I mean, you sing any old way, but they can do lots of things with all that stuff, make you sound different. But I think they just called in another girl. One who can sing but ain't famous like me. Somehow, it don't seem fair, do it?''

Dobe chuckled, then looked at her troubled face and shook his head while he took the ribs off the grill. ''Ever hear of con games, Sharleen? Almost anyone can play 'em.''

46

''Miss Irons?''

If she heard her name one more time today, she would cut someone's throat. She answered the steward without looking up from her notes. ''What?''

''The captain asked me to tell you we'll be landing in Oakland in fifteen minutes. Is there anything I can get for you?''

''No,'' she snapped. ''Just make sure my car is waiting.''

''I've already called ahead. It'll be on the apron as you deplane.''

April waved the steward away, made a few last entries on the page, and closed the leather-bound book. She looked around the cabin of the Cessna Citation to the only other person on board and beckoned to her. The woman came immediately and stood beside April. ''Yes?'' she said, simply. No ''Miss Irons,'' April noticed. At least this one was learning. ''Did you get him?''

''No. I left three messages that you wanted to speak to him, but he hasn't returned your calls. His secretary said Mr. Shields was working on a scene with Miss Moore and wasn't to be disturbed.''

''Does he know I'm coming?''

''Yes, since yesterday.''

April shook her head, then handed her secretary the notebook and snapped, ''Type this. I want it by the time we get to the set.'' She watched the woman move forward, sit down at the word processor, and begin to type. A hundred words per minute, but what the fuck was her name? she thought. April had been through three or four of these bitches in six months and couldn't remember one from another. A thousand bucks a week to type and place phone calls, and they couldn't take the heat. Not one of them. Well, the next one's going to be a man, she told herself. Like the old queen Samuel Mayer had. In his fifties, on top of everything, and loyal to a fault. Except they don't make executive assistants like that anymore.

April looked down onto the Pacific coastline, and saw the waves pounding the nearly empty beaches. Somewhere down there, on one of those beaches, was the cast and crew of *Birth of a Star*. Fucked up and out of control. All of them bending under the pressure.

Michael had been whining to her on the phone all week. "I'm not going to take a dive on this one, April. I can't even get to see the dailies. No one can, for the last three weeks. Sam has that flunky kid leaving the set every night with them and a fucking security guard. They've started to call the kid 'Tsar of All the Rushes,' security's so tight."

She knew that. Sam had stopped sending them to her, too. And she was the fucking producer! "What's your read on this, Michael?" she had asked.

"What's *my* read? Jesus Christ, April, you have a director just out of the gate who's taking a week to set up a two-character beach scene—the fucking beach is *already there*, and he's three weeks behind schedule. *And* over budget. Performances suck, morale is worse. And *no one* gets to see the dailies. Plus, he's holed up all the time with the dumb bitch. What's that tell you? If this film goes down the tubes, I'm fucked!"

Everything had gone wrong. Michael fucking Jahne. Sam fucking me. Sam fucking Jahne. Michael giving it to Sam for fucking Jahne. Christ, they were all skittish. Michael was the bankable star; the movie rode on his back. Also, he had to be asking himself, Is this my last romantic lead, or only my second to last, or third to last?

And Jahne Moore, nervous as a cat. Well, of course. Her *first* film. Would the transition from the little box to the silver screen work? April had seen personal lives fuck up her deals before, from the Julia Roberts–Kiefer Sutherland breakup to getting caught with a Madonna–Sean Penn deal on the table. But she'd never had a film where the female costar had fucked the male lead *and* the director. And certainly not when she, April, had *also* been fucking the director.

She gritted her teeth. Sam Shields and she had come to an understanding: she had forgiven the dalliance with Crystal Plenum, but before she signed him to direct this turkey, she had made it clear that from that point on she expected loyalty and continuity.

Now the shmuck was sleeping with Jahne Moore, and April would lose face. Not to mention money. Sam had dipped his wick and lost control. Control of himself, the crew, the project, the budget.

April was coming to fix all that. Everyone would be punished.

The plane banked to the right, and the seat-belt sign came on. April noticed that her secretary fastened hers but kept typing. Now, if she could just get that kind of work out of the artistic assholes she was on her way to see, she'd have a movie. Maybe not a box-office smash, but at least respectable return on investment.

They taxied to a stop outside the private terminal. April stood up, smoothed her skirt, and motioned for her secretary to pick up her briefcase. She walked down the lowered steps to see the black stretch limo pulling up. The back door opened, and a young man stepped out, holding the door for her. It wasn't Sam. She couldn't believe it. April strode over to the door and looked at him. He smiled, a light mist of perspiration forming on his upper lip. "Good afternoon, Miss Irons," he said, as she was about to lean forward and step into the car.

When he made a move to follow her into the back seat, she paused, turned, and looked him over from head to toe. "Who the fuck are you?" she snarled.

The skinny kid jumped back. "Joel Grossman, Miss Irons." He spoke quickly. "Sam's assistant director, Miss Irons. We met in L.A. I mean, I was at the meeting when Sam hired me and I saw you, Miss Irons."

This was as good a place as any to start meting out the punishment, she thought. "What do you keep saying my name for? Afraid you're going to forget it?" She ducked into the car and sat, not moving over to make room for him.

"May I join you, Miss . . . I mean, do you want me to ride in the front?"

"Am *I* supposed to move?" she asked. He didn't answer. Instead, he closed her door and ran around to get in the other side. The secretary got in the front, next to the driver.

"Okay," she said, when he'd got in and closed the door, not looking at him. "What are the problems, and what are the solutions? In twenty-five words or less."

"No problems, no problems," he hurried to explain. "We're just a little bit behind because of the weather. Other than that . . ."

"You got ten more words left. Better talk to me straight." Just as I thought. This asshole is going to try to make a fool out of me.

"Well, Miss Irons," he said, really getting into it now, "you know what an artist Sam is. Everything has to be perfect. In that way, he's a lot like Oliver Stone—he's dragging it out of himself, relying on personal experience. . . ."

Oliver Stone! Why not quote Oliver Hardy? She held up her hand. "Just tell me one thing. Was it your idea for you to meet me today, or was it Sam's?"

The kid's face dropped. "It was, uh, Sam's, Miss Irons."

She flicked the switch on the intercom to the driver. "Pull over. Right now."

The long black car came to a quick halt on the shoulder of the highway back to town. April turned to the kid. "Get out," she said, looking into his eyes. "And tell Sam he should never send a boy to do a man's job."

"But, Miss Irons, we're on a highway! It's three, four miles to the next exit." She saw his lower lip begin to quiver.

"You're an AD. Be resourceful. Now get the fuck out of this car," she told him. She hated it when they made her have to do this. But, goddamn it, I got forty million bucks riding on my ass, she reminded herself, and this little shithead is going to fuck with my head? "Out!" she repeated.

Joel stumbled out, his face imploring her.

"Shut the goddamned door. I'm in a hurry."

The set on the otherwise deserted beach was chaotic. Goddamn it, the set costs were astronomical. And what for? They were shooting the ocean, not some dotty Ferdinando Scarfiotti folly. Klieg lights were on all over, but no cameras were running. How much was *that* costing her? Another indication that this film was getting away from Sam. If he couldn't keep the crew running smoothly, he wasn't going to be able to make a film.

Where was he? Busy playing with Jahne Moore's clit? The movie was the only important thing right now, she reminded herself. Not Sam, not who was fucking who. Just the movie, and her forty mil. Well, not *hers,* but gotten on her name from the sons-of-bitches at American National Bank and Trust. She thought of Sam, wasting her money and gritted her teeth again. She would *never* allow her credibility to be undermined by *anyone,* whether she was fucking him or not.

She sat in the car for a few minutes, waiting for the location manager to notice the only goddamned limousine on the beach and come to her. Finally, he did. "Get Sam," she spat through the open window, then rolled it up in his face as the old guy started talking.

Another ten minutes; then Sam knocked on the door. This was the part she hated the most—wiping asses. She didn't mind it so much with actors. They approached life events as if they were movie roles. They were like troublesome children. But directors—they believed that *life* was a fucking movie. "Get in," she said, not bothering with preliminaries. "I haven't been getting dailies lately, and you haven't returned my calls." She watched as Sam brought back his head and stared for a moment at the ceiling of the car. "No bullshit, now, Sam. I mean it."

Sam began to shake his head. "I don't know, April. It's just not coming together."

"Well, *make* it come together," she snapped, forcing herself not to speak through clenched teeth. "If I had been getting the dailies, I might have been able to help you sooner." And saved us all time *and* money, for chrissakes. "Why haven't you been sending me the dailies?"

Sam put his intense look on, the artistic–fucking–New York–theater–turned–Hollywood–director look that she was beginning to despise. They forget that this is a *business*. The *movie* business. It's not art. It's money. "Jahne's not coming across on the screen. I've been working with her—really hard—and she puts out a lot of energy, but . . ."

April dropped the sympathetic-ear shit. "I already know she puts out. If you can get her to do that, then, goddamn it, get her to come across."

"April, don't think I don't have total commitment to this project. Jahne and I . . ."

"Let's get this straight. I'm your producer, no matter how well we fuck. Do you get that? I'm your *boss,* and right now I don't give a shit what you do with your dick except when it interferes with my money. Your spot in bed can be filled with just a phone call. So don't talk to me about total commitment. You know, when Barbet Schroeder's movie was about to go into turnaround at Cannon, he showed up at his boss's office and threatened to cut off a finger with a jigsaw. They let him continue. Are *you* that committed? Me, I'd *help* you cut off body parts, and not just fingers. As your boss, I'm telling you that your job and your future can be taken care of that easily too. So don't get confused. You're working now. For me." She allowed her voice to return to normal. "Why are you three weeks behind schedule and two point six over budget?"

"Mostly the weather. We haven't had sun in seven days. I was hoping we'd get some sun this afternoon, but it doesn't look like it."

"Then what?"

"Then . . ." Sam shrugged his shoulders.

April felt like choking him. He had no plan B? Why

had she let him talk her into filming this on location? "You wanted to play God, so you became a movie director. But this isn't a stage, Mr. Off Broadway. This is the movies—the great outdoors. So, when you can't shoot outside, shoot interiors. Christ, do I have to tell you *everything*? Okay, make sun. You have fucking kliegs on, and you're not even shooting. You're over budget and you're going to tell me about *sun*light?"

"Wait, it's not only that. Michael's been giving me a lot of shit. He's playing temperamental."

"You're fucking his snatch. What the hell do you expect?"

"Jahne and I . . ."

"I told you, *I don't give a fuck.* Except it's costing *me* money. Now, what's the holdup on shooting this beach scene? It's James and Judy walking on the beach together, the next-to-last scene in the movie. What's the *problem?*"

"Michael is only five four."

"So was Alan Ladd. So what?"

"But Jahne is five six. Plus heels. Plus hair."

"Yeah, so?"

"Well, we needed time to come up with a solution that would allow us to shoot long shots front and rear. We finally got it. We had a ramp built the length of the beach. I think it's going to work."

"I'll go you one better, Sam. It had fucking *better* work, because all you've got is tomorrow." She pointed to the door, dismissing him. "I'll be here at six in the morning, rain or fucking shine, Sam." She paused, turned to him, and looked him in the eye. "Oh, and Sam: another thing. You had best show up in my hotel room tonight. I don't care if you can't get it up, but I won't be left looking as if you prefer some television starlet to me."

On the way back to the hotel, she laid her head on the cushioned headrest. Another migraine. The doctor said it was stress-related. Fucking shmuck. *Life* is stress-related. She wondered for the millionth time why she hadn't picked Bo Goldman for the project right after he came off *Scent of a Woman*. She had barely got into the hotel room when the phone began ringing.

"April, I heard you were on the set, but you didn't come to see me." It was Michael. This one was hurt Michael. Well, *you* didn't come to see *me*, she thought. And *I* sign the checks. Instead, she just sighed.

"I have a lot on my mind, Michael. And a major migraine. I had to get back here and lie down."

"Migraine? I know an ancient Chinese cure for migraines. Want me to come over and show it to you?" His voice was syrupy.

"This is a forty-million-dollar headache, Michael. I don't think the ancient Chinese had a cure for anything that expensive. I'll see you on the set in the morning. That's six A.M., Michael. We're doing that scene, sun or no sun." She thought of the six million bucks he was getting for this and gritted her teeth again.

"Of course I'll be there. I've been there every day, ready, willing, and able." His voice dropped, sexy. "But, hey, April, this is *Michael*. I can cure *anything*. And I happen to be free tonight."

"You've *never* been free," she said, and hung up.

The next morning, April was on the set before Michael, Sam, or Jahne. She spoke to the lighting director, who then pulled in more lights, and had reflector boards positioned around the beach. Sam was the first one on the set. "I see you've taken to directing?" he said.

"You sound surprised, Sam. As if it's a rare talent or something." She turned to him before he could respond. "Let me put it straight to you. You're not doing your job, so someone's got to do it. Either you do what I tell you today, or I'm going to get someone who will. Do you understand me?" He paled, nodded, and began to walk away.

"And, Sam," she said, still not finished with him. "What's with Jahne and all that makeup on her legs? Is she trying to cover leprosy, for chrissakes?" She saw Sam look over at Jahne's trailer, where the actress was walking toward them, her leg makeup thicker by inches than the rest of the body makeup.

"She's nervous about this scene. She wants to look right, so I gave her permission to do the makeup her way. I think it calls for it."

"I hope you're right, Sam. That one's a judgment call. And you're being paid for your judgment. I just hope that's not your dick talking."

Michael was walking quickly toward them, his hands thrust deep into the pockets of his robe. April braced herself, but she was in no mood for his bullshit today. If he didn't like getting turned down last night, fuck him.

"What's the look for, Michael? You've got a face like a man who's found out he has something that can't be cured." Let *him* start off on the defensive, she thought.

Michael ignored her, and walked up to Sam. "What the fuck is that?" he asked, indicating the length of wooden boards running along the beach. "Is that a fucking ramp?"

"Yes, Michael. It's the best way we could compensate for Jahne's excessive height." April could see Sam sweat. Pussy. He'd never manage Michael *that* way.

"I'm not walking on any fucking ramp. You can forget about it."

"We got the lighting just right, the crew and cast is ready to go. I want this scene shot today, Michael. We've lost too much time on it as it is." April had moved to stand next to Sam in front of Michael.

"Fuck you," Michael said, turning his attention to her for the first time today. *"I'm* the one that's carrying this dog on my back. And I'm not going to lose my dignity by subjecting myself to walking on any fucking ramp."

April had a movie to make, and investors, and a forty-million-dollar budget that was getting out of hand. "But, Michael, how do we do the long shots?"

He took a couple of steps back toward his trailer, then turned and looked at them. "Dig the bitch a trench!"

47

Jahne sat in her trailer, waiting to be called for the next take, writing to Dr. Moore. Because, after all, she had no one else to explain anything to. Mai's death had hit her harder than she could have imagined it would. She wasn't sleeping, and the resulting bags and swollenness were making photography a nightmare. And her almost constant crying wasn't helping.

> I know you're going to think that you told me so, but even if you did . . .

She paused. She had everything she'd ever wanted. A great career and the man she loved. But did she? It was still hard for her to believe that she had Sam now, again. That he loved her, held her, wanted her. She still felt his hands run over her body, caressing it. His mouth against hers, on her neck, her breasts, her shoulders, her belly and lower, even lower.

> He loves me, but it doesn't feel like I'm there. Or maybe it's more that he's not. When he touches my face, it's not *my* face. Well, what I mean is, of course it's my face, but it's not the face I had before, when he didn't love me.

In a way, it felt as if each caress were a blow. Each time Sam stroked her face, he might as well have slapped it. Each time he traced her profile with a loving finger and marveled at her perfection, she trembled under his hand as if he wielded a weapon. How could it be? she asked herself over and over. He *is* what I want. He is what I *always* wanted, and now I have him. At last, I am loved.

But, somehow, some part of her couldn't take the love he so openly offered. It was clear to her that Sam adored her. She saw, firsthand now, what she used to observe other women receiving. She remembered her New York friends Chuck and Molly, and how Chuck had been almost sick with love for Mol. She thought of all the pretty girls, the actresses and dancers she had known, and their ardent lovers, men who followed their women with hungry eyes, who seemed drawn to them like pins to a magnet, doting. And she remembered her envy, and how bitter it felt to know that she would never be in their sorority, that she had never inspired, and would never inspire, that kind of passion.

She thought, then, of Neil. Mary Jane's one conquest. Yet his desire had shamed her—even sickened her, in a way. She felt that he had only loved her out of desperation and loneliness. He had so few other options that being "chosen" by Neil had felt to her like a condemnation, not a compliment. It was official acceptance into the Losers' Society. It was admitting that not only were you unlovely but you accepted the fact and would lie to yourself as you settled for another such as yourself, another awkward, funny-looking, unlovely person. Your lie would be that you truly loved one another, but the truth was that you had run out of choices, time, and hope.

But was that perception true? Or had it come from her own self-hate? Hadn't Neil been the man who truly knew her, who really approved of her? Who accepted her true self? *She* had been the snob, she had been the one afraid of a plain mate.

She had escaped that fate, she told herself fiercely. Mary Jane, that unlovely lump of a woman, was dead, and Jahne Moore should now lie beautifully, gracefully, beside her handsome, lanky, successful lover and luxuriate in his caresses. She was one of life's winners now, and if she had had to purchase the spoils, they still belonged to her, the victor. The past was dead, the present could be delightful, and the future even more promising. Why did it all feel so empty? She just had to get over Mai's death and her own morbid attitudes.

There was no doubt in her mind that she was having a breakdown of some sort. Too bad she couldn't do it in the privacy of her own home. Now over two hundred people depended on her mood, her looks, how she'd slept the night before. This morning, Jerry, in desperation, had daubed Preparation H under her eyes to reduce the swelling. Every one of her pores was discussed, like NASA scientists studied moon craters. And Sam depended on her ability to concentrate, to emote. But she couldn't do it, for chrissake. She seemed almost paralyzed, split into two or more selves. Was this schizophrenia? Or, for a person who had been, still was, two people, was it normal? And what was any normal person's reaction to the pressures she was under?

Each night, when Sam made love to her, she'd cry. At first, he was touched, and tears came into his own eyes. But it had been over a week now, and her tears continued. Lovemaking, the only thing she had found comfort and release in, had become a nightmare of tears.

And Michael was making each take an absolute nightmare. It was becoming almost impossible to stand on her mark beside him, let alone act as if she worshipped him. She despised him. She'd never seen a man be so petty about a rejection. Of course, she reminded herself, she'd never had the luxury of rejecting a handsome man before. But his nastiness was way out of proportion. After all, it was *he* who had deceived *her, he* who had not told *her* about Sharleen, or Lila. Why should *he* hate *her?* He'd cheated on her, dropped her, and insulted *her.* Why had he been surprised by *her* slap?

Well, whatever his reason for hating her, he did, and it was scary. He did small things to trip her up, odd line readings that threw her off her cue, movements that prevented her from hitting her mark. And now that she was so fragile; now, since Mai's death, he was even more heartless. This morning, he had called her a "puffball," alluding to her swollen face.

But the scariest thing of all was this feeling she'd get with Sam. When he looked at her, when he'd reach out and stroke her. She'd look at his face—the very look she had longed for, that look of adoration, of love—and she'd feel . . . jealous. Then the tears would begin. It was crazy. She'd feel jealous of Sam's feelings for her, Jahne. Because now that she, Jahne, had his love, she still wanted it for Mary Jane.

God, it was crazy. Had Mai's death unleased all this, or was it the pressure of the shoot, or was it the affair itself? Oh, God, whatever it was, it wouldn't let her sleep at night, wouldn't let her relax. It left her so tired that she could barely concentrate.

Jerry, her makeup man, was sitting in the alcove by the mirror, smoking a cigarette and waiting to do what he could for her. She put down the pen and picked up another Mounds bar. She had begun to have a craving for candy: this after almost four years of going without any desserts or sugar. But the craving was irresistible. Each bite seemed a comfort. Until, of course, she tried to struggle into one of the costumes that Mai had worked so hard on and found the zipper stuck. She knew she'd gained at least five pounds. It shouldn't matter—it wouldn't matter in normal life—but the camera was merciless, and every bulge, even the smallest, would show.

Mai had worked so hard on each piece, perfecting the lines of every one, camouflaging the tiniest imperfections. Now, Jahne realized, she was ruining Mai's last work. Was she doing it because she was angry at Mai for dying? Or because she was so desperate for comfort? Whatever the reason, she was driving both Wardrobe and herself crazy.

She finished the last bit of the Mounds bar and licked the dark chocolate off her fingers. She picked up the letter to Brewster again.

> I've been so tempted to tell Sam everything, but I don't know that it would improve anything for me, and it might make things worse. I suppose what I want is not a change in Sam's present behavior but a change in his past. I want him to have loved me then like he loves me now.
>
> Too bad you couldn't do surgery on the inside of me as successfully as you did on the outside.

Oh, it was impossible! Jahne crumpled up the letter, threw it in the wastebasket along with the envelope from Dr. Moore's last note. She'd write to him later, when it made more sense, when *she* made more sense.

There was a knock from outside the trailer. "They're ready, Miss Moore," Joel's annoying little voice called. Jahne walked out to Jerry.

"I'm ready for my close-up, Mr. DeMille," she told him grimly.

Minos Paige stood outside the trailer. He was wearing a dark-blue jumpsuit. Over the left-hand pocket it read "Cinema Sanitation" in orange chain stitch. He waited until Jahne Moore was called to the shoot, then knocked politely on the trailer door. "Sanitation," he said. "Can I vacuum up now?"

The makeup guy let him in. Minos carefully began to Hoover down the rug, then wiped all the visible surfaces of the trailer. The silly-ass makeup pouf sat there the whole time. So Minos just emptied the wastepaper basket into his big plastic garbage bag and walked out the door.

Later, in the van, he had the time to go through the rumpled tissues, the candy wrappers, the unpleasant flotsam and distasteful jetsam, until he found the gold: the envelope, postmarked New York, return address Dr. Brewster Moore.

48

Lila snapped up the phone on the first ring. For the new season of *3/4*, she had not only snagged the lead, she had a new trailer with three phone lines. Phones that, unfortunately, never stopped ringing.

"Miss Kyle, I'm sorry to bother you, but you got a visitor out here." It was Security, at the front gate of the lot.

She waited. "And I'm supposed to guess who it is, right?"

"Oh, no, ma'am . . . It's Minos Paige. . . . I woulda gone through your secretary, only the guy says I should call you direct. Seeing as how I seen him around before,

I figured it was all right. I mean, he ain't no fan or wacko, you know? He says he got business . . .''

"Send him to me," she said, and slammed down the phone. She held her hand on it for a moment, trying not to get too excited. Paige knew not to come to the studio unless he had something really big. Otherwise, he was to send his reports to her at home. Lila sat down at the vanity table and began to brush her hair—long, slow strokes. She started to braid it, changed her mind, and disentangled it again, then resumed the methodical brushing.

"Yes," she said to the knock on the door, and turned to face it when Minos walked in. He waved a manila envelope in his hand, and smiled. "It took you long enough," she said.

Minos dropped his hand and the smile. "It's only been a little over a month, Miss Kyle."

"I mean from the front gate. What did you do, go on the studio tour?" She held out her hand for the envelope, but Minos turned and sat down without being asked, holding the envelope on his lap. Okay, we're going to play some games now, Lila thought. She was in no mood, but thought again of the possible contents and smiled. Officially, she would be judged for the Emmy by last season's performances, but she knew everyone would see the new show before voting. And now, if there was some juicy stuff to take some of the shine off the other two . . . "It's been a very long day, Mr. Paige. You must forgive me. Would you care for something to drink? Coffee? Perrier?"

"No, thank you. I figured you'd want to hear all this in person, so that's why I came to the studio. Don't worry. I haven't worked this lot in a while, so not very many people would recognize me. So few old-timers left." He settled himself more comfortably in the chair.

This is where I get the bit about how hard he had to work, and how his fee barely covers it, Lila thought. Well, he better have something, or else this creep is out on his ass for wasting my time. Lila leaned forward, her elbows on her crossed legs. "What have you got?" she asked, still smiling.

Minos smiled back, evidently very pleased with himself. "What do you want first? The good news, or the very good news?"

Goddamn him! "This isn't a surprise party, for chrissakes. Spit it out."

Minos got the picture. "Jahne Moore," he said, looking down at a small notebook he'd flipped out of his pocket. "Real name, Mary Jane Moran. Born in Scuderstown, New York, September 22, 1958. She was . . ."

"What? *When* was she born?"

Minos jerked his head up, then looked back at his notes. "September 22, 1958. In Scuders—"

"Jesus Christ! That makes her . . ." Lila thought for a moment. "That would make her almost *thirty-eight years old*. You got that all wrong." Lila sat back, folding her arms across her chest. Minos said nothing, just opened the manila envelope, reached in, and took out a sheaf of papers. He handed Lila the first one. "Exhibit A," he said, a smug look on his face.

Lila took the photocopy from him. It was a birth certificate, all right. For Mary Jane Moran, born September 22, 1958, Scuderstown, New York. So what? "But how do you know this is Jahne Moore?" she asked, handing back the photocopy.

Minos shook the rest of the typewritten papers in the air. "High school diploma, yearbook with picture, nursing-school diploma, unemployment book from New York City, depositions from kids she acted with in some church-basement theater workshop . . ."

"For Mary Jane Moran. But what about Jahne Moore?" Lila was having a hard time holding in her excitement, and her fear. "What do you have on *Jahne Moore?*"

"A legal name change and deposition from a lawyer in Albany. Pissed off over some probate deal that's soured on him. But wait, it gets better. Interview and files from a nurse in a plastic surgeon's office in New York. It seems our Jahne Moore is a real Cinderella. She got ahold of some money and had herself done over. The grandmother died just before this, so maybe from her. Had herself carved head to toe. Took two years. According to this nurse, she went from an ugly, overweight mouse, to a twenty-four-year-old sexy beauty. Money can do that for you." Minos paused, his expression changing. "Speaking of money, I've taken the liberty of promising this medical source a large payment. Seeing as how the *National Questioner* would outbid you if they knew about it, I put you out on the limb. Not by name of course."

Lila snatched the nurse's deposition from his hand and scanned it hungrily. Medical records. Pictures! Befores and afters! It was all here. "She went to this plastic surgeon, Dr. Moore? Was she related to this doctor?" Lila asked Minos.

"No. Nurse says she probably had the hots for him, though. Who knows, maybe they traded tit for tat, you should excuse the expression. He was her Henry Higgins. You know, like in *My Fair Lady*. Anyhow, the nurse showed me the records." Minos kept talking while Lila devoured the typewritten pages. "Made her appointments as Mary Jane Moran. That was her biggest mistake. She shoulda started with the alias *first, then* the surgery. Typical amateur. His records even show her present name and address right here in L.A." Minos handed Lila a folder. "So," he said, "that's the 'good.' Ready for the 'very good'?"

Lila didn't have to answer, couldn't answer. There was something better, juicier than *this?* She tried to digest it all, but realized that she couldn't. Not right now, at least. Just take it all in for now, she told herself. Then decide what to do. Slow down.

Lila could smile without forcing it. "Minos, I'm impressed. Now the 'very good.' " She settled back to listen, although she was sure he couldn't top this. Jahne Moore, carved like a duck out of a piece of soap. Soap melts, she thought, then brought her attention back to Minos' words, which now, strangely, had a very calming effect on her. This must be how alcoholics feel after their first drink in a long while: peaceful, like the world is really okay. "I'm ready," she told him.

Minos turned gleeful. "You're not ready for this. Listen: Sharleen Smith, from Lamson, Texas. Has a brother, Dean. . . ."

"You mean a *boyfriend* Dean," Lila asked, almost afraid to breathe. She'd heard about Dean.

"No, a *brother*, Dean Smith," Minos said. "Two years younger than her. They've been passing themselves off as boyfriend and girlfriend for the last few years. But the mother says no, they are her kids all right."

"Their mother *admits* this? Where's the mother now? How do you know it's the truth?" Lila felt the words rushing out of her.

"I traced the mother to New Orleans. She was a drunk and a whore before she started getting money from Sharleen. Now she's just a drunk. Sharleen keeps her out of sight. Packed her off to New Orleans for some mysterious reason."

"You don't have to be a detective to figure out why she packed her away, for chrissakes, Minos. Her kids are fucking each other."

"Yeah, I know, but that's not what I mean. There's more to the story, but I didn't have enough time to get into it that deep. I figured I'd get back here to give you what I found out so far." Minos handed Lila two snapshots. "Got these from the mother's house."

Lila looked at the pictures. It was Sharleen all right. Maybe she was eight or nine years old. The little boy must be Dean. They were standing with some white-trash couple in front of a trailer.

"How's that so far?" Minos asked.

Lila sat back, the papers and snapshots on her lap. Unbelievable. Had any incest perpetrators ever won an Emmy? Lila smiled. "You've done very well, Minos. I'll go over this all tonight, then call you tomorrow. I might want you to do some more for me, depending." She stood up to let him know his time was up.

Minos didn't stand. "And the money, to the nurse?"

Lila smiled. "Worth every dime, Mr. Paige. Don't worry about a thing. We'll talk tomorrow." She shook his hand, then closed the door behind him.

Lila stood there, all the power she needed in her hands. I did it, she thought. I finally did it. I got both of them.

Now Lila knew the Emmy was hers. She went over to her dressing table and picked up the old sepia photograph she kept there in a silver frame. Thank you, Nadia, Lila said to herself. Thank you. Now I got both Candy and Skinny out of the way. It took a very long time, but they're both dead now. And I get my *own* show.

She'd been so pleased she'd forgotten to ask about Jughead and his threats.

Lila had just finished rereading the papers Minos had left her, savoring every word, and put them back in the envelope, when the door to her trailer banged open. She jumped up and stared at the figure in the doorway.

"What are *you* doing here? How did you get on the lot? I gave specific instructions . . ." Lila's voice trailed off as she picked up the phone to call Security and rip that guard out another asshole.

"Lila, Lila, Lila. Don't overact. I always told you, hold *something* back." Theresa O'Donnell began pulling off her long white gloves, finger by finger, as she stepped into the room, then sat in the chair Lila had just vacated at her vanity table.

Gloves in California, Lila thought. Leave it to her mother to develop an affectation that other people *wouldn't* copy. Who was she playing today? Miss Piggy? Now that Lila was past her first shock, she could cope. "Isn't it a little dangerous for you to be out of your coffin in daylight?" Lila asked, putting the phone down before Security answered.

Theresa turned to the mirror and began to examine her makeup. "We take our chances, darling. *You* know that."

"You've taken a big chance today, then, because I'm going to have you kicked out on your ass." But Lila didn't pick up the phone again. And she wasn't sure why not.

She heard Theresa's throaty laugh. "Lila, I *own* a piece of this lot. They don't kick stockholders off their own property. And *no one* kicks Theresa O'Donnell out of *anyplace*." Theresa was still looking in the mirror, now considering her hair.

Lila took a step closer to her mother. "What do you want?"

Theresa sighed and turned to face Lila. "There's been a terrible misunderstanding that I need to clear up. I was offered a part on *Three for the Road*, then had it suddenly pulled out from under me. Paul Grasso said it would present too many conflicts. I said to him that he *couldn't* mean with my *daughter*—she's such a *professional*. But he seemed to think that you didn't want me on the show." Theresa slapped the long gloves against one hand. "So, here I am, darling. You have *got* to clear up this misunderstanding with Marty, tell him you *do* want to work with me. I'm *so* looking forward to us working together, Lila. It's something I've always wanted. And you, too, of course. So, call Marty. I'll wait."

Lila had feared this day, knowing that it would come, but not knowing when. "Get out," Lila simply said.

She watched Theresa's face tighten; then a smile returned once again. "Jack Warner taught me something, once. I've never forgotten it, used it to negotiate every contract I ever signed. Never issue an ultimatum unless you hold all the aces." Theresa leaned back on the table on one elbow, and crossed her legs at the knees. "I see you had a visit from Minos Paige, Lila. What was that little creep doing here? You're not thinking of doing business with the worst piece of scum in Hollywood, are you? You'd want to think twice about that."

Lila kept her eyes from falling on the envelope still resting on her vanity table, too close to Theresa for Lila's comfort. What was in there was for Lila only. The last person she wanted to share the dirt with was her mother. Because somehow, Lila knew, her mother would use it for her *own* benefit.

"How do *you* know Minos Paige?"

"I know everything. *Everything*, Lila. *Remember* that." Theresa laughed again, like she didn't have a care in the world. That always made Lila nervous. That meant that Theresa *didn't* have a care in the world. "Once, when he was very young, Kerry found out some smarmy little jealous actor put a private detective on him. Your father was—how should I put it?—vulnerable in several areas, but not stupid. So Kerry got one of his friends and a couple of prostitutes: a sixteen-year-old male hustler who looked twelve, and a dead ringer for the young Shirley Temple. You couldn't fuck with Shirley Temple and get away with it.''

Lila could see Theresa was having a good time, going down memory lane. But Lila wasn't in the mood. ''If this is your way of saying goodbye, I'm bored already.''

Theresa ignored the remark. ''They got this guy with chloral hydrate in his drink, took him to a hotel, stripped him, and photographed him in every position imaginable with the two kids. The next day, Kerry had the pictures delivered to the guy's house, and left them in a sealed envelope with his wife. Then he called the guy and told him what he had done, and where the pictures were. The guy beat it home just in time. The wife had a letter opener at the flap as he walked in.''

''Why are you telling me all this?''

''Because it's important for you to know your heritage. And to remember that what you can do to someone else, they can do to you. Or anyone can. My point, Lila, is that two can play the game. You see, I think that, if you really thought about it, you'd see how it would make much better sense for you to have me as your co-worker, rather than your enemy.'' Theresa motioned to the envelope on the table. ''I've got some of those at home. Dozens. And if I have nothing to lose, maybe . . . who knows?—maybe I'd even open them up and pass them around.''

Lila felt the chill run the length of her body. *''You're* in those envelopes at home, Mother. That stuff pertains to you, too.''

Theresa shrugged. ''Let's keep this short and sweet, Lila. You want to find out someone's secrets but keep your own? Here are my terms: I do the season-opening show *and* a miniseries with you.''

''Miniseries! I am not . . .''

''I'm not *asking* you, you ungrateful, malicious little bitch. I'm *telling* you. Get a deal out of Marty DiGennaro. You could if you tried. Whatever little secrets

Minos is tracking down for you will look like nothing compared to yours."

"They won't just crucify me, Mother. They'll crucify you, too."

"Better public crucifixion than private oblivion. So, consider next week the deadline. Sign on the dotted line, bitch. Or I'll blow your whole scene wide open. And I have nothing to lose. No television show, no movies, no powerful man in my life." Theresa paused. "But *you*, you have lots to lose, don't you, Lila?" Lila watched her mother stand up and begin to pull her gloves on. "You want that Emmy, don't you? Ask yourself that. And if the answer is yes, then call Marty DiGennaro. And tell him how much you love me."

Theresa grasped the door handle in her hand. "And if you decide you have nothing to lose, well, then it will be back to just you and me. And maybe Kevin. One happy family." Then she walked out the door and closed it softly behind her.

Lila sat down before her knees buckled under her.

49

Now that Flora Lee was gone, Dobe was with them, and Sharleen didn't have to work on 3/4, she was actually beginning to feel good. She spent long afternoons in the garden, weeding, and she put up tomatoes, canned some peaches, and made an unbeatable three-bean salad.

Dobe was going to have to leave again, but, though she'd miss him terribly, Sharleen was so grateful to him that she could hardly resent his going, or his need to live his own life. It was just that she felt he was the only person who she could lean on, and when he left, she knew she'd feel very alone.

Tonight they were having a goodbye dinner, and the talk was casual but fun. Dobe told them half a dozen funny stories, while Oprah sat, content as usual, superior to the gamboling puppies.

"Hey!" Dean spoke up. "I saw a new license plate today. 'North Carolina, First in Flight.' Does that mean they're chicken? I wouldn't be proud of that."

Dobe smiled and explained about Kitty Hawk. "Good name for a cat," Dean said.

After Dean helped Sharleen clear, Dobe stacked the dishwasher while Sharleen mopped down the table—she didn't like to leave a mess. Dean took all the dogs out back. It was then that Dobe started talking business—not his business, but hers.

"What are you investing in?" Dobe asked.

"I don't know," Sharleen told him. "Lenny takes care of all of that stuff."

"Buying any land?"

She shrugged. "We bought this place, but I don't think we bought any other land." Somehow, she felt uncomfortable talking about this with Dobe, as if it were wrong, or maybe dangerous. "You had enough to eat?" she asked, trying to change the subject.

"Sure did, and it was good, too. You're a good little cook, Sharleen. But let me ask you another question, Sharleen. You still got that idea of havin' a ranch someday?"

She didn't want to talk about this to Dobe. Somehow, she knew it would lead to trouble. "Yeah," she said reluctantly. "Me and Dean would like that someday. When we got enough money." It was once she said the word "money" that she realized what felt wrong: talking to Dobe about money made her feel as if, maybe, he was talking to her the way he did to those people he sold the fake gas pills to. "Let's go outside," she said. And wandered out into the darkness. She hoped that would be enough to change the subject.

"You lookin' for a partner?" Dobe asked. For a moment, she didn't understand. "A partner in your ranch?" he prompted. "Someone to scout out the real estate, maybe to get it started for you till you come out later."

"I don't know, Dobe," she said, and felt her heart grow heavy in her chest. Oh, God, she should have known that Dobe's help would have a price. Like everyone else out here, he was looking to make some money

718

off her. Somehow, Sharleen felt it would be easier if he just asked her for money instead of trying to scam her out of it.

"Listen to the way I see it, Sharleen," he was saying. "The longer you wait, the higher land out in Montana is going to cost. But I met a guy, got about four hundred acres that he'd sell to me for a hundred thousand dollars cash. And it's beautiful land. But after I finish this shoe deal, I only got about fifty. Now, if you go in as a partner, we could either split the land or live on it together. There's a river there, Sharleen, that's so beautiful you would hardly believe it. And a house. Needs some work —kind of rough, you know, like how a single man lives —but it's sound. And there's a view from the front porch that would just about break your heart."

Sharleen felt as if she didn't need to have her heart broken—again. Her daddy had broken it. Flora Lee had broken it, and now Dobe was. Could you have a heart broken three times? Well, she knew how it felt: real bad, real sad, and real tired. It seemed like everyone but Dean expected nothin' but money or work out of her. Tears flooded her eyes, and she turned her head so Dobe couldn't see her in the darkness. The only light was from the dying coals of the barbecue. She stood there silently for another moment.

"Well, I guess it's not something you'd chose to do right now," Dobe said, and she could hear the disappointment in his voice.

He had helped them, back when they needed help worse than they ever would again. She remembered standin' in the road, outside Lamson, scared and tired, afraid of the police and without a place to go. Even now, she could recall the comfort of sinking into the air-conditioned back seat of Dobe's big old sedan.

"Sure, Dobe," she said quietly. "Me and Dean would love to be partners with you. I'll ask Lenny for a check tomorrow."

"You sure?" he asked.

"Sure I'm sure," she said, but she knew her voice lacked conviction. Well, like Lila said, Sharleen knew she wasn't a very good actress.

If Dobe noticed, he didn't show it. He stuck his hand out, took her own, and pumped it. "You won't regret it, partner," he told her. "I really think I got us a hell of a deal lined up. Uh, excusin' my French."

She nodded. "Great," she said.

"So, mind if I tell Dean?" he asked. "I didn't want to bring it up in front of him in case you didn't like the idea. But now that we're . . ."

"No, let's not tell him until the deal's all done," she interrupted, looking out into the darkness for Dean and the dogs. "He gets so excited, and so tired of waitin'. Let's just surprise him later."

"Anything you say, partner," Dobe smiled.

50

April Irons' visit had shaken up the crew, but it had shaken Jahne even more deeply. She knew there were problems with the film—maybe there was nothing but problems. Still, she only thought of April as Sam's ex-lover. He had explained there was no longer anything between them, but Jahne was not so sure.

And when, on the night of April's visit, for the first time in weeks, Sam didn't come to her room, she'd been hurt and suspicious. He told her it was only business, but she could tell from the looks of the crew that word was out. Mai would have told her the truth. No one else would. Had Sam spent the night with April?

Has it started again? she asked herself. I've gotten difficult and emotional. Is he going to cheat on me, lie to me, the way he lied to Mary Jane? I'm dependent on him, she thought. Exactly what Mai told me not to be. Is he with April? Does he care for her? Is he touching her?

That night, she'd driven herself nearly crazy, and the fiasco on the beach the next day only made things worse. Sam took her aside and told her he'd worked all night. She chose to believe him, and after the crew dug a ditch in the sand, she walked through it and the scene as best she could.

That night, Sam had been even more passionate, and had promised her again and again that there was nothing between him and April.

"Jesus," he finally moaned. "I wish this shoot were wrapped. I want to go home."

But Jahne, though she desperately wanted the movie to end, had no home to go to.

Jahne had always heard that wrap parties were wild, outrageous farewell bashes, but the party at the end of the *Birth of a Star* shoot wasn't even cheerful with relief that the pain was over. Michael's misbehavior, Mai's death, and April's wrath had combined to make this a hell trip for everyone. Jahne had, as she knew she was expected to, bought gifts for all the crew: carryall's with *Birth of a Star* and "Love and Thanks from Jahne" embroidered on them. Sam made a little speech, but Michael showed up only for a few moments, and April Irons, Seymore LeVine, and the suits didn't show up at all. That was a relief, but still, the party was an ordeal that was best when it was over and she and Sam were free to leave the nasty little world of gossip and tension that the set had become.

Before editing and looping began, Sam had decided to take a few days off and drive down the coast. Jahne wasn't expected back on the set of *Three for the Road* until the end of the next week, so they'd holiday a little. She'd never needed a rest so badly in her life. As he tossed her bags into the trunk of the 300ZX, she felt her spirits lift for the first time since Mai's death. They got into the car, waving goodbye to Jerry and the others who were still left at the hotel, and then Sam gunned the motor.

"Why," he asked, "why did I ever think I wanted to be a director when I grew up?"

"Oh, doesn't everyone?" Jahne replied. The famous joke around the Industry was the one about Mother Teresa dying and being received in heaven by God and a host of singing angels. "You were so wonderful, so good, down on earth,'' God says to her. ''I want especially to reward you. Isn't there anything you wanted to do that you never got a chance to?'' She begs for no special treatment. But God is equally insistent. ''Name one thing you've always wanted,'' He insists. ''Well,'' Mother Teresa finally admits, ''I always wanted to direct.''

Now Jahne smiled at him. ''You and Mother Teresa.''

''Yeah. We have so much in common,'' he laughed.

''Well, you were both christened.''

''How did you know that?'' Jahne realized Sam had—back in New York—told her a long funny story about the ceremony. Something she, as Jahne, just couldn't know.

''Oh, I just assumed you were. Wasn't everyone?''

''Was your family religious?'' he asked.

''Not really.'' Whenever questions about *her* earlier life came up, Jahne reverted to the shortest casual answers. She certainly didn't want to seem secretive, but she was always afraid she'd be caught in a contradiction if she said much. As she had always done for her stage characters, she had imagined a past, complete with an army dad, a housewife mom, and a peripatetic youth. Not enough time at the various bases to put down roots or make lasting friends. And then there was the tragic car accident, so she didn't have to contend with questions about living family members today. In fact, since she was representing herself as in her twenties, she didn't have much of a past to account for. She smiled, remembering her New York friend Molly's take on why men preferred younger women: they didn't have as long a story.

The only problem was that she wasn't a stage character and this wasn't supposed to be acting. This was her real life today, and she had everything she wanted. Except, of course, for the irony that she could never *be* herself. A day, an hour didn't go by in which she wasn't tempted to tell Sam everything, but now she was in too deep. She had told so many lies. Wouldn't he hate her for lying? And wouldn't he feel a fool to have believed them? And maybe a cad to have put her in the position to lie?

So she did her best to ignore her feelings and keep up her charade. Beneath all that, though, wasn't she still hoping, waiting, for him finally to look at her and see her, *know* her? The Bible referred to carnal possession as a man "knowing" a woman. Now that they were lovers, didn't Sam know her?

"Did your folks make a big deal about Christmas? Mine didn't. I was always jealous of other kids for that."

"No. Baptists don't, really."

"I thought you said they were Methodists."

She smiled, but her stomach tightened. "Well, Dad was. But Mom was Baptist." She paused, a bit unnerved. They really hadn't had long periods of time to talk, what with shootings all day and lovemaking all night. Suddenly the car felt confining, claustrophobic instead of cozy. "What was the best Christmas gift you ever got?" she asked.

It was always surprisingly easy to turn the conversation back to Sam. He did love to talk. About himself, about movie-making, about the theater, about books, about the difference between Jung and Freud, about, well, about everything. And it was almost always interesting. But, Jahne had to admit this time around, it was also narcissistic. Sometimes she had the feeling he appreciated her intelligence, her self, more as an audience, a vessel to understand him and be filled by him than as a discrete entity.

In fact, sometimes she saw him as a sculptor, a creator, always trying to mold. He had created plays, he now created movies. She had to admit, when she was Mary Jane he had done a lot to mold her taste, her opinions and views.

Jahne turned to enjoy the view from the coast road. It was, really, a breathtaking drive, and the day was a good one for it: sunny and mild, and because they'd gotten an early start they'd get to see the sunset before they found a place to stay that evening. Tomorrow they might get as far as San Simeon, Hearst's castle.

The weather was cool enough for her to wear one of the big Donna Karan sweaters she liked, a huge creamy-white turtleneck, and she had the matching cardigan thrown over her shoulders. It was too warm in L.A. to get to wear them much.

"Pretty sweater," Sam said. "It suits you."

It pleased her that he noticed, but she no longer allowed men to affect her taste in clothes. Mai had taught her that. Poor Mai. Well, poor me. Jahne sighed.

"What is it?" Sam asked.

"Oh, I was thinking about L.A. I've gotten a new place there. A more secure one. La Brecque helped me pick it out. It may be safe, but I don't like it nearly as well as my old rental. It seems so grown-up. I was hoping that Mai would move in there with me." She stopped, her lips trembling. No, no more tears today, she told herself. Mai would want me finally to have some fun. "It's too big for one person. It's impersonal. It's cold."

"I'll help you warm it up," Sam offered, a wolfish grin on his face.

"You'll be my first guest," Jahne told him.

He took his eyes off the road, surveying her warmly, then reached across the gearshift and took her hand. "I'm honored," he said, and there was no humor in his voice, only passion. He moved her hand to his cheek. She felt the thrill move down her arm, across her chest, and down to her center.

Mai was gone, Neil was gone, Molly was gone, her mother was so long gone. There was only Sam to love, to be loved by. And at that moment, she loved him so much it hurt.

51

I might as well be into fucking astrology, April thought bitterly to herself as the limo pulled up to the nondescript brick building in West L.A. where forty million dollars was, at that very moment, about to be lost. She could predict the future. Not a horoscope: a horrorscope. April and the stars. That was her life. Reading the stars and trying to predict the future. This project hadn't been hard to pitch to the suits. Remakes they understood. Top stars they understood. It was forty-million-dollar failures they had trouble understanding. And it didn't matter how many winners she'd brought in. One fucking failure and the pricks would start in again with how she didn't understand the realities of the marketplace, or how as a woman she was only good on small pictures, soft pictures. Well, fuck them! If the picture worked, every one of them would be claiming credit, but if it failed, they'd all point to her and say, "I told you so."

April got out of the car and stared up, not to the stars but to the second floor, where carnage was already taking place.

Up there it was like a confrontation between the Crips and the Bloods—two of L.A.'s most vicious teenage gangs. Testosterone amok. None of the stupid bastards knew what to do, and all of them so scared that the only position was a defensive one. April sighed.

When she opened the door to the conference room, it was much as she had expected: the half-empty paper coffee cups, the smoke, the yelling. Michael McLain held the floor.

"Well, what the fuck are you going to do—send it out for a week to Billy Joe's Pitcher Show in West Des Moines, then slap 'Recent Theatrical Release' on the videos and sell them in Asia?" Michael turned to her as she entered, and under the rage she clearly saw the fear. She sighed. She would have to find a way to turn his desperation into part of her solution.

"Hello, gentlemen," she said dryly, and took a seat. Seymore LeVine looked at her, his eyes almost weepy. Afraid his daddy was going to yell at him. Michael sighed but nodded hello. But Sam could hardly bring himself to look at her. She felt his shame, but from long experience she knew it wasn't shame over the ridiculous bungle of this film. It was sexual shame—that "Oops, you caught me" crap that some men do. What a shmuck! As if a couple of orgasms one way or the other mattered, compared to this forty-million-dollar mountain of shit. Jesus Christ, *she'd* sleep with Jahne Moore if it would fix the picture.

"What's going on?" was all she said.

"The end of our lives as we know them," Seymore moaned. Everyone ignored him.

"We are discussing how the genius director wasted a multi hundred thousand feet of film to take home movies of his girlfriend," Michael spat out. "A girlfriend, I might add, who can put out anywhere except on the screen."

"She never put out for me," Seymore mourned.

"Michael has been impossible to direct." Sam spoke for the first time, ignoring the other two. "That, and a certain—well—woodenness in the way Jahne sometimes comes across, has . . ."

"Okay, never mind the 'who shot Jahne,' " April said harshly. "The point now isn't that it's shit, or why it's shit, or even whose fault it is that it's shit. The point *now* is how to save it." April was calm. She was always at her calmest after everything was lost and her back was to the wall. It was the time *before* all was lost that was agonizing to her. Now she could take over.

"We have to save it," she repeated.

"Impossible," said Michael, and April could see Sam wince.

April sighed. Sam was like a spooked horse: his eyes were wide, showing too much white; he'd take off in any direction, just to get away. Michael was impossible. He was also scared, but angry, too. And even at his calmest, Michael was not what one could call a problem solver. And Seymore . . . Well, he was just Seymore. Laslo, the cinematographer, and Bob, the editor, were along for the ride.

But there was a great deal that could be done in editing. The right music, some new dialogue looped in, a voiceover . . . and, if worse came to worst, a few new scenes could be shot. It would be expensive, but perhaps . . .

"We can turn this around," April told them.

"Impossible!" Seymore repeated.

"Look, have a sense of proportion. Eliminating infant mortality in Calcutta is impossible. *This* is only fixing a movie." She stood up, smoothing her leather slacks. Nineteen hundred dollars at North Beach Leather, and the sons-of-bitches rode up into her crotch.

"We'd have a better shot at infant mortality," moaned Seymore. At the studio they called him "Seymore Problems."

726

"Thanks for the backup," she told him, then paced to the window and drew back the curtain. There was no view. "Okay, there's no point to a remake of a great movie unless it *adds* something. I mean, look at *His Girl Friday* and *Front Page*. When Hildy became a woman, it *added* something to the remake."

"Yeah. Sex. *And* Cary Grant. We got nothin'," Seymore sighed.

"You've got me," Michael said.

"I repeat: we got nothin'," Seymore groaned.

"Well, Cary Grant is dead!" April reminded them.

Seymore rolled his eyes. "Even Cary Grant couldn't save this one," he said.

"Jesus Christ, Seymore, would you shut up!" Michael yelled. He looked over at Sam. "Well, *you're* the genius writer-director. What next?"

"Tighter cutting will help," Sam began. "It's too slow. And if we refocus on the love story . . ."

"Piss on the love story." Adrenaline was pumping through April's body. She'd been in this spot before, but each time it felt new. Each time it felt as if this time, *this* time, she wouldn't be able to pull it out and she'd lose it all. Lose the money, lose the job, lose power, lose face. But, just as she had each time before, she felt the solution dangling only slightly out of reach. She only had to be smart enough not to blind herself to it, and to be brave enough, once she saw it, to try for it, and strong enough to make it happen. Goldwyn could do it. Selznick had done it again and again. Capra, despite that motherfucker Harry Cohn, had triumphed. Please, she prayed, more to that pantheon of those dead heroes than to some Yahweh Hebrew-school God, please, let me see the way.

"I want to see the dailies. Every one. Every take. I want to see the out-takes. I want to see every fucking millimeter of film you've shot, and I want to see it forwards and backwards. *Everything*."

52

Jahne returned home—well, back to her empty house—alone after the long day of work. This season, *3/4* was not going to be a picnic. Jahne was overworked and lonely, and Sam was as busy as she was, wrapped up in postproduction. Apart all day, seeing him only at night, both of them exhausted—this was real life, but it felt more like a nightmare. Sam had told her to trust him—trust him about the script, about her performance, about his loyalty and love—but she seemed less and less able to do so. It felt as if each night was a trial, and each day she'd shift through the evidence and her suspicions.

Sam had promised tonight that he'd join her later. She set the table, and put out some of the dinner that her housekeeper had left.

She ate some salad and half a cup of cottage cheese, then showered and got into bed. She'd have the rest of her dinner later, when Sam got back. The cat curled up in her armpit, purring. "You didn't have a good day, either?" she asked it, as it began to knead her arm, preparing to sleep. Jahne fell asleep to its soothing mechanical hum.

It was later, much later, when she awoke. She didn't have a watch on, and there wasn't a single clock in the new house, except for the one on the oven timer. Jahne pushed the cat aside, rose, and paced the empty, darkened living room, afraid to find out just how late Sam was. It was like the night on location when April had shown up and Sam had never come to her. This must be how it begins, she thought. The lateness, followed by the lies, followed by the arguments, followed by the accusations and the denials. She was stupid and childish to think that this time it could be different, that this time he would not only love her but be faithful. She had let this happen to herself. She had promised herself that she wouldn't trust him, that she wouldn't love him. She had promised Mai the same thing. Oh, if only she could talk to Mai!

But what good would that do? Mai had told her what kind of man Sam was and what kind of danger she was in. But she hadn't listened. She had chosen this foolish movie despite her agent's warnings. She had alienated Marty DiGennaro, as well as Monica Flanders and Sy Ortis. She had probably messed up her career.

She looked around her at the lofty, darkening room. It was like a tomb, and she hated it. Perhaps La Brecque and his people had vetted it, perhaps there was an alarm system and a patrol to check on her, but she felt like a target here, exposed and alone. Without Sam, she hated to be in the house. She passed by the dining room, saw the set table. By now the salad had wilted on the plates, and the ragout would be vile. She shivered and climbed up onto the sofa, wrapping herself in the throw that draped its back. Time seemed to crawl by. It must be past one. He hadn't called. Perhaps he simply wouldn't show up. Perhaps she'd never hear from him again. Like with Michael McLain. After all, the movie was finished, except for some looping. Maybe she was no longer necessary.

When she heard him at the security gate, she knew her anger was mixed pathetically with relief. Then there was the sound of his car on the gravel, his footsteps on the walk, his key in the lock. She sat, motionless, and listened as he called out her name softly and walked down the hall. He must have checked the bedroom, then the kitchen. At last, he stood in the archway to the living room, where she could see him.

"Oh, here you are. I'm sorry it went so long," Sam said as he walked into the room. He seemed haggard, the circles under his eyes darker than ever. "We just had a lot we had to go over." He looked at Jahne and he winced. "Why are you sitting in the dark? You're angry, aren't you?"

"You're hours late, you didn't call, and you ask me if I'm angry?"

"I'm sorry, babe. I forgot to call from the office, and then the goddamned car phone wouldn't work. It just kept cutting out. I figured by then that I'd be here in a little while anyway.''

"There are pay phones."

"Oh, Christ, Jahne! In L.A. no one but a junkie uses a pay phone! Give me a break. I'm really getting crushed out there! I have a lot on my mind. I admit it was rude and thoughtless, and I'm sorry, but it's not like we were going out or anything.''

She stood up. "No, we weren't going out. We were just going to have dinner and make love. Nothing worth telephoning home about. And now dinner is ruined.''

"Oh, that's all right. I had a quick bite with April.'' She saw him wince again as he realized that what he had said would worsen her mood. He sighed. "Jahne, you don't seem to understand the pressure I'm under. It's not going to be easy to finish this movie the way we both want it to be finished. I have to stay on good terms with April. We simply had a lot to talk over, a lot of planning to do.''

"What else did you do with April?" she asked. "Let's just get the cards laid out on the table. You're not playing solitaire, you know. This is at least a two-person game. Or is it a *ménage à trois?*''

"Oh, for God's sake, Jahne. April is the *producer*. Don't you understand that?''

"Don't you understand that I'm not stupid and I'm not blind? This time, I won't close my eyes while you humili- ate me in front of . . .'' She stopped and turned away from him, biting her tongue. Sam had never humiliated Jahne Moore, she reminded herself. He had humiliated Mary Jane Moran. She strode across the wide, empty floor to the window, staring out into the darkness. She felt him come up from behind her. She didn't turn to him.

"When have I ever lied to you?" he asked, his voice husky with hurt. "When did I ever humiliate you?''

She wheeled to look at him. "Don't tell me that you haven't slept with April Irons.''

"Jahne, I told you. That was long ago.''

"I want the details. When did it begin?''

"On my first trip out here. She was trying to buy *Jack*

and Jill, and I was holding out because I wanted to direct it."

On his first trip out to L.A., she thought. He was sleeping with Mary Jane—with me!—in New York, and April Irons in L.A. She remembered his apologetic phone calls to her in that dingy New York walk-up. Had he called her from April's bed?

"Well, it seems you didn't hold out for long."

"It was a complicated situation, Jahne. I wanted to sell the play, but I also wanted to direct it and get a part in it for a friend. I had never negotiated for those stakes. I won a couple of hands, and I lost one. We sealed the deal in bed. It was all very heady. You know, the limos, the palm trees, the ass-kissing. Feeling that for the first time in your life you're at the very center of the universe. For once, I was sought after; for once, I had the power. I don't know. Maybe I thought an affair would give me some leverage. It didn't."

All that time he was commuting, she thought. Comforting me, fucking April Irons. Commiserating with me, but sealing his deal in bed with her. Using jet lag as an excuse not to make love. And at the time I blamed myself. She felt her face flush. She wanted to slap him, to hit his face over and over and over. But how could she ever explain?

"Get out," she whispered. "Get out right now."

53

April spent most of two days and three nights watching all of the film. Calling it a bomb would be polite. If she had the choice between releasing *Birth of a Star* or *Hudson Hawk*, she'd go with the Willis movie. After all, *he* had a mother who would pay to see it. Both Jahne Moore's and Michael McLain's parents were dead. And so would she be, if something wasn't radically altered.

For a moment, only a moment, she thought of the great pleasure it would give Bob LeVine to fire her. She threatened him and his job security. He'd love to return her to the subworld of indy producers. She shivered. Christ, it did sound like the title of a horror movie.

Well, the hours of shit that she'd been watching was a horror all right. Michael's performance was angry, even when it shouldn't have been. And Jahne Moore was simply another beautiful face. She read her lines intelligently, but, somehow, the two together made nothing happen.

The film kept running, but April closed her tired eyes. She rubbed the lids, careful not to stretch the skin further. She'd had an eye job only two years ago, and didn't want to go through another for at least five more. In the darkness, with her eyes closed, she could hear both the dialogue and Seymore's snores.

Actually, the dialogue sounded pretty good, she thought. Then she opened her eyes, saw another take, and closed them again. But once again, the dialogue sounded good. It sounded . . . hot. Well, anger was as good a sexual fuel as any, and there had been plenty of anger on the set. Too bad they'd been filming a love story instead of a Schwarzenegger vehicle. What she needed was Mankiewicz to doctor this up. To keep the heat. Too bad he was dead.

She stopped, held herself absolutely still. What was it that Mankiewicz had said? Something about the first guy who found a way to show fucking on the screen would become a billionaire. Or was it Goldwyn? Well, it didn't matter. She kept her eyes closed and simply listened. And then the idea came, slipping in as if it had always been there. The little chill that accompanied it, the thrill, the metallic taste in her mouth. Yess!

Carefully, like tonguing a very sore tooth, she felt her way around it. There was risk. But they had always seen this film as a way to contemporize a great old love story. Well, they just hadn't gone far enough! This was the nineties, for God's sake. It was time. Let's show the world a tender love story—a violent, tragic one—and let's show the lovers on the screen. Not porno actors, but stars you knew, stars you loved, real stars making love on the screen. Not a slap and a tickle, a quick frontal shot, but the real thing. Okay, a little soft focus here and there, but let's give the people what they want. Let's have every woman in the audience wet, every man stiff as a board. And so what if Michael was getting old? They'd use a body double, they'd fake it, they'd cut and intercut.

And she thought they could get both audiences: the young ones that would go to a movie half a dozen times, *and* the aging boomers. Yes. Kids, gonads pulsating, would take their dates. Twice. After all, Jahne Moore was their biggest wet dream. While the boomers would feel nostalgia. The women had made Michael a teen idol twenty years ago, and the men had watched him as a role model and had grown old with him. There was life in the old dog yet. And, by extension, in them. They'd eat this up. And everyone would go home and rip one off. Then, later, what would it do in home-video release? Oh, my God! What wouldn't it do?

It all worked. It sounded great! Of course, it required a certain amount of daring. Not since *Last Tango in Paris* had a major star done sex. Even Michael Douglas in *Basic Instinct* had held back more than a little. But McLain was desperate. And afraid he was losing it. It would have stud appeal. April knew she could sell it to him.

It was Jahne Moore who might prove a problem. April smiled. The body-double clause that had cost her so much legal time and effort! Sy Ortis' stupid clause! It would allow her to cut and splice anything she wanted to. Why, she could have the body double dress like a chicken and bark like a dog if she wanted. And if the close-ups showed Jahne Moore's face, well, that was the magic of Hollywood. Of course, it might upset Miss Moore, or Sy Ortis, or Marty DiGennaro. Maybe it would lose the bitch her Flanders Cosmetics contract. It might even upset Sam to see what looked like his girl spread-eagled on the screen. Good thing she, April, had retained final cut. Sam could take it or walk, she couldn't care less. Her smile broadened as she stood up.

"Gentlemen," she said, "I have an idea."

54

After she threw him out, two days without Sam, two nights alone, were more than Jahne could bear. She walked through her days, an automaton, and sat up for the nights. What had he done to her, and what had she done to him? She got a copy of *Great Expectations* and read again about the mad Miss Havisham and her heart-cold ward Estella. Then she lay in bed and sobbed. Who had she avenged? What had she proved? How and why had she done this to herself? At last, hopeless, she called him on Friday, and he asked her to come over to his place on Saturday night.

They spent the evening together, making love as if they'd been separated for years, not days.

She agreed that she'd been irrational, that what was in the past was over, and that she believed him when he told her there was nothing between him and April. She went to sleep in his arms, the only way she could sleep now without waking with nightmares, always of the past.

But, like a crusty scab, the past was something she could not stop herself from picking away at.

Now, this sunny Sunday morning, Sam lay stretched across his living-room sofa. He looked exhausted. She knew postproduction was not going smoothly. Still, they would have this quiet time together.

Sam put his hand into his pocket and held it out toward her. "I have something for you," he said, and when she saw the glittering in his hand she thought, for a moment, of Michael McLain's gift. But this was no diamond. It was a key, Sam's key.

"For you," he said. *"Mi casa, su casa."*

She took it. "Does this mean we're pinned?" she asked, and laughed to hide the depth of her feelings.

"Do kids *still* use that expression?" He was reading the *L.A. Times* and sipping fresh-squeezed grapefruit juice that he had picked up at Mrs. Gooch's. As usual, he had opened first to the sports section. She watched him as he scanned the columns looking for his basketball fix. Jahne clutched the key. He had never given his key to Mary Jane. She stared at him. He must have felt her gaze, because he looked up. Another tribute that only an exquisite woman would receive from Sam: he'd even interrupt his fanatical sports-fan pursuits for her.

"You know how I know that I'll never be a real Angelino?" he asked. She shook her head. "Because I could never, ever love the Lakers." He turned back to the sports pages. "You'd think, with all the displaced New Yorkers out here, they'd give better coverage to the Knicks," he grumbled. He cocked an eyebrow at her. "Did I tell you that you look better in my sweats than any woman I've ever known?"

Demurely, she tucked her legs up under herself and pulled the stretched-out gray shirtfront over her knees. "And have a lot of women modeled your sweats?" she asked. She tried to sound casual, and succeeded, but she cursed herself for asking.

"I've had my share." Sam smiled, looking over the scores. Don't start, she told herself. But she felt the wave of curiosity and rage grow. Where had he spent the last few nights? In whose bed?

"Sam, how many women have you really loved?" she asked.

He looked up from the paper. "Uh-oh. Is this going to be an 'I'll-show-you-mine-if-you-show-me-yours'? Because I don't play that game, Jahne. And if we did, I'd win, because I'm a lot older than you are." He paused and looked her over appreciatively. "Although I imagine there was a long and distinguished line of high school boys who broke their hearts over you. Not that I want to hear about any of them. After all, I'm more than a decade past *my* sexual peak."

"Not that I could tell."

"Ah, you bring out the best in me." He went back to the scores.

She should read the arts section, take a look at the book reviews, and give it up. Just leave it alone, she told herself, but she couldn't. It was as if all those years of unspoken jealousy, all those horrible years as Mary Jane, when she lived on crumbs and closed her eyes to everything she couldn't bear to see, couldn't afford to see, were spilling out now. "I don't want to hear about your conquests. I just want to know who you *loved*."

He frowned, lowering the newspaper. "Now, at last, you're sounding your age." He put down the sports section, got up, and came to her, seating himself on the arm of the big chair she was in. "What do you want to know that for?" he asked her, his voice gentle. "Isn't it enough to know that I love you? Jahne, I'm working so hard to make you look good in the movie. I'm championing you. Don't you know how I feel?"

"You were married," she said. It sounded like an accusation, even to herself.

He rolled his eyes and sighed. "Yes, I was married. I thought I loved her at the time, but now I realize that we were both too young to know who we were, let alone who we loved."

What was she looking for? she asked herself. She didn't know, but she couldn't stop. "How old were you?"

"Oh, about your age," he laughed. "But you have your head on a lot firmer than I ever did." He reached over and stroked her hair. Then he put a hand on both sides of her face, turning her head gently back and forth. "Yep, this head is definitely on firmly."

But this wasn't enough. She had to know. She had to hear it. "If you didn't love your wife, who did you love?" she went on, relentlessly.

"Jahne, there are questions I've never asked you. I felt you didn't want to talk about them. That was all right with me. Can't you feel the same?"

"You mean my scars?" she asked. "That's different. They have nothing to do with you. But who you love, *how* you love, does have to do with me."

Sam stood up, turned away, and reached for his glass of juice. He took a swallow, then wiped his mouth with the back of his long, graceful hand. She thought he was ignoring her question, closing the subject, and she felt both irritation and relief. Then he spoke. "I once loved a woman named Nora. She was crazy, I was crazy, but I did love her.''

Jahne felt her heart begin to beat harder. Was that it, then? Had he *never* loved Mary Jane? "Did she love you?"

"Who knows?" He shrugged. "She said she did, but she left me for the producer of my first play. I guess she figured producers cast more often than playwrights." He gave her a lopsided grin. "She was right."

She couldn't smile at the joke. "Who else?" she asked. Please, God, she prayed silently, please, God, let him say he loved Mary Jane.

"I loved a woman in New York. Another actress."

Thank you, God. Oh, thank you. But then it occurred to her that it might not be Mary Jane he was thinking of. It could have been anyone. Bethanie Lake, for all she knew. Jahne felt her heart flutter, then beat even harder. "What was her name?"

"It's not important now." He got off the sofa arm and knelt on the floor in front of her, putting his two hands on her shoulders. He looked deeply into her eyes. "I can honestly say that I never loved anyone the way I love you. No contest. Nothing even close. I feel blessed to touch you." He moved his hands up to her cheeks and lifted her face to his. "Do you believe me?"

So, there it was. The Lord had given, and the Lord had taken away. If he had loved Mary Jane, he was negating it now, even as he told her that he loved her. Tears filled Jahne's eyes.

"Oh, Jahnie, don't cry. I knew I shouldn't have played your stupid twenty questions! I swear that I've forgotten every one of them. They don't matter. There's only you." He drew her from the chair and circled her with his arms, rocking her as if she were a child. "There's only you," he said.

Jahne stood on the set of *3/4* with all the lights turned on her, Marty and the crew all staring, the cameras rolling. "Perfect," Marty was saying. "You are perfect." But then it was Sam's voice coming from the darkness behind the light. "Perfect," he said clearly. She was naked, but she stood there proudly, admired by all of them.

Then, "Are you crazy?" Lila shrieked. "Look at those scars! Look at them!" And as they looked, Jahne could feel the scars growing red, glowing. Then, in her shame and horror, she felt her breasts begin to sag, her thighs to bulge, her stomach to hang, her ass to droop, and the men, Lila, and the audience all began to laugh. Neil was there beside her, dressed as a magician. "Ta-da!" he chortled, as he waved a magic wand. "Before and after. After and before."

Jahne woke from the nightmare in a sweat.

Sam slept beside her, but Jahne was terrified. Her breath came in gasps, but Sam didn't awaken. Quietly, so as not to disturb him, she got out of bed, left the room, and went into the cold white marble bathroom. It was enormous, vaster even than the one at the Beverly Wilshire, with a big Jacuzzi, built-in makeup drawers, recessed lights, an enclosed toilet, and a bidet. Jahne shivered in its coldness.

Jahne flicked on the light, blinked, and saw herself, reflected in the floor-to-ceiling mirror. She approached it more closely, scrutinizing her face, the face she had bought. She stared into her eyes, her own, unaltered eyes. But in the light of the new bathroom, it seemed to her even her eyes had changed. She couldn't bear to look at them.

She flicked off the light and wandered into the high-ceilinged living room of her new house. It was impressive. The white tile floor seemed to stretch endlessly into the dining room, the long hall, and through to the kitchen. Jahne drifted toward the glass doors that led out to the pool and garden. The moonlight poured down, one of the few smog-free nights in L.A. Jahne stood and looked out to the perfect terrace, the perfect topiary trees, the perfect Roman pool, the perfect everything. And, La Brecque had assured her, all perfectly safe. Little or no chance of madmen intruders, fans breaching the walls, photographers telezooming in on her.

Too bad she didn't like the place. It had nothing to do with her, it had nothing to do with her taste, who she was, or the way she wanted to live. It was forced on her, like her fame, like her new life. And it was grand, but no place she wanted to be. She sighed. Her feet were very cold on the tiles of the floor.

Then Snowball, her sleek black cat, rubbed up against her leg. When they had arrived at the house after their trip, Sam had admired everything but Snowball. Back in New York, he had never really liked Midnight, either. The city cat used to pounce on his chest at night and wake him. "Why do women have cats?" he'd grumbled. As if sensing that, Snowball had kept away, but now he nuzzled Jahne's left foot, as if that would warm her. She scooped him up gratefully and went back to the bedroom.

Sam was awake when she entered. "Where were you?" he asked, out of the darkness.

"I had a dream. It woke me, so I just took a look around."

He held his hand out to her, tried to pull her onto the bed. "I had a dream, too. It was about you," he murmured. He tugged at her and she stumbled, almost falling over him. Snowball jumped out of her arms, tried to gain a footing, and took off across Sam's chest. Sam shrieked with surprise and pain at the scratch.

"Oh, no, Midnight!" Jahne cried. "I'm so sorry, Sam. I was holding the cat."

Sam was silent for a moment, then longer. In the darkness, she became frightened. "Are you all right?" she asked. He said nothing; then she heard him move, fumble for the light, and the room was ablaze. She blinked in the sudden glare, saw the scratches across his chest, the blood just beginning to ooze up. But it was his face that scared her.

"Not Midnight," he said. "That isn't the cat's name."

"What did I call him?" Jahne asked. But she knew. The dark, her voice, the cat had all conspired at last to give her away.

Black cats named Snowball, white ones named Midnight. Contrary Mary. "Who are you?" he whispered.

She sat, frozen, at the side of the bed.

"Who are you?" he demanded again, and moved across to her, a hand gripping each of her shoulders.

"This has all happened before, hasn't it? A cat pouncing on me in bed. Except it wasn't a black cat named Snowball, it was a white one named Midnight. *Who are you?*"

His voice had risen now, and he stared deep, deep into her eyes. Eyes from which she'd removed her deep-blue contact lenses. "Oh, my God," he said, and she saw the recognition come to his face. But "Who are you?" he asked again.

She felt as if her world were coming apart, as if she were spinning out of control. "I don't know," she whispered.

They sat opposite one another, on either side of the kitchen table, the overhead light unbelievably harsh. The clock ticked loudly. A quarter past three in the morning. Sam was pale, his mouth compressed to a colorless line.

"When did you decide to do this?" he asked again.

They had been going around and around. Jahne had never been so tired. She had tried to answer all his questions. Despite her rage, she felt, somehow, guilty. Well, she should have told him. She should have let him make the decision, not forced this on them. But she was tired of all his questions. She had told him the story, all of it, and now he was asking her to repeat, to clarify. Like he was a lawyer, or something. But she owed him at least this, she told herself, and took a deep breath. "In the winter. After you left."

"Hey, don't make it sound as if those things were related—our breakup and your surgery."

"They were, though."

"Jahne . . . Mary Jane . . . you made a decision to slice up your flesh, and you can't blame it on me!"

"Oh, can't I? Why not? Didn't you always let me know I wasn't pretty enough? Didn't you?"

"That's a complete lie! Goddamn it! I never said a word about your looks."

"I didn't say that you *said* anything. But you let me know. You slept with all the pretty ones. Because I wasn't enough. Not the way I was. And then Hollywood agreed with you, and you left me. So I decided to change things. Don't you dare rebuke me for that."

"It was all in your head. We broke up because it was over, that's all."

Jahne stood up. She felt herself trembling all over, and a heat in her belly and chest that she recognized for the pure rage it was. "Don't you dare lie to me about that!" she roared, and her own voice filled the kitchen. "I've slept with you, and I know the truth. Mary Jane never got a word, never a goddamn word of praise. But Jahne . . ." She took a breath, lowered her voice and began to imitate his during lovemaking. "You're so beautiful. Yes, Jahne, yes. God, I love your legs, your breasts. You're so perfect. You're . . ."

"Shut up!" he shouted. Her mimicry had been eerie. He jumped up, striding to the door.

"Where are you going? Don't you dare leave now."

"Goddamn it! Don't tell me what to do!" He tripped over the chair at the counter, and it clattered to the floor. He continued to move toward the door. Jahne knew that if he walked out now she would kill him or she would die. She picked up the heavy pottery bowl from the center of the table and hurled it at the door. It smashed against the wall, leaving a deep scar in the door frame. The shards flew around the room and skittered on the floor. She hadn't missed his head by much. He turned back to her, blinking his eyes. Was that fear she saw there?

"Don't turn your back on me," she warned him. "Don't lie, and don't take me for granted. I'm not the same woman you abandoned in New York, you son-of-a-bitch."

"You've lied to me. What do you want me to do, ignore it? I don't even know who the fuck you are. I can't ever trust you again."

"Big fucking deal! Like you haven't lied to me daily. About the part in *Jack and Jill*, about Bethanie Lake, about April Irons, about who was going to play opposite me in *Birth*, about whether the script was any good . . ." Despite her determination not to, she began to cry. Because she knew that, in part, he was right. Who was she? The aging, abandoned Miss Havisham, raging in her rotting bridal gown, or was she Estella, the cold revenge? It felt as if she was both, and couldn't contain them. It

741

felt as if victimized Mary Jane and the new Jahne were tearing at her own guts. She moved to the counter, picked up the vase of anemones, and threw them across the floor. The release felt necessary. She wiped her arm across the counter, smashing the pitcher, the crystal glasses. Because either the glassware or she was going to be smashed. She turned to him. Sam still stood in the doorway, frozen by her outburst. He was not a violent man.

"What do you want from me, Jahne? What the hell do you want?"

"I want you to love me."

"But I did love you! And you do this."

"Well, see how it feels. I loved you more than anyone in my life. You weren't just a walk-on in a cast of thousands. You don't know what it felt like, loving you and knowing I wasn't enough. Not perfect enough. Not pretty enough. Not young enough."

"So you decided to teach me a lesson? Jesus Christ, it's macabre. The Revenge of the Stepford Wife. That's not your nose, that's half of your ass, and that's a plastic chin. All the time we were together, you were laughing at me. I was groveling at your feet, and you were laughing."

She looked up at him. "Laughing is the last thing I was doing," she said.

Then, there, under the unforgiving glare, in the shambles that had been her kitchen, she realized the enormity of her problem: he was the only man who could heal her pain. If he could love her now, knowing who she had been and what she had done, he could heal the split in her. His absolution, his understanding and acceptance, his love would be the blessing of total acceptance. If he forgave her, she could forgive herself. If he loved her, she could love herself.

And if he couldn't, she realized that all she had been would blow away, be gone forever. And she could never trust that any man who loved her new incarnation was not betraying her old one.

A fear, deeper and colder than any she had known, slipped like a knife into her belly and froze the anger. She shivered. Her future, her life, depended on Sam's seeing the truth, owning it, and being able to come through this with her. He had loved her, he did love her. He must continue to love her. If she stopped, right now, and made him realize that here, at last, their better selves could meet, there was a chance that both of them could win. "Please, Sam. Please," she began. "I know you're hurt. I'm so sorry. But this is important. Really, really important." She started walking toward him, her bare feet numb to the broken glass beneath her soles. Tears ran down her cheeks. "Don't just blame, Sam. Because, if you do, I won't be able to forgive you." Jahne continued to walk toward him and to sob, but Sam, pale as death, didn't try to console her. He merely shook his head.

"How could you?" he asked. "Mary Jane, how could you?"

Oh, God, it seemed hopeless. All at once, she felt the glass beneath her feet, and the pain that began to throb. She looked down. Blood was mixing with the glass shards on the white ceramic tile. It didn't matter. It wasn't important. What was important was getting him to understand. How could she explain the self-hate, the desperation, the ambition that had driven her? How could she defend having her flesh vacuumed, cut, and stapled, having her skin peeled from her tissue and relocated? How could she explain giving up sensation in her nipples for sensational breasts? How could she explain dropping her friends, her life, and doing all this? How could she explain, to the only person that she wanted—that she needed—to understand, how could she explain what it had felt like to be plain, aging, an invisible, undesirable lump of a woman? How could she tell him? She must gain his compassion. How could she do this? she wondered. But also, how could she not?

Sam looked at her again, with horror and disgust. "How could you do this to me?" he asked.

Infamy

I wouldn't do nudity in films. To act with my clothes
on is a performance; to act with my clothes off is a
documentary.
—JULIA ROBERTS

Facing the press is more difficult than bathing a leper.
—MOTHER TERESA

It's all fantasy that if you're considered attractive you
have a perfect life and there's no dark side.
—MICHELLE PFEIFFER

Infamy

So, you hate Sam Shields, right? He's like all those bums you've had in your own life, all those men who left you, who lied, who weren't there for you in the end. But remember, like all those bums, Sam Shields feels like he's the one with an ax to grind, he's the one who's gotten a raw deal, the one who has been disappointed, the one who was betrayed.

After the scene in the kitchen, Sam reeled out of Jahne's house as if he were drunk. He could hardly believe that the woman he had loved, the woman he had risked his career for, had betrayed him in this way. Jahne was Mary Jane. It was unbelievable. It was ghoulish, a Stephen King horror. She had fooled him, made a fool of him. With a kind of sick fascination, he tried to remember conversations about their past. How often had she laughed at him, how often had she caught him in lies, evasions, and half-truths?

Inevitably, defensiveness set in. After all, he'd been caught posturing, foolish for months. But how much longer had she worked at setting him up for it? He was, perhaps, not all that he should be, but she, she was crazy and malevolent. What kind of woman would dream of such an act? And what kind would actually achieve it? Well, Reader, how would you answer that question?

Sam sat in the darkened screening room watching the new rough cut of *Birth of a Star*, squirming nervously in his seat. It worked. Well, it worked in a way. It certainly wasn't the movie he had envisioned *Birth of a Star* to be. It was more like *Blue Velvet* meets *Akkbar*. But it did work.

He and April, Laslo and Michael, along with the body doubles, had flown to Hong Kong to work for nineteen feverish days on the new scenes for the film. Joy Wah Studios—''Where Hollywood Comes to Get Oriented''

747

—was a film factory that turned out dozens of action and porn films for the Asian market each month. They had technicians and special-effects crews that worked fast and cheap. And now their efforts had transformed the movie.

Sam lifted one of his hands to his temple. He had had a merciless headache for a week or maybe more. Nothing seemed to help. Perhaps it was the food or water in Hong Kong, maybe it was staring at the moviola editing screen for hours, but even the daily massages and the Chinese acupuncturist hadn't helped.

Sam had worked day and night to save the film. Well, to save his ass. After the new scenes had been written and shot, after the more difficult splicing had been done, only then could he leave the scene of the crime, return to L.A. with the rough cut and his headaches.

He hadn't sold out, he told himself fiercely. The film was different from what he'd intended, but not necessarily worse. In fact, the first version of the film, as he had originally envisioned it, was a failure, stillborn. He'd always had reservations about the stupid melodrama. He even now wasn't sure if it was his forced revisions, Michael's hostility, or Jahne's flat performance that had miscarried, but, whatever it was, the film as it had been was a certain failure. Now, with the music laid in and a little more tightening, this *Birth of a Star* had a chance. That it was the costliest sexually explicit mainstream film ever made, he had no doubt. That it would make back its cost, he was almost certain. But whether it was any good or not, he was still not sure.

He had left for Hong Kong furious with Jahne. He had not spoken to her before he left. But, in the few hours that he had to himself there, he stared out the floor-to-ceiling windows of the Regent Hotel at the magnificent view of the Hong Kong harbor and tried to fit pieces back together. He had loved Jahne—perhaps he still loved her —and now he knew why. She had been able to please his eye, as only a beautiful woman could, while caring for him in the way that Mary Jane had. She had the passion of the plain. Mary Jane had made him feel comfortable, and worshipped. He did not have to strive to please her.

She had given him the acceptance of a mother, while Jahne had given him the sexual thrill of a girl the age of a daughter. Had he been judged harshly for wanting that? Wasn't that what all men craved? The security of unjudgmental love without the boredom? Sexual temptation without challenge or the threat of abandonment? Jahne had all the maturity of a forty-year-old woman in the body of a teen. And the vulnerability of both.

Back in New York, he had been ashamed of Mary Jane, and ashamed of his dependence on her, but he knew now that he *had* loved her. And if she was someone he would never have introduced to his parents, or felt comfortable with at a Hollywood party, that was human, wasn't it? Anyone could understand that. He shifted uncomfortably in his seat, the images on the screen torturing him. Jahne's face, Jahne's body looming up at him. Overpowering him.

He also knew that he had loved Jahne. *And* had been proud of her. Surely she could tell that, and she would have to be the first to admit that as Mary Jane she had not been a partner he could show off with pride. The knowledge felt like a weight in his gut, but it was the truth, for good or ill. He was ashamed, and the shame made him angry. Now he just had to decide what to do about it.

Had Jahne made him a laughingstock? Did jerks like Molly and Chuck and that little rat Neil know and laugh at him? At his shallowness, and his stupidity? Who else thought he was a fool? All of Hollywood? He sighed. Had she done it all in spite? Or had Jahne loved him? Surely M.J. had. Had she gone through this transformation out of love, or revenge? The fact was, despite this horrible trick, despite this betrayal, he did still love Jahne. And perhaps, just possibly, they could work something out. Later. After he had done what he could to salvage *Birth*.

Now, returned to L.A., he holed up in editing rooms and guarded the screenings. No one but Michael, Seymore, and April could gain entry. He'd keep coaxing it into shape. Only then would the suits get to see it. But it would all be kept under wraps. And he would not speak to Jahne or see her. He would let her sit this out alone. She'd caused him enough grief for right now.

In the meantime, word had already appeared in the trades that the movie was in trouble. April was furious. "Those fuckers could bury us before we have a chance," she screamed. "We won't be able to get distributors to even *look* at it." She'd ordered Marketing to move up the opening of the film and to have a quick roll-out to eleven hundred theaters. Jahne, Laslo, none of the others, not even little A. Joel Grossman would get to see it. Sam shook his aching head. Poor A. Joel. He was a lost man anyway since Adrienne had coupled up with Michael McLain. Losing a love could do that to a man. Sam had to smile, despite the pain in his head. The smile increased his pain, and he winced, staring at the scene on the screen. The scene was as intense as his headache.

He knew it was the pressure, the guilt, and the anger. But he also knew he wasn't doing this to Jahne, to Mary Jane, out of anger or revenge. Not that she didn't deserve it. But he was going to work that out between them. No, he was doing this to the movie because he had to, to keep control of the project. To keep his career viable. As April told him plainly, if he didn't, someone else would.

And, after all, he told himself, looking up at the screen, it wasn't so very bad, what he had done. Adrienne's body looked beautiful, and the cuts had been seamless: far more seamless than the work that had been done on Jahne's own torso. She would see herself as perfect. Everyone would see her as perfect.

After all, wasn't that what she and every woman really wanted?

Michael McLain leaned back into the softness of the sheets and smiled. And it wasn't even for the camera. Things had taken a definite turn for the better. Shooting had ended a week ago, and it had been, no doubt about it, a real pleasure. Although there had definitely been a certain—how shall we say—awkwardness about stepping out of the scene when his body double took over, Adrienne, the girl who was doubling for Jahne Moore, made it clear that she only had eyes for him. So, even if his stomach wasn't washboard-flat anymore, he still had what it takes. He reached out and patted Adrienne's bare ass, pushed against his back. She had stayed on with him to vacation for a week in Hong Kong. A week of shopping and sex. He loved doing both with her.

And he loved what he had seen in the dailies. The stuff wasn't just hot, it was beautiful and hot. In fact, it was *gorgeous* and *very* hot. The best stroke film ever made. Laslo and that shmuck Sam had figured out some clever angles and approaches. Not since *Don't Look Now,* when Donald Sutherland went down on Julie Christie, had sex looked this good on the screen.

And they had made it as easy for him at the studio as they could. They had a cadre of Oriental girls who powdered and massaged him, who sprayed him with glycerine to imitate sweat, who deferred, who bowed. They even had a "fluffer," the pretty, slender girl who ensured his erection.

Yes, it had worked, and it looked to him as if the rough cuts would work. It was risky, of course. But if Nicholson could have a career coup frugging as a fat Joker in *Batman,* and Lancaster and Kirk Douglas could get away with mooning the audience with their wrinkled old asses, surely Michael McLain could bow out as a leading man with lovemaking: bold, graphic lovemaking on the silver screen. And after that, he was history. He was going to get out of the picture business and into something with dignity.

Maybe he'd finally get married.

2

In her twenty years of life so far, there were a lot of things Lila had hated, but working with her mother definitely topped the list. She'd had to watch the old bitch arrive every morning as if *3/4* were *her* show, greeting all the crew by name (how the fuck did she learn their names so *quickly*? Lila didn't know any of them after more than a year), seeing Theresa preen her pulled and lifted old face for the makeup man and consult with the boom operator. It all made Lila sick with rage.

Worst of all had been watching her with Marty. Marty had been surprised when Lila had told him she'd changed her mind, that she would allow her mother on the show, but he'd jumped at it. Lila watched him work with Theresa. Jesus, he didn't have to suck up to the Puppet Mistress. But he deferred to her, he laughed at her stupid jokes, he gave serious consideration to her suggestions about lighting and camera angles.

Lila had felt her rage boiling to the surface, but she swallowed it down over and over again, until she felt as if she might scream. Her mother had made the deal clear —she had made her devastating threat crystal-clear. So Lila raged in silence. And along with the rage, she felt something else. It was jealousy, she admitted. She was jealous when Marty paid attention to anyone else. All during the hiatus, she had had him to herself. She knew she would have to share him with the other two. Bad enough, but sharing him with Theresa was unbearable. She found herself watching them through narrowed eyes, biting the inside of her cheeks. After the first two days, her mouth had been a bloody mess.

The only comfort she had during all of it was the gossip that *Birth of a Star* was a shambles. Lila plowed through the trades and the columns looking for the latest inside scoop. She had been delighted when Minos called and gave her a full report about the infighting between the director, the producer, and the stars. And she was even more pleased when Marty told her that he had heard it was a total bomb and being rushed into release before distributors could back out.

So, with her mother's segment almost finished and in the can, she could focus on the upcoming Emmys. She wasn't worried about Sharleen wresting an Emmy from her. It was only Jahne that Lila worried about. Well, a bomb at the box office shouldn't affect the Emmy award, but she knew it did. She smiled and prayed *Birth of a Star* would be released before the voting took place. It should have been the movie that made Lila a star, but if it was the one that brought Jahne Moore down, that would be some compensation.

It took almost two weeks, but at last the unbearable business with Theresa had ended. Going home that evening, for the first time Lila managed to smile at Marty's jokes. She'd agreed to have dinner with him, though not to stay over. She never slept at his house. Sally was getting used to the 2:00 A.M. drive back to Malibu.

"It wasn't so bad, was it, Lila?" Marty asked her, and she knew he was referring to the work with her mother. They had not spoken one word about it during the two weeks of shooting.

"Bad enough," she told him curtly. "Thank God the script didn't demand I had to act as if I loved her. If I could do *that*, I'd deserve an Oscar, not an Emmy."

"First things first," Marty told her. "The Academy will see this show right before the voting. And you were good, Lila. Really good. It will help." He smiled. "I think we're going to break some records when this is televised. No one gets more than a thirty-percent share. Not even *Murphy Brown* after Dan Quayle's remark. But I think we'll top that."

"What did *M*A*S*H*'s last episode pull?" she asked.

"Over eighty, but that was before cable fragmented the audience."

"I want ninety."

Marty laughed, until he looked at her and realized she wasn't joking. "If we pulled ninety, Les Merchant and Hyram Flanders would pay whatever it took to have us both canonized. My mother would love it. A saint as a son. For a Catholic, that's better than a doctor." Lila didn't smile. He decided to change the subject. "Someone is having a birthday soon," he said. "And have I got a surprise for her."

God, she hated it when he got cute. "So what?" she asked.

"How do you want to celebrate it?" he asked. "The town is yours."

"I'd like to see a screening of *Birth of a Star*," she told him.

He felt the cut. Jesus, she knew how to get to him. He

still regretted that *he* hadn't gotten the rights, that a movie *he* should have made had fallen into the hands of barbarians. And he also knew how tight security would be over the prints. Lila had a knack for picking the only things he couldn't deliver as the only things she wanted. "Why bother?" he asked, with a casualness he didn't feel. "It stinks."

"How do you know?" she asked. "Have you seen it?"

"No, but . . ."

"I want to see it," she told him. "That's what I want for my birthday."

Sally did it. How, Marty didn't even inquire. After all, Sally was still connected, and it was best not to delve too deep. Just appreciate that the cans of film, each marked *Birth of a Star,* were all ready for the private screening, along with the rest of the evening's props: the perfectly set dinner table, the gladiola, the candles, the fire that crackled in the fireplace and took the chill off the air conditioning, as well as the tiny velvet box that sat, waiting, on the mantel shelf.

Marty wasn't a vain man. Looking so ordinary—that's the most truthful he was capable of being about his looks —he usually dressed in a perfunctory way. But this evening, he was doing the full treatment. At Lila's insistence, he had started using a personal trainer, and had had a full, hard session with him today. He looked at himself in the mirror, naked after his shower, and was pleased with what he saw. Lila, it appeared more and more, was good for him. The training was beginning to pay off. Flat stomach, tighter skin. Even the slightest bulge of biceps on his skinny arm. Not bad.

The most difficult indulgence in vanity he had to accept was the hairdresser Lila had insisted he use tonight. If she had to put herself through such preparations, why should he be able to get away with less? she had asked. She was right again, although, with her beauty, any professional assistance she got was really only framing. The ministrations *he* needed came more in the category of camouflage.

But enough of that. He *was* happy. He turned from his

full-length mirror, and held up the tux from Bijan Lila had bought him. He began to dress, each layer making him more excited, since everything he now wore was personally selected by Lila, including the silk underwear that brushed so gently against the head of his penis. The sensation was more than just pleasant. It was a taste of what was to follow, after the screening, during their oh-so-private party. Marty shivered. Scenes from their nights together flashed on him at all sorts of times during the day, leaving him sweaty and enervated. No woman had ever thrilled him, enthralled him like this. He was her slave. And tonight he would prove it.

He had come up with the perfect birthday gift. It sat wrapped with a crimson satin ribbon on the coffee table. And he knew it would make Lila happier than anything else would. It was a script—a script so perfect for her talents that she would have to love it. It would be his gift to her. And, after next season, they would make the movie together, even if it meant delaying *3/4*. Even if it meant canceling the fucker. He thought of Sy's screams, of the network's reaction, of Flanders Cosmetics going ballistic, but he only smiled. That's what Hollywood lawyers were for.

Lila looked down at the big box that Robbie had set on the table. She hadn't seen him for a long time, but he looked as pudgy and pathetic as ever. "Well, happy birthday to me," Lila said, smiling.

"I had to wait until she was on the set. Then Ken decoyed Kevin to get him out of there. There was no other way. I don't know what she's going to do when she finds out they're gone." He was sweating, his bland, round face a mask of concern.

Lila just snorted. She had to get ready for her date with Marty—there were a lot of preparations for their evenings together—and she had no time for this wet, fat fuck. It had taken him months to bring over this tribute, so it might well take her that long to forgive him. But her eyes glistened as she looked at the box.

"Well, okay," she told him curtly. "But I've got things to do now. I'm going out."

"Anyone I know?" Robbie asked brightly. Yeah, like I'm going to confide in you, she thought.

"Maybe," she answered, as noncommittal as a confessional priest. She walked to the door and opened it. "See you," she said, indicating his way out.

"Don't you have time even for a coffee?" he asked. She hated how needy he sounded; it made her angry, not sympathetic.

Lila didn't have a lot of insights, but she knew she was the type who took advantage of and despised weakness.

"Not even a quick espresso!" she said brightly and shut the door on his hopeful face.

Lila settled back on the sofa of Marty's screening room. Dinner had been perfect, and now they'd screen the purloined copy of *Birth*. She knew she'd set him a challenge, and she knew he'd rise to it.

"Roll it, Sally," Marty said into the intercom, and then dimmed the lights. The credits had not yet been cut into the beginning.

It began predictably. Michael McLain meets the bitch. He's successful. She's a nobody with talent. He helps her. He's on the slide, but she worships him. It was okay, but nothing special. She heard Marty shift restlessly in his seat. Good. He didn't like it.

Then Michael, up on the screen, bent in to Jahne. "Prove that you trust me," he said, and his eyes, for the first time, came alive. There was a quick cut to his hand on hers, then a dissolve, and his hand was now on hers again, but she was stretched across a bed, and he was holding her arms down as she gave him head! Lila gasped. You couldn't quite see everything, but the act was clearly implied. And then that close-up of her mouth and the cut to his thrusting hips from behind, and again her mouth.

Michael, on the screen, moaned, and Lila thought for a moment she heard Marty moan as well. Then Jahne's hands broke free and clutched at Michael's bare rump, as if she couldn't get enough of him.

"Jesus Christ!" Marty gasped.

"Worship me," Michael was grunting, and the scene faded out.

The story unfolded, and there was another scene, now with both of them in a public doorway, Michael opening her buttons, pulling up her skirt, taunting her, and doing her from behind, oblivious of the occasional passersby. Then she turned to face him, wanting more. Jahne was gorgeous, her legs perfect, wrapped around him like a monkey. It was unbelievable. Her perfect breasts bobbed before his mouth and he gobbled at them.

Lila felt as if she were hypnotized. This stuff was porn —it was filth—but it was beautifully shot. And it was sexy. Very, very sexy. Wasn't it? Lila could never be sure. In the dark she quickly reached across to Marty and put her hand on his crotch. She pulled it away as if hot coals had burned her. "You have an erection!" she cried, jumping up. It was a fact and an accusation.

"Lila, I . . ."

"You like her! You want her!"

"Lila, don't be silly. It's only a movie. It's a sexy movie. I . . ."

"Goddamn it!" she cried. "You have a hard-on for her. You think she's more of a woman than I am, don't you?" Her voice had risen to a scream. Behind her, the images of Michael and Jahne continued to couple. "You do, don't you?"

"Sally, please, turn it off," Marty said into the intercom. "Then you can go." He turned the lights on and looked at Lila. It was the first time she'd ever appeared possessive. "Lila, the hard-on was an automatic. Good porn will always get a rise out of me. I'm visual, Lila. But this is a desecration. *Birth of a Star* was a classic. It shocked me to see Jahne in a porn movie. I had no idea . . ."

"Do you want her?" Lila asked.

"I only want you. No one but you," he said.

Lila collapsed onto the sofa and began to sob. "She's going to get all the attention. She's going to get the Emmy and an Oscar."

"Are you crazy? In this Puritan town? April must have been desperate. They'd never have gone for it otherwise.

I mean, what kind of rating will it get? This is no PG-13. The Network will go nuts. They'll evoke the morals clause. And Flanders will go crazy. Jahne can kiss that contract goodbye.''

"Really?" Lila wiped her eyes. "You think it won't go over well?"

"Jesus, Lila! One of America's sweethearts going down on Michael McLain?" Marty laughed. He walked to the console table at the side of the room and picked up a package. "Not to worry, darling. She's history. Meanwhile, look what I got you for your birthday." He handed her the script.

"What is it?" she asked, suspiciously.

"Just the best vehicle for a young actress that I've seen in ten years. And it's for you. We can film it before next season. I've got a green light from Paramount already."

Lila jumped up off the couch and ran across the room to him. "Yes!" she cried. "Yes!" And she hugged him tightly.

"Happy birthday," Marty told her.

"Oh, thank you!"

This was it! This was it! She'd be bigger than Jahne Moore and Sharleen Smith. That she could be certain of, even before this movie was shot: Marty had never done anything second-rate. It was Oscar-nomination stuff, for sure. And now, with the promise of this film and the Emmy all but guaranteed, now she *knew* she'd be the biggest thing to happen in this town in years. And, sweetest of all, she'd be bigger than her mother. Bigger than Theresa O'Donnell had *ever* been. She shivered to think she almost hadn't responded to Marty's advances, and almost turned down both him and the chance for this role. She reached out and squeezed Marty's arm.

Only Marty was powerful enough to do this for her. Only Marty would care for her enough to do it. Perhaps their affair wasn't perfect. Perhaps he wasn't someone she even wanted to touch, but he was good to her. He took care of her as no one ever had. Tears flooded her eyes. "I love you," she whispered.

"Good," he said simply. He covered her hand with his own for a moment and then stood up and walked to the fireplace. "There's something else here for you," he said, and came to her with the little box. He held it out to her.

Lila took it and quickly flipped open the top. Inside, the white satin only enhanced the sparkle of a huge marquis-cut diamond.

"Twelve-carat. Perfect clarity. Perfect color. Perfect. Just like you," Marty said.

Lila stared at the ring. It caught the rays from the dying fire and refracted them in a thousand points of light across the ceiling and walls. The ring was so grown-up, so Republican, but so breathtaking. Lila could not take her eyes off it.

"You're going to marry me," Marty told her.

3

Jahne couldn't eat, couldn't sleep. The scene with Sam had been awful, once he realized who she was. He had been more than angry, he had been enraged. And she had felt strangely guilty. Guilty for lying, guilty for loving him still, guilty for letting him love her. He had stormed out, shocked and hurt and angry, but he had called five days later, five long days later, during the day, when he knew she'd be out, and left a message. He said that he'd be working hard on the movie, that he'd have to go to Hong Kong for special effects and some reshooting and would be gone several weeks. But that he'd been doing a lot of thinking, that he wanted to see her and would call her as soon as he returned.

He still had not called. And she had been stupid enough to think that time would allow a healing, would allow him to join his love for Mary Jane to his love for her today. But did she want him to? Did she still want a man so selfish, so narcissistic, that he could only see her through himself? She thought again of his immense nerve, thinking that she had done all of this for him and to him. What an ass!

Yet a small doubt had entered her mind. She'd done it to grab a chance, a last chance to succeed on her own terms: to act, to pursue her career, her craft, her calling. Or had she?

Lying in bed, sleepless night after night, she was tortured by the idea. Had she done all this to get Sam back? Or to get back at Sam? Both ideas appalled her. She'd never imagined herself so needy, or so angry, that she'd go that far for either love or revenge. But maybe she had.

She roamed the big, empty house at night, lights off. The rooms felt empty, so empty. Tomblike. Oh, she could play Aida, bricked into the grave alone. That was how abandoned she felt. But abandoned by whom?

Over and over, she felt herself drawn to the mirrors in her dressing room. There, at the marble counters that were pristine and cold as a mortuary table, she stared at her own face, at the face she had bought. A face Sam said he had loved.

The face had given her power—power over Pete, and power enough to get the Melrose Playhouse part, power to be selected by Marty, power to entrance Sam. But what real kind of power was it, the power that these lips, this nose, the line of this jaw had given?

It was only clear to Jahne how very powerless she was after the breakup with Sam and the resumption of *3/4*. It was clear that things had changed on the set. What little weight her opinion had earlier carried was now completely usurped by the new closeness between Lila and Marty and the ill will her absence for the beginning of the season had bred. As far as *Birth* went, since the scene with Sam, Jahne had clearly been cut out of the editing process. It wasn't only that her calls were not returned and her services no longer needed; Jahne Moore couldn't even seem to get a screening of her own film. It was incredible. The International offices informed her that both April Irons and Sam Shields were unavailable: both were out of the country. She called Seymore LeVine and got the same stonewalling, tried Sam's number at his house. No answer, no matter what time of day or night she called. She left no message. What was the use? It was all out of her control.

Lila, on the other hand, appeared to be in complete control. Jahne's part was even stupider (and smaller) than before, while Lila stole almost every scene, got every punch line and every close-up. Sharleen walked through her part humbly, but Jahne found it humiliating. And Sy Ortis was no help. No help at all.

"What can I tell you?" he wheezed into the phone. "You made your bed. Marty doesn't appreciate ingratitude. You screwed him with *Birth*, now he screws you. What can I tell you?"

"You can tell me how I can get a screening of *Birth of a Star*, for God sake!" Jahne snapped. "I don't have a clue to what's happening."

"You're not alone. Apparently it's in big trouble." His voice was heavy with satisfaction; his silent "I told you so" hung in the air. A part of Jahne knew that he was right, had been right all along, but for all the wrong reasons. I'll fire him, she thought, but the idea of getting a new agent when *Birth* bombed frightened her. No one but a hungry bum would want to pick her up then, and if Sy was also a bum, he was at least a well-connected, *powerful* bum.

"I guess you were right, Sy. Meanwhile, try and get me a screening," was all she said before she hung up the phone.

Jahne felt as if she were falling apart. For once, she didn't have to worry about her diet: she couldn't eat. Slipping into her jeans, the ones Mai had sewn for her, she found they gapped at her waist. There were hollows beneath her cheekbones, and darkness under her eyes. And still she hadn't heard from Sam, had seen nothing of *Birth*.

On the set, Pete approached her one afternoon. "Are you okay?" he asked. They hadn't spoken in months, except for "hello" and "good night." She looked up at him from her folding canvas chair; he was as young and simple and straight as he'd always been. I must really look bad if he's noticed, she thought.

"Not so great." She tried to smile, but it didn't work well.

761

"Can I do anything to help?" he asked. She had to turn her head away from the kindness.

"No. But thanks." She watched as he started to walk away, and then it occurred to her. "Pete. Wait. Isn't your dad a projectionist?" she asked. He nodded. "Do you think he could get me a screening?"

You might say that Jahne Moore walked into the screening room for *Birth of a Star* a virgin. Two hours and ten minutes later, both her eyes and her cherry had been popped. She watched herself—or someone cut and pasted to appear to be her—fucked half a dozen times in as many positions and costumes by a younger, slimmer Michael McLain. She watched what appeared to be her right breast, ten feet wide on the screen, squeezed by his hands in close-up. She watched what appeared to be her nipples inflate, watched his lips surround them, watched her own face in close-up react to the sensation. She watched as she appeared to kneel to take it doggy style, her perfect ass a heart-shaped invitation. She watched as a leg—supposedly *her* leg—reached up around Michael's neck and caressed his cheek, only to be joined by her other, first framing his face with her calves, then opening wide as a protractor to accommodate him. She saw the sheen of sweat on her arms, her back, her thighs, the dampness on a perfect curl of what was represented as her pubic hair.

She sat beside Pete in the private screening room and she saw the film that *Birth of a Star* had become. It broke all the boundaries between "popular entertainment" and "soft porn." And it wasn't soft at all. It was a film that she had not made, yet her face was up there, the illusion of her body was there for everyone to see: to see and watch her being made love to, watch her achieve orgasm, watch her be violated. Watch her capitulate. How had it happened? she wondered. How had it happened to *her*?

She felt actually dizzy. The beauty of Laslo's photography, the lush music, the perfect settings, all of it cushioned this violation. But a violation it was. How had they even managed to do it? It certainly wasn't either her own scarred body or Michael's aging one up there. What tricks had April and Laslo and Sam resorted to?

Pete shifted uncomfortably in the seat beside her. He cleared his throat. Once he whispered, "God!" Then he was silent. She wondered if he had an erection. She didn't want to know.

Then a small thrill of horror passed over her, like an exquisite chill. How many men would get a hard-on from this? How many men would jerk off to her image? How many strangers would fuck her in their minds, in the privacy of their own homes? One of La Brecque's warnings sounded in her ears: "You can't seem accessible. It's the accessible ones who get killed." Well, how accessible was a woman who was publicly fucked? And how would she get any respect in the community? How would she ever graduate to real acting jobs, the kind she craved? How would she even show her face? How had this happened?

She thought Sam had loved her. But this, this was not love. This was rage, betrayal, and rape. She stared at the moving images on the screen.

At last the horror ended. The credits rolled as Michael's character walked into the waves. Pete's father must have flicked on the lights from the control booth. Pete looked over at her, blinking in the glare.

Jahne stood up, reached for the arm of the chair, and vomited onto the vacant velvet seat before her.

"So what do you want to do?" Howard Taft asked Jahne. Howard was the best entertainment lawyer in L.A., and the most expensive.

"Sue them. Stop them. Get the film burned."

"Fine. So what do you *really* want to do?"

"*Sue* them. *Stop* them. *Get the film burned*."

"Miss Moore—Jahne—that's all well and good, and I know all about artistic differences, but we're talking International Studios here. We're talking April Irons. We're talking *Bob LeVine*. We're not talking about people who roll over nicely when hit with an injunction. Not that we could even *get* an injunction."

"Why not? They . . ."

"Your contract clearly states that . . ."

"But I didn't know they would do *this*. Don't I have a right to control my own face, my body . . . ?"

"Not according to your contract. You requested the body double. You insisted on secrecy and no credit for the body double. They're doing that. You can't sue them for keeping to your contract."

"But then who *should* I sue?"

"Your agent, I would say. But not if you want to work again." Howard took off his steel-rimmed glasses, removed a spotless white handkerchief from his breast pocket, and began to wipe the lenses carefully, his kind gray eyes watching her all the time. "Listen, I'd love to take your money. And there might be some, some . . . *softening* of the final cut that I could wangle, but a suit, I promise you, would be costly, *and* disastrous to your career . . ."

"Fuck my career."

He paused, shocked. And there was very little that shocked a Hollywood attorney. He licked his lips, clasped his hands together on his perfectly clear desk. "Well, I can see you feel strongly now, but later your feelings may change. This suit would be longer and more costly than Cliff Robertson's. Worse than Art Buchwald's. The studios cannot afford to give up their right to use your image. You clearly signed the body-double agreement. And suing on this would end your options. . . ."

"I don't need those kinds of options."

". . . and would ultimately accomplish nothing. April Irons and a squad of bankers put fifty million dollars into this film, and you cannot stop it from . . ."

Tears rose in Jahne's eyes. The feeling of powerlessness that she had been trying to deny again swept over her, draining her energy, leaving her weak and helpless. She began to cry. "Then there's nothing I can do?" she whispered.

"Here," Howard said, extending his hand, his immaculate handkerchief still in it. "You can wipe your nose."

* * *

When Jahne left Howard Taft's office, she was too enraged to go home, too angry to stand still. She felt if she didn't keep moving she might hit something or break something, or even explode. Perhaps she had no legal options, but she had personal ones. She got in her car and began driving.

She was breathing hard by the time she reached the canyon road. She snorted at herself. L.A. makes you soft, she thought, but she felt anything but. She felt harder than she had in her life, hard as steel, as a diamond, and just as ready to cut. If he was here in L.A., she'd find Sam. If he wasn't, she'd . . . She pulled into his driveway.

She found Sam's key, buried deep in her bag. Why did women, why did she, shlepp around so much crap? Makeup, hairbrush, comb, mirror. The burden of being a woman. She tried, quietly, to fit the key in the lock, but her hands shook. She took a deep breath, steadied herself, and, with both hands, managed to slide in the key, turn it, and open the door.

He was there, thank God, and he appeared to be alone. Not that she gave a rat's ass. He could be going down on April Irons while Crystal Plenum was giving him head and she wouldn't care. Not anymore. He was alone, though, lying on the sofa, a washcloth over his eyes, a script lying open on his chest. Some fresh hell of a movie for some new woman he would ruin.

"You lousy piece of shit!" Jahne screamed.

He jumped up from the sofa, threw the script or whatever it was he was reading aside. "Jesus! Oh, Jesus, Jahne. Mary Jane. Oh, Jesus. You frightened me! Listen, I know what you're going to say. . . ." He was breathing like he'd run a marathon. Good. She'd scared him. Fine. She wanted him scared.

"No, you don't, you lying cocksucker."

"Hey." He stood there, breathing hard, his hands extended in a palm-down, Buddha-calming-the-waters gesture. "No need for . . ."

"Don't you *dare* tell me what there's a need for *or* how to behave. You're a lying bastard."

"You're the one who lied! I . . . ."

"I've seen it."

He had the grace to pause for a moment. She watched as he tried to slow his breathing. Old actor's trick. Fuck him and his tricks. "Jahne, I had no choice. The film hadn't come together. I'd failed April. I failed *you*. This was the only way to get to roll the dice again. And it works, Jahne—Mary Jane—" He fumbled for a moment. "Once you get over your, your . . ."

"Disgust?"

"Surprise. Once you get over your *surprise*, you'll *see* it works. The way I directed you . . ."

"Directed me? You *pimped* me. You pimped me as if I were a twenty-dollar whore. Now don't insult my intelligence by telling me I'm going to like it! And it wasn't *me* you were directing. I wasn't informed or involved with any of this. It was a couple of body doubles, Michael McLain, and a tube of K-Y Jelly!"

"What good would it have done to ask you? You wouldn't have agreed. And we were not exactly in the negotiating mode."

"We aren't in that mode now, either."

She had to pause for a moment as she felt her anger drain out of her. She dropped her bag to the floor and, in her weakness, would have sat down. But she didn't want to be weak in front of him. She wanted to be strong, angry, and scary. She narrowed her eyes and lowered her voice. She began to walk toward him, and was gratified to see him back away. "You betrayed me, and, like a fool, I blamed myself. The first time, back in New York, I thought, if I'd been prettier, or kinder, or sexier, or more understanding, you wouldn't have run off with Bethanie, sold my part to the highest bidder, and never even bothered to speak to me again." She had circled him around the sofa. He continued to back away. "I blamed myself! But what's your excuse now? Now I *am* prettier and kinder and sexier. So what the fuck reason have you got for betraying me *this* time? You know I wanted to be a serious actress. You know how important this picture was to me, to my career. . . ."

Sam's back was against the adobe wall of the fireplace. "Always you!" he yelled. "Always you and what *you* want, how *you're* hurt, how *you* feel, what's important for *your* career. What about *me*? I thought you loved *me*. But you never even told me who you were. You tricked me into loving you, and it was *my* career on the line here. Think I'd get a shot at a lot more pictures if fifty million bucks went down the toilet on this one? Did you think about how *I* felt? *I* had to save the picture. And I have.''

"But at what cost, Sam?" She stared at him. Surely he'd admit what he had done.

"Look, *Last Tango in Paris* didn't hurt Brando's career."

Oh, God. He was hopeless. "No." She laughed bitterly. "Men gain status by fucking women on the screen. But how did Maria Schneider do? Didn't she wind up a suicide?" She turned, picked up her bag, and started to walk away, down the hall to the door.

"I love you, Jahne. I wanted to marry you."

She stopped, her heart pounding. Then, slowly, she turned around.

"Well, this is a great time to tell me, and a great way for me to find out. Why does your proposal sound like a weapon?"

"Oh, don't give me any holier-than-thou shit, please. If your face wasn't like a blank billboard on the screen, I wouldn't've had to do this. Christ, I worked with what you had, limited as it was."

"So, it *is* all my fault."

" 'Fault' is a word for children."

"I'm hearing 'fault' from you. And I'm not hearing an apology, or remorse, or even any guilt. Only that what you did was okay, was necessary. You're comfortable? You're glad you did this to me?"

It was the only moment when he paused. He had been looking at her, his eyes angry, opaque, and direct, but now, for the first time, he looked down, turning his head toward the bedroom, but not seeing the bed they had once shared. Then he looked back.

"I didn't betray you," he said. "I never told anyone about your scars."

"Well, congratulations," she told him, threw his key on the floor, and walked out.

Jahne stood there in the harsh sunlight outside Sam's stupid fake Santa Fe–adobe house and realized she had no place to go, no one to talk to, no one to tell about this horror.

If only Mai were alive. If only she could go to Mai's and have a glass of beer and cry and laugh with her. She got into the car and began to drive, accelerating until she was doing seventy on the canyon road. Where could she go? Who could she go to? She knew that the mausoleum she now called home was impossible. She would die if she went home.

There was only one place left. She drove east, toward the Valley. After forty minutes, she pulled up to the gate, and the security guard recognized her. He greeted her, then buzzed the house while Jahne sat in the car and waited. Please, God. Please, let her be home, she prayed. The guard hung up the phone and told Jahne that Sharleen would meet her at the door.

Jahne drove up the driveway. Sharleen called out a greeting as she walked toward Jahne's car. She leaned onto the car door, smiling. "Well, hi there. Good to see you."

Jahne burst into tears, tears so violent she had to put her head down on the steering wheel, clutching the wheel tightly with both hands, just to keep from falling completely apart.

Sharleen was at Jahne's window. "Why, Jahne, honey. What's happened?" Sharleen opened the car door for Jahne, but Jahne couldn't move. "Come on, honey," Sharleen said, gently tugging at Jahne's hands on the wheel. "Get out of that car and come inside."

But Jahne, at least for the moment, could only clutch the steering wheel, sit there, and shake and cry.

4

The bedroom was filled with sunlight when Jahne opened her eyes. It had been two, no, three days now that she had been staying quietly here at Sharleen's. Bless Sharleen's heart, and bless her boyfriend's heart, too, Jahne thought. Dean might not be real bright, but he was sweet as could be. It was relaxing just to sit beside him.

Sharleen had called Marty and the *Three for the Road* production manager for Jahne and reported Jahne sick. Then Sharleen had a doctor come in, "jest to make it look kosher." She left for work each day without even waking Jahne, who felt she could sleep for a month. It wasn't until about ten that Dean would knock timidly on the door each morning and bring in a glass of fresh juice and a cup of steaming coffee. After Jahne had drunk both, he'd bring the dogs in—Jahne laughed when she met Cara and the other namesakes, but she liked the golden retriever best.

"I don't have no favorites," Dean told her. "It wouldn't be right. They could tell, you know." Then he lowered his voice. "If I *did* have a favorite, it would be Oprah, my friend's Lab. But that's only right, 'cause I knew her the longest."

After her juice, Dean would help Jahne establish herself under a tree in the garden, and he'd spend the rest of the morning working on the grounds, weeding the enormous vegetable garden, playing with the dogs, mowing the lawn on a tiny tractor, pruning back some fruit trees. Jahne just sat back on the lawn chair, at first too tired to read, too tired to think, too tired even to be sad.

The abundance of the garden reminded her of the van Huysums at the Getty. Abundance. But real and natural in season. She shook her head. Her life so far had been the opposite: the meagerness of New York, the waste of her life in the theater, the emptiness of her success out here in L.A. All of it had been a fruitless search for something she could not find: love, and warmth, and abundance.

She'd made a botch of it, there was no doubt. She'd picked a man to love who had no love to return. A shallow, selfish man. She'd abandoned her friends, she'd pursued the dictates of her own ego and vanity, and it had given her so little in return. Her face on magazine covers. Her image on a flickering TV screen. Money. Fame. But she'd never been to Europe, she'd never had a baby, she'd never ridden a horse, she couldn't speak another language. She'd never skied, or camped out in a wilderness, or taken a cruise, or gone to college. And she'd helped no one, not even herself.

God had given her talent, and Brewster Moore had given her beauty, and hadn't she been almost as blind and selfish as Sam Shields, wasting her gifts?

Sam. The thought of him was enough to make her cry, or laugh. Sam had never understood her, never truly tried. Both as Mary Jane and as Jahne, she had ignored that. He had taken comfort from her nurturing, he had been titillated by her beauty, but he had never known her. What had he given? A few words of praise. A hug. A caress. Crumbs. And she, always a fool, had accepted crumbs and thought they were a banquet.

Now, under the tree in Dean's garden, she had a horrible, chilling thought. Hadn't she, somehow, planned it all —the surgery, the success, the reunion with Sam—all in the hopes that he, alone of everyone—would see through her new flesh to her old heart, recognize her love, recognize and heal her? She thought again of the Bible, where the euphemism for sex was "knowing." "And Abraham went with the woman and he 'knew' her." Sam had never known her at all. And wasn't that what she craved?

She understood his temptations now: ambition overcame his morality and judgment. Well, hadn't it overcome her own? She had wanted Sam, and agreed to make a bad movie to get him. And she had felt triumph at achieving her ambition: in luring Sam into her bed. At possessing him, the way a spider must gloat over its mummified prey. How often had she gloated over his sheet-wrapped form, sleeping in her bed? But had she known Sam? Clearly not.

A goal achieved is only admirable if it's a worthy goal. Who had said that to her? Mai? Brewster? Neil? Molly? Only the people who had a sense of values, who knew the difference between empty, selfish vanity and real achievement. But did *she* know the difference? It didn't appear that she did. She couldn't simply call herself a victim. She had been a willing victim, the wood that threw itself into the fire. She'd given Sam warmth and it had consumed her, leaving nothing but ashes.

Sam had betrayed her, April Irons had manipulated her, Sy Ortis used her, Monica Flanders exploited her, but hadn't she allowed it? She'd used her beauty, flaunted it for money in the Flanders ads, used it to get work on a questionable show like *3/4,* and agreed to bare it—or let another woman do it for her—in *Birth.* She'd sold herself like a commodity, so could she blame others for doing the same?

Jahne lay under the tree and thought difficult thoughts.

At noon, Dean came to interrupt her. They would have lunch together. Dean would bring in the salad fixings from the perfect rows of baby lettuce, tiny radishes, sugar peas, and miniature carrots. Jahne washed them and he'd chop them up, one day adding tuna and the next day pasta. Then they sat out on the patio and ate, drinking two or three fresh lemonades along with their meal. Yesterday Dean had turned to her and smiled. "It's nice to have someone to eat lunch with," he said.

"It is."

"Guess you eat with Sharleen most days."

"No. Usually I eat alone in my trailer. I can't afford to eat much. I used to eat with . . ." She swallowed. ". . . an old lady friend of mine, but she died." Poor, dear Mai. Jahne missed her so.

"So how come you don't eat with Sharleen now?"

"Oh, we get too busy. Or we don't eat at the same time, because we're in different shots. Or she has other work. Or I do." Or because I've been a condescending snob who didn't know who my friends were, Jahne told herself.

"You like your work?"

"No."

"That's bad. It's really bad if you don't like your work. I worry 'cause I don't think Sharleen likes her job, neither. And I think it's too hard."

"Well, they pay us a lot of money, so it should be hard, I guess."

Dean shrugged. "I don't think you should do it if it's too hard and you don't like it. I think that's probably why you're sad."

"You're probably right," Jahne told him.

The first night she was there, Jahne found herself waking from a horrible dream, Sharleen beside her, gently shaking her arm. "Git up, honey, it's just a nightmare, it ain't real."

Jahne gasped for air. What had it been? The knives again? Or was it the one where she was on the set, naked, with the crew and the cast laughing and laughing and laughing? She pulled air into her lungs and felt her heart pushing against her chest. It felt as if it might tear out of her.

"It's okay, honey. It's okay," Sharleen crooned. Grateful, Jahne reached for her hand.

"I'm sorry," she whispered. "You need your sleep. I'm sorry I woke you."

"Want a glass of water? Or maybe I should get you some warm milk? When Dean has bad dreams, I make him some milk."

"No, just stay with me." Jahne felt as if she were five years old. She clung to Sharleen's hand, to Sharleen's warmth, as if she might drown or freeze without it. She shivered under the bedclothes. She couldn't bear to feel this lonely anymore. It was too big a burden to bear, having nobody know you at all. "Sharleen," she said, "can I tell you something?"

Sharleen sat on the side of the bed and patted Jahne's hand. "You surely can," she said. And then Jahne poured out the whole sorry story about Sam and New York and *Jack and Jill* and Brewster and Pete and Mai and Michael and *Birth* and all of it. Sometimes she cried, and other times she could hardly bear to whisper it, but at last she finished.

Sharleen held her hand all through. She still did, and now she patted it. "Why, you poor child. I think you must be even more lonely than I am." And Sharleen bent toward Jahne, gathering her up in her arms. "You poor, poor child," she crooned, and rocked her friend until Jahne, at last, fell asleep.

Jahne felt better after that. She spent the morning with Dean and the afternoon alone in her room, avoiding the strong sun. But, though she felt better, she couldn't avoid her thoughts. She couldn't help replaying over and over again the images she had seen of herself flashing on the screen. And she replayed her relationship with Sam. All of it, from that first spring in New York when he cast her in *Jack and Jill* to the grimy winter he left her, to their time together on location. All of it.

And, while she was at it, she looked at the rest of her life. It didn't make sense, and now she was determined to figure out why. She'd accomplished what she had wanted to: she'd gone from a woman no one remembered to a girl impossible to forget, and she had all the money she needed, plus a lot more fame than she wanted.

But in the last three years, with few exceptions, she hadn't met anyone that she wanted to know. Now Mai was dead, Raoul was back home in South America, and Dr. Moore had his life in New York. She was totally alone, and, except for Sharleen and Dean, there was no one here she trusted, no one to be kind to her. And, in days or weeks, she'd become notorious. Maybe Sharleen and Dean would want nothing to do with her when this monstrous pornographic picture came out. Surely even unflappable Brewster would be shocked and disgusted, as she was.

She was relieved when Dean knocked on her door at the end of his day. In the evenings, the two of them made dinner and waited for Sharleen. Then they watched a video, or the two women talked while Dean watched a tape of *The Andy Griffith Show*. It was simple, and routine, and warm. Jahne began to rest, really to relax for the first time in longer than she could remember. It was like going home, home to a home she had never known.

And slowly, slowly, Jahne began to feel a little more human, as if maybe she could go back and face her life. Maybe.

But on Thursday evening, when Sharleen turned to her as they sat side by side on the sofa and said, "I think you better come back soon," tears unexpectedly filled Jahne's eyes. Suddenly she felt as if this place, this time, was the only bit of peace there was.

"Oh, honey. Don't cry. It's jest that Marty is shootin' so much around you, and he was already kinda mad about your takin' so long on the film. . . . Well, and you know Lila. She don't miss a moment to blame you *or* me when *anything* goes wrong. When I blew a line today you know what she asked?" Jahne shook her head. "She asked how come blondes can't make frozen orange juice. Because the can says 'concentrate.' " They both laughed. Then Sharleen sighed, "And Sy's callin' me three or four times a day."

Jahne took a deep breath. "I'm sorry I've been such a bother."

"Hey, no bother at all. Me and Dean *like* havin' you. You're like family. Why don't you stay on with us instead of goin' home? We can go in to work together."

"Yeah! Why don't you stay, Jahne? It would be great havin' two sisters, even if I can't have lunch with you no more. But, then, Sharleen can," Dean said.

"Oh, could I? Just for a little while longer, until *Birth of a Star* opens? So I can weather that storm?"

"Well, of course you can!" Sharleen told her. "And who knows? Maybe it won't be as bad as it seemed." She smiled. "Anyway, nothin' worse can happen to either of us!"

She was wrong.

The security phone rang, and Sharleen answered it. Both Jahne and Dean were out in the back, playing with the dogs.

"Security gate. There's a visitor here without an appointment. Should I send him up?"

"No. I'll speak to him."

"Is Jahne Moore there?" a man's voice asked.

"Who is this?" she asked.

"Tell her Sam Shields is outside."

Sharleen bristled. "I don't think she wants to see you," Sharleen told him.

"Who is this?" he asked.

"A friend of Jahne's. A true friend," Sharleen said.

"Look, I'm in no mood for theatrics. Or moralizing. It took me a long time to track her down. I want to see her."

"Look, yourself. I know how you treated Jahne, and I know the kind of man you are. Why, I've had men like you after me since I was eleven years old. Men who only cared about the outside, about how I looked, not who I was. You don't deserve a girl like Jahne."

"Look, she's going to want to see me. Go ask her."

Reluctantly, Sharleen put the phone down and went out to the yard. Jahne was running across the lawn, holding a rawhide bone, the three dogs chasing after her. Dean stood in the sunlight, laughing. "Jahne," Sharleen called. "Jahne." Her friend looked up. "There's someone here to see you."

Jahne squinted into the sun. She walked toward Sharleen. "Who is it?" she asked.

"It's Sam."

Jahne stopped. Sharleen looked deep into her eyes. Would she succumb? Would she fall again? Sharleen looked at her without saying a word. For a moment, the two of them stared at one another, silent. Then Jahne spoke.

"Tell him to go away," she told her friend.

Later that night, Jahne wrote to Dr. Moore.

I can't remember ever feeling as dependent as I do now. Not even on you, during that long, hard time in the hospital. Like Blanche DuBois, I am reduced to depending on the kindness of strangers. And I am afraid that even they and you will judge me harshly when you see that awful film I've made.

I know it's a lot to ask, but if you could take some

time off, could you come out for a visit? I'd come to N.Y. but I'm already in a lot of trouble on the set. I'll understand if you refuse, but I'd love to see you.

It was only after she had finished the letter and sealed it that she remembered something odd Dean had said that evening when he welcomed her to stay: something about how it would be great to have two sisters.

Had he said "sisters"? she wondered as she turned off the lamp. How strange. And then she fell asleep.

5

Skin Flick
Hits Big

**DESPITE OR BECAUSE OF ITS
GRAPHIC SEX, "BIRTH" REVIVAL
BREAKS BOX OFFICE RECORDS.**

In a stunning exception to the old Hollywood rule that "dirt doesn't pay," the Michael McLain–Jahne Moore remake of "Birth of a Star" has drawn not only critical praise but also hordes of ticket buyers. An unexpected audience of aging baby boomers, mixed with the teen and young-adult market hot for a romance flick with no holds barred, has exceeded all expectations. . . .

—*Daily Variety*

Lila crumpled the trade bible and threw it across the room. Damn! She picked up the *L.A. Times*.

"THE SEXIEST WOMAN IN THE WORLD!" screamed the banner headline across the top of the entertainment section. There wasn't even an interview to go along with pages of pictures of Jahne Moore, just the usual PR blather. The bitch was so smug she wasn't even doing publicity!

Somehow, in her mind, the success of Jahne Moore in *Birth* completely negated Lila. It was like she was back to square one. Despite its rating as an adult picture, it had opened to record box office and was now number two, with a good chance at being number one. It had done thirteen million last weekend. Worse, everyone was talking about it. How it had broken nearly every taboo, yet was also commercial. It brought every jealousy crashing back down around Lila's head. Just when she thought she had the Emmy in the little black velvet bag, tied up with gold braided tassel, this . . . this insult had to happen to *her*. It wasn't fair. *Something* had to be done.

She looked at another crumpled bit of newspaper. There, buried on a back page, was the announcement that should have been at the front of the whole damn newspaper:

DIRECTOR AND STAR ANNOUNCE
UPCOMING NUPTIALS

Jesus, against all her better judgment, just to keep up with Jahne's newsworthiness, she'd told Marty yes, and *this* was the publicity it received? Aunt Robbie said he could guarantee great coverage. Well, buried on page 24 of the *L.A. Times* and getting a paragraph in *Milestones* was not coverage. It was a fucking insult. After all, *she* was Hollywood royalty. She was Kerry Kyle's daughter. And the daughter of the Puppet Mistress, who, for all her faults, at least had been a star.

The phone rang. Lila rarely answered it, letting the service do her screening, but she was expecting Marty's call. She lifted the receiver.

"Are you crazy?" the voice rasped. "Are you completely fucking crazy?"

Lila considered, for a moment, hanging up on her mother, but the power of the Puppet Mistress held her on the line. "Shut up," she managed.

"I just read the *Times*. You can't get away with this, Lila. You've gone too far."

"Just shut up. I can do what I want. And when I need your opinion, I'll send you a ballot."

"Lila, *this* you can't do. Marty DiGennaro isn't Kevin. It will ruin us both."

"Shut up! I gave you the goddamn show, didn't I? It airs next week. Now, keep the fuck away from me. That was our deal. Leave me alone, or I swear I'll get Marty to cancel the program." Lila was almost spitting with rage. She wished she could kill Theresa, once and for all.

"Lila, listen to me. You can fool some of the people all of the time, and all of the people some of the time . . ."

"Yeah, but I can't fool Mom. Right? Well, fuck you, Mom. Fuck you and Aunt Robbie and Kevin and Candy and Skinny and Estrella and all of you. You didn't worry about that twenty years ago, did you? Don't bother to worry about it now. I warn you: leave me alone!" She slammed the phone down onto the receiver. It took less than a moment for it to ring again. Lila snorted and looked away. It would be a cold day in Malibu before she answered it again. She stood up, shaking with anger. First Marty nags her into saying yes, then Jahne's movie is a hit, the season premiere is overshadowed, and her engagement gets no coverage. Now this!

She *had* to win that Emmy, and she had to show the Puppet Mistress once and for all that she, Lila Kyle, was not to be fucked with. She stood there, breathing hard, almost dizzy with rage, and considered her options. It was time for a no-holds-barred attack on all of them. She didn't need anyone but Marty. And she would marry him. She would.

She looked down at her hands to find they were shaking. She felt murderous. And then she thought of the box. The "birthday present" peace offering that Robbie had brought. It still lay on the table, waiting for her. She smiled grimly, turned around, and went into the kitchen. She scrabbled through the utility drawers for a sharp knife. A very sharp knife.

* * *

Minos Paige couldn't exactly say he was surprised at receiving another call from Lila Kyle. Very little surprised Minos, certainly not the insatiable need of the denizens of this town to one-up each other. But he was surprised at Lila's carefully worded instructions. It was a good thing he hadn't been taken by surprise, because, if he had, he never would have worked out the fee that he did, the fee which was exactly quadruple that which he had originally gotten from Lila. But, then, this piece of work was at least four times as valuable to Lila as his original work had been. *That* he was sure of.

Minos didn't have to stop for a minute to think about how he was going to follow Lila's instructions. Minos had his priorities straight, knew just who to call and in what order. As he dialed the phone, he smiled to himself. The last job Lila had given him was for peanuts, took him all over and more than two months to finish. This assignment, for the most part, would take minutes, and would be done mostly by phone. Ah, fate.

When I answered the phone in my office, it was to hear a monotone I knew too well. "Guess who this is with some very good news," he said playfully to me, Laura Richie, a woman who very few men played with.

"Kevin Costner, and you're having my baby."

"Laura, it's better than that. And I swear, you are the first person I'm telling. I'm not doing this strictly for money, Laura. I'm doing this because you've been good to me in the past. So, get out a bunch of sharp pencils, and a long pad. All you gotta do is listen and write."

The totally one-sided conversation with Minos took less than fifteen minutes. I have a tape of the whole thing. Every now and then, during his narrative, you can hear an uncharacteristic gasp come through the line from me, and once I say "Holy shit!," but, other than that, he did all the talking. I do repeat "Her brother?," parroting his words, but that's it. I asked only one question when he was finished. "You got any paper on this, Minos?"

"It'll be coming over your fax machine in exactly five minutes."

"Pictures of the surgery?"

He laughed. *"For that, you have to pay,"* he said.

"How much for an exclusive?" I asked.

"More than you and Kitty Kelley combined could afford. No exclusives. I'm calling the Enquirer, *the* Observer, Entertainment Weekly, People, *and* Time *in the next twenty minutes. But you are the first one to hear. Make hay while the sun shines."*

Before he hung up, he did have to get in a commercial. *"Now, remember, Laura, you owe me. And you can't use my name in publication."*

"If you got the paper, I don't even want to know your name. But if I ain't paying for this, who is?"

"John Beresford Tipton," Minos laughed, and hung up.

6

SHARLEEN SMITH IN INCEST NEST

The shocking story of the star who sleeps with her brother. Inside this issue of the National Observer

THE SEXIEST WOMAN IN THE WORLD? WHO IS THE REAL JAHNE MOORE?

PLASTIC TO THE MAX. THE FULL STORY OF JAHNE MOORE AND HER TOTAL FACIAL AND BODY SURGERY. A complete report by Laura Richie. IN THIS ISSUE OF ENTERTAINMENT WORLD. AVAILABLE AT NEWSSTANDS NOW.

The phone hadn't stopped ringing. Sam felt as if he'd kill himself if he heard one more "b-b-b-r-r-i-i-i-n-g." Every yellow journalist in the country wanted to interview Sam, wanted to know what it felt like to sleep with

Jahne Moore. Yesterday, after lunch at Le Dôme, they shouted questions at him in the parking lot. "Did she feel the same as she had before the surgery?" "Did you do this as a publicity stunt?" "How do you think this will affect *Birth of a Star* box office?"

His secretary was going crazy. Sam had disconnected his home phone. He'd been reamed already by Bob LeVine, who couldn't believe Sam had unknowingly cast a female Frankenstein in their sex film, and had threatened to sue. LeVine was ready to throw Sam off the lot. He'd heard from his agent, who couldn't believe he hadn't known all along, and who insisted Sam hire a PR firm for damage control. And now there was the inevitable phone call from April. He'd ducked two of them, but he knew he couldn't put it off indefinitely. Oh, Jesus! What would she say? What would April try to do to him? He lifted up the receiver.

"Hello, April." He tried to keep his voice calm, his tone matter-of-fact, but he himself could hear the quaver. "Sixteen million," she said.

"What?"

"Sixteen million! We did sixteen million in box office this weekend. I just got the word. They had to run midnight shows of *Birth* to accommodate the crowds. Sixteen fucking million! It was a freak show."

Sam, speechless, could only nod in agreement.

O'CONNOR ANNOUNCES TEN-CITY TOUR TO HEAL THE NATION; CALLS FOR FAMILY RESPONSE

New York, NY. Yesterday, in his Sunday sermon at St. Patrick's Cathedral, Cardinal O'Connor, the Archbishop of the Roman Catholic Archdiocese of New York, announced to his parishioners and the media reporters brought out by his press release that he denounced television and particularly *Three for the Road* as an example of what the worship of the golden calf of Hollywood had done to the country. After denouncing *Murphy Brown*, *Cheers*, and a host of other shows he went on to proclaim that his Christian Family Tour would heal the hurt caused the people of America by the charges of Sharleen Smith's incest and the sexually explicit new film starring Jahne Moore that has rocked the nation. He asked the parish to join in his prayers for the costars of the popular program, then added that all three were guilty of "provoking lustful thoughts." The Cardinal invoked St. Joseph, the Patron Saint of the Family, to intercede in the country beset by confusion over lack of family values. "What happened to Disney World?" the Cardinal asked in his heated oration. "To *Mary Poppins?* Instead, today we have Hollywood, and Jahne Moore and Sharleen Smith. Something is very wrong in a nation that ignores all that is holy and beautiful in the example of the Blessed Virgin and turns instead to idols with feet of clay (CONT. ON PG. 6)

Jahne felt as if she was under siege. This is what it must have been like behind the walls of a medieval city during war. She had taken the phone off the hook, Gerry La Brecque had sent in three more security guards, and now the Beverly Hills police had stationed a cop car outside to try and control the traffic. She couldn't go out, she couldn't be seen, she couldn't go anywhere, and staying home was unbearable.

It was spooky. After only a couple of weeks of the media blitz following *Birth*'s release, this new exposure had come about, and the snowball had gathered enough momentum to become an avalanche. She felt flattened under the load. Who had leaked her medical history? Had Sam betrayed her in an even deeper way?

The irony that the nation's newest sex goddess was man-made wasn't lost on her or on the media. She didn't have the courage to read most of the trash that was being published, but she did tune in to *Entertainment Tonight*, only to see John Tesh interview Miss Hennessey, Dr. Moore's nurse. They had an old "before" photo of her, a Polaroid that had been shot in Dr. Moore's office. She looked horrible.

"Oh, my God," she moaned.

Then they began the exposé on Sharleen. It was awful. A sneering, smirking Jukes-and-Kallikaks-oh-those-hillbillies-can't-be-trusted number. Jahne felt sick. She remembered the slip that Dean had made: something about how he could have two sisters. Well, what if it was true? Who was she, Jahne, to judge? She picked up the phone, plugged it in, and dialed Sharleen's private number. Of course, she only got a busy signal. Well, she'd have to go over there. If Sharleen needed her, she owed it to Sharleen; and, anyway, she wanted to help. She's my friend, Jahne thought. They both are.

MEMORANDUM

TO: All Employees of Sy Ortis and Associates
FROM: Sy Ortis
SUBJECT: Press Leaks

Anyone discovered to have leaked any item about Sharleen Smith or Jahne Moore, or any item about Three for the Road, will be terminated immediately, and prosecuted for breaching client confidentiality.

If any part of this memo is unclear, please contact Miss Hancock in Public Relations for illumination.

S. O.

Jahne had managed to get through the barrage of press and over to Sharleen's. They sat now almost barricaded into the living room. Sharleen looked even paler than usual, but otherwise seemed to be holding up. Jahne sat beside her on the sofa, her hand in Sharleen's. Two of the PR staff from Sy's office were buzzing around in the kitchen on the phones, and an attorney was screaming at his paralegal, both of who seemed permanently camped out in the dining room.

"Jahne, are you mad at me?" Sharleen asked.

"Why would I be mad?"

"Because you told me about your secret, but I didn't say nothin' about mine."

"Hey, Sharleen, it wasn't a trade. Friends don't work like that."

"We're still friends?" Sharleen asked, a tear escaping from under a long eyelash and running down her pale cheek.

"Of course we are," Jahne said, and squeezed Sharleen's hand.

"Well, it's a real hard feeling, knowing that everyone despises you."

"It surely is," Jahne said, and tried to smile. Her lip trembled, but she didn't cry. So what if everyone hated her. This was the risk you took. After all, she told herself, you didn't just want this, you *paid* for it. And it looks as if I'm going to keep on paying for it, she thought wryly. She also thought of Brewster Moore. In the maelstrom of all that had happened to her in the last months, she had come to realize that aside from Mai and Sharleen it was only Brewster's quiet talks at the hospital in the dead of night, only Brewster's letters, that seemed to have any substance. But she hadn't heard a word from him since her last letter. Surely *he* had not betrayed her. Was he being accosted by journalists even now? Would he despise her for the publicity and bother she had caused him? She shrank down onto the sofa. Somehow, the thought of being despised by Brewster was more than she could bear.

Sharleen Smith's Father Talks About His Years in Prison
By Clint Roper
Special to the *Dallas* Independent

Dean Smith, Sr., father of *Three for the Road* costar Sharleen Smith and her half brother, Dean Jr., met with this reporter and talked freely of Boyd Jamison, the boy the senior Smith has been found guilty of murdering outside the Smith trailer in Lamson, Texas, more than three years ago. He also confirmed reports of the incest between his son and daughter.

In the three-part series which begins this Monday, the Independent probes into Mr. Smith's allegations that Sharleen could have saved him if she had appeared at his trial, that he only killed the boy in self-defense while protecting his daughter from Boyd's sexual attack, and that he loves Sharleen despite her sins and begs her to contact him.

He hasn't heard from wife, son, or daughter since the time of the murder, and says he misses and loves them all. He claims that his drinking provoked him, but that he's cured of his habit, through the intervention of Christ. He has been sober since admission to prison. It is a tale that only a certain kind of Texan could love, a tale fit for a J. R. Ewing. In the annals of family dysfunction, the Smiths of Lamson, Texas, are one for the books. . . .

"I still can't believe Daddy is alive," Sharleen murmured. She felt drained of all energy, as if she would never move off the Herculon-covered sofa again.

"We don't have to see him, though, do we?" Dean asked. His eyes were big, the way they got when he was scared. Funny how nothin' scared Dean exceptin' their daddy. Maybe his fright got all used up when we were kids, Sharleen thought.

"No. I guess we don't. But he's sayin' we're bad kids. And so's everyone else."

"I don't understand," Dean said, standing beside the sofa she was lying on. He held up one of the newspapers from the pile in front of him. "I don't understand."

"I know you don't, Dean, honey. I know."

"But why are they so mad? I only hit him 'cause he was hittin' on you. And I'm glad he ain't dead, but I'd kill him again if he hit you."

"That ain't why they're mad."

"Why, then?"

"Because of what we do at night. Because of how we sleep together."

"But we *always* sleep together," Dean said. "Why are they mad now?"

"Well, I guess they didn't know till now."

"Does that mean you won't get the prize?"

For a moment, she didn't know what he was talking about. Then she remembered the Emmy. "I guess it does, honey." Dean hunkered down next to her. He dropped the paper and stared at her.

"Does that make you sad?"

Sharleen nodded. "But I ain't so sad as I'm ashamed." Though she tried to stop it, a tear escaped and slid down her cheek.

"Oh, Sharleen! Please. Don't be. It's like the time that Opie met the man who worked on the power lines. And he told everyone about it, but Andy thought he was makin' it all up. So he made Opie apologize for bein' wrong and lyin', even when he wasn't. But then Andy met the power-line man. So he came to see it Opie's way. We didn't do nothin' wrong, Sharleen. They'll come to see that."

Sharleen took his hand and shook her head. "I don't think so."

"Why not?"

"Because that was Mayberry. This is Hollywood."

First Photos: Jahne Moore
Before and After

In this week's issue of the *National Questioner* are the exclusive photos of Jahne Moore's miracle surgery. See how surgery can take a woman from being a thirty-four-year-old, overweight, mousy woman to a twenty-four-year-old beauty with the body of a goddess. EXCLUSIVE!

"Jesus Christ!" Marty could hardly believe it! First there had been the rescheduling problems with Jahne

Moore over *Birth*. Then the problems with Lila and Theresa. Then Jahne calls in sick for a week. Now both Sharleen and Jahne were in the epicenter of the biggest scandals since Fatty Arbuckle and the Coke bottle. Didn't they all understand he had a show to shoot?

He had suspended shooting for a week. Les Merchant was going nuts. It cost the Network almost the same amount not to shoot an episode as to shoot one. Meanwhile, Sy was constantly on the phone with new reports from the press, new outrage from the sponsors, and general fear and loathing.

Marty listened to the sound of phones going crazy and unanswered outside his office door. He lifted his hand to rub the bridge of his nose. He had a Headache from Hell, and he was afraid it wasn't going away anytime soon.

Sharleen Smith's Mother Busted for Prostitution

THE LOS ANGELES TIMES

NEW ORLEANS, LA. Flora Lee Deluce, the mother of Sharleen Smith, costar of *Three for the Road*, was arrested last night for prostitution in a motel on Route 101, also known by the locals as "Mattress Mile" because of the profusion of motels that rent rooms by the hour.

At first the police weren't aware that Mrs. Deluce was Ms. Smith's mother, and the booking was regarded as routine, the result of a regular stake-out by the police of the Sun Star Motel.

Mrs. Deluce, while declining to comment on her relationship with her daughter, did say the arrest "was a frame-up. I didn't even have my teeth out when the cops crashed in the door."

Sharleen Smith's meteoric career and the accusation of an incestuous relationship with her brother have cast the spotlight on all aspects of her life. Neither Miss Smith nor her spokesperson had any comment to make.

Arraignment is scheduled for 2:00 P.M. today in St. Charles Parish Courthouse. Fifty dollars bail was paid by an associate of Mrs. Deluce, who declined to be named or interviewed.

"What a family!" Sy Ortis screamed into his car phone. He could barely manage to get enough air into his lungs to do it. "Is there one member of the Smith family who hasn't been jailed or broken a commandment today?"

TOP TEN REASONS WHY WOMEN NO LONGER WATCH *THREE FOR THE ROAD*

—FROM *Late Night with David Letterman*

10. Their boyfriends don't make them anymore
9. Their brothers don't make them anymore
8. So they don't have to hate themselves in the morning
7. They're not into motorcycles
6. Their mothers won't let them
5. Their fathers won't let them
4. Their priests won't let them
3. They prefer NFL highlights
2. They can't afford the surgical bills
1. They prefer *Bride of Frankenstein*

BIRTH *TOPS IN BOX*

Jahne Moore's *Birth of a Star* once again topped all other releases in box-office performance, bringing in $83 million in the less than a month since its release. . . .
—*Hollywood Reporter*

Sharleen was sitting in the living room, hunched over, a blanket covering her shoulders. She heard his voice before she saw him, and turned around. "Dobe!" she yelled, and jumped from the recliner, dropping the afghan. "Dobe Samuels, what are you doing here? Why, you look better than a warm stove on a cold night."

"And you look like something the cat dragged in," Dobe told her. "What in the name of the living God got you tucked away in this dark hole?"

"I told him you been sick, Sharleen," Dean said. "I told him you were cryin' and all."

"Well, what the hell have you got to cry about, I'd like to know?"

"Oh, Dobe. It's really been terrible. The newspapers and television people won't leave us alone, and then the news about Daddy in prison. Dean and me both been sick about it. Plus Flora Lee's been . . ."

"People make their bed, Sharleen. Only can do so much for them. You, on the other hand, you never done nothing bad to no one that I know about. So why are you holed up here like some kind of outlaw on the lam?"

She only shrugged her shoulders. Dobe shook his head. "Sit down, you two," he told them. Sharleen sank back down onto the recliner. Dean took a seat on the floor with the dogs. "Now, listen up. Ain't no incest going on here. Never was, never will be. Flora Lee ain't your mother. . . ."

"I know that. Dean's only my *half*-brother, but . . . but that don't make it only half wrong."

Dobe interrupted her with a brusque wave of his hand. "Dean ain't your brother at all. Flora Lee told your daddy he was, but it wasn't so. And there's a birth certificate that proves it. Flora Lee was carrying Dean before she even met your daddy. He's a Deluce, her first husband's boy. Well, her only husband. She never even married your daddy. He was only a port in the storm."

Sharleen sat there quiet for a minute. "Dean wasn't my daddy's son?"

It was too much to grasp. All the secrets, all the shame, for so long. And for nothing. The surprise and the relief flooded her, and she began to sob. "It's all been so hard. So hard. Lila bein' mean, and then Mr. McLain, and the album, with Mr. Ortis lyin' to me and makin' me a crook.

And Marty so hard to work with now, and me so slow. Then this. I can't . . . Even if it ain't true, I just can't go to them Emmys and then to Ara Sagarian's party with all them people laughing at me, whispering about me and Dean behind my back.''

"What do you care what a bunch of misfits and perverts have to say about you? Why should you care what *anyone* thinks of you?''

"Did you read some of them stories? They would make you vomit. I wonder why Momma never told me this. Woulda saved a heap of worryin'. I hope Momma wasn't upset if she found out what they been saying, wherever she is. It would kill her dead, and that's the truth.''

"Don't you worry about your momma. Truth wasn't really her strong point, Sharleen." He watched the tears course down her cheeks. Then he shook his head and sighed. "Honey, I got something for you. But, before I give it to you, I gotta ask that you don't question me 'bout how I got it or nothin'. We got a deal?''

Mutely, Sharleen nodded.

"Okay, then, honey. You never told me much about your growin'-up years, but I got a powerful strong imagination, and I ain't stupid, neither. So I thought you might need these someday." He went to his bag and took out an envelope of papers. He handed the sheaf to Sharleen.

"Your birth certificate. And Dean's. See, Sharleen, Dean's not your brother. Dean ain't your blood kin at all. These are just copies; you'll find the originals in the lockbox at the bank. You got the key I gave you.''

"But how . . .'' she began, remembered her promise, and stopped, then abruptly sat down. "Dobe, I just can't believe this. I just got to ask, is this for real? Not some fake papers, like a fake driver's license?''

"No, this is strictly legit. And the newspapers will be gettin' a copy of this as soon as you want them to. Plus, you can sue 'em for slander.''

"Dobe, you got all the proof here I need?''

"Well, I think I got it all, Minos a Paige or two." He chuckled.

"Where's the missing page?" Sharleen asked.

"Oh, probably in the hospital, minus a few teeth."

Dobe shook his head. "Just a little joke. Now's not the time to go into it. You got everything you need here to disprove everything. Most important thing is, you know the truth now, and there isn't anyone out there who has the right to judge you. You go and marry Dean if you want to. I know you, Sharleen, and you're a real good girl. A fine girl. So stop your cryin'."

ROBOACTRESS?

The disclosure that Jahne Moore is the product of expert transformational surgery has hit Los Angeles, the entertainment capital of the world, like a ton of pâté de foie gras. In a town with the largest per-capita number of plastic surgeons— or "transformational specialists," as some now prefer to be called—everyone is looking over her (and his) shoulder, waiting for another disgruntled nurse or lab technician of one of the multimillionaire surgeons to make public another list of names.

Many in the Hollywood community are considering going public about their cosmetic surgery before someone takes it into his (or her) mind to tell all. As names are being named, and reporters are being deflected from one big name to another, a small but radical group of surgery-philes have reacted to the public outcry against this type of elective surgery. Raquel Welch, the national spokesperson for the group known as America the Beautiful, asked, "What's wrong with a nip and tuck? Or a full-body make-over, for that matter? I have nothing but respect for Jahne Moore. It's just like using any other cosmetic device. Men think nothing of using a blade every day to improve their looks, but as soon as a woman tries to do the same thing, she's branded a fake."

Michael Jackson, Michelle Pfeiffer, and Cher have each called a press conference to talk about the impact of the media's negative coverage of a private issue. "It's a form of rape," Cher said.

"He's Not My Brother"

SHARLEEN SMITH ISSUES DENIAL

In a new twist to the ongoing *Three for the Road* scandals, Sharleen Smith today in a public statement denied a blood relationship to Dean Deluce, known as Dean Smith, her alleged brother. She provided birth certificates and a written statement from Deluce, who declined to be interviewed.

Asked whether she would sue those publications that may have slandered her, Miss Smith told the assembled media, "I think enough damage has been done."

Lila rolled over onto her stomach. Around her, the stack of torn and wrinkled newspapers and magazines defaced the otherwise immaculate room. A breeze blew in at the window, rifling the neat pile of carefully scissored clippings before her. If she felt cheated out of publicity on her engagement, at least she was compensated by this avalanche of bad press burying Sharleen and Jahne.

Right now she was being cheated out of filming the next *3/4* episode. Marty and the Network had suspended filming for the next week while they decided what to do. If Marty knew it was Lila who had started this shit storm, would he be angry? She had sympathized with him, and then suggested that they fire and replace Sharleen and Jahne. He was going to take it up with Les Merchant at the meeting next week. Lila felt cheated that she couldn't go to that, either, but a girl could only do what a girl could do. She smiled to herself.

And she wouldn't be cheated out of the Emmy, that she was sure of. Voting was taking place next week, and no one in the Industry would vote for a monster or an incester. No matter, or because of, whatever monstrous surgery and incestuous secrets they had of their own. She had the Emmy for sure, and maybe *Three for the Road* would become her private show.

7

Since Dobe had appeared like an avenging angel with the good news, Sharleen had felt happier than she had in a long, long time. It wasn't just that she no longer had to be afraid of exposure. And it wasn't just that she no longer was a sinner. Dean wasn't a murderer, and while her daddy wasn't dead, it was good to know he was safely put away. And if having the spotlight of fame on them had given them this knowledge, it was almost worth it. And reading about Flora Lee's degradation was sad but not surprising. Sharleen would send her money, but make sure she didn't bother Dean again.

The best part of the news, she realized, was that she and Dean could be together. That there was nothing wrong about them loving each other the way they did.

The news was so good, so big, so *enormous* that it would take some getting used to. She had sat down with Dean and spent some time trying to make him understand. They sat outside, in the safety of the night darkness. Night was the only time they could go out into the yard without being photographed.

"Dean, I got some good news to tell you. You ain't my brother."

He looked up at her with pained eyes. "I ain't?"

"No. Momma lied to us and Daddy about it."

"But I *want* to be your brother."

"No, you don't, Dean. 'Cause brothers and sisters don't sleep together." For a moment, Sharleen longed for some romance from Dean. For him to give a pretty speech about how he loved her, how he needed her, and for him to woo her with gifts and flowers. But Dean spoke only through his eyes. She could see how he felt. She sighed.

"Dean, you want to stay with me always?" she asked.

"Sure, Sharleen. You *know* that."

"Well, I was thinking that we could get married. I could be your wife instead of your sister." Dean was silent for a moment.

"Can't you be both?"

"No. It don't work like that."

"Well, then, let's get married." It wasn't a romantic proposal, but it was real, and dependable.

"You mean it, Dean? You want to?"

"Sure do. We could still keep the dogs, right?"

Sharleen smiled and took his hand. "We surely could."

And there, in the dark behind their house, in the midst of their beautiful garden, she was flooded with such love for him, such a deep and full and pure swell of love, that she thought, for a moment, she might not be able to go on living. Her heart seemed so full it might burst, and she stood drinking in the fullness and the pain. Dean was imperfect: she knew he wasn't what most other women looked for in men. But he was what she loved and what she wanted. His goodness, his clarity and pureness were the most important things in the world to her. He was her anchor and her compass, and he had always been the mechanism that helped her steer a clear path through dangerous waters.

Sharleen woke up on the day of the Emmy awards full of joy and gratitude. Copies of the birth certificates and appropriate statements had gone out to the press. And, inevitably, a new avalanche of publicity had started. The awards would still be a horrible ordeal. But, after breakfast, Dobe insisted that she should go—and go with Dean.

"But I *never* take him to business stuff."

"No reason not to now."

"But he'll hate it."

"So do you. But he's a big boy."

"Dobe Samuels, I don't want no award, and I don't want to go to no party where everybody will look at me like I'm a freak. All I want . . ." She paused, thinking her words out very carefully. ". . . is to live quiet, in the country like, on a ranch with horses for Dean, and a bunch of dogs, and lots of trees and open fields and lakes and hills. And kids running around, all over the place. They don't got to be mine. Just some kids got no place else to go. And *no* other people. Just you around, close by. And no fancy stores, or fancy parties, or gossipy magazines. I just want some peace and quiet for Dean and me. To be left alone, and never to have to wear a formal dress again." She paused, imagining it. "You ever been square dancin', Dobe?"

"No. Never stayed in one place long enough to learn how."

"I'd like to learn. I always wanted to, but never got around to it. Now, if Dean and me had a nice country place, we could learn square dancing, and have some real fun. And maybe we can afford to do that soon." She didn't want to make Dobe feel guilty about the money she had given him, so she shut up.

But Dobe didn't seem to even remember about the money. "All that's possible, Sharleen. And sooner than you think. Now, all you've got to do is show up tonight like you own the world, and, believe you me, ninety percent of them bastards—excuse me, honey—ninety percent of them will actually believe you do. No matter what anybody's been saying or writing. 'Cause, to make it in this town, one of the things I learned, you act as if you don't give a rat's ass about nobody, and they eat it up."

Sharleen was beginning to hear Dobe, and had to agree with him, for the most part. She usually did, because he usually was right. "But I'll still feel like a freak in a sideshow."

"Well, honey, to be really honest, that's exactly what you've been, since the first day you set foot in front of that there television camera. And so is every other one of them television and movie stars. All freaks. But you're also one of the sweetest and most beautiful women in

795

America, and you can go anywhere and hold your head high. Most of them women gonna be there tonight would trade places with you in a Tennessee minute, publicity and all. Maybe even *because* of the publicity. Shows you how sick some of them really are. This ain't the real world, Sharleen. Don't make that mistake. It ain't even Planet Earth. We're on some separate planet that spins around the sun backwards, at ten times the normal speed. Hell, a woman gets old in this town in two or three years, instead of two or three decades. This is a town out of joint. Only you and I know that. Every one of them other jerks thinks this is heaven.'' Dobe paused, seeing Sharleen was beginning to feel better. ''And not one of these Hollywood people could shine your boots, and that's the truth. Maybe Jahne Moore. Sounds like she got some backbone, but not one of them others. Remember that.''

Sharleen's eyes filled with tears. ''Dobe, you're one lovely man. You deserve the best there is in this life. But I'll only go on one condition: we get another ticket and you come, too. Okay?'' She waited until he nodded. Was that a blush she saw? She rose, kissed him on the cheek, and started to leave the room, to go upstairs to get ready for the awards.

''Sharleen,'' Dobe called, ''after tonight, after all this mess is over, you and me have to have a really good talk. I know some things that I think you're ready to hear, but we've talked serious enough for one day. You get ready now. I'll save the rest of it until all this is all over.''

Sharleen ran back to Dobe and kissed him. Perhaps Dobe had talked her out of some money, but it didn't matter now. He was a good friend, one who had proved his loyalty, and she loved him.

''Thank you for everything,'' she said, and went to get dressed for the awards.

Jahne woke up on the morning of the Emmy awards with a bad case of the shakes. She'd taken two Xanax tablets the night before, but that didn't explain the tremors that shook her. And she simply wasn't able to get organized or to focus. She keyed in Sharleen's phone number, and her hand shook so badly that she misdialed twice. When Sharleen answered, Jahne just managed to croak out a "hello."

"Come on, Jahne. It ain't so bad," Sharleen said. What? When they had last spoken, Sharleen had agreed that life was shit. What had cheered her up so?

"Are you going?" Jahne asked. She didn't need to explain. Sharleen knew what she was talking about.

"Yes. And I'm going with Dean. What about you, Jahne? Come with us. There was nothing wrong in what you did."

"I don't know. Who would I go *with?* Sy said he could set something up, but I haven't agreed. And then Gerald La Brecque offered to take me. But that's too much— being so desperate that you have to go with your paid bodyguard."

"Oh, Jahne. Come. Come with us. I'll ask Dobe to take you. He's a good friend. What do you say? We can't let Lila have *all* the glory."

"I don't know. I'll call you back." Jahne hung up and paced up and down the living room. She shivered. This house was always cold. She hated it.

Could she face the barracudas tonight? Could she afford not to? Lucky Sharleen, to be rescued. No one could rescue her. And what would she wear if she went tonight? It wasn't such a frivolous question as it sounded. The only point to showing up would be to demonstrate that she looked good, felt good, was good. But could she manage to *look* good? Without Mai, she had no guide, and no confidence in her own choices. Let's face it, she told herself, when Mai died, you lost both your best friend *and* your sense of style.

It all seemed like so much trouble, too. Finding the right dress, getting her hair done, the manicure, the pedicure, the leg waxing, the makeup, the perfume, the jewelry, the whole thing. She was exhausted just thinking about it. And then, then, the ordeal began—being watched and judged by thirty or forty million people. She imagined the cameras closing in, the commentator recapping the scandal, the audience at home straining their eyes, looking for a telltale scar. And how the cameras would pan the audience, seeking close-ups of the losers when the winners' names were announced.

"No way," she groaned, walked back to her bedroom, and threw herself back into bed. She shook two more Xanax into her palm and swallowed them dry.

It was more than an hour later when the phone rang. She picked it up, almost as if it were a snake that might bite. "Hello," she murmured, hesitant.

"Jahne? Thank God. It's Brewster."

"Brewster? Oh, God, Brewster. It's so good to hear from you." Warmth flooded her. It was a physical feeling. "Brewster. Hello," she repeated.

"Are you all right, Jahne?" he asked. The phone clicked and spit with static. He must be calling from far away. South America, she thought. Wasn't he making a clinic trip there? It was so good of him to call. "Are you all right?" he repeated.

"I'm just so embarrassed, Brewster. It sounds stupid, but it feels terminal."

"Which terminal?" he asked. "Jahne, I can hardly hear you. What terminal did you say?"

"Life is terminal. Oh, Brewster, I feel so bad! Nothing has worked out the way I planned. I got a second chance and I wasted it. I simply couldn't swing it." Her voice wavered. Even to her it seemed weak and far away.

"This connection is awful," Brewster cried. "It keeps cutting out on us. What did you say about swinging?"

"Brewster, aren't you ashamed of me? That horrible movie, and now this tabloid blitz. Are they driving you crazy at the office? Did I ruin your life?"

"More to the point, did I ruin yours? Are you okay, Jahne? You sound so far away."

"Do you still like me, Brewster?" she asked.

"Of course I do. Jahne, I . . ." His voice faded out.

"Brewster? Brewster, are you there?" There was another wave of static, then the line was dead. Stupidly, she shook the phone in frustration. "Brewster? Brewster?" she cried. But he was gone. She began to sob, but in the weak, disheartened way of a hopeless child. Oh, God, Brewster was gone. She couldn't talk to him. She sobbed on, her nose dripping, and picked up the quilt to wipe her face. Then the security buzzer sounded.

She lifted the intercom. "Brewster Moore. Are you expecting him?" the voice asked. She shook her head to clear it. How had Brewster called on her security phone? "Yes," she mumbled, and hung on. Or should she hang up? Were they patching him through?

The doorbell rang. She reached for her robe and barely managed to struggle into it without dropping the phone. But Brewster didn't come onto the line. The doorbell rang again. "One minute," she yelled, but she knew that whoever it was couldn't hear. Could she put the phone down? Should she hang up? Would she lose Brewster's call?

She left the phone on the bed and tried to run to the door. But the pills affected her balance. She ran into the side of the night table and nearly fell. "I'm coming," she yelled, righted herself, and managed to get across the living room, down the gallery, and to the enormous front door. She threw it open.

Brewster Moore stood on the doorstep, a suitcase in his left hand, his raincoat bunched over his right arm. Brewster. Brewster was right there.

"Aren't you in Honduras?" she asked.

He stepped into the foyer. "Aren't you in trouble?" he asked, and then he dropped his things and they hugged one another.

Later that day, after she had bathed, after Brewster had fed her lunch, after he had helped her wash her hair and she'd picked out a dress and managed to pull herself together—after all that, they sat side by side in the limo. "There is no way," Jahne said to Dr. Moore, "that I could face any of this tonight without you. Thank you for coming all this way, just to take me to the awards and the party. If you couldn't make it, I wouldn't be going."

"You'll excuse me, Jahne, but I wouldn't have missed it for the world. You don't know this, but there are a lot of people—men as well as women—who are going to be very nervous when they see me tonight. You won't be-lieve who's been calling me in New York, since my name came out connected with you. Now that you've been 'outed,' everyone's afraid.''

Jahne looked at him. "What do you mean?"

"Do you really think you're my *only* celebrity client? You weren't a celebrity then, of course. But, Jahne, I've spent years doing corrections of other surgeons' mistakes for some very rich, very famous people. It wouldn't have been ethical of me to have gone into it with you when we first developed our professional relationship. Or even now. But everyone will be afraid that I'm out here to do a book deal, or TV, or to somehow go public." He took a sip of the white wine he had poured. "And, considering what these bastards have done to you, and said about me, well, it's a very tempting idea. Do you know I've been approached—just in the last forty-eight hours—by Laura Richie, *and* every publisher in the English-speaking world, just to tell all? They're offering obscene amounts of money. Tempting, real tempting. The money would pay for the work on a lot of kids like Raoul. They'll be coming to you, too—don't be surprised."

"Ha! I'll never talk to another bloodsucking journalist as long as I live. I wish I could just run away. Start over somewhere." She laughed at herself. "Does that sound familiar?"

"Yes, but it doesn't sound so stupid. Maybe you should do just that. Go back to New York." He reached out and took her hand with his own. His hand was small, but warm and surprisingly comforting. She gripped it tightly.

"What for? To act? That's a laugh! Now the gape factor is high enough for me to star in some Broadway revival—people would come to stare and see if they could spot the scars. Might as well join a carnival sideshow. No, New York theater is over—for good, I'm afraid. But I'll worry about my career dilemma later, when I have more time. Now I'd rather appreciate the moment—having you here." Jahne managed a smile. "But right now I have to face all those beautiful barracudas."

Dr. Moore laughed. "Some of whom once were *ugly* barracudas, before they came to me," he pointed out. "So what? And don't you think you're showing a lot of class and a certain *je ne sais quoi* by showing up with your surgeon? Sort of sticking it in their eye."

Jahne laughed at that. "But no one knows *that* about *them,* and now everyone knows everything about *me.* My age, my previous and present weight—they've seen my 'before' pictures, interviewed girls I went to high school with, dragged out the affairs I had with Pete and Michael McLain. I'm humiliated."

"Well, I'm no psychiatrist, but by now I think I know something about people. When they see who you're with tonight, they're going to treat you like Princess Diana. *Before her scandals.* Make no mistake, I know details of people's lives that make your puny little problems look like a pimple against their cancerous growths. And if it gets too bad for you, if you get the last-minute heeby-jeebies and don't want to get out of the limousine, I'm fully prepared to show you some of the pictures I brought along with me from New York. From my files. I know, it's unprofessional, but I hate hypocrites. Jahne, as I tell all my patients, it's only going to hurt a bit, then it's over."

Lila stretched her arms above her head, her legs flexed down the length of the satin sheets, then reached to her face and removed the eyeshades. She winced as she opened her eyes to the harsh afternoon light. That was the bitch of a Malibu house—the harsh west light. Too much sun, even with the curtains drawn. Lila rang for the maid, had her bring fresh-squeezed orange juice, and slowly—very slowly—open the curtains. She didn't need any other help. As always, Lila would tend to her own toilette.

She lay motionless, sipping the iced juice intermittently, trying to figure out how she really felt about the night that lay ahead. The Emmy was *this close.* She could feel its heft in her hand, the coldness of the metal against her warm palm. Right now, squiggling her toes between the sheets, she felt delighted, as if she were Cinderella that first morning she'd awakened in the palace. After all, Marty *was* a prince in Hollywood, and she a princess.

Their wedding and new movie together would mark the start of their reign.

Lila shifted a little in bed. Of course there would be a lot of risks, but they were worth it. She'd already told Marty that she insisted on her own room, her own bed, and privacy. Yet, if her antics could keep him satisfied, he had nothing to complain about.

And if she didn't marry Marty, what was there for her?

A chill wind blew in off the Pacific, turning her skin to gooseflesh. She felt the good mood begin to bleed away, as it did whenever she thought of marriage, but she refused to let it. She *would* be happy.

Lila knew there was a lot to do, but for the next few minutes she wasn't going to do anything but gloat about the waiting prize she would receive tonight, and what she would say in her acceptance speech. Maybe she would mention her costars, just for spite. She laughed.

Then the phone trilled by her bedside. She cursed the interruption, but answered anyway. "Yes," she simply said, her usual telephone greeting.

"Lila, darling, I'm so glad I caught you in." It was me. "Laura Richie here. I hope I didn't disturb you, but I wanted to be the very first to congratulate you on the Emmy. No one deserves it more."

"Thank you, Laura. I'll always remember you for this. Congratulating me for something I haven't won yet. Now, that *shows real confidence."*

I laughed. "Nonsense, darling, what are friends for? Anyhow, it's in the bag. Why, anyone with half a brain knows you are a shoo-in. Everyone, my dear, is saying so. And I do mean everyone." I was trying to get enough stuff to write tomorrow's column in advance. Tricky, because sometimes you have to tell a secret or get caught in a lie, but necessary when you have to be in three places at once.

"Laura, you'll have to excuse me, I must run. They're screaming for me downstairs. Photographers, Network publicity people. The house is simply teeming. Of course, I won't tell them a thing. I'll save every detail just for you. After all, you're my oldest and dearest friend in Hollywood."

Lila slung the manure just the way her mother did. "I'm not so old, dearie, but thanks for the vote of confidence," I said. "Do you know who's presenting the award?"

"No. Do you?"

I ignored her. "Are you going with Marty?"

"Of course."

"And have you two set a date?"

"Not yet, but you'll be the first to know."

It was the last time I ever spoke to Lila Kyle.

Michael McLain lay on the lounge at his pool, applying yet another layer of sun block. How to achieve that perfect color of brown masculine health without destroying his skin's elasticity forever? Such a riddle. He hated to have to resort to bronzer, so he paid particular attention to the sun on his face today, changing his face's position every fifteen minutes to make sure the tan came out perfectly even.

Ara's party tonight would be both pleasure and torture —sort of like fucking a woman who had an exquisite body but an ordinary face. Which, in fact, was what he would be doing in a little while. His date tonight was, after all, Adrienne.

Birth of a Star had given him the boost that he had been needing for a while. It would prolong his life. He'd done it again! Still, he wasn't stupid or naïve. While it was by no means his swan song, he realized that this was the top of the crop of the older man parts he would be offered. He could see Stewart Granger–type made-for-TV-movie roles looming in his future, and he was not about to end his exceptional acting career playing old but-still-attractive John Forsythe roles. Not Michael McLain.

No, it was time to move his public image to a whole new level. He liked being on the A list and wanted to stay there forever, the way Greg Peck and Jimmy Stewart had. So it was time, at last, for the inevitable. What was the one thing newsworthy Michael McLain had never done with a woman?

Marry one.

After all, it was the nineties. A time of family values. Hadn't Adrienne told him she'd missed a period? No D&C this time. He'd marry her. Have the baby. Be a dad. What a way to spend his sixth decade.

He shifted his face in the sun and stopped the smile from making dangerously aging wrinkles. Yes. Right after the Emmys, he'd leak the info that Adrienne was the body in *Birth*. After she had a smidgen of facial work. Then announce that he was going to marry her. Wouldn't *that* make headlines?

Theresa O'Donnell walked out of the shower and wrapped a bath sheet around her sagging body. She couldn't be bothered putting on a robe. She was tired, and her evening's work had not even begun. She walked into the dressing room and picked up the Lycra bodysuit that Estrella had laid out for her. It was specially made for her in Paris and worked like a whole-body girdle. She powdered herself down and began the arduous task of wiggling into it, a sausage struggling into its casing.

At last she finished and, exhausted, sat down at her mirrored vanity table. She very nearly groaned as she looked at the wreck that stared back at her. Vanity table, indeed! It was a holy crucifixion to look at the ruin that had been her face. The Loveliest Girl in the World! Well, once she had been.

Where once she had a chin she now had several. And the hollows under her eyes had long ago turned to bags. Well, she'd turned into a bag. Her hair, never her strongest suit, was thinner than ever. Forty years of coloring and perms had had their way. She snatched up a wig cap and stuffed the straggling gray ends into it, fastening the skintight nylon to her head by viciously stabbing in hairpins.

She began to coat her sallow skin with the Estée Lauder base she used. She daubed the natural sea sponge across the wrinkles on her forehead, the puffiness that had become her nose.

"Ah. Transformation time," Kevin said as he walked in with two glasses of gin. He looked over her shoulder into the mirror. There were no longer any secrets from Kevin. Now he was bitter because she was going to the Emmys and Ara's party with Robbie and not him. Because she'd be on TV presenting the Best Actress award while he was left home watching. She took the glass from his hand, drank it down, and picked up the makeup sponge again.

"Can I get you a trowel?" he asked.

"Very clever. I told you, I'm not speaking to you until you return Candy and Skinny."

"I don't have them. But I think I know where they are."

Aunt Robbie arrived at Theresa's at four. "Where is she?" he asked Kevin, who nodded up the stairs to Theresa's bedroom, then shrugged his shoulders. "Has she had anything to drink yet?" he asked.

"I don't know and I don't give a shit."

Robbie moved to the stairs. At Theresa's door, he stopped to knock, but, knowing he wasn't going to get an answer, opened the door and walked in.

"Jesus Christ," he said to no one in particular. The room was in shambles. Even with the curtains drawn, the dim light showed piles of clothes heaped everywhere, the bed stripped of linen, a stained yellow pile on the floor, and a bloated, whitened heap of a human being stretched out full-length, as if dead, across the sill of the bathroom door. She was naked, and dirty, and her gray hair had the coated, greasy look of a street-woman's. This is what becomes of a legend most often, he thought. Robbie wouldn't let himself feel the sadness that throbbed in his chest. There was too much work to be done.

Robbie pulled back the curtains, and the room sprang into light. Theresa groaned and turned her head.

Robbie pulled Theresa off the floor. He called to Estrella. The maid arrived and gasped. "Grab her black dress and iron it. Meanwhile, find a pair of her long white gloves, and shoes." Estrella began to sort through the debris, mumbling to herself. Robbie called out to her, "And thanks, Estrella. She's lucky to have you."

"And you, too, Mr. Robbie. No one else would come to take her to a party anymore. You a good friend."

"I have no friends," Theresa cried. "No one cares about me."

"Goddamn it, Theresa! Pull yourself together!" Robbie grabbed her by the shoulders and shook her. "You've got an appearance."

"No. Not anymore. They'll find out. They'll all find out." She mumbled. Robbie wondered what the hell she was going on about.

"Theresa, you've got to sober up, and you've got to go. If you don't show up, you're finished forever. This is live net. We are going tonight. You and I. Goddamn it, Theresa, I want to go to this party."

"But, Robbie," Theresa began to cry. "I can't go. I'd be humiliated."

"Not if you're sober you won't."

"But Lila will be there," Theresa wailed. "With an Emmy." Theresa stopped crying and looked around. "She'll kill me, Robbie," she whispered.

"Ridiculous! When has Lila or anybody scared you?"

"She was such a lovely baby, wasn't she? Kerry could never have raised a son. I didn't want a son. A daughter was just right."

"Certainly. Perfect. Now, start to get ready for your hairdresser."

"But she'll kill me. Like she killed Candy and Skinny." She was wailing now.

Robbie had listened to the rambling, but didn't try to make much sense of it. Until she mentioned the dummies. He felt a tug of guilt. Well, it had been necessary to get this truce signed. Still, what was she talking about? The dummies were gone.

"What are you talking about, Theresa?" The star shrank into the middle of the big bed, and Robbie wasn't sure if she was shaking from alcohol withdrawal or fear.

"I did the right thing, didn't I, Robbie? I raised a girl. A lovely girl. Only now she hates me. I should never have done it to her," Theresa whispered.

"What?" Robbie asked.

"The way I raised her. Then hating her because she was so young, so beautiful. And that ghastly episode I shot with her. She hates me for that. She wants to kill me. Like she killed Candy and Skinny. She killed my other babies."

"Theresa, what *are* you talking about?"

Slowly, as if each movement was painful, Theresa crawled to the edge of the bed, then got off it, fell to her knees, and began to scrabble about under it. Neither Robbie nor Miss Wholley had had time to evacuate the horrors under there, and God knew the last time Estrella had tried.

But instead of empty bottles, or old mateless shoes, Theresa pulled out a long white box. A coffin, really. Then another. Two actual coffins, perhaps for children's burials. Robbie shivered and saw that Theresa was shivering, too. Whimpering, she flipped open the lids.

Robbie looked inside. Skinny had been decapitated, her head chopped to kindling. Candy had been defaced by a thousand vicious stab wounds. Both dummies were nude, their bodies smeared with paint, or maybe someone's blood. And each of them had perfect little sets of male genitalia nailed to the appropriate parts on their torsos.

Neil Morelli had not received an invitation to Ara's party. No surprise. But he had been surprised to hear from Roger after so long a silence. And to speak to him over the television set, not the car radio, as he usually did. He, Neil, was getting closer to the center of things. Neil was very glad Roger had called. He needed to ask him so much, needed to know so much. And, with failure and humiliation weighing on him like a ton of bricks, Neil knew Roger would understand—and help. Neil now knew who was to blame for his failure—all those who traded on their celebrity names and family connections.

He had at first been hesitant to tell Roger about whose

ultimate responsibility all this humiliation was, of his plan to go to the Emmys, get into them somehow. But Roger had been so kind, so, well, fatherly, he began to tell him everything, and, to Neil's great relief and surprise, Roger not only agreed with Neil's appraisal, but approved of Neil's plan, and gave him exact instructions on how to carry it out. In fact, it was Roger who told him about the theater manager who did the hiring of the ushers for the Emmy show. Neil had run off and applied for the job for the evening of the Emmys—for tonight—and gotten it, even though he'd had to lie and swear that he had a tuxedo. It was Roger's doing that he got the job, Neil was convinced, of course. Roger must have spoken to the manager on his behalf.

Roger also told him not to worry about the tux, and gave him the tip about the tuxedo department at Saks, and how easy it was to put one on under his regular clothes in the dressing room and walk out. The tuxedo department was the least busy department in the store, so there never were any salespersons or security guards lurking about. Walking out with the formal wear under his baggy jeans and windbreaker had been a breeze. Even the brazen act of grabbing a dress shirt and bow tie from a display near the door seemed easy, with Roger watching over him.

The other items Roger had told him to get were as easily acquired, some of them through the guys at the cab company. He wasn't exactly sure how or when he would use all this stuff, but Neil wasn't going to question any of Roger's directions. Because Roger told him that he—Neil Morelli—was going to host the awards show. Just like Billy Crystal did the Oscars. He, Neil, would be as famous, as admired, as loved. Roger had thought of everything so far, right down to the suspenders. This was a man on his side, probably the only man who had ever looked out for Neil in his life, and that included his degenerate gambler father. No, Neil was going to do everything Roger told him to do. Roger understood. Roger would help him set things right.

Neil adjusted his tie in the mirror of the bathroom, and wished he had a full-length mirror to admire the full effect of the tux. But wouldn't you know it? Roger called just then, and, as if he could read Neil's mind, told Neil how great he looked, and—this brought tears to Neil's eyes—how proud he was of him. Then Roger told him to sit down and go over the seating arrangement for the auditorium the manager had given each of the ushers, and told him to memorize where the key people were sitting. Roger also went over the physical plan of the theater, and told him the exact spot where he should be standing, and the exact time, to get the best view of the award presentation.

Neil got it all, put the sheet of paper back into his inside pocket, spit on his hand and smoothed his hair, then opened the door and walked down the street toward the bus. On the way, he heard Roger's voice come from behind him, not through a radio or an amplifier like usual, but over his shoulder, like a guardian angel. "Timing is everything," Roger said. And Neil didn't have to turn around to know that Roger was with him and, as always, was absolutely right.

Sam Shields had definitely risen on Ara's Hollywood-heat barometer. This year, he had not only an invitation to go, once again, as April's escort, but his own invitation as well.

Since *Birth* had succeeded, he was a popular boy. No doubt about it. Two hits in a row. April wanted him to sign a three-picture deal, but so did Columbia. He had options now.

He also had a new Armani tux, and a Thai silk custom-made dress shirt. He slipped into the jacket and shot his cuffs. He'd look like a winner tonight.

But he'd see Mary Jane—Jahne—tonight, too. It was traditional for the Emmy winners to drop by after the award. Of course, he could leave early. But he *wanted* to see her. After thinking it over, Sam was ready to forgive her. He wanted her back. And being turned away at Sharleen's gate had only made him more eager.

And, after all, didn't she owe everything to him? Sam shook his head at the irony. Mary Jane couldn't get cast in a soap commercial, couldn't get a part off-off-off-

Broadway, until he had given her the break in *Jack and Jill*. And she'd gone through the surgery for him. Because of that, now, tonight, Jahne Moore just might be walking away with an Emmy award. And perhaps an Oscar in the future. Sometimes Sam could see the amusement in the way things evolved in this town. Just as he could at this moment.

But he had his public persona to think about. Tonight, after the awards ceremony, if Jahne showed up at Ara's, Sam would be there. He couldn't—*wouldn't*—not be there; that was out of the question. How was he going to handle his encounter with Jahne, in front of the entire Industry, in front of all the media people? That's what he had to decide.

And how was *she* going to handle it? Sam hoped, for no other reason than that it would make things easier for him, that Jahne in fact did win the Emmy. At least she would be in a good—no, an elated—mood, and their connection could be swift and gay. Oh, he remembered all the things Mary Jane used to say about awards, and award shows, and award winners. But that was back before she had a spitting chance of getting nominated for one, never mind actually winning one. Would Jahne still be as equanimous as she once had been about these things, and not let her loss make her turn on him, bring unwanted attention? He doubted it.

But his final thought, the one that helped him get into the shower and ready for the night, was that Jahne Moore must have loved him a lot to go through all that she had for him. Even if she turned him away at Sharleen Smith's. Somehow, he was sure that they'd get back together. Because, really, who else had ever loved him like that?

Monica Flanders waited impatiently for Hyram to pick her up. Hyram's wife, Sylvia, still resented not being invited to Ara Sagarian's party. Or perhaps she resented Hyram's going with Monica. For the invitation was for Monica—always for Monica.

She took one last look at herself in the mirror. Tonight she would get more publicity and free advertising from the awards program than ever before. Whoever won, they wore *her* makeup. And the commercial they were running would announce it. Just so long as it wasn't that surgery girl. She would be canceled, but definitely. Unless, of course, she won.

Monica patted her wig into place and then clipped on her diamond earrings. They were so big—eight-carat emerald-cut perfect stones—that they hurt her ears, but pain was the price you paid for beauty.

Tonight one of her girls would win the prize. And she would win, too. Flanders Cosmetics was sponsoring the Emmy show. Sales would boom tomorrow. What an idea this whole *3/4* business had been! Despite the scandals. Or because of them. Best idea she'd ever come up with.

Paul Grasso took another sip of his vodka and tried for the third time to tie the fucking formal black bow tie. What's wrong with the clip-ons? he thought once again.

Tonight was a good night for Paul. He had finally made it, without Glick after all. He didn't like to remember last year: sneaking into Ara's party through the bushes. Tonight he was going to see his discovery Lila Kyle get an Emmy, then go on to Ara's Emmy party, where the real shakers were going to be, shoulder to shoulder. Like at the roulette tables at Vegas. Only the heavy hitters stood at the table. The little guys, the assholes with their twenty-dollar chips, stood around the outer edge. And not for very long, either. Either they made a hit the first time at the table, or they were on the move again, looking for the next win. The whole secret was to stick with it, play it out—all night, if you had to. Like in this Hollywood game. Eventually, if you stayed with it, luck turned your way, and you were being back-slapped by the other heavy hitters.

Tonight Paul Grasso felt like a heavy hitter. And he was in the mood for some back-slapping. If only he could get this fucking tie tied.

It didn't seem right to Sy that he had all three Emmy nominees as his clients and not one of the bitches had asked him to escort her tonight. So he'd settled on Crystal, who was having a shit fit because she hadn't received her own invitation. Well, maybe they could use the party to jump-start her stalled career.

Of course, Sy didn't need any of the *3/4* girls to get into the awards ceremony or Ara Sagarian's party. This much he had done on his own. But it would have been a nice gesture on their part, considering. He was the one, after all, who got the three of them made into the hits they are. And stood behind them during the scandals. Only Sharleen had ever called him to thank him for the Emmy nomination. Jahne had written him a cool note. And Lila was out in fucking Siberia; he heard shit from her. Surprise.

But he could afford to put all that behind him. Tonight was a big night, probably the biggest night in his career. Tonight he owned everyone and everything, because all three of the big ones were in his stable. Tonight he even owned Ara Sagarian himself, not that he was such a prize. It's about time Ara moved over. Next year, Sy thought, I'm going to have an Emmy party at *my* house. *The* Emmy party. If I'm really bigger than Ara Sagarian ever was, and that's the word around town, then I might as well have the full coronation ceremony, and all the perks that go with it. So, next year it would be Sy Ortis' party, A list and then some.

Sy hadn't let on to anyone, of course, but all this tabloid stuff was turning out to be a boon to the reputation of his girls. Yeah, everyone's *cojones* were in an uproar, but he knew that the minor squall over Sharleen and Jahne would pass, and in its place would come a torrent of new interest. And with that, of course, higher ratings.

So Sy wasn't ambivalent at all about showing up at the celebrations tonight. One of his girls was going to walk away with an Emmy, that much was guaranteed. He didn't really care which one, but kind of hoped that it would be Sharleen or Jahne—they could use the positive press, and, in light of the tabloid mess, it would go a long way toward balancing things out.

But whoever got it would be Sy's. And that no one could take away from him.

The way Sy figured it, the only way he could lose tonight was if there was a nuclear holocaust. Other than that, he was already the winner. The very best, the absolute very best that could happen would be that there would be a three-way tie. Sy chuckled. About as much chance of that as a nuclear holocaust.

But he could hope, couldn't he?

April looked into the mirror and grimaced. Yes, lipstick *had* smeared onto her two front incisors, as it so often did. When she was a kid, some of the children at school had teased her, calling her "werewolf girl." Stubbornly, even now, she'd never had them filed down. They came in handy when she had to tear out the throat of her next victim.

Carefully she wiped off the offending makeup. Yes, she would do some throat-tearing tonight. Sy Ortis and Marty DiGennaro were about to participate in her favorite little game: retribution. Because, after all the chips she'd called in, it was certain that *Three for the Road* wasn't going to win a goddamn thing tonight. The bad publicity on the bitch Jahne hadn't hurt, nor had the exposé on that Jukes-and-Kallikaks brother-and-sister act, but she was pretty sure that she could have neutralized the thing anyway. Her pressure on Warren Lashbeck and the Industry censorship committee was tightening the pressure on Les Merchant, head of the Network. He might be pushed into canceling the show. She couldn't trust anyone to do what they promised, of course. Still, if there was one thing she was dead certain of, it was this: that rats in Hollywood knew what to do about a sinking ship.

Tonight, after almost eleven years, she'd get to fuck up Marty DiGennaro and Sy Ortis as badly as they'd fucked her all that long time ago.

Marty DiGennaro hummed tonelessly to himself as he fit the opal cabochon stud into his shirtfront. It was a habit that used to drive his ex-wife nuts, but he never thought about her anymore. He almost hoped that he would run into her this evening, with Lila clinging to his arm. His ex was petite and dark, not really an impressive woman. Lovely in her way, certainly, but not stunning. Not Lila. No one was like Lila.

He kept trying to push in the stud, but something wasn't working. Either the buttonhole was sewed closed or the damned stud was defective. Shit. Marty was a detail person, and he loved the detail of dressing. The opal shirt studs had once belonged to Gary Cooper. Marty had bought them, as discreetly as possible, from the estate of a past mistress of Coop. Sally had been upset, said that opals brought bad luck unless they were your birthstone, but Marty loved them. He was wearing them for the first time tonight.

Well, they were bringing bad luck now. He checked the time, then called to Sally for help. He would wear the opals, damn it. Because he was a man who had made all the good luck he'd ever need. He had a ravishing fiancée who never looked at another man, a string of Oscars a mile long, and a new, hot career in television, which he, single-handedly, was turning around.

"Sal!" he called, impatient. "Hurry up and bring a scissors."

As Sal walked into the room, Marty jerked at the stud. It spun out of his hand, arching across the room, and fell on the marble saddle at the bottom of his dressing-room door. As if in the slow motion of one of his films, Marty watched the opal shatter, sending gleams of iridescent color across the floor.

"Goddamn it!" Marty cried.

"Maybe it can be fixed," Sally said, and knelt to begin gathering the shards.

"Forget it!" Marty told him. "Once it's broken, it's broken."

Ara's guests began to arrive, and though he was tired—well, almost exhausted—from all the preparations, now it all seemed worth it. Not bad for an old man, he thought. Here he was, a man that should by all rights be dead, or at least retired and living in Palm Springs, here he was, giving yet another successful party, with only the *crème de la crème* of the Industry present.

He laughed at his little pretension. *Crème de la crème,*

my wrinkled Armenian *vorick,* he thought to himself. Stars, star-makers, star-fuckers, and star-breakers—all grasping, back-stabbing cutthroats.

But, he reminded himself, most of the media clout in the nation was gathered under one roof tonight. He was still a player. A major player. A man of power, surrounded by the tastemakers, the trendsetters, the wavemakers. All under one roof. *His* roof.

He smiled, nodded, and limped forward to greet his first guest.

"Don't forget who you're dealing with," Theresa snapped at Robbie when she'd asked for a simple glass of sherry and he refused. "I just need a little something to calm me down."

"Theresa, right now you have enough Valium in you to float you higher than the Goodyear blimp. You don't need another thing."

Theresa couldn't give up so easily. As if Valium could ever take the place of vodka. "You don't seem to grasp one very important fact here. I'm under *incredible* pressure. In a little while I'll have to go out there and face her. And show myself to all those people. Live. Jesus. I haven't done live in a hundred years."

"You'll be fine. It will all go fine," he assured her and patted her shoulder.

"I was just saying to—who was it? Warren Beatty? No, it was Annette. No, April Irons! That's who it was, April." Crystal Plenum almost had Ara by the lapels, standing very close. "I was saying to April how Ara Sagarian never seems to age. What's your secret, Ara? You could make a fortune if you sold it."

Crystal felt pretty desperate, and her desperation showed. She knew what it was like to enter a room and make an impression. And she knew that she had and hadn't.

Crystal's face hurt. If she had to smile at these fucking assholes, these insulting, insufferable assholes, for even ten more minutes, she would have facial spasms. Joel Silver was here. So was Larry Gordon. Dawn Steel looked great—where did she get that dress? God, Crystal was ready to stoop to being a Disney whore if she had to. They were famous for buying up fading stars cheap and resuscitating them. So, smile nice at Dawn. She remembered what her first movie director had told her. He had said that some actors and directors thought the most difficult thing to do on cue was cry. He had disagreed and said it was laughter, not crying, that was the harder for actors to manage realistically. He was right. Laughing at people's little jokes at her expense was almost more than she could bear.

Then she saw him: the son-of-a-bitch! In tiny steps—all her dress would allow—she walked up to Sam Shields. He was surrounded by some of the powers in the Industry, but she ignored them.

"Aren't you going to say hello?" she asked.

He looked up and smiled—one of those useless polite smiles she'd been getting from people lately.

"Hello, Crystal."

She looked him right in the face. "I just wanted to say thank you. Thank you for ruining my career. And I wanted to give you this." And then she spat at him.

Elizabeth wandered with Larry. Warren sat, laughing, beside Annette. Kevin Costner and Cindy chatted with Marvin Davis. Joe Pesci stood in a corner, sharing a bottle of Evian water with Jack Nicholson. Steven Seagal ate sushi beside one of the monitors. Scott Rudin threw a napkin at Paula Weinstein. Rob Reiner stood beside his wife, one of the famous Singer sisters.

Now the thirty-five-inch screens scattered around Ara's house were all forgotten, save one. The screen in Ara's library seemed to be the only one the guests were watching, as if sharing the one screen made them all feel more a part of the audience. Ara sat in the middle of the guests. On the screen, the emcee was introducing Theresa O'Donnell, who was smiling and opening the envelope. There wasn't a sound in the room, as if everyone had a personal stake in the outcome of the Emmys. Ara smiled to himself. He did, too. Yes, anyone, just so long as it wasn't Lila Kyle.

Theresa tore at the envelope, pretending she was having trouble getting it open, prolonging the tension. She opened the envelope, took out the card, and said, "The winner is . . ."

9

Jahne had taken her place on an aisle seat, with Dr. Moore next to her. She had forced herself to sit back in her seat, and tried to breathe deeply. Brewster sat beside her, his hand holding hers tightly. And it was not just comforting, but a clever career move: it was as if she were laughing at the bad press, flaunting her doctor at them. She seemed unashamed.

As the evening wore on, there were a lot more losers than winners. The audience was restive. Self-loathing and fear seemed like a palpable force. Winners glowed, but every loser had to sit in a pool of failure, everyone watching and judging. She told herself she could rise above it all.

But could she? It was hard to sit there, in this room filled with the best and the beautiful, and know that she was being watched and judged, perhaps most of all. Would she get the Emmy? Did she care? She was certain that neither Sharleen nor Lila could act. She was not so certain that the rest of her peers saw things that way. And she found that, oddly enough, she wanted to win tonight. Not because she thought these contests mattered, but because, right now, she needed a vote of approval.

When she arrived at the theater, Sharleen had looked up to the monitor, only to see her own face turning from the camera. She had quickly looked away, back to Dean. On the other side of her sat Dobe—Sy had managed the extra ticket. "I never been on live television before.

OLIVIA GOLDSMITH

Don't it make you nervous?'' she asked him in a whisper,
her throat dry.

"Sure do. Afraid some people we sold gas pills to
might be tuned in.''

For a moment, she turned to him with frightened eyes.
Then she saw he was jokin' with her.

"They never bother no one, Sharleen. They're too embarrassed by their own greed and stupidity. Now, hold
your head up high, girl. You're on TV, and you got
nothin' to be ashamed of.''

"I'm ashamed that I ever doubted you," she admitted.
"I thought I'd never see you again after I gave you that
money.''

"But you gave it to me anyway, didn't you? How
come?''

"I couldn't say no to a friend, Dobe.''

"And I noticed you haven't asked me about our
spread.''

"It's okay if you lost the money, Dobe. I just didn't
want to lose *you*.''

"Lost the money? Well, hell, do you think I'm a dang
fool? I didn't *lose* the money. But I didn't buy us any
land in Montana.''

Oh, good. He was going to confess. Sharleen felt relieved. It was the one thing that had stood between them.
"That's all right, Dobe. It's water under the bridge.'' He
was welcome to the money. She just didn't want him to
lie to her about it.

"Great. I'm glad you aren't disappointed. Montana
was full of yuppies and Hollywood jerks. Turned the
whole damned state into a fern bar.'' She nodded. It was
all right. She loved Dobe and she always would. As if
he knew what she was thinking, he smiled back. "Yep,
Montana's been ruined. So I bought us the nicest piece a
land in Wyoming that you ever laid eyes on!''

Her mouth opened in surprise. "Did you really,
Dobe?'' She turned to him, her face shining. Happiness
flooded her.

"Of course I did! You never doubted me, did you?''
He grinned at her slyly. "Got all the papers back at the

house. Nine hundred acres. Not too shabby. Halfway between Daniel and Halfway.''

"Halfway?"

"No, not *in* Halfway. That's the town to the south. Daniel's to the north. We're halfway. Kinda like the who's-on-first joke. Anyway, I'll show you on the map tonight. Now, wave to the people at home, and then settle down and pay attention to the man onstage. They're announcing the Best Actress award. No matter what happens, I want you to keep that look on your face when the winner is announced.''

The master of ceremonies had gone through all the oddball categories, the ones only family and friends of the nominated sat at the edge of their seats for. He presented the penultimate award, for Best Actor in a Dramatic Series, then said, "And now the one we've all been waiting for: Best Actress in a Dramatic Series. And to present it, someone who might have a preference. Ladies and gentlemen, Theresa O'Donnell!''

"The Loveliest Girl in the World" theme song began and Theresa tottered out. Was she drunk? She read the nominees' names from the cue screen, then the inevitable, "The envelope, please.''

Lila felt paralyzed. The PMS here! To present the Emmy. No. No. She was totally prepared to win. But not for this. Oh God, not this!

And what if she lost? All at once, the possibility swept over her. She reached her hand out to Marty's beside her and almost crushed his in her clawlike grasp.

"Jesus, your hands are cold!" he said, and then the master of ceremonies, Johnny Burton, handed the envelope to her mother.

"And the winner is . . . Lila Kyle!''

10

The theater audience gasped as if it were one person, then burst into applause. Hey, no one bought drama the way actors do. The camera picked up Lila's face as it broke into well-rehearsed surprise, then the broadest smile she had ever done, on- or offscreen. She kissed Marty sitting next to her, jumped up, and, holding up her long dress to ensure she wouldn't trip, ran up the aisle and to the podium. She felt the hammering of her heart, and the heat of the lights. She seemed to be moving as if through water, as if in a dream, all in slow motion: each step up to the platform, across the stage.

She faced her mother, who clutched the Emmy in her own claws. Lila reached for the statuette. Theresa stared at her glassily. Lila pulled at the award. But Theresa didn't let go. Lila tugged. Theresa hung on. But Lila would have it. It was hers. Everything would be hers from now on. And at last her mother gave in. Lila held the award to her chest. The crowd went wild.

She had never stood before a crowd like this. Well, after all, she wasn't a stage actress. Now, standing in front of this audience, the *crème de la crème* of her world, she felt the applause, and she felt the love they had for her. Oh, it was indescribable, it was what she had dreamed of, night after night. Love. Pure love. Love that didn't sully, love that didn't touch her, but that surrounded her like a warm bath, like a mother's breast. She could feel the applause, she could feel it across her erect nipples, against her stomach, and lower, somewhere lower.

"Oh," she gasped into the microphone. "Oh. Thank you!" she managed to say, her prepared speech disappearing somewhere out of her head. "Thank you all." The audience, tired of the usual long-winded speeches and faked sincerity, responded to her pure feeling. The applause began again, building and swelling until it beat

FLAVOR OF THE MONTH

against her. And Lila felt something build and swell within. The applause seemed to carry her, the approval to build and to release her.

And, for the first and last time in her life, Lila felt the exquisite tingling that became a wave, a deep, powerful wave that made her shudder and brought her, right there on the stage at the podium, to orgasm.

It took a few minutes for the applause to die down, and, in those few minutes, Lila wept. From relief, from joy, but most of all because this was the first time since that party, so many years ago, that she had won applause from an audience. My mother hit me then. She was jealous then. Is she watching and jealous now? Lila shivered in her triumph. Since then, before this magical night, Lila had only performed in front of a camera, cut off from reaction, from response, without the benefit of applause. Tonight she realized what she had been missing. And wanted more.

She gathered herself, though she still trembled. Then, carefully, ignoring Theresa, she stepped from around the podium to take one more bow, to still the audience, yet at the same time to milk every glorious moment of it. Lila bowed and stood in place, the Emmy in her hands in front of her.

It was the happiest moment of her life. And the last.

11

The crack came from the back of the auditorium, and Lila pitched forward, the Emmy dropping from her hands and rolling several feet forward until it came to a stop, teetering just at the edge of the stage. It took the camera crew almost four seconds to realize something extraordinary had happened. Lila Kyle had dropped completely out of the frame. Mitch Goldman, the Emmy-show producer, who was back in the control booth, barked an order to Camera 1. "Give me a long shot," he yelled.

821

Lila was revealed, lying prone across the front of the stage. "Is the bitch drunk like her mother?" Mitch asked. "Did she trip? Get me a close-up, Bobby." A dazed murmur had gone up from the crowd. Was this a gag? An accident?

Johnny Burton was the first one to Lila. He touched her, then looked at the red stain that had already begun to spread across the back of her dress to his hand.

"She's been shot," he shouted. "Get a doctor up here!"

"Fuck this live TV," Mitch Goldman groaned.

Everyone surrounding Ara in his living room gasped as Lila fell. They all stood, paralyzed, as still as statues. No one even blinked, all eyes fixed to the screen. What was going on? Lila had just been named winner . . . was taking her bows . . . and suddenly keeled over. On the screen, Johnny Burton was leaning over her. His voice took over the room once again, breaking the silence. "She's been shot."

Ara's first thought was that it was shtick. Then, after the briefest silence, someone screamed.

"Oh, my God!" Michael McLain cried out. Several women screamed. "Is she dead?" someone yelled. Everyone was up, pushing closer to one of the screens. Véronique Peck was sobbing. "Hush! Quiet so we can hear!" Michael Douglas told the crowd. In the pandemonium, only Ara, unnoticed, continued to sit in his chair.

Sam had only just managed to come back from the men's room. He'd regained his composure after the incident with Crystal when he heard the commotion and looked up at the screen. He heard the announcement about Lila and gasped.

My God! Sam thought. What about Jahne? Is she safe? If she had won, would she have been shot?

And all at once a longing—the strongest feeling of his life—washed over him. My God, what if she were dead? What if I could never see her, never hold her, never love her again?

In that moment, he realized he would never love anyone but her.

Robbie couldn't think, couldn't put two words together, so he didn't try. He reacted instead, gathering up the collapsed form of Theresa and moving quickly out of the green room and to the auditorium exit. Lila! Was she really hurt? No, it's only television. It can't be real. Theresa's having an attack. Got to get her out of here. Jesus, where's the car? He screamed for the driver as he made it through the door. The driver was nowhere to be found. But somehow Robbie would get to the hospital, where both his girls needed help.

Sy Ortis stood in the middle of the room, the spot he had maneuvered himself into, right next to Ara, so he could be where he belonged, in the center of everything, ready to receive the congratulations. Now he didn't move, couldn't move. Lila's been shot? He put his hand on his chest for a moment, then dropped it to his pocket and his inhaler. But his breathing was fine. He looked at the screen. Lila's been shot. Jesus Christ! An Emmy, *and* national TV coverage of her shooting. Sy would never cease to be amazed by that woman. She must have set it up. He remembered what the bus crash had done for Gloria Estefan. If Lila survived this—and Sy didn't for a minute think she wouldn't somehow—she was going to be the hottest actress around for years to come. A definite cover next week on *People*. She'd own this fuckin' town.

The room was swirling now. There was no way Ara could stop it, even when he closed his eyes. When he opened them again, he saw everything through a rose light, like the jelly lights on a stage. Red. He knew it. He had felt it coming. The stab of pain, then the pain receding, giving him a moment to breathe. He tried to stand, to call out, but couldn't. Then the searing red-hot pain again, in his head, down the side of his body. Ara tried to open his mouth to call out for help, but all that came out was a long stream of drool. He fell back into the chair, grateful for the relief of the semiconsciousness that was falling over him.

Ara remained seated, with the crowd swirling around him, around and around like a merry-go-round. His head hurt. No, it was worse than "hurt." It felt as if his brain would split. He decided to sit there until everything stopped. And then, for him, it did.

"Oh, no, that poor girl." The blonde starlet next to Paul Grasso was in tears, her head lowered to rest on Paul's shoulder. Paul shrugged it off.

Marty, he thought. What about Marty DiGennaro? They hadn't said anything about him. It seemed, as much as Paul could make out, that Lila was the only one hurt. The scene on the screen had already shifted to a news-room set, and the newsman was speaking in a strained but clear voice. "Word has just reached us that this was a terrorist act of the International Anti-Nepotism League. Police are still trying to identify the shooter. The FBI has been called in."

Paul turned back to the blonde starlet, who now was only sniffling. "I discovered Lila Kyle," he told her.

"Wait a minute," Michael McLain called out to the crowd. "Shut up. Let's hear what they're saying," he warned everyone, pointing to the TV monitor. Adrienne was by his side, as she had been all evening, only now she was clinging with both hands, bunches of his formal jacket in each of her fists. "It's okay, honey," he told her, charmed by her dependence. "That's miles away. You're safe here." Her belly was already protruding, making a pleasant mound that she now pushed against him. He patted it, then brought his attention back to the screen. It *was* Lila Kyle, he thought. Shot. Yes. It's been confirmed. What was this league? Christ, now the assas-sinations of movie stars would begin. He thought of the psychopath in prison who kept writing to him. The army of loners carrying copies of *Catcher in the Rye*. For him old threats would probably be joined with the threats of women fans once he announced his engagement to Adrienne. He turned to Adrienne to lead her out of the room. There was no sense staying here. Not with his fiancée in her delicate condition. As he led a grasping Adrienne to the door, he thought that it could have been worse. Lila could have been shot *before* the award. Then that bitch Jahne Moore might have won it by default.

Someone said, "Who's Auntie Nepo . . . You know. That woman they said."

"Nepotism," came the answer, "is when you get your job through family ties."

"Holy shit," Seymore LeVine yelled out. "They're going to kill us all."

12

Neil Morelli calmly turned away from the stage, not even waiting a moment to get a reaction. After all, Roger had told him what to do, and Roger had told him he wouldn't miss. When they hadn't called Neil up to replace Johnny as master of ceremonies, Roger had calmed his rage, Roger had explained the change in plans. Neil let the gun hang loosely from his arm. He began calmly walking down the left aisle, toward the stage, toward the lights, toward Johnny, who was now holding the crumpled body of Lila Kyle in a sort of gender-reversed pietà. Calm. Neil felt perfectly calm, because now the worst was over.

The screams seemed distant. It wasn't that he didn't hear them. Half the auditorium was screaming, and the other half was either ducking under the seats or running for the exits. But the pandemonium seemed distant, unrelated to him.

He had gotten within fifteen feet of the stage before they tackled him. He felt the blow from behind, crumpled to his knees, and hit the floor, but there was no pain. Roger had told him there would be none. The gun was wrested from his hand, but Neil didn't need it anymore, anyway. What he needed was some air. His lungs felt curiously empty, with the pile of squirming bodies on top of him. It wasn't pain, exactly—Roger had promised no pain—but it was a lot of pressure. Then it lifted, and he felt the wrench as his arms were tugged together, behind him, but he was too busy trying to fill his lungs to mind the bite of the handcuffs on his thin wrists.

When he was jerked to his feet, the lights and cameras were there, as Roger had assured him they would be. Neil smiled. He *wasn't* a loser. Far from it. Now he'd be a star. The Deliverer. He would set everyone free from the wretched system. No more handing on from mother to daughter, father to son. And Roger had predicted all of this. Roger had chosen him. Neil had had his fears and doubts, but he had triumphed. He'd completed his mission, except for the speech.

People were shouting questions at him, at the five men who surrounded him. Neil just smiled. "I represent the International Anti-Nepotism League," he shouted. "Death to those who defy us." And then he launched into his comedy monologue.

13

The scoop of a lifetime comes only once to each of us, and then only if we're lucky. Did Woodward and Bernstein know what they had discovered as they checked out that break-in? I don't think so. I do know that the news of Lila's shooting was enough to make me bribe a rented-limo driver with $210 in cash and my Rolex to abandon his client at the Emmy awards and drive me to the hospital.

The streets around the hospital were mobbed, swarming with police black-and-whites. Their red bubble-gum lights spun eerily, bouncing off the strained faces of onlookers. The ambulance was losing precious moments, waiting for the police to clear a path. The police finally got the screaming ambulance through, and it pulled into the bay giving onto the emergency room. The back doors were pulled open, and medical personnel pulled the stretcher onto the walkway and ran it through the doors of the ER. I could just see Marty DiGennaro walking beside the gurney holding an IV bag aloft, the tubes a tangle.

The entrance to the emergency room at Cedars-Sinai was a madhouse. Another ambulance was pulling up. I didn't know it at the time, but in it rode the earthly remains of Ara Sagarian. From the midst of the growing throng, I could now see not only Marty DiGennaro but also Theresa O'Donnell at the head of the crush, pushing their way through the crowd of reporters and gawkers, trying to get in the doors of the hospital.

Theresa O'Donnell was behind the stretcher. I don't know where she'd come from. She stepped haltingly, her eyes scanning the watching faces. "It's okay, Miss O'Donnell. Just police and hospital workers." A police officer gallantly offered his hand, and she followed the stretcher through the doors, Robbie Lymon holding her by one arm. A woman in a business suit and an identification tag showing her to be a hospital employee, said to Theresa, "Follow me, Miss O'Donnell."

Another gurney came trundling down the pike. "What you got?" one of the ER specialists called out.

"Stroke. DOA," the paramedic yelled.

"Park 'im. We got a live one!" And that is how Ara Sagarian was left: parked, dead, in the hallway of the ER for the next five hours, while the drama of the living played itself out around him.

The group surrounding Lila continued on, through a gauntlet of police holding back the throngs of people who, like maggots, came to feed on the flesh of the fallen. Camcorders whirled from behind the wall of police, and reporters screamed out questions. The last question Theresa heard through the noise and confusion, just before they turned down a corridor, was, "Is she dead or alive, Miss O'Donnell?"

A nurse, her white uniform sharply contrasting with the black of Marty's tux, opened the door from inside and, while holding off the pushing crowd, pulled first Marty, then Theresa O'Donnell and Robbie into the lobby. By now my elbows had ensured that I was right

827

behind those three, but I knew that, like the other media people, I would have to stand outside, my nose pressed to the glass of the doors, waiting like all the other news-hounds and -hens for crumbs of information.

It was then that I got my lucky break. Literally. The door, pushed violently in, swung back, and bashed me in the nose. And I am an easy and copious bleeder.

Inside the hospital, it was still pandemonium, but the guard saw the blood and waved me in. Nurses and hospital personnel had already converged on Marty, Theresa, and Robbie, guiding them off to a quieter corner. "I'm with their party," I murmured to the charge nurse, and, checking out the jewelry and the blood in a single apprais-ing glance, she seated me with them. I surreptitiously lowered my head between my legs to make sure the bleeding continued. It had already made dramatic smears on my yellow silk blouse ($316 at Giorgio's), and I made sure it was all over my face, too. The emergency room is no place for personal vanity.

The charge nurse had already begun ministering to Theresa, who was loudly moaning, clutching the Emmy statuette. Marty sat silent, his hands dangling emptily between his skinny legs. He looked catatonic. And Rob-bie Lymon was sobbing loudly.

A doctor came out through the double doors of the treatment area and asked for Lila Kyle's next of kin.

"Right here," Theresa moaned.

"And I'm her aunt. Uh, uncle," Robbie corrected him-self.

"I'm her fiancé, doctor," Marty DiGennaro said, standing up.

The doctor looked strangely at Marty. "That patient in there cannot be your fiancée," he said. To all of us he added, "I need to speak to a blood relative or a legal spouse. Is there anyone here?"

Robbie spoke for Theresa, who was still moaning, held up on one side by the nurse. "This is the mother, doctor. Miss O'Donnell."

The doctor spoke directly to Theresa. "Miss O'Don-nell," he said, "we don't know exactly what's happened, but you needn't worry. The patient that was brought in is *not your daughter. Of that I can assure you." Theresa went weak in the knees, and her collapsed hulk was beginning to slip out of Robbie's and the nurse's grasp, but I noticed she held onto the Emmy. "Nurse," the doctor barked, "get Miss O'Donnell to one of the examining rooms." A hospital suit came over and began to lead Theresa and the nurse away, though Robbie trailed after her, down the hall.*

Marty, speechless up to now, at last found the words to speak to the doctor. "What are you talking about? Of course that's my fiancée. I saw her shot. I came with her in the ambulance."

"That's a physical impossibility," the doctor snapped. "It can't be Lila Kyle."

"Why?" Marty snapped.

"Because the patient you brought in, the one with a gunshot wound, has a penis."

14

The sign on the doors said "No Admittance. Hospital Employees Only." A lone hospital security guard stood in front of those doors, his hands behind his back, his stance military. The woman nodded to him as they passed through; Theresa and Robbie were finally shown into a secretary's office, then into a larger, tastefully decorated inner office, the nameplate on the door announcing ownership: "Dr. Robert Stern, Chief Administrator." Robbie didn't know what the hell was going on. What had the doctor meant, that Lila wasn't shot? That she had a . . . It was unthinkable. Robbie had seen her on the stretcher. Theresa seemed to have pulled herself together and had a whispered discussion with the doctor and an officious woman.

"I'm Ms. McElroy," the woman who had guided them finally said, once they were safely in the office. "Dr. Stern has been advised of the situation, and insists that you be given the privacy of his office for as long as you wish to use it. A doctor from the emergency room will be in to speak with you as soon as the patient's situation has been completely appraised. Right now all I can report is that the patient is still alive. I'm sorry, Miss O'Donnell. I wish there was more I could tell you. But it won't be long now."

She offered the usual refreshments, and gave Theresa a telephone number at which to call her directly if they needed anything, or had a question. She also opened the bottom drawer of Dr. Stern's desk and showed them the private telephone, the number only she and Dr. Stern would have. This was the only phone Theresa should answer. Ms. McElroy unplugged the desk model, and advised Theresa to replug this phone if she needed to make any outgoing calls. Only Dr. Stern's private phone was to be answered during this emergency.

When Ms. McElroy opened the door to leave, another security guard was standing there. As the door was closing behind her, Theresa could hear the efficient young woman giving him instructions.

As soon as the door closed behind them, Robbie threw himself down onto the leather chair, stunned into silence. Theresa began to walk around the room, opening and closing cabinet doors until she found the one she was looking for. She selected a bottle of excellent brandy from Dr. Stern's stock, then, with bottle and glasses in hand, flopped onto the leather sofa across from Robbie. She pulled off the bottle top, poured a full glass of brandy for herself, and, still with bottle in hand, drank hungrily from the glass until it was drained. She finally put the glasses and the bottle down on the coffee table, breathing as if she had been holding her breath under water.

"Keep it together, Theresa. And tell me what the hell is going on."

"Don't say one fucking word to me, do you understand? I was a good little girl all night, and did exactly what you wanted me to do, right? Well, the party's over. I deserve a drink, under the circumstances. And I'd advise you to have one. You're as pale as a ghost. I don't need you fainting on me now, for chrissakes."

Theresa poured herself another water tumbler of

brandy, and began to sip this one. Her face was set in a grim but distant look. "Well, there's no hope now."

"You heard what Ms. McElroy said. Lila is still alive."

Theresa shook her head, snapping out of her reverie. "I'm not talking about Lila. Can't you think about *me* for one minute? What *I'm* going through? *Now* what happens to me? To my future?"

Robbie stared at Theresa for a moment, then there was a sudden, insistent knock on the door. Theresa could hear the security guard questioning someone, then the guard opened the door and let in a young doctor.

He was nervous *and* officious, as well as in a hurry. His white coat was bloodied, and he carried a sheaf of papers in his hands. He walked into the room and spoke directly to Theresa without preamble. "I must talk to you —alone." His tone was insistent.

"Is she alive?" Robbie asked.

"Yes," he said to them both. Then, to Theresa, he repeated his demand: "We must talk."

Theresa let her breathing slow, then said to the doctor, "You can discuss anything in front of Mr. Lymon. He's one of my oldest and dearest friends. What is it, doctor?" She asked as if she had no idea what was coming.

"Lila Kyle is *your* child? You are Lila Kyle's birth mother?"

"Yes," Theresa answered.

"Then I have to ask you to sign the corrected permission-for-surgery sheet. Like the one you signed before, but this one states the gender correctly."

The doctor paused again, this time to look at Robbie, then continued: "You are, of course, aware of the genital sex of your child."

Robbie could hardly believe his ears. "What? What the hell is that supposed to mean, Theresa? What's he talking about?"

Theresa waved her hand to silence Robbie, then answered the doctor's question. "Yes," she said curtly.

"So you know that Lila Kyle is, in fact, a male, and not a female."

"Yes," she said again.

"What?" Robbie screeched, but they ignored him.

"Needless to say, that changes nothing in the approach we take to saving her—uh, his—life. But, for obvious legal reasons, we did need this clarified. Please sign the amended form, Miss O'Donnell. We have a lot of additional surgery to perform."

Theresa scribbled her name at the bottom of the page. "What are her chances?"

"That's too early to tell. I'm sorry. But we're doing everything we can. So far, it appears that it was only one bullet wound, but it has nicked the aorta. I have to be honest with you, Miss O'Donnell. It's touch and go, I'm afraid. I'm not going to offer you false hope, just my promise that we will do everything we can for him."

"And, doctor, the . . . other information. How long will that remain confidential?"

He paused at the door. "Any aspect of Miss Kyle's condition can only be made known by a hospital spokesperson, in this case Ms. McElroy. So, officially, there will be no press conference until we know something more. We will not mention the gender reidentification at this time. And until you have been advised." He looked at Theresa directly now. "Unofficially is another matter. This is a major piece of information. I can only say that I rely on the integrity of the staff, and hope that you can feel the same way. The mob of reporters and fans outside is overwhelming." Then he left Robbie and Theresa alone.

Robbie, who had remained silent, pushed himself up from the sofa. "What the fuck does he mean, 'gender reidentification'?"

Theresa gulped from her glass. "I always wanted a girl," she murmured. She spoke as if to herself. "There was no way I could have raised a boy."

"Answer me," Robbie demanded.

Theresa jerked her head erect. "Don't take that tone with me. I've got enough to deal with now without having to deal with an outraged faggot." Robbie didn't respond. "The baby had a problem. A testicle hadn't descended. You know Kerry. He couldn't cope with being married, never mind playing the father to a son. Jesus, we only got legal for the publicity. The studio forced it. You know that better than anyone."

"And?" Robbie asked.

"And what? We had our drunken nights together, I got pregnant, and Kerry returned to you, or whatever young man he was fucking at the time. When I told him I was pregnant, he laughed so hard I thought he was going to have a brain hemorrhage." Theresa continued to drink from the glass of brandy, replenishing it even before the glass was empty. "When he got used to the idea—when *we* got used to the idea—we began to talk about the little *girl* we were going to have. It was what we both wanted. We didn't even consider having a boy."

"But you did," Robbie said.

"Technically, yes."

"Technically! *Technically?* What the hell do you mean? Was there a question?"

"Not actually. But with the testicle . . . Well, I tied a string around the other. It atrophied. No problem. And I raised Lila as a girl."

"So how did you . . . Lila's birth certificate says 'girl.' I've seen it. How did you do that?"

"Oh, you remember Dr. Carlton. That old quack. He would do anything you told him to do. He got more people in Hollywood amphetamines or morphine than any drug dealer today could handle. He did abortions, which were illegal in those days, and even repaired bullet wounds that were never reported to the police. Anything. He was the Industry's very personal physician. He attended me at the Westlake Maternity Home. So, when he told me it was a boy, I simply told him he must be mistaken. I had a girl. And I expected the birth certificate to reflect that fact."

"And Carlton did that for you? He had Lila registered as a girl?"

"Of course he did, for chrissakes. He tied off the testicle. And gave hormone treatments when the time came. And it cost me a bundle."

"Jesus Christ! My God, Theresa! What did Kerry say about it?"

Theresa laughed. "You might not know this, but the night Lila was born, Kerry was at one of Ara's all-night, all-boy sex orgies. He didn't show up at the hospital to see me or the baby until all this was taken care of."

"But how could he never have known?"

"Why, would he have found out when he changed her diaper? Or gave her a bath? Don't be such an ass, Robbie. You knew Kerry better than I did. He wanted no part of me, or the baby, or a happy home life. He didn't even want any part of you, as I remember, when it looked like you wanted more than the occasional fuck. Kerry didn't want to be tied down. Not to anyone. So it became our secret. Lila's and mine."

"But Estrella?"

"Estrella was bought and paid for. She knew what the deal was from day one. It was either live with it, and with all the comforts my life-style could provide her, or back she would go, to that thatched-roof *casa* in the desert of Mexico. What would *you* have chosen?"

The brandy was beginning to have its effects on Theresa. Her eyes filmed over. She sank into a low leather chair. "She was such a pretty little girl. All round and soft, with beautiful eyes, and lovely hair." Theresa seemed to get lost in the memory for the moment. "We never thought about it again. When it came time, Carlton started her on hormones. He got her a breast implant in Mexico. She has a perfect set of tits. Lila never complained, never questioned any of it. She was happy as a little girl. The penis was tiny. Hardly noticeable. We forgot, most of the time, that she had been born male."

"She wasn't very happy the day she moved in with me! Jesus Christ, Theresa, you robbed her of her sex. You neutered her! You crippled her. No wonder she hates you," Robbie spat.

"This has nothing to do with that," Theresa screamed. "She hates me because I didn't help her career. But I knew something like this would happen. You can't have a private life, a secret, and be famous. Not anymore. I knew, somehow or other, she'd be exposed."

"You mean that *you'd* be exposed. You're the author of this little tragedy." Robbie took a gulp of his own drink. "Theresa, you make Joan Crawford look like Mother Teresa."

"How dare you! It's not like I beat her, or tied her to her bed. She had a perfectly wonderful life. Everything a child could want."

"Except her identity."

"Her identity? What about mine? What difference did it make to a squalling infant whether it wore a dress or pants? None. But it made all the difference to me, and my career."

"Your career," Robbie snarled.

"Yes, my career. Without it, there would be no pretty dresses, no big house, maids, private schools. None of it, without me. Then she had to go out and fuck it all up. With *your* help, I might add."

"How did she fuck it all up?"

"She had to go and become an actress. She couldn't marry the guy I had picked out for her, make her life simple. No, she wanted to be a *star*. She only did it to compete with me. Since puberty. She's always wanted to compete. Except look what that has done to me. Now I'll have nothing. People will laugh. No one will understand. I'll never work again. I'll never be able to go to another party."

"What about *Lila?* What's going to happen to *her?*"

"Nothing's going to happen. She still has Kerry's trust fund. And she's got the millions she'll made out of this series. And the Emmy. I hope they don't fuck up the Emmy for her. Isn't all that enough?"

The phone rang in the bottom drawer. Theresa looked at Robbie, for him to answer it. He just shook his head. Theresa wobbled to her feet and lurched across the room.

"Yes? Certainly. I'll be waiting." She turned to Robbie. "That was Ms. McElroy. She just wanted to let me know the doctors are coming to give me a report, that I should let them in."

The double rap was soft on the door. Theresa finished what was in her glass, then stood in the center of the room. Robbie opened the door, and two doctors in surgical greens walked in.

"Miss O'Donnell," the older doctor began. He took a step toward Theresa and reached for her hand. "I'm afraid we have very bad news. I'm so sorry. We lost her."

Theresa stood there silently for a moment. "What do you mean, 'lost'?"

"Lila Kyle is dead, Miss O'Donnell. He died during surgery."

Robbie made a choking noise, but started walking toward the door as if to leave. Theresa screamed, "Robbie, don't leave me. I need you." But Robbie didn't even slow his steps.

15

Jahne heard the shot, saw Lila crumple like a puppet with its strings cut, but it was the silence, that moment of eerie, terrible silence, that let her know something was horribly wrong. Then the screaming started.

Afterward, Jahne wondered what she would have done without Brewster. He got her up and out of her seat; then, somehow, in all the screaming, pushing, hysterical crowd, he united her with Sharleen, Dean, and Dobe. "Keep them here," he told Dobe. "I'm a doctor. I have to see if I can help."

He made it up to the stage by walking on the seat backs. Dobe kept the three of them together, sheltered by a column. Jahne watched as celebrities tore at one another to get out the exit doors. Then Brewster was back, breathless but calm.

"He's been apprehended. It's all right. Some nut with a grudge, apparently. They've taken his gun. It's all right. We're all safe, as long as some actor doesn't kill us as he stampedes over us out the door."

"Is Lila okay?" Sharleen asked.

"I don't think so. A chest wound. Serious, but maybe not fatal."

"Oh, God! It could have been either of us!" Jahne shuddered. Sharleen began to cry.

Then, at last, Gerald La Brecque's staff reached them.

There was a lot of talk then about security exits and conspiracies and snipers, but Jahne stopped listening. She had started to shake again, the way she had in the morning, except this time she couldn't stop. She wasn't afraid, not exactly, not of some sniper. She suddenly felt afraid of *everything,* the theater, the stage, the security guards, the crowds, the lights, the noise. Her shaking got worse. She tried to say something, but found that she couldn't speak.

"Jahne's sick!" Dean said, and she felt a wash of gratitude that he had noticed. Then Brewster had his coat off, around her shoulders, and his arms made a safe circle for her. She closed her eyes, and he murmured something, and she kept her head down on his shoulder, and somehow they got out of the theater and into a car and there was the noise of sirens, and lights flashing from the police cars, or cameras, she couldn't tell which, and then there was darkness.

Brewster stayed with her round the clock for the next two days. They were at the Beverly Wilshire, and in a corner suite. The house had been thought too dangerous, until the truth about the assassin became clear. Brewster talked to her and read to her, but mostly she napped. He kept the TV off and allowed her no calls or newspapers, but on the second day he told her all about Lila. Jahne listened, in shock and amazement, and cried.

"A man? She was transsexual?"

"No, not medically. She was still intact. Probably impotent. Asexual."

She began to cry again. "It's all so sad." He held her hand until she fell asleep. Jahne felt she could sleep for a month.

Brewster didn't let her up out of bed except for trips to the bathroom. He called Room Service, let her speak to Sharleen, but he kept everyone else at bay. It was a relief.

Finally, she pushed herself up in bed and managed a smile. "You're a wonderful doctor," she said.

He shook his head. "No, I'm a wonderful nurse. So are you, for that matter."

Jahne thought back to how long ago it was since she'd been a nurse. It felt like decades.

"Are you feeling better?"

"Much better. I still can't believe it, but I'm okay. Really."

"Well, there's someone who wants to see you. He's been camped outside in the hallway for two days. I didn't feel comfortable about sending him away."

"Sam?" she asked, and felt herself blush. Brewster nodded.

"Do you want to see him, or should I send him away?"

Jahne sighed. "I already sent him away once. I better see him. I'm sorry."

"Don't be. It's your life, Jahne. You don't have to apologize. You don't owe me anything." He turned and went to the door.

I must look like shit, Jahne thought, and then got angry at herself. Oh, God, who cared about looks? Sam? Well, he didn't matter to her anymore.

She looked up. Sam had silently entered the bedroom.

"You're all right? I couldn't believe it. I had to see you. You're all right?" She nodded. Sam approached the side of the bed. "God, when I saw the murder on TV, I realized that it would kill me if anything happened to you. Mary Jane, I . . . I don't know what you need to hear to come back to me, I don't know what you want me to say, but I know that there is no one, absolutely no one on earth that I want to marry except you."

"Marry?" She was speechless. "Marry you? I never want to *see* you again."

"Oh, I know you felt that way before *Birth* hit as big as it did. But surely now you see that it was necessary to . . ."

"Are you crazy?" she asked him. "Have you gone completely crazy?"

"Listen, we've both done things we aren't proud of. But it's not too late. . . ."

"That's where you are two hundred and ten percent wrong. It's *years* too late," she told him.

"Jahne, everything you said, every word, was true. I've been doing some thinking. Some real thinking. And

I know what I want now. I want you. No one but you. Let's forget everything else." He took her hand. "Life's too short to waste."

She looked at him. What had she loved about him? His looks? His selfishness? His easy, shallow style? His facile wit? How shallow had she been to care about this man?

"You're right," she said at last. "Life *is* too short to waste. That's why I won't spend another minute with you."

It wasn't until the third day that Brewster let Jahne watch the news herself. There was a special segment of *Entertainment Tonight* that focused on the shooting. Jahne watched clips of herself and Lila and Sharleen arriving for the Emmy awards, then she saw the close-ups of them in the audience. It was macabre. Who would want to watch this awfulness play out? Why was the audience tuned in? To watch the death of an idol? A false idol? Poor, poor Lila. It made Jahne sick. Literally sick to her stomach. "Well, as a doctor, I'll give you the remedy that my mother always suggested," Brewster smiled. Then he called Room Service.

She was drinking from a glass of plain old ginger ale when she saw, for the first time, the apprehension of the gunman. And there, on the screen, was a close-up of Neil Morelli.

16

Jahne said goodbye to Brewster at her front door. The idea of an airport farewell reminded her too much of her last one, with Neil, back in New York. She shivered.

"Are you cold?" Brewster asked, and she smiled at his concern. It should be winter, after the killing frost that had descended upon them all, but Hollywood was heartless, and the air was balmy.

"No. I'm fine. I will be fine." She stopped. She wasn't

too certain of that, so why lie? "Listen, Brewster, I don't know how I'm ever going to thank you. . . ."

"Well, I think you just did." He was looking down at his feet.

"No. You deserve something more than just words."

"I *do* need these shoes resoled," he said, then shrugged at his attempt at a joke. "Hey, this is what friends are for," he said. And he raised himself on his toes and kissed her, just once, and very gently, on the lips. Then he was gone.

Jahne went back into the house, her lips tingling. She hadn't kissed anyone since Sam, and it felt good. A tiny bit of the grimness lifted. But then she remembered Lila. Her lips were cold by now. Jahne picked up her cat, settled herself on the sofa, and began to write a list. She had a lot to do.

When the phone rang, she couldn't decide whether to answer or not. But La Brecque's security guy did it for her. He stood at the door to the living room and called out to her, "It's some guy called Sam. You want to take the call?"

Jahne sat, frozen. What in the world did he want now? She shook her head—not at the guard, but at herself. "I'll take it," she told him, and reached for the extension beside her.

"Mary Jane? Jahne? Is it you?"

"Yes. It's me."

Sam was silent for a moment. "Listen, this is business. I know how you feel about me, but I think we have a lot to talk about. Among other things, I'm just signing a three-picture deal with Paramount. And I want you for the lead in my first film for them."

Now it was Jahne's turn to be silent. Hollywood! She almost snorted. It was the town where the devil disguised himself as a producer and offered a three-picture deal. Who *was* this guy at the other end of the line? Who had she thought he was, and who did he think she was? "Sorry. Homey don't do that no more," was all she said.

His voice deepened. She heard the actor bring in the strings. Was he acting, was he crazy, or was he just the most insensitive man in America? "It can be the way it was. I'm working on the script, and it's good, Jahne. Really good. It's about a race-car driver who nearly loses the woman he loves because he can't give up racing." He paused. She didn't say a word. "Look, I know it sounds juvenile, but it doesn't play that way." He stopped to take a breath. And, for the first time in this amazing conversation, Jahne thought she heard his true voice.

"We could be good together, Jahne," he said.

Gently, she hung up the phone.

17

They wouldn't stop playing the goddamn song. Sy Ortis swerved, almost hitting a lamppost as he fumbled for the Blaupunkt radio dial, but it didn't matter what station he listened to. Since the shooting, they were *all* playing the Kinks' tribute to female impersonators. Next that stupid cocksucker Al Yankovic would do a parody actually called "Lila." But, really, there wasn't much that could be added to the original.

Not surprisingly, the Early Artists management offices were going batshit. Sponsors, the press, the studio—all of Hollywood, it seemed, wanted to cash in or cash out on *Three for the Road*. And that old *puta* Laura Bitchy had actually had the nerve to call him at home, at night, on his private number, to ask if he had ever seen either Jahne Moore or Lila in the nude.

When Sy Ortis reached Reception, the little fool at the desk had a copy of the *Informer* lying there, an obvious pastiche photo on the cover with a screaming red head-line that said, "The Scandal to End the Road Show."

"What are you planning to do after you work here?" Sy asked the girl.

"I don't know," she said, blinking.

"Too bad, because you don't work here anymore," he told her. He grabbed the paper off her desk, then crumpled it and tore it to shreds before he threw it to the ground and walked over it. He slammed through the swinging glass doors on down the hall. His secretary stood waiting. "Any word from Mr. DiGennaro?"

"No. He's still under sedation. But there was a call from the hospital. There's been a change in Miss . . . I mean, Mr. Kyle's condition." She paused. "I mean, the fact is, he's dead."

"What the hell do I care?" barked Sy Ortis. "The bitch—I mean the son of a bitch—was as good as dead anyway." Christ, he couldn't breathe! Sy got into his office and began to scrabble through his desk drawers, looking for another aspirator. His chest felt as if it would burst. If he wasn't careful, he'd wind up in the morgue at Cedars, next to that freak. He tried to count, just to get his breath. As he did, he saw the pile of pink message slips lying beside his multibutton phone. He rifled through them. All clients, soon to be ex-clients, he guessed. Of course, every one of the *niños de las putas* was calling in to "discuss management issues." Of course. There was no loyalty, no sense of history, with these children of pigs. They'd be calling Mike Ovitz, CMI and CAA and all the other agents so fast that phone lines would be melting.

Everything was falling apart! Marty was having some kind of breakdown, the Okie blonde was a pervert, Jahne Moore was a surgical trick, and fuckin' Lila Kyle was a man! Over at the Network, they were going crazy. Les Merchant was threatening to cancel the show. Hyram Flanders was homicidal, and all the other sponsors were bailing out. Christ, he'd be lucky if the merchandisers didn't sue his ass. Well, they probably would. This would cost him millions!

But it was worse than that! Hollywood was a town built on hype, but it was a town that believed its own. When you were hot you were hot, and when you were not you were *frío* to the max. Christ! Sy winced. What would those gringo cocksuckers at Morton's be saying about him this Monday night? He almost writhed in his chair as he thought about it. Their little grins as he walked by their tables, the concealed laughs. Jokes about wet-backs and chicano-ry! Oh, he could hear it all now.

Damage control was necessary. Lots of it, and fast. But wasn't it too late for the spin doctors? Well, he could salvage Jahne Moore. *Birth of a Star* was still a hit, a big one. She could eke out another major part. The curiosity factor was high on her. That TV script he'd read last month about the prostitute who adopts the two kids. It could work. Meanwhile, they'd sue the *Informer,* and that bitch Laura Richie. No, suits took too long and cost too much. He wrinkled his brow and took a prophylactic suck on the aspirator.

He had it! He'd call Hefner. This wasn't for Christie. He'd go right to the top. A centerfold. And not one of those soft-focus stills from the film. Fresh, hot meat. She'd show them *everything*. And then they'd put her, quick, into another TV film. The bitch would do what he told her now, if she wanted to survive. This shit worked for Madonna, didn't it? Then there was the Smith family. Apparently Dean wasn't the hillbilly's brother, so they would sue all those tabloids on Sharleen's behalf, and maybe she could get engaged—or, better yet, married. It should get the church and the Moral Majority assholes off his back. That just left Lila. With her dead, maybe *Three for the Road* could go on, once Marty snapped out of it. Or even before, with another director. And the Kyle freak would be replaced. After all, finding fresh meat in Hollywood wasn't hard. Only a week ago, he'd decided to drop Sharleen and Jahne. Now he'd drop Lila and keep the other two. With two of the three in place, the show had a good chance of survival.

So, really, the only problem left was Marty. He was drooling and babbling, all right, but so what? A few weeks at the rest home and he'd be in the pink. And maybe, Sy Ortis thought, maybe even *Marty* can be replaced. Okay, the ideas, the format, all of it was his, but it was established now. Maybe that kid, the AD from *Birth*—what was his name? Joel Something. He could do it. After all, what was there to do?

For four more days, days of siege, Sy managed to hold Early Artists and himself together while they were buffeted by the media, by the Industry, and by the Network and sponsors. Every bastard whom he had ever screwed felt it his duty to call in and be counted. Every son-of-a-bitch in the Industry had something smart to say. Well, fuck 'em all. The audience last night for *Three for the Road* had broken all records. As Sy had promised Hyram Flanders that it would. So now all Sy needed to do was find a way to replace Lila and Marty and keep, as they say, the show on the road.

The phone intercom buzzed. "Miss Moore is here to see you."

"Okay." *Madre de Jesús*, he was in no mood for this twat who always had fuckin' opinions and attitudes. At least today she should be under control. He'd seen them, the Talents, when they first were hit with the realization that what the public giveth it could also take away. Look how humbled Crystal had become. And—he smiled to himself—he liked his Talents humbled; humbled and scared. It made them a lot more respectful. Until, of course, they were panicked, and then they'd turn on their own young and eat them alive.

Jahne Moore would be concerned but not panicked, he figured. She'd probably calmed down from the surprise of *Birth*, she'd realized by now he was right about it being a hit, and the opportunity to continue on *3/4* with, perhaps, an expanded part would keep her in line. Plus, the *Playboy* or *Penthouse* spread he'd just about lined up (with a bonus to him, of course) would silence this plastic-surgery rumor. It was a good strategy. She'd finally appreciate him. Sy put down his respirator, ready to calm an upset and frightened Talent.

Except she didn't look upset or frightened. She looked beautiful as ever, but also calm. She was wearing a pair of those goddamn jeans with a plain white sweater, but he couldn't help thinking, for a moment, of what was under it. He smiled, but she didn't return it. What was wrong with this *puta*?

"Hello, Sy," she said, and sat across from him. "I'm here to exercise my option."

"What option?"

"To drop out of *3/4*."

"What?"

"I'm out, Sy. You put it in the contract. Now I'm using it."

What the hell was this shit? Sy narrowed his eyes. "I know you have a lot of other offers flowing in. In fact, I've read a few properties, possibilities, but let's not throw up the baby with the bathwater."

"Out, Sy. Throw *out* the baby with the bathwater. But never mind. I'm quitting. Quitting 3/4, movies, cosmetics ads, mall openings. I'm out of the business."

Sy's secretary stuck her head inside the door, ignored Jahne, and said to Sy, "Your wife's on the line."

"Which one?" Sy snapped.

"Sandra."

"Not which *wife!* Which *line?*"

He punched the blinking light the secretary indicated among the bank of other blinking lights. "What?" he shouted. "No! Don't you DARE GO TO THE CLUB. DON'T SPEAK TO ANYONE. NO. ESPECIALLY NOT ANNE." Anne was his wife's friend, married to a reporter on the *L.A. Times*. "So, *be* lonesome!" he told her, and hung up. He turned back to the Moore bitch.

"Listen," he said, as calmly as he could manage. "You're still upset about *Birth*. About the violence. The death. You're overreacting. I understand. You're sensitive. You're an artist. But you must look at this as a challenge."

"Forget it, Sy. I'm out of here."

"Jahne. Listen. I have a great idea. A way to show them all. I've talked with Guccione. We'll show them that these rumors are all jealous lies. Exaggerations. We'll do a layout. Eight pages. Bob says he'll shoot it himself. And you'll be gorgeous. Spectacular. Bigger than ever. And you'll have your choice of parts."

"Good. I'd like to do Cordelia."

"What part was that? Did I see that script? What's the working title?"

"*King Lear*. We could pick up the option cheap."

"Very funny. I've heard of *King Lear*. Shakespeare doesn't play. Except that Mel Gibson vehicle."

"Hamlet?"

"Whatever. Anyway, Jahne, don't talk this way. We got a lot invested in you now, and I know this is just a stage you're going through. Bad publicity hurts. But you'll get over it. We'll just counter it with this layout."

"Show them my goodies?" She laughed and shook her head. "Forget it, Sy."

"I'm not sure that you understand what I'm trying to say. Listen, *everyone* out here has had a little cosmetic work. It's nothing to be ashamed of. I realize you might not choose to do this normally. And normally I wouldn't recommend it. But we're talking about extreme damage to your career here. And a tastefully done layout in a fine magazine . . ."

"Sy, *Penthouse* isn't a 'fine magazine,' and Bob Guccione is the Antichrist." Jahne paused, and then she smiled at him. "Anyway, it wouldn't work. The scars are too obvious."

"The scars? Wait. What are you telling me?" Sy Ortis cried, his hand clenching around the aspirator he clutched. "Are you saying all this bullshit is *true?*"

Jahne looked at him directly. "Yes," she said. "It is."

"So you're scarred all over. Like a Frankenstein?" Sy Ortis asked, his high voice almost a shriek.

"I don't like to put it that way, but, yes, the scarring is extensive."

"So, no *Penthouse.*"

"No *Penthouse,*" Jahne smiled.

"What the fuck are you smiling for?" Sy spat at her. "The three of you were dream meat. God, now it's a nightmare! Do you know what this does to you?"

Jahne shrugged. "Ends my career as a sexpot?" she asked, and giggled. The bitch *giggled.*

"How about ends your career completely? Don't you see? The illusion is gone. They'll look up at the screen and wonder, 'Where are the scars?' They'll be watching for clues. They'll be mesmerized. No producer, no director will want you."

Jahne laughed.

"What the fuck are you *laughing* about?" Sy screamed.

"I think it's funny. A TV exploitation show that created the three sexiest women in America. What you so candidly call 'dream meat.' One is a Frankenstein, one sleeps with her brother, and the third one was a man. Not much left there to exploit, huh, Sy?"

18

There was never a funeral like it. Not Rudolph Valentino's, not Jean Harlow's, not even Marilyn Monroe's compared to the carnival-cum-media-orgy that Lila Kyle's funeral became.

There was no one to do it for her except poor, heartbroken Robbie Lymon. Theresa was drugged out, Sy Ortis was bummed out, Marty was freaked out, and Ara Sagarian was out-and-out dead. Loved by millions, reviled by millions more, Lila had no one to pick out her casket and arrange the memorial service but an old camp follower of her mother's.

Robbie had the body dressed in a lavender Bob Mackie dress—if she had chosen to be a girl in life, she'd also be one in death, he said—and a frightening picture of Lila in the casket, her red hair clashing with the lilac-colored dress, was printed on the cover of half the magazines of the world. There were close to a thousand funeral wreaths and flower arrangements sent.

Thousands came to see her. "They were her fans," Robbie said, weeping. "She loved them." The problem was that not all of them loved her. One woman tried to wipe the makeup off her dead face. Another began speaking in tongues before the casket. The funeral home finally put Lila behind a glass viewing wall. It gave her a sort of Snow White–in–the–glass–coffin look.

Worse than the ones that reviled her, though, were the ones who came to worship at her shrine. Hundreds of young men (and some not so young) showed up in full Lila Kyle regalia, including high heels, makeup, and the de rigueur long red wig. Some screamed and fainted at the sight of her corpse. Others sobbed. Many had to be helped out. But, once they had viewed her, they raced to the end of the seven-block-long line to do it again.

Thousands of teenage girls showed up, too. Somehow, they didn't seem to mind the gender-bender revelation. Perhaps they even liked her more for it. After all, David Bowie had dressed almost as extremely and built a following twenty years before. And this was the nineties. The girls wailed out their pain in a constant keen of adolescent screaming.

There were close to two hundred cars that tried to make the long run to Forest Lawn. The scene at the gravesite was bedlam. And, with all the people there, the only one who had actually known Lila in life was her aunt Robbie, who had to be carried from the grave.

19

Small things. If he kept his mind on small things, on tiny little things, Marty knew he was okay. A patch of sunlight reflecting off a wrinkle of the snow-white sheets. The shadow of the bedside lampshade on the wall. The taste of the sliced banana on his corn flakes.

Slowly, Marty, in bathrobe and slippers, moved to the window that looked out over the beautifully manicured grounds. It must be Japan, he thought. Everything was so perfect, so neat, it had to be Japan. But then he remembered, and moved away from the window.

He heard the now familiar key in the lock, and saw the nurse—what was her name?—come through the door. "Hi, how are you doing today, Mr. DiGennaro?" She picked up his breakfast tray and walked toward the door. "You did very well today. Your appetite is coming back." She closed and locked the door behind her, leaving him in the silence of his thoughts once again.

He sat in the reproduction–Queen Anne armchair that overlooked the garden below his window. Oh, no. Now he was upset. Tears filled his eyes, then slowly slid down his cheeks. He often sat here, in this clean and quiet room, and cried. He still had not figured out why, exactly, so he just let himself cry.

The hospital bed had been made earlier, the fake-Aubusson rug vacuumed, and the Sheraton-style chest and bedside tables dusted. All this while he was at water therapy, before breakfast. He was impressed with the service here. A good hotel. No trouble in the world couldn't be alleviated by a stay in a luxury hotel. Wherever it was. If it wasn't Japan, was it England? No. Too sunny for that.

He continued to sit on the brocade-upholstered chair and cry. Sometimes, every now and then, like now, just before medication time, a tiny window would open in his mind, and he'd remember. Lila. Lila was dead. And then he'd cry. Lila had lied to him, he remembered, the tears now flowing faster. And Lila was a man.

She didn't have to lie. He would have loved her anyway. But that made him a homosexual, and he was sure he wasn't that. Still, they could have found a way. They *did* find a way. It would have been okay, if only Lila hadn't lied. Lied and died. It made an ugly poem, buzzing in his head. She shouldn't have lied and died. They could have worked it out, just the two of them.

But now, Marty knew, it wasn't just the two of them. He was the laughingstock of Hollywood, and pitied by everyone. It was the pity that hurt the most. Or perhaps it was knowing he would never see Lila again. No, it was the fact that he could never work again, never create beauty on a screen again, that really hurt the most.

Lila lied to him. And now she was dead. Lied and died.

Soon the nurse would return with the pleated paper cup of pills and the glass of water. Soon, soon, and then the tears and memories would stop.

Usually Marty remembered none of this. Usually he

couldn't pull up a past event, a memory. Not even when Sally came to visit. He knew he knew Sally, but he couldn't remember how, or from where.

And not remembering anything, not knowing what had brought him to this place where he lived behind a locked door, that was exactly the way Marty liked it.

20

Monica Flanders towered over the crouched form of her son, Hyram, who sat at his desk. At four feet eleven, it was not easy to tower, but Monica achieved the effect spectacularly well.

"First we find out the blonde is sleeping with her brother. . . ."

"He wasn't really her brother, Ma," Hyram began.

"Oh, excuse *me*," Monica said icily. "She recently found out he wasn't. I feel *so* much better. *Then* the world discovers that the brunette is a monster." She took a deep breath. So did Hyram.

"Not a monster, Ma. Just a plastic-surgery patient. You yourself . . ."

"I myself never looked like she did," Monica snapped. "She was a nothing. A mess. *She* represents Flanders Cosmetics?" she snorted. "And if that wasn't enough— a pervert and a lump—now we add a freak. A cross-dressing female-impersonator transvestite queer *faygele* to convince women to wear our lipstick. Perfect, Hyram. Perfect. Great idea you had."

"Mother, the show this week got the highest rating *any* show ever got. It's . . ."

"It's a freak show, is what it is. And fuck the ratings. Fuck the *ratings,* Hyram. Tell me about *sales.*"

"Well, you have to expect a little dip . . ."

"Hyram, you really are an asshole. Even considering the possibility that you could take over for me is the only big error of judgment I ever made. Except, of course, for this fiasco. Don't you get it, Hyram? The line is over.

Finished. No woman will ever buy that shit again. We sell dreams, Hyram, not nightmares. The party, as they say, is over."

"But we have close to a hundred million dollars invested in that stuff."

"Take your losses like a big boy, Hyram."

"Mother, are you crazy? We'll get a replacement for Lila Kyle. We'll change the print-ad copy. We could even get rid of the other two. But we *have* to keep the line, Mother."

"Pull our sponsorship. Cut our losses. Start over on this one, Hyram."

He stood up. "Forget it. I'm not going to eat this loss. Not in my first year as president. Mother, I mean it: I'll fight you on this. I'll take it to the board. I'll press the issue, Mother. They won't see it as you do."

"Yes they will, Hyram. And they'll remember who brought this idea to them. Don't do it. You'll be sorry."

But he did. And then he was.

21

Jahne sat on the veranda of Sharleen's house, among the wrapped furniture and crated kitchenware. The two friends had been silent for some time. The sun was setting over the smog of the Valley, creating a spectacular sunset.

"It's the pollution and dust that make the colors," Jahne said.

"So, then, even dirt is good for something."

"And I thought all that garbage written about us was useless."

"Hell, no. We wrapped our dishes with a lot of it. And in Wyoming we'll use it for starting fires and mulching the garden." Sharleen grinned. Then she looked back at the sunset. "Sure is pretty. Nice to know there's a chance for one every night." She sighed. "I still can't believe that Lila is dead. She ain't gonna see another sunset. I mean, it's all so weird. I still can't believe she was a man.''

"Well, I guess she wasn't, really, was she? I mean, she had some of the equipment, but that didn't make her a fireman, if you know what I mean."

"Speaking of mean, now we know why she was. I guess she was a really unhappy person." Sharleen shook her head. "What did her mother *do* to her?"

"I want to know what *Marty* did to her. I mean, she had to be pretty good at faking to make him think she was a woman. I've sometimes faked my orgasms, but not my gender."

"Huh?"

Jahne looked at Sharleen. "Haven't you ever faked an orgasm?"

"Uh-uh. Well, why would I do that?" Sharleen asked. "What's the point?"

"Oh, to take the pressure off you, or him. To end it if it's boring. To, well, you know." Jahne found herself looking into Sharleen's blank face.

"I surely don't. I haven't slept with many guys, but I never faked how I felt in my life. It would be like a lie, and at a very bad time to lie."

"I think you're right, Sharleen, but I think most women do."

Sharleen shook her head and shrugged. "I don't understand about sex," she said.

"Join the club."

"I felt so ashamed about me and Dean for so long, it's hard to get used to it bein' okay. Plus, even when it wasn't supposed to be the right thing, it always *felt* like the right thing. Sometimes it was the *only* thing that was right."

"You'll get over the guilt. Just keep telling yourself he's not your brother."

"Well, even if he *isn't* my brother, he still *feels* like he is," Sharleen said. "That's what I like. That we're like blood kin, you know? We really *know* each other. But now I ain't ashamed. I know what other people still might say, and think, but I don't care. I really don't. Because I *ain't* shamed. What we done, what we are, felt right. It *is* right.'' She looked up at Jahne.

''What *you* think is the most important thing, Sharleen,'' Jahne said.

''Well, yes, but I'd like you to understand.'' She paused. ''See, it's like this: Sex with men, with other men, always felt like there was two different kinds of us in bed. Their kind and our kind. Even with Boyd, and then with Michael McLain, it always felt like it was a kind of two-part contest.''

Jahne thought of Michael, of Sam, and nodded.

''Well, with Dean it don't feel like that. It don't feel like his turn and my turn. It don't feel like no contest. It's just *us*. . . . We're *both* us, both the same. It ain't as excitin' as with Michael, I admit that. And for a while I got confused. But now I know one thing: it may not be the way sex is supposed to be, but the way it is with Dean is the way I like it.'' Tears stood in Sharleen's perfect eyes as she searched Jahne's face.

And Jahne, all at once, was hit with such a strong wave of . . . of envy, she realized with a start of surprise. Because the strife, the battle, had always been there, between her and her lovers. The battle for possession, for dominance, for freedom. The battle of the sexes. And because always, following the excitement, there had been disappointment, loneliness, or betrayal. Always. They were never really on my side, she thought. Except maybe Neil. Neil was on my side, but he wasn't exciting enough, pretty enough for me. I never slept with him. And now it's probably too late for Neil. And maybe it's too late for me.

She looked at Sharleen, up front and beautiful as she'd always been, simple and straight and right as rain. She thought of all the advice she'd given Sharleen, of how she'd condescended to her, and she very nearly blushed.

''What are you going to do?'' Jahne asked Sharleen.

''I reckon me and Dean are goin' to take up my friend's offer. We're goin' to move out to Wyoming with Dobe. He and us are partners on a big spread he bought out there. Dean and me'll get married later.''

''So, you'll just walk away without looking back?''

"Why, sure. And feel lucky. It could have been you or me got shot."

"But won't you miss it? All the excitement, and the attention . . . and the money?"

"Oh, heck. It ain't ever the way it seems. *You* know that. Seems that there ain't much money. So much went in taxes and fees. And there's such a big mortgage on this place that lots went on interest and what all. Seems that only Mr. Ortis made money. I won't miss him. And I missed my stepmother more once I found her than I ever did when she was gone. I'll miss the *idea* of fame some. Wouldn't be human if I said I wouldn't. But I won't really miss any of this. . . ." She turned to look out the window at the hills spread below them. Then she looked back at Jahne. "I'll miss *you*," she said, "but I hope you'll come to visit."

"I will," Jahne promised.

"What about you? You stayin' on?"

"I have a few things I still have to take care of."

"And then what?"

"Then I don't know."

"You'd always be welcome on the ranch, Jahne."

"Thanks." Tears filled her eyes. She probably didn't deserve a friend as kind as Sharleen, but she was grateful she had her. She'd better lighten this up, or else she'd be sobbing all over the two of them. "So," she said, "no more Crimson, Cara, and Clover."

As if she sensed Jahne's mood, Sharleen tossed her head and whistled. "Oh, hell, sure there is. We're takin' the three bitches with us!" She laughed, and turned to stroke the head of the first dog that ran to her side.

22

Jahne dressed carefully, as if for an important audition. But what role is it that you are trying out for? she asked herself. Good friend? A bit late for that. You haven't played that role opposite Neil in a long time. Lady Bountiful? Isn't that a laugh? You've never been a lady, and for the last year at least you've been spiritually and emotionally impoverished. What Neil must need is a real good psychiatrist and an even better lawyer, not some one-trick pony. Well, at least you can write a check. That might help him, though he may be beyond help now.

Probably Neil won't even have a clue as to who I am. He won't know that I'm Mary Jane. Well, that I *was*. And why should he when you don't? she asked herself. He might not even agree to see her. She surveyed herself in the full-length mirror of her marble bathroom. She wore a becomingly casual pair of the jeans Mai had made for her, and the big sweater that she had worn with Sam on their vacation in Northern California. She stared at her reflection in the mirror: tall, willowy, her perfect face a shining oval, her thick, lustrous black hair cascading down from her widow's peak, her lips full, her face a valentine. She still was amazed by her own looks. She looked like one of the people who'd always looked down on her. Back in New York, so many people had. Except Neil. She sighed.

Another one of the privileges of fame, Jahne thought as she walked down the green-tiled hallway of the Los Angeles County Jail. Only relatives and attorneys are allowed access to prisoners. And, of course, the occasional reporter willing to pay out a few bucks. Or a movie star.

"A close family friend" was how she had put it, and the prison official asked for nothing except the autographed photos she had been smart enough to bring, along with two tickets to a sneak preview of something or other that she'd received a week ago. He had looked her over carefully, and she was certain he was looking for the grisly scars. Well, he'd get a full report from the hefty female guard who'd searched her *very* thoroughly before she allowed Jahne to cross through the barred doors onto this corridor that led to the visiting room. Jahne had to announce herself as "Jahne Moore," of course. Would Neil even speak to her?

She left the security room, dressed neatly again, and began to walk down the hallway. She winced at the unbelievably harsh overhead lights, the green-checkered tile, the institutionally two-toned walls.

She entered the small, private room the guard pointed her to. It was almost completely filled by a scarred wooden table and four mismatched chairs. Neil was sitting in the fifth, his narrow back turned to the door, dressed in an orange jumpsuit. He turned to her, his face more feral than ever, his eyes more deeply sunk and hooded. He surveyed her, not moving a muscle of his body or face.

Then he stood. "Veronica!" he said, and as he held his arms out to her, his eyes filled with tears.

It was hard to believe that he recognized her so quickly, despite the surgery, the time, and the dislocation of this strange venue. But perhaps that was the magic of love. Neil had loved her, had known her, and he still did. She hugged him, then took a seat next to him at the table.

"I'm sorry that it took me so long to find you," Jahne was explaining. "I looked. I really did. But your number wasn't listed and I . . ."

"That's okay, Veronica," Neil told her sweetly. "I forgive you."

He seemed normal, if a little subdued. How do you talk to an old friend who has become a murderer? Should she avoid the issue?

"What happened?" she asked gently.

"They made a mistake. It was all wrong."

"What do you mean?" He'd been filmed by a dozen

cameras doing the deed. Surely he wasn't going to claim innocence.

"I wasn't supposed to be Jughead. I was supposed to be *Archie*. The one everybody liked. That was the mistake. But it's fixed now. Roger fixed it. It wasn't my fault the girl was shot. Someone screwed up. Johnny Burton. He wasn't supposed to. I was. Master of ceremonies. Me. Forgive me, master." He looked at her, his mad eyes glittering into hers.

"I'm sure you'll be forgiven," she whispered.

"Great!" he shouted into the air. Then he turned to her again, a crafty look on his face. "And then I'll get my show back? Because I can't take too much more of this shit. Not being recognized, getting no respect. I can't take too much more." His voice had risen; now, abruptly, he put his head down on his arms and began to weep. "You don't know what it's like," he cried. "You don't know how it feels to be so close, so close to that love. And to lose it. To lose it all."

"I do, Neil. I do."

She patted his shoulder as softly as she could. They sat together as he wept.

"I'm so sorry. What do you need?" she asked. "I'll get you anything they allow you to have."

"I have everything I need." He lifted his head from the table and wiped his eyes.

"What about a lawyer? I could help with . . ."

"My sister's girlfriend is a lawyer. Diana. And there's Roger. Roger will take care of everything."

"Neil, I want to help. I . . ."

His face changed from a vacant, soggy smile to an animal snarl. "Not Neil!" he yelled at her. "Archie. I'm Archie now. Really popular. Everyone likes me."

"Okay. Okay, Archie," she said, to calm him down. His face had scared her. Was he crazy? Did he really recognize her? "So, Archie, are you treated well here?"

"Treated well? Hey, I'm the most popular guy at Riverdale High. I was elected president of the senior class. Reggie ran against me, but *I* won. It was unanimous. Even Reggie voted for me in the end."

Jahne tried to laugh at the feeble joke, but it wasn't

easy. "Archie, I'm just so sorry about everything. About your show getting canceled, and about the . . ."

Neil sprang up, overturning the chair. Jahne jumped at the sudden movement, more startled than frightened. The door opened fast, and a big black male prison guard stood over them. Neil looked over at him. "Hello, Veronica," Neil said. Then he held out his arms, and his eyes filled with tears.

As Jahne walked down the corridor, away from Neil and his broken mumblings, she had to use all her acting strength not to sob out loud. He hadn't known her. He didn't know what day it was, or what had happened. Apparently he had started calling *everyone* Veronica, or so the assistant warden said. He was locked into his own private prison of pain. His guilt was even worse than his madness, and, from time to time, when he came out of the paranoid fog of his delusions, the pain and terror in his eyes were worse than the ravings of his conspiracy theories. For the first time, Jahne could see why people sought the comfort of madness.

There in the prison corridor, the long enfilade of barred doors ahead of her, Jahne felt her own eyes fill with tears. How long would Neil be sentenced to a life behind bars? Or no life at all? She felt sick, and dizzy. Oh, God, it had all gone so wrong! She knew that Mary Jane and Neil had had a great deal in common: Both of us were born without the appropriate physical gifts. And both of us had the brains and sensitivity to know it. We've both spent half a lifetime overcompensating. But, in the end, Neil had failed, and he couldn't live with who he was. A skinny, funny, weasel-faced guy without an audience, without a friend. A murderer. Jahne took a shuddering breath. "Oh, Neil, how could you?" she whispered.

But how close to her own murder had she been, back in Scuderstown? She wouldn't forget that time after her grandmother's funeral. After her own failures and rejections had made her almost as crazy as Neil had become from his. Neil, failing, had only been different in deciding to turn his anger outward, to kill another instead of himself. That was what men did. Women killed themselves. Which was the greater sin?

She stopped, leaned her long, slender body against the wall and felt herself trembling all over. Because, she realized all at once, she, too, was guilty of murder. She had killed Mary Jane Moran back in New York, more than two years ago. Mary Jane had died under Brewster's knife just as surely as Lila Kyle had died from a bullet. She had ended Mary Jane's life, sentencing her to death for not being pretty enough, successful enough, to live.

Poor, pathetic Neil. Poor, motherless, unloved Mary Jane.

23

Sam Shields slid into a seat on the aisle so that he could stretch out his legs. He'd forgotten just how uncomfortable regular movie-theater seats could be. He only saw films at screenings or premieres now. When was the last time he'd actually paid to see a movie, the way civilians do? Certainly not since he'd moved here. Maybe not since New York, with Mary Jane.

His mind jumped away from the thought. He was getting good at that. Move on to the pleasant, to the present. *Birth* was in its seventh week of distribution, and it had already passed the hundred-million-dollar mark. He would make more than three million on it, and was moving out of the canyon rental to his first real home: a soaring space tucked behind the Hotel Bel-Air. Meanwhile, he'd become the most popular boy in town. Everyone from everywhere was clamoring to have him direct their next film. He'd already met with Rob Reiner at Castle Rock, Mark Cannon from Columbia, and Stanley Jaffe at Paramount. It was nice to be popular.

The theater darkened, and the trailer began. Sam watched the preview, until a couple stopped at his seat and asked to pass into the row. He stood up. He loomed over them. They were already chubbing up, the way middle-class Americans did. The two of them, in their late teens or early twenties, settled into seats only a short distance from him. Well, you wanted audience reaction, he reminded himself. Now you'll get it really close at hand. The guy offered his date some popcorn from a paper bucket the size of a snare drum. Sam turned back to the screen.

The music swelled, and the establishing shot with the LAX sign opened the film, *his* film. The audience, a pretty large one for an afternoon in Burbank, was still settling in, murmuring to one another and shifting in their seats. Then Jahne's image flashed on the screen, and that argument with the cabbie where Michael steps in and rescues her. It went fairly well. The audience laughed at Jahne's put-down, though he didn't get the second laugh out of them with the quick cut to the cabbie. April had been right about that.

April wanted him for another project. And why should he say no? So far, they were batting a thousand, and although she still wasn't giving him final cut, she was negotiating. In the wake of *Birth*'s success, all the bad blood between them seemed to have washed away in the tide of cash. Offers from the other studios looked promising, but wasn't the devil you knew better than the one you didn't? Not that April was a devil, exactly. Where had that image come from? I have not made a deal with the devil, he told himself.

Birth was unfolding on the screen, and though he had seen it a hundred or five hundred or a thousand times, he was here to feel what it was like when it played to what Sy Ortis would call "the Regulars." And it seemed to be playing well. Jahne and Michael—Judy and James—had just kissed for the first time on the big screen. As James stripped off Judy's blouse, Sam heard the intake of breath from the crowd. Obliquely he glanced at the couple to his right. The guy had his mouth partly open, staring, mesmerized. Then his girlfriend reached over, took the hand that wasn't in the popcorn bucket, and placed it on her own breast. Sam felt a jolt. Did people—regular people—still neck in movies?

He turned back to the screen. Jahne *did* look beautiful.

His own empty hand cupped, as if, just once more, he could circle it around her breast. He watched as the scene played. And he could feel it work its magic on the audience. The theater was completely silent as James began his symbolic devouring of Judy.

It works because all my impotent love and rage is cut into it, Sam thought. I did love her. I do love her. And now, when I can have almost any woman I want, I'll never have another who loved me before I succeeded. Now they will always love what I can do for them, and what I have done as much as who I am. He looked over at the couple beside him. The guy had discarded his popcorn and was holding the hand of his girlfriend tight against the crotch of his jeans. Sam felt a stab of loneliness so acute that he almost lifted his own hand to his chest.

The love scene ended, and Sam watched the camera pan Adrienne's pale bare back and ass, Michael's tanned hand lying along the beautiful curve of her hips. The illusion was perfect: it was Jahne up there, Jahne exposed. And after the fight scene, in the drunken fuck, it was Jahne who was pinned, Jahne who was mauled. Sam heard a guttural grunt from the guy beside him as, on the screen, Michael pulled off his trunks to ravage his target: a woman, any woman, Every Woman, who could serve as a receptacle for him.

Sam could feel the heat from the screen igniting the audience. "Give it to her," someone called out, and "Fuck the bitch!" a deeper voice yelled, and there was a moment of silence, then a high-pitched giggle. Sam felt nausea sweep through him. Yes, he had meant to arouse them; yes, he had tapped his own anger; but what, exactly, had he done?

He watched the film, and he listened to the audience. He saw then how he'd used his own rage—at his mother, at his ex-wife, at Jahne, at April—and had used Michael's, to carry the movie. This was no love letter, he saw. The hot scenes were hot, all right, but the undercurrent was anger and fear. Oh, they were not love scenes.

No. The drowning male character struck out at the female through sex. He didn't love her. He fucked her. Just as this film fucked Jahne.

Sam sat there, alone in the dark, and watched what he had done to Jahne, and then what that did to the audience.

24

Sharleen closed the door of the house behind her and jumped in the King Cab of Dobe's new truck. Dean was in the back seat with the four dogs, each of them fighting for his attention. She slammed the door of the cab and breathed in the delicious scent of new plastic, metal, and upholstery. "Okay," she nodded to Dobe, and they drove through the gates, Dean twisting in his seat to wave to the security guard looking after them as they drove away.

"You going to miss any of this, Dean?" Sharleen asked.

Dean was silent for a moment. "Yes," he said, the sadness causing him to speak softly. "My garden."

Dobe looked into the rearview mirror and caught Dean's eyes. "How would you like a farm, not just a garden?"

"How big?" Dean asked for about the three hundredth time.

"Nine hundred and thirty-two acres."

Sharleen laughed for the first time today. "That's as big as some state parks," she said.

"Not much compared to them big suckers' places. You know, Ted Turner and those types. But it's just about the prettiest land I ever saw."

Dean was shaking his head. "I don't know about them other farmers, but that's a big spread. I can't do it all myself. I'll need some help."

Sharleen turned in her seat to face Dean. "We'll help you, Dean. Right, Dobe?"

"Sure. That's why I'm going, to get out into the air, do some honest hard work." He laughed, and Sharleen caught him looking at her out of the corner of his eye.

"It will be that, Dobe. Honest *and* hard."

"Can't think of a better way to live, Sharleen. Honest and hard."

"Does it have an orchard?" Dean asked.

"Not yet, but it will. If you want one."

"And we'll get a horse," Dean said. "Are there trails?"

"We'll get *three* horses, and there's plenty of trails."

Sharleen thought again about all that she was leaving behind and what she felt. Leaving this isn't hard, she thought, as the truck with the few belongings she cherished barreled out of California to Wyoming. She now had everything she wanted. A ranch in Wyoming, Dean, Dobe, the dogs. There would be good, real work, and fun, too. And no people for miles around, Dobe had said.

No television. Or VCR. No interviews, no parties with dressed-up people who said they liked you when they really didn't. No newspapers, no magazines, no scandal sheets blaring out people's shame. No shame, no lies, no secrets. And not much money, either. Sy's accountant had explained about management fees, and legal fees, and taxes, and the agency's percentage. It didn't leave much. But they owned the land, and the furniture that would arrive in a day or two, and that was more than most people had. More than she'd ever expected to have. Leave all this to them as wants it, she thought, as they crossed the state line. It hadn't made her happy, only sad and lonely. And none of it was real, she thought. Except the pain.

"Look!" Dean called out.

"What?" Sharleen asked, bringing her thoughts back to the present.

"An *Idaho* license plate. Guess what it says," Dean said, his face bright with a grin. He couldn't wait to tell them. " 'Idaho,' " Dean quoted. " 'Famous potatoes.' Ain't that a funny tag?"

Dobe laughed. "Sure 'nough is."

"Famous potato," Sharleen said through the ripples of laughter. "Sounds like me."

And then the only sound in the truck that was taking them away from Hollywood—the clothes and parties, the self-indulgence and fame, the security guards, the money, the special privilege, of having everything except privacy and peace of mind—the only sound, as the wheels of Dobe's new truck passed the state-line marker, was the sound of their laughter.

25

Giving it all up wouldn't be *too* hard, Jahne thought as she folded clothes into one of the suitcases that lay open on her bed. What was it she was losing? After all, she'd never, except for the time with *Jack and Jill*, gotten to play the parts she wanted. First it was all the "character" parts, now it would be naked airheads. Moaning, jiggling, naked airheads. She threw a disgusted look at the pile of scripts that had been submitted to her. The women that Hollywood wanted: runaways, whores, victims; desperate, dependent women, and teenagers in trouble. The women that *America* seemed to want.

Yes, she could give it up. God, *why* had she wanted so much to be an actress anyway? That was a question with an answer too sad to ignore. She thought of Neil. Like him, she was a kid who had never had anyone's approval. And who had never had a family. I was a natural for it, she thought. The roar of the greasepaint, the smell of the crowd; the sense of family in a troupe, the attention of an audience, meager as those sometimes were. All I really wanted was someone to look at me and approve. I was so tired of not being looked at. She shook her head and folded a white silk blouse, stuffed it into the suitcase, and shook her head again. No one had ever seen her, except perhaps Neil, and she hadn't believed *him*, hadn't cared enough about *his* good opinion. Would anyone's approval ever fill the void in her? Would more of Sam's love, more of the critics' raves, a larger audience's applause, would any of it have made her believe she was good enough? She doubted it.

With real pain, an actual hurt deep in her chest, she thought of all those kids back in New York, suffering to be seen, to be heard, to be *liked*. And the even more pathetic grovelers out here in L.A., desperate for a taste of fame, willing almost to die for a chance to be flavor of the month. Well, she'd had it, and someone else could have it now. She was sick of it. She had wasted herself, gone on a quest for a grail that was vulgar.

Still, it hadn't been all bad judgment on her part. Rather, it had been bad judgment foisted on her by every TV show, every magazine, every movie she'd ever seen. Be pretty, be popular, be attractive, be sexy, be wanted, to be desirable. Well, she thought grimly, she was desirable now. There wasn't a man in the country who couldn't jerk off to living, moving pictures of her imitation orgasms. And soon she'd go into international release. Today Scuderstown, tomorrow the world. She almost had to laugh at the irony. She had wanted to show them all. Show her grandmother, show the girls back at Scuderstown Regional High, show the casting agents and the producers in New York, show everyone how good, how very good she was. Well, her grandmother was dead, she couldn't remember the names of her high school classmates, and New York never cared about anything.

Meanwhile, all she appeared to have shown was her genitalia, to any of the population on earth who could afford a VCR and a two-dollar rental. She had shown them how good she was at counterfeiting orgasms, a trait that almost every young girl would find useful, but hardly what she had originally had in mind. She shook her head at her own bitterness.

While she was facing home truths, she'd better face another one: Acting had also drawn her because she had been so afraid to live. Afraid of sinking into the day-to-day routine of a job, a husband, a family. She thought of Sharleen and her bravery: going out to Wyoming to live everyday life. Could Jahne do it? Playing a role was so much easier than living. Well, to hell with this idea of showing other people's feelings so that a numbed audience could have a few of their own. No, she'd *do* things from now on, not *act* them. Michael McLain had certainly taught her the difference between acting a hero and being a villain.

Villains. There were so many out here, all of them posing as heroes. Sy Ortis, Les Merchant, Hyram Flanders, Bob LeVine, Michael McLain, Marty DiGennaro. And Sam, of course. All selling dream meat. She looked at the picture of her and Sam which still stood on the table beside the bed and shook her head again before she pitched it into the wastepaper basket, frame and all. It had been taken in Santa Cruz. That was only a few months ago. Back when she thought he could love her. Back when she thought he was worth loving.

One more home truth: Ridiculous as the charade had been, she was glad she'd gone through it. She'd longed for him, been rejected, and burned with her humiliation, a sort of culmination of all the humiliations of fat, sad, serious, smart, sensitive, plain girls. But, unlike them, at last, she'd had the chance to transform herself, and then to feel his longing for her. Still, the ending was the same. NOTHING HAD CHANGED. Beauty didn't protect you from betrayal. Hadn't Mai told her that? Hadn't Brewster Moore? Well, fuck it, then! Who needed beauty? It was only another trap for women. The silken trap, the desired trap, the exalted trap, but nothing more than a trap with trappings.

She stalked into the bathroom, ready to pack her toothbrush, deodorant, and that host of products that were lined up there, promising to make her more lovely, younger, softer; to bring out her hidden beauty or to hide her flaws. She looked up to the mirror, at her face: her sculpted, expensive, symmetrical, perfect face. And, once again, she saw her eyes, her old eyes, those eyes of a little girl left alone with her mother's blood in a hospital corridor. The eyes of a betrayed and abandoned child. They stared out at her, trapped behind the face that she now wore like a mask. Once again, she had hurt that little girl; once again, she had forced her to be hurt.

"I'm sorry," she gasped, and found herself crying aloud. "I'm so sorry about what I did to you." The image in the mirror blurred through her tears but, desperate that she would lose touch with the child, her younger self, she rubbed the tears away.

"I'm sorry I hated you," she choked. "I'm sorry I caused you so much pain." She thought of those years of rejection she'd forced herself to go through in New York, of rejection by directors who wouldn't cast her, by men who didn't want her, of starving herself, of the agony at the hospital. "I'm sorry," she gasped again. "I believed them, not you." She looked into her own eyes, warm, brown, unchanged, and still so sad, so frightened. "I'll never do it again. I promise you. I'll never believe them again."

She turned to the jars and bottles arranged along the vanity. She picked up a bottle of Visible Difference Night Repair. It was a pretty bottle, and fit smoothly, seductively, into the palm of her hand, like a pearl tucked in an oyster. But pearls were actually poison that the oyster had ingested, then coated with its own secretions.

"No more!" she said, and threw the little bottle against the marble floor. It smashed, sending tiny, diamond-bright shards across the floor. She picked up the one next to it. Système Anti-Age Crème de Jour. Where did they get these names? She flung it across the room, where it crashed against the marble baseboard and split open, its heavy white contents oozing onto the floor. She picked up the eye creams next, and the special hair conditioners, then the hand creams, the moisturizers, the makeup base, the blushers and their sable brushes, hurling them all across the room. She stamped on blusher, crushing the color into the white marble, pulverizing it. Then she broke open the eye-shadow colors, one after another. Glimmering Violet. Misty Mauve. Opalescent. She threw each one as if it were a grenade, breathing hard as they all smashed against the wall and fell to the floor. That wasn't enough. They had to be crushed for the lies they represented. "Use me and you'll be beautiful." "Paint me on your eyelids and you'll be loved." As she pulverized them, a bouquet began to blossom underfoot.

"Pretty poison," she murmured and, lifting a bottle of Youth Dew Eye Make-Up Remover, poured its oily contents onto the floor. Then she smashed the empty bottle. She was out of breath, but she couldn't stop, didn't want to stop.

All her life, it seemed, she hadn't been pretty enough. She had lost jobs, men, and her self-esteem because she didn't look enough like the impossible pictures in the magazines, on the movie screen, on television. And even when she became pretty, even beautiful, even when she *became* one of the women on the screens, in the magazines, she had learned that *they* weren't perfect enough, that she still wasn't perfect enough, without special lenses, without careful makeup, without a full-time hairdresser, a stylist, a trainer, starvation diets, facials and manicures, an artful cameraman, a legion of specialists to perfect the illusion. No wonder there wasn't a single woman in America under forty who was satisfied with her looks. No wonder women were risking cancer to increase their breast size, no wonder they were anorectic, and bulimic, and crazy. Hollywood, Madison Avenue and the media, and men—all of them had conspired to make women hate themselves for not looking like Lila Kyle, a six-foot-tall postadolescent boy with a huge pair of silicone knockers.

Jahne looked into the mirror again. Worst of all was that she had helped spread the lie. She'd had the surgery, she'd starved herself, she'd denied her appetites, her age, her face. I helped them, she thought. I helped Marty and Sy and Seymore and April. I helped them push product, push image. I helped Flanders Cosmetics with those endorsements; I helped to sell the lie. And I was loved for the lie. Which means I was never loved at all.

"No more," she cried, and picked up a Chanel lipstick, Ultra Violet, and smeared it across the mirror. As she scrawled "NO MORE," the stick broke, and she threw it away from her, picked up another, and continued until it broke, too. Then another, and another, until the huge mirror was covered with "NO MORE"'s in a rainbow of colors and the floor was littered with the broken remains of two dozen lipsticks. Jahne turned to the perfumes.

It wasn't enough to be ashamed of your looks. You also had to be ashamed of your smell. Don't smell like a woman. Smell like lilacs, or tuberoses and eucalyptus. Smell like citrus, or musk with a slight hint of lavender, or violet-scented talc. Put on deodorant, then perfume, then douche with the smell of country flowers, then slip in a perfumed panty liner and powder yourself fresh as a daisy, lovely as a lily bouquet.

With a single movement, she wiped the expensive perfume bottles off the counter and onto the floor. The crystal flagons crashed, then crunched noisily underfoot. The scent rose up, thick as a wall, and nearly sickened her. "Yes!" she cried. It smelled like a whorehouse, and it should. It was appropriate. She had sold and been sold. Pimped by Hollywood, pimped by April, pimped by Sam, by Sy Ortis. "But no more!" she cried, the smell clawing at her throat, nauseating her. She picked up the remaining face powder, the brushes, the cover sticks, the tweezer, the eyebrow pencils, the mascaras, the lip liners, the eyeliners. She broke what she could, scattered the rest, tore open the drawers, and found more: eyelash curlers, makeup sponges, rollers, mascara cakes and brushes, pancake lip glosses. She pulled out the entire drawer and emptied it onto the floor, smashing what she could.

By now it was a punishment to stay in the room: her eyes were stinging from the stink, and she was gagging. But she had to finish the job. She grabbed the next drawer, emptied it, and smashed the contents. There were the hot rollers, the hair gel, the mousses. There was the honey-almond facial scrub, the cucumber skin toner, the strawberry facial masque. Enough fruits and nuts and vegetables to feed a Honduran village for a week, enough alcohol to get them drunk for a month, enough cotton balls and pads to keep them clothed for a year.

She was taking her breaths in jagged, sickening gulps. She surveyed the filth of the ruined room. The desecration was complete: her pristine bathroom, that temple to feminine allure, was splashed with the muck that she and every other woman in America had been taught they needed. "No more," she said, and stepped backward, closing the door.

Jahne lay on the sofa in her huge, empty living room. Living room? This mausoleum? No, giving this up wouldn't be too hard. But what did she do next?

She thought back to New York, to the time before *Jack and Jill,* to her life with Sam, to the breakup. She thought about Molly and Chuck, about Neil before he lost it. And she thought about those two horrible, lonely years she'd spent getting cut and pasted back together.

Did she wish she'd never done it? Did she wish she'd maintained her identity as Mary Jane?

She couldn't say yes to that. She was glad she'd gone through it. Not for anyone else, but for *her*. Never having had beauty, she would have always craved it. She would not have known that no amount of it was ever enough. If she hadn't gone through with the surgery, she'd never have experienced all of this. She thought she'd known the differences in life for a beautiful woman and an ugly one, but she'd had to experience them. She was glad she had.

And now she was sick of the world that perpetuated those differences: that made the shape of an eye and the tip of a nose so much more than a genetic hat trick. She was sick of a culture that worshipped youth and beauty only so that it could humiliate, humble, and control all those without it. But Hollywood's mania, America's mania, was spreading all across the globe. America exported its vision of culture the way Japan exported televisions.

So where could she go? Where was safe? And what would she do once she got there?

Jahne could hear the phone ringing at the other end of the long-distance line. Please be home, doctor, she prayed. Please be home. She wondered what Brewster Moore's apartment was like. Did he sleep in a single bed, or a double, or even a king? Did he sleep alone? Please, God, she prayed, let him sleep alone.

"Hello?"

"Brewster? It's Mary Jane." Thank God. It was a good connection. She could hear him take in his breath. "Did I wake you? I'm sorry."

"That's all right." He paused. "I haven't spoken to Mary Jane in a long time."

"I know. Neither have I, really." She stopped. How could she explain? How could anyone, even he, understand what had happened to her: who she had been and who she had tried to be and who she was now? "Something has happened. I mean, I feel like I've changed, that . . ." She sounded ridiculous. She listened to the silence on the line and for a moment became afraid that he wasn't there. "Brewster?" she asked.

"Yes, Mary Jane?"

"When do you go back to Honduras?"

"Not till next month."

"Do you need a nurse?"

"Do you need a job?"

"No, but I want one. I want one very, very much."

Was he going to laugh at her? Was he going to think she was a dilettante, a ditz with a new role to play? All at once, she felt this was the most important call she'd ever made, the most important audition of her life. She closed her eyes. "I know it's kind of sudden," she began, "but something has happened to me. I think I've been building up to this for a long time."

"I think you have, too," Brewster said.

"I think I could still nurse. I mean, I'd have to study. I've forgotten a lot. And I don't know any Spanish, except what Raoul taught me. . . ."

"Wasn't that mostly curses?"

"Yes. I could call you a monkey's whore."

"It may come in handy."

She took a deep breath. "I could help with the kids. I know I could. Not in surgery, maybe, but postop. And counseling, maybe. I could help the ones with no faces. I could look at them. I could *see* them, Brewster. I know I could. And that makes all the difference. Having just one person who can see who you really are." Tears filled her eyes. "Can I come, Brewster?" she whispered.

"Welcome aboard," he said.

"Brewster? It's Mary Jane." Thank God. It was no...
ated connection. She could hear him take in his breath.

"Did I wake you? I'm sorry."

"That's all right," He paused. "I haven't spoken to
Mary Jane in a long time.

"I know. Neither have I, really," She stopped. How
could she explain, how could anyone even understand what had happened to her who she had been? "I, she-
who she had wished to be and who she was now. "Something has happened, I mean, I feel like I've changed..."
...She sounded rebellious. She listened to the
silence on the line and for a moment became a child that
he wasn't Tom...? Brewster?" she asked.

"Yes, Mary Jane."

"When do you go back to Honduras?"

"...first till next month."

"Do you need a nurse?"

"Do you need a job?"

"...No, but I want one. I want one. Very much."

Was he going to laugh at her? Was he telling to think
she was a dilettante, a dirty suitor new role to play? After
...once she felt this was the most important call she'd ever
made, the most important decision of her life. She closed
her eyes. "I know it's kind of sudden..." she began. "but
something has happened to me. Maybe I've been hunting
up to this for a long time."

"I think you have, too," Brewster said.

"I think I could still nurse, I mean. I'd have to study.
I've forgotten a lot. And I don't know any Spanish, except what I recall taught me..."

"Wasn't that mostly curses?"

"Yes, I could tell your monkeys wine...
...many come in handy."

...she bones deep inside. "I could help with the kids, I
know I could. Not in surgery, maybe, but photos. And
counseling, maybe. I could help the ones with no faces. I
could look at them, I could see them, Brewster. I know I
could. And that makes all the difference. Having just one
person who can see who you really are..." Tears filled her
eyes. "Can I come, Brewster?" she whispered.

"Welcome aboard," he said.

Obscurity II

———————————— • ————————————

Are you kidding? I would trade it all for anonymity
again.

—KEVIN COSTNER

In the future everyone will be world-famous for fifteen
minutes.

—ANDY WARHOL

Fifteen minutes of that was more than enough.

—JAHNE MOORE

Obscurity II

Laura Richie here. Of course, I was there all along, reporting the facts, getting down each detail of the story. And what a story! I can't take the credit for making it up, but I can get the credit for writing it all down. Who could make something like this up? All of America worshipping at the shrine of the three false sex idols: one involved with her "brother," one a Frankenstein, and the last one a man! It was a story that used too many exclamation points, and I myself try to be sparing with them. Well, you know what they say: truth is stranger than fiction. You can't say that you didn't get good value for your twenty-three dollars. (Or six ninety-nine in paper.)

It has taken me more than three years to do the research and to fit all the pieces together. I don't suppose I'll get the Pulitzer, or a MacArthur grant, but it's a hell of a job of reporting, nonetheless. And if the critics, as they inevitably do, lambaste me as petty, small-minded, and vicious, I may shed a secret tear as I endorse my next royalty check. I already banked a seven-figure advance, and gave Nancy, my secretary, enough of a bonus for her to put down a large deposit on a nice little condo in San Diego. She's retiring next month. I tell her she won't be able to take doing nothing all day, but she just laughs and says she's going to try. She says she only wants to live through the typing of this final revision of this, my final book. I, too, am tired of the dirt, of the secrets, of the scandals that America loves to read about. Maybe, in my heart, I believe what my critics have said. Mine was a small and dirty contribution to literature.

But you, gentle Reader, you bought the book. Thank you. Perhaps you can explain to the critics and the reporters and sociologists this American fascination for gossip about the rich and famous. I don't have a clue.

But I knew this story would sell like cellulite remover in the spring.

And don't think it was easy, ferreting all this out. Even for me, Laura Richie, gossip columnist extraordinaire. *Lila, of course, was dead, the poor thing. She or he wasn't talking to anyone. After that insane funeral, they had her cremated and the ashes interred at Forest Lawn, in the crypt with her father. Then I had to wait. And wait. Because, without Theresa, I didn't have Lila's story, and without that, I had nothing.*

Well, I admit it was a little ghoulish, but, see, I know celebrities. Once addicted to the hot white light of fame, they find it impossible to live in the darkness. In the end, bad publicity becomes better—much better—than none at all. Look at Zsa Zsa Gabor.

Theresa stayed in seclusion for months, but after the tabloids calmed down, after the worst of it blew away, after Robbie left and she had no one to perform for, no audience to watch her suffer, Theresa got bored. Very, very bored.

So, in the end, Theresa talked. A lot of what she said was lies and cover-up and garbage, but some of it was the truth. Then her maid, Estrella, for a price, told me what she knew. It was after that that Theresa finally went into the hospital. Not the Betty Ford—she was too far gone for that—but Cedars-Sinai. Cirrhosis. Terminal. She died last spring.

Robbie got himself into Al-anon and now runs a Twelve-Step bookstore in Aspen. He claims a celebrity clientele. And Kevin—well, once I found him, I couldn't stop him from talking.

Early Artists, of course, fell apart. Sy Ortis' three key clients had bitten the dust, Michael McLain was gone, and the others left in droves. So Sy took his money and went to that Valhalla of all ex-agents—independent-producer status. His phone calls don't get returned.

Ara Sagarian, after he was found abandoned in the hallway of the hospital, was buried the same week Lila Kyle was. His obit was dwarfed by the media attention paid to Lila. In death, as in life, she crushed him.

It took a long time to track down Sharleen and Dean. They seemed, at first, to have disappeared off the planet. But we finally got a line on them by checking out her companion on TV at the Emmys. Once we got his name, Nancy and I did a lot of searching and found a real-estate transaction in the Butler County, Wyoming, records. Then I went out and spent four weeks in a deadly motel in the middle of nowhere to get a chance to talk with Sharleen. But that didn't help, because the locals didn't know her, or if they did, they wouldn't talk. The funny thing was, after the first couple of weeks of hating it, I started to like it out there. It wasn't like L.A. It was a clean place.

But I wasn't rich enough to take a permanent vacation. In fact, I was just about to give up on the story and start on the Douglas family when my own incompetence got me in the door. And it was through Dean that it happened. I took a drive out along the dirt track that led to their ranch. It was fenced at the entrance and there wasn't any way to get in. I knew that; I'd already been out there a dozen times, so I'd taken to driving by and up the mountain road, just for the view. It was beautiful, unspoiled country.

Well, the ruts got the tire, and after a while I noticed I was driving on a flat. A real flat, on a mountain road, about twenty miles from nowhere. And I was in heels.

Let's face it, I'm not a wilderness kind of gal. Lucky for me, Dean found me. Sweet as ever, he took me home. I had lunch that day with the three of them on their ranch. In a month, I had their story.

With Minos, it was much easier. Money talks, nobody walks. I found out a lot of the basics from Minos, after a friend of mine at the LAPD placed a couple of calls. I got my info. Minos still has his license. Everybody's happy.

Ricky Dunn's next movie bombed, and then he married Kiki Mansard, the new Crystal Plenum. When her career took off he was arrested twice for DWI and then for hitting Kiki. Shane, his P.A., apparently did not serve as his mouthpiece at the arraignment. Now Shane's working in the music industry. Ricky isn't working at all. So maybe Michael McLain's instincts on that were right.

But in other ways, Michael's instincts sucked. It took him more than fifty years to marry and to father a child, and he was had twice. Of course, before he got divorced, Michael McLain was claiming his wife Adrienne was a virgin he met at her convent-school graduation. I scouted down Mrs. Godowski, and a couple of six-packs unloaded a lot of resentments. We had the story on Mrs. McLain, but I never used it against Michael. It was only when Melvin Belli took on the case for Adrienne that Michael himself began squawking. Because, as I always say, community-property laws can surely make strange bedfellows. Michael needed everyone to know that his wife had been a whore before he met her. Even Michael McLain knows it's better to look like a woman's dupe than to be poor. It seems that Adrienne had an affair with A. Joel Grossman the whole time she was married to Michael. The child, apparently, was A. Joel's. Since the divorce, he and Adrienne are living together on Michael's money, and A. Joel is teaching film courses at Cal State.

Crystal Plenum dumped Sy. Then, by luck, she got a hot little script from some indie and her last picture, River Road, had legs as good as her own. She's back on top. They say she's a shoo-in for the Oscar.

Les Merchant watched his network slip back to number three; then he watched as the stockholders allowed him to be replaced. Bob LeVine was dumped from International, but his son, Seymore, was the money behind River Road, and he's moved into the big time on his own.

Success has many fathers, but failure is an orphan. There was no one connected with the Three for the Road debacle who was willing to admit it. And just last month poor Marty came out of the hospital, only to go into retirement.

Benny Eggs finally caught up with Paulie Grasso. Or perhaps I should say Paulie's gambling did. He's living in Seattle or a city a lot like it and was willing to talk to me for what he once would have called "chump change."

Monica Flanders died in her sleep, but not before a bitter proxy fight had ousted her son Hyram from Flanders Cosmetics. By the way, Monica looked terrific at her funeral.

April is doing fine. Anyone who reads the trades knows that. She gave me several interviews, now that she's the new queen of the studio. As the new president of International, she's redecorated Bob LeVine's old office in a masculine maroon color.

And Sam Shields? What happened to him? Well, he made two flops, but it looks like his latest is going to be a hit. At least, that's the word on the street. And you've probably read that he and April are about to become engaged. A real love match.

Anyway, the last bits and pieces of the story I got from my husband. Yes, that is one more piece of gossip for you. Consider it a wedding gift from my new husband and me to you. Not that the public is very interested in the private life of writers, even one such as I. But I did get married, at this late date. When I met Dobe Samuels, I knew he was one of a kind. And so, in a way, am I. Reader, I married him. And he was worth waiting for. Sometime just before you read this, in a very private ceremony, I became Mrs. Dobe Samuels.

Brewster Moore and his wife attended. He has never spoken to me about any of this, and once the book is published I will welcome the opportunity to see if he has any comments to make. But his wife told me more than a few things. Mary Jane likes her privacy, and she says she has plenty of it in Honduras, except when her adopted son, Raoul, is home with his friends from school. But she was willing to talk, she said, to atone for her sins. And maybe because she had to talk to someone, just once, to make sense out of the whole thing.

She and Sharleen are still close friends, though they only get to spend part of their summers together on the ranch. Sharleen doesn't ever leave it. And I don't think I will, either. After this book sale, Dobe and I are buying another three thousand acres. He figures if we plant two thousand trees a year, we can add more ozone to the atmosphere than all my books used up. Evening up our karma. He believes it isn't a bad way for me to spend my declining years and my increasing wealth. And he says three thousand acres ought to hold us all.

He also says he won't allow reporters or celebrities on any of it.